Heart's
Blood

By Jenn Gott

The Beacon Campaigns
The Lady of Souls
Fixing Fate
Heart's Blood
Whispers of the Ice

Hopefuls
The Private Life of Jane Maxwell
Who's Afraid of Amy Sinclair?

THE BEACON CAMPAIGNS • BOOK THREE

Heart's
Blood

JENN GOTT

HEART'S BLOOD

This is a work of fiction. Names, characters, businesses, places, events and incidents are either the products of the author's imagination or used in a fictitious manner. Any resemblance to actual persons, living or dead, or actual events is purely coincidental.

ISBN 979-8-4258-7407-8 (hardcover)
ISBN 978-0-692-61472-3 (paperback)
ISBN 978-0-9908914-3-7 (ebook)

Heart's
Blood

Chapter One

PRAXIS FELLOWS LET herself out onto the narrow ledge that ringed the outside of her tower, smoking a cigarette and holding both a letter and a telegram. The telegram she had read—the letter, she hadn't. She stuffed both of them into the band of her maroon suspenders as she edged her way along the ledge. It wasn't the smartest place to be walking: the ledge was scarcely wide enough for both of her feet, and there was one part where the mortar was beginning to pull away from the wall, but it was nearly two o'clock in the afternoon by that point, and only the front side of the house would provide her with any shade. Her blanched Yandosian skin already wanted to recoil at the onslaught of the oppressive sunlight, and so she hurried her steps along as fast as she was able.

Which was, admittedly, nowhere near as fast as she'd like. Her right fingers stretched outward, and a sturdy length of cord attached to a harness-like glove pulled taut; the cord fed up her arm, held in place by a collection of leather braces and straps, and then down the length of her body until it finally connected with a set of gears on her hip. The gears, then, initiated a series of motions that carried the command down through a sturdy metal support system that lifted her heel and guided her foot forward one pace. All of this was done within a few seconds, the system refined and reconfigured until, in theory, it should provide her with a near-normal speed and range of motion, but Praxis really hadn't gotten used to the new setup yet. Until recently, she'd been managing with a haphazard system of pulleys, and though it had served her well enough for the two and a half years since the injury that had lost her control of much of her leg, it had been somewhat . . . crude.

Besides, she'd needed something to do, and her work only kept her so busy. Her lab was a train ride and a walk away, and even during the weeks when she slept there, eating little and working all hours, she would find herself awake in the middle of the night, just futzing. A pair of singed-off eyebrows had convinced her not to touch her choate-salt experiments in this half-asleep state, at least, and so her idle mind had turned next to cannibalizing Abramm Haverdash's engineering designs for anything that might be adapted to serve the use of her leg. And so.

Unfortunately, this meant that the control system was entirely new, and Praxis found herself in the position of having to relearn all the tricks that she'd used to move herself about. By all accounts, the new system was far superior: the glove was more streamlined, the motions of her fingers enabling finer motor control than the flex of her wrist; she could even disconnect the entire system with a click of her thumb, to free up use of her hand. Which would be great, except that she'd become so practiced with the old wrist brace that so often now she found herself getting up and flexing her hand in those motions instead.

She did not forget today. She stretched her fingers, first one and then another as she eased around the broken pieces of ledge. *Be careful,* a voice in her head said, not her own but dearer to her than if it was. "Shut up," Praxis muttered, the usual reply that she'd always given the real owner of the voice when she knew that she was being called out. Despite the words being only in her head these days—either through her imagination, or ringing loudly while she read Kaedrich's steady stream of letters—old habits died hard.

Praxis reached the front of the tower at last, breathing a gentle sigh of relief as she stepped into blissful shade. She looked out over the grounds and gardens below, squinting despite wearing her black-tinted spectacles. It was one of those noxiously beautiful spring days, the flowers blooming in a riotous assault that covered the sloping hills, and the grass so green that not even a gem could glow brighter. Valinda Vandervoon, the mistress of the house, was taking tea on the patio below the tower with one of her guests. Baby Jillus bounced and cooed and made spit bubbles on her knee while Garen, the toddler, sat ripping up grass nearby with reckless abandon. Praxis scoffed. She spat out her cigarette onto the ledge beside her, grinding it down with her battered shoe, and pulled the letter and telegram from her suspenders. At least no one had spotted her yet.

The letter had arrived that morning, the telegram just an hour or so ago. Praxis unfolded the telegram and read it again, despite the fact that it was only two sentences and she knew exactly what it said. HOME THIS EVENING. THE ANSWER IS NO.

No. The word rolled itself around in Praxis's mind, tormenting her, enraging her. No? How could the answer possibly be no—in what universe, under what sort of god or gods a person might believe in, in what circumstances could the Board possibly have shoved their heads so far up their own backsides that they could even theoretically *think* of answering "no"? Praxis tossed the telegram out to be caught by the winds, and then with a flick of her fingers a spark of conjured flame jumped out and attacked it, disappearing in a satisfying little puff of light and smoke.

She should probably get around to reading the letter, then. She had put it off long enough, and it might help to cheer her mood, if she was lucky. But even having decided that, the envelope stayed in her hands for a few minutes longer, unopened.

The letters came two, sometimes three, occasionally four times a week, without fail. All neatly addressed, postmarked from Monfort, the scripty words written with an elegant flourish. In these last several months the quality of the paper had improved, obviously a new batch from a different stationer than before, though when Praxis held them up to her face they still smelled faintly of chesterwood soap. Praxis slid her finger beneath the flap and drew the letter out, tucking the envelope with great care into the pocket of her pinstripe trousers. She leaned back against the wall of the tower, still warm from where the sun had been hitting it all morning.

My dear Praxis . . .

A mighty caw broke over the countryside, and Praxis looked up in time to see a flash of iridescent blue and silver tumbling through the clear blue skies. It turned over in the air and dove toward her, barreling straight into her chest with a frenzy of happy chittering. Wide eyes and mousy ears flashed across her vision as the small creature nuzzled against the bottom of her chin. "Yes, yes, I'm here," Praxis muttered, but when she reached up to pet the creature it turned and dropped something out of its small paws, and Praxis found herself holding a dead canary.

She heaved an exasperated sigh. "Brex!" Praxis hissed. "How many times? No. More. Canaries. They're caged up as *pets*, not some sort of personal buffet!"

But the animal, Brex, ignored this scolding as he clawed his way up onto Praxis's shoulder, chittering and rubbing against her face the whole way. Praxis scowled down at the lump of yellow feathers cradled in her hand, and quickly glanced at the patio to make sure that she hadn't been loud enough to draw attention in her chastising. The merry scene below continued on, oblivious, and so Praxis stuffed the letter back into her suspenders and grabbed Brex off of her shoulder. She held him up in front of her face, looking him as directly in the eyes as he would allow when he wasn't twisting his head this way and that, nipping playfully at the very fingers that held him. "Fine, fine—but if you're going to keep killing them, will you *at least* have the decency to eat them somewhere else? Valinda is pissy enough with me these days without you leaving telltale feathers all over my pillow in the morning."

Whether any shred of this made sense to the animal or not, it was impossible to say, although now he had apparently caught a whiff of his prize and was squirming and reaching with his impossibly tiny paws toward her other hand. He chittered low in his throat, thrashing, and Praxis tossed both of them off of the tower—the canary began to drop, and Brex dove and snatched it out of midair, careening off into the distant treeline with a happy squawk.

Praxis shook her head, watching him go—and that is how she spotted a figure coming up the lane.

Discerning any kind of identifying features from this distance was impossible, but it was too early to be Quaith Vandervoon returning— and besides, he would have taken a carriage from the station. So Praxis watched with idle curiosity as the man (probably), clad all in black, worked his way up the gravel road. He seemed in a great hurry, though he was unusually preoccupied with his surroundings. He kept glancing back over his shoulder and shading his eyes to peer down the lane. When he reached the gates that surrounded Brindlewood Hall, he stopped. From this vantage point, blocked by the greenery running wild over the walls, there was nothing to betray his actions next, except for a subtle fluttering of leaves and vines as if teased by a stray gust of wind. And then, to Praxis's surprise and offense, the gate swung open just enough for the man to scuttle through.

He froze, spying the party set up on the patio, but as no one seemed to be paying him any mind, he slunk back into the shadows. Pressing himself close to the wall, he moved with a disturbing ease through the layers of vines that twined their stems around him.

He could only be a wizard. The ability to get through the locked gate, the lack of notice, the way that the natural surroundings accepted his presence and let him pass without effort—there was no other explanation.

Which meant trouble. Because even setting aside the growing suspicion of magic throughout the country, and in the area surrounding Brindle in particular, there were no other wizards nearby that might be choosing to pay a friendly visit to Praxis.

It was his great misfortune, then, that Praxis should happen to be outside on exactly that afternoon, from exactly that height, looking out in exactly that way. So as he rounded the corner and disappeared from sight, she did the only logical thing to do.

She jumped off of the tower.

It had been a while since she'd exercised that particular magic, and her balance was different now. Her fall was not quite the gentle dip that it should have been. She plummeted about half of the height of the tower before she found her center, a sharp cry of alarm ringing out from the patio. As she caught herself, Praxis looked over, where Valinda's guest was staring wild-eyed, her hands clamped in front of her gaping mouth. Praxis gave them all a jaunty, two-fingered salute as her feet graced down on the carpet of soft grass. "Afternoon," she said, even as Valinda scowled in her direction, fingering a piece of red lace that ringed the collar of her dress.

Praxis did not stick around to start an argument or to be repri-manded, so before either of those things could happen she had struck out for the side yard, her fingers stretching and curling with every hur-ried step. Happy laughter and claps of childish delight from Garen followed her as she rounded the side of the house, disappearing from their view.

It took only a moment to reorient herself to the new vantage point, and to spot exactly what she'd been looking for. To anyone else, perhaps, the challenge might have been greater, but Praxis had spent plenty of time in her life looking for things that didn't belong, and was quite accustomed to finding them. She set off at once, toward (mercifully) the shade of a large yew tree behind the garden shed, where the figure had paused as if to catch his breath. He turned as she drew nearer, but he made no means of attempting to hide, and as she got closer and closer she spotted something familiar in the countenance of his bearing, until at last he came fully into view.

Praxis stopped. "What in the seven hells are you doing here?" she asked. "And skulking about like a petty thief, no less? I would have expected a grander entrance than that."

Don Eagleburns swept off his hat, tucking it underneath one arm. His fat face was flushed, his bristly mustache puffing from exertion. But it wasn't the Don's beady eyes or arrogant scowl that distressed Praxis as she regarded him—those were things that she was used to. No, what unsettled Praxis as she stepped in closer, letting herself take refuge in the overhang of the tree's wide branches, was the state of the man. His fine suit was covered in dust, the hems splattered with mud, a tear running down the length of one sleeve. His hair was all helter-skelter atop his head, and even his mustache seemed somehow disheveled, all the whiskers out of place. Despite her inherent dislike of the man, Praxis found a flutter of worry running through her gut. "Something's happened," she said.

Perhaps most distressing of all was the fact that Don Eagleburns offered no sniping retort to Praxis's statement of the obvious. Instead, he merely nodded, as he continued to catch his breath. "The news," he panted, "the news, I take it, has not reached you yet?"

Praxis shook her head, instantly thinking of the letter. Perhaps it had, and she'd just been so wrapped up in savoring the words for later that she found herself now sadly ignorant. But no, whatever the trouble, if it was something truly serious then Kaedrich would not have opened the letter so calmly; so it must have happened since then, if indeed it mattered at all.

Don Eagleburns reached back to steady himself against the trunk of the tree. "The Society has been . . . dissolved."

He watched her to judge her reaction to this news, but though it was clearly a shocking turn of events, Praxis found herself oddly let down by the declaration. "Oh," was all that she said on the matter.

Don Eagleburns looked on, incredulous. "'Oh'? '*Oh*'! I tell you that the oldest institution of magic on the whole continent has been forcibly disbanded, and all that you can say is 'oh'?"

"Well, I would say that I'm sorry, but that would be a lie."

The Don reared back, his face somehow horribly broken. "Even you cannot be that bitter."

"I'm not *bitter*," Praxis snapped, and . . . she wasn't, not really, that much was true. Even though the Royal Society of Magic had rejected her, then been forced through a quirk of their own rules to accept her, then shoved her aside and snubbed her and wedged her into a position far inferior to her talents, then banned her over a simple, *harmless* misunderstanding with a lord from the Crescent, *and* forbade her to practice magic in the whole of Durland, she could not honestly say that any of this had turned her *bitter*. This much, she had more or less expected.

Though it was clear the Don did not believe her, he at least had the mercy not to argue the point to her face. Which . . . actually, was almost more upsetting than the news of the Society's disbandment. Don Eagleburns and Praxis had never gotten along, not once, especially since he'd been at the forefront in pushing for her dismissal from their halls, and to have him be cordial now made it feel as if the world was listing to one side, not quite balanced.

"That still doesn't explain what you're doing *here*," Praxis said finally, even if just to break the silence.

The Don shook his head. "Believe me, it wasn't my first choice. But it's chaos for us back in Monfort. They've arrested the Premier, and most of the rest of the Dons. I was lucky enough to already be outside of the city when the news came, but even I barely escaped with my life."

This, at least, finally seemed to make some impact on Praxis. She stepped back. "You . . . cannot mean to tell me they've gotten violent."

The laugh that escaped the Don now had a tinge of hysteria that raised the hair on the back of Praxis's neck. "I don't expect someone like you to understand, but Monfort's a different place these days," he said. "Suspicion against magic is running rampant, and the Crescent grows more aggressive toward it with each day. It . . . is not outright prohibited, not yet anyway, but you can't imagine the scrutiny that we've been under." Here Don Eagleburns paused, gnawing fervently on his lower lip. "You . . . realize that you must not tell anyone that we've spoken."

"Do I?" Praxis said. She crossed her arms. "I don't think that I *must* do anything that you ask of me, anymore."

The Don sneered. "Good gods, woman. Do you think that this is easy for me, turning to you for help? What do you want me to do, beg?"

"Oh, 'help' is it? Is that what you're doing? See, it seems to me that you are, in fact, trespassing." She clucked her tongue. "And you, a wanted man."

"Listen, Miss Fellows," the Don said, narrowing his eyes, "you go ahead and be flippant, if it makes you happy—I really don't give a damn right now. But you *will* listen to what I have to tell you, and you *will* take this matter seriously."

Praxis shrugged. "So far, at least, 'this matter' doesn't seem to be of very great importance to me. I fail to see why I should grant it any sort of gravity."

"Fine. You don't want to care about the Society, or me, or any of us, that's fine. But I don't think that even you will want to stand idly by as people are being abducted for Perlandra-only-knows what evil purpose."

"Abducted?" Praxis scoffed. "Oh, please. What sort of nonsense is this?"

"This 'nonsense' is the reason why the Society was disbanded in the first place," Don Eagleburns said. "We were investigating. We . . . got too close."

Despite herself, Praxis raised an eyebrow in curiosity. "Go on."

But the Don shook his head. "I will not go into the particulars with you, not yet. Not unless you promise me that you're going to do something useful for once and help us."

"I don't know what you expect me to do about it," Praxis said. "Even if I were inclined to go nosing about in something that clearly doesn't concern me—"

"When have you ever *not*?"

"—there is, if you'll recall, the small matter of me being banned from the city, on official order. Society or no, it's my understanding that this was a legal decree."

Don Eagleburns rolled his eyes. He reached into the vest pocket of his evening jacket, still dressed for dinner from the night before, and pulled out a piece of paper folded into thirds. "You mean this one?" he asked, shaking it out.

Praxis's eyes went wide as she snatched it out of his hands. She turned away and stepped several paces aside, blocking his view as she skimmed the words swimming in front of her. Her own name, a brief recount of the particulars leading to the Society's decision, the officially worded notice stamped and sealed along the bottom. The paper shook in her hands, the corners fluttering. "You . . . you can't just *take* this."

"Before the order went into effect, I was a high-ranking member of the Society's ruling council," Don Eagleburns said. "I assure you, I could just *take* about whatever I damned well pleased."

"But that doesn't make it binding," Praxis said, turning. She held the paper out. "I mean, the Crescent must have a copy of this. They won't just ignore it because the original is missing."

"Miss Fellows, despite the direness of our straits, I do have *some* friends left in Monfort. A small amendment to the record books, and your banishment is as if it never happened. Believe me, right now, there are far more pressing matters for the Crescent to attend to than the expunged record of one long-forgotten, nobody wizard."

For a moment she could only stare, the order for her banishment still held outstretched between them. The paper felt so frail, nothing more than a scrap, and yet like a trained dog that can now run free, Praxis hesitated, uncertain. For so long the idea of her returning to Monfort had been an iron door, barred shut from the other side, a thousand complicated locks and wards standing firm between her and the capital city, and now . . . now it stood open, gaping. Beckoning.

Praxis's heart fluttered, stirring from a long slumber in her chest. Kaedrich was in Monfort.

She lowered the paper. Don Eagleburns was just standing there, waiting for her to respond. This man, who had been the source of so many ills that Praxis had suffered, both directly and indirectly. This man, who had been the champion of her exile from the start. This man, who had flounced into Brindlewood before and cast himself about as if he owned it and everything—and every*one* inside—now held his hands open as if attempting to show himself disarmed. "We need a wizard, back on the inside," he said. "Much as I am loath to admit it . . . you are more qualified than any of the junior members still allowed to roam free."

Praxis huffed. "That's not exactly ringing support, for someone that you're hoping to conscript."

"I don't need your support," the Don said. "And I don't think either of us expects you to like me. All I need from you . . . is to do the right thing."

"The right thing," Praxis said. Her throat closed up around the words, and she had to look away from his hideously arrogant face. An ache flared in her wrist, heat trapped underneath the skin like a scarred tattoo. Praxis touched it idly with her thumb. She had never really taken much interest in what "the right thing" even was, and *Don Eagleburns's* face certainly wasn't going to stir any feelings of moral duty. But she did find herself fingering the corner of the letter that was still stuffed into her suspenders, almost exactly over her heart. Kaedrich would do the right thing, would never even question it. What had she chided Praxis with, once, what felt like a lifetime ago? *Just be a decent human being for once.* Praxis still didn't know if she was capable of that, despite all of her efforts, but she did know one thing: that Kaedrich would want her to try.

"Where do you suggest that I start?" she asked, turning back to the Don.

I WISH THAT words could capture the beauty of Monfort in the springtime, Kaedrich had written in her last letter, *for it is every bit as lovely as everyone says. Last year, if you'll recall, we had a freak weather pattern that left the city rain-soaked all throughout the blooming season, and so this is really the first time that I've been able to appreciate the majesty of the city in full blossom, and Praxis . . . it feels as if everywhere you look, there is even more wonder to be found.*

Kaedrich Mannly leapt to the side, dodging just in time to avoid being trampled by a passing carriage. Mud splattered up across the bottom of her trousers while a cry of "watch it!" rained down over her head, but she only raised her hand in a friendly wave as she darted through the crowded street. Safely on the other side, she drew an apple from her pocket, the skin bruised along one side, and began to shine it across the sleeve of her plaid suit jacket. The smell of muck and steam filled the air, the streets washed a dull gray as the crowd chewed through it about their business. Kaedrich ducked underneath the haul of lumber that a couple of workmen were unloading from the back of a cart, and smiled as she passed by a shop window with a handful of bedraggled halva blossoms blooming in a narrow window box; their smell was damp and nonthreatening.

My studies progress much as normal. We're moving on to level three fencing, and my marksmanship is improving by an accuracy range of half a percent a week, according to the latest results from Fillsby. Trials are coming up in a few weeks' time, and I actually qualify for participation this year, so study is extra intensive. You've probably seen the Trials themselves during Crown Day, when you lived here, but the actual ascension ceremony for the winners is so much more involved, and I have to memorize it all in case I qualify for the next level. I'm not supposed to talk about it, but did you know, there's an actual hedgehog involved? Silly, I know, but what's to be done? They do love their rituals at Falconridge—I swear there's a new one for every accomplishment. "Pride in the Teachings, Humility of the Faith," they like to say, as if that even makes sense.

"Kaedrich!"

Kaedrich turned on the street corner, her foot already hovering over the intersection. She grinned as Marlick jogged through the crowd, and she raised her hand in greeting. "Good afternoon," Kaedrich said, as the young man caught up with her.

Marlick shook his head, his freckled cheeks flush with exertion. The others, Marlick and the rest of the men at the Falconridge Academy of Arms, had long since tired of teasing Kaedrich about her meticulous manners. It had been Kaedrich's first stumble, upon arrival: she had no idea how much the company of men expected their compatriots to drop all formality when they thought they were alone among equals. Marlick caught up with her, his head level with her shoulders, and gave her a hardy slap on the back, man to man. Kaedrich held her breath, feeling the weight of his stocky hand laying against her. Every time, she always worried: Would he notice the bindings, wrapped across her back as they held her chest in place? Would this be the moment when all was lost?

But as always, he dropped his hand and fell easily into step beside Kaedrich as they crossed the road, dodging horses and scampering urchins both. "Did you hear?" Marlick asked. "A bunch of us are gathering at Cross Street—apparently, Havil's father has gotten a new motocarriage and he's brought it into town to show off."

"Is this going to be anything like when he tried to show off the automaid?"

Marlick laughed, throwing his whole head back. "You never know. You coming?"

"'Course I'm coming," Kaedrich said. They skirted around a thick gaggle of girls, barely old enough to fill out the dresses they proudly flounced down the street in. Marlick spun on his heel as he passed, walking backwards to keep up with Kaedrich. He ran his hands through his neatly trimmed ginger hair, watching the girls with a twinkle in his eye.

He sighed. "Oh, to be a man about town."

"They're too young for you, Marlick."

"Yes, but soon they won't be," Marlick said. He turned, unhappily stuffing his hands into his pockets. "And it still won't do me any good."

"Perhaps your father will relent, when he sees how much progress you've been making as an armsman."

Marlick made a face. "You know that he won't. He's only allowing this"—he gestured at the Falconridge patch sewn over his breast pocket—"because mother insisted. *All* men should know how to defend themselves, you know, in case there's another war." He rolled his eyes. "What good is being able to fight going to do me if I'm stuck inside a temple all day?"

"Maybe if your congregation gets rowdy, you can beat them into submission."

Marlick laughed, turning the corner in sync with Kaedrich's steps. But then his face clouded over, like it always did when the conversation turned to the future. "I just don't know how to make him understand. *He's* married—*he* has six children. You would think that he would get it! I mean, what man doesn't?"

"It may not be *so* bad, being an Attendant."

"Right," Marlick said, snorting under his breath. "I forgot who I'm talking to. I'm sure *you* wouldn't mind swearing off the ladies—it's not like you even know what to do with them anyway."

Kaedrich stumbled, catching herself quickly. Her face had flushed, but she hoped that Marlick's typical, pale understanding of dark skin would hide it from his notice. "I like women just *fine*," Kaedrich said, a little more staunchness in her voice than she perhaps intended. "I'm just . . . particular."

And it *was* true, not that it would help her much. To her surprise and fascination she had discovered more than a year ago now that her inclinations did not run only toward men as she'd previously believed— which you would think would help her pass as a man herself, and at times it did . . . but she could only ever go so far. She dared not encourage the affections of any woman who did not know her true identity, for what if the worst should occur? What if said lady dared to fall in love and wished to marry Kaedrich, believing "him" to be a man? As for confessing . . . it did not bear thinking about. Only Praxis knew the details of her circumstance, and Praxis . . . well, what were the odds of that happening? It was folly to even consider.

I miss you, as always, Kaedrich had written, on a page that she didn't send. *I wish that circumstances were different, and that you were not prohibited from living in Monfort. The time that we spent together—assisting you in your research, our wild adventures to "save the day" . . . all of it I would take back in an instant if you asked me to. I know that it was best for me to come here, and I appreciate your support, both financial and otherwise, that makes this opportunity possible, but—*

This was the point where she had stopped, her pen hovering over the paper, reading over the last few lines. She'd written it without thinking, and now that she caught up with herself she couldn't believe what she was about to say. Kaedrich had taken the page out, copied over the words that had preceded this. She had held the original draft over the fireplace, intending to burn it, but instead she found herself taking it back to her desk and folding it up. It lay now, pressed between the pages in the middle of a book, locked in her bottom drawer. She did not know what she planned to do with it.

But soon enough they had arrived, Marlick and Kaedrich, at the Cross Street pub that had become the favorite meeting ground of this mismatched group of friends that she'd collected. She had surprised even herself, to find a place in the middle of it all. They waved and exchanged greetings, waiting underneath the sign.

"I thought Havil was supposed to be here," Kaedrich said, and Lucan rolled his eyes.

As both the oldest and highest social-ranked member of the group, it was Lucan's unofficial role to be disdainful about everything; a job that he was happy to accept. Everything about Lucan, from his bronzed gentleman's tan to his coppery-blond hair to his heroic jawline, was polished and perfect. He would never tolerate disorder, so what he was even doing with the rest of them was somewhat of a mystery. Lucan was leaning against a lamppost, and he brushed a speck of nonexistent dirt off of his perfectly knotted red cravat. "Are you honestly surprised that he's late?"

"He'll be here," piped up Tristy, in the corner of the group. The only woman there—apart from Kaedrich, and that really didn't count—Tristy was well known to have a crush on Havil, and dared not tolerate anyone speaking ill of him. She leaned over to peer down the street, her thick braid sliding across her back and hanging nearly down to her knees. Her hair was so deeply brown that it usually looked black, but today in the spring sunshine, an underscore of red caught the light.

"Oh, yes," Lucan said, waving his hand about sarcastically, "because we all know that you're a fantastic judge of his character."

"You're such a jerk," Tristy said, wrinkling her sandy-brown nose as she turned back. "I don't know why any of us bother putting up with you."

Lucan grinned. "It's because I'm so good with a *sword*."

Tristy rolled her eyes, a quiet "ugh" escaping her lips.

Kaedrich tried to throw Tristy a sympathetic look. There were times that she felt a certain commiseration between the two of them, the only girls at a boys-only club, although of course it wasn't like that, not really. In Tristy's eyes Kaedrich was just another one of them—quieter, perhaps, and certainly less coarse than the rest of the gathering that she'd gotten herself involved with from the Falconridge Academy, but still a man all the same. Sometimes Kaedrich liked to entertain herself by imagining what would happen if she did confide in Tristy, but how could she even begin to broach such a subject? Besides, that would then require Tristy to lie to the rest of the group, a thing that seemed terribly unfair to simply throw upon a person without permission. Kaedrich watched while Tristy reached up, fixing her earring that had gotten twisted around as it brushed her shoulder.

They had just started to argue about whether or not they should head inside and get started on the drinks, when the cheerful beeping of a horn came barreling up the street. All the conversation in front of the pub came to a stop as they craned their necks for a better look around the traffic. Several passing horses snorted and quickened their step, their drivers attempting to rein them in, and soon a gap had been created down the middle of the lane, and there was Havil, as promised.

He sat proud as a peacock on a seat atop the motocarriage, a pair of wide-lensed goggles strapped to his brown face with what looked like far more bits of leather than were strictly necessary to accomplish the job. His fluffy curls stuck out in fifteen extra directions, fluttering in the wind as he approached, and Kaedrich felt a pang in her chest. Havil had let his hair grow as long as he could get away with, as a man, a glorious natural halo that Kaedrich dared not emulate for herself. Potential gender issues aside, Kaedrich was clawing her way up from the bottom, whereas Havil's family had made their mark in the days of the revolution. He could afford to show pride in their shared heritage, pride that would rob Kaedrich of her status if she dared follow suit.

Still, she made herself muster up enthusiasm as he approached, shouting and waving with the rest of her friends, as if there was any chance that Havil hadn't seen them.

Havil took a hand off of the controls for a second to wave, but then the beast of a machine began to veer to the left, and he hurriedly grabbed hold of the sticks and levers in front of him. The whole thing looked terribly overcomplicated. It was narrow, its six wheels in tight sets of two all down the length of its sleek body. A steam engine lay embedded in the front of it, belching smoke out of two little stacks coming off of either side. Coal and steam filled the air with the smell of industry and innovation. Havil rode immediately behind the open engine, using his levers and gears as he maneuvered slowly up to the curb in front of the Cross Street pub. "There, you see?" he asked triumphantly as he set a lever in place and the whole thing began to hiss and steam as it shut down. "What did I tell you?"

"It's amazing!" Marlick said, rushing forward as Havil jumped down, and it was only then that Kaedrich saw that there was room behind him for a single passenger, and that Havil had taken full advantage of this.

Lyana Lebule, grinning from ear to ear. Her hand was clamped to a hat on her head, keeping it fixed in place as they'd been traveling, and for a second it seemed that she'd almost forgotten that, since they'd stopped, it was no longer needed. She turned to the assembled gathering, her eyes immediately alighting on one in particular. "Kaedrich! Oh, I did so hope that you would be here today!"

Kaedrich forced a smile, but Lucan was already glowering as he looked back and forth between the two of them. He rushed up to the side of the motocarriage, lowering his voice but not enough. "Lyana, what are you doing here?"

"I was *invited*, dear brother, but thank you so much for welcoming me," Lyana said. She undid a little latch on the short door by her shoes, and Lucan reluctantly held out his hand to assist her in climbing out of the vehicle. Her day dress, a fine silk ensemble of powder-blue and cream, was covered in flecks of soot; but she didn't seem to care, breezing straight by her brother. Lucan's jaw set tight as Lyana made a beeline for Kaedrich, who had subtly tried to maneuver to the back of their small group.

"Don't you think it's the most wonderful thing?" Lyana asked breathlessly. "I was just on my way to the shops on Garland Street when Havil came driving by on this marvel! Well! Imagine my delight when he invited me for a ride in it."

"That's amazing," Kaedrich said. She held herself stiffly, several paces back from Lyana at least, but it wasn't anywhere near distant enough as far as Kaedrich was concerned.

Either Lyana didn't notice, or else she didn't care. It was hard to tell with her, sometimes, whether she was ignorant or simply determined, and lately it had been getting harder and harder to keep her at bay. And it wasn't that Lyana wasn't nice—she was, with such a talent for conversation once you got her onto an interesting topic—and you couldn't fault her beauty. Her delicate nose had just enough of an upturn to be adorable, her eyelashes naturally thick. She had her brother's coloring, shiny as a new brass penny, all wealthy tan and honey-blond curls, artfully arranged. The truth is that it was mostly she that had made Kaedrich put such a strict rule in place, though Kaedrich could hardly dare voice that to anyone else.

"Well, what say you all?" Havil asked, cutting through the general chatter as he clapped his hands together. He glanced at Tristy. "Who's up for a ride?"

There was a brief clamor, and a bit of scuffling as they tried to figure out a fair order to who would get to go first and next, and too late, Kaedrich realized that this would have been the perfect opportunity for her to escape Lyana's clutches—but the moment was gone, and soon Marlick was clambering aboard, belaboring that he was not allowed to try the controls for himself. "Maybe next time," Havil said, in a voice that clearly wasn't as sure as his words.

"Eh, bugger that anyway," Lucan said as the contraption veered off and wound through the knot of traffic. "Time for a drink."

"Hear, hear," Tristy said. She wound her arm through Lyana's as if they were the dearest of friends. All girls together.

Lyana turned back. "Coming, Kaedrich?"

"Actually . . . I'm sorry, I've just remembered, I have to get back home," Kaedrich said.

Lyana frowned. "So soon?"

"I'm afraid so. I, um . . . forgot that I promised Mrs. Davish that I'd clean out the—the attic. This afternoon."

"The attic?"

"Yeah, it's . . . gotten full of . . . bats," Kaedrich said. She tried not to wince at the stupidity of her own excuse, and Tristy was smirking at her in a way that clearly indicated she did not believe it for an instant. Kaedrich didn't care. If it would manage to get her away . . .

Lyana nodded, looking deeply thoughtful. "You are such a good man, to help out your landlady like that."

Lucan snorted. "It's fine if you're the sort that *needs* a landlady, I suppose."

"Yeah, so," Kaedrich said. She was already backing down the street. "I should get back. Sorry, everyone."

"Oh, but I've just had the most delightful idea!" Lyana slipped her arm free of Tristy, and clapped her hands together. "Kaedrich, I've been meaning to drop by and see my old nanny, Miss Tendershins, and she lives on Danver Street; that's just a few blocks down from Woodland Alley, isn't it? Why don't you walk me there? It won't take long—surely it's on your way."

"I—"

"Since when do you ever care to visit old Nanny?" Lucan asked, hanging back out of the door to the pub.

"It's always nice to start," Lyana sniped. She fixed her grin on Kaedrich, already stepping up and taking her arm, as if the matter was settled. "Shall we be off?"

Kaedrich glanced from Lucan's sour face, to Tristy's full cheeks as she tried to bite down her own amusement, to finally Lyana as she beamed expectantly up at Kaedrich. *Blast,* Kaedrich thought, as her shoulders sagged. What other choice did she have, really? Social politeness was of the utmost importance in Monfort, and to be seen snubbing a Lebule, the daughter of a member of the Commoner's Arm of the Crescent, would not do anyone any favors. Kaedrich drew herself back to her normal height. "Of course," she said. "It would be my honor."

Chapter Two

THE TROUBLE WAS that Kaedrich *did* like Lyana, although she harbored no romantic attractions toward her. How could she, she thought somewhat resentfully, when all of her affections remained so fixedly set? She was trying, she really was, to put aside her feelings toward Praxis, and she felt that she'd been making great progress. Maybe this was healthy, she decided, stretching her long legs as she walked arm in arm with Lyana down the busy streets, underneath the trundle of the inner-city train circuits. Distract herself with the idle affections of someone else, warm the cockles of her heart that they might one day find another direction to point themselves in.

So it was that, despite the rocky beginning, their walk proceeded with a pleasant air. Their conversation soon turned to Kaedrich's studies, which were far from limited to the curriculum that the academy doled out. She had learned to read only as an adult, and since then had found herself with a voracious appetite for books. Not a day went by that she wasn't studying *something* new—chemistry, philosophy, history, the great works of poets throughout the ages, it didn't matter. She loved it all, loved knowing every scrap of it.

That particular week, it turned out, she had just finished reading a novel by Roran Sellick, a definitive work from the time of the revolutions, when Durland finally drove the Marcovallan Empire back across what was more or less their original border.

"Oh, I loved his earlier works," Lyana said as soon as the subject came up. "But I'm afraid I'm not familiar with that one."

"Really?" Kaedrich asked. "I've been working my way through his entire collection, and I've never met anyone else that seems to really like them at all."

Lyana laughed. "That's probably true, I'm afraid. He's not exactly a popular favorite these days. Oh, but my nanny, you remember, she used to read them to me every night when I was a child."

"Your nanny? Reading Sellick, to a child?"

"It's true, I swear! I loved them. Oh, I didn't *understand* most of what was going on, but there was something about the language he used, the *sound* of the story. I could just picture the royal palace, and all of the princesses and knights bedecked in their finest."

Kaedrich smiled. "He did seem somewhat obsessed with the royal family."

"Didn't he just?" Lyana shook her head. "Of course it's terrible when you take into account his part in the revolution, but I didn't know about any of that at the time. I just thought it was terribly romantic, all of his characters dashing about, trying to keep hold of their empire as it threatened to fall to pieces all around them."

"It must have been a terrible time."

"Nanny Tendershins tells it quite well, herself," Lyana said. "Did you know, her mother was part of the group that led the revolts in Commons Square?"

Kaedrich raised an eyebrow. "Just how old *is* your nanny?"

"Too old, I'm sure she would say," Lyana said with a laugh. "Though if you like, you can ask her about it yourself. We're nearly there."

Which is how, despite some of her better judgment, Kaedrich came to spend more than an hour dawdling on her way home that afternoon; and how, when all was said and done, she agreed to let Lyana walk with her the rest of the way back to her apartment. Lyana was going to borrow the novel, the one she'd never read. It was all quite harmless, and though Kaedrich knew the dangers in potentially letting Lyana get her hopes up, she was not going to refuse the girl her interest in the book that Kaedrich was already done with.

Of course, later she would come to regret this. But she had no way of knowing, as she walked along, the sun beginning to stain the sky pink, just how things would transpire when she arrived.

"I'll get the book and be right back down," Kaedrich said, drawing her key from her vest pocket.

Lyana nodded, much to Kaedrich's surprise. Then frowned, much *not* to her surprise. Lyana began to cough, just one or two politely at first, then louder and with a bit more vigor. "Oh," she said, patting her chest. "Oh, I do apologize—it appears that I am quite parched out. Do you mind, can we just step inside for a minute for a glass of water, or lemonade or something?"

Kaedrich hesitated, turning the key over in her hands.

Lyana smiled. "I promise that I won't stay but a minute longer than necessary."

"All right, all right," Kaedrich found herself saying. "One glass, and then you're going."

"Deal."

They continued their conversation on the way up the stairs, past the first floor that belonged to Mrs. Davish's suites, and the second that housed a Tjalavan couple, all the way past the turn and up the narrowing stairs to the third, a two-bedroom flat that Kaedrich shared with Marlick. Fleetingly, Kaedrich wondered if she'd taken so long that Marlick might have beaten her home, and this was her first flicker of worry—what would he think if he had, and saw Kaedrich bringing Lyana in like this? However, there was no way to ask her to turn around now, and so when Kaedrich got to the top she pushed the door open, revealing their small sitting room beyond.

Marlick had, in fact, returned first, and he was not alone. He perched in the wide windowsill at the front of the flat, while the guest had taken the sofa, her back to the door. White-blond hair, cropped short but sticking up in back, led way to a slate-blue overcoat; and at the sound of the door, Praxis Fellows turned around in her seat.

Kaedrich froze in the doorway, one arm outstretched to hold open the door itself, while the other—dear gods, the other lay neatly along the small of Lyana's back, as she'd been guiding her in. She quickly dropped both of them, nearly tripping over herself as she stumbled farther into the sitting room. "Praxis! I—what are you—how did you—when?"

"It's nice to see you, too," Praxis said. She stood with surprising ease, working her way around the sofa. She fluttered two breezy kisses across Kaedrich's cheeks, and then stepped back as if appraising her. "You're looking well."

Kaedrich forced herself to breathe. She thought that she'd been keeping the impression of Praxis alive in her mind, but now Kaedrich realized how faded it had become with time. Having Praxis right in front of her again was familiar and electric, lighting up dim memories left and right.

Her Yandosian accent, the clipped vowels and drawn-out *L*'s, pooled around Kaedrich like a rich perfume. Her smile slayed as it tentatively broke free.

"Praxis?" Lyana asked from behind Kaedrich. "From *Brindlewood*?"

Praxis raised an eyebrow, turning her attention on the girl as if only just now noticing her presence. "You've heard of me?"

"Oh, indeed! Kaedrich has told us all so much about you—you're the one that he was working with before he came to Monfort, isn't that right? The *older* woman with the crazy designs."

Kaedrich winced, squeezing her eyes shut. If there was any justice in the universe, then Perlandra would hear her silent plea and open up the floor beneath her, allowing her to be sucked down into the depths of the world and not have to face another minute of this. Apparently luck was not to be on her side, because the house remained stubbornly intact. So she heard Praxis laugh, but it wasn't until she dared to peek an eye back open that she saw Praxis spread her arms. Her sleeves pulled back, the stark lines of a black tattoo contrasting on one wrist, the angry red of a scar on the other. "That's me," Praxis said. She turned to Kaedrich. "Old, you say?"

"I never said *that*," Kaedrich squeaked, although of course the damage was done.

Lyana, however, would not be swayed. She shoved her way past Kaedrich, all of her sights set on the Yandosian woman. "Yes, I've heard that you're *quite* the wizard. But then, I suppose you would be, given all of your many years of experience."

"I'm sure that it looks that way to a child," Praxis said, her smile never once leaving her face, "but I assure you, experience can be gathered quite quickly if one is adept."

"Oh, come, don't tell me that you're vain. Spinsters surely don't care about a thing like age, anymore, do they?" She glanced Praxis up and down, from the top of her mussed hair, to the extremely battered men's trousers with a long row of buttons running down the side of each leg, to the scuffed-up wingtips that had seen better days a dozen times over. "Or their looks, it seems?"

"Let me find that book for you!" Kaedrich said, jumping between the two of them as she shoved past toward the corner with her writing desk. She hurried to the pile of books sitting on the corner, not even seeing the titles as she looked at the writing stamped into their spines. All that she could think about was that Praxis was here, in this apartment, in this *city*!, and how was such a thing even to be?

It was, given the circumstances, the easiest thing for her to fixate on, though it wasn't what she really cared about.

Her interruption, however, did not seem to have served to do much interrupting. Praxis was smirking at Lyana now, Kaedrich saw when she glanced nervously over her shoulder. "Yes, I can see why my appearance would make you hostile, my 'dear,'" Praxis said, her accent slipping smoothly into an aristocratic pitch, and now Kaedrich knew Lyana was in trouble, "but unlike some people, I'm afraid that I do not have to get by on looks alone in order to win people's affections."

"Which is a good thing, indeed, apparently."

"Ha!"

"Here it is!" Kaedrich shouted, wrenching the blasted book from somewhere in the middle of the pile. The rest of them toppled, sliding this way and that across the desk and spilling to the floor, but Kaedrich ignored it and hurried over, pressing the book firmly into Lyana's hands.

Which turned out to be a mistake, for she wrapped her own hands around Kaedrich's, still clutched tight to the book. Lyana smiled, positively simpering with delight. "Oh, thank you, *dear* Kaedrich. You're always so kind to me."

"Erm . . . yes. Well, I, I, I—I hope you enjoy it, please don't hesitate to keep it for as long as you like I have plenty I'm sure, yes, well this has been wonderful but I believe you'd best be going before it gets too dark!" She said all of this in a mad rush, half of the words probably not even making it out of her mouth, as she guided Lyana as quickly as she was able to back toward the open door.

Lyana hesitated at the threshold, her mind no doubt reeling forward as she searched for any excuse to delay her departure. A frown crossed her face before she hurriedly recovered herself. She fixed her best smile on, clutching the book to her chest. "Perhaps we could get together tomorrow, and discuss the story further? Say, over tea?"

"Fine, good, sounds perfect," Kaedrich said, barely listening. "Until then!"

With one final glower in Praxis's direction, Lyana departed, the door shutting fast on her heels. Kaedrich leaned against it for one moment, trying to gather what strength she could, kicking herself repeatedly for having been so foolish as to allow Lyana to return with her in the first place. She turned only when Praxis chuckled behind her.

Praxis. Kaedrich's mind was still reeling at the sight of her, standing there in the middle of the apartment's modest sitting room, the light from the sunset pouring in through the windows and tinting her hair golden red. She hadn't seemed to have changed at all, not a single day added to her face. "You're . . . really here," Kaedrich said.

Praxis shrugged. "Seems that way."

A cough sounded from across the room, and both Praxis and Kaedrich started at the noise. Marlick was unfolding himself as he got down from the wide windowsill, a smirk toying about his face. "Well, I think that I'll be heading out for a while," he said as he edged past Praxis. He paused, extending his hand. "Pleasure to meet you, Miss Fellows."

"And you, Mr. Darbury."

Marlick nodded, then turned and made his way to the door, easing Kaedrich aside. "Good luck," Marlick murmured as he hurried out and shut the door behind him with a conspiratorial wink.

Silence hung in the air, so quiet that Kaedrich feared her thundering heart and shaky breath would betray her. "You're really here," she said, again.

"Yes, I believe that we've established that."

"But . . . what are you doing here—and *how*? Praxis, you can't—"

"I can, and I should, thank you," Praxis said, snipping the ends of her words. "My ban has been lifted. I thought that I would come and visit."

Of course; Kaedrich should have realized earlier. Though she wasn't privy to many of the details that had led to Praxis's banishment from the capital city, she did at least know enough to understand that it had been the Royal Society of Magic that had seen fit to do it. "I see. You mean because of . . . what's happened."

Praxis inclined her head, not quite a nod but close enough. How strange: the news had broken not three days prior, and of course Kaedrich had heard a great many bits of detail and gossip about exactly what had led to this shocking turn of events, but never once did she consider the impact that it might have on the boundaries of where Praxis might now be free to travel. Monfort had always been the one place where Praxis never was, never could be; it was Kaedrich's alone to explore and adapt to, Kaedrich's alone to conquer her own small corner of, Kaedrich's alone to define for herself her place inside of it.

She realized that she had fallen silent once more, but Praxis didn't seem to care. Instead, she turned and made her way back to the sofa, settling into the exact place that she'd been when Kaedrich first arrived. Kaedrich frowned, watching her movements—her hand was barely even shifting. "Did you change the design of your pulleys?" Kaedrich asked, coming around to the front of the sofa.

Idly, Praxis glanced at her hand, which she'd laid on the armrest.

Indeed, the bulky brace that she'd always worn was gone, replaced by an odd-looking sort of "glove": her fingers were not encased in fabric like they would be in a normal glove, but rather caps dotted three of her fingers, and tight wire ran in a guided path to gather in a complicated device at her wrist. Praxis shrugged. "I needed *something* to do while you were away."

Kaedrich perched on the edge of the windowsill, so recently vacated. "That almost makes it sound like you missed me," she said. A familiar softness billowed in her chest, a loosening of all the tension of her muscles. She was trying not to smile, but a smile kept twitching along the edges of her mouth.

"Nah," Praxis said, "I wouldn't go that far." She glanced up quickly, before returning her attention to watching the stretch and pull of her fingers as she tested the tension along each of her lines in turn. Her visible fingernails, Kaedrich noted with some curiosity, were oddly well-tended, trimmed and buffed smooth.

Praxis cleared her throat. "You, um. You seem to be doing well."

"I am. You've been getting all of my letters, I assume?" Kaedrich gave her a significant look; Praxis herself wrote only rarely, and even then the missives were always brief and remote.

"I have," Praxis said softly. "And I'm glad that you're so comfortable here."

"Well, the classes are interesting," Kaedrich said. "And I like the instructors."

Praxis raised an eyebrow. "But?"

"'But' nothing," Kaedrich said, startled. "I wasn't going to—"

"I know that you weren't *going* to say anything, but it sounds like there's something there anyway. Unless you're going to tell me that I'm reading you wrong."

Kaedrich stared, mouth slightly agape as she was still paused from the interruption of her sentence. No one in her Monfort life even tried to read behind what she was saying to them, much less with any kind of accuracy. Kaedrich glanced down at her hands, shrugging. "It's not really anything, it's just . . . I don't know. The academy is fantastic, don't get me wrong, I love it here—but it's just a little strange at times. Most of the students are either training up to be guardsmen in the service of some noble, or else they're noblemen's younger sons who want to feel as if they have some sort of military background without having to actually serve anyone."

"And? Are they rude to you because you're black or something?"

"No, there are several of us enrolled," Kaedrich said. A tiny frown creased between her eyes. "People are happy enough to let us defend them as guardsmen; it's defending ourselves that they tend to get up in arms about. It's just . . . I'm there because I want to know how to protect myself and the people around me. It's not like I ever *want* to have to use these skills—they teach you how to kill people, which . . . come on, could I ever do that? So then, I think about it, and my being here almost seems like a lark."

"There are no requirements of attendance, you know. I checked."

"I know," Kaedrich said, nodding. "I know. I just feel like a fraud sometimes. I mean, who am I? I'm nobody."

Praxis rolled her eyes. "Kaedrich, you have just as much right to be there as anyone else. More so, I'd say, because you actually care about what you're learning—even if you don't plan to use it. The rest . . . Oh, stuff the rest. If anyone doesn't like it, they can go hang."

Kaedrich smirked. "Yeah, that's easy for you to say. You actually *are* upper-class," she added, when Praxis gave her an annoyed, puzzled sort of look, "so you can dismiss them as much as you want without fear of reprisal."

"You think?" Praxis asked with a snort. She shook her head. "Then you've obviously never met my mother."

PRAXIS THOUGHT THAT she'd been bracing herself, preparing herself, but the flood of emotions that had struck her when Kaedrich had walked into the room was nearly overwhelming. It was good, in some ways, that Kaedrich had brought in that flippy little wisp of a girl, all white smiles and deep golden dimples, just so that Praxis had someone to spar with and distract herself while she'd tried to regain her footing. Her barbs were not as well-rehearsed as they should have been, so long had she been out of practice at attempting to maintain both disdain and false-politeness (normally, these days, she contented herself with just being rude), but it served the job well enough. By the time she was gone Praxis had settled somewhat, and the longer the evening wore on, the more she had let down her guard. Being in the company of Kaedrich again was like slipping into a hot bath after an impossibly long day, and soon the teasing and the gentle barbs had begun to flow between them once more.

They talked for a couple of hours, mostly Kaedrich, reiterating all the details of her life that she had already shared over the course of a hundred letters. Names and places, routines and habits, books that she'd read, people that she'd met. On some level Praxis knew that she should probably not be "wasting" all of this time here, that she had things to accomplish, information to scuttle out, people to attempt to track down—but she didn't care, not a single bit, not while she was here in this sitting room, listening to the one voice that she'd wanted to hear more than any other for a long year and a half.

She found herself drinking in everything, every nuance of the room, of Kaedrich herself. A sofa and two sitting chairs were more or less facing the window, positioned for ease of conversation, while a tiny dining table was wedged into the corner to her right. A writing desk was in the opposite corner; papers with Kaedrich's neat handwriting littered every surface, but always contained in neat piles, never spread hither and thither the way that Praxis would have left them. There was one painting tacked to the wall, hanging over the fireplace that stood near the writing desk, a ship at sea with a bright blue sky contrasting against the stark white sails.

And Kaedrich, oh! Kaedrich. It seemed to Praxis's trained eyes that Kaedrich had grown stronger and more defined, her long limbs flexing with a restrained sense of power and grace that she'd lacked when she'd left. Her face, too, seemed sharper, her eyes more watchful and aware of the smallest movements. To say nothing of the crisp suit that she'd bought for herself, deep green plaid with a purple-brown shirt, her shoes cared for and polished, a neat little bow-tie folded expertly at her neck. Her old familiar pin, the symbol of her faith in Perlandra, was still tacked to her lapel, but even that seemed to have been given a professional polishing job, and gleamed like new. And when Kaedrich moved her arms, a flash on her shirtsleeves caught the light, tiny green cufflinks made out of emerald. Praxis smiled, noticing them.

When her business for the Society was done, Praxis wondered, how could she possibly bring herself to journey back to Brindlewood? When Kaedrich was here, happy and content; when Praxis had the option of staying in this city that she'd once called a home? She had not journeyed to Monfort with the intention of staying—so much of her junk was still crammed in the tower of Brindlewood, and she still had promises to keep to the Vandervoons—but now, sitting here, warm and snug, Kaedrich right in front of her again, was it even possible to consider leaving?

The simple answer, of course, is that no, no it wasn't. This had settled in her mind before the question had even coalesced, the certainty of her answer laying thick over every other consideration. Kaedrich was back in her life, and unless Kaedrich herself declared a wish for it to be otherwise, nothing was going to keep Praxis that far away from her again.

So it was absurdly easy after Kaedrich's flatmate, Marlick, returned, sputtering profuse apologies that Kaedrich assured him were unnecessary, for Praxis to accept their invitation to stick around for dinner. And during the course of the modest meal, the best that two bachelor "men" could provide on short notice, when the question came around of where Praxis was going to be staying, it was altogether too easy to not fight Marlick's suggestion that she'd be welcome to stay here.

Kaedrich very nearly choked upon her food. "Here?" she asked once she'd managed to regain a tiny bit of her composure, though she still had a wild look about the eyes. Praxis tried not to smirk, helping herself to another drink as Kaedrich sputtered. "But . . . we don't have a spare bed."

Marlick leveled a significant look in Kaedrich's direction, which Praxis clearly wasn't supposed to see. "Kaedrich, surely you'd be willing to do the gentlemanly thing and offer the lady yours."

"Oh, no," Praxis cut in, setting her glass back down. Though Kaedrich had, at times, been forced through circumstances not to unwrap her chest bindings overnight, Praxis knew how uncomfortable it always was for her. "If you insist upon my staying, that's fine, but I've done far worse than sofas before, and no doubt will again. Though I can easily afford a hotel."

"And what sort of reputable establishment would have you, at this time of night?" Marlick said, still ignoring Kaedrich's death glares shot across the table. He leaned around to see the clock, his stocky bearing nudging the edge of the table. "It's nearly midnight by now."

"Is it?" Praxis asked, glancing at the same modest clock posed atop the mantel. She shrugged. "I'm used to late hours—I hadn't noticed. Of course, if Kaedrich doesn't want me to stay, I'll—"

"I didn't say that." It was spoken softly, more to the table itself than the people around it, though Praxis heard. It was the only thing that she'd cared about since the subject began.

Praxis shrugged. "One night, I promise, and then I'll book a hotel in the morning and be out of your way."

There was little more to say after that, and so, in the morning, Praxis found herself walking along the streets beyond the view of the little apartment. She had risen with the dawn, scrawled a fast thank-you note on the back of one of Kaedrich's letters to her, still in progress on the writing desk, and left it pinned to the pillow of the sofa. Outside, she'd stood on the sidewalk in the first light of day, donned her tinted spectacles and deerstalker cap, turned up the collar of her overcoat, and set off into the city.

Outwardly, the streets of Monfort had changed very little in the five years since Praxis had last set foot in them. Even at this hour the city was alive with delivery carts of all kinds, and servants rushing back and forth as they retrieved early morning supplies for their households. Shop boys swept the walk in front of their establishments, and bakers filled the windows with steaming loaves that fogged the glass, and yawning young girls arranged fresh-cut bouquets of flowers in street-side stalls. Everything was the picture of ideal city living, and yet underneath it ran a current so subtle that it could almost be missed.

It was hard to put a finger on, and indeed at first Praxis didn't really notice it. She walked with her head down, keeping to herself, lost in her own calculating mind. She managed to get a good six blocks away from Kaedrich's apartment, when she stopped to light herself a cigarette. Praxis stood in the middle of the bustling sidewalk, underneath the shady overhang of the inner-city rail lines, and groped at the various pockets of her coat until she found one, half-smoked already and bent in the middle. She shrugged; it would do. She raised it to her lips, snapping her fingers to ignite the end. The first flutters of smoke were already curling into her mouth when she froze, an eerie chill settling over her like a thick fog. Nothing had changed, not really. The street bustled on much the same as before, except that now Praxis had noticed what was missing: there was not a single piece of magic being done anywhere within sight. All the everyday sorts of little uses that had woven their way into the fabric of daily life were conspicuously missing, while in their place flutters of red invaded the fashion choices of every rank and station within view.

And now she was drawing several curious looks.

She ducked her head and hurried on, Don Eagleburns's words ringing loudly in her mind. *It . . . is not outright prohibited, not yet anyway.* And yet, they had dissolved the single institute devoted wholly to its study and practice. When he had first told her it had seemed like a wonderful joke, the perfect revenge on those that had turned their backs on her. Only now was she beginning to feel the first creep of dread that must have driven Don Eagleburns to seek her out. Instinctively, she touched the lump of the heavy pendant buried underneath her shirt. It was nestled between her breasts, the chain warm against her skin. Praxis didn't normally wear it, preferring to leave it tucked away in her tower back at Brindlewood Hall, but somehow, at a time like this, it didn't feel right to leave something like the Beacon of Souls behind.

At Jerrison Street, she hailed a hansom. Much as she might have preferred to walk the whole way, to better reacquaint herself with the feel of the city, a certain sense of haste had settled over her. And so, direction duly given, she sat back and took in the rest of the city through the relative safety and shelter of her cab.

Monfort itself was sliced up and divided, as any great city, into a number of sections. It spanned three-quarters of a ring that surrounded Abbney Bay, the upper slopes of what was left of an enormous crater that had reshaped the coastline eons ago. (The last quarter, lower than the rest, lay underneath the glimmering water of the bay itself, partially separating it from the Violet Seas.) The highest peaks housed the wealthy and the powerful, everyone that had reason to want to look down upon the rest of the masses, while the banking and commerce districts, the courts and the Crescent and the seats of government, those lay nestled directly on the coast of the bay itself. Between them, in a narrow slice that kept getting choked by both halves surrounding it, was the middle, working class of the city, everyone that made it really run. The shop owners, the bankers, the members of clergy, the teachers of moderate esteem, all crammed together and further divided and subdivided by class and rank within their station, all complicated enough to give Praxis a headache. It was one of these districts that her driver led her into, slowing in the middle of a narrow, sloped lane with houses crammed thick on each side.

But it was really only one house in particular that Praxis had any interest in, and she strode up to it as bold as brass, and rapped the knocker.

One of the narrower houses of the row, it was wedged firmly between the walls of its neighbors, as if it could no longer bear the burden of standing tall on its own. It was nondescript, small and brown, lacking any of the towers and spiral rooftops of the larger houses along the crest. The tiny patch of grass next to either side of the front walk was green and well-tended, although a piece did appear recently ripped up in the corner. Praxis frowned at it, as she waited for an answer, and then she took in the rest of it with a more curious eye: the window with a pane missing and neatly patched with wood, the vibrant red geraniums growing thick in all of the newly installed window boxes, and metal scrollwork letters tacked up beside the door. *P. V. Weevish,* they said, and below them someone had obviously yanked off the rest of the title, for all that was left was the ghostly imprint of something that had been there forever, now missing. *Chief-Clerk, R.S.M.*

"Hmm." Praxis leaned back, checking the upper-floor windows for any signs of life, when a flutter of motion caught her eye. The neighbor to the left, peering through the curtained window, her eyes popping in alarm at being caught as she dropped the fabric back in place.

Praxis knocked again. She crouched down, propping open the mail slot. "Hello?" she called into the empty foyer beyond. "Hello?"

"If I've told you once, I've told you a thousand times!" came a voice from inside, shifting in volume as its owner obviously moved from room to room, "I had nothing to do with any of it! Please, please, just—"

Praxis straightened up as the footsteps grew louder, and the door opened up in her face.

"—leave me alone!" Weevish finished. He was a squat little man, still in his dressing gown, his white hair all askew atop his head, what little was left anyway. Moon-shaped spectacles rested on the edge of his bulbous nose, and he stared open-mouthed at the sight of Praxis.

"Good morning," Praxis said, as Weevish's eyes bugged out. "I'm—"

The door slammed in her face.

Praxis raised an eyebrow. She leaned in, knocking with her knuckles this time upon the seal of the door. "Hello? Mr. Weevish? My name is Praxis—"

"I know perfectly well!" he shouted, ripping the door open again. "But I have no business with you! None!" It slammed in her face once more.

"Might I ask why not?" she called, leaning in toward the door.

The door opened. "You may not!" The door slammed.

"How are you even certain that you know who I am? You might be mistaking me for someone else."

"Ha!" came a shout from inside. The door opened. "Ha! As if there could be any doubt. *Praxis Fellows*," he sneered. "I drafted the order for the council on you, you know. Your file at the Society is four inches thick! Four! The amount of *paperwork*! No!" he declared, his voice raised extra loud as he addressed the rest of the street, "I have nothing to do with wizards these days!" He shook his head. He slammed the door.

Praxis sighed. She crouched back down, propping the mail slot open once more. "Then are you also aware of the plot going on somewhere at the Crescent?" she asked, although the only answer that she got was Weevish's hands coming down and attempting to shut the flap closed on her. "The disappearances? And how, just as the Society was beginning to investigate, they were suddenly disbanded?"

She got no answer, only more pressure weighing against the mail slot.

"Mr. Weevish, I'm here under the advisement of Lord-Don Eagleburns." This last part she said with great pains, although he did insist that if she had any trouble she must not hesitate to use his name. Grumbling, Praxis dug something out of her coat, holding it in her open palm. The

Don's signet ring, the Society seal stamped proudly on the front, his own initials worked in around the emblem. Praxis shoved it forcibly through the mail slot, where she heard it land upon his tile-work with a cheerful *ping!* Whether he bothered to retrieve it, she couldn't say.

She gave him a minute, just to see if she had managed to change his mind. "Please," she said, taking care to keep her voice down, "it's important that I speak with you. Eagleburns recommended you personally."

Another minute, ticking by in silence. Somewhere in the distance a dog was barking, and the clatter of a carriage passed by in the street behind her.

The mail slot snapped open, Weevish's narrow eyes peering out with great suspicion. "I've never admitted this to anyone," Weevish said, his voice barely a whisper, "but I have *never* liked that man. Not since he first applied as an apprentice. Arrogant, nasty, pompous little—" He stopped himself, taking a deep breath. "You must never tell, of course."

Praxis smiled. "You have my word; and for the record, I quite agree. Unfortunately, he *is* right this time, isn't he? There is something going on. Something terrible?"

Weevish didn't answer straightaway, his eyes darting left and right as he took in the view beyond Praxis. "Whatever you think you know," he said, "I promise you that it is only half of what is really at stake here."

"Then you'll help me?" Praxis pressed. "Please?"

Weevish shook his head. "You don't want to get involved. Go back to wherever you've been buried, Miss Fellows. I promise you that you don't want anything to do with this."

"Much as I might love to heed your advice, that . . . really isn't an option anymore," Praxis said. She sighed. "In truth, I am far too nosy to ignore something like this."

"Hmph. Well, that's a rather silly reason to go charging into something beyond your powers to control."

"You're probably right, but it's worked out for me in the past. Please, can we not just talk like normal people? Will you allow me in?"

"No," Weevish snapped. He threw the ring back out through the mail slot, and Praxis scrambled to catch it. "You must not come in. You must never be seen coming to my home again, do you understand me?"

"But—"

"Meet me in the old quarter, by the burned-down temple. There's a pub at the corner called Willy's. Eight o'clock this evening. If you're really stupid enough to want to see this through."

Praxis let out the faintest sigh of relief as she tucked the Don's ring into her pocket. "Thank you."

Weevish huffed. "Don't thank me, girl. This is not a favor, I assure you. Now get away! Quickly, before they suspect!"

"Well, *fine*, then!" Praxis shouted as she stood up. Weevish's eye still peeped up at her through the mail slot, and she gave him a sly wink. "If that's how you're going to be, then I'll just have to find someone else!" And she turned and stormed off, past all the spying eyes of the windows around her.

Chapter Three

Sweat ran freely down Kaedrich's face and neck, tracing lines down between her shoulder blades and soaking through the bindings around her chest. All of her muscles ached, but she kept pummeling the training dummy, throwing all of her weight into each punch. How long she had been there, she couldn't even begin to guess.

It would have been better if she'd just stayed asleep. She'd woken from the most remarkable dreams—the details were lost to her, in the world of the waking, but she opened her eyes with a grin and happy sigh, and nuzzled farther down in her pillow. She hadn't been ready to get up, everything in her quiet bedroom peaceful and still. Her head felt light and free, as she stretched and rolled over onto her back, and then the memory of the day before hit her all at once. Her eyes had widened, and she'd thrown herself from her bed, dressing as quickly as possible. A knot of both apprehension and delight had lodged firm in the pit of her stomach, and she kept leaning toward the door to the sitting room, trying to determine if anyone was awake yet.

Only when she finally did open the door and step through, she found that nobody at all was around. Praxis's sofa was empty, a note pinned in place. *Kaedrich,* it read, *I've gone out. I'll be booking a room at the Crestview Hotel if you care to get in touch. -P*

Kaedrich tried to tell herself that she was not disappointed by this, no, not at all, that would be silly. That it was just as well, because she had plenty of things to do that day. And this was true, and with a jolt she realized that she was probably going to be late already.

So she'd run out the door, racing through the familiar streets, cutting across town. The door to the Monfort Daily Witness slammed as she scrambled in. "Kaedrich!" someone barked; she didn't know who because she ran on, waving an acknowledgment behind her.

"Kaedrich!" her boss shouted as soon as she dashed into his office. "Where have you been? We haven't got all day!"

"Sorry, sorry!" Kaedrich said. In the corner of the office was a rickety tray table, a stack of papers piled so high that the whole thing listed to the right. She snatched the top sheet off, a list filling the entire page. "What have we got today?"

Mr. Bundling, her boss, scoffed as he settled behind his own, much larger desk. "Start with the one on Pennbrook's."

Kaedrich nodded, shuffling through the stack of papers. Several toppled off, crashing in a haphazard mess on the floor, and when Kaedrich lunged to grab them she jostled the tray table, and the rest went crashing down with her.

"Kaedrich! What in the darkness is wrong with you this morning?"

Now, more than two hours later, pummeling the training dummy, Kaedrich gritted her teeth as she remembered it. She'd been sent home about half an hour later, having spilled coffee, smeared ink across an entire page, and tripped over a box. "Listen, I don't know what's gotten into your head today," Mr. Bundling had said, "but whatever it is, you're useless here. Get out. Come back when you're ready to work."

Kaedrich threw another punch, her whole arm aching upon impact. The safe tang of sweat and furniture polish hung thick in the air.

"Ah-ha!" came a voice from somewhere behind her. "I knew it! The clear signs of a woman!"

Kaedrich whirled, her heart racing even harder than it had been just from her workout. Marlick was striding up the length of the training room, a wide grin spread across his freckled face. "You thought you could keep it from me, didn't you?" he continued.

"I—" Kaedrich started, a thousand excuses vying for her attention.

"There's no point in trying to deny it," Marlick said, still walking, "I can spot it anywhere. Only a woman would make a man hit old Cheery here *that* hard."

Kaedrich glanced back at "Cheery," the boys' nickname for the training dummies, relief pouring off her as thick as her perspiration. She gave a nervous laugh, trying to calm her unsteady heart. "Is it that obvious?"

"Well, I say this as a man of some experience when it comes to the vexations of women," Marlick said. He had finally caught up with her, and now his grin was as broad as ever.

"Since when?"

Marlick waved this off. "So. Now the truth comes out. I always wondered why you never seemed to take to any of the advances thrown your way—but I admit, I never suspected that it's because you already had someone."

Kaedrich blushed. "I don't . . . *have* someone."

"Ah," Marlick said with a knowing nod. "So it's like that, is it? What's the matter—too scared?"

"No." Kaedrich shook her head. "This is ridiculous. You're seeing it all wrong, I'm not—we're not—I mean, it's never . . . it's never going to be like that." She took a deep breath as she turned away from him, back toward the dummy. Another punch, a clean uppercut straight into the dummy's chest. Cheery wobbled slightly at the impact, its smiling head seeming to shake at her in silent, disbelieving laughter.

Marlick clucked his tongue. "Kaedrich, Kaedrich, Kaedrich. Don't be a fool. Okay, I . . . don't really see the appeal in her, myself, but taste is a funny thing—anyway, you should strike while you can! There's no telling how long this opportunity will last!"

Another punch, another round of jeering mirth from the part of Cheery. "There's no opportunity," Kaedrich said, throwing her arm into it. "You're imagining it." Kaedrich hesitated, her glove still firmly lodged against Cheery's cheerful face. "And that's even assuming that I wanted to try courting her, and I don't."

"*Courting?* Who said anything about courting?" Marlick asked. He snorted. "No, that's clearly a bad match right there. And anyway, I don't think that your friend is really courting material. But there are *plenty* of other ways to enjoy the company of a woman, you know."

Kaedrich scowled in disgust. She threw herself away from the training dummy and began to rip off the lacing of her gloves, pulling at the rope with her teeth to get it started. "I should have expected as much, from you," she said, as she started to make her way toward the far wall.

Marlick's footsteps hurried after her. "I'm only trying to look out for your best interests!" he said. "Besides, I'm not exactly at liberty to pursue those kinds of indulgences—you are! If I was in your shoes, I wouldn't waste a single chance."

Kaedrich ripped off first one glove, then the other, tucking them underneath her armpits as she carried them back to the bench. There was a towel waiting for her, and a clean shirt and a waistcoat and her suit jacket. She worked out in a thick, sleeveless undershirt that covered her bindings but didn't breathe very well, feigning a family heritage that taught modesty for all, and because no one knew any better, no one questioned it. "Aren't you supposed to be encouraging me to follow the path of Perlandra or something?" she asked as she dropped her gloves and began to mop the sweat off of her brow. "You know, home and family and choosing a good, sturdy wife? That sort of thing?"

"I have it on the best authority that such a life is vastly overrated," Marlick said. "Besides, I'm not swornbound yet. I don't have to preach any of that until I'm an Attendant."

"Lucky me."

"Look, I don't know how it is where you come from," Marlick said, and Kaedrich was lucky that she already had her face buried in the cloth, because she could not contain the snap glower that Marlick's casual insinuations brought forth, "but around here, when a man starts receiving attention from a lady he desires, he doesn't just throw it away."

"I'm not—" Kaedrich started, but the sound of approaching footsteps cut her off. She dropped her towel as Lucan and Havil rounded the corner.

"—but that's exactly what I was trying to explain!" Havil was saying. He was swinging his hands wildly through the air as he spoke, walking backwards ahead of Lucan.

"Watch where you point that thing!" Lucan snapped. He smacked the end of the fencing foil that Havil had tucked underneath his arm. "Oh, hey," he added, spotting Kaedrich and Marlick.

Kaedrich nodded. She was already gathering up her shirt, and she slid it on with her back to the group. She was grateful for the interruption, and hoped that talk would now move to whatever Havil had been going on about.

Alas: "So, listen," Marlick began, crossing his arms over his stout chest, "Kaedrich and I need someone to settle a dispute."

"We really don't," Kaedrich called over her shoulder, but even she could see the flattened interest piqued on Lucan's smooth face, the curious spark of excitement bubbling in Havil's eyes.

Marlick ignored her. "Okay, so say there's a woman—"

"Yes," Havil said, and Lucan smacked his arm.

"—and she's *clearly* interested in you—"

"Yes."

"—then you'd be a fool to ignore her advances. Right?"

"Is this a trick question?" Havil asked.

Lucan narrowed his eyes. "Is it my sister?"

"No," Marlick said, "and no."

Lucan shrugged. "Then yes. Obviously."

Marlick smirked. "See?"

"Well, wait, wait," Havil said, suddenly looking nervous. "You didn't say: is she attractive?"

"Yes," Kaedrich said, while Marlick said, "Not bad."

And then the whole group stopped. Kaedrich had finished buttoning the rest of her shirt while they were chatting, and had been listening to their boys-will-be-boys banter with only half an ear out; she'd answered without thinking, as she slid the first of her emerald cufflinks into place. When she'd realized what she'd said she froze, and now, a beat later, she turned stiffly to see the rest of the group. They were grinning at her with various levels of effort not to.

"Oh ho," Havil said.

"This is new," Lucan said.

"Apparently it's not!" Marlick added, jumping in as gleefully as a puppy. "Our friend here has just been hiding her away somewhere."

"What, like in a basement?"

"Oh, good gods," Kaedrich muttered. She jammed the other cufflink in place, fixing it quickly, and then draped her tie loose across the back of her neck. Her vest and jacket she threw over her arm, moving off quickly as she began to knot her tie.

Laughter and three sets of footsteps hurried to follow her. "No, no, this is too good," Havil was saying, the first to fall in line with Kaedrich. Out in the hallway, they began to pass a handful of other small groups, mingling outside of the various class- and practice rooms. Suddenly, Kaedrich regretted her decision to come here—she could have found someplace else to work off some steam, surely?—but it was too late.

"Look, can we please move on?" Kaedrich said. Her cheeks were burning fiercely as they walked. "It's not what you think, I promise."

How many times were they going to make her say it? She had thought that it was bad enough before, when they would rib her mercilessly whenever she declined to flirt with someone at the Cross Street pub. She quickened her pace further still, pounding down the main stairwell, while the trailing conversation continued without her. Falconridge Academy was an old mansion, all dark and masculine, wood panels everywhere, and lots of hanging swords. Their cheerful voices bounced easily off of the high ceiling as they clattered down to the main floor.

"No, but seriously," Havil was saying; he had fallen back a little, giving up on getting anything further out of Kaedrich, "you saw her? She *actually* exists?"

"I swear to Perlandra herself! Never would have believed it when she showed up at our door yesterday, but there she was, in *trousers* no less! Not that she seemed to care, with her ice face. Yandosian," Marlick added, seeing the slight look of confusion that Havil sported.

Lucan gave a low whistle. "You have your work cut out there, Mannly: those ones are frosty nearly to the core."

Havil raised an eyebrow. "Nearly?"

Lucan grinned. "Oh, I'm not saying there's *no* heat buried in there."

The rest of them burst out in a low, rude laugh, but Kaedrich just grunted, slipping her arms through her suit coat as they reached the bottom of the stairs. She buttoned it up, smoothing out the front so that the Falconridge patch on her breast pocket lay flat. "For the last time, can we *please—*"

But her thought was cut off as she rounded the corner, and found herself nearly colliding with a pile of papers. "Whoa!"

The papers jerked aside, several fluttering off the top. "Gentlemen!"

Kaedrich skittered to a halt, the weight of several other men slamming into her back as their jovial chatter died underneath the towering figure of Director Tarlock.

"I—I'm sorry, sir," Kaedrich sputtered, instantly ducking to retrieve the pages scattered on the floor. Her head was pounding, the flush and stress combining to a roaring pain clamping down like a tight helmet.

As if this day hadn't already been bad enough: Director Tarlock himself, head of the entire academy, leveling Kaedrich with a withering stare. His clean-shaven jaw shifted, his teeth clenched. Every line of his face was primed to cut down nonsense. How much of their conversation had he heard, as they had bounded chaotically down the stairs? The rest of them hadn't exactly been making an effort to keep quiet.

Kaedrich's shoulders curled as the director snatched the papers out of her hand. She winced, ready to begin sputtering further apologies, when Lucan folded Kaedrich expertly out of the line.

"Tarlock, my sincerest apologies," Lucan said, all polished and old-boys. His voice was as smooth as his combed-back hair. He nodded at the pile in Director Tarlock's arms. "Can we get someone to help you with that?"

Director Tarlock shifted the weight of his papers. Kaedrich caught a glimpse of the crest sewn into Tarlock's own jacket, done in gold thread to indicate his status. "That will not be necessary," Tarlock said. "Surely you boys have better things to be doing . . . ? Mannly, Darbury, don't you have Trials coming up?"

The admonishment wasn't spoken with a particularly harsh tone, though to Kaedrich it may as well have been decreed from an angry Perlandra herself. Kaedrich forced a shaky nod, her eyes trained somewhere in the vicinity of Director Tarlock's knees. Even his *trousers* looked as if they did a hundred push-ups every morning, not a single thread out of line, not a single crease daring to cross them.

"Oh, I'm sure they're well-prepared," Lucan said. He patted Kaedrich cheerfully on the back, for extra emphasis.

Director Tarlock harrumphed under his breath.

The thing is that it was fine and well for Lucan to brush this off and pretend like nothing had happened. To him, nothing probably *had* happened, after all; he hadn't been the one to physically crash into the academy director, and he had already been initiated into the Talon bracket the previous summer. But there was more to it than that. It was the way that Lucan exchanged polite nods with Director Tarlock as he began to move on, the way that Lucan called out after, to insist that Director Tarlock bid Mrs. Tarlock a "hello" for him. The way that Director Tarlock's eyes had narrowed almost imperceptibly, looking at Kaedrich after Lucan had vouched for her. The way that the standards were always just a little higher for Kaedrich, despite the fact that both she and Lucan had their tuition fully paid in advance at the beginning of each semester. And now—! If he had heard the teasing the others had been laying thick on Kaedrich, what would he think now? That Kaedrich was going to let herself get distracted? That she wasn't going to be working as hard, fixated on the idea of wooing some random Yandosian?

Kaedrich closed her eyes, letting out a quiet groan as she leaned her forehead against the smooth paneling of the hall. She worked harder than all of them, Lucan and Marlick, even Havil, probably harder than all three combined, just to keep a measure of respect around this place. It was so hard to gain and so easy to lose, and she knew, breathing in the smell of the fresh polish, that she had just dropped several hard-won notches in the director's esteem.

She had been right, this morning: she should have just stayed in bed.

By PRAXIS'S ESTIMATES, she still had at least three more hours to go before Kaedrich would have some free time.

The letters had recounted Kaedrich's schedule in so many bits and pieces that it was difficult to be certain of anything, but Praxis had spent more hours than she cared to admit, even to herself, trying to stitch together a sense of Kaedrich's normal routine. Pages littered her laboratory and tower back home, scrawls of Praxis's scratchy handwriting: *if marksmanship lessons end just before sunset in winter,* they would start, trailing off as Praxis had set it aside and reread a passage or two, mulling over the time it would reasonably take to get from the edge of the city's ring—where the academy was nestled—up the steep hill and into the shopping district, where Kaedrich had mentioned going next. Her letters were scattered with clues, which Praxis had culled and mused over, looking at this way and that. These days, she thought that she had the basics of Kaedrich's routine fairly well established, and often, back at Brindlewood, she'd find herself marking the time against whatever she'd assumed Kaedrich would be doing at the moment.

Now, it was a more conscious effort. Praxis's short visit with Weevish had been wrapped up too early, leaving the entire day spread out before her. She did not dare to consider crashing in on Kaedrich's apartment again, not so soon anyway. Especially when Kaedrich likely wouldn't even be there, but even if she was—Praxis knew that she was treading on delicate ground, showing up so unexpectedly. So after she'd made her way slowly out of the middle district, stopping at a street café for a cup of coffee and a stale cigarette, she had done her best to kill a few hours.

She'd visited the headquarters of Orange Rail Lines.

This had gone about as well as she had expected it to. Quaith Vandervoon had, after all, been here just two days earlier, making the same request. Though his had been presented as part of his official, biannual meeting with the Board of Directors, and Praxis was merely showing up on their doorstep.

"Yes," Praxis had said, leaning heavily on the desk of the unlucky clerk that happened to get stuck dealing with her, "I get that I don't have an appointment, but surely they cannot *all* be so busy that no one has five minutes to spare."

The clerk, a timid-looking man in a cheap tweed suit, leaned across his cluttered desk and adjusted the battered wooden name plaque that Praxis had brushed up against. *H. L. Murran,* it read, in letters obviously hand-carved by someone with more pride than skill. He glanced up nervously, his eyes skittering back to the desk almost the instant after they'd met Praxis's face. "It's not that I don't understand your position, Miss . . ."

He did this a lot, Praxis was beginning to realize: start a sentence and then just let it trail off after his opening point, as if the rest was either obvious, or so complicated that he grew weary just considering it.

Praxis sighed. "Look, this is not complicated. You go into their offices, and"—she pointed behind him, where a row of doors overlooked the bustling pit of clerks and typing and filing that Praxis was currently mired in—"you tell them that Praxis Fellows would like to further discuss the engine designs proposed by Quaith Vandervoon during their last meeting. You *do* know who Mr. Vandervoon is, don't you?"

It was a cheap tactic, a low-slung sting that the poor clerk probably didn't deserve. But if he was offended by the idea that he might not know the name of the man that owned the entire railroad that he worked for, he didn't show it. Murran blinked at Praxis, his narrow face and pointed nose reminding her unnervingly of a mouse sniffing about the room.

"Did I mention that I have a letter from him?" Praxis said, knowing full well that she had. Several times. But she withdrew it just in case, on the off chance that the clerk either didn't believe or didn't trust her, and she waved it in front of him.

At least this note was genuine, penned by Quaith before she left, when Praxis had been hastily stuffing together a suitcase and ignoring the rest of the household. There had been plenty of times when Praxis had needed Quaith's authority, and simply . . . created the credentials that she'd needed. She felt somewhat proud of herself, that she'd taken the time to acquire the real article, and the fact that it was getting her nowhere was only making her angrier.

Murran idly picked a pencil off of his desk. He spun it by the point, or at least he tried to, but it didn't even make a complete circle before it flipped out of his awkward fingers and disappeared underneath his desk. He jerked in surprise, and almost looked as if he was considering diving underneath to get it, but one steady glower from Praxis stilled him in his chair. He slouched farther down in his seat, instead. "I'm sorry, miss. They said . . ."

"Yeah, I'll bet they said," Praxis muttered. But at least now Murran had confirmed that the Board was not, in fact, all out—merely avoiding her.

Praxis settled herself heavily in the creaky desk chair across from Murran. The infuriating thing is that this time, for once, they actually did have something important to discuss. Normally, Quaith's meetings were all one-sided: the Board would tell him how things stood, the Board would inform him of their plans, the Board would dismiss him at the end of the day like some errant schoolboy. Thus formally appeased, Quaith would duck his head and return dejectedly to Brindlewood Hall, where Praxis would again have no progress to report to cheer him up.

She tried not to blame herself. Quaith had inherited the railroad when he was but fifteen, and had never been prepared for the task of running it. His father, a brilliant businessman, had built the company up from literally nothing but a handful of promises and the dreams of his tinkering friend, Abramm Haverdash. The fact that Quaith had never figured out how to stand up to the Board of Directors and take charge was not Praxis's fault; and neither, she kept telling herself, was the difficulty that she'd faced over the years in trying to finish off the half-formed dreams and designs that Abramm had left behind when he'd died.

Possibly there was no answer. The schematics that he'd begun were wild and grand visions, complete overhauls of the engine designs that had been the backbone of all of Durland's rail lines for decades. Even assuming Praxis could crack the process he'd obviously dreamed up for improving the heat transfer of the choate-salt that powered all of them, there was no guarantee that any of the designs would work in the real world. They were wild and impressive, streamlining and in many cases completely reimagining the process, and though Praxis wasn't an expert at engineering, even she could see that they were far beyond the technological level that Durland was currently operating at. For sanity's sake, some of his wilder scribblings described proposals for a type of ship that could be lifted through the air!

The Board knew this, they must have, so Praxis wasn't exactly surprised when they had shelved the designs years ago rather than invest money in exploring them. She had been brought in on Quaith's own expense, his one wild act of rebellion against the Board's wishes.

And Praxis actually *had* made some progress in the last few months. She'd finally landed on a formula for the choate-salt that, while it didn't quite come close to the expectations of Abramm's calculations, did improve the engine efficiency by a significant margin. Her small models had flourished underneath the improvements, and what she needed now was more: more funding, more space, more resources than what Quaith could provide on his own. And while normally Praxis would be more than willing to throw her own money at the problem, her funds had been devoted almost entirely to paying for Kaedrich's academy, and when she'd gone to dip into her bank accounts recently to make up the difference, she'd discovered to her shock that she'd managed to make a significant dent in what had looked for years like an inexhaustible resource.

So it had come down to this: the Board needed to approve before they could move forward. But the Board would not approve, not for Quaith. And not, she was finding, for her either.

She left the offices nearly three hours after she'd entered them, walking out flanked by the burly forms of two security guards that had been called after she'd gotten tired of waiting and attempted to *make* herself an "appointment" with the Board directly. They hadn't been enough to force her to leave, of course—a single burst of conjured flames would have been enough to win a direct fight—but for once her better judgment had won out. Praxis had backed down, rather than escalate the situation to that level of conflict and violence.

Now, with the midafternoon sun beating down on the sett stone streets of Monfort's business district, Praxis turned up the collar of her slate-blue coat and crammed her tinted spectacles on her face, setting off for points unknown. She had left her contact details with Murran, not that she expected anything to come of it, and the sad fact was that she had nothing else of particular importance to do with the rest of her day.

With no other reason to guide her path, Praxis started to make her way along the curl of Monfort, heading in the general direction of the hotel that she had technically already checked in to the previous afternoon, before she'd even gone to see Kaedrich. And this is how, quite by accident, she ended up running into the outskirts of a protest.

She didn't even realize what she'd stumbled into, at first. The outer edges did not appear much different from those of a crowded day, and Praxis's memories of the exact beats and rhythms of the daily streets of Monfort life were, after all, several years out of date by now. Even once the crowds grew thicker, the energy more charged, Praxis was so lost in her own thoughts that it took her a minute to register the change. By the time she did look up—and even then, only because of someone sideswiping her as they shoved by—she was already in the middle of it.

Praxis did not especially like crowds in the best of times, and so a flutter of apprehension passed over her, realizing what she'd stepped into. She had no way of knowing what the protest was about, but regardless of the nature of these people's grievances, she did not exactly relish the idea of finding out the hard way. She considered whistling for Brex; he'd been freely wandering the skies over Monfort ever since they'd disembarked the train, and no doubt would be more than willing to rejoin her if she needed him. But that seemed a bit of an overreaction, at least before anything had actually *happened*.

Instead, she tried to simply extricate herself from the situation. Her first inclination was to backtrack, but there were several problems with this—something she realized as she turned around and faced an equally thick mass of bodies behind her as had been before her.

She shut her eyes for a second, breathing in deeply. It was fine, she had to remember that. The assembly was not out of control, and while there were quite a number of red accessories poking out of coat collars and fluttering freely from hats, the Lanali support (and therefore anti-magic sentiment that inevitably followed) did not seem to be the focus of the gathering.

Which was good, but also slightly troubling in and of itself: if not protesting the free expression of magic in Durland, then what *were* these people so riled up about? For while it was clearly a peaceful protest on the surface, Praxis could feel the bristling frustration that radiated off of these people like waves of heat. She suspected that it would not take much of a spark to set them off. Clenched jaws and raised fists surrounded her in packs, sharp edges and harsh syllables dominating what few snatches of individual conversation she could make out over the general clamor.

And then, down the street, a tiny gap opened up in the crowd. Praxis took it, stumbling for a second as she began to flex her wrist instead of her fingers, but quickly catching up with herself. It was deeper into the center of the group, but also more directly in line with the street that she needed in order to reach her hotel.

But as she drew closer to the center, the purpose of the protests became a little more clear. Groups had erected small platforms out of whatever random supplies had been nearby, and the nearer toward Commons Square she drew, the more people had stepped up to vocalize their grievances. And with it, Praxis felt a certain amount of loosening in the tightness of her chest. It really wasn't anything extraordinary or surprising—most of the protest seemed to be centered around economic difficulties, and poor decisions on the part of the Crown in recent years. All she had to do, then, was inch her way out of the mass of bodies, and that shouldn't take too much longer now that she was passing the heart of the crowd.

She almost let herself believe that she had caught a stroke of luck. Unfortunately, no sooner had she decided that than a bottle went flying over the protesters heads, a flaming rag wedged deeply into its neck.

Chapter Four

$\mathcal{T}$HE CLATTER OF daily life along the streets of Monfort was often so loud and chaotic that a lot of things could go unnoticed. Once, Kaedrich had nearly stumbled over a lost child sobbing for his mother, barreling straight into the poor boy simply because she hadn't heard his cries. Between the horses and carriages, between the hawkers and bell criers, between the people hailing for taxis and yelling at shop boys, between the general conversations that sometimes shouted to be heard, any extra sound had to fight its way through a thick sea of noises.

Several people around Kaedrich winced as a loud caw, like that of a mighty bird of prey, split across the skies of Monfort. One woman gasped as the sight of a small, iridescent blue and silver creature came tumbling out of the sky; but to Kaedrich, the sound and the sight of it only brought a grin to her cheeks. She caught Brex easily, snatching him out of the air just before he could careen into the top of Kaedrich's chest. The woman that had cried out shook her head in disgust, turning and striding off, but today Kaedrich didn't care.

Today, this was exactly what she needed.

"Hey, little fella," Kaedrich said, nuzzling Brex's soft, downy fur against her cheek as the creature chittered happily. Brex rubbed his tiny face along Kaedrich's, sniffing and snuffling as he took in the changes in Kaedrich's scent since the last time they'd seen each other.

The memory of that day still tended to bring a knot to Kaedrich's stomach. She and Praxis had just recently returned to the mainland after thwarting a particularly twisted scheme of Pon Lanali, the aftereffects of which had sent Kaedrich's head reeling. Lanali had somehow tapped into a magic to create what Praxis had later called a "vacant," a creature brought into the world to fulfill a single purpose. In this case, she had crafted the vacant to look like an older version of Praxis Fellows herself, who claimed to be returned from the future via the power of one of the Beacons. This was just after Kaedrich had begun to realize that her feelings toward Praxis were not quite as . . . platonic as she had thought, and to say that the telepathic vacant had taken full advantage of this was an understatement. The woman had spun such an elaborate picture of the future, everything that could (and, as far as Kaedrich knew at the time, definitely *would*) happen between the two of them, that when Kaedrich found out it had all been a lie . . . she hadn't taken it well.

This was when she had decided to come to Monfort. Tuition at Falconridge was an open offer that Kaedrich hadn't yet given Praxis an answer on, but she gave her one easily after that. Kaedrich had needed space to clear her head, to figure out which of her feelings were a result of the vacant's mind games, and which had been genuine. She knew even then that it was the best decision, but that didn't make the parting any easier. She had stood in the train station, handing over Brex's cage, feeling the whole time as if her chest was going to collapse in on itself. Each step as she had walked away had been a monumental effort. Twice on her way to the train, she had almost changed her mind.

Even once she had arrived, the first several days hadn't exactly gone according to plan. For almost three whole weeks, Kaedrich had questioned the wisdom of her choice, every heartbeat telling her one thing, every lucid thought telling her another.

But things had gotten better. She had to remind herself of that suddenly, standing in the middle of the open street, Brex's gentle, trilling purr vibrating across the skin of her cheek. Kaedrich stopped and buried her nose in Brex's thick fur, breathing in his soft musk. And now, look: Brex was here again. *Praxis* was here again. And despite the stress of the day that she'd had so far, this one thought brought a sense of calm to swaddle her up in.

Kaedrich laughed, nudging Brex's nose aside as it continued to dig around at the crook of her neck. "I know—I missed you too, buddy." She pulled Brex away, peering at the creature's mousy ears and wide eyes. He looked the same as he had the last time she'd seen him, the familiar ring of shock-green fur around his snout lending way to nothing but shimmering blue and silver. Velvety wings stretched out happily in the sunshine as Kaedrich scritched her fingers down the length of his spine.

It was a lovely moment, one of those perfect little bubbles where you just want things to stay exactly the same forever. The afternoon sun was out, warming Kaedrich's cheeks, the benign smell of halva vines and fresh leaves tinting the air, and as far as Kaedrich was concerned, time could just pause right there for a few hours. She let out a deep breath, moving over to sit on the lip of a crowded fountain. A girl playing nearby looked over, spotting Brex, and just as she was creeping forward, an eager look on her face, everything shifted all at once.

It might have been a policeman's whistle that first disrupted the scene, or it might have been a shout pounding down from farther up the city. Or it might have been a bristling tension that rippled through the milling crowd. Or a cold breeze, suddenly pouring over the city from the plains to the north.

Or maybe it was nothing tangible, or maybe it was a combination of all of these things, all mixing together at once. But either way, the whole street seemed to pause for a second, reacting to this. And Brex's head snapped up, ears poised and alert, and Kaedrich knew, somehow, before he even vaulted out of her hands, that he was going to.

Something had happened, that much was clear. But now, a cold douse crashed over Kaedrich, because now, as Brex tore into the air and zoomed in the direction of the growing shouts, Kaedrich knew that whatever that something was, it involved Praxis.

IF THERE WAS one change that Kaedrich was always happy she'd made since coming to Monfort, it was this: every morning, or nearly so, she took the time to go for a run.

Kaedrich had always been a fast runner. Between her and her twin brother, the real Kaedrich, it had never been a contest. Kaedrich (then Kaedriella) had longer legs, and had never once gotten tired of using them. The family story was that Kaedrich had learned to walk first, and Kaedriella had responded by learning how to *run* the next day—skipping the tedium of walking altogether.

Over the last several years, ever since the twins had been taken from their home, and Kaedrich had died in the effort of their escape, Kaedriella hadn't run anywhere near as much as she used to. She'd run that night, that terrible night, all the way through the darkness until the sun began to streak the sky. She didn't think that she'd ever be able to *stop* running. Once she did, collapsing at the edge of a farmer's field, it seemed for a long time as if she'd never be able to start again.

But here in Monfort, something had changed. It wasn't just that she was training so hard at the academy, and having strong legs was an asset. One morning, less than a week since her arrival, she had woken up before the dawn, anxious and restless, and running seemed like the only thing that would quiet her mind.

So it was that it didn't take her long to find the source of the commotion. She barreled up the street, her legs pounding the setts as she darted through the scrambling crowds, and before she knew it she was down near the Council's Crescent, and Commons Square.

Of course, it made sense now. Protesters had been gathering in larger and larger numbers at the Square for weeks, and while things were normally peaceful, lately there had been a number of these little eruptions. The only thing that she couldn't immediately understand was what Praxis was doing here, but that didn't really matter at the moment. Kaedrich knew how these sorts of things went, and she knew what was coming next.

She was just lucky she had beaten most of the police in their arrival.

"Praxis!" Kaedrich called out. She couldn't see her yet, but she knew that she had to be here somewhere. She had seen Brex diving into the crowd from above. Kaedrich ducked a swinging elbow as she shoved her way through a mad rush of bodies. Shouts flew thick overhead, along with several bottles that went crashing into the sides of the Crescent; they exploded with a shower of broken glass and fresh flames, licking up the wall wherever the liquid of the bottles had splattered. A *crack!* sounded somewhere nearby, the stale air of gunpowder twisting through the crowd. Kaedrich took a deep breath, smelling for any trace of flowers, and reassured herself when she found none. So that was good: she wouldn't die here, in the chaos.

Not that she was expecting to, but she was always aware of it, on some level. Years ago, Kaedrich had struck a magical bargain to grant her temporary access into the land of the dead, and the price that she'd paid was that her death became a fixed point in time. Nothing she did would help her avoid it, not even if she saw it coming—but Kaedrich did have a slight advantage. She'd found her darkened display, the moment of her death preserved in the land of the dead. It was hidden from view, but the shadows could not contain the smell of it: an exotic flower, which Kaedrich had never encountered in life, mingled with the tang of gunpowder.

It was odd, perhaps, but Kaedrich had lived with it for a long time now, and she'd come to take a certain comfort in this predictability. Danger felt somehow removed, when she would plunge in and find those smells missing.

She was well aware, however, that this did not protect her from getting *injured*. Nor did it protect anyone *else*—namely, certain nosy wizards who liked to go snooping where they didn't belong. Kaedrich jerked to the side as one of the bottles went flying straight past her head. It struck a statue of a man on horseback, and Kaedrich had to leap back to avoid the shower of flames. "Praxis!"

If anyone could hear her at all, it would be a miracle. The odds of Praxis herself hearing it were basically nonexistent, and Kaedrich knew that, even as she shouted for her again, and then again. She scanned the crowd, which was imploding in on itself as half of the people inside seemed to be fighting to get outside, and half of them seemed to be pressing in deeper. Several people were picking up stones and scraps now, hurling them over the heads of the crowd. "—how *that* feels!" someone screamed, right in Kaedrich's ear. She winced, thrown off-balance as someone crashed into her from the opposite side, and it was in this moment that the crowd parted just a fraction, and she saw a slice of a familiar slate-blue coat.

But then the crowd surged and shifted again, legs cutting off the view just as Kaedrich hit the street. Her shoulder crashed into the ground, and she rolled aside only just in time to avoid being trampled. She lurched to the side, grabbing a cane that someone had dropped in the chaos, and launched herself into a sprint. Kaedrich burst through the wall of people, sweeping over the spot where Praxis was crouched on the cold street.

"Back!" Kaedrich shouted, swinging her cane at a particularly thick crowd of people that were running forward, near to Praxis. "Get back!" Another swing, and a circle opened up around Praxis. Brex swept in, flying a tight circuit of the perimeter, his claws and teeth bared.

"Kaedrich! What are—?"

"Thank me later," Kaedrich snapped. She ducked and helped Praxis back to her feet—it seemed that something of the new system to control her leg had been damaged, and though she could walk, it more closely resembled a drunken stagger.

At least Praxis had retained enough sense not to use too much obvious magic in fending off the mad rush of people around them. Kaedrich took a small comfort in this as she passed Praxis the cane, even if her next thought was a flutter of panic at seeing a deep cut running straight across Praxis's forehead. Praxis reached up, probably intending to heal it, but Kaedrich retrieved her handkerchief and pressed it fast against Praxis's injury. "Not here. Don't argue, just follow me," Kaedrich said as she passed the job of holding the handkerchief in place over to Praxis. She wrapped her arm protectively around Praxis's shoulders as she turned her attention to the challenge of getting them out of the crowd.

Police whistles were drawing in fast now, along with the whinny of horses to announce the arrival of the Crown's royal guards. Kaedrich's attention flew from one end of the chaos to the other, trying to spot the most likely means of a successful escape.

It wasn't particularly graceful, or the most direct route that they could have taken. But in the midst of the situation, they had little options. Kaedrich guided them through the throng, ducking into whatever gaps presented themselves. Most people were bolting now, unwilling to be around once the arrests began. The guardsmen were shouting, ordering people to stay where they were—one of them had retrieved a pistol, and actually began to take potshots at some of the retreating backs. Kaedrich darted to the side, dragging Praxis along with her.

There was no way they were getting all the way back to Crestview Hotel, where Praxis was staying, and Kaedrich's apartment was even farther away. But there was one place. She jerked them aside, ducking away into a side alley just off the edge of the square.

"What in the seven hells was all that about?" Praxis asked, as soon as they were out of the worst of the crowd. A number of people were also pouring down this direction, shoving their way roughly past the pair of them as they staggered forward.

Kaedrich just shook her head. She didn't normally approach the theater district from this direction, and she needed to pay attention to the back of each building if she was going to find the correct one.

"Here—down here," she said finally. She turned both of them around, retreating down a short set of steps to a basement-level door. Kaedrich pounded furiously, sending a silent prayer to Perlandra that Tristy would be home.

No one answered, though, and Kaedrich gritted her teeth. She pounded on the door again, muttering underneath her breath.

Praxis, meanwhile, was peeping her head up over the lip of the street. "Kaedrich . . . ," she started, an obvious sharp edge of nervousness to her voice. Her Yandosian accent was slipping in, the "aed" sound of Kaedrich's name even more chopped than usual. A police whistle cut down the alley, which was fast emptying out.

And then, mercifully, the door was thrown open from the inside. "Kaedrich!" Tristy cried, as Brex swept past her head into the room beyond. "What in the darkness—?"

"No time," Kaedrich said. Tristy jumped out of the way, and Kaedrich led Praxis inside.

Brex was waiting for them, flying a tight circle around the ceiling, chittering madly.

Tristy snapped the door shut behind them, drawing the bolt firmly into place. "Please tell me that thing isn't carrying some disease," Tristy said, and Brex squawked in protest.

Kaedrich shuffled across the room, her mind running in a thousand different ways at once. The answer came automatically, "He's harmless." She knew without having to turn around that Tristy was glowering at the lot of them, but she decided to ignore this for the moment.

"Here," Kaedrich said, easing Praxis over to a worn but comfortable chair in the corner. "There, that should do for now." She took a deep breath and a step back, her head light from the adrenaline.

Brex fluttered down, settling easily in Praxis's lap. Praxis was looking up curiously at Kaedrich now, and she wasn't the only one. Tristy had moved to the side, just far enough to be within Kaedrich's field of view, her arms crossed over her chest. Kaedrich knew she probably owed them both explanations, but it felt impossible to know where to start just then.

"I'm sorry," Kaedrich said, for lack of any better opener. "I didn't know where else to go. We got caught up in the protests."

"Yeah, I kind of gathered that," Tristy said. She glanced back and forth between Praxis and Kaedrich. "The question is what either of you were doing there in the first place. I don't know about *you*," she said, pointing directly at Praxis, "but Kaedrich, you know better than to get involved with them."

Despite herself, Kaedrich felt her cheeks warm. "I . . . wasn't."

"And I don't even know who they *were*," Praxis snapped. "So whatever judgment you're trying to make about me right now, I'd appreciate it if you'd stop."

"Oh, sure, insult me in my own dressing room," Tristy said. "That's a sure way to endear yourself to someone you've just met."

Kaedrich winced. "Tristy—"

Tristy threw her hands up. Her braid swished behind her. "No. I don't have time for this. I'm due upstairs. You two settle whatever it is you need to settle, but by the time I get back, I expect you both to be gone. I can't afford to get involved in anything. Understood?"

Kaedrich nodded. She hadn't stopped to think about the time, and in their rush she hadn't even noticed the fact that Tristy was already dressed in her stage costume—a skimpy dress of silks that she hated, because it showed off the curve of her belly and because she wasn't even from the right culture to be wearing it, but her manager had insisted that she looked "close enough." *Oh gods,* Kaedrich thought suddenly, *What is Praxis going to think?* Kaedrich couldn't help but see the room afresh now: gauzy curtains strung in dipped patterns across the stretch of the ceiling, every spare bit of floorspace devoted to racks of costumes covered in feathers and shimmering faux-silks. There was a vanity in a corner, the tabletop full of thick makeups and strong perfumes. A single daybed rested in the other corner, although Kaedrich suspected that it served as Tristy's regular bed as well—she could never have afforded a separate apartment on the pitiful excuse for a salary that the pub upstairs gave her each night.

Tristy walked off in a huff, layers of thin skirts swishing in time with her hair. The skirts were hitched up higher than normal fashion allowed, showing what was often considered a scandalous amount of calf and ankle, which Tristy wrapped in bright ribbons that spooled up from her slippers. The door clicked shut behind her.

"It's not—we're not—" Kaedrich started, and then she stumbled to a halt.

"You don't have to explain; I'm not your mother." Praxis had already peeled the handkerchief off of her forehead and was pressing her fingers against the cut, sealing it up underneath her touch.

"I know, but . . . we're friends. Tristy and me. We haven't . . . she doesn't even know."

Praxis raised an eyebrow, watching Kaedrich evenly.

Kaedrich bit her lip, curling her shoulders forward. Praxis was right: she didn't have to explain. But she could also see perfectly well how it might look, Kaedrich knowing exactly how to get here, barging in on someone that she was obviously close to. It didn't matter, of course. Praxis was entitled to think whatever she wanted.

Kaedrich sighed. She walked over and sat on the wobbly stool in front of Tristy's vanity. Her elbow knocked several bottles together as she leaned against it, but she didn't even care.

"So, what's with the protests?"

"What, you really don't know?" Kaedrich asked. The idea almost struck her as funny. She had just assumed that Praxis had gone on purpose, that she was nosing about where she probably shouldn't be. The idea of her just happening to stumble across the most volatile part of Monfort at the moment was almost incomprehensible.

Praxis drew her hand away from her forehead—the skin was smooth underneath, if still streaked with patches of bright red blood. "In case you haven't noticed, I wasn't exactly in the position to be up to date on the latest gossip until very recently."

"Then what are you doing here?"

"Excuse me?"

"In Monfort," Kaedrich said. "If you're not here because of . . . well, everything that's happened recently—with the Society, and the protests, and everything . . . then why?"

Praxis frowned. "I came to see you, of course."

"Okay, now we *both* know that's not true."

"Why?" Praxis snapped, "I can't visit simply for the sake of visiting?"

Kaedrich sighed. She ran her hand across her face. This wasn't going even remotely the way that she'd wanted it to. "I didn't say that . . ." And of course, Kaedrich would have loved to believe that there was no other reason for Praxis's visit. But her wishes and fantasies did not shape reality, and no matter how much she wanted to accept this idea at face value, she knew Praxis too well.

There was always something more.

Praxis heaved a weary sigh. "All right, *fine*, so . . . maybe there's a second reason why I'm here, too, but that doesn't mean that I wouldn't have visited *anyway.*"

And there it was. Kaedrich felt the sting of it, numbed only because it was expected. But that was fine, of course it was—it's not as if it mattered anyway. She drew herself up straight upon her stool. *The first rule of combat is that half of the battle is won with your face,* she thought, her inner voice echoing one of her instructors' favorite mantras. Kaedrich felt herself start to frown, puzzled by the idea that she'd remember something like that now, but caught herself. *Half the battle.* Her face relaxed.

"And this other reason is?"

"Oh, it's nothing to do with the protesters," Praxis said, waving her off. "That really was just bad timing on my part."

"Okay, then what *does* it have to do with?"

Gods, Kaedrich had forgotten just how difficult it could be sometimes, to get a single honest answer out of Praxis's mouth.

Praxis hesitated. She leaned over, lifting up the cuff of her trousers enough to examine a little bit of the mechanism she'd wrapped her leg in.

"Praxis."

She prodded at a gear by her ankle, fingers pinching in to adjust the tension by hand.

"*Praxis.*"

"Please don't ask me," Praxis said. She dropped her work, wincing as she sat up. "Seriously, please just . . . just don't get involved. I don't want you involved."

The first hints of a flush began to creep into the edges of Kaedrich's cheeks. Of *course* Praxis didn't want her getting involved. It shouldn't have been a surprise, and yet it was. It shouldn't have stung, and yet it did.

Kaedrich took a second, took a breath. Patience and composure, equally valuable as swords and strategy—that was another lesson, one Kaedrich had learned well and many of her classmates had not. She willed the blood to retreat from her face, forced her hackles to settle.

It would be one thing if it was just a matter of privacy. Kaedrich could easily respect the idea of Praxis keeping things to herself because they were too personal (though they both knew so many of each other's secrets that even that would be a little silly). But Kaedrich knew better by now. No, this was clearly something that Praxis *wanted* to discuss, but was holding herself back from. Kaedrich had seen that look too many times, in too many places. And, frankly, she was getting tired of it.

"I thought that we would be past this by now," Kaedrich said, and when she got nothing in response save for a quizzical look she added, "Hiding things to protect me? I mean, what was the point of sending me to the academy if not to prove that I could handle myself?"

Praxis sat back, eyes wide. "You think that's why I've been paying for this?"

"Honestly, I don't really *know* why."

"But . . . I told you: when I first offered, I said that you've always wanted to know how to defend yourself. You *wanted* to go!"

"I know," Kaedrich said. "And I'm happy I did, I'm not arguing that. It's just . . . if even *this* doesn't prove—"

"Kaedrich, you never had to prove anything to me."

"You say that, but you still don't trust me enough to tell me what's going on."

"I—" Praxis started, and then abruptly stopped.

Once, when Kaedrich was Kaedriella and the twins were very small, a pigeon had gotten into the cottage where they had all recently started living with their mother's new lover, Trimmis. Kaedrich and Kaedriella had shrieked with delight as they'd chased it around the tiny rooms, the bird squawking and shitting all over the place as Trimmis ran for a blanket to pin it beneath. By the time he got back, though, the twins had cornered the bird in an open cupboard. They had been delighted by the experience, thinking it a marvelous game, and it wasn't until Kaedriella had seen the trapped bird's face that she'd understood. It stared out at them, its small chest heaving, beady eyes darting for any possible escape route.

It wasn't entirely dissimilar from the look that Praxis was giving her now. Pinned beneath Kaedrich's level gaze, she squirmed in the seat of her chair, discomfort radiating from every twitch of her muscles. By turns, Praxis picked at her nails, studied the ceiling, cleared her throat, and scritched the top of Brex's sleeping head.

When she did finally speak, she addressed her comments to a blanket folded across the armrest of her chair. "I'm not trying to shut you out from this. But you've built yourself a comfortable life here, and I didn't come to mess it up for you." Praxis's thumb idly traced her scar as she spoke, the irritated-looking circle and the triangle that she had once said was supposed to represent a wing, though she wouldn't say why.

The silence that followed was absolute, or at least it felt that way to Kaedrich. Intellectually, she knew that there must still be the stomp of constant footsteps on the ceiling, a sprinkling of music slipping in from upstairs, the faint whistle of wind against the not-quite-sealed windows. But to Kaedrich, someone may as well have boxed her ears. She was just as unbalanced, her head spinning with what she knew had been the fatal blow of the conversation. She had forgotten her instructor's other favorite: *block where you least expect it.*

Kaedrich could think of nothing to say to this, at least not immediately. She hadn't thought about it before, but now she realized that she had just assumed, the instant she'd spotted Praxis back in the apartment, that this was the beginning of another one of their insane adventures together. She was partially right: whatever Praxis was up to, it would probably drag her in deeper than she'd intended, it would probably be dangerous, it would probably spiral into some madcap series of events that she'd be lucky to escape unharmed. The difference was that, for once, Praxis wasn't just automatically dragging Kaedrich in behind her. That for once, Kaedrich may have had something else going on in her life, something worth protecting, even if it meant sitting this one out.

She wasn't sure how she felt about that, and the discomfort it brought made *her* want to squirm in her seat. But she kept herself steady and still, one arm resting on the vanity to ground her in time and place.

"Well . . . you really should try to be more careful," Kaedrich said finally. "Monfort isn't a safe haven anymore, and just because you're the Lady of Souls, that doesn't mean that you can't be killed."

"I will."

Kaedrich nodded. "Right, then."

They waited in Tristy's dressing room for another few minutes after that. In near silence, except to establish that, yes, it was probably long enough for the square to have quieted by now, and yes, despite that it would probably still be a good idea to let themselves out through the building rather than straight back into the alley. Neither one really looked at the other when they could avoid it. Praxis washed her forehead with a cloth that Kaedrich found for her, their hands lingering for a second too long as she passed it over.

Praxis was probably taking Kaedrich's silence on the matter as an agreement to stay out of Praxis's business, and several times Kaedrich took a breath, almost ready to argue the point. But she always caught herself at the last second. It wasn't that Kaedrich necessarily *did* agree that she was better off staying out of it, but she could not quite bring herself to dismiss that Praxis might have been right. That there were things in Kaedrich's life worth protecting, that what she'd built shouldn't necessarily be thrown aside. And until she was sure, she wasn't going to jeopardize things by being too curious.

So she led Praxis up through the theater, skirting around the bar and the stage in the corner where Tristy was dancing someone else's native dance, and out to the front steps. In the dwindling afternoon sunlight, they made noises about arranging to meet up for an ordinary coffee and breakfast . . . sometime. They shook hands, all professional and courteous. And when Kaedrich stuffed her hands into her pockets and set off down the street, she knew without even turning back that Praxis was heading in the opposite direction. She heard the flutter of Brex's wings, once, or maybe it had just been her imagination; but then a shrill whistle cut up the lane, and the fluttering darted off.

Which was fine. In fact, it was probably as it should be.

Probably.

Pon Lanali sat alone in the room for a long time after her guest had departed.

In and of itself, this wasn't unusual. The Pon, while having graciously opened up her house to the needs of her most loyal followers, was fond of solitude and often spent many hours sequestered away from the attentions of her devotees. The places that she chose for being alone varied from week to week, day to day, but by this point everyone was used to her numerous quirks, her routine of meditations and special posing, her midday nap—her temper whenever someone new dared to cross the threshold. In the manner of children, the people in Dreamfield House had learned to sense when their parental figure needed space, and no one dared to approach unless the circumstances were truly dire.

This particular evening, she had already suffered through one dire interruption, and now she stood at the window, looking out at the grounds, and tried to figure out how to proceed from here.

The news wasn't good.

But it also wasn't surprising.

Lanali considered the situation as the sun began to sink below the distant horizon. From the house's position at the crest of the hills, you could see all the way out into Abbney Bay and the Violet Seas beyond. The harbor was dotted with tiny ships, colorful sails darting to and fro like butterflies flitting from place to place. The lip that made up the hills of Monfort sloped down to and underneath the water, creating a ridge just along the edge of the bay—there was a gap only twelve feet tall for vessels to pass over, and so no large ships could maneuver across it. This left the waters surrounded by Monfort's embrace open to leisure sport only, and the nobility of the region had taken to it with gusto. Not a day went by that the bay wasn't filled with the little ships, acting so self-important, preening and posturing for everyone else to see.

Lanali's lip curled up as she watched the sailing ships far below. She detested the water, and sailing in particular. It reminded her too much of where she came from, and everything she had fought so hard to escape.

She reached up and snapped the heavy velvet curtains shut. Then, turning on her heel, she marched out of the room.

The halls of Dreamfield House were bustling, and almost immediately the Pon was accosted with someone trying to get her attention. Lanali stopped, clasping her hands together and swaying side to side in greeting, a motion that was mimicked right back to her. Despite the dire situation, there were still images to uphold, still devotion to maintain. Her followers were like a garden, and only careful tending would maintain the beauty of everything that she had cultivated.

"My Pon," this follower began—he was a tidy man, a banker or a solicitor, she couldn't remember which, "when you have a moment, there is a matter in the solar that requires your attention."

Lanali smiled beatifically from behind her black lace veil. "Indeed. Will attend in a moment, please."

Gods, Lanali was getting tired of the stilted speech that she'd adopted in the early days. It made sense at the time, when she'd needed to be seen as exotic, though by now its time had passed. She'd been trying to phase it out, but such a process had to be done gradually—as if she was finally learning the quirks of Durlish grammar—so as not to arouse suspicion.

The tidy man nodded, so fast that Lanali might have feared for the safety of his frail neck. "Yes, my Pon. Thank you, my Pon. I will await you there."

"Do, please," Lanali said, already moving on down the hall.

She passed through the house, nodding at those that looked up, pausing to exchange her clasped greetings with those that approached. Thankfully, most of her followers were absorbed in worshipful meditations, kneeling in small clusters as they chanted low melodies to themselves. The corridors were thick with burning incense, the walls covered in sweeps of red bunting. The occasional bust or painting provided the only décor, art that she had specially commissioned: scenes of war and death and torment intermingled with idyllic depictions of forests dappled in light and poppy fields. None of the pictures venerated—or even showed—the Pon herself. She had considered it, but ultimately ruled it out. She did not want anyone to accuse her of trying to position herself as the head of a cult of personality, even if that was in some ways exactly what she was attempting to do.

Rule four: if the story is all about them, they'll never question it.

Lanali went up the stairs, where the air was thinner and the halls were quieter. She burned no incense here, since hardly anyone spent their time in the libraries and studies that made up most of the third floor. Slowly, Lanali was removing books one by one, for what was the point in reading them? If you lived here, you had direct access to the great Pon herself—she was the only source of wisdom and guidance that most of these people trusted anymore, having lost faith in gods and governments alike. It would have been sad, Lanali supposed, if it wasn't so incredibly useful.

The fourth floor was even more empty, mostly servants' quarters long since abandoned. Everything in the house was tended to by the followers themselves, their way of paying back to the collective group. Only on this level did the air finally clear of all the burning scents, and Lanali paused at the top of the stairs to take a deep breath. True, she did regularly drink a tonic of merriweed and mallen extract to counterbalance the somewhat soporific effects of the poppy oil that her incense had been soaked in, but that didn't mean that she enjoyed the smell. Stepping up here, she felt more clearheaded than she had all day. She supposed that must be why he'd chosen this place for his quarters, for she could think of no other reason to shun the immaculate luxuries of the rest of the house.

She strode down the narrow hallway, heels clacking against the uneven wood slats.

Only one of the rooms was occupied these days. It was at the end of a long hallway, as far from the rest of the household as possible. Lanali had never been here before, but she knew from rumors where she would find it, and so find it she had. The door was cracked open, a slice of candlelight cutting into the otherwise darkened corridor.

Lanali did not bother to knock as she let herself into the room. She shut the door swiftly behind her, and only the sound of it clicking into place drew the attention of the room's single occupant.

Tol lifted his head, annoyance instantly replaced by shock at the sight of the Pon.

He leapt to his feet. "Lanali!" He lurched forward, around the lip of the writing desk that he'd been sitting at. His foot caught the corner of the desk, dragging it along with a loud screech of metal on wood floor.

By the time he collected himself, Lanali had already crossed the room. There was little furniture: the desk, a bookshelf, a chest. A tree, growing straight up out of the floor. Its upper branches twisted against the slant of the ceiling. The sturdiest branch, however, came out of the middle of the trunk and protruded just far enough into the room to accommodate the girth of an enormous pod hanging down from it like a teardrop ready to fall.

Lanali stopped just short of it, reaching out to run her palm along the supple surface of the palla pod. "I can't imagine why you go through such effort to maintain this," she said, even as she parted the gap running as a seam down the belly of the pod and climbed in.

She had to hitch her skirts way up around her knees just to scramble through the opening, and even once inside, it felt as if she was wearing far too much clothing for it. It was as if there was suddenly too much bustle and lace, the high collar of her dress choking her as her back curled against the rear wall of the pod. It wasn't as if Lanali ever found the palla pods of their shared homeland particularly comfortable or enjoyable anyway— why would you want to curl up on yourself like a babe in the womb, when you could sprawl out luxuriantly on flat mattresses like the rest of the world?—but this was ridiculous. She was drowning in here, smothered to death by her own clothes.

"Here, please, my Pon, take my seat," Tol was already saying as he helped her back out of the pod. Lanali straightened up, brushing out her skirts. She nodded crisply, settling at Tol's little writing desk as he easily replaced her in the palla pod bed.

For a moment, there was silence. Tol would never rush her, and while Lanali knew that she was wasting time, she didn't really want to admit the problem out loud, not yet. She took a moment to remove her veil, resting it smack dab in the middle of the writing desk. A single candle, used down to a mere stub by now, burned gently in the corner. Lanali twisted her fingers above the flame, teasing a thread of fire out from the rest.

"I've just heard a disturbing rumor," Lanali said finally. The thread of fire twisted harmlessly over her hand, weaving in and out between her fingers. "It's possible that Praxis Fellows has been spotted in Monfort."

She waited to see how Tol would react to this, but he didn't say anything on the matter at first. When Lanali looked over he was just sitting in his palla pod, one leg tucked up comfortably against his chest, the other trailing out, his foot swinging freely over the floor.

The timing of this could not have been worse. Lanali finally had just about all the support that she needed to make her move. Lord Hendril, her stooge in the Governance Council, had just managed to finish getting his committee to approve the appointments that would fill the last seats in the Commoner's Arm—all of them staunch proponents of the Pon's teachings, all of them loyal to a fault. They would begin their terms as soon as the Council returned from spring recess, in three weeks time. Lanali had that long to finish tying off the loose ends: perfecting her magical experiments, swaying the last voice in the King's Court of State, her final arrangements with Captain Montrey. She did not have time for this distraction.

"Well?" Lanali snapped. "Didn't you hear me?"

"I heard you. I'm just not surprised. I told you, years ago, that my research suggested that the only reason why she didn't ever return to Monfort was by decree of the Society."

Lanali bristled. "So this is *my* fault?"

"I'm not assigning blame, my Pon. This was one of the risks of encouraging the vote for their disbandment. We cannot lose our heads now that the Fellows contingency has come to pass."

The flames over Lanali's hand flared, burning themselves out in a single burst of light. She clenched her fingers through the lingering wisps of smoke. She glared at Tol, but he just stared back at her, calm as an ocean breeze. He'd been growing his hair out for the past couple of years, the braids that used to just brush his shoulders now teasing several inches down the top of his chest. His hands were clasped casually around the knee that was drawn up in front of him, a simple line-drawing tattoo of a curling wave stamped onto the back of his left hand.

There was a time that he would have withered underneath such a look from Lanali—and not just because she was the great and venerated Pon. No, he had been there from the beginning, when Lanali was just Frel, a little waif of a girl lost in the scattered islands of Aul. She didn't have anything in those days, no power or respect, no money or property, and yet when she commanded him to follow her, he'd listened without a second thought. He did not dare to question her wisdom, even when she'd had none.

"Very well," Lanali said; it felt like breaking a standoff. "If you're so prepared for this contingency, then tell me what you're going to do about it."

Tol shook his head. "Oh, that's easy." He stretched his arm out, tracing the line of a scar that marred the otherwise flawless skin of his elbow. When Tol clenched his fist, as he did now, the scar bulged out like a vein. "We kill her, of course."

Chapter Five

KAEDRICH STOOD ON the front steps of the Lebules' townhouse, struggling to catch her breath before the door opened.

She couldn't believe that she'd forgotten.

Actually, she could—she just didn't like to accept it. Quite apart from her desire not to hurt Lyana's feelings, she hated to consider what this would do to her social standing if Lyana decided to take serious offense—a distinct possibility, and one Kaedrich wouldn't be able to blame her for, if it came to pass. Kaedrich waited, her chest heaving, her legs burning, and all the while she was chewing her lip down to the base.

If Marlick hadn't come home and reminded her . . .

She hated to think about it. It was bad enough to run here hours late, racing the setting sun as she dodged traffic through the city streets; if she'd forgotten completely, and had run into Lyana the next day, or the next, or dear gods a *week* later, Kaedrich did not think that any apology would have been enough. Which had been a distinct possibility. Kaedrich had been settled behind her desk, half-buried underneath a mountain of work that she'd neglected over the last day or so, and she hadn't even noticed the time as Marlick arrived back. When he asked her how "it" had gone, Kaedrich had started, instantly remembering the protests, her conversation in Tristy's dressing room. It wasn't until

Marlick had expressly mentioned Lyana's name that Kaedrich remembered setting up an appointment over tea, in her haste to get Lyana from her apartment the previous day.

Had it really only been the previous day? It felt as if Praxis had already been here for a month.

The door cracked open. A gray-faced butler peered down, a pair of pince-nez perched on the bridge of his nose. He took barely a single look in Kaedrich's direction before he turned his interest to a lamppost across the street. "Yes?"

"Can you tell Miss Lebule that Kaedrich Mannly is here?"

"Does this Mr. Mannly have a card?"

Kaedrich was already patting down her pockets, before the question was even asked. The butler waited, idly watching the comings-and-goings of the street. Kaedrich had ordered a small set of calling cards from the stationers about a month before, when she'd gone in to buy replacement stationery for her letters. She didn't think that she'd ever have much use for them, but with her association with Lucan now turning somewhat toward friendship, it had seemed a reasonable course of action.

And it was—assuming that she'd remembered to bring them.

Which, of course, she hadn't.

Kaedrich winced, slumping as she realized that a pile of them was still wrapped neatly in a bundle in the drawer of her desk. "Blast," she muttered under her breath.

The butler was stepping back, one hand already poised to shut the door. "If there will be nothing else . . ."

"No, wait!" Kaedrich stuck her hand out, blocking the door. "Wait, please, I have to talk to Lyana."

"Not without the proper protocols, you won't."

"Fine," Kaedrich said. "Fine, just . . . just hang on, one second."

The butler raised an eyebrow, his hand still on the edge of the door. But he waited, as Kaedrich rummaged again through the pockets of her suit coat. She held up one finger, wait, as she pulled out a tiny leather notebook and flipped it open. With a pencil stub that was wedged in the top, Kaedrich scrawled out a brief note: *Kaedrich Mannly, come to beg Lyana Lebule's forgiveness.*

She ripped the paper out, folded it crisply in half, and pressed it into the butler's hand.

The butler stared at the scrap of white, incredulousness easily readable on his open face. "You cannot expect *this* to—"

"Please just give it to her. Let her decide."

The butler tutted, shaking his head. "Wait a moment," he said, easing the door over. "I do not imagine that the lady will be inclined to accept you, but I will . . . present it."

"Thank y—" Kaedrich started, but the door clicked shut in her face.

Kaedrich let out a low breath, whistling through her teeth. Fresh flowers bloomed in boxes to either side of the door, taunting her with their perfume—but they were not *her* flowers, the ones that would carry her into the arms of death. Kaedrich looked away from them. She stuffed her hands in the pockets of her suit coat, and stepped back to the farthest edge of the front stoop. From here she could crane her neck up to see the upper windows, one of which was probably Lyana's bedroom. If she could figure out which one, could she come back later, somehow get Lyana's attention? Kaedrich scoffed at herself—what did she think that she was going to do, throw a stone and serenade Lyana from the streets?

A flutter of motion caught her attention, a curtain ruffling from one of the windows that she'd been spying. Kaedrich ran down the steps, moving up the street to the left to get closer.

But there was nothing else. The curtain lay still beyond the glass, and even if it was a person rather than, say, the family cat, they were gone now.

She was just reaching the bottom of the front steps again when the door opened once more. The gray-faced butler looked down at Kaedrich as if she was something unpleasant that had been scraped off of a shoe and left on the stoop as a commentary of the family. But he nodded, and stepped aside to allow room for Kaedrich to slip past. His pince-nez, Kaedrich noted, were gripped firm between his fingers, and as Kaedrich entered the main hall the butler drew out a stark-white handkerchief and began to clean the lenses aggressively. He paused only long enough to close the door behind Kaedrich, and then he was off, his shoes clicking against the immaculate tile of the foyer.

It didn't take long to reach a drawing room. It was smaller than the one in Brindlewood, but equally if not more beautifully appointed. The gas lamps had already been lit, giving the room a purposeful, cozy air, and a fire crackled merrily underneath the mosaic-tiled hearth.

Lyana was perched on the edge of the sofa, her attentions fastidiously buried in the spine of a book. She was all that Kaedrich saw, as she stepped into the room, already beginning. "Lyana, I'm sorry, I didn't—"

And then she stopped, spying a man tucked away at a writing desk in the corner. Older and expertly styled, his white hair swept back in exactly the same fashion that Lucan wore. He was engaged with the process of writing, his attention apparently on his work, but Kaedrich found her apology drying up in her throat. She wasn't expecting an audience.

Lyana glanced up, folding the book lightly around her finger. "I believe that you had something you wished to say to me, Mr. Mannly?"

Kaedrich drew her attention away from the man in the corner. If she focused on Lyana, perhaps she could pretend they were alone? It wasn't, after all, as if she had any particularly personal secrets to reveal; still, the extra listener dragged on her mind.

"Um, yes," Kaedrich said, smoothing out her vest. She folded her hands neatly in front of her, then realized it probably looked slightly feminine, and switched them to resting idly at her back.

If Lyana noticed any of this, she made no motion of it. She appeared, if anything, slightly bored by the whole exchange, and while normally Kaedrich might be encouraged by the idea of losing her interest, she had no desire to offend.

"Lyana—Miss Lebule—I am truly sorry that I was not able to make our appointment this afternoon. I ask that you consider extending your legendary generosity in my direction. I, um . . . I realize that my extreme tardiness is inexcusable, but . . . circumstances—"

Lyana gave a dainty huff. "'Circumstances.' I'd rather not hear excuses, if it's all the same to you. I'm disappointed, Kaedrich. I thought that you were a man of your word."

"I am," Kaedrich said, lurching out of the guiding hand of the butler, who had stepped forward. Kaedrich shot him a quick glare before she turned back to Lyana. "I was caught up in the edge of the protests in Commons Square—I did not mean to neglect—"

"What?" Lyana had nearly dropped her book, and now she scrambled to retrieve it. She deposited it hastily on a frilly end table, her wide eyes sparkling once more when they next returned to Kaedrich.

Blast.

"Oh, but you didn't get hurt, did you?" Lyana asked. She scooted to one side, reaching out to lead Kaedrich to sit beside her. Kaedrich tried to keep her knees from knocking against Lyana or one of the many tables sitting within easy reach. Lyana gripped Kaedrich's hands. "I heard about what happened! Oh! You're so brave to be standing here as if it was nothing at all!"

Kaedrich winced at the praise. She stole a glance at the man at the writing desk, but he did not apparently care about this turn of events. She could not say the same for the butler, but there was nothing to be done about that now.

"It's . . . really nothing," Kaedrich said. "I wasn't really *involved*, I was just . . . in the wrong place at the wrong time. I wasn't hurt."

"Of course not! No man studying at Falconridge would ever be caught unprepared—would they, papa?" This last question she directed over her shoulder, where the man at the writing desk gave a grunt that didn't seem to indicate either agreement or dissent.

Kaedrich nodded. "Right, well . . . I'm relieved there are no harsh feelings."

"Oh, not at all! On the contrary, I feel simply terrible that you were out there defending yourself and those around you, and here I was feeling jilted! And you missed tea; oh, there must be something that we can do about that. Won't you stay for dinner, instead?"

"I . . . ," Kaedrich started, but then her tongue simply froze up inside of her mouth. She found herself looking expectantly at Lyana's father in the corner, perhaps waiting for him to swoop in and declare that the whole idea was a terrible breach of form. She was suddenly hyper aware of the cheaper material of her suit, the fact that her emerald cufflinks were the only ones that she wore day in and day out, of the minor scuff on the toe of her shoe. Surely, if Mr. Lebule would only turn around, he would immediately forbid it? "I would hate to impose," Kaedrich said finally, the only thing that she could think to say.

Lyana laughed. "Nonsense. We're having no other guests for dinner —we're not even bothering to change this evening. I'm sure that it would be fine. Wouldn't it, papa?"

She turned once again, twisting to see over the back of the sofa.

Finally, finally, Mr. Lebule looked up. He did not even bother setting his pen down, glancing only barely in the direction of the two of them. When he saw Kaedrich, his eyebrow quirked up, and Kaedrich breathed a silent sigh of relief.

But, to Kaedrich's shock, Mr. Lebule only shrugged. "I suppose."

Lyana turned back, beaming, her hands clasped happily in front of her. "I'd say that's settled then!"

"Yes," Kaedrich said. She felt her shoulders begin to sag, and forced them back in line. "I suppose it is."

A LOT OF things went into making up the smells of Monfort—everything from horse shit to baked bread, from wet dogs to ladies' perfumes— and the smells varied up and down the great slopes that led from the rim to the bay. But cutting underneath it all, laying the foundation for every scent that would come later, was always the smell of the bay itself. The salt water had a particular edge here, attributed by most to the flora that grew nestled in the curve of the harbor. It was a tang that most people described as a kind of honey-lime mix. It was the first thing that visitors commented on, and the biggest thing that people missed when they moved away.

This pleasing bedrock did not make it over the lip of the ring of Monfort, however, and the ragged slopes that cut down to the plains beyond were full of their own special aroma: stale dirt and sweat, cheap whiskey and the tonic they splashed on cheaper whores; and if the season was right, the nose-curling stench of sugar beets being pulped and boiled twenty miles away.

Luckily for Praxis, the season was not yet right. She had experienced that particular horror once in her life, and that was more than enough.

The pub called Willy's took some time to find. Even when she did stop someone to ask for directions, more often than not they only led her in a circle, as the layout of the old quarter was notoriously twisted up on itself. It was as if someone had thrown a ball of yarn on the floor, sketched out the pattern, and then laid the roads to match. So it was well after eight when Praxis finally spotted the place, noticing it only because the loose sign that was sitting half out of a rain barrel started with a *W*.

It was a pitiful excuse for a pub, but around these parts that didn't stop it from being packed. Praxis elbowed her way through the crowd, holding her breath when she passed some of Willy's riper patrons.

Weevish was nowhere to be seen.

Praxis took a few more turns around the room, spying as best as she could underneath low-brimmed hats and the occasional outdated cloak, and mentally checking everyone off in turn. Too fat, too young, a woman, missing a hand. After three circuits, she was almost ready to go up to the bar to ask a discreet question or two when she spotted it: a single white Cloak and Crowns piece, resting on a high piece of wood that ran along the wall as a support beam.

She palmed it and made her way back outside. She did not even have to look closely at it to tell which piece he'd left. The curve of a serpent's head was unmistakable—the Spymaster, one of the pieces from the board's Court of Intrigue. Praxis wasn't sure entirely how to take the symbolism of Weevish's choice, but she knew that it was not chosen at random. The piece was one of the most valuable and dangerous ones in the game, so much so that if you were able to turn an opponent's Spymaster into a traitor, you were almost guaranteed to be the winner.

But while the piece was obviously supposed to send Praxis a message, she knew that the *real* message was buried somewhere deep inside. Now the only thing that she would need was a private corner.

Fortunately, such shady nooks and crannies were in plentiful supply in the old quarter. Most streets did not even have a single lamp to their name, and those that did were usually not lit. Praxis tucked herself into the shadows in a gap beside Willy's, and held the Cloak and Crowns piece to her face. "Praxis Fellows," she whispered to it. "And . . ."

Praxis frowned. A puzzlebox letter was opened with the names of the recipient and the sender, and never once had Praxis bothered to learn Weevish's first name. But he must have known that, too, surely? She remembered the name plaque in front of his house, *P. V.* She only had one chance to get it right, or else the piece would turn to ashes.

She took a deep breath. "Chief-Clerk Weevish," she said on a whim, and leapt back as the serpentine Spymaster began to glow hot in her hand. She nearly dropped it out of instinct, but she made herself clutch it tighter, even as the piece began to burn into her skin. Praxis bit her lip to keep from crying out, the familiar smell of charred flesh starting to fight through the stench of the street. As if in response, the heat underneath her wrist turned over and raced faster along its tight design.

And then, in a flash, it was over. The Cloak and Crowns piece turned cold, and Praxis dropped it onto the streets, clutching her hand against herself as she rode out the remaining pain. Only once it had subsided a fraction was she able to uncurl her fingers. She summoned a flame with her free hand, just large enough to see by, and held it gently over the white expanse of her palm. There, in searing red letters, unfamiliar handwriting made up a single word: *tandalla.*

It was Yandosian, and Praxis had to admit that she was impressed by the effort. The rough translation was something like "timepiece," although instantly she understood that Weevish had not meant just any clock.

Praxis sighed; it was a long walk back to the crest of the city, and she had already been on her feet most of the day. But she knew that she was going to have to play his game if there was any hope of getting the information that she needed out of him, and so Praxis scooped the Cloak and Crowns piece back up and set off. She ran one hand over the other as she walked, the skin of her burned palm first warming and then cooling as her magic healed up the damage.

The clock tower was the oldest structure in Monfort. Originally part of a great temple or monastery or something else that was lost to the winds of time. Most of the building had long since rotted away, leaving only the tower itself as a testament to what had come before. How the people of that era had even managed to build it was something of a mystery—they had no other mechanical traces in the structures that they'd left behind, and there was great speculation about where the rocks that made up the structure had come from, how they'd been transported, how they could have raised them all of the way up to the top of the tower.

Praxis had read about it when she'd first come to Durland, and like most people had gone to see it for herself shortly after arriving in the great capital city. She'd suspected magic to be at work somewhere, somehow, but when she'd gotten out of the carriage and walked across the soggy green to stand at the base of the ancient tower, there was no trace of magic to be found in the lifeless stones. She'd known it even before she'd rested her hand upon the cold surface, before she'd stepped inside and seen the suspension system that slowly rotated the clock's hands. It was impressive, sure, the cleverness and resources needed to make it work. But it was normal craftsmanship, of normal life, and therefore had held no interest to the younger Praxis.

This time she found herself slightly more appreciative—or at least she could feel that she would have been, if she wasn't tired and sore and covered in the finest layer of sweat. By the time she trudged up the last step to the crest, she was cursing out Weevish and his skittish paranoia with every breath, and by the time she yanked the thick oak doors open and let herself inside, she was questioning whether any of this was even worth her effort.

And that was before she saw the steps inside the tower.

Tall and impossibly narrow, like every old staircase, they were just at the limits of how far Praxis could maneuver her harnessed leg. She ground her teeth together as she trudged up one step after another. The soft click of the gears that ran along her harness echoed out in the empty tower, a gentle underscore to the puffing of her breath, the scuffle of her shoes, the ominous creak of ancient chains as tied-up stones bobbed up and down, shifting the clock inexorably forward. They said, in this one book at least, that the weight of the stones was precisely balanced to shift back and forth, one rising and then the other; they said that even the faint layer of moss that had grown up over the centuries had slowed the clock by three minutes.

Praxis paused about halfway up to catch her breath and undo some of the row of buttons along the side of her trouser leg for greater maneuverability. She watched the stones as they bobbed oh-so-slowly on the ends of their chains. Somewhere far down below, Praxis knew, they were attached to other chains in an intricate system that was tethered to an underground water supply that fed the whole process, but here there were only the stones. Back and forth, perfectly balanced. When they would pass, the sides slid together, the surface worn down as smooth as glass. They brushed with barely a whisper.

By the time she reached the top, she was in no more mood for games. So it was a good thing that Weevish was there, finally. He stepped out of the shadows dressed all in black, a long, flowing coat and a large-brimmed hat badly attempting to obscure his features. Praxis threw the Cloak and Crowns piece to him, and he scrambled to catch it. "Was all this really necessary?" Praxis asked.

Weevish clutched the Spymaster to his chest. "You can never be too careful, these days."

"I think you can."

"That's because you still don't really know what's going on here lately. Are you sure you weren't followed?" Weevish ran across the tiny platform that topped the tower, peering out from behind the face of the giant clock. The darkened spread of Monfort sprawled far below, sloping away. Dots of light ran in trails along the affluent streets, black shapes moving in the far distance.

"Satisfied?" Praxis asked, looking over his shoulder. "Now, are you going to tell me about the disappearances, or are we going to play hide-and-seek all night?"

Weevish shook his head. "The disappearances," he scoffed. "The disappearances are only half of the problem, Miss Fellows. The bigger issue is what happens when the people *show up* again."

Praxis held up a hand. "Hang on a second. Eagleburns dragged me all the way out here because people were going missing, and now you're trying to tell me that no one is *actually* missing?"

"They were." Weevish swept his hat off, mussing the brim nervously as he began to pace around the top of the clock tower. "We started receiving reports months ago—people would go to work, or out for an errand or a drink, and never make it back. At first, we dismissed it as normal rabble-rousing; these people were from the old quarter, and we just assumed that they were turning to us because the constabulary wasn't bothering to take their problem seriously. There didn't seem to be any evidence suggesting the disappearances were magical in nature, and the Dons . . . were not exactly eager to speculate that magic even *could* be involved in something like this, given the current climate."

Praxis huffed. "Yeah, it *is* generally in their nature to protect their own image before they concern themselves with actually helping people."

"I'm going to refrain from commenting on that matter. Anyway: we were content to ignore the matter until it happened to one of our own."

"What, she actually managed to snag a wizard?"

Weevish raised an eyebrow. "'She'?"

Praxis waved her hand dismissively. "Oh, I just assume that it's got something to do with Pon Lanali these days."

"The Pon?" Weevish asked, utter confusion written plainly on his face. "What does she have to do with anything?"

"It doesn't matter right now. You were saying?"

Weevish shook his head. "Right, well . . . It was a junior apprentice, barely even a member really. Near as we can figure, he'd gone out to make a certain . . . liaison . . . and no one saw him for two weeks."

"Maybe he was just having a *really* good time."

"Miss Fellows, if you're not going to take this matter seriously—"

"Relax, Weevish. It was a joke."

Weevish's face pinched. "In that case, I must say that it was in very ill taste, given that the poor soul is now dead." Weevish paused, waiting to see how Praxis would take this declaration. She said nothing, staring blankly as if the matter didn't mean anything to her, and after a moment Weevish cleared his throat and continued. "He was behaving strangely as soon as he returned. Sullen, erratic. He would go through periods where he was all but mute, and then suddenly swing into wild rages of lunatic rantings. He kept . . . he kept clawing at his chest," Weevish said, absentmindedly pawing the fabric of his own shirt. "There were times where it looked as if the poor fellow was attempting to rip himself apart. And then . . . one morning, he was just dead. Lying in a pool of his own blood."

"What, did someone stab him?"

"No . . . we think it was vomited up. There were traces of something metallic mingled in the blood, and we suspect he ingested something, mercury perhaps, and made himself deathly ill."

"Mercury?" Praxis asked, eyes narrowing. "It was silver colored?"

"From what we could tell, yes. Why—is that significant?"

Praxis cradled her left arm against her chest. It was noticeably heavier than her right, one of her forearm bones having been replaced by one made of a magically crafted silver. "Do you have any samples of the blood or the metal left?" she asked, ignoring Weevish's own question. "Is his body still around?"

"They burned it," Weevish said. "When they seized our assets, and disbanded the Society."

"Oh, I'll bet they did." Praxis turned away, running her hand through her hair as she tried to figure out the significance of this new information. There was no direct reason that she could think of why Lanali would have been able to start cracking the magic of the group known only as the Silvers, but that didn't mean that it wasn't possible. Any magic that could be figured out once could be figured out again, and Lanali did have plenty of time to study the Silvers up close after they'd all ended up on the city of barges. But if she did manage to recreate the success of Deeter Vaulsk's magic . . . Praxis shuddered at the very idea. She knew firsthand the kind of power that would allow Lanali to wield.

"Miss Fellows, is there something that I should know about this?"

Praxis turned on her heel, leveling her gaze at Weevish. For once, she made no effort to mask the apprehension on her face. "How much do you know about the Silvers?"

Weevish grimaced. "Thankfully very little. I only met the ambassadors once, at a state function that the Society hosted before the anti-magic sentiment got *too* strong. Nasty sorts, I imagine, but I assure you, they couldn't have—"

"Wait: You've *met* some of them? There are Silvers here in Monfort?"

"Well, of course," Weevish said. "Ever since Vaulaine was legitimized, there's been a permanent posting of two ambassadors. Surely even *you* must have known that."

Praxis glared at him, but did not otherwise deign the comment with a response.

"But as I was saying, there's no way that they were responsible. They're strictly prohibited from practicing magic within Durland's borders, and our trade agreements are far too important to them to risk over some petty scheme. No, Miss Fellows, we aren't investigating the Silvers."

"*You* can investigate—or not—whatever you wish. I'll do as I please."

"*No,*" Weevish said. He grabbed her arm, so sudden and strong that Praxis could only boggle at it for a moment. "You have no idea what you're meddling with, Miss Fellows. The entire Royal *Society* was disbanded because we were too brazen with our curiosity—many of us are either dead or imprisoned, and if we're not then we're under virtual house arrest. They are watching our every movement. That, with all of our resources and influence behind us. You're supposed to be smart: whoever is really behind this, what do you think they would do to a single individual? You'd be gone before you even asked a single question."

"Your concern for my well-being is *touching*," Praxis said with a sneer. She drew her arm away, wrenching it from his grip. She did not outright state that she was going to ignore his advice, but nor did she offer assurances to the contrary. Instead, she brushed her jacket off, as if Weevish had sullied the sleeve already covered in stains and burn marks. "Did you find anything else out before they stopped you?"

Weevish shook his head. "I don't know—I wasn't kept that well informed."

"Oh, that's helpful."

"But I *can* put you in touch with someone who does know," Weevish said. He drew a slim card from his pocket, ivory stock with red and silver enchanted ink shimmering brightly enough to be legible even in the dark. "This man was assigned to help the Don that was investigating."

Praxis plucked the card out of his grip. "It would be better if I could speak directly to the Don himself."

"Yes, I'm sure we'd all like the chance—and if you find him at the bottom of the bay, please don't hesitate to ask him anything that you'd like."

"Point taken," Praxis said. She tucked the card away, so fast that it may as well have been sleight-of-hand. "Anything else I should know?"

"I would tell you not to do anything stupid, but I doubt that would make much difference."

"Now you're getting it." Praxis extended her hand, and after a brief hesitation Weevish hurriedly shook it. "So if I need to get in touch with you again . . . ?"

"Don't," Weevish said. "Take tomorrow to assess the situation, and then return to Willy's. I'll leave another puzzlebox letter the morning after next; you can brief us on your plan then. Under *no* circumstances are you to seek me out directly, do you understand? I will not be bullied on this point," he added hurriedly.

Praxis smirked. "I'll see what I can do," she said, and then she started toward the stairs before he could do more than offer a derisive snort in her direction.

And now, Praxis thought, clomping down the narrow staircase, *the fun begins.*

Chapter Six

 *I*T WAS REMARKABLE, Kaedrich felt, the sheer number of changes that could happen within the span of a single day. Two mornings ago, everything had been normal. Kaedrich had woken up early, gone for a run, returned to the apartment long enough to change and eat a fast breakfast, and then dashed off to work without the slightest idea that anything unusual was going to happen that day.

Then yesterday, Praxis was back, and from the moment Kaedrich had opened her eyes it was as if the world had come alive, like she had been seeing only half of the colors before and now everything was bright and as it should be. Kaedrich's life was completely upside down, but mingled in with the upheaval was a sense of almost inevitable change, like the beginning of something was looming just at the horizon.

And then there was *this* morning.

Kaedrich parted the curtains in her bedroom, taking in the dingy little street that ran behind the house. The sun had not yet risen, but even in the predawn darkness she could see the shifting fog, thick as soup. Faint traces of raindrops made wavy streaks across the windowpane. Her sigh hit the window and fogged it up, hot breath condensing against chilled glass.

It was fitting that the weather had turned so sour. Kaedrich crossed to her chest of drawers, pulling out the thick fabric strips that changed her from Kaedriella into a copy of her brother. She roughed them up quickly between her hands, trying in vain to bring some kind of warmth to them before she'd have to put them on. As she tossed them aside and began to unbutton her nightshirt, she closed her eyes.

This was a mistake, because every time that she did so now, she kept seeing glimpses of her dinner with the Lebules. Lucan's white knuckles as he gripped his glass so hard that it shattered; the wide, pitying eyes of Mrs. Lebule, seated across from her; the row of various silverware spread out on both sides of her plate—she *knew* these rules, she was certain of it!—and the sudden flush of embarrassment when she'd found herself holding the wrong fork.

Kaedrich's nightshirt hit the floor and she stepped out from the pile, passing by the single mirror that she kept in her room. The reflection caught her eye and she started at the sight of herself. She spent so much time and effort trying to hide her body that the sight of it in its true form was becoming disturbingly unfamiliar. Kaedrich paused in front of the mirror. She reached over and turned her bedside lamp up just a little.

This is what she could never show anyone, then, her greatest secret laid bare. It had been so long since she'd attempted to judge her appearance as a woman that she didn't even know where to start these days, but she supposed that it would suit her fine. Kaedrich ran her hands down the subtle curve of her sides, cupped her modest breasts, fluffed the triangle of hair between her legs. She stared at herself, honest and unabashed, and she considered how each of the Lebules would react, if they ever learned the truth. For Lyana, Kaedrich saw disappointment and offense in equal measure, her hopes cruelly dashed upon the shores of Kaedrich's womanhood. Mr. Lebule had barely paid Kaedrich any mind as a man so, while he would no doubt remove her from his house and forbid her return, she doubted that he'd be likely to even remember her face. Mrs. Lebule's charity had been laid thick, and no doubt this would only increase her insistence upon Kaedrich's needing all sorts of help—mostly spiritual, correctional, the type of things that required intense prayer and repentance. As for Lucan . . .

A cold shiver ran down Kaedrich's back and she hurriedly turned away, snatching up her bindings from their pile on the bed. After the night before, it was best not to think about Lucan at all, much less in the context of him viewing Kaedrich as the woman she actually was; his words had been cruel enough when he thought he was dealing with someone close to an equal.

Sometimes, mostly in the dead of night, Kaedrich did think about what it would be like to drop all of the pretenses. Oh, not here in Monfort, certainly—she could never, did not dare. But in some ways it would be much simpler to accept the hand that life had dealt her, rather than constantly hiding several of the cards up her sleeve and hoping that nobody would notice. She would lie there and imagine it, a life where she disappeared from Monfort—where she returned to the quiet of the country or a modest city like Quorral, her childhood home. Growing her hair back out, putting on dresses, finding a husband. Raising children. Kaedrich frowned down at herself, at the slowly flattening chest as she pulled the fabric tight. What if she was causing some sort of damage, binding herself together every day? If she ever did want that other life, was she sabotaging her ability to feed her own babies? Would she even know *how* to be a woman again, after all of this time studying men's postures, their loping gait, the way they sat with their knees spread proudly?

It was a folly to consider, though. The basic fact is that Kaedrich had worked too hard at this life to trade it in. Despite the setbacks, despite the hard work, despite having to face people like the Lebules and play their social games and dance how they expected her, she could not abandon it. She probably didn't even want to.

And so, mind set, she finished dressing, checked the smoothness of her bindings, put on the rattier of her two pairs of shoes, and set off into the morning gloom.

Only now, out on the nearly empty streets, the events of the night before were once again seeping in to haunt her. She had managed to partially distract herself, but perhaps that had been a mistake; when they returned now, they roared full-force into her mind.

She shouldn't have stayed for dinner.

Kaedrich stood in their home, pinned in place just the same as the butterfly specimens that Mrs. Lebule had out on display in the drawing room. Lyana had given her the full tour of the main floor as the two of them waited for the rest of the Lebules to assemble, and it was there, leaning in stiffly to peer at the stilled wings, that Lucan had come in. Kaedrich heard the door, caught his reflection in the glass of the butterfly display cases. She was acutely aware, suddenly, of Lyana's hand resting lightly on her arm, of the warmth as Lyana leaned over to point out one of her favorite specimens. Kaedrich straightened up so fast that she clonked against Lyana's chin, and a rapid series of sputtered apologies masked Lucan's departure from the room. Lyana hadn't even noticed him.

They didn't see each other again until dinner. Kaedrich tried to catch his attention just before they were all seated, hoping to explain, but then a servant was ushering Kaedrich into a chair, and the Lebules were trilling with greetings and the beginnings of stories about their day, and there was nothing to be done but sit and wait it out.

For a while, it had seemed as if Kaedrich was going to luck out. While she had been greeted politely by Mrs. Lebule, and there was of course the occasional attempt by Lyana to draw her into the topic at hand, no one else seemed particularly eager to engage Kaedrich in conversation. She ate stiffly, responding only when directly addressed, and as the first course turned into the second, and the second into the third, she found herself breathing a little easier. Surely, she reasoned, if anything was going to happen it would have happened already?

Now, the morning drizzle steadily soaking through her clothes and her shoes pounding against the street, she felt every bit the fool for her earlier optimism, her almost youthful naïveté. She shut her eyes, trying not to remember it.

It wasn't working.

"It would do the city a world of good if they did *shut them down," Mr. Lebule said, before stabbing at a bite of veal. "Nothing good ever comes out of those establishments."*

"But papa, how are they any different from your clubs?" Lyana asked. Kaedrich glanced up, immediately concerned for her, for she was clearly trying to rile her family. Apparently they were used to it, however, as they barely even paid attention.

Lucan raised his glass in a half-toast. "I, for one, would be happy if the Council made the move. Of course," and here he took the time to shoot a pointed look at Kaedrich, sitting across the way, "that would leave some of us with nothing to do with our weekend nights."

If he was trying to catch Mr. Lebule's attention, it had certainly worked; he actually paused in his eating, resting his knife and fork in a perfect X across his plate. "Mr. Mannly? Do you have some experience with those houses?"

Kaedrich wished more than anything that the question hadn't been so direct. Instantly, a picture of the Scorpion's Stable filled her head: the basement-level entrance near Tristy's playhouse, the thick layer of smoke that lent a permanent haze, the rough laughter that tore through it on regular intervals. It wasn't a horrible place, no, but in the wave of false piety that the Pon was spreading, it did not do to be seen coming and going through the doors. And it's not like she went on a regular basis. But occasionally her work at the newspaper ran a little slow, and rather than dipping into her savings (what little there was, anyway), she had sometimes resorted to filling her coffers by winning a few hands of Fiddler's Dash. She'd learned the game over a year ago, and it turned out that she had something of a knack for it—more often than not, she left a winner. But it wasn't as if she made a habit *of this, though how would it sound to people of the Lebules' standing if they found out at all? Lucan only knew because Kaedrich thought that she could trust him—she thought that they were* friends.

Kaedrich cleared her throat, and reached for her wine glass as if to water down a cough that had come on. Everyone was looking at her now, even Lyana, though her eyes had a slight sparkle on the edges, as if somehow this made Kaedrich just a little dangerous. "I would hardly call it 'experience,' no," Kaedrich said, the best cover that she could think of that wasn't an outright lie.

There were so many things the next morning that she thought of, instead, everything that she wished she could have said and hadn't. In the cold drizzle, even lying felt better. It wasn't as if her entire life wasn't already a lie, so what difference did one more make?

Praxis was right, at times Kaedrich really was just too "noble." Praxis wouldn't have thought twice about making up a lie, especially to people like the Lebules. In fact—

No. She was the last person that Kaedrich should be thinking about right now. The whole *point* of coming to Monfort in the first place was to get Praxis out of her head. Kaedrich took a deep breath, feeling the chill of the morning air as it spread down into her lungs, feeling the stream of raindrops and sweat as they cut tracks down her skin. She tried to listen to the slap of her shoes, until she realized that all that she was hearing, instead, in the one-two, one-two rhythm was *Prax-is, Prax-is.*

Kaedrich stopped at the street corner, surprised to find herself having returned to her starting point, her run already behind her. She barely remembered it. As she slowed to a light jog, heading back to the apartment, she decided that it was good that she was going to work next. She needed something concrete to focus on, something beyond the mess that her social standing had become. She paused in front of her building, wondering how it was possible for it to look so normal while everything inside was beginning to topple.

Must be nice to be a building, she thought to herself, as she bounded up the front stairs two at a time.

*   *   *

So she went to work, but the problem is that Bundling wasn't even there.

"I'm sorry, Kaedrich," the secretary that manned the front desk said when Kaedrich came back out of Mr. Bundling's empty office, "as far as I know, nobody's seen him all morning."

Kaedrich drummed her fingers nervously on the secretary's counter. "Are you *sure*?"

"No," the secretary snapped. "I'm not *sure*. Do I look like I keep tabs on everyone in the building? Do you have any idea how many eyes I'd need to do so?" She sighed as someone hurried over, dropping another thick stack of pages on top of her already overcrowded workspace. She was nice, Kaedrich knew, but also knew that there were times when she should be left well alone. First thing in the morning was a buzz of activity in the crowded offices, more so than usual even, and so Kaedrich retreated back to the tiny room that she normally shared with Mr. Bundling.

She waited around for another hour, in case he showed up late, but eventually it became obvious something had drawn him away. The problem was that Kaedrich really didn't have anything to do without him there. She had been hired on to take Mr. Bundling's notes and translate them into a rough draft of an article, not to help out with his investigation, or even make suggestions. The few times that Kaedrich had tried to take initiative had been slapped down immediately.

With nothing better presenting itself, she eventually left (making sure to position a note in the middle of his desk, where he'd be sure to see it and know that she'd been there), and since she had the extra time for once in her life, she decided to spend some of it putting in additional hours at the academy. Crown Day was now less than a fortnight away, which meant that Falconridge's Trials were coming up. This was the one time of year when people were tested and promoted up to the next levels, and though Kaedrich felt reasonably confident in her actual skills, there was so much more to it. Falconridge loved its rituals. They dressed everything up in ceremony, with special clothes, special weapons, even complicated chants and body paints and lines scribbled on the floor. It was all a little ridiculous, but since you could not fault the school for its defense instruction, Kaedrich supposed that she could deal with a little bit of ridiculous.

At least she wouldn't have to do any of this nonsense in front of the crowd. While the actual Trials themselves took place as a public event, designed to be witnessed, Falconridge saved the ascension ceremonies for their own private halls, days after the fact.

Nonetheless, it needed to be rehearsed. Which is how she found herself pouring oil down the length of a curved sword, trying to make sure the liquid pooled into an impossibly tiny bowl rather than where it wanted to go: namely, all over the floor.

"Blast," Kaedrich muttered, as a stream dropped off the edge of the blade and splashed all over her bare foot. She had learned weeks ago to take off her shoes first, lest she spend the next several days trying to mop all of it out of the creases and folds of the leather.

Marlick, working across from her, had a somewhat more colorful expression of displeasure, when he poured his own oil too quickly and the liquid splashed up and caught a piece of the hilt. He lurched in a vain effort to try to maybe catch the excess, which only resulted in the whole bottle falling from his grip; it landed on the floor with a heavy *thud*, though thankfully did not shatter.

Kaedrich laughed, more at the situation than at Marlick. She snatched one of many rags that she had sitting nearby and tossed it over to him. They were the only two in the tiny classroom, standing underneath a high window, in a waxing and waning pool of sunlight as it struggled to break through the clouds.

"I don't know why we even have to bother," Marlick grumbled. "This is such a waste of time."

"I hate to break it to you, Marlick, but if you don't like rituals, then you're not going to have a very fun time as an Attendant."

Marlick snorted. "Don't I know it." He looked up from his work. "Do you know that my father's been making me rehearse my oaths already? Like I don't have enough to worry about right now? I keep telling him that you only say them once—I'll write them on my palm if I have to. But oh, no. Apparently it's a point of *pride*."

Kaedrich shrugged. "Attendant Hillish used to recite his every year, during Good Summer's Sunset."

"Hillish?" Marlick asked. "You grew up in *Quorral*?"

"I . . ." Kaedrich paused. She tried to speak of her childhood as little as possible, and gave details even less. If she hadn't been so distracted trying to get this oil to pour just right, she might not have even said anything at all. "We . . . we were only there for a few years," she lied.

"Yeah, but still—Kaedrich, my cousins lived there. You might have known them!"

Kaedrich purposefully fumbled with her bottle, just to buy her some time as she gathered up the rag that she'd been using. "Oh, I doubt that."

Though even as she said it, a part of her was already spinning back.

She'd thought that the name "Darbury" sounded familiar when she'd first met Marlick, but had dismissed it without much consideration. She had fuzzy impressions now, a family with a bunch of children, all ginger-haired and wild.

But Marlick was not so easily dissuaded. "Why not? They lived up near—"

"There you are."

Kaedrich looked up. She never thought that she would be so happy to see Lucan again, certainly not so soon after last night, but now he appeared in the doorway like a shining agent of Perlandra.

Unfortunately, Lucan did not appear nearly as relieved to see Kaedrich, despite the fact that he had apparently been looking for her.

He folded his arms across his chest as he leaned against the doorframe. His hand was still wrapped in a bandage, and Kaedrich hoped that the shards of glass hadn't done too much damage.

"Well?" Lucan asked. "Aren't you going to thank me?"

Kaedrich blinked. "Excuse me?"

"For solving your Lyana problem."

For a second, Kaedrich could only stare. Lucan's face was every bit as hard as it had been the night before, when he'd all but eviscerated Kaedrich at the dinner table—the gambling admission had been just the beginning, though he did have to quickly start making things up. Kaedrich frowned. "Wait, you . . . that was an *act*?"

"Oh, no, I really was pissed to see you there. But then later I realized that you couldn't possibly expect to be able to achieve anything with her, since you'd never get the family's permission to court her. And you don't strike me as the kind of man who would sully her honor by using her without formal consent." He narrowed his eyes. "I am right, aren't I?"

"Of course!" Kaedrich blurted. Her relief felt so strong that for a moment she was worried that she'd have to sit down; she couldn't believe that the social fallout she'd been envisioning all night and all morning had now just . . . disappeared, like dew burning off of the grass. Despite the stress that it had caused her, Kaedrich shook her head, fighting against a grin. "*Thank* you."

"I feel like I'm missing something," Marlick said, chiming in for the first time. He set his sword and oil down, looking curiously between Kaedrich and Lucan.

Kaedrich cringed. She'd managed to avoid Marlick when she'd gotten back from dinner, and she was always gone from the apartment before

Marlick woke up in the morning. It wasn't that she was necessarily trying to hide what had happened from him, but she was grateful when he hadn't asked as they'd started practicing for the Trials.

When it became apparent Kaedrich wasn't going to be immediately forthcoming, Lucan grunted his disapproval. "Lyana invited Mannly to stay for dinner last night—but I managed to dissuade her interest. She shouldn't be nosing about so much anymore."

"Wait, 'shouldn't'?" Kaedrich asked, suddenly nervous. "Did she *say* that she was giving up on me, or are you just assuming that she *will*?"

"Oh, she will. No respectable young woman would want a man courting them who's slummed around in seedy gambling houses. I don't know why I didn't think to tell her sooner."

Kaedrich groaned, remembering the way that Lyana's eyes had sparkled at the idea. "Lucan . . . she doesn't *want* society's approval—or your family's. That's the whole *point*. I fear that you've only gone and made me more attractive to her."

Lucan waved his hand, giving a *pshaw* of dismissal. "Nonsense. Anyway, since when are *you* the expert on women?"

Kaedrich bit her lip, just barely restraining herself from bursting out laughing at such a statement. Besides, the situation on the whole was far too grim to warrant such merriment. She gave a frustrated sigh, knowing she would never get anywhere in trying to argue this matter with Lucan.

Awkwardness hung in the air like a bad smell that everybody was being too polite to comment on. Kaedrich glanced at the ceremonial sword in her hand, the bottle. Where did that leave the state of their friendship now, her and Lucan? Of all the new relationships that she'd formed here, theirs had been the most complex. Lucan wasn't the easiest person to get along with, at times gregarious to the point of flamboyance, at times so sullen it was difficult to get two words out of him—and in the span of a day she'd gone from this fragile state, to thinking that their friendship lay ruined beyond repair, to relief when she found out that it wasn't. But now the relief had curdled as if it had laid out underneath the sun for three days, and she had no idea what was to come next.

All things considered, it was a good thing then when another pair of footsteps came clacking down the hall toward their little practice room. Most of the academy was empty rooms in one way or another, an endless sea of open space for men to throw punches or each other. Compared to most, this little room was nothing but a closet, though until Lucan had showed up it hadn't felt like one.

He turned now, the approaching shoes breaking whatever moment had passed over the three of them. Lucan slipped down the hall, murmuring an acknowledgment to whoever was approaching as they passed, and then in an instant it was Director Tarlock filling up the doorframe.

"Sir!" Kaedrich and Marlick jumped to attention in unison, though Marlick wasn't quite as prepared for it as Kaedrich; the bottle of oil slipped from his hands, spitting an arc as it tumbled until he caught it somewhere near his knees.

Kaedrich winced in sympathy. She thought for sure Director Tarlock was going to reprimand him, or at the very least level a withering look of displeasure, and yet when she glanced back she found with surprise that he wasn't looking at Marlick at all. All of his attention was fixed on Kaedrich, the corners of his eyes wrinkled just enough to show that he had zeroed-in his focus.

A lead ball settled in Kaedrich's stomach, as surely as if she'd swallowed one of the cannon balls from the downstairs display. "Sir?"

"Mr. Mannly." Director Tarlock raised his hand, flicking his fingers up. A folded piece of cream paper sat pinched between his middle and forefinger. "A message has come in for you."

Kaedrich probably should have found it odd that Director Tarlock himself was bothering with something like this, but at the moment she did not. The sight of the paper had sent a jolt of panic through her, for she could see it in an instant: Praxis, in trouble; Praxis, hurt; Praxis, lying dead on the streets because Kaedrich didn't get her message in time. Kaedrich snatched the paper, all thought of propriety gone, and turned her back on Director Tarlock as she hastily unfolded the missive. Her heart was pounding, feeling as if it had clawed all the way up her throat and into her mouth, and for a moment the words just swam in front of her, vague and disconnected from reality. But it wasn't Praxis's familiar, scratchy handwriting that filled the space, nor did any words like "help" or "hurt" or "danger" fly up at her, and so after a moment of staring at the looping letters she was able to collect herself enough to force her eyes to read it properly.

It was neither from Praxis, nor in any way about Praxis. It was from Mr. Bundling.

Kaedrich read it quickly, frowned at it, then read it again. She folded it and tucked it into her pocket, and when she turned around she found that Marlick and Director Tarlock were still in the room with her, staring at her with apprehension and quiet displeasure, respectively.

A few minutes later she was running along the crowded streets once more. She had made her excuses, just barely remembering to take the time to put her sword and oil away, to stuff her socks and shoes back on. Kaedrich slipped on the sett stones of the Monfort streets, still damp from the cold drizzle that had settled over the capital. She was lucky the academy wasn't that far from the Crescent, that she didn't need to waste time or money trying to book a hansom or skip across town on the overhead rail lines that rattled back and forth along the great curve of the city. And yet, as she rounded the corner and the heart of the political center came into view, Kaedrich feared how long it was going to take her anyway.

The streets were packed. Far more than the usual protesters that had taken up residence around the Council's Crescent, this assembly was a mix of revolutionaries and gawkers alike. They were jammed in shoulder to shoulder and hip to hip, everyone trying to worm their way through in one direction or another.

Kaedrich only caught bits and pieces as she forced her way through. The tension level alone was enough to spike her own sense of apprehension. No one seemed to really want to say anything, and the whispers that flew in short bursts were cryptic at best. For a normally gossipy people, this was perhaps the most disturbing thing that they could have done. By the time she finally did burst through the last layer of the onlookers, she had almost forgotten that she was supposed to be meeting Mr. Bundling at all—the need to get to the front, to see whatever was going on for herself, had become an overriding force.

If the arms of the ring of policemen cordoning off the area hadn't stopped her, the sight that lay beyond them surely would have. While a thick swarm of official-looking men in a variety of official-looking uniforms did their best to block the scene from view, there was simply no way to hide it.

Three people—no, three *bodies*, for these hardly qualified as people anymore, not in this state—were staked on the outside of the Crescent. Nailed directly into the walls with massive spikes that ran straight through their upper chests, the bodies hung like rag dolls, dotting the gaps between a handful of second-story windows. Soaked in blood, their skin turned to ribbons that hung off of their arms and legs and caught the occasional breeze. Someone had laid a tarp out along the front steps of the Crescent to catch the drippings.

Kaedrich forced herself to look down from the sight of it, and found herself catching the eye of Mr. Bundling.

He was standing in the thick of a copse of royal guards, notebook out, engaged in hurried conversation with the captain. When he spotted Kaedrich he paused for just a second, then snapped his attention back to the captain as he scribbled something fresh in his notebook. He listened, scribbled, nodded, scribbled some more. His glasses had slid down his short nose, caught on the stubby upturn at the end. Mr. Bundling pushed them up, and they just slid down again. He ran his hands nervously across his slicked hair, thinning at the temples, and nodded again at something the captain said. Then the captain was stepping off, following after a subordinate that had come to collect his attention, and Mr. Bundling was tucking his pen behind his ear, flipping his notebook closed. His beady eyes narrowed in. He came straight up to the line of policemen holding back the crowd, tapped the shoulder of the one nearest to Kaedrich. "This one's with me," Mr. Bundling said, and the policeman nodded and shifted just long enough for Kaedrich to duck underneath his linked arm.

Mr. Bundling snapped his fingers, beckoning Kaedrich to follow. He was just as tall as Kaedrich was, though his back was perpetually stooped as if he was walking against a stiff wind. He plunged deeper into the cluster of guards and policemen milling around the square in front of the Council's Crescent. "Sir," Kaedrich began, trotting to keep up, "what's happened? Who are those . . . ?" She swallowed, the image of the bodies sending a fresh wave of vertigo through her. She did not need to finish.

Mr. Bundling shook his head. "Nobody knows, not yet. They appeared early this morning—but never mind that."

They stopped walking, stopped talking. They were in a relatively quiet corner of the square now, tucked off behind a statue of a long-dead general. Mr. Bundling set down his notebook, the one that he'd been scribbling in when he was talking to the captain, and withdrew a second one from the inner pocket of his suit jacket. It was identically made, but the difference between one and the other was staggering: this second notebook was bulging at the seams, straining against a leather cord wrapped tightly around it. Bits of papers and the corner of a photograph or two stuck out at odd angles, and the pages had been thumbed through so much that the edges looked soft. Mr. Bundling began to untie the cord.

"Kaedrich, you've done a good job for me so far, but I think that we both know that you've been underutilized." He glanced up, the notebook free of the cord now, but still held shut in his hands. "If I asked you to take care of something important, do you think that you could do it?"

Kaedrich raised an eyebrow, not sure if she should be flattered by his trust, or insulted by the idea that it was a question. She made herself nod. "I'm sure I could."

Mr. Bundling didn't do anything at first. Clearly, he was still working out whether or not he believed this.

Oh, if only you knew, Kaedrich thought. She, who had been to the land of the dead and back. Something important, sure.

Without further comment, Mr. Bundling abruptly looked down and flipped the heavy notebook open. He cradled it in both hands, taking care not to let any of the loose slips of papers flutter out. With his thumb, he turned the pages, flipping past scratches of lists, obsessive trails of thought that were crammed in at odd angles, bits and pieces underlined or circled here and there. Finally he found the section that he was looking for, and drew out a single sheet of paper. Kaedrich read it upside down. *Lord Wellen, half-past three o'clock, 24 Evington Park.*

"I need you to take a meeting for me," Mr. Bundling said. His face puckered inward, as if even the words themselves were physically distasteful. He gave a tiny sigh that came out more as a snort. "Ordinarily, I would never dream of sending someone in my place, but Jemson is insisting that I handle this crisis myself, and I have no way of rescheduling with my contact. I'm going to give you a letter of reference," he said, picking up his original notebook again and tearing out a page, "and I don't know if it's going to be enough to get him to talk to you, but it's the best that I can do under the circumstances. Find him; show him the letter. If he's still willing to talk, I want you to write down everything that he says."

Kaedrich nodded. She looked again at the name and address, now pressed into her own hands. The name was vaguely familiar to her, though she couldn't place from where. She certainly didn't know him, not with his address. Evington Park—one of *the* most elite neighborhoods in all of Monfort, if not the top spot itself. It ran along the very highest ridge of the peak of the city.

A knot twisted in Kaedrich's stomach. "Sir, if I may . . . who *is* this gentleman?"

Mr. Bundling snorted. "Nobody as important as he used to be," he said. He folded up his letter and dropped it straight into the breast pocket of Kaedrich's suit jacket, as if Kaedrich was his son and he was tucking away some pocket money for sweets. "He's a wizard," Mr. Bundling continued, when Kaedrich still didn't look reassured. "One of the few left standing after the collapse of the Society, but that doesn't count for what it should anymore; rumor has it that his entire staff has up and quit on him. I wanted to contact him days ago, when he first reappeared, but he refused to see me. Now he's reaching out, and I need to know why."

"Of course, sir," Kaedrich said. "I won't let you down." She hoped that if she sounded confident enough, he wouldn't worry. Not that it was a difficult assignment, but the location made her more apprehensive than she should be. Kaedrich held out her hand.

Mr. Bundling's face twisted up for a moment before he grudgingly accepted Kaedrich's handshake. "Don't screw this up for me." He jerked his head in the direction of the rest of the square. "Now get out of here, or you're going to be late."

Wellen, Wellen, Wellen.

Kaedrich turned the name over in her mind as she trudged up the long and switchbacked streets to the crest of the city. The longer she sat with it, the more certain she felt that she'd seen it somewhere before—and *not* just from the society pages, his parties and engagements splashed all over for everyone to be jealous of. But then where?

The fact that he was a wizard didn't help her narrow it down. Nor did his prestigious social ranking. So many members of the Society used to belong to Monfort's elite, and not just the Dons that ran the show. Magic was once regarded as a gentleman's art, and in the early days after Durland had thrown off the shackles of Marcovallan rule, a number of families with strong magical bloodlines were elevated to nobility. The wizards had played a key role, after all, in seizing back Durland's freedom. It seemed only fair to give them some status, some say in how things were run. The Society was established out of the ashes of a former organization, from the days before Marcovalla took over, in order to ensure that the magical community remained "respectable."

Kaedrich still couldn't believe that they were gone now.

She didn't have any personal stakes in the matter either way, of course, but . . . for something that old, that had once been so venerated, to slowly fall to the gutters of public opinion . . . and then to have been forcibly disbanded! It felt unstable, like the ground itself wasn't as solid as she'd always believed it to be.

And then there was the matter of Lord Wellen himself. Mr. Bundling had said something about when Lord Wellen had "reappeared," so did that mean he'd been missing for a while? Was it related, somehow, to the other disappearances that had been reported and ignored?

Not that Kaedrich was supposed to know about that, technically. Mr. Bundling was normally very careful with his papers, but he'd dropped one in a rush out the door about a week ago, and Kaedrich had picked it up. Oh, she'd intended to just leave it on his desk for him. Snooping had never been her intention. But this particular paper was jam-packed with Mr. Bundling's hand-scrawled notes, lots of arrows and exclamation marks to indicate importance. And maybe some of her time with Praxis had rubbed off, because Kaedrich found herself reading it, right there in the office.

Soon she'd needed to sit down, her head swimming with uncertainty. It seemed that Mr. Bundling was discreetly following a string of disappearances, mostly centered around the old quarter—there were references to missing police reports, misfiled or lost, as well as a series of names now half scratched out, dates listed neatly beside them in two or three different colored inks.

She'd shoved the paper into a stack on his desk after that, wishing that she'd never seen it. She had tried her best to forget about it, but it came back to her now as she walked. She edged around a group of workmen carefully maneuvering a piano out of the back of a large delivery cart, turning it all over in her mind. Disappearances, and now people staked up to the front of the Crescent? Even if they had absolutely nothing to do with each other (and there was no reason to assume that they did), what kind of city was this turning into? Monfort was supposed to be a bed of enlightenment, a monument to how far Durland had come since the violent days of the revolution.

Of course, that reputation was established *before* the great ghost crisis more than two years ago. She supposed that, given the circumstances, it might not be so shocking, really. All sorts of things had changed since then: whole swaths of people had turned from the teachings of Perlandra as a general crisis of the spirit had quickly swept the country in the wake of the disaster; Pon Lanali, having claimed sole credit for saving them all from the disaster, had grown exponentially in popularity; people were questioning everything from the government to the role of magic in society; the protests had sprung up. Kaedrich supposed that it all made sense, that people were only reacting to a horrible situation that they didn't fully understand. *She* had the advantage of having been there, of seeing for herself exactly what had happened as it happened.

Kaedrich snorted, thinking that—to imagine her trip in the land of the dead as any kind of advantage was not an angle that she'd ever considered before, though . . . in some ways, it absolutely was. She understood what had happened; she hadn't felt helpless, sitting at home as ghosts broke through the barriers between the living and the dead, ripping people's souls out of their mortal bodies. Granted, they'd been returned to themselves in the end—but what must that be like, Kaedrich wondered, to live with that experience day in and day out, and not even really know what it meant? Was it any wonder that times were so tumultuous now, that people were pointing fingers at nearly everything and everyone, looking for someone to take the blame for their nightmares?

She turned a corner, nearly to the top of the slopes of Monfort. She'd been living here long enough that she was barely even out of breath. On the upper levels, the streets widened up and traffic settled down into a gentle trickle. The gaps between houses had been growing for several blocks, and now they had enough space between them for proper gardens, for rows of delicate flowerbeds and the occasional duck pond. The gardens put off specially crafted perfumes, mingling with the citrusy-sweet smell of the bay. Houses were set back from the main streets, the view of the world beyond the city peeking out here and there between hedgerows and trees. Towers with twisting spiral rooftops littered the skyline. Kaedrich found the street she was looking for easily enough, and now she turned her attention to the numbers formed out of wrought-iron bars at the gates of each walk.

The gate to number 24 was already open. Kaedrich reached out, running a hand gingerly along the top bars. Every other gate in the row was snapped shut, not necessarily locked but distinctly latched, and Kaedrich wasn't sure what to make of this. It might have been nothing, but these days, she kind of doubted that. She breathed in, but the flowers growing in Lord Wellen's garden were benign. Still, Kaedrich paused at the entry, glancing both ways up and down the street. Nobody was around, save for a single maid three doors down, out sweeping the front walk, but neither did anything appear amiss. Birds chirruped happily in the trees, and the sun was optimistically trying to poke its way through the thick cloud layer. The maid was whistling to herself, the tune carrying just enough for Kaedrich to catch one or two notes before they slipped away.

Still, Kaedrich stayed on guard as she made her way up the front walk. Her training let her know where to look for a potential attack, all the tiny little shadows that hugged a house like this, and the line of the upper roofs, and the windows hidden by shut curtains. But it was still fine, it was all fine, as she climbed up the steps, and it was fine as she rang the bell, and it was fine as she waited.

She waited.

Silence met the chiming of the doorbell. Kaedrich frowned. If Lord Wellen really wanted to give Mr. Bundling information, then wouldn't he have been home at the appointed time to provide it?

Then again, perhaps he just didn't know how to answer his own door, given the lack of a butler to do it for him. Kaedrich pressed her finger into the fat button of the doorbell again, and then grabbed the heavy brass knocker and tried that for good measure, as well.

She waited.

If she stood there much longer, she knew that she would start attracting attention. Even if the rest of the houses appeared quiet, Kaedrich knew perfectly well that they were abuzz inside with busy servants all too eager for something to gossip about. She was going to have to leave soon, regardless of the importance of her meeting. Kaedrich leaned over, trying to steal a peek in through a nearby window, and it was at this exact moment that the door whipped open.

Kaedrich jerked up, startled and embarrassed at having been caught snooping. Her voice was already forming apologies, all of which died in her throat when she found herself face-to-face with Praxis.

"I should have known," Praxis said, cutting off the myriad of questions before Kaedrich even had a chance to sort through and prioritize them, much less ask them. As Kaedrich stood there gawping, Praxis leaned out, stealing a fast look around, before she retreated back into the foyer and yanked Kaedrich inside with her.

The door slammed shut, the sound echoing out into the quiet streets. The maid, three doors down, glanced up briefly, a puzzled look on her face, before she shrugged and went back to her sweeping.

Chapter Seven

$\mathcal{P}$RAXIS SHUT THE DOOR, then planted her hands on her hips. "How in the seven hells did you find me?"

Kaedrich didn't answer her at first. She stood there, blinking, staring Praxis up and down, as if she'd never seen her before. "You . . . you changed your clothes."

"What? Oh." Praxis glanced down, running her hand briefly across the new vest that cinched in around her waist. What Kaedrich said was partially true: Praxis had on a peacock-blue cotton shirt and a vest with a pattern across it that resembled the green-and-gold pattern of the same bird's tail, though her trousers were the battered brownish pinstripes that she'd had for years. It was going to take the tailor a lot longer to stitch her new pairs to accommodate Praxis's special-ordered open sides with the row of all of those tiny little buttons holding them together, and she still hadn't picked out a coat—though her shoes were new. Still, it hardly seemed worth mentioning at this point, and she tried to ignore that she hadn't planned on seeing Kaedrich until she'd picked up the rest of it. Praxis shrugged. "It's a work in progress."

Kaedrich frowned. "Work in . . . ? Praxis, what are you talking about? What are you even *doing* here?"

"Those are two very different topics," Praxis said. "Which one would you like me to address first?"

"You can't just let yourself into someone's house!"

Praxis rolled her eyes. "Actually, I *can*, it's quite easy. What I think you mean to say is that I *shouldn't* just let myself into someone's house, and we both know how likely I am to listen to that."

Kaedrich pressed her lips together in a firm line, not pleased at all but not arguing the point either. An entire back-and-forth dance had passed between them, unspoken, and on the other side there was nothing to do but move on.

Praxis turned, already stalking back toward the sitting room that she'd been searching before the doorbell had rung. They rounded an empty cage in the foyer, claw marks marring the polished stone floor inside of it. In addition to his household staff, it appeared that Lord Wellen had recently had to give up his falcat as well—which meant that, despite still being technically allowed his home and his title, his social ranking had taken a plummet. Praxis noted this, tucking it into the corners of her mind.

She breezed into the sitting room. "Kaedrich, I told you that I didn't want you getting involved in this. You have a *life* here—you should be living it, not chasing after me." As soon as she said it, she realized that it was a poor choice of words. Praxis flinched. "I mean, not *me*, but—"

"What are you talking about? I *am* living it—I'm here for my job! You're the one that isn't supposed to be here."

"A job?" Praxis said, ignoring the question of her own motives. She looked over her shoulder to find that Kaedrich was standing in the doorway, because of course she'd followed. "What job?"

Kaedrich shrugged, already looking away. She picked up a useless statue on a useless end table, flipping it over as if maybe the underside would save her from this line of inquiry. "My job. I'm sure I've mentioned it."

"No," Praxis said. "You haven't." She tried to keep the ice out of her voice, but even she could hear the way that she'd clipped her vowels down to their barest essence, a holdover of her Yandosian accent.

"You must have just forgotten it. I wrote a lot—too much, maybe. You can't be expected to remember *everything*."

A flood of Kaedrich's words came back to her, then, a thousand different bits and pieces of the letters. Praxis would lie on her bed and read them over and over again, the imagined sound of Kaedrich's voice lulling her to sleep as the rising sun crept up the walls of her tower. When she shut her eyes, even now, the first thing that she saw was a string of Kaedrich's handwriting.

"I didn't forget any of it," Praxis said. "Not a single line."

When Kaedrich looked up, Praxis looked down. She steadied herself against the mantel of the fireplace, the room and Kaedrich both to her back. Those letters had been Praxis's lifeblood over the last year-and-change, and the idea that they might have meant nothing to Kaedrich, that she'd dashed them off without the slightest thought, was almost more than Praxis could bear. She gulped down a silent lungful of air, once, twice.

"All right," Kaedrich said finally, "so you're right, I didn't tell you. I didn't think that you'd understand."

Praxis nodded, the biggest response that she could muster. Kaedrich was right—she didn't understand. If it was money Kaedrich wanted, she could have just written. Did she think that Praxis wouldn't have sent her more? But even beyond that, Praxis felt the loss of something stable, all of her carefully crafted charts of Kaedrich's activities now jumbled and useless. Praxis used to think that she could picture where Kaedrich was sometimes, and she'd imagine her going along about her business. Oh, Praxis knew that she would always get the details wrong, no matter how much Kaedrich conveyed in her letters; the imagination just wasn't that accurate, so much nuance lost to interpretation and reinterpretation. She saw it now for the fantasy that it really was. Just a childish daydream, no more real than when she would finally set the letters down and shut her eyes, imagining that Kaedrich hadn't gone away at all, that she was tucked into the crook of Praxis's arm, the tight curls of her hair just tickling Praxis's nose.

"Fine, so what is your business here, then?" Praxis said. She twitched her fingers, shifting her weight as she moved away from the mantel. She pulled open a drawer in an end table and shuffled through the papers there, just for something to do.

"I'm supposed to meet with Lord Wellen. Well—technically Mr. Bundling was supposed to meet with him, but he sent me in his place because—"

"Bundling?" Praxis turned, scowling. "Erstan Bundling? The newspaper reporter?"

Kaedrich shrugged. "What of it?"

"Erstan Bundling," he'd said, extending his hand in Praxis's direction. "Monfort Daily Witness."

Praxis turned her collar up, already stepping away. "I don't talk to reporters."

"Then it's going to be difficult to tell the world your side of things, isn't it, Lady Praxis?" He was jogging after her, out into the gentle blanket of unexpected snow that had settled on the jailhouse steps overnight.

Praxis shook her head. "Nothing. But, Kaedrich, please tell me that you don't have anything to *do* with that worm."

"He's a good man . . . more or less."

"He's a muckraker."

"Then I guess you're down in the muck these days," Kaedrich said, "because he's investigating these disappearances same as you are."

Praxis raised an eyebrow. "I never said anything about disappearances."

"Really? You're going to try playing that game now? I'm not an idiot, Praxis. I'm here because Lord Wellen disappeared and now he wants to talk, and instead I find you. You really want to stand there and tell me that you're not here looking for the same things?"

There really was nothing to say to that without outright lying, and so Praxis wrinkled her nose and did what she always did when Kaedrich cornered her. "Shut up."

Kaedrich laughed. "Gods, you know . . . I've kind of missed hearing that."

Praxis ducked her head, biting down on the smile threatening to break free. "Shut up."

"Okay, but since we *are* on the same page," Kaedrich said, not shutting up, "don't you think that maybe we should drop the pretenses? I take it Lord Wellen wasn't here when you arrived—do you have any idea where he's gone? He was expecting Mr. Bundling, it was really important, and I find it odd that he would have just popped out for a cigarette and a quick walk."

"No," Praxis said, though exactly which part of this she was saying "no" to remained unclear. She tucked her hands into the pockets of her slate-blue overcoat, wrapping her hand around a fountain pen that she'd plucked from the front stoop. Carefully, she drew it out, keeping it clenched tight in her fist. "Though I think that I might know where we'll find him. You say that he was expecting Bundling personally?"

"That's right."

The fountain pen had been sitting on the front steps when Praxis arrived, resting in the middle of the doormat as if it was a delivery waiting to be picked up. Praxis had pocketed it immediately, because of course she had.

While she'd considered the idea of it being a puzzlebox letter, she hadn't given the idea much time because she did not know what purpose leaving a message would have served. Now that she knew that Erstan Bundling had been coming to call . . . this was a test, Praxis was sure of it.

You didn't need to be a wizard to *receive* a puzzlebox letter, only to create one, though the ensuring burns that it left on your hand certainly made it less problematic for wizards.

Praxis held the fountain pen up to her lips now, still held tight in her fist. "Erstan Bundling and Lord Wellen," she whispered to it. Her hand clenched down on the burn as she fought against crying out, though she could see that Kaedrich wasn't fooled by her stoicism. As soon as the heat began to recede, Praxis dropped the fountain pen, letting it clatter to the floor.

Kaedrich ducked to retrieve it, not realizing yet that it was useless at this point. She scooped it up in her handkerchief, careful not to touch it.

"It's not dangerous," Praxis said.

"Looked that way from here."

"It's not dangerous *anymore*, then." Gingerly, she uncurled her fingers, flexing the tendons of her hand as she spread her palm for both her and Kaedrich to see.

Monfort Zoo, neat letters seared into her palm read, *four o'clock, the fountain.* The writing was blistered and angry, and Kaedrich looked stricken by the sight of it.

"Gods," Kaedrich said. "Couldn't he have just left a note like a normal person?"

Praxis clicked her thumb, cutting the tension of her gears. She ran one hand over the other, working as much of the healing touch as she could through the fitted, mechanical glove. "Notes can be intercepted."

"This was, too. Technically."

"Technically," Praxis conceded. Her palm still stung, but the burns had been healed now, white lines of new flesh leaving the faintest whisper of the message.

"Oh, blast!" Kaedrich said suddenly. Her attention flew to the mantel, a fat-bellied clock shaped like a jungle cat. "I've got to go—I'm going to be late."

Praxis grabbed Kaedrich's sleeve, even as Kaedrich was spinning toward the door. "Don't you mean *we've* got to go?"

"Praxis—"

"No. I don't know exactly what Bundling's interest in this matter is, but I know that mine's important. And since I helped you, I think that you owe me the courtesy of inclusion, don't you?"

Kaedrich hesitated, gnawing on her lower lip. She glanced once more at the clock, no doubt weighing the potential trouble against the pressing time. She took a deep breath. "I don't think—"

"Perfect, then it's settled," Praxis said. She twitched her fingers and headed for the door, backtracking toward the foyer before Kaedrich could decide to protest.

THE FANCY LITTLE booth at the entrance to the zoo gleamed golden in the late afternoon sun. Praxis bought the tickets, insisting that Kaedrich keep her money.

"I can afford this, you know," Kaedrich said, her billfold still in her hand. Praxis had already handed over the money, though, and they were moving on almost before the words were out of Kaedrich's mouth.

Praxis passed one of the tickets over, already stamped for a day's entrance. She wasn't looking at Kaedrich. "Yes, I'm sure you can."

"Are you still upset about the job?"

"I'm not upset about anything," Praxis said. She waggled the ticket, and Kaedrich took it with a sigh and stuffed it into her pocket, along with her unspent money.

"I just don't like being dependent on you, that's all."

"Kaedrich, you don't need to explain yourself."

This is probably true—she didn't *need* to explain herself, no. She owed Praxis for many things in her life, but none of it entitled Praxis to demand an account of Kaedrich's own, independent decisions. But Praxis *wasn't* demanding it, that was the thing, though Kaedrich could tell that something about the situation had hurt Praxis's feelings.

Not that she was showing it. As they left the main gate behind them, Brex darted in from the skies and Praxis scooped him and kissed his tiny head, cooing at the creature for a moment as he nuzzled her cheek.

Kaedrich turned away, pretending to consult with a posted map of the zoo. Really, she just didn't want to watch as Brex tucked himself happily against the curve of where Praxis's neck met her shoulder. How odd, Kaedrich thought, to experience a flash of jealousy for essentially a household pet, and yet she wasn't going to lie to herself. The tenderness with which Praxis cradled Brex, the softness of her voice as she murmured something into his silken fur. Kaedrich forced herself to actually consult the map, tracing the nearby paths for any sign of a fountain.

How was it possible that she was still in love with Praxis? A year and a half. That should have been enough time to get over somebody. A year and a half of filling her time to the brim, of classes and friends, of work and independent studies, of card games and nights at the Cross Street pub. A year and a half to let herself admire the handsome men and pretty women both, though neither was an option for her in her current form—but still, she could watch. She had watched, she had made herself watch. And what had she seen? Wizards that either lacked Praxis's skill, repressed their talents, or both. Men that liked to joke, but weren't as funny as Praxis's biting sarcasm. Women with perfectly lovely smiles, women with faces like paintings, women that should have been pretty, that *were* pretty, rows and rows of them, all different shapes and sizes, all different shades and attitudes, and all of them lacking some indelible *spark* that transformed Praxis's features into something beyond mere surface beauty. More than once Kaedrich would find herself studying one of them, any one of them, perhaps even listening and nodding along as Marlick or Lucan or Havil would expound upon this or that part of her body, and all that Kaedrich could drum up was a restless, heavy *sadness* that hung off of her like an oversized coat. Whenever she tried to show interest, even just for the purpose of making herself do so, she always found these women falling short in one way or another: not as smart, not as clever, not as endearing. They failed before they even began, for the simple fact that none of them would ever be Praxis.

Now here was the genuine article, Praxis herself in Monfort at long last, and yet in some ways that was almost worse. When they were separated by distance, Praxis had been reduced to a string of memories, dreams, and the infrequent letter, and in this space Kaedrich could attempt to compartmentalize her. She could focus on her lessons for now, because she could write to Praxis about it later. She could draft a version of Mr. Bundling's latest article over dinner, because she could dream of Praxis after she went to sleep. And slowly, bit by bit, she could attempt to ween herself of these habits, so that eventually she wouldn't need to use Praxis as a reward at all, eventually she would be able to go an entire day, a week—two weeks?—without thinking much about her.

But then Praxis had appeared, so suddenly, and all of Kaedrich's efforts lay in a heap. She knew that every day she was backsliding. By rights, Praxis's presence should have made things better. She was *here*, she was real and whole again, she was close enough to touch; which was exactly the problem. A year and a half, and it had made no difference. They had barely spent any time together since her arrival and already Kaedrich was finding herself drifting off in conversations more and more, wondering, would it really be *so* bad if she admitted how she felt? Kaedrich harbored no hopes of it being reciprocal (the last time, when she'd almost blurted it out, had done a fantastic job of dispelling *that* idea), but just getting it off of her chest, wouldn't that be better? Like soul-bearing in a temple of

Perlandra, by speaking the truth aloud and having it be witnessed, might this cleanse her of the weight of it, wrapped so tightly around her ribs that at times she could barely even breathe?

With a loud chitter, Brex took flight once more, dragging Kaedrich back to herself. "Just don't eat anything!" Praxis called after him, eliciting one or two odd looks from the people milling nearby.

"Come on," Kaedrich said. She took Praxis by the elbow and guided her into the snaking path of the Monfort Zoo.

Within moments, they'd reached the fountain. It lay in the center of the entire zoo, the central hub where all the different paths finally came together and twisted apart again. A circular pool at least as large as the cottage where Kaedrich had grown up, the fountain was about two feet deep. Statuary of all sorts of waterfowl—everything from swans and cranes, to things that Kaedrich had never been able to identify—stood out of the water, streams pouring up from their mouths or the tips of their upturned wings.

They stood around the perimeter of the central hub, scanning the crowd. The air was thick with the smell of animals and candied treats. Kaedrich shaded her eyes, while Praxis dug out a deerstalker cap from the deep pockets of her coat. She shoved it on her head, the bill shading her face, the untied side flaps hanging loose and blocking partial view of her cheeks. She was already wearing her signature tinted spectacles, had been since they'd set off for the zoo.

"It would help if we knew what he looked like," Kaedrich grumbled.

"We'll know him when we see him."

"I wish I could be sure of that." She dug a pocket watch out of her suit coat, popping it open. It was already nearly ten minutes past four— what if they were too late?

Praxis glanced over, snorting at Kaedrich's fidgeting. "He's not going to have given up *that* quickly."

"He might have."

"He wouldn't." Praxis waved her hand dismissively. "These Royal Society types, they're all the same. If he went through the effort of arranging this meeting in the first place, then he's not going to just give up on it. Not if it means that he gets the opportunity to bore someone senseless with his own perceived brilliance."

"It's a little more complicated than that, Praxis."

"Not to him, it won't be. Trust me. He'll show. He's going to be late on purpose, just to make us wait."

Kaedrich shook her head. She wasn't at all convinced that Praxis was right, but at this point there was little other option than to wait and see. She tried to distract herself from the knot of worry that had twisted up her stomach, the concern over what Mr. Bundling would think if she botched up her first real assignment from him.

Praxis, meanwhile, was settling in for the long haul. She flexed her fingers, sidestepping until she could lean against a nearby signpost. Colorful arrows pointed in several different directions over her head, spread out like branches of a tree. Lions, one read, while another pointed toward The World of Birds. Praxis kept her collar high and her hat low. She reached into the pocket of her trousers, and in doing so, her coat pulled back. Her new vest shone in the light, gold thread embroidered in a delicate pattern of feathers with dots in them that looked like wide, unblinking eyes. They seemed to be fixed on Kaedrich, dozens of them pinning her in place.

"Why *did* you buy new clothes, anyway?" Kaedrich asked.

Praxis turned, peering over the top of her spectacles. "Are you saying I didn't *need* some new clothes?"

"No," Kaedrich said, remembering the rumpled, stained, and at times threadbare state that most of Praxis's laundry had been in a year and a half ago. She doubted that time had improved matters. "But . . . I would have thought that you'd just buy the same things."

Praxis shrugged. "Yeah, well, I didn't."

"Right, but *why*?"

"Aren't you always the one telling me that I should put more effort into my appearance?" Praxis snapped.

"Well . . . sort of. Though I usually meant in terms of, you know . . . baths."

"I *bathe*."

"Not as much as you should."

"Oh really?" Praxis held her arm out, wrist upturned. The outer wisps of her tattoo stuck out from between the straps of her contraption, catching Kaedrich's eye as Praxis positioned her wrist almost directly underneath Kaedrich's nose. Praxis motioned for her to take a sniff.

Kaedrich raised an eyebrow, but she dutifully leaned over and inhaled—gingerly at first, knowing Praxis's history. But while soot, smoke, and a little bit of sweat still no doubt clung to Praxis's battered coat, there was another scent undercutting that layer, stronger as Kaedrich's nose got closer to her skin.

The lemony tang of chesterwood soap, the same type that Kaedrich herself always used.

It was a common enough soap, cheap and plentiful, but it wasn't the kind that Brindlewood Hall had always stocked their upstairs bathrooms with, and it certainly wasn't anything that would be provided in a hotel like the Crestview in Monfort; which meant that Praxis had gone out and purposefully bought some herself, or . . . maybe she had nicked some of Kaedrich's, when she'd stayed on the couch that first night.

Kaedrich wasn't sure which option made her dizzy where she stood—not that either of them *meant* anything, she told herself firmly—but she steadied herself against the same signpost that Praxis was leaning on.

Praxis, meanwhile, had withdrawn her arm with a mild, wordless grumble. Pink edged its way into her cheeks, creeping past the barrier of her hat's earflaps, and she turned away. But the flush ringed her neck, too, which she had presented while she ducked her head, fumbling with something in front of her face.

When she lifted her head a moment later, a bent cigarette, already half-smoked from earlier, was pinched tight between her lips.

Kaedrich jerked back. She snatched the cigarette before she'd even realized that she was going to, throwing it against the interlocked stones of the path and stomping down hard.

"Hey—!"

"Since when do you smoke?" Kaedrich asked. Already she felt slightly bad about lashing out like that, knowing surely that she'd just been rude, but another part of her didn't care.

"I don't know, a while. What difference does it make?"

There wasn't a concise way to answer that, and so Kaedrich didn't know what to say, at first. The Attendants preached for abstaining from all sorts of vices and pleasures, most of which Kaedrich had no particular problem with, for it wasn't as if she was going to follow Marlick and take up vows. (Nor had she been a particularly *devout* follower for a while now, and realizing this made Kaedrich flinch and self-consciously touch the pin on her lapel.) If not that trite explanation, though, then what was she left with? Kaedrich's grandmother, Perlandra bless her soul, had smoked more than anyone that Kaedrich had ever known, so much in her later years that her apartment was always filled with a thick haze that burned Kaedriella's eyes and left her breathing a little unsteady for an hour or two after leaving. When she had succumbed to a coughing sickness the year that the twins were nine, nobody had ever spoken a word of blame on the smoke, but Kaedriella hadn't liked it ever since. In the years that followed, even Trimmis's pipes, once a symbol of warmth and childhood storytelling, had begun to lose their charm.

"I just . . . ," Kaedrich started, because Praxis was watching her carefully now, waiting. "It doesn't seem like a good idea. I can't explain it, okay?"

Praxis glanced at the ground, the smudge of paper and dried leaf already flicking away in the shifting breezes. "Okay," she said finally.

"What?"

She turned back to Kaedrich. "I said 'okay.' I'll give it up."

Kaedrich frowned. "What, just like that?"

"If it means that much to you, then yes," Praxis said. Her face was steady, and even half-hidden by the tinted lenses, Kaedrich could tell that there was no trace of mockery in her expression. "Just like that."

There was nothing that Kaedrich could say to this, and so she didn't. She was acutely aware, suddenly, of the marginal distance that separated their shoulders, the tiny pocket of air between them that they both drew breath from. *Just like that?*

If Praxis was at all moved by the exchange, though, she didn't show it. Her attention had already shifted back to the crowds milling around the fountain. Peals of children's laughter rained down from somewhere nearby, the squawk of a bird, the bark of a dog. The general susurrus of bickering families and questions asked back-and-forth by a group of visitors from Syll. Praxis regarded it all with the same kind of detachment that she always wore, and Kaedrich studied her face, trying to read if there was *anything* hiding beneath the surface.

After a moment or two, Praxis tapped Kaedrich on the elbow. "To arms, soldier. Your quarry approaches."

"Huh?" Kaedrich dragged herself back to the present, to the fountain. She looked at the people that circled nearby, but all of them looked like interchangeable pegs in a game board. "Where?" she asked, squinting into the sunlight.

Praxis jerked her head, though she kept her attention down somewhere in the vicinity of her shoes. "See the gentleman with the rather unfortunate squared-off jawline?"

Kaedrich's attention immediately landed on a young aristocrat standing idly by the far edge of the fountain: a bronze gentleman's tan, midnight-black hair, a perfectly tailored suit that wasn't *quite* paired correctly with his tie and his gloves. He did have a sharp jawline, but Kaedrich would hardly have described it in quite that way.

"I think most ladies would have called him 'handsome,'" Kaedrich said. For he was, in a classical way; he looked like a painting of an ancient god, or an actor that might play a king.

Praxis made a nasty sound under her breath. "Are you serious?" She was staring at him openly now, her whole face drawn up in disgust and disbelief.

"What makes you so sure that's even him?" Kaedrich asked, hoping to change the subject.

Praxis shrugged. "Well, either that's him, or it's someone that Lord Wellen likes so much that he took the time to commission a painting of him for his dining room. Which, hey, no judgments here, but somehow I think that if his flag flew that direction he wouldn't display it so proudly, you know what I'm saying?"

Heat flooded Kaedrich's cheeks. "Um. Yeah, okay, I guess that makes sense."

"So?"

Kaedrich blinked. "What do you mean, 'so'?"

"Are you going to approach him, or what?"

"*Me?*"

Praxis rolled her eyes, her whole head clonking back against the signpost in exaggeration. "Yes, you. You're the one he was expecting, aren't you? Or, well . . . you know, Bundling, but same thing in this case."

While technically true (and obvious, now that she thought about it), Kaedrich hadn't quite worked through this part of the meeting yet in her head. The shift in time and place, the appearance of Praxis; it was all enough to send whatever plans she may have been making to the winds. And, well . . . a part of Kaedrich had just assumed Praxis would take control of the situation, now that she was involved. The fact that she was standing back instead, that she was letting Kaedrich be the one to step up and make the decisions was . . . odd.

"I'm not sure how to approach him," Kaedrich said finally.

"Oh, for sanity's sake—you're not trying to take him to bed or something. Just walk up to him, tell him who you are and who sent you, and see what happens next."

Kaedrich nodded. "Okay . . . Okay," she said, more to herself than to Praxis. "I, um . . . Just, stay here, all right?"

Praxis snapped her fingers, then drew them to her lips for a fast kiss— a gesture that Kaedrich assumed meant something to Yandosians, like crossing one's heart or buttoning one's lips. "Where else would I go?"

It wasn't as reassuring as Praxis probably intended it to be, but it would have to do.

Kaedrich set off, taking a wide track around the perimeter of the fountain. Lord Wellen did not even look at her as she approached.

His slightly mismatched suit made it look like he had tried to dress as if for dinner, with full black tie, top hat and crystal-topped cane.

Kaedrich cleared her throat, but Lord Wellen did not turn. He was examining the statuary in the fountain, metal waterfowl positioned in what someone clearly thought were natural-looking poses. Lord Wellen reached out and ran a finger down the beak of a sculpted crane.

"Excuse me, sir," Kaedrich said.

Nothing.

"Sir? Lord Wellen?"

Still nothing.

Kaedrich sighed. "My lord, my name is Kaedrich Mannly, and I've been sent by Mr. Bundling to meet with you." As she spoke, she drew the letter of reference out of her jacket and held it right in front of Lord Wellen's face, breaking his line of sight with the metal waterfowl.

Lord Wellen snatched the note from Kaedrich's hands and threw it—unread—into the waters of the fountain.

"*Excuse* me, I—"

"You tell Mr. Bundling that if he values my information, he shouldn't insult me by sending *someone else* in his place," Lord Wellen said. He turned to Kaedrich directly, the first time he'd done so—he was clearly hoping to look intimidating, but unfortunately for him, Kaedrich was at least two inches taller. Lord Wellen was forced to look upward, though that didn't stop him from leveling Kaedrich with what he must have thought was a thoroughly withering stare.

What he didn't know, of course, is that Kaedrich was used to Praxis's bursts of austere superiority, and that he (alas) did not hold a candle to her icy glares.

So Kaedrich met his look with a practiced smile. "I assure you, Mr. Bundling would like nothing better. However, he is presently detained on important business. I'm afraid it's either me . . . or nothing."

"Then it's nothing," Lord Wellen said. He turned to go, but was stilled when a bone-white hand suddenly clamped down on his shoulder from behind him.

"What's the rush, Wellen?" Praxis asked. She slid up beside him, her arm still clapped firmly around his shoulders as if they were the dearest and most informal friends. Kaedrich had spotted her coming, approaching calmly while Lord Wellen had been turned toward Kaedrich.

So much for staying put, Kaedrich thought, though she had to admit that at the moment she didn't really mind.

Praxis reached up to remove her tinted spectacles. She took her time, drawing attention to a thick signet ring that lay cozily on her finger. It wasn't something that she normally wore—it was far too gaudy and masculine, if Praxis was going to wear jewelry at all—but it clearly meant something to Lord Wellen. He kept staring at it, as Praxis folded her spectacles against herself and tucked them away neatly in a pocket of her coat. Her face was still mostly in shadow from the brim of her deerstalker cap; however, it did nothing to hide the look that she gave Lord Wellen now. It was not haughty, as his had been, and yet somehow her cold disinterest struck a more intense fear of reprisal than anything Lord Wellen had to offer.

"What do you want?" Lord Wellen asked.

"The Society has questions for you."

Lord Wellen snorted in a poor attempt to hide his apprehension. He looked back and forth between Praxis and Kaedrich, as if he couldn't quite figure out how his meeting with Mr. Bundling fit in with the Society's interest. "I had nothing to do with that," he said finally.

Anyone else might not have noticed the tiny flicker of curiosity that Praxis wiped from her face in an instant, but it did not escape Kaedrich. Praxis shrugged. "Then you have nothing to worry about."

Lord Wellen shook his head. "No. I will not be punished for something that I didn't do."

"Don't be stupid," Praxis said. "No one is talking about punishing any—"

"No!"

It happened too fast for Kaedrich to react, though Praxis tried to. Lord Wellen slid from her grasp and leaped aside, turning back toward them as he did so; he shouted something that Kaedrich didn't catch, and then the next thing she knew a blast of frozen air had flung her off of her feet. She saw a flash of Lord Wellen as her eyes widened in shock: his hat knocked to the ground, his cane extended as if it was a magical staff in an old story. She saw a burst of flames that was probably Praxis's attempt at retaliation before she, too, was lifted from the ground. Then it was just the sky, clouded over in a haze as Kaedrich went flying backwards, and a flare of pain and cold as she landed on her back in the splash of the fountain.

Chapter Eight

PRAXIS STILL HAD most of her head in the water when Kaedrich sprang to her feet. There were probably apologies (it sounded like there were apologies), and there was definitely a hand on Praxis's upper arm, attempting to help get her back to her feet. Praxis threw the help off, though, as she pushed herself up just enough to sputter, "Don't waste time with me—get after him!"

There was clear hesitation, that much Praxis could see even in the bottom of Kaedrich's legs, the only part of her visible from where Praxis was floundering in the fountain. "Praxis—"

"Just go!" Praxis threw her hand out, thinking more about shoving Kaedrich away from her than anything else, and ended up getting her coat sleeve tangled in the foot of an iron bird.

By the time she managed to free herself, Kaedrich had already leaped out of the fountain. Praxis caught a small glimpse of Kaedrich's plaid suit coat, disappearing around a corner as she all but flew in chase of Wellen.

Every inch of Praxis ached as she dragged herself up. A nearby zoo employee had rushed over in the ensuring commotion, and Praxis waved off his concerns. She had managed to tip herself back into a somewhat undignified squat, one hand grasping the neck of a metal crane, its wings spread as if it was about to take flight.

She wished that she could do that, right about now. Spread her arms, soar over the heads of the cluster of gawkers that had gathered around the fountain to whisper excitedly over what they'd just witnessed. Though at the moment, Praxis would have easily settled for following in Kaedrich's example and running full-tilt after Wellen. She hated being stuck back here, struggling to free her drenched pants from the turn of gears around her knee, under open scrutiny of the assembled crowd. The zoo worker had at least decided that Praxis appeared all right, and was doing his best to try to get everyone else to step back and give her some room.

Someone was talking about sending for the police.

Praxis whipped her head up. "No. No police—I'm fine. Look, see?" She grabbed her sopping hat from where it was floating in the water and pulled herself up, motioning wide to indicate her general health, despite the ringing pain in the back of her head and the bend of her elbow. "It was a misunderstanding. Everything's all right."

"But it was magic!" someone—a young woman, smushed into the crowd—shouted. "I saw it!"

"Yes, which is not illegal," Praxis snapped.

The woman's face twisted up. "Not *yet*."

"All right, all right," the zoo worker was saying. "Come on now, clear out, everyone. Nothing more to see here."

Praxis trudged to the edge of the fountain, ignoring the nasty looks that the onlookers kept shooting her. Most of them were listening to the instructions of the zoo employee, though one or two took the time to spit in Praxis's general direction first.

She ignored them. Crammed her dripping hat back onto her head and plowed straight through their ranks. They broke apart as she marched out of the junction where the fountain was, scurrying as if she was dangerous. As if they had any idea how dangerous she could be. Whatever Wellen was trying to hide, it must have been important if he was willing to risk an open display of magic like that.

Praxis shook her head. She held herself tall, trying to look as dignified and purposeful as a woman dripping a steady trail of fountain water could manage. She pulled her coat closed over her chest, wishing that she could do up its front buttons with only one hand.

It was easy enough to follow the trail of both water and startled looks that Kaedrich had left behind. Praxis kept a constant ear out for shouts of alarm or outcries that might indicate Kaedrich was in trouble, but so far there were only the shriek of monkeys and small children, the chirrup of exotic birds, the low murmur of conversation rising up in Praxis's wake. Down a gently sloping path, past cages that rose up on either side like buildings along a city street. Trees and flowers bloomed thick beyond the black bars, but Praxis barely paid any attention to the sights around her.

She had reached a quieter part of the zoo now. No other visitors hung around in the path that Praxis turned down. At the end of the path was a small building, the reptile house. The door was left open, still swaying a little underneath the force of having been thrown wide. Praxis let herself inside, blinking as she adjusted to the sudden darkness. Only the glass enclosures on either side of the halls were illuminated, splashing sickly yellow in large blotches on the scuffed wooden floor.

A flash of light lit up the far end of the corridor, a sharp yelp trailing fast on its heels. Praxis was off in an instant, her fingers nearly tripping over themselves as she barreled past the glass enclosures. While she had known that she would never get herself out of the fountain in time to catch Wellen, she was now cursing her earlier logic; why had she not expected that he would turn violent? What terrible straits had she thrown Kaedrich into without the slightest thought to her safety? A hundred sickening images flooded her as she threw herself around the corner, the scar in her wrist flaring with heat.

"—*don't* want to hurt you," a voice said, but it was not Wellen that had the upper hand when the scene unfolded before her. Praxis stumbled to a halt. Kaedrich had the wizard pinned against one of the glass enclosures, his cheek mashed up in a twisted grimace, his arm wrenched up behind his back. How in the world Kaedrich had managed to get the drop on a trained wizard was beyond Praxis at the moment, and at first she could only stare.

"I told you," Kaedrich continued, "I only want to talk. You have nothing to be afraid of." Her steady voice was somehow terrifying and soothing all mixed up in one, such a perfect blend that Praxis couldn't help but be impressed. She bit her lip, studying the expert lock of Kaedrich's arms, the assertive stance of her planted legs.

Wellen winced. "You have a rather aggressive definition of 'talking.'"

"You attacked *me*," Kaedrich said, though she was already releasing her hold on him; apparently she had made her point. She stepped back, allowing Wellen (after he slumped against the glass in a brief sigh of relief) to gather himself together. Kaedrich's attention flicked to Praxis for just an instant, the tiniest hint of a grin toying at her mouth.

Wellen, meanwhile, was clearly rattled. A fresh bruise was just beginning to blush on his hideous chin.

Most ladies would have called him "handsome."

Praxis looked away. *Fine, whatever,* Praxis thought to Kaedrich, *but the question is: do you?*

She shook her head, shooing such nonsense from her thoughts. By the time she looked up again, Wellen was back to scowling at Kaedrich, and Kaedrich had crossed her arms in front of her chest, just waiting.

"Look, whatever it is you want from me," Wellen said, "just tell me and be done with it."

They spoke at the same time: "Your message to Mr. Bundling," and, "What are you protecting?"

Kaedrich glanced sharply at Praxis. Praxis could all but hear the reprimand in her head, *Don't provoke him,* but Praxis would be damned if she was giving up that easily. Information that Wellen had already chosen to tell to a reporter would no doubt be interesting to some degree or another, but information that he wanted to keep to himself, well—that was far more likely to be useful.

Wellen's mouth twisted up in distaste. "I'm not *protecting* anything. Except, perhaps, the Society's reputation, which you can see has taken quite a beating these days."

"And which you, of course, had *nothing* to do with," Praxis said. It was a stab in the dark, but she saw it hit her target. A slight bristling of Wellen's shoulders, the tightening of his brow. Though he shook his head most adamantly, it wasn't hard to see through his defenses. Guilt was gnawing at him, as obviously as if it was made manifest, a looming creature to chew upon his bones.

"I would never have done anything to harm the Society," Wellen said. "*Never.* Under any circumstances."

Praxis gave a soft *hmm,* noncommittal and unconvinced. "That's what we all like to think of ourselves."

"Enough," Kaedrich said. "Lord Wellen, you had something that you wanted to tell Mr. Bundling. I suggest you start there."

Wellen shook his head. He stepped just a few feet down the hall— Kaedrich hovered nearby, ready to spring to action if he decided to make a run for it. He wasn't trying to flee, though. Instead, he settled on a nearby bench. He leaned his cane beside him, staring somewhat bitterly at the topper of it, a crystal the shape of a falcat's head.

"Any time now," Praxis said, and this time both Kaedrich and Wellen shot her a nasty look. Praxis shrugged.

"There's a growing threat in Monfort," Wellen began, "and everyone that gets too close to figuring it out is being taken down."

"Yeah, that much we know," Praxis said.

This time, her sass actually earned her a swat on the shoulder from Kaedrich. "Ow!" Praxis muttered, rubbing at the spot while Kaedrich shook her head. The set of Kaedrich's jaw was wound tight, someone clearly fed up with not being listened to despite multiple reprimands. Praxis couldn't help it; she glanced away, momentarily cowed. A yellow lizard was crawling up the glass pane beside her, darting after some insect or another.

Wellen let her admonishment hang in the air for a bit too long, Praxis felt, but after a few moments he did continue. In the most unexpected way possible: "We found them."

Praxis whipped her head up; Kaedrich was already watching with wide, steady eyes.

"There's a pub, down in the old quarter," Wellen went on. "Lord Don Trommel and I, we tracked down the movements of everyone that had disappeared. The victims of this plot had nothing in common— *except* that they all made the mistake of visiting the same grubby little pub."

"And somehow the police *didn't* notice this?" Praxis scoffed. "You really expect me to believe that?"

"I am not interested in what a woman *believes*, miss, only what we *know* to be fact. Indeed, it would be a severe mark against their investigative services, *if* these visits had taken place the night the individuals in question disappeared. However, it took more than a little digging to discover this pattern. Some of them hadn't been there in days, even weeks."

"If that's the case," Kaedrich said, "what makes you think that it's related at all?"

"Elementary-level deduction. My mentor, Lord-Don Trommel, Perlandra rest his eternal soul, was a great believer in the lessons to be learned in a careful examination of the world around us. There are patterns that surround us every day of our lives, if we're only dedicated enough to open our eyes to them."

Praxis snorted. "Yeah, I've read his rantings on the subject. Unfortunately, those same 'patterns'—as you call it—can also be interpreted to prove the exact opposite. It's all charades; whoever gets the biggest reaction from the audience is the winner."

"You may have read it, then, but you clearly didn't understand it."

"Sure, because *that's* the only reason I could disagree with it."

"All right," Kaedrich said, talking over Praxis. "But you said that you found them. So you went to this pub?"

Wellen's eyes flicked away. There was a snake in the enclosure across from him, fat and lazy, coiled around a piece of a dead tree branch. "I did," he said slowly, watching the snake. "The Don stayed behind, but . . . but I did."

"And . . . ?"

Wellen's face soured. "I don't think that's relevant. What you need to know—what Bundling needs to print—is that the Society has been looking out for people's best interests, even at the expense of our own institution. I will not stand by and have us branded as cowards and traitors."

Kaedrich frowned; Praxis groaned. *"That's* what you care about?" Praxis asked. "Not what's going to happen now, or what these people are up to next—but protecting the *image* of an organization that doesn't even exist anymore?"

"The Society will *always* exist," Wellen snapped. He turned, glaring directly at Praxis. "So long as there are those of us who know the truth of the good work that we did. We will not be stamped out that easily. I will not let us be."

"Yeah, charming sentiment," Praxis said. "Now, why don't you cut the shit and tell us what really brought you here?"

Wellen scoffed. "I have no idea what you're talking about," he said, as he turned away.

Praxis clicked her gears back into action as she stepped forward. She cut between Wellen and the snake enclosure. Kaedrich edged over nervously, as if she was afraid of what Praxis might do next.

However, for once Praxis had no intention of being snide and abrasive. Instead, she sat on the bench across from Wellen, leaning forward and resting her elbows on her knees in a nonthreatening pose. "Listen, Wellen, I promise you that your guilt is not going to go away just by ignoring it. Whatever you've done—"

"I haven't done anything," Wellen said. His voice had gone both soft and strained, so desperate to cling to this delusion.

"Whatever you've done," Praxis repeated, taking each word slowly, "you have an opportunity now to help set it right. Believe me when I say that those are rare, if not impossible, to come by. You reached out to Bundling—a part of you wants to do something good. Don't waste this chance."

Wellen was still frowning, still not looking at Praxis—but at least he wasn't arguing with her. She left the silence hanging between the three of them, giving Wellen the time he needed to wrestle through his hesitation. Praxis risked a glance up, and found Kaedrich looking at her with a surprised, soft expression; however, Kaedrich quickly looked away once Praxis spotted her.

"At least tell us about the pub," Praxis said after a moment. "Where is it?"

Wellen leaned forward. He pinched the bridge of his nose as if the question had physically pained him. "I . . . I don't remember," he muttered to his shoes.

Praxis raised an eyebrow as Wellen looked up. He looked so young, all of a sudden, more like a schoolboy than a member of an esteemed institution of magic. His face was open, desperate, pleading with his eyes for someone to forgive his transgressions.

"I don't remember," he said again, louder and more sure of his words. And then it was like the wall had finally crumbled, the truth that he'd been holding in now bursting forth. "Please, I don't—I don't know what happened. I went to the old quarter, I was heading for the pub, and then . . . and then . . ." He shook his head. "It's just a blank. The next thing I remember is being at home, three days later, with my valet tendering his resignation, and hearing news that the Society is in ruins."

He blubbered a little around the edges of his words, like Praxis had somehow become his nanny or his mother and he wanted nothing more than to lie his head down in her lap and sob about his troubles. Praxis bristled, and sat up straight. Okay, so she'd wanted the truth, and had tried to use softness to get it for once, but this really was taking matters a bit too far.

Kaedrich, meanwhile, was obviously torn. Pity for the man was splashed across her face, but her normal impulse to be kind was hampered somewhat by her need to maintain a stoic, "masculine" presence. It would have almost been funny—their roles somewhat reversed by circumstance—if Praxis didn't find the support role so damned annoying.

"Are those literally the only things that you can remember?" Praxis asked. "Going out . . . and then waking up? Nothing in between?"

"No. Nothing."

"And what about when you try to remember the name of the pub? Or finding out about where it was located? What happens then?"

Wellen scrunched up his forehead. "It's . . . fuzzy. Like there's a haze across the details, and they've all gotten sort of smudged up in my mind. I've—I've tried to sort it out. I know how it looks—like I had something to do with what happened. But I swear I didn't. I wouldn't."

"It's all right," Kaedrich said. She patted Wellen on the shoulder, the most that she would bring herself to do. "We believe you."

"I don't," Praxis said. When they both looked at her—one a stern glare, the other a hurt snarl—all Praxis did was shrug. "If you don't remember what you've done, then you cannot guarantee *what* your actions were, good or bad. As much as you'd like to believe the best in yourself, the fact that you're so worried about your actions suggests that even *you* know it's possible that you broke under pressure. So the question is: what information did you have that was so valuable that someone would want to steal it from you?"

Despite himself, Wellen huffed dismissively. "Obviously, whatever was needed to help bring the Society down. If that's the story that you'd still like to entertain, despite my assurances to the contrary."

Praxis smirked. "Really? One man, not even on the Dons' council, and they're able to disband the entire Royal Society of Magic? I hate to bruise your ego—"

"I doubt *that*."

"—but the Society was disbanded via an order of the Governance Council. No. Your role, I suspect, was something else."

"Then by all means, *enlighten* me," Wellen said. His lip curled into a sneer as he spoke, his obvious distaste of Praxis's accusations finally blotting out whatever perceived womanly comfort he thought he was getting earlier.

"Would you like me to? It's not going to be pretty."

This was clearly not the answer that Wellen was expecting. He sat back, studying Praxis with no small amount of anxiety. "What did you have in mind?"

Praxis hesitated. Admitting what she had in mind meant admitting that she'd *had* the idea in the first place, and this was not something that Praxis was in a rush to do. It was a tricky bit of magic, hard to learn of its existence and harder still to get details about how it worked. Praxis had never tried it, but she'd been the recipient of it once.

That was more than enough for her tastes.

But at the moment Praxis had no other leads to investigate, and clearly Wellen had gotten himself involved in *something* nasty. So it was probably worth the risk, and probably worth the distaste in her mouth as she said to Wellen, "All that you need to concern yourself with is that I can do it." (She hoped.) "Oh, and that you won't be physically harmed by the process in any way. Beyond that, it's up to you to determine how badly you want the truth."

Wellen didn't answer right away. He sat there chewing his lower lip for a while, a nervous tic that Praxis was surprised wasn't beaten out of such a high-born gentleman at a young age; but perhaps he was just regressing under the recent strain.

Praxis stood up, giving him some time. She clicked her thumb and moved off to more closely examine a huddle of turtles sunning themselves in the warmth from the heat lamps. Their lacquered shells were peeling at the edges, scutes preparing to shed.

Kaedrich sidled up to her just as Praxis was resting her fingers against the glass. "You want to tell me what you're planning?" Kaedrich asked. She kept her voice low, her face turned partially away from Praxis to imply that she wasn't really paying attention.

"It's fine," Praxis said, matching Kaedrich's tone. "Don't worry about it."

"I'd have an easier time doing that if you didn't have such a broad definition of what constitutes 'fine.'"

The faintest hint of a smile tugged at Praxis's mouth. "It's safe."

"That isn't what I asked."

And that was a good thing, because it was a lot easier for Praxis to lie when Kaedrich didn't put her directly on the spot. Praxis gave a half-shrug of indifference.

Thankfully, she was saved from having to answer Kaedrich's questions by the sound of Wellen taking a breath. "All right," he said, and Praxis was already moving. Magic was sparking at the back of her eyes, trying to break loose and shoot down her arms; the eagerness of it was combining with her anxiety in the pit of her stomach, making her queasy and a little unstable as she took up her position on the bench across from Wellen once more. Tiny sparks were dancing from finger to finger, and Praxis had to physically clamp her jaw in her efforts to hold it back.

None of this passed by the notice of Wellen. His already nervous face went pale underneath the mask of his gentleman's tan.

This was one of the points of concern that had entered Praxis's mind: the raw amount of magic she'd be revealing to him in order to break through the fog in his memories. Magic ran on fuel, like anything else, and Praxis had been born with a moderately high amount of it swimming through her veins—but it was the theft of life force from others that had vaulted her onto another level entirely. Normally, she kept it tapped at a mere dribble of what she was capable of. Which was fine: reading memories at all was a little-known skill, but it did not require great sums of energy. Digging up *forgotten* memories on the other hand, and ones that had been purposefully buried, at that . . . This was going to need a stronger force than she liked to let out at once.

Which meant that he was going to see, and it meant that he was going to be able to talk, if he so chose.

Praxis hesitated for a second, but the damage was already done. Her magic was all but ripping itself from her, so eager to be put to the test, and Wellen was staring at her now as if he'd never seen her before, as if she'd somehow changed into a creature worthy of equal parts awe and terror. "What are you?" he asked in a whisper.

"Someone who's on your side today," Praxis said, as she reached across and laid her fingers against Wellen's temple.

She did not even need to tell her magic to go. It was all that she could do to shape it as the energy ripped out of her. Wellen's eyes bugged in alarm, and Praxis couldn't blame him for being afraid of her. She was ripping into his mind, tearing through his recent memories as if she was a pack of wild dogs going crazy over a nest of scared rabbits. A jumble of images flooded her: walking to the zoo in anticipation of this meeting; the twisted look on a valet's face as he left the house for the last time; a letter penned by a lady's hand, now stained with tears; an enormous and empty kitchen, and absolutely no idea what to do with it; a collection of empty wine bottles on a table, Wellen's wretched face reflected back in the glass as he swept them angrily away. A black fog, voices occasionally peppering through.

It was here that Praxis focused in. The minutia of the rest of Wellen's life fell away, and the haze surrounded Praxis, thick and smothering as a room full of smoke. She felt Wellen mentally flinch. The haze crackled and stung as if it was electrically charged. Praxis had to fight to keep her muscles from seizing up on her; her magic *wanted* to shut down at the touch of it, *wanted* to retreat to a safer distance. *Oh no you don't*, Praxis thought to it. *You're the one that was desperate to come out and play.*

A scream broke through first. Wellen's whole body convulsed in sympathetic harmony, his face scrunched as if reliving whatever pain had brought the sound out of him in the first place. Traces of white-hot pain sparked up the tether of Praxis's magic, and Praxis hurried past them, rushing to a different point in the hazy memories. She held herself back, both emotionally, and as much as she could physically, without breaking the connection between them. There was a *crack*, and a splash, and— Praxis tipped her head, straining to hear. The faintest whispers, shifting in the dark.

"I promise you, you will tell me—"
"If I could just—"
"It was clever of you—"
"Stop, stop, stop, stop, sto—"

The voices overlapped each other, as jumbled and out of step as a clumsy waltz. The smell of hot metal, sweat, and fear clung to the back of Praxis's throat as she listened. She pushed her magic further, trying to clear the haze. The image of the world would not resolve itself, everything coated black as deep as the mines of Yandosia, but the voices—the voices were peeling themselves apart, one by one. There was one of them, a man's, that filled Wellen's head more than the rest: deep and honey-sweet, as warm and inviting as a tropical breeze.

"You've noticed them too, then?"

Praxis's mouth twisted up. Tol. It was no less than she expected, but confirmation of it hit her like a punch to the gut. She narrowed in, following the thread of what he was saying, tracing it all the way back to the beginning.

"It's all right," Tol continued. *"There are plenty of us, all around the city, that have noticed. It was clever of you to track them here—did you manage that all by yourself?"*

Wellen flinched, and the memory skipped forward like a needle hopping across a wax record. Tol laughed next, the dull roar of a pub underpinning his mirth. The feeling of a hand slapping Wellen across the back transferred from Wellen to Praxis, and she jerked forward slightly under the impact.

The memory slid forward again. It was slippery underneath her mental grasp, gliding like silk through her fingers. Impossible to hold on to for very long.

"You bastard!" This voice belonged to Wellen himself. It resonated deep in his chest, fury and humiliation burning underneath his heart. *"You said that you would help me!"* They were somewhere else now, somewhere colder and slightly damp. Or . . . no, Praxis realized, it wasn't colder than the pub had been—what he was feeling in the memory was an empty fear, a hollowness in the pit of Wellen's stomach. It was a sensation that Praxis recognized, for she'd felt it once herself, in a prison in Marcovalla.

Wellen had been in a room with a magic suppressor.

Praxis's own blood took a slight chill. She shouldn't be surprised that Tol would have been willing to sneak back into Marcovalla to collect one of the damned things—though not being able to shield himself from the effects as he brought it back would have made the journey far less appealing than it would be otherwise.

But if anyone was going to be stupid and crazy enough to pull something like that off . . . it would be Lanali, via her right-hand stooge.

A crack of pain brought Praxis back to herself. She'd allowed her own mind to wander, and she'd missed several moments of the hazy memories that she'd been dredging up in Wellen. She felt his perceptions as his cheek burned like a branding. The heat pulled back. In real life and the memory both, he started to whimper.

"I promise you, you will tell me what I need to know."

Tol's voice echoed in from a safe distance—outside of the range of the magic suppressor, no doubt. Judging by the heavy breathing nearby, he'd probably roped in some thick-necked barbarian to handle the up-close-and-dirty work of tormenting poor Wellen.

Praxis's jaw clenched. *Coward,* she thought.

Another jolt of pain, and the memory slipped forward again. Everything in the room was quiet, only the rasp of Wellen's empty sobs breaking up the stillness. Shame and remorse coursed through him, and Praxis's scar flared at the influx of such familiar feelings. *"Please forgive me,"* Wellen was whispering to himself, a nearly-silent prayer thrown into the haze of his memory. *"Please forgive me, please, please, please forgive—"*

"How exactly did you find this?" Tol asked, and Praxis perked up. If she wasn't mistaken, it was the first time that she'd come even remotely close to hearing fear in Tol's voice.

But before Wellen even had a chance to answer, the memory slipped once more. Wellen's voice, deadened as if resigned to his traitorous fate. *"Tomorrow, at the eastern corner of Truly Park. He'll leave a puzzlebox letter with the exact address."*

"What names?" Tol asked.

"Lord-Don Trommel and Lord Ecklebaan Wellen. He'll be expecting me at noon."

"No!" Wellen shouted, though this time his voice came from the present. He ripped Praxis's grip from his head, and her magic snapped as if a cord had been broken. She stumbled back, off-balance as the world settled back in around her. Wellen had leaned forward, his head between his knees as if he was going to be sick. He took several deep breaths, and Praxis swore that she could hear the words "I wouldn't, I wouldn't," slipping out from his lips.

"I'm sorry," Praxis said, and for once she meant it, but Wellen held up his hand: stop. He sat up stiffly, though he still wasn't looking at either Praxis or Kaedrich.

"I trust that you have what you need?" he said. He gripped the top of his cane as if grounding himself.

"We have what we need," Kaedrich said, speaking for both of them. Praxis didn't argue, though in truth she dearly wished to have another few moments. If she could get the memory to back up just a bit, find out what Wellen had found . . . But she didn't dare intrude upon his thoughts against his wishes, not under Kaedrich's watchful eyes anyway, and he was clearly in no mood to cooperate further.

Wellen nodded. "Then I'm going home," he said. Only now did he look up, meeting each of their faces in turn. "Don't follow me immediately. Wait five minutes. You never know who's watching."

Actually, we do, Praxis wanted to say, though she kept her tongue. A small part of her had been hoping that somehow Lanali wasn't involved in this, but she knew that was an unrealistic wish. Praxis turned away, chewing this new information over in her mind. What had he found? Damn his pride, and damn his pain. For all of his guilt and blubbering, for all of Praxis's efforts, they were really no better off than they'd been before.

Chapter Nine

So they waited five minutes, per Lord Wellen's request. Which, in the grand scheme of things, was not a whole lot of time—barely an instant, really—but in the suddenly cramped quarters of the reptile house, the lights blaring hot inside of the glass enclosures, it felt like an entire lifetime.

There was a lot of silence, and Kaedrich had nothing to say.

Well, no. Kaedrich had a lot of things to say, too many things to say, but all of them felt as dangerous as the python that lay just beyond the glass by her elbow.

She was used to people looking at Praxis in fear, but somehow in Lord Wellen's case it had been different. Praxis hadn't done anything obviously threatening, and even the type of magic that she had used ended up being helpful—so it wasn't the type of spell *itself* that had sent terror down Lord Wellen's spine, so much as something intrinsic in Praxis herself.

Kaedrich wasn't sure how to feel about that.

A part of her was arguing with Lord Wellen in her head: of course Praxis wasn't dangerous (well, not *really* anyway), of course she only used her abilities in the defense of good. Of course she was a good person, a decent person, deep down, underneath all of her layers of scowls and ice. Kaedrich knew this, in the core of her soul, even if Praxis herself didn't.

And yet.

Even as she argued, she could not deny the objective truth. There was something raw and untamable in Praxis. In many ways she was a force of nature, like fire or an approaching storm, too large to be confined by ideals of purely "good" or "bad." Kaedrich knew this, saw this, and the knowing of it made her chest ache. Because this is what she loved. And she knew that she probably shouldn't, but that didn't make it any less true.

Praxis cleared her throat, and Kaedrich hastily looked away. Back at the python, coiled fat around itself near the water bowl that was shaped like a rock with a dip in it.

"Well, that wasn't exactly what I was hoping to get out of this meeting," Praxis said.

Kaedrich nodded. Right, right. Lord Wellen, and disappearances, and things that actually mattered. "At least you got something. Though I'm not sure what I'm going to say to Mr. Bundling."

"I still can't believe that you work with that man," Praxis said. "Honestly, Kaedrich. I thought that you had standards."

Kaedrich flinched. "He's a good man. Well . . . most of the time—but how many people do you know who *always* do the right thing, anyway? Every single time? In every single situation?"

"Just one."

There was something in the way that Praxis said this that made Kaedrich glance up. Praxis was just watching her, looking . . . almost *sad*, and it was this more than the open scrutiny that made Kaedrich turn away again. "Anyway," Kaedrich said, then fell short because she had nothing really to add. She picked at the seam of the enclosure in front of her, the line where the glass fitted into the wall, running her thumbnail in the slight groove.

Praxis leaned on the glass beside her. "What *is* your job, anyway? Are you some kind of . . . reporter now, or something?"

"Not exactly." Kaedrich shrugged. "You see, Mr. Bundling, he . . . well, he likes *investigating* a lot more than he likes actually writing everything up. So throughout his career, he's hired . . . assistants."

Praxis raised an eyebrow.

"It's not like *that*," Kaedrich added hastily. "It's strictly business. Mr. Bundling makes an outline—a detailed outline—touching on all the points that he wants his articles to cover. Then we—well, it's really just me, now, he only keeps one of us on at a time—but we draft up a copy of his articles."

"So you do the work for him."

"No . . . I mean, yes, technically, some of it. It's complicated. He gives me revision notes, and when it's the way he wants it to be, he still goes over it himself, you know, makes it sound more 'like him.' Then it goes to print." Kaedrich shrugged again. Somehow, saying it out loud like that, it did sound a little odd, and Kaedrich felt her shoulders start to curl just a bit forward.

Praxis shook her head. "It sounds to me like you're doing all the work, and he's getting all the credit."

Heat flared in Kaedrich's cheeks. "It's not about who gets *credit*," she snapped. "It's about . . . being part of something. Helping the world, in some small way. Did you know, when the Board of Abbney Gas and Lighting was caught embezzling funds, it was Mr. Bundling that found out about it? Without him, it never would have become public. They might have still been getting away with it to this *day*." Kaedrich sighed. "What?"

"What do you mean, 'What'?"

"That look. And don't say, 'What look?', because we both know that you did it."

Praxis had started to take a breath, but she shut her mouth and twisted it into a mockery of her usual scowl, instead. "It's nothing."

"Uh-huh."

"Really, it was nothing. It's just . . . I don't know, I think I forgot just how idealistic you are." Praxis glanced at her hands, as if the mechanical glove that she wore suddenly required a detailed inspection. She shrugged. "And I think . . . I think maybe I missed that."

It was a good thing that Kaedrich was already more or less steadying herself against the enclosure, because otherwise she might have collapsed outright at Praxis's admission. As it was, she merely wobbled, flattening her hand against the glass. Her throat went dry, but her palms made up the difference.

No, it wasn't much—and it wasn't as if Praxis had actually admitted to missing *Kaedrich*, so much as Kaedrich's idealism, but in Praxis-speak that was . . .

To be honest, Kaedrich wasn't really quite sure what it was. But it *felt* important.

She could tell her. Here, now. There was something about the reptile house that felt confessional, like maybe there was some lingering effect of whatever magic Praxis had used to try to suss the truth out of Lord Wellen, some lure that pulled buried thoughts to the surface. Kaedrich swallowed, trying to get her voice back. "Praxis—"

A distant crack broke the air, a scream trailing fast on its heels. Praxis and Kaedrich shared the briefest glance. "Was that—?" Praxis started.

"Gunfire," Kaedrich said.

She bolted, her long legs carrying her out the door almost as soon as the word had escaped her lips.

The air felt cool after the confined space of the reptile house. It spurred Kaedrich on, through the same paths that she'd chased Lord Wellen down not long before. Their isolated area of the zoo quickly gave way to the more popular attractions, and soon Kaedrich found herself needing to slow, edging her way hastily through an ever more rattled crowd. A couple of quieter shrieks were filtering their way back now, along with one girl sitting on the edge of the planter just sobbing her eyes out—someone else was rubbing her back, trying to shush her, though he was clearly disturbed by the experience as well. And in an instant, Kaedrich understood the distress: a body was sprawled on the tight-knit paving stones of the zoo's walkway, half of his face blown clean off. Kaedrich lurched to a halt, bile rising in her throat. A spray of red ran up the bars of the lion's cage, the beast inside all bristled up and pacing anxiously back and forth. It was a horrible spectacle, a gentleman dead at their feet, the man's hand still grasping his cane, which—

A chill jolted through Kaedrich. The cane was topped with a crystal falcat's head. Lord Wellen's cane. Kaedrich's stomach seized, and she made herself look away from it. She whipped her gaze up, scanning the crowd. It appeared to be a normal assemblage of people, both noblemen and the upper-middle class mixed together in what was supposed to be an afternoon of fun and frivolity, now all gaping downward in horror, or burying their faces in the shoulders of their companions to avoid looking at it. A handful of zoo employees, too, in their distinctive sage-and-tan uniforms that were cut to look like something one might wear out on safari.

And one man, near the edges of the crowd by now: head down, hat low, moving off as if he didn't have the slightest care what was going on around him. The crowd parted, just enough, and Kaedrich caught a glimpse of the man's hand, buried deep in the pocket of his long, gray overcoat.

Without thought, Kaedrich charged after him. No flowers hung in the air, and so Kaedrich shoved her way roughly through the crowd, occasionally toppling someone here or there—ordinarily, she would be beside herself with apologies, but as it was she did not have time. Her commotion had momentarily drawn the attention of the man that she was chasing, and he picked up his own pace now, discretion apparently be damned.

Kaedrich hurried forward, but unfortunately the crowds were work-ing against her. They sprang up thick and fast, parting seamlessly for the man that she was chasing and then oh-so-coincidentally coming together in tight knots in his wake. They were too random of an assemblage to all be working together, but Kaedrich had seen Praxis manipulate crowds so that everyone just happened to want to be out of her way at the ex-act right moment, so . . . Kaedrich was chasing a wizard of some skill. She gritted her teeth as she veered around a mother whose toddler had bolted in front of Kaedrich, stopping her short. "Excuse me, pardon me," Kaedrich kept saying, but the man in gray was getting harder and harder to see.

Silently, Kaedrich cursed herself for not having brought along her gun. Not that she would have wanted to fire it in a crowd full of women and children and elderly couples—it's just that a bullet was quickly becoming the only thing likely to catch up with him at this point. She couldn't let him get away.

That's exactly what was going to happen, though, and Kaedrich let out a small cry of frustration as she realized this. She could not call out to him, she could not shout "thief" or "stop" and point him out (for no one would believe her, against him), she could not shoot him even if she'd wanted to. She tried surging forward, and as expected, someone carrying an overlarge sack of animal feed chose that exact moment as the perfect time to cross her path. Kaedrich swerved, and tripped over a small rock.

She scooped it up. It was a last-ditch effort, the man's head nearly swallowed by the crowds now, but Kaedrich hopped onto a nearby bench and tracked his progress for a second or two. Just before he rounded a corner, Kaedrich threw the rock.

The man stopped, whirling to glare at Kaedrich. He raised his arm, shielding his face. In that moment his sleeve pulled back, just a little, enough for a flash of silver to catch the light. Not a piece of jewelry, however—it was difficult to tell in that brief moment, but the metal appeared to be *part* of his arm, blooming like a rash across his skin.

Kaedrich's blood ran cold as the rock struck the man's sleeve. It bounced off harmlessly, and the man shot Kaedrich another glare, this one laced with superiority. The man reached up, tipped his hat sarcastically in Kaedrich's direction.

He was gone before Kaedrich could even get down off of the bench. A large family had arranged themselves smack in front of the bench while Kaedrich's attention was turned, and she had to struggle to find enough room to escape. In the end, she had to scramble through a planter to the right of the bench, practically climbing the bars of the gazelle cage in order to work around them. She hopped down and ran to the corner where she'd last seen him, but it was too late by that point. "Blast," Kaedrich muttered.

So she followed the thickening foot traffic back the way that she'd come. Panic at the fate of Lord Wellen had given way by this point to gruesome curiosity, and despite the efforts of the zoo employees to keep everyone back, there was only so much they could do to tame the crowds. A press of gawkers had formed a wide circle around the scene, and Kaedrich was almost there when someone grabbed her roughly by the elbow.

"Best not get too close," Praxis muttered in her ear. There was a tug on Kaedrich's arm. "This way. Act sickened by what you've seen."

That was easy enough to do, although at the moment Kaedrich had more pressing concerns than her own horror at the death of Lord Wellen. "Praxis," Kaedrich started, keeping her voice low, "the man—the one that shot Wellen—he . . . I swear that part of his arm was *silver*."

"Not surprising."

"Not—!" Kaedrich sputtered. She threw her hands up. "When were you going to tell me that the Silvers are involved?"

"*Quiet!*" Praxis hissed. She cast a furtive glance around, her head down and her gaze shaded by her deerstalker cap. Her grip on Kaedrich's arm as Praxis wrenched it down was firm as a vice. "They're not *involved*, not exactly . . . not if I'm right."

"And what's *that* supposed to mean?"

"It means that we shouldn't discuss it here. I promise that I'll fill you in if you really want to know, but for now can we concentrate on getting out of here, please?"

Kaedrich fell silent, neither agreeing nor disagreeing. The main gates weren't far at this point, and so she concentrated on maneuvering through the crowd.

Unfortunately, they were already too late. Over the tops of people's heads, Kaedrich could just spot the gates being clanged shut, a contingent of police officers and a handful of royal guards talking to zoo officials and securing the area.

"I suppose they want to make sure whoever did it can't escape," Kaedrich said, speaking low in Praxis's ear. Never mind that he had already *gotten* away. A flash of guilt coursed through Kaedrich—if she hadn't chased after him, might he have been in less of a hurry to clear the area?

"We need to find someplace to hide," Praxis said.

"But we didn't do anything wrong."

Praxis snorted. "You think that's going to stop them?"

There was no argument to this, and so Kaedrich didn't offer one. She followed Praxis's lead as they casually folded themselves back into the crowd, which was now rippling with new irritation and excitement and gossip over the closing of the gates.

"I don't suppose you have a plan about where we should go," Kaedrich said after a few minutes of what felt like aimless wandering.

"Not really," Praxis admitted.

Kaedrich sighed. "Yeah, I didn't think so. All right, this way." She grabbed Praxis's sleeve, tugging her down a random path that they had almost passed by now. They kept their pace even, their heads high. Kaedrich wasn't even sure this was going to work, but it felt better than standing out here in the open. At the end of that path, they turned down another: shorter, less public—and a dead end.

Well, almost.

They were along the edge of the zoo by now, a high stone wall cutting off their exit. To either side were large enclosures, bored and lazy animals nibbling at feed scattered along the bottom of their cages.

Kaedrich glanced behind her, making sure no one else was with them. The pathway was mercifully empty, with only Praxis, looking at her with a puzzled expression.

Puzzled gave way to shocked when Kaedrich grabbed the bars and hopped up, like a child eager to get as close to the animals as she was able. She reached up, stretching as high as she could. Her fingers traced the upper lip of the bars. There was a tiny ledge ringing the top, hidden by a decorative front. Filth and cobwebs rained down, and Kaedrich twisted her face to avoid getting it into her eyes. She sidestepped, still feeling her way in the dark above her head.

"What in the world are you—?"

"Just keep a watch out, will you?" Kaedrich said. "Hang on, I think I've almost—there!" She grinned.

A heavy chain was tucked up in the hidden depths. Kaedrich tugged, wincing at the noise as it rattled and clanged its way down the bars. She scrambled to catch it before it crashed all of the way to the ground.

It was a short chain, just wrapped around two of the cage's bars. In the middle of the chain was a heavy padlock, and Kaedrich turned it around and motioned it toward Praxis.

Praxis did not question it. She touched the padlock, and a second later it clicked open. Kaedrich hurriedly removed it, unlooping the chain from around the bars—and then she swung the bars inward, revealing a previously hidden door, like something to a prison cell.

A tiny laugh of amazement escaped Praxis before she could stop it. "How did you know?"

"Long story," Kaedrich said. She took one last glance down the empty path before slipping through, and then she held out her hand to help Praxis inside. A moment to ease the door shut, another moment to string the chain back and tuck it all up out of sight again. The animals inside of the enclosure with them—a family of sleepy zebras—didn't even pay attention to them as they hurried to a far corner. The Monfort Zoo had gone through a partial effort to make their cages feel natural and lifelike, and so a handful of artificial trees and rocks had been arranged like stage props. Kaedrich lifted up the corner of one of the rocks, her heart pounding—gods, if she was wrong about all of this . . .

But thankfully, the inside was a hollow pocket, a façade of lumber and tarp and plaster paint. Just large enough for two people to crawl underneath.

BY THE TIME a soft rapping could be heard against her door, Lanali was already shouting over it. *"Enter!"* she snapped in Aul. She dropped her arms, wriggling out of the depths of the dress that her lady's maid was currently assisting her with.

This was, she had to admit to herself, one minor aspect of Durlish affluence that she was not especially thrilled with. In Aul, nobody helped each other to dress unless you were an invalid or otherwise unable to do the job yourself. Granted, the clothes were much simpler—everyone wore pants and shirts, various colors and textures and cuts of course, and they had unisex suits with formal short-sleeved jackets and pieces of neckwear that were kind of like ties. Lanali didn't miss the *styles* of her homeland, just like she didn't miss the beds, or the food, or the music . . . but still, trying to adjust to letting someone else do up her corsets, arrange her hair . . . it hadn't quite *settled* yet with the Pon.

Her lady's maid swiftly pulled the yards of fabric out from underfoot, tucking it over her arm with such precision that she could have been a soldier folding a flag. She straightened up, towering over Lanali; Lanali watched in the mirror as the maid's eyes shifted to a corner of the reflection and bugged out in alarm.

The maid whirled, already squeaking in protest as Tol stepped through the doorway. She started to throw the dress back over Lanali, but Lanali raised her hand in a single, demure gesture, noble and Pon-like. By the tides, Lanali was still wearing three layers of undergarments—where, exactly, was the harm?

"Will manage," Lanali told the maid. "Gratitude. Please later return, with summons."

The maid forced a nod, though her face was pinched. She bowed and turned, carrying the dress away to launder or mend or whatever it was that happened to finery once it was out of sight. Lanali caught a glimpse of one last glare cast down at Tol's head as the maid passed, but otherwise she did what was asked of her.

The door shut gently in her wake.

As soon as she was gone, Lanali began yanking pins out of her hair and throwing them down on a nearby vanity. She wore it down, loose curls caressing her shoulders, but she did defer enough to Durlish modesty to wear the sides twisted back in elaborate loops and braids. She grabbed a brush and ripped through her locks, too angry to even look at Tol.

"You told me that you were going to kill her."

"Did I say that I was running straight out to do the deed in haste?"

Lanali let out a soft "ugh" under her breath. "Yes, that's all very *patient* of you—but in the meantime, I've just had reports of a confirmed sighting. Would you like to know who she was talking to?"

"Lord Wellen," Tol said, as calmly as if reciting the lunch menu.

Lanali turned only long enough to glare at him. He was standing as unruffled as ever, hands folded neatly in front of him. He met Lanali's gaze openly, not even having the decency to blush at her relative state of undress.

"I don't have time to play these games," Lanali said. She threw the brush down and stalked over to her open closet, as if she had any idea what was even inside of it, as if she'd ever hand-selected one of her new spread of dresses.

"Our business *is* games."

"Not anymore. I have a meeting with the captain of the royal guardsmen in an hour, and a dinner with Lord Braynish after that. We're too close to leave anything else in play at this point."

Tol chuckled. "How is 'mern' Braynish these days?"

"Are you even listening to me?" Lanali asked. She ripped a dress at random off of its hanger, throwing it across to Tol; he caught it without even flinching. "I want her dead! You promised me her death!"

"And so she will die," Tol said. "Do not mistake my patience for idleness. But if you think that charging her in a brazen attempt to catch her off guard will work—"

"It will *work* if you rain enough hell down faster than she can handle." Lanali jerked her head upward and roughly to the left, in the general direction of Tol's room. "How's your little science project coming along?"

Tol gritted his teeth. A muscle near his elbow flexed, the scar twitching as if in anticipation. "I've had great success so far," he said, weighing each word carefully before laying it out by her feet. "But we shouldn't bank everything on it—not against someone of her skill."

"Her 'skill'?" Lanali asked, already bristling. "Is that a trace of *admiration* in your voice? Do I need to remind you who we're dealing with?"

Tol merely shrugged. "It's never smart to disrespect your opponents. She's proven herself an able wizard."

"She's gotten *lucky*."

"Perhaps. That is not to be discounted."

Lanali huffed as she turned away. A full-length mirror caught her disgust, the sneer crinkling her nose. She smoothed her face out; she would not be ruffled, not tonight. Her expressions needed to be flawless in her meetings, her mind free of concern. "Her luck ends tonight, do you hear me?" Lanali said. She waved her hand, as if it didn't matter. "Take whoever you need—some of the new recruits. Use the weapon. Bring her down."

Tol was smirking in the reflection, his mirth and disapproval peeping over the top of Lanali's shoulder. She shifted, just enough to cut off his view.

"It won't be enough," he said.

Lanali shrugged. "Make it enough." She leaned in toward the mirror. "And send the girl back in, will you? Something needs to be done about my hair."

IT WAS TWO or three hours before Praxis deemed that the zoo had cleared out enough for them to make their escape. Though she'd burned half a dozen discreet air holes in the top and sides of their fake rock, the air of their hiding place had long since gone stale. The musty smell of hay and large animals hung ripe in their faces, baked to their fullest by the warm rays of the setting sun. Sweat coated Kaedrich's skin, a tacky layer that acted like glue to her slowly drying clothes. She wanted to take off her suit jacket, or at least open up the collar of her shirt, but she dared not do either. Her legs were scrunched in front of her, the steeple of them pressed parallel against Praxis's. There was no room under here for personal space.

They had spoken only a little since coming in here. A handful of whispered remarks—are-you-okay's, and do-you-think-they're-gone-yet's. They did not risk their voices carrying. They did not risk the zebras getting spooked, or acting oddly and drawing attention.

It was dark by the time they finally crawled out. Kaedrich gulped down fresh air as she stood up. Her legs were cramping something fierce, and it took several moments of shaking out her foot for the pins-and-needles numbness to go away. Brex squawked at them happily as soon as they appeared, swooping in from a nearby perch, but Praxis shushed him and sent him flying again almost immediately.

Getting back out of the enclosure was no more difficult than getting in. Praxis kept an ear out, her senses on high alert as they stole into the darkness of the zoo. She motioned her intentions to Kaedrich: stop, go, left, stop, right. Kaedrich would have thought that, given the fact that someone had been *murdered*, there would have been a lot more night patrolmen on duty—perhaps even joined by a temporary police force, on loan from the nearest station—but the zoo was oddly quiet. They hurried through without incident, avoiding the few guards that were around. Animals snuffled as they passed, or snored in large huddles from the middle of their enclosures. The night air had turned chill, or perhaps it just felt that way to Kaedrich after being trapped under the rock all evening. The hairs on the back of her neck were standing on end. Something was very wrong here, some calm that Kaedrich didn't trust.

And yet, their escape was textbook. When they approached the main gates, a solitary patrolman standing vigil, Praxis gave a light whistle, and Brex dove at him. The patrolman yelped, swatting at the blur that nipped playfully at his face. He ran aside, trying to duck out from underneath Brex's lovable assault, leaving just enough time for Praxis and Kaedrich to let themselves seamlessly out of the gate.

They strolled down the main path from the zoo entrance with nary a backward glance, chittering filtering down from above them that sounded oddly like laughter. With a click and a whistle, Brex was off, hunting some innocent animal he'd spotted, and leaving Praxis and Kaedrich to blend back in with the main traffic of the streets without so much as a hiccup in their operations.

So Kaedrich tried to shake it off. She had more important things to worry about at the moment, anyway—like where in the world she would find Mr. Bundling at this time of day, to report in on everything that had happened. She figured that the best bet would be to head back to the square, see if he was still getting any information on the dead bodies staked up in front of the Crescent, and when she turned down the appropriate street, Praxis followed.

Which was nice, in some respects, and yet . . . after so much time spent in silence, the air between them had thickened. Kaedrich shifted, trying to get her suit to lie better against her rapidly cooling skin. This was what it was like, she decided: keeping all of her secrets from Praxis felt as if she was constantly wearing a dampened suit, chafing against her at the slightest movement.

"So, are you finally going to tell me now?" Praxis asked.

Kaedrich stumbled, her feet catching on nothing. "T-tell you?"

"Yeah," Praxis said, frowning. "The 'long story'? How you knew exactly how to get into the zebra cage?"

"Oh! Oh, that, yeah—I, um." She took a deep breath, trying to calm her heart rate. "Well . . . basically, it boils down to this bet? Something that Lucan got himself into in the Cross Street pub, and . . . you know what, maybe it's better if you don't know," she said. "I don't want to tarnish your impression of him before you've actually met."

"No, no—now you *have* to tell me," Praxis said. She had moved up until she was right beside Kaedrich now, and in the passing streetlamps the grin that she flashed was dazzling.

Kaedrich flushed. "No, it's . . ." She cleared her throat. "Anyway, shouldn't we talk about something that actually matters? Like what you managed to get out of Lord Wellen?"

The grin was gone. Strips of light and dark passed over Praxis's face as they walked by the shops and homes leading toward the center of Monfort. Kaedrich tried not to think about what Praxis had to do in order to get Lord Wellen to share his information with her, and tried to focus instead on the fact that they had learned something. That was the important part, she told herself. Maybe if she thought it enough, she'd start to believe it.

There was a long moment of silence after that. Long enough for Kaedrich to assume that Praxis had decided to be her usual secretive self, boxing Kaedrich out of their investigations to "protect" her. Kaedrich's mouth twisted up in disgust; but then, out of nowhere, Praxis took a breath.

She told her.

She told her everything—what the magic was; the layers of resistance that Lord Wellen had put up in an instinctive effort to keep her out; the fog in his memories, thick and pervasive. And everything that had happened, every word that Praxis could remember, every pain that he'd felt and transferred to her.

By the time she was done, Kaedrich's stomach was twisted up in a dozen different kinds of knots. The magic that Praxis was using was particularly disquieting—okay, so she'd explained that it wasn't the ability to simply pluck things from a person's mind at a distance, like the "vacant" that had posed as Praxis's double, but . . . it was close enough to make Kaedrich's skin crawl.

"We should tell Mr. Bundling," Kaedrich said finally.

Praxis scoffed. "What good is *that* going to do?"

"He can get the word out. He's already investigating—I'm sure that once he hears about all of this, he'll be only too happy to publish. People have to know what's happening, Praxis. They have to be able to protect themselves."

"Oh, yes," Praxis said, rolling her eyes. "Let's do that, why not? Cause a mass panic. I suppose you want to tell him that Lanali is behind it, too?"

"You make that sound like a bad thing."

"Because it *is*." Praxis sighed. She and Kaedrich separated for a moment, jostled apart by the crowd leading up to the Crescent. Chants from the center of the square could already be heard even here, two or three blocks out.

"We can trust him," Kaedrich said.

"Fine," Praxis said. "Fine, you want to trust him, then trust him. Tell him everything. See what good it does you." She scowled, moving *again* around a knot of protesters hurrying forward. "Gods, do these crowds get thicker every day?"

"They do, in fact," Kaedrich said, elbowing her way through. There were at least as many people here now as there had been earlier—maybe more. That tended to happen, too, the evening driving them out in greater numbers. As if the events of the day had simply been too much, and now whatever was holding them back from joining in had finally broken. They gathered around makeshift fires when the nights were cold, their faces looking angrier than usual in the harsh shadows of the lamps and the flames.

Praxis ducked to avoid someone's arm. "You'd think they'd have better things to do than stand around shouting."

Kaedrich darted aside, dragging Praxis to avoid the spiteful glare that one or two of the people around them had cast in their general direction. "Perlandra's breath, Praxis, keep comments like that to yourself," she muttered.

"What? Don't tell me that anyone here actually believes they're going to *change* something."

"*Praxis.*"

"I'm just saying, the Governance Council isn't even in session right now. What's the point?"

Kaedrich shook her head. She scanned the crowd jostling around her as she squeezed farther and farther toward the Crescent. Bodies shifted in the dark, the night turning everyone unfamiliar. Mr. Bundling could have been anywhere, and Kaedrich took her time, trying to peer into people's faces without drawing attention to herself.

The bodies had been taken down by now, the police and royal guards reduced to their normal patrolling levels. A lamp over the main doors revealed a faint smudge of red, presumably from before they'd laid down the tarp, the only indication that something had happened here. Well, that and the odd quiet that still hovered over the innermost layers of the protesters, the way that they kept ducking their heads and talking furiously to one another. But Kaedrich supposed that was to be expected.

It was probably nothing, but Kaedrich kept glancing skyward, relief blooming in her heart whenever she spotted the flash of Brex's silvery fur in the moonlight. Things had been getting tenser for weeks now, and Kaedrich had no intentions of being here when things finally reached the breaking point.

Because there was no doubt in her mind that there *would* come a breaking point, no matter what cynicism Praxis chose to cling to. The very air of Monfort was thick with unrest these days—it could not sustain itself forever.

There was no sign of Mr. Bundling. Kaedrich tried not to be concerned about this, as they made their way out of the thick of things. Thankfully, all was quiet as they returned to the bustle of everyday life, protests leading way to people going about their nightly business. Never had Kaedrich been more grateful for street hawkers and evening newspaper sellers, for people sweeping manure out of the way in front of wealthy gentlemen and ladies. Kaedrich's mouth watered as they passed by first one restaurant and then another, the smell of frying meat and well-seasoned sauces pulling like a tether on her ravenous stomach. At this point, she wanted nothing more than to go home and change, chew through whatever meager food was lying around. Kaedrich shifted; her clothes were stiff from having dried against her skin, and now it felt like her bindings were starting to give. She tried to look discreetly downward to make sure she was still all "in place," and so she wasn't really listening when Praxis said, "I guess today's been kind of ridiculous, hasn't it?", nor did Kaedrich really think when she gave her reply: "I wouldn't have minded so much if I had gotten time for lunch—I haven't eaten anything since this morning."

"Oh . . . Let's get dinner, then," Praxis said, and now Kaedrich was paying attention.

She stopped. Praxis stopped.

"Dinner?"

It didn't mean anything, Kaedrich reminded herself. It was a gesture of friendship—not even that, hadn't Kaedrich just expressed her own hunger? One flowed somewhat naturally from the other.

Praxis shrugged. "Why not? There's a nice-looking restaurant just across from my hotel."

This was the wrong thing to say, though Praxis probably had no idea. Why would she? Instantly, Kaedrich remembered the last time that she'd followed Praxis to a restaurant: the smell of the lilies that Kaedrich had bought, the way that her sweaty palm had soaked through the paper wrapper around the stems. That was the night before Kaedrich had left.

"I . . . I should really go by Mr. Bundling's office," Kaedrich said. "I still think he's our best way forward."

"That's fine," Praxis said, ignoring Kaedrich's discomfort, "we can meet after. There's probably a wait for a table, anyway. I'll go ahead, get us a good spot—you can catch up when you're done."

Kaedrich sighed. "Praxis, I fell into a fountain, remember? I look awful, I can't—"

"Nonsense, you look fine."

"I do *not* look 'fine,'" Kaedrich snapped. "I'm a mess. My legs are cramped from hiding, I'm filthy, I'm miserable—I just want to get this done so that I can go home and *change*."

The irritation fell as quickly as it had risen. Shame rushed in to take its place, as Kaedrich saw her words hit their mark. Praxis's face slackened, her usual wall of ice back in place; it was only once it returned that Kaedrich realized it hadn't been there a moment before.

Kaedrich reached out, but Praxis shifted so naturally out of reach, brushing her hair aside as if that was the entire purpose for her motion.

"I'm sorry," Kaedrich said, "I didn't—"

"No, it's fine, of course it's fine. It was a stupid suggestion. I don't know why I even said it."

"You know what, maybe I was wrong. I probably *should* eat. I mean, it's not like there's much in the way of dinner waiting for me back at the apartment."

It was a weak cover, and they both knew it. Praxis shook her head. "Go home, Kaedrich," she said, already moving off.

"No, but—" Kaedrich started. She lurched forward, grabbing Praxis's free hand.

Praxis stopped, glanced down, glanced up. Her fingers were cold, probably from the chill of her slow-drying coat. Kaedrich remembered the first time that she'd fully held Praxis's hand, as Praxis hauled her up from the grass; she'd been surprised by Praxis's warmth, so sure that someone from the frozen south would be herself only partially thawed. It was a silly assumption then, just like it was silly now to assume that nothing about Praxis would ever be different. This wasn't the same restaurant, this wasn't last time. She had *invited* Kaedrich this time—would it have really been so dangerous to say "yes," just this once?

But before Kaedrich could say anything, Praxis slipped her hand away, and Kaedrich knew that the offer had passed. "Tomorrow, maybe?" Kaedrich asked. It felt so important to snatch it back, suddenly, whatever intangible air that she'd lost.

One of Praxis's shoulders rose and fell with casual indifference, slaying Kaedrich's heart and hopes both. "Maybe. Sure. If there's time."

Kaedrich glanced down. There was no point in arguing, and she said nothing as Praxis started off down the street once more. Kaedrich waited until she was out of sight before whirling around, slamming her fist into the side of a nearby building. Pain flared in her knuckles, but she bit down on it, refusing to cry out. The act startled a nearby couple, strolling arm in arm, and they hurriedly crossed to the other side of the street, eyeing Kaedrich nervously the whole time.

"Gods *dammit*," Kaedrich muttered to herself, harsher language than she normally allowed herself to use. What was the point of being pious now, though? She punched the wall again. Her fist stung, half a dozen tiny scrapes just beginning to bloom droplets of red, and Praxis was still gone. Kaedrich tried to tell herself that it didn't really matter, because it's not like Kaedrich was going to say anything. That the dinner would have changed nothing, not even relieved the burden of secrecy from Kaedrich's heart. That it was probably for the best.

And all of this may have been true, to some degree or another, but it did nothing to stop the ache lodged deep in her rib cage. It did nothing to quell the feeling that she'd just lost something precious. Kaedrich leaned her forehead against the brick wall that she'd just been punching, regret locking her up. If she stayed here, then maybe if Praxis changed her mind . . . ?

Her mouth twisted up. It was a foolish sentiment—Praxis never changed her mind. Kaedrich shoved herself away from the wall in disgust, and turned on her heel. She still had to check in with Mr. Bundling. Kaedrich made herself walk off, made herself look straight ahead instead of constantly checking back over her shoulder. She left the street behind, with its gentle bustle of foot traffic, the rattle of the rails overhead, the shouts as people hailed hansoms or hawked their wares. No one that was left even heard the subtle click of gears a few minutes later, edging toward the street corner. They approached, stopped for a moment.

The sounded receded again, unheard, back the way that it had come.

Chapter Ten

"Stop," Mr. Bundling said. He held up one ink-stained hand, whorls of black tracing hedgerow-paths across each of his fingertips. "I can't print this."

Kaedrich sputtered to a halt. She wanted to say *You're joking,* but she knew that Mr. Bundling wasn't joking. Even ignoring the fact that Kaedrich had never known Mr. Bundling to crack a joke at all, one look at his sharp face, the straight cut of his brow, the angry bruise blooming underneath his left eye, and it was clear that humor was the last thing on his mind. Mr. Bundling pushed his glasses up his nose, and they slid right back down again.

Maybe Praxis was right, maybe it *was* a mistake to try to get Mr. Bundling involved. Kaedrich had been so convinced, during the walk back to the Daily Witness, that it was the right thing to do, but now . . .

She sat down heavily in the chair on the far side of Mr. Bundling's desk. She'd been on her feet as she talked, bursting into his office as if the world was on fire. The story had spilled out of her so fast that her words were practically tripping over themselves. There was no time to sit. There was no time to *think,* even—Kaedrich knew that she was babbling, and while a part of her worried that she was giving too much away, another part of her couldn't stop herself. She told him the whole story, more or less. The meeting with Lord Wellen, of course, and everything that Praxis had relayed of his experience; but she'd also told him about Pon Lanali. The truth, going back to the beginning. It felt like it had happened a million years ago. Kaedrich wondered, briefly, why she'd never done this before, why she'd never tried to fight the tide of Lanali's support—but then she realized that she *had* tried, that she'd told everyone who would listen on her trip back to Brindle, and at Brindlewood Hall. Nobody had believed her. By the time she'd moved to Monfort, she'd stopped trying.

Kaedrich tried now. She had no idea if Mr. Bundling would believe her any more than the valet or the maids or the gardener had, but it felt desperately important that she try. Maybe this, finally, would be the turning point. Maybe Mr. Bundling's story would spread, the truth finally brought to light.

But no. The hand, a clear and present signal. *Stop. I can't print this.*

It was the valet all over again.

Mr. Bundling made a noise of disgust. Kaedrich looked up, worried that she was in for a reprimand, but instead Mr. Bundling was looking at her as if she was a puppy that he'd just kicked. He tossed his pen down onto his desk; ink splattered from the tip, staining several pages of an open book, as well as the corner of a formal-looking envelope bearing the distinctive turquoise seal of the Crown.

"Kaedrich, think about what you're asking me to do. Lanali is the people's *savior*. You want me to turn around and claim otherwise? Without *proof*?"

"But Lord Wellen—"

"Is dead," Mr. Bundling said. "If he was still alive, or if we had a written admission of everything that he'd suffered at the hands of this . . . Tol, did you say?"

Kaedrich nodded.

Mr. Bundling shrugged. "Well, maybe then we would be having a different conversation. As it stands, all that we have is your word on the matter. *Your* word, Mr. Mannly. Which, forgive me for saying so, but that doesn't amount to much in the eyes of the public."

"There's Praxis."

Kaedrich kind of hated using Praxis like this—taking advantage of her station in life, the power that her family wielded in Yandosia. It was the first time that Kaedrich had ever purposefully tried to use her connection to Praxis for a boost, and it left Kaedrich feeling oddly squirmy in her chair. But, personal discomfort aside, if it got the job done, then Kaedrich would be willing to live with it.

Assuming Praxis agreed to go on record, but Kaedrich could worry about that later.

Mr. Bundling sucked in his cheek, chewing the inside thoughtfully for a moment. He was studying Kaedrich as if seeing her for the first time again. He held up one finger. "I doubt that Lady Praxis would be willing to do something like that," Mr. Bundling said. He added another finger. "And even if she was, she's been publicly discredited here in Monfort. Or didn't you know that she *attacked* her former patron?"

"I did," Kaedrich said, though that wasn't her first thought. Her first thought ran hotter through her mind, bringing a flush to her cheeks. *What did he mean by "Lady" Praxis?* Yandosians *had* no nobility, though now that Kaedrich thought about it . . . Gods, was this the level of courtesy that she was supposed to give Praxis, and all of this time Kaedrich had been going around publicly claiming a very *intimate* form of address with her, instead?

No wonder Mr. Bundling was giving her such an odd look.

Kaedrich cleared her throat. "But surely the word of *Lady* Praxis still has to be worth something. Her actions don't diminish her rank."

"No," Mr. Bundling conceded. "That's certainly true. That would be enough to get people to listen, but unfortunately, her actions would make it more likely that they'd assume that she's started making up non-sense. She could easily discredit your claims, rather than bolstering them. And . . ." Mr. Bundling paused, frowned. "Privately, I have it on good authority that Lord Levington has changed his story. I have no doubt that he'd come forward with it—true or not—in the event that Lady Praxis tried to breathe a single word against the Pon. Thus disgracing both her *and* anyone foolish enough to give her space in the newspaper."

"You can't be suggesting that we sit and do nothing," Kaedrich said.

She knew Mr. Bundling well enough to be sure of *that*. True, it's not as if they were fast friends (why should they be?), nor had Mr. Bundling ever taken Kaedrich under his wing as a mentor and master-of-trade to a raw and budding talent. But they'd shared an office for a year now. Kaedrich had watched his process, as he listened for stories and pursued them with the determination of Brex on a hunt. Mr. Bundling *wanted* to do good in this world. Why else would he have refused the various editorial positions that had sometimes been offered to him, why else would he want to be out there on the streets day and night, why else would he sometimes give up all sleep and forget to eat, trying to piece a puzzle together? The far wall of Bundling's cramped office was covered with a street map of Monfort, nearly falling apart now from years of pins being stuck all over it as he tracked the line of a story from one corner of the city to the other.

The map lay empty now. All of his notes about the disappearances, every trace of what he was looking for, lay tucked out of sight.

And he was staring at Kaedrich, his hands folded neatly over his desk. A tight, empty smile sliced his face. Kaedrich went cold. It occurred to her for the first time that Mr. Bundling was *scared*. Not just for his reputation at the newspaper, should he move forward with the story before he had solid proof; his terror ran deeper than that, masked and stamped down so much that maybe even he didn't realize it was there—but it was. She found herself studying the bruise underneath his eye. He'd claimed, when she had first burst in here, that he'd gotten in the way of a swing that one of the protesters had meant for a royal guard, but Kaedrich was forced to question the truth of that.

"Listen," Mr. Bundling said. His voice had turned friendly, as if they were old pals. He pushed his glasses up his nose where, for once, they stayed put. "I'll tell you what—I'll keep an ear out. Okay? And maybe, you know, if anyone wants to come forward and corroborate what you've said, or if I find anything out that supports your version of events, well . . ."

Kaedrich waited. Mr. Bundling's fingers twitched, as if he wanted to unfold them and drum them heavily on his desk.

He shrugged. "Well . . . if that happens, we'll see what happens then. If anything happens then. In the meantime, I'd like you to drop this subject. Not just around me—it's best if you keep these sorts of accusations to yourself. Do you understand me, Mr. Mannly?"

She didn't.

Or rather, she did—but she understood too *much*. It could be that he was trying to warn her off, to protect her from something dangerous that he understood more about than he was willing to admit. Or it could be that he was hinting the opposite: that Kaedrich *should* nose about on her own, ask questions, try to bring in witnesses that Mr. Bundling (for whatever reason) was unable to gain direct access to. Perhaps he thought that her association with Praxis meant that she had more connections than he'd previously believed. Or maybe he was trying to signal that he couldn't be trusted, that she'd already said too much. Maybe the office wasn't safe. Maybe he wanted to discuss the subject in greater detail later, somewhere they could talk without fear of being compromised.

Or maybe he just meant what he said. That he was going to keep an ear out, and until then it was safer if Kaedrich kept to herself. That was the trouble with having spent so much time with Praxis and her sullen glances, her layers upon layers of unspoken meaning. Kaedrich was used to looking for depth, but what if there was nothing underneath?

Mr. Bundling had leveled Kaedrich with a heavy stare as he waited. His glasses slid, infinitesimally, down the oily slope of his nose. *Do you understand me?*

Kaedrich nodded. It felt like the only acceptable answer.

"Good," Mr. Bundling said. He pushed his glasses back up and turned his attention to the papers spread across his desk. There was a fat stack with ink still gleaming, and he dropped it unceremoniously in front of Kaedrich. The papers landed with a *slap* that made Kaedrich jump. "In the meantime, you can start there."

"Now?" Kaedrich asked. She looked from the papers, to the clock that sat on a corner shelf, back to the papers again. Even if she hurried, translating Mr. Bundling's dense outline into a coherent thought process was going to take hours.

Mr. Bundling frowned. "I'm sorry," he said, not sounding sorry at all, "do you have someplace more *important* to be right now?"

Kaedrich swallowed down the lump in her throat. She pictured a restaurant, generic and alluring. Somewhere in the back of her head, she'd begun to wonder . . . if she showed up . . . if Praxis had gone without her . . .

Kaedrich shook her head, chasing the image away. "No."

Mr. Bundling nodded. "Good. I'll expect a draft by the morning. Now, if you'll excuse me, I'm going to head out—my understanding is that the body from the zoo still hasn't been correctly identified." Mr. Bundling grinned, slick and a little unnerving, as he stood up. "With any luck, I'll get the story before anyone else has time."

Kaedrich grimaced, but made no attempt to argue. She scooped the pages of Mr. Bundling's outline into her arms, shuffling over to her rickety tea table in the corner. The door was already shutting behind him as Kaedrich sat back down. Ordinarily, Kaedrich would carefully sort through each page one piece at a time, absorbing the whole of what Mr. Bundling was going for before she ever dared begin setting words to paper—yet now, she couldn't even get herself past the premise for the headline, scrawled in fast letters over the top of the page. *Royal Guard Implicated in Death of Top Protest Leaders; Officials Deny All Involvement.* The hairs on the back of her neck stood on end, remembering the people that she'd seen staked to the front of the Crescent. She read the line over and over again, but it was other words that kept ringing round and round her mind. *Do you understand me?*

She did. Even if it was not what Mr. Bundling had meant, she understood.

This was too big now for her to ignore.

THE RESTAURANT PROBABLY *was* as good as it looked, though Praxis hardly noticed.

She sulked all through dinner. They had seated her at a table for two, tucked out of sight in a corner, where Praxis fastidiously refused to look at the empty chair across from her. She ate her meal without tasting it, mindlessly drank her coffee, and tried and failed and tried and failed *not* to picture what the evening could have looked like. If Kaedrich had said "yes." If Praxis hadn't taken the rejection so harshly, or had relented when Kaedrich tried to change her mind.

The invitation had been a lark. It was out of Praxis's mouth before she could question herself, and she had seen Kaedrich's hesitation immediately. By that point, though, what other choice did she have but to push onward? Backtracking would have made it seem as if it mattered, but more than that . . . it *did* matter, dammit. Once Praxis had said it, she had envisioned it, and once she'd envisioned it she couldn't resist. Praxis was not, generally speaking, a brave person when it came to expressing her emotions, and so it's not as if she had ever imagined that this was the night, that they would sit down and the whole truth would come tumbling out of her. It didn't have to be that. The idea of having another quiet evening with Kaedrich was enough. Listening to her voice, her laughter. No business to discuss, no schemes to bicker over.

Instead, she'd eaten in silence, only the clink of her knife and fork to keep her company. The other sounds of the restaurant washed over her as a disinterested tide. A piano was playing in the middle of the room, conversations drifting in and out of hearing range. Trills of laughter, both fake and genuine, punctuated the restaurant as high notes in a song that Praxis didn't want to hear.

The last time that she'd been in a restaurant had been one of the worst mistakes of Praxis's life. It was just after returning to the shores of Durland, having thwarted another one of Pon Lanali's mad schemes, and Praxis was only trying to pay back a favor. They'd been helped quite a bit by one of the people they'd met, and the thing that he wanted in exchange was a good steak dinner—a thing that he never could have afforded on his own. It was a small price to pay, and seemed harmless. Praxis left Kaedrich back at their hotel room, intending only to be gone for only an hour or two. And everything had been fine, until Kaedrich turned up right behind Praxis's chair, wanting a word with her; and the *look* on her face . . .

Praxis wasn't stupid. She knew how it looked, being out like this. The fine table spread, the romantic lighting. It wasn't her fault that the best place for a good meal was dressed up like that, and she'd *wanted* to explain herself right then and there.

She hadn't, and that was the mistake. Kaedrich had left the next morning.

Praxis almost didn't go to the restaurant tonight. Going with Kaedrich would have been one thing, but going by herself . . . The only reason that she'd done so, in the end, was the simple fact that she was hungry and it was convenient. She told herself that it didn't matter, that avoiding restaurants for the rest of her life was a stupid reaction and she had to get it out of her system now, before it became a physiological condition. But now she wasn't so sure that she'd made the right choice.

Halfway through her meal, they seated a couple at a nearby table. Praxis kept her attention on her plate, though it did nothing to deflect the honeyed tones of the couple's banter as they settled into place and reviewed their menus. Praxis stabbed at her dinner as the woman practically purred in response to something the man had said to her.

Gods, was it really so difficult? If Praxis could master the Triad of Light spell, if she could traverse the ruins of Kal Z'har, if she could journey into the land of the dead and trap the freed Beacon of Souls for herself, then how was *this* the thing that stymied her? Her feelings were straightforward, even if she refused to give name to them. There was even a sliver of a chance they might be reciprocated, though Praxis kept herself from assuming too much on that regard—she was not, after all, an unbiased judge when it came to gauging Kaedrich's moods, her pauses. So how was it, Praxis asked herself as she stood and left a handful of bills on the table, how was it she could not bring herself to flat-out *say* anything?

The hotel stared at her from directly across the street, but Praxis couldn't face it. Eating alone, going "home" alone, sleeping alone. She turned instead, curling her fingers as she stalked off into the tide of foot traffic that was still going strong. She had no particular destination in mind, nothing to *do* to fill up all of this free time, but she knew that she needed to keep moving. Sitting around in her empty hotel room would do her no good at all.

Her sour mood followed her for the rest of the evening. As she walked from one end of Monfort to the other, couples arm in arm all around her; as she took in a meaningless song-and-dance show at a music hall;

as she stood along the shore and watched the stars, each twinkling light mocking her in its cheerfulness. It followed her all the way back to her room, finally, well after midnight. Praxis crossed the room, fingers flexing, to pop open the window so that Brex could return whenever he liked. She paused for a moment, breathing in the night air, and considered whistling for him, but what would be the point? He was lovely company, sure— but he wasn't the company that she wanted. She stared at the street below without really seeing it.

If there was a click, it was so quiet that Praxis didn't consciously hear it; still *something* made her turn around, and as she did so, the crack of a gun suddenly filled the tiny space of her hotel room. Praxis flicked her free hand, deflecting the bullet; but without any sense of where it was coming from or exactly what part of her it was heading toward, it was difficult to direct its trajectory with her usual skill. The bullet veered off course and bit through her hip.

She did not cry out, but the force of the impact did stagger her. Praxis fell back against the windowsill. In this marginal pause she heard the weapon rearm, and a single footstep as the interloper let himself out of her wardrobe.

Tol. She should have expected as much. Praxis snapped her palm open, fire springing to life. She lurched to the side as he took aim once more, and she threw a burst of flame toward him.

He doused it easily enough, which was just what Praxis had expected— in fact, she was counting on it. The momentary effort that it took gave her enough time to conjure a larger, unformed burst of flames, to stand between the two of them. Tol flinched back, as she was hoping that he would, though he did not waste time. He fired the gun through the flames, even without being able to see. Praxis batted the bullet aside with a flash of light, realizing only too late that the action itself had probably given something of her position away.

Why did Tol even *bother* with guns? To a wizard, such weapons were crude at best, slowing down their attacks with their cumbersome need for ammunition and the time it took to recover from the kickback.

As much of a curiosity as it was, though, Praxis gave it little thought at the time. She dodged another shot, and then another, and then Tol apparently had to stop and reload. Praxis took the opportunity to make for the door. She had intended to shape the free-form fire into a standing figure, a puppet she could use to attack Tol, but between clutching at her hip and flexing her fingers to guide her other leg forward, she found herself with a frustrating lack of hands.

She was almost to the door when it burst open. In poured two additional men, their faces hidden by heavy cloaks of deep crimson. At the sight of them, Praxis's arm gave a sympathetic twinge; a ringing flared through her mind, like two pieces of metal clashing together. Praxis grimaced. She released hold on her wound long enough to toss random flames in their direction, as they, too, opened fire. Praxis darted and ducked, trying to backtrack her way to the window. She whistled shrilly toward the open sky, and then she dodged another bullet, two—it hardly mattered at this point. The room was filling with smoke now, which Praxis willed not to drift out into the night air. Tol was shouting something at the other men in a tone that sounded authoritative, and Praxis took the temporary distraction of their reshuffling to make a mad rush for the window.

It was true that the harness on her leg made it impossible to outright *run* anymore, but she had made it a habit to practice moving as fast as she could, and it paid off now. Praxis flicked her free hand, and the flames leaped higher, the men shouted louder. She heard the comforting shriek of Brex, a mad flutter bursting over her head as she reached the window.

This was no time to worry about being dainty. The window was open, yes, but not yet large enough. Praxis threw a fireball at the remaining glass and it shattered outward, raining onto the street below. As Brex dealt with her assailants, Praxis all but threw herself out of the window, tipping head over heels as she began to fall toward the street.

It was safe to say that her encounter had not gone unnoticed by this point. Before she fell, she'd heard many additional voices pounding toward her hotel room, and in the street beyond, a tiny crowd was gathering to watch the flaming room high above them. These gawkers probably thought that they were safe, well out of harm's way, and so the screams that met her as she sped toward the sidewalk were no doubt as much out of fear for themselves as out of concern for her.

She slowed herself just before she struck the ground, but not quite as quickly as she'd intended. The slap of stone knocked the wind out of her, and her arm twisted painfully underneath her collapsing weight. Praxis gritted her teeth together as she struggled back to her feet, throwing off the occasional offer of help from the people gathered around—what few had regained their senses enough to approach. She whistled for Brex, saying nothing to the people nearby as she hurried in a stagger away from the scene.

By now, several people were shouting for help, and somewhere in the distance Praxis could hear the whistle of the police, blaring into the night in short bursts. Praxis hurried off, throwing herself into the mercy of the shadows as she ducked into the narrow gaps between buildings.

But she would never escape if she left a trail of blood, and so as soon as she'd deemed herself out of the immediate danger zone, she sagged against a wall and prodded at her hip. Brex fluttered in from the distance, landing anxiously atop her head. Praxis winced as her fingers found the gash. She took a deep breath, shutting her eyes. Healing magic was elemental, so basic that Praxis felt sometimes like she could do it in her sleep, and she reassured her racing heart that soon everything would be fine—or fine enough, anyway, given the circumstances.

So when a flare of heat tore through her hip instead, Praxis cried out with such ferocity that Brex took flight, squawking madly. She jerked her hand back, as if somehow her hip had lashed out at it instead of . . . what? Healing magic did not just spontaneously *not* work. With a shaky hand, Praxis made herself touch the gash again, discovering to her annoyance that it was at least a centimeter longer than before, and deeper as well. She took another breath. Tried again.

Again, a flare of heat struck her side, her hip now feeling as if it was itself aflame. Only the fact that she'd experienced it before kept her silent this time, but nothing suppressed the panic beginning to flutter in her chest. If she couldn't heal herself . . .

She did not know any first aid. It simply hadn't been necessary before. Praxis lurched down the alley, being mindful of the noises around her, the distant blaring of whistles still crying out into the night. She clamped her hand across the wound—that was something that people did, right? She didn't know why, but she knew that she'd seen people clutching at their bloodied bodies before. But what to do, where to turn now? The idea of going to a *doctor* was out of the question, given the circumstances—and what would a doctor be able to do, if Praxis herself could not? Her heart was racing madly now, all of the options collapsing in turn.

Except for one.

Praxis took a deep breath. True, she did not exactly relish the idea of dragging Kaedrich into whatever it was that she'd stumbled into, but what other choice did she have? And really, in Praxis's heart of hearts, was there actually any question as to where she'd turn? She was panicked, and hurting, and scared senseless as she stumbled down the night streets of Monfort.

There was no other place that she *would* go.

* * *

KAEDRICH WAS SLEEPING, and then suddenly she wasn't.

It was hard to say what, exactly, had woken her. She lay still, instantly alert, her ears pricked against the sigh of the night. She tried to tell herself that it was nothing, her mind running away with her.

Yet if that was true, then why could she swear that she heard the whisper of a second breath? It was so faint that it might not have been there at all, except that Kaedrich was certain it was. She held her own breath, listening even harder, and—yes, there. A tiny sigh, the scrape of a shoe.

It used to be that Kaedrich sometimes thought that she was being overcautious, keeping a loaded gun tucked underneath her pillow—not anymore. Moving slowly, so as not to draw any attention, Kaedrich shifted her hand farther up the bed, fingers grasping until they'd wrapped themselves around the cold metal. Another scrape of shoe announced her intruder creeping closer.

Hesitation is death, one of her instructors was fond of saying, and so Kaedrich did not hesitate. She yanked the gun out and sat up in one wild motion, turning until she faced the door. She took aim as the flap of wings of a small creature burst into the room and began to flutter about the ceiling, chittering anxiously.

The figure at the door shifted, a patch of moonlight catching as if on itself.

"Praxis?" Kaedrich whipped her gun aside. She sighed as she tucked her gun away, then reached to turn on the gas of her bedside lamp. "Perlandra's breath, Praxis, I almost killed you. You can't just go sneaking up on—oh gods! What *happened*?"

Praxis shook her head, as if she was either too tired or it was simply too much to go into. Either could easily be the case: she was leaning back against Kaedrich's closed door, drained of what little color she normally had, her eyes half-shut. Her left hand rested on her hip, blood coating all of her fingers and leaking down her leg.

A jolt sent Kaedrich scrambling out of bed. She vaulted across the few feet separating them, grabbing Praxis just as she began to slide to the ground. "Easy, easy," Kaedrich said, worming herself underneath Praxis's shoulder. She clamped her own hand over Praxis's, increasing the pressure that was applied to the wound. "Come on, this way." She eased the two of them forward, Praxis's feet dragging behind them as they approached the bed.

"I'm sorry," Praxis mumbled, her speech slurred and so heavily accented that it was difficult to make out the words. "I didn't know where else to go."

Kaedrich ducked out from underneath Praxis's arm, letting her slump onto the mattress. She guided Praxis until she was lying on her side, and ran a hand across her blanched face. "You'd be in *more* trouble if you hadn't come here," Kaedrich said. She rushed across the room to where a small wash basin stood. A pitcher of fresh water was next to it, and Kaedrich gathered up both of them, tucking a handful of clean towels underneath her arm first. A new bar of soap was already wrapped in the towels, and Kaedrich hastily set it all down on the floor beside her bed.

She knelt down in the middle of it all, pushing aside the long sweep of Praxis's coat. Brex squawked from somewhere near the ceiling, diving until he collided with the pillow by Praxis's head. He butted his head up against her cheek, and Praxis tried to mutter something reassuring to him, her lips buried in his downy fur.

It would have been nice if someone offered reassurance to Kaedrich, though she didn't waste time belaboring this point. "I'm assuming there's a good reason why you haven't just healed this," Kaedrich said as she lifted Praxis's hand off of her hip. Blood trailed from Praxis's fingers, and Kaedrich tried not to let her stomach twist up too badly at the sight of it.

Praxis winced, sucking air in between her teeth as Kaedrich peeled the fabric away from the bloody gash in her side. "I don't know. I don't know—I tried, but . . . I think it made things worse. Something's wrong with it, I can't—"

"It's okay, don't worry about it. I've got you, you'll be fine." Kaedrich only hoped that it wasn't a lie. She had already undone a couple of the upper buttons, giving her just enough access to Praxis's hip to see what she was working with. She was more grateful than ever now for the academy's thorough curriculum, which included basic first aid and wound treatment. The course had made her sick at the time, but now she dipped easily back into her memories, sifting through the lessons. The wound in front of her *looked* awful, but a quick assessment made the knot in Kaedrich's chest loosen just a little. "It looks like a flesh wound. You should be okay, but we'd better get you to a doctor. I'll just—"

"No," Praxis said. She grabbed Kaedrich's wrist, and the fast motion disturbed Brex, who squawked and fluttered back up to the ceiling. "You take care of it."

"Me? Praxis, I don't know if I can. I mean, not properly."

"You can. Please."

Kaedrich shook her head, but she already knew that she'd do what Praxis asked. The look that Praxis had given her, open and scared and desperate all wrapped up in one—Kaedrich would never refuse that look, not if she had a choice. She turned back to the task at hand, and Praxis released her grip, settling back on the pillow.

She didn't want Praxis to panic, so she didn't question her on how this had happened, though she dearly wanted to. She wanted to demand explanations for their own sake, and she also wanted a distraction from what she was doing. She did none of that, however, just focused on what needed to be done. It was almost possible to detach the process from the reality of it: Kaedrich tried to pretend she wasn't patching up Praxis's hip, just that she was treating a wound, trying to pass a test at the academy. She started to sing under her breath. Not loud enough to be overheard by Marlick or any of the neighbors below, but enough to steady her nerves, enough to get Praxis's shaky breath to smooth out into a gentle rhythm.

> *Said the stars above: "My love, my love,*
> *Do you see the seas below?"*
> *And the seas, they sigh, for the days gone by*
> *They were something to behold . . .*

In this fashion, then, the time passed. The moment wrapped them both in a bubble, looping without end. They had always been here, they would always be here, and yet somehow at the moment that was all right. Even Brex calmed down, nestling into a watchful post on the headboard. When Kaedrich would reach the end of the song, she would just start it back up again. It was the first one that had popped into her head, something that her mother used to like. She hadn't even thought about it in years, and why she had latched onto it now, only the gods would know.

When she finally finished, her voice trailed off and she blinked, surprised at herself. Like waking from a dream, Kaedrich found herself strangely disoriented. A fresh bandage lay in front of her, neatly applied, and Praxis was breathing deeply, her eyes shut. For a second Kaedrich could only sit there, watching Praxis's face as her side rose and fell, rose and fell.

Kaedrich rebuttoned the side of Praxis's trousers—as much as she could anyway, though several of the buttons had been destroyed when Praxis was hit—and then pushed herself to her feet. She gathered up the towels, now soiled, and returned everything to their proper places. It took several minutes to clean up her own hands, but she was in no rush. It was no doubt the middle of the night by now, but what were the odds that

Kaedrich could get back to sleep after all of this? It seemed such a foreign concept, unrecognizable and alien.

Praxis was still sleeping when Kaedrich was done, Brex still standing a firm watch over her. Kaedrich opened up her wardrobe and pulled out an extra blanket, which she gently spread over Praxis. Then she straightened up, looking about the room. She had already been asleep when this had started, her chest bindings tucked neatly away; she didn't feel comfortable going out to the rest of the apartment, but likewise, she didn't just want to stand sentry for the rest of the night.

"Sit with me for a while," Praxis said suddenly, as if she had read Kaedrich's mind. Her eyes were blinking open as she shifted her head to better look up.

Kaedrich shook her head. "I thought you were asleep."

"I can't sleep." Praxis reached out, as if she was going to take Kaedrich's hand; but then she saw the drying blood all over her own, and pulled back. "Sit with me? Please?"

There was no question. "Of course."

Kaedrich started to crouch back down to the floor, but Praxis's frown stopped her. "What are you doing?"

"I don't exactly have a chair," Kaedrich said. "In case you haven't noticed."

"There's room next to me."

Technically true, although (Kaedrich's eyes flicked to the sliver of open mattress that ran down beside Praxis) not nearly as much room as propriety would demand. Then again, when had propriety ever been much of a concern between them? And what even *were* the rules here? To the outside world, Praxis shouldn't even be in Kaedrich's bedroom, though if anyone knew that they were both women they would assume a bond of sisterhood and excuse it easily. Of course that assumption wasn't entirely accurate either, so did that mean that it once again became inappropriate? Kaedrich pinched the bridge of her nose. It was the middle of the night and she was too tired to care about this sort of nonsense, and so she rounded the foot of her bed and sat down on the other side.

She *did* make sure to sit up straight against the headboard, however. Her long legs stretched down much of the mattress, and Kaedrich crossed them at the ankles. Every move that she made felt like it was teetering dangerously close to the edge of a cliff, even as she tried to tell herself not to make too much out of this, because *this* was nothing.

No sooner had her weight settled out in the mattress than Praxis shifted, rolling half onto her back. She winced as she slithered backward, closing the pencil-thin gap that Kaedrich had purposefully left. Kaedrich held her breath, petrified, as Praxis leaned against her, her head making a pillow out of Kaedrich's hip. Praxis's eyes were still closed and her hand drifted, searching, through the air until Kaedrich took hold of it. Then Praxis drew it toward her, their fingers interlaced as she tucked the bundle of hands underneath her chin.

Kaedrich couldn't move, couldn't say a word. Not that Praxis seemed to expect anything. Immediately upon settling in, her breathing had begun to deepen and slow, as if the stress of everything that she'd been through was finally leaving her. Even Brex crawled forward and bedded down in the curve beside Praxis, tucked on top of Kaedrich's pinned leg; he yawned widely, folding his wings and his paws into a tight bundle around himself. The three of them, piled into a single heap, with Kaedrich sitting highest and keeping watch.

Tomorrow would come questions and explanations. Tomorrow, whatever had happened to Praxis would have to be faced head-on. Tomorrow, their lives would probably get more complicated. The day ahead loomed already on the horizon, but for now Kaedrich leaned against the headboard, suddenly exhausted. For now a warm peace had cloaked the bedroom, and Kaedrich reached over carefully to turn down the lamp. Brex's snores were already swirling up toward the ceiling, and even in the dark Kaedrich could see the shock-white of Praxis's hair, smushed up against Kaedrich's side. Kaedrich kept her eye on it, as she let the moment wrap itself around her. She counted the rise and fall of Praxis's breath, one, two, twenty, forty, until her mind slid underneath the heavy cloak of dreams and she, too, was asleep.

Chapter Eleven

THE FIRST THING that Kaedrich heard was merry laughter.

She awoke to find herself slumped along the top of her bed, contorted as if she'd been sitting up and then had slid sideways until she was laying more or less across her pillow. She pushed herself up, frowning, squinting in the bright light. With a jolt, she realized that it was well past when she normally got up, and Kaedrich threw herself out of bed and scrambled for her clothes, her bindings—only to trip on an overcoat that lay in a heap in the middle of her bedroom floor.

A slate-blue overcoat, Praxis's overcoat. Kaedrich caught her balance on the table where she kept her wash basin, and the whole of the night before came flooding back to her. The basin still had a tinge of red about the water. But if Praxis was gone, her coat abandoned, did that mean— gods, had whoever attacked her caught up with her somehow? Kaedrich vaulted across the room, heading for the door, and then another snap of laughter came in from the other room.

It was the twinned sound of Marlick and Praxis, underscored by the chink of breakfast dishes, the playful chitter of Brex. Praxis's voice came through the door, muffled but still distinct enough, as she made a reprimanding sound like she was gently trying to pry Brex away from something.

There was no emergency, no need to panic.

Still, Kaedrich threw her bindings on in record time, and stuffed her legs down a random pair of trousers, tucking in her nightshirt; nowhere near a proper outfit for the day, but enough to be seen in the context of her own home. She cracked open the door and toed into the sitting room, uncertain of exactly what kind of situation she would find there.

Sunlight caught against Praxis as she stood from the table, lending her a reassuringly healthy glow. She had actually freshened up, her hair still damp, her clothes smooth and tucked. Her new shirt and vest were cinched in at the waist, leading way to a pair of Kaedrich's own trousers—Kaedrich flushed slightly at that, though there was of course no reason why she couldn't borrow them, given the circumstances.

"*There* you are!" Marlick said, startling Kaedrich. Kaedrich jumped, turning to see Marlick standing in the open doorway that led to their tiny kitchen alcove. He leaned against the doorframe, a grin splayed open on his face. "I thought you were going to sleep the whole morning away—not that I'd blame you. I'd want to sleep, too, if I'd had the company of a beautiful woman in my bed."

"Er, no, it's not—" Kaedrich started, her face already burning, but Praxis waved her hand.

"Now now, don't embarrass him, Marlick," she said. She came straight up to Kaedrich and slid her arm possessively around Kaedrich's waist. Kaedrich froze as Praxis leaned in as if to kiss her cheek—which she did, though a fast whisper landed itself in Kaedrich's ear as well: "Just play along."

Play along, sure—as if Kaedrich's brain could even figure out *how*, given the fact that it had completely jammed up at the light breeze of Praxis's lips against her ear. She stood there, rooted in place, heart pounding wildly, as Marlick and Praxis continued the conversation without her. Play along? She couldn't even get herself to sort out what the words drifting through the room were saying, much less be able to contribute. Praxis's arm was still hooked around her waist, and Kaedrich realized with a start that somehow her *own* arm had ended up curled counterpoint around Praxis.

Playtime over.

Kaedrich jumped away from Praxis as if she'd discovered that she'd just put her hand on a hot stove. Muttering some lame excuse about the time, she darted back into the relative safety of her bedroom. She shut and locked the door, leaning her head momentarily against the wood. Only when her breathing had settled somewhat did she allow herself to cross the room and open her dresser.

She had just pulled off her nightshirt when the click of her door sounded. "So, listen—"

"Praxis!" Kaedrich snapped, grabbing up her shirt and clutching it in front of her. "Gods! I'm trying to change!"

"No, no, it's fine, look! See? I'm not looking, I promise."

Kaedrich glowered over her shoulder, and sure enough: Praxis was standing just inside of her room, the door already firmly shut behind her, her free hand clamped over her eyes. "That's not the *point*," Kaedrich said. She sighed in resignation. "My door was *locked*."

"Oh." Praxis shrugged. "I thought that was because of Marlick."

Kaedrich shook her head, even though Praxis couldn't see it. "Remind me to talk to you sometime about *boundaries*."

They both just stood there for a minute, not speaking. On the plus side, at least Praxis wasn't arguing about the need for Kaedrich's lecture, but neither was she apologizing for barging in the way that she had. Instead, she was posted like a sentry by the door, her hand clamped almost comically over her face.

"So, are you going to get dressed, or what?"

Kaedrich frowned. "I thought you couldn't see anything."

"I can't. But it doesn't sound like you're moving, and that's kind of, you know, part of the process."

"You realize that's pretty creepy of you to say, right?" Kaedrich asked, but she did make herself turn and drop her nightshirt into a modest laundry pile. Her skin felt prickled and on edge, and she couldn't shake the feeling that somehow Praxis knew what she was doing even without apparently seeing it. Still: she *did* need to get dressed, and she doubted that she'd be able to convince Praxis that shutting her eyes wasn't, you know, *enough*.

"Okay, so what did you want?" Kaedrich asked finally, as she selected a shirt.

"I thought that it was important that we talked. I wanted you to know that I didn't give Marlick that idea—about us. He caught me as I was coming out of your room, and he drew his own conclusions."

"And you didn't think to correct him?"

Praxis was silent for a moment. "I didn't . . . I don't know, I guess I didn't really want to? It's probably best that he believes it, since that keeps uncomfortable questions to a minimum. Plus, it gives me an excuse to crash here for a while without him objecting."

"Here?" Kaedrich turned. She was tucking the hem of her shirt into her trousers, the front buttons already done up.

Praxis shrugged. "I can't exactly go back to my hotel. You don't mind, do you?"

Kaedrich glanced down at herself, verifying her modesty. "You can open your eyes," she said, ignoring the question. She still hadn't picked out a vest, done up her sleeves, gotten a tie, but these things didn't exactly require privacy. As Praxis dropped her hand, Kaedrich turned back to her dresser, already rummaging in the drawers. The box where she kept her cufflinks fit perfectly in her hand, and Kaedrich tried not to think about when she'd first worn these. Praxis had given them to her, slipping them into place while Kaedrich stared, dumbfounded, at the expertly cut emeralds.

She plucked them out of their box, pinning them in place with automatic precision.

"Kaedrich?"

"Mm?"

"*Do* you mind? If I stay here, I mean. I won't do it if you're unhappy with it."

Kaedrich glanced up, catching Praxis's eye in the mirror. Gods, she really was *trying*.

Before Kaedrich could say anything, though, Praxis winced, clutching at her hip.

Kaedrich was there before Praxis could tell her not to bother. She guided Praxis to sit on the edge of the bed. "Have you changed your bandage this morning?" Kaedrich asked, and even as she said it she realized that Praxis never would have—did she even know how? Kaedrich shook her head. "Never mind. Lie down—I'm going to fix it up, and then I want you to visit a proper doctor, first thing this morning."

Praxis shook her head. "No doctors."

"Did I ask for your opinion?"

"I told you last night—"

"I don't care," Kaedrich said. "I patched you up enough so that you wouldn't bleed out on my floor, but I'm telling you flat-out, I don't know that I did the best job in terms of properly letting it heal. You're *going* to see a doctor, and you're *going* to do as he instructs you to take care of it. Unless you can suddenly fix it this morning?"

Praxis frowned.

"Yeah, I didn't think so. Come on." Kaedrich tipped Praxis's shoulders, making her lie down on her side. The exact same way that she'd been the night before. There was a tiny bloodstain on the carpet by the bed, that Kaedrich had been too tired or too worn-out to notice.

Kaedrich straightened up, grabbing the blankets that were still scattered loosely all around the bed. She tossed it at Praxis. "I'll give you a minute—slide your trousers down and find some way to make yourself decent. Let me know when you're done." Then she rounded the bed, returning to her dresser and her own preparations. She dutifully kept her attention away from the mirror, going so far as to grab the edge and tip it down toward the floor.

She was fully dressed—vest and tie, suit coat, polished shoes—by the time Praxis indicated that she was settled. Kaedrich grabbed some fresh bandaging from a little box underneath her bed and came back around, kneeling in front of Praxis.

"So are you going to tell me what happened now?" Kaedrich asked, peeling away the old bandage. Fresh blood oozed out between congealed lumps of old blood, sticking to the bandage.

Praxis took a deep breath, trying not to move her hip in the process. "It was Tol."

"Tol?" Kaedrich shook her head. "Great. I suppose I should have guessed as much. What did he do? Did he say anything?"

"No . . . he was hiding out in my hotel room. Snuck up on me when I was opening the window for Brex."

"What, seriously? I thought you could . . . I don't know, I thought you could *tell* if someone was in the room."

Praxis winced, hissing a breath in through her teeth as Kaedrich dabbed at the gash.

"Sorry," Kaedrich said. She waited a moment, and when Praxis didn't say anything more, she added, "Well?"

"Yeah, I . . . can tell that, usually. But obviously I didn't."

"Obviously."

"Shut up," Praxis said. "I was distracted, all right?"

"By *what*?"

Praxis frowned. "Are you almost done?" she asked instead.

"Almost." Kaedrich let the subject drop, though she kept turning it over in her mind as she finished with Praxis's new bandage. She didn't like the idea of them knowing of Praxis's whereabouts so quickly. Kaedrich was well aware that Lanali's influence had spread throughout most of the city, but this . . . How many people even knew that Praxis was in Monfort? Okay, so Praxis wasn't exactly in hiding, and it's not like she'd been trying to conceal her appearance when out in public—still. She'd only been in the city for two days, and already Tol had tracked down her exact hotel room?

Suddenly she wasn't sure she wanted Praxis going out at all, even to do something as useful as visit a doctor. Of course Praxis would stay here, now, if for no other reason than for Kaedrich to be able to keep a better eye on her.

Praxis cleared her throat. She had twisted her head and was staring unfixed at a point on the ceiling, her fingers idly twisting the end of one of her short locks. In another context, she might have been a young girl laying about as she dreamed of a handsome boy. "So, um. How did your meeting with Bundling go?"

Kaedrich's mouth twisted up at the memory.

"That good, huh?"

"Could have been better . . . He won't act. Not unless he has *proof.*"

"Coward."

"You can't really blame him," Kaedrich said. Even though she kind of did. "It would mean putting his own neck on the line, to stand up like that."

Praxis snorted. "I won't say, 'I told you so.'"

"You kind of just *did.*"

"True."

Kaedrich fell silent. She gnawed on her lower lip as she considered her next words. "I did . . . *try* to convince him that you might be willing to—"

"Nope."

"You don't even know what I was going to say."

"Yes, I do. You want me to go on record, recounting everything that we know." Praxis sighed. She dropped her arm. Her fingers rested on Kaedrich's wrist, as Kaedrich pressed a fresh bandage in place, although it wasn't clear if Praxis had meant the touch or not. "They wouldn't believe me, anyway."

Kaedrich licked her lips, trying to bring some moisture back to her suddenly very dried-out mouth. "For what it's worth, Mr. Bundling agrees with you. And . . . I'm not even sure if *he* believes us."

"Seven hells, why is this so hard for people to accept?" Praxis asked. "Do they really buy her whole more-honorable-than-thou routine?"

"Nobody else has seen what we have, Praxis. It's not unreasonable."

Praxis waved her hand in dismissal. Kaedrich's wrist felt cold and empty without her. "Yeah, but so what's supposed to count as 'proof' in a situation like this, anyway?" Praxis said. "*My* word isn't enough. *Your* word isn't enough. What do they expect me to do? Break into Lanali's home and collect a journal that she's just *happened* to keep this whole time, *All of My Evil Plans Laid out in Detail*?"

A giggle escaped Kaedrich. "That would be convenient."

"Wouldn't it, though?"

Silence fell between them. Kaedrich was almost done, the bandage neat and clean on Praxis's hip.

"Should we try it anyway?" Kaedrich asked after a moment. "Breaking into her house, I mean."

"*Gods* no," Praxis said. She propped herself up on her elbows, keeping herself twisted so that her hip didn't move. "I've suggested some crazy things over the years, Kaedrich, I know, but I swear, I do not want to hear you say something like that again. We can snoop around the city all we want, and if we can find the location of wherever she's holding people, that would be one thing. But attacking a wizard in her own territory . . ." She shook her head. "Only a madman would try it. You'd need inside access to even breach the perimeter."

"Okay."

"Seriously, I need to hear you *promise*," Praxis said. She reached out, pinching Kaedrich's elbow, desperation pouring off of her. "*Promise* me that you won't try something stupid on your own. Please."

"I promise," Kaedrich said, and when Praxis still didn't look convinced, Kaedrich grinned. "Oh, come on. You know that I wouldn't do anything stupid without you."

She still didn't look entirely convinced.

Kaedrich plucked Praxis's grip off. "Done." She pushed herself to her feet, gathering up the scraps, as Praxis lifted her head to examine the crisp white cloth that had been left behind.

"You know, perhaps you missed your calling," Praxis said, prodding gently at the bandage on her hip.

"Hardly. And don't think that flattering me is going to get you out of having it looked at by a professional."

Praxis sighed wearily, flopping her head back onto the pillow with great drama. "Yes, madam. I would never *dream* of such a thing."

"Liar."

"True," Praxis said, smirking. She reached out, grabbing the cuff of Kaedrich's suit coat. By the time Kaedrich glanced down, Praxis had already taken hold of her hand, squeezing her fingers tightly together. She wasn't looking at Kaedrich's face, focusing instead on the grip between them. "But truthfully, I . . . am grateful," she said. The words were so faint, as if she had to squeeze them out of her lungs one at a time. "For everything. I don't deserve to have you on my side."

Kaedrich leaned over, tipping Praxis's chin up so that she couldn't avoid looking at her. "Even if that was true," Kaedrich said, looking Praxis straight in the eyes, "I'd be there anyway." She gave Praxis's hand another squeeze as she straightened up. "Now, come on. I believe you have a doctor to see, and I have to get to work. But I'll have you know that I expect you home in time for supper."

Praxis rolled her eyes, but somewhere hidden behind her feigned annoyance, a smile fought to break through. "So this means that I *can* stay?"

"Yes," Kaedrich said. She dropped Praxis's hand and went to the door, but hesitated before she actually left. She took a deep breath, staring at the polished wooden slats. "And for the record, Praxis . . . you don't need to ask. You already know how to let yourself in . . . and you can *always* stay once you do."

THERE WERE FEW things that Tol disliked more than being kept waiting, especially after the night he'd just had. Nonetheless, there he was.

He sat in a stiff chair across from the empty desk and tried to make himself as comfortable as he could. To say that the evening prior hadn't gone well was an understatement of the most extreme proportions. Setting aside for a moment the simple fact that Praxis was still alive (whereabouts unknown), the entire operation had gone *sloppy*.

Though at least Praxis had gotten struck. Tol tried to take comfort in this. Given that most wizards had no clue how to handle wounds and illnesses when they couldn't use healing spells, there was still a chance that she might develop an infection and die. Tol reached over and touched the scar on his elbow; he hadn't been much better prepared to deal with it himself, when he'd first encountered it, and that was a mild version compared to what he'd treated his own weapons with. A bullet had grazed his arm in Marcovalla, and though it had healed over at the time, the wound had reopened a few days later. And then a few days after that. And a few days after that. It had taken him ages to figure out how they'd done it, but he had, and he'd managed to improve upon their technique—the wounds that *his* weapons inflicted couldn't be closed by magic at all.

So that was *one* small mark in their favor, though the situation was still wildly out of control. Tol grimaced. If he had been alone, he might have been able to contain the damage, but Lanali had insisted that he take two of her "recruits" along with him. They'd just finished passing all of her tests, their loyalty absolute, and now all that remained was to see how they handled themselves in the real world. Now Lanali's men lay in the city morgue, something Tol was going to have to waste time correcting.

But not yet.

First, he had to figure out where Praxis had disappeared. He'd spent the whole night scouring the city, following first a trail of blood and then his own intuition and the magical impressions around him, but ultimately coming up empty. He needed a new approach, for wandering the city aimlessly would get him nowhere. And so that morning Tol had scrubbed his efforts, returning instead to the source of the original rumor, the first sighting of Praxis, to see if there was anything new that might be gleaned, anything that their source hadn't thought to volunteer. Even the smallest details could be useful, and so few people thought to include them.

The door to the office opened, and Tol slid off of his chair and stood, turning to greet the man as he entered. "Mr. Tarlock," Tol said, extending his hand with far more grace and respect than this man deserved. Tarlock, in Tol's esteem, was one of those men who valued themselves far more highly than they ought. Look at him: pressed and polished into a fine suit, the academy's coat of arms stitched in detail over his breast pocket. They claimed that their crest contained the profile of a falcon head, but Tol could spot the fraud straight off—the distinctive beak was all wrong. The academy had originally belonged to Tarlock's father, established after the withdraw of Marcovalla; if the family was willing to get such a simple detail as their own symbolism wrong, then what did it speak of their worth?

"I came as soon as I could," Tarlock said by way of a hello. He accepted Tol's handshake, his grip crushing against Tol's. "Forgive me, I did not know that you were coming in this morning." He rounded his desk, motioning for Tol to sit before he dared to settle in himself. "How can I be of service?"

Slightly appeased, Tol returned to his seat. He didn't like the way that his height became obvious, sitting directly across from this man. It wasn't just their height, though the difference was significant even for a Durn; Tarlock was as fit as a doberman, his muscles coiled and controlled.

Tol would never hope to make up the height difference by sitting up straight, and so he leaned back instead, affecting a posture of languid disinterest. "The Pon wishes more details about your report," Tol began. "About Praxis Fellows."

Tarlock sucked in his cheeks. "I'm not sure that there's much more that I *can* detail, alas. Regrettably, I did not set eyes upon the woman myself. As I stated, it was something a group of students were discussing."

"What did they say?"

"The usual things men say about a woman," Tarlock said with a shrug. "You know how boys are. Apparently she appeals to one of them, though from what I've heard, I cannot gather why."

Tol had been listening with only half an ear, not even sure what it was that he was waiting for. He raised an eyebrow at this, however, as a faint memory nagged at him. He looked over sharply. "Which student? What does he look like?"

Tarlock blinked, obviously startled by Tol's interest. "Um ... tall fellow, skinny. Dark. Hardly anyone of note."

"Name," Tol said, snapping his fingers. "I need his name. Address, too. Anything you have on him." He got to his feet, and Tarlock hurriedly followed suit.

"I ... yes, of course." Tarlock hurried around the desk, poking his head out into the outer office and snapping something at his secretary.

Tol paced around Tarlock's office as he waited for the appropriate file to be gathered. His mind was already racing, ideas crackling with potential. Every time that he'd dealt with Praxis before, there had always been a man with her—Tol had long assumed that he was a servant, but now that he thought about it, Praxis did seem to have an oddly deep concern for this man. Tol smirked, rubbing his hands together.

Tarlock returned a moment later with a slim file. Tol snatched it without ceremony, flipping it open.

"I really don't see what this has to do with anything," Tarlock said as Tol scanned the few pages inside. "Mr. Mannly is a nobody—he has no connections."

"Oh, really?" Tol had already taken in the top lines, committing the name and address to memory, but it was something much farther down the page that drew his attention. "Then why is it that his funding for this prestigious institution of yours is coming from none other than Praxis Fellows herself?"

"*What?*"

Tarlock leaned over, trying to read out of the file, but Tol snatched the top paper out and folded it neatly in half. He handed the rest of the file back to Tarlock, shoving it at his chest.

"I'll be taking this," Tol said, folding the halved paper in half again and tucking it neatly into his coat pocket. "Thank you, Mr. Tarlock. You've been most helpful."

Chapter Twelve

PRAXIS WINCED, cradling her hip as she stepped into the back of the cart. As Kaedrich had insisted, Praxis had spent the better part of the morning at a doctor's office—who had jabbed her with needles, prodded at her as pain flared through her hip, *tsked* at Kaedrich's "shoddy" job of bandaging Praxis up, and asked far too many questions about exactly how and when and *why* someone had shot at Praxis. He would not shut up until Praxis, in a fit of disgust, threw even more money in his face. The doctor glanced at the bills as they fluttered into a scattered pile across his lap. He raised an eyebrow. He said nothing else, not until the matter was done and it was time to regale Praxis with a whole litany of things that she should and shouldn't do whilst tending to the thick and chaffing bandage now strapped to her side.

Which left only one other matter to attend to—and, all things considered, Praxis would have preferred staying at the damned doctor's for a few more hours over *this*, but . . . Here she was, anyway.

The cart was driven by a dark-skinned man who was smoking a fat cigar when Praxis approached. He stood beside his cart, leaning against the wheel. He and Praxis were several miles outside of Monfort's city limits, in an empty stretch where the ground flattened to nothing, and wheat and corn and prairie grass shot up quick in the spring and swayed as tall as anybody. The road was like a path through a forest, and the cart and the man were pulled off to the side, butted straight up against a wall of rustling, vibrant green. The grassy smell of residual harvest magic leached out of the soil. Pollen and dirt spun dances in the air, and Praxis sneezed as she approached.

"Bless you," the man said. He spoke in a drawl, and he barely took the cigar out of his mouth. Then he turned, without another word, and climbed up to take his place in the driver's seat. The cart was narrow and, lacking other options, Praxis had to content herself with finding a place among the empty wine barrels that were on their way back to the vineyards.

She settled in, and sneezed again. Her nose was running, and she wiped it off on the sleeve of her coat.

The cart wound outward at a steady, if somewhat sedate, pace. Birds sang, insects hummed, and Brex occasionally darted in and out of view overhead. The grasses and crops swayed and sighed in the breeze that tickled the air across the back of Praxis's neck. Praxis reached up and untied her deerstalker cap, pulling the flaps down to hang across her ears and cheeks. There was no place to hide from the sun here, and she made sure to keep her collar high and her tinted spectacles on firmly. Her hands she tucked into her sleeves. Anything could burn out here, in the open sunlight.

Eventually, they arrived at their destination. An old country estate, huge and square and brick. The face of it was covered in vines, blue halva blossom buds dotting the green. A sprawling lawn surrounded the building, the grass overgrown with weeds that crept onto the gravel drive and poked up through the rocks. A statue near the front door was cracked in half, held together with nothing but some wayward vines that had crept away from the house.

Weevish was standing on the front steps, waiting for her. He rushed down to the cart as it pulled idly up, gravel crunching underneath the wheels.

"You could have just given me the address," Praxis said as she began to climb down. Weevish held his hand out to her, as if he was a butler, though Praxis ignored it.

"It's safer this way, for all involved," Weevish said.

This may be true, but it didn't make Praxis's trip any more pleasant. She'd been following a string of clues and cryptic notes all over Monfort, like some sort of bizarre treasure hunt, ever since she'd left the doctor's office that morning. Now it was creeping toward noon, and Praxis's hip was screaming at her to *sit down already*.

". . . all assembled, they're just waiting on you," Weevish was saying, as Praxis realized that she'd been lost in her own world.

"Love what you've done with the place," Praxis said as they reached the front door. She peeled a long strip of decaying paint from the frame.

Weevish's face pinched. "Yes, well . . . we *are* supposed to be keeping a low profile. The Dons didn't want someplace that would draw attention to them."

They passed into the front hall, and Praxis laughed. "Sure, because a house of this size is very discreet."

"There is such a thing as *standards*."

Praxis snorted, but did not comment. Soon he had led her through the house, deep into the depths of the private living quarters, far beyond the range of where guests would normally be entertained. He opened a door to a study or a small library, motioning her inside.

A handful of wizards sat around in front of a fireplace, drinking and acting as if this was just another day, as if they weren't all exiled and fearing for their lives. Some of them she recognized, and some of them she didn't. Don Eagleburns was there, of course, as well as someone that she knew on sight to be Don Trew, formerly of the Governance Council, though she'd never met him before. Two younger gentlemen, trying hard to smoke as much as their elders, and a withered man with papery skin who looked old enough to be even Weevish's grandfather. They lounged on the sofas and chairs, legs crossed, arms sprawled, taking up as much space as they were able. Praxis only barely resisted rolling her eyes at them. Gentlemen were the same the world over, she decided—the sky could be collapsing, and the most it would get out of them was to ring for a servant to tell them to make it stop.

Weevish coughed politely, but Praxis didn't wait for him to announce her. She strode into their midst, cigar smoke curling out of her way as she went. She cut a straight line through their idle chatter, planted herself in front of the fireplace, and turned to face them with one hand on her hip.

"Wellen is dead," she said, skipping the preamble.

The reactions to this were subtle, and varied. Don Eagleburns frowned into his drink, tipping it as if somehow the green fog pooling off of the liquid held answers to life's great mysteries. One of the younger gentlemen paled in obvious dread, while the other held back a self-satisfied sneer at Wellen's expense. Don Trew clucked his tongue in detached pity. The ancient wizard, meanwhile, leaned in toward Praxis, holding a pair of pince-nez up to his face as he studied the length of her trousers. "Who in Veracy's name are you?" he asked.

Praxis regarded him with the same look that one usually reserved for a dead roach found belly-up on the dining table. "Praxis Fellows."

"Who?"

Don Eagleburns cleared his throat. "I told you, Trimbly. The wizard that I called in, to . . . look into this matter."

The ancient wizard—Trimbly, apparently, and a Lord-Don if his signet ring was to be believed—narrowed his eyes. He was still peering intently at Praxis's legs. "I thought you said that you were contacting some fellow you knew."

"Fellows," Don Eagleburns said. "I said *Fellows*."

"She's *not* a fellow."

"Yes," Praxis said, snatching the pince-nez out of Don Trimbly's grip. "Thank you, I hadn't noticed that particular detail."

Don Trimbly looked up, his whole face contorted. He plucked the pince-nez away from her. "In my day, women didn't speak back to their betters."

"Neither do I."

Don Trimbly harrumphed. He sat back in his chair, crossing bony arms over his spoon-curved chest.

Don Eagleburns held up his hand. "It might be better if you get on with what you've come here to tell us," he said. "You say that they've caught up with poor Wellen now, too?"

Praxis stuffed her hands into her coat pockets, leaning casually against the hearth. The hem of her coat fluttered into the outskirts of the flames, unburnt. "I don't know that I'd waste too much of your sympathy on him, considering that he ratted out Don Trommel and probably betrayed the whole of your investigation to the very people he'd been sent to expose."

As expected, this was met with overcompensated skepticism. Don Trimbly's frown deepened, if such a thing was possible, and Don Eagleburns shook his head. Don Trew huffed. "Lord Wellen? Betraying us? I'd sooner believe in glimmer fairies."

"Hear, hear," one of the younger gentlemen said. The smarmier looking one, Praxis decided in an instant. "There isn't a man among us who would give up the secrets of our order." He looked around at his compatriots, who naturally all nodded in brash agreement.

Praxis didn't even try to avoid rolling her eyes. "Shall we put that to the test, then? Since you're so confident? I'm sure that if I dug *really* deep, I could find it in me to hand you over to these people."

Lord Smarmy's nose wrinkled. "There's no need to be crass, *Miss* Fellows."

"That's Lady Praxis to you, *boy*."

Though technically without a badge of nobility (Yandosians lacking in such a concept on paper), this was nonetheless the most "appropriate" form of address in the Durlish language—and not one that Praxis brought out or often insisted upon. In fact, she usually cut down anyone that dared to use it, but not today. Not for Lord Smarmy. She watched as her words hit the young man, as he glanced at Don Eagleburns for confirmation or denial. Don Eagleburns's mouth was a tight line, but he nonetheless forced out the barest of nods.

"Anyway, we have much more important things to discuss," Praxis said. Having made her point, she did not need to harp. "The basic fact is that they know that you've been nosing in *deep* on this matter, and I wouldn't be at all surprised if they suspect that you haven't dropped it even with the disbanding. You should pull everyone else out of Monfort, immediately, for their own safety."

Praxis made a point of looking straight at Weevish as she said this. Not only was he the most likely to listen to her, in this room of arrogance that clouded the air like the cigar smoke, but she wanted him to know that his own safety was a concern. He wasn't a bad sort. Not compared to the rest of them.

He nodded, and Praxis flicked her attention away.

"That seems an overreaction," Don Trew said.

"Well, what do you expect?" Smarmy added. "Even a great *Lady* is susceptible to the hysterics of womanhood."

Praxis laughed under her breath. "Boy, are you *trying* to get yourself in trouble?"

Smarmy drew himself up. "The name is Drawling, thank you. The Honorable Brythard Drawling III, Baron of—"

"Yeah, yeah," Praxis said, waving her hand. "Don't bother; I won't remember anyway."

"Can we please return to the matter at hand?" Don Eagleburns asked, talking over the intake of breath that the smarmy young Drawling was already taking. Don Eagleburns shot him a silencing glance before returning his attention to Praxis. "Miss Fellows, you were sent to investigate. Have you actually discovered *anything* of consequence? Did you manage to learn anything from Lord Wellen? Before . . . ?"

Praxis shrugged. "Nothing that I didn't already know, on some level. I was hoping to find proof that the people disappearing are being turned into poor copies of Silvers, but it seems that Wellen wasn't chosen for some reason. But listen, that's not important. You fools are ignoring the larger issue here. You're all in terrible danger—and while I can't say that I give a rat's ass what really happens to any of you, I'd never hear the end of it if I didn't warn you about this: There's a new weapon in play. One that prevents healing magic."

For once, the room was silent. Praxis looked at all of them in turn: Weevish, gone slightly green around the edges; Don Trew, pinching the bridge of his nose in obvious exasperation; the smarmy Drawling, still smarmy as ever, and his young and thus-far silent companion who was staring at his family signet ring; Don Trimbly, with his face twisted up all shriveled and sour; and Don Eagleburns. Eagleburns, the one man who was staring openly at her, his face for once free of doubt.

"You must be mistaken," Drawling said. He glanced at the others, no doubt hoping that someone would back him up on this. "Nothing can prevent healing magic."

Drawling's silent friend glanced up. He shrugged. "Not so long as you act in time, no," he said, his voice barely more than a whisper.

"Indeed," Don Trew added, somewhat unnecessarily.

Praxis nodded. "For once, I understand your skepticism. Believe me, if I hadn't experienced it firsthand, I wouldn't have accepted it either."

"Is that so?" Don Trimbly said. He sneered, his words dripping with contempt. "And where, exactly, is this wound that you couldn't heal?"

"None of your business," Praxis said.

"And the manner of this weapon?"

"A bullet."

"Ah," Don Trimbly said. He smacked his lips and sat back, obviously satisfied. "No doubt, yes. Bullet wounds can be quite tricky."

"Not in my experience," Praxis said. "Believe me, I know. This was something . . . else. Something new, and something that you should all take very, *very* seriously."

A loud, wooden-sounding *tock* echoed through the room as Don Trimbly clicked his tongue. "Nonsense. Obviously, the advanced healing arts are simply beyond you. It's not surprising—very few wizards can handle the exchange of energy required to—"

Praxis flicked a single finger. Don Trimbly gasped, along with all the other men in the room—all save for Don Eagleburns, who swore like a sailor as the tip of his left index finger dropped to the floor. It bounced once, twice, and Praxis stepped over it as she moved to Don Eagleburns's side. He was screaming now, having leapt to his feet, but Praxis ignored him as she grabbed the remaining stub of his finger tight inside of her fist. Though she was loath to waste perfectly good spells on the likes of him, she nonetheless fed her magic down until it twisted around his severed digit.

Within moments she was releasing him again, a fresh fingertip gleaming untanned and baby soft in the candlelight. She kicked the stub of the old one into the fire.

She turned back to Don Trimbly. He'd gone pale, his papery lips slightly parted in shock. "I know how to use healing magic," Praxis told him. "It didn't work."

"You could have demonstrated that some *other way*," Don Eagleburns grumbled from behind her.

Praxis shot him a glare over her shoulder. "Be grateful that it wasn't your nose," she said, her voice low and dangerous.

Don Eagleburns gulped. "You see?" he asked the room at large. "You see now, why we banished her?"

Though he spoke with bravado, the tremor in his voice betrayed him. Most of the rest of the men glanced into their drinks, reluctant to agree with him under Praxis's icy stare.

Praxis let his hang in the air for a while, like a bad smell. Go ahead, let them take her in. Let them believe that she was crazy and dangerous—so long as they did not deny the power crackling off of her, always keeping the smoke of the room at a comfortable distance. It was the only thing they understood, the only thing they would ever respect.

"You don't have to like me," Praxis said eventually. "In fact, I'd kind of prefer it if you didn't. You don't even have to trust me, or believe me. I really don't care, do you understand? But make no mistake: if any of you stay in Monfort, you're putting your lives at risk. Now," she added, straightening her coat, "I've said what I came here to say. It's up to you if you want to be stupid or not."

They said nothing, but that was fine. Praxis left, the smoke swirling back to take her place.

THERE WAS NO more putting it off: Tol returned to Dreamfield House.

He hadn't wanted to return until he had something to report, and he couldn't exactly report anything when the only thing that had happened is that he'd failed to kill Praxis Fellows. Now, though, it was different. Because now he knew where Praxis was staying.

The mere fact that this "Kaedrich" was associated with Praxis wasn't, in and of itself, damning enough. So Tol had taken a lovely stroll through the whole of Monfort, crossing from one side to another, until finally he made his way to a narrow little building in Woodland Alley. And then he'd known. Praxis may as well have put out a large sign, *I am Hiding*

Here, for the number and strength of protective wards that she'd cloaked the building with. There was no way that Tol would be breaking through them without a plan, and there was no way that he'd be able to make a solid plan on zero sleep and little food, already nearing midday. And so, satisfied that Praxis would likely be staying put for a while, Tol hailed a carriage.

It pulled up now in front of Dreamfield House, or as close to the front as the driver could manage, anyway. Tol leaned out the window as the carriage slowed, two doors down from Lanali's townhouse. A cluster of three other carriages already blocked access—large, bulky things, designed for carrying cargo rather than people.

He hopped out early, paid the driver. A string of volunteers, faithful devotees of the Pon, were busy unloading objects and bringing them in through the great front doors of the house. Tol hopped up the front steps, observing the proceedings with a cool detachment. He stood just inside of the foyer, where the bustle continued unabated. By the look of things, someone passing by on the street would think that a family was just moving into the house, though Tol knew better. He and Lanali had been waiting impatiently for the Council of Assets to clear their request, and frankly their timing couldn't have been better. He watched as someone carried a painting by, then a shoe, then a vase. Many of these items were covered with a fine layer of what looked like a cobweb of ice, ethereal with the faintest glow, and the volunteers wore white gloves as they carried them into the building.

Tol turned away from the bustle. He started to let himself up a nearby flight of stairs when a voice called out to him, "Tol! Tol, a moment, please!"

Davil, the household's butler, approached the base of the stairs. Tol acknowledged his presence with a stiff nod.

"Sir, the Pon has left a message that you're to report to her the moment you return," Davil said. "She is most anxious to see you."

Tol sighed. He was hoping that he'd have a chance to freshen up before Lanali realized that he was back, but no doubt Davil would send word of his arrival immediately, if Tol did not report in himself. He waved off Davil, sending him back to his duties; he was overseeing the unloading of the carriages, and he happily returned to work, making note of the various items as they queued up in the foyer.

There was only one place that the Pon would be, in the midst of all of this fuss. Tol headed for the basement.

The room had been cleared five days before, almost immediately after the successful dissolution of the Royal Society. Tol squeezed through the thick crowd of workers, down the narrow steps into the cavernous space below. Already, half of the shelves that they'd brought in had been filled, with no sign that the move was slowing down. Lanali's followers packed the narrow aisles, unboxing and sorting as they filed papers, scrolls, bottles of a thousand shades.

When Tol had suggested that they request control over the contents of the Royal Society's property, he had no idea just how *much* stuff they'd managed to accumulate over the years. Some of it they'd already gotten hold of, and some of the buildings were in the process of being transferred outright to Lanali's ownership. But it was one basement in particular, crammed full, that had caught Tol's attention as he poured over their accounts and catalogs, and it was the contents of this one that was slowly filling their own basement now.

It took Tol a few moments to find Lanali, though in the end all he had to do was follow the shouts. She was standing in a corner, barking orders as a handful of people set a rather large crate on the floor. One of the people nearby was Lord Hendril; he had planted himself directly at her side, repeating her instructions as if he'd thought of them himself. Lanali was ignoring the young lord, however, and Tol couldn't help but smile at that. The volunteers had just busted out the crowbars when Lanali glanced over, her eyes narrowing behind her veil as they settled on Tol.

She paused, midsentence. They did not need to speak for her to understand the message that Praxis Fellows was still alive—it was written plain enough on Tol's slack face, if you knew how to read it. Lanali's mouth tightened into a hard line.

At the sudden halt of instructions to parrot, Hendril glanced down at Lanali's veiled figure. He followed the line of her attention easily enough, a faint scowl marring his otherwise flawless features.

It was fair to say that Tol and Lord Hendril had never gotten along, not really. He was perhaps Lanali's first true follower, and in the beginning they had used his wealth and influence to gain greater audiences, spreading the Pon's messages to the rest of Monfort's social elite. Later, he had still proven useful, though only after Tol had arranged for various circumstances to roll in his favor, lending Hendril stewardship over his young nephew's title and estates and granting him a seat in the Crescent. So it wasn't that Hendril didn't have his purpose. No, the source of their thinly veiled animosity was much more basic than politics and power: about a year ago, Lanali had decided to allow herself the pleasure of a lover, and had taken *Hendril* to her bed.

The basic fact of that was enough to incur Tol's loathing, and Hendril returned it when his new status was still not enough to unseat Tol as her right-hand man. They had engaged in a variety of petty jabs and attempts to get rid of the other ever since.

"Tol," Hendril said, bristling even as he spoke. "Do you have any idea how long the Pon has been waiting to hear from you? I can't believe—"

Lanali raised her hand, and though she spoke not a word, she cut off his sentence in an instant.

Tol smirked openly. Because he knew that it would enrage Hendril, and because he knew that Hendril would be able to do nothing about it, and because Hendril was already angry about the fact that he didn't have the slightest clue what business Tol had been sent out on.

"How soon can you try again?" Lanali asked. She spoke in their native Aul, because nobody else here understood it; yet she also spoke in generalities, because she did not trust their word about that.

"Soon. I've already tracked down her new nest."

Lanali nodded. Tol drew out the sheet of paper he'd taken from Kaedrich Mannly's file. He wanted to show her, to put her mind at ease. The paper slipped from his grasp as he was taking it out, however, and fluttered to land by his feet. The quartered sheet landed on its spine, flopping partially open like a book just being cracked. Tol ducked, intending to retrieve it, when Lanali shouted at him, *"Stop!"*

Tol froze, half-bent. He glanced up, and found Lanali staring at the paper, her eyes so wide that the whites clearly popped behind the shadows of her veil.

"Out," she said, in Durlish. She still had not taken her eyes from the paper. "Everyone. Out!"

Her followers jumped, startled into submission. Hastily, they put down their charges and began to shuffle as a single mass toward the staircase and the door beyond. Only Hendril remained where he was, stubbornly clinging to his place at Lanali's side. She took her eyes away from the paper only long enough to turn and glare up at him, murderous rage contorting her face. "Out."

Hendril hesitated. Clearly, he'd thought (or at least hoped) that since Lanali's command apparently did not apply to Tol, nor would it apply to him. He glanced once in Tol's direction, perhaps hoping that the Pon might next order his departure as well, and yet when a moment passed and this did not happen, there was nothing for him to do about it. He slumped his shoulders, bowing graciously at Lanali. "My Pon," he said, and then he shot a glower at Tol and headed out.

They waited for a long time in silence, just the two of them. Long after the sounds of the last footsteps filed out, long after the door clicked shut behind them. Tol had straightened up as soon as Lanali had ordered the departure of her followers, and Lanali had returned her attention to the paper almost immediately after dismissing Hendril, and in this manner they waited.

"Do you see it?" Lanali asked finally. Her breath was faint against her veil, her hand nervously clutched at the top of her chest.

Tol looked at the paper, still resting half-opened against the side of his shoe. There was no point in lying. "No."

"It is a white bird."

Tol sighed. When he regarded the paper again he had to admit that, sure, from a different angle perhaps the *V* of the folded sheet could be taken as a symbolic pair of wings, but it would be a stretch to see it like that. "No it isn't," he said, and he snatched the paper up before Lanali could argue the point.

Lanali gasped, as if Tol had just desecrated something sacred—or as if she'd expected it to explode upon being touched. Either was equally likely of a delusion, as far as Tol was concerned. Not that he expected to ever be able to convince Lanali of that. A year and a half ago, just before Praxis had foiled their last great game, Lanali had seen a disturbing number of instances of what she called the "white bird"—in clouds, in the foam on expensive coffee, in the pattern of soap bubbles. These signs had distressed her then, but she'd plunged ahead anyway, refusing to "heed their warning," as she puts it these days. Now, when she spoke of it at all, it was with a bitter twist of her tongue.

She strode across the tiny gap between them, grabbing Tol's wrist. "I will not allow her to ruin this," she said.

"We won't. I promise. But this—" Tol jerked the paper, pinched between his fingers. "This means *nothing*. You have to stop worrying about it."

Lanali laughed, a single bark of humorless mirth that echoed through the basement. "You say that, and yet you have failed to deliver a satisfactory result. *Once again*, I might add. Tell me, which one of you should I believe? Your *words*, that I taught you how to spin—or the *signs*, which might have saved me last time?"

Tol gritted his teeth. "I will deliver her," he said, barely snarling the words out.

"No," Lanali said. She'd plucked the sheet from Tol's grip before he realized what was happening. The paper whispered as she unfolded it, already turning away from him. "This is where she is?" she asked, skimming the information. "With this . . . Kaedrich Mannly?"

"Yes. You can be certain of it."

"Hmm." Lanali folded the paper again, tucking it away somewhere in the hidden folds of her skirts. "In that case, your business with this matter is done. I will send someone else to handle the final end of things."

"What? You can't!" He darted forward—to do what, he did not know—but Lanali stepped easily out of his way.

Lanali laughed again, longer and colder than the last time. "You dare to tell your most venerated Pon what she can and cannot do? Tol." She clucked her tongue. "Do not think that my love for you will keep you safe, if you decide to cross me."

Tol froze, as sure as if Lanali had cast a spell to encase him in ice. On the one hand: rage burned through him, deep and primal, that she would dare to threaten the only other person in the world that knew her secrets. On the other: her *love*. That was what she'd said. Tol had never once heard her utter the word, not in any context that he could recall, and here she had chosen to attach it to *him*. He felt himself stop and shut down, two contradictory halves of him fighting a silent war; a war that stole control of all of his body, all of his mind. All of his heart.

When Lanali recalled the rest of her followers a few moments later, the bustle filing back into the basement as if nothing had happened, Tol was still standing there, exactly as she'd left him.

Chapter Thirteen

PRAXIS EASED THE door open in silence, taking in the great room beyond. It had probably once been a library or an over-large study, back when the academy was nothing more than the prestigious house of an old family. Now, though, it was clearly a practice room of some sort: devoid of all furniture save for a handful of seats around the perimeter, the polished wood floor and paneling matched to create the open air of a ballroom. Tall windows broke up the far wall, brilliant midday sunlight pouring in and catching the glint of swords and shields that were mounted all over the walls. It also caught, in bits and pieces, the single weapon that was being wielded in the room. Light flashed as Kaedrich lunged, then disappeared with a retreat and a well-practiced turn.

Praxis leaned against the wall for a while, taking in the show. She hadn't yet had the opportunity to see what all of her funding had gotten her, not really, and now that she did she felt her chest swell with pride. Kaedrich cut through a series of exercises with military precision. Her movements were fluid and graceful, obviously anticipating each new attack well before she got into position. Only the faint squeak of shoes announced her movements. Though she'd likely been practicing for a while by this point, a thin sheen of perspiration on her toned arms, she did not appear breathless. Watching her was like watching a ballerina, her sturdy muscles propelling her in twirls and leaps as she crossed the vast expanse of floor, back and forth and back again. Praxis couldn't help but smile.

She waited until it appeared that Kaedrich had finished with one routine, in the almost infinitesimal pause as she decided on her next course of action. That's when Praxis began to clap.

Instantly, Kaedrich whirled at the sound. Her sword was raised and ready, her eyes snapping to position as if she'd already known where to find the person who'd interrupted her. Except that whoever it was she expected to find there, it wasn't Praxis; Kaedrich's eyes widened, and she lowered her weapon. "Praxis!" she hissed. "What are you doing here?"

Praxis smirked. "What, a woman can't visit her lover?" Memory of their ruse for Marlick's sake had clung with Praxis all morning, as she'd sought out medical care, as she'd stolen into her ruined hotel room to quietly remove her luggage and dig one of Tol's bullets out of the wall, as she'd met with the Dons. She was probably enjoying the lie a little more than she should, but never mind.

Kaedrich ignored this. She rushed over, grabbing Praxis by the elbow. "Are you crazy? Visitors aren't even allowed beyond the foyer, and no one beneath their second year is permitted to be on this floor. If they catch you—"

"I'll be escorted from the premises," Praxis said. "Probably told never to return. Believe me, I've had worse. Besides, it's worth it to see all of this." She brushed easily by Kaedrich, moving to the center of the open room. She flexed her fingers to turn on point, taking it all in slowly. "It's good to know that my money has been well spent. You're learning a lot."

As Praxis had hoped, this earned her a blush from Kaedrich. "Thanks. I'm hardly an expert yet, but yeah . . . I'm getting the hang of things."

"Of course, it's *one* thing to be able to wave a sword around by yourself. I wonder how you'd fare against an actual opponent."

Kaedrich shrugged. "I can hold my own."

"Can you now?" Praxis asked with a grin. She spun around, her eyes landing on a rack of swords. "Let's find out!"

"What? Praxis, no, you can't—you can't actually be asking me to spar with you."

Praxis raised an eyebrow as she glanced over her shoulder. "Oh? Why, because I'm a *woman?*"

"Because you're *hurt,* for one thing," Kaedrich said, ignoring the subtle joke entirely.

Pain flared in response to Kaedrich's observation, but Praxis waved the concern off. "My hip is doing fine, thank you. Your doctor stitched it shut and padded it up—yes, I did go."

"That's good, but it doesn't mean that you can't still damage it."

"Bah. Let me worry about that," Praxis said. "Come on. You can't honestly tell me that you're happier just running through exercises."

"No, that's true . . . ," Kaedrich said, her voice trailing off. "But you're not exactly trained—not really, anyway. And . . ." She glanced meaningfully at Praxis's right leg. Though her harness was hidden by trousers, Praxis acutely felt the tightness on her thigh, the only part of her leg where she still had sensations.

"And yet," Praxis said, brushing the thought away. "I'm willing to bet you that I can still get the first strike in."

Kaedrich snorted. "I doubt that."

Praxis laughed. "Okay, now you *have* to fight me." She was in front of a display of swords now, perfectly gleaming steel with leather and bronze trimmings. She put her hands on her hips, surveying her options. "Don't forget, good sir, that I am still a wizard. Training is little help when your opponent can sense your movements before you even—"

But in the next instant she froze, because in the breath that it had taken her to reach for one of the swords, three things had happened in fast succession: a series of rapid, shrill whistles had broken out through the room, almost like an alarm sounding; a sudden wave of vertigo had struck Praxis from behind; the subtle but distinctly present point of a blunted sword had pressed itself in the gap between her shoulder blades.

She twisted to look over her shoulder, hardly daring to believe it. Beyond the length of the blade at her back was the length of Kaedrich's arm, and beyond that was Kaedrich's face, wearing a broad, self-satisfied grin.

Kaedrich tipped her head, still grinning. "Didn't you know? The monks of the Syll monasteries discovered decades ago that specific frequency sounds will disrupt a wizard's ability to concentrate on their surroundings." She swung her weapon away, staking it against the floor, her free hand tucked neatly behind her back. "Which means that you're dead, *and* that you owe me. But don't worry—I'll let you try again. If you think you can."

"You realize that's cheating, right?" Praxis asked. She grabbed one of the swords at random, giving it a light swing as she moved a few feet into the room.

"No," Kaedrich said, "that's fighting intelligently." She, too, backed off, putting a handful of paces between the two of them. She bowed at Praxis, the formal acknowledgment of her readiness. Then she folded her hands over the hilt of her resting sword, just waiting.

So Praxis took the first move. True, she did not know much of advanced sword fighting, but she'd managed to convince one of her older brothers to give her basic lessons when she was about nine or ten, and she'd always been good at the fast strike. This particular trick was Yandosian in nature, and she doubted that Kaedrich had heard of it: it involved a feint to one side, and an upward thrust when you'd expect a straight blow. Once she'd learned it, it had always served her well in sparring with her brothers, and she anticipated the same success here.

Unfortunately, she had barely moved before Kaedrich darted aside—heading straight into the opening that Praxis was trying to keep hidden. Her motions were a blur, and Praxis's magic failed her again as Kaedrich cut underneath her arm, coming up suddenly behind her. Kaedrich's arm wrenched Praxis's own back, and a blade was to Praxis's neck before she'd realized what was happening. Praxis gasped, in shock and at the sudden jerk of her muscles both.

"Want to know the best part about the whistles?" Kaedrich asked. Her breath was right in Praxis's ear, Praxis's body held tightly against her own. "The disorienting effect lingers for a while on a wizard that isn't prepared for it."

And then Praxis was released, as suddenly as she'd been pinned. The heat of Kaedrich moved back, a wave of cool air rushing in to take its place.

Praxis rubbed at her throat as Kaedrich rounded back to face her. "They certainly teach you a lot of tricks here."

"Not tricks," Kaedrich said. "Tactics. And yes, they teach them very well."

"What, like this?" Praxis threw her arm forward, a whip of flames darting out from her fingertips; the end wrapped itself around Kaedrich's sword, and with a fast snap of her wrist Praxis yanked it from Kaedrich's grasp. The sword went flying, caught with ease in Praxis's outstretched hand. She waved both of the swords at Kaedrich, one in each grip. Now it was her turn to grin. "Oh, I'm sorry, were you unprepared for that? What are you going to do now, smarty?"

Kaedrich gave a little bow of concession. "Nicely done. All right, I guess you have me." She stepped back, spreading her arms wide. "Let's leave the weapons behind then. Go ahead: take your best shot."

Praxis frowned, lowering the swords. "Excuse me?"

"Well, I know that you don't need swords to attack, I've seen it often enough. So why don't you give it a go?"

This was true enough, and yet the idea of lashing out against Kaedrich with magic . . .

"What, you . . . you honestly expect me to hit you with a fireball?"

"Oh, not at all," Kaedrich said, shaking her head. She smiled, a far more wicked curl of her lips than anything Praxis was used to. "I expect you to try to hit me, and fail."

Praxis bit down on a grin, though it felt like half of it probably escaped anyway. The smile alone had done her in, snaking across the room and seizing her chest, teasing and enticing. Praxis dragged her attention away, ostensibly to lean the swords against the nearby rack.

Kaedrich just waited. She kept her arms spread, presenting Praxis with an easy, open target. Praxis took her time. She set down the weapons and stepped slowly into the middle of the room while Kaedrich pivoted to keep a direct line toward her. "Any time, now," Kaedrich called out.

Praxis took a deep breath. Though she trusted Kaedrich to know what she was doing, it was still difficult to get herself to click open the spark of magic, tease the heat down toward her fingers. As the flames sprang to life in her palms, she kept the temperature as low as she could.

The first throw really wasn't very heartfelt. It veered wide, missing Kaedrich easily. The fireball struck the floor, puffing into a harmless trail of smoke.

"You can do better than *that*," Kaedrich said. "Come on, now. Really *try*."

Praxis didn't say anything, though her next shot was a little more concentrated. And then the next one, even more so. A little more. And then, somewhere between attempts five and six, Praxis realized that with each new attempt, Kaedrich was actually managing to twist aside with a frustrating ease. It wasn't only that Praxis's efforts weren't all they could have been—Kaedrich just seemed to know where each volley was coming from, and even with the speed that they approached, somehow found a way to not be there at the very last second.

The next one Praxis threw, she threw with real effort. Still, Kaedrich dodged aside. The next two she threw together, and Kaedrich ducked and swerved at the same moment. Always, with each new level of dedication that Praxis piled on, it did not work. Soon, despite herself, Praxis found the flames coming rapidly, and Kaedrich darted and wove between them— faster and faster, even as Praxis began to step in a wide circle around her. If she wasn't concentrating so hard on her target, Praxis would have been impressed; instead, frustration mounted as her efforts kept failing her, as Kaedrich moved like a slippery fish, until suddenly Kaedrich darted forward.

One second Praxis was on her feet, and then the next she wasn't. Her head spun from the flip, her back and hip shouting at her in protest as she landed hard on the open floor. Praxis blinked, trying to make sense of what had just happened. Kaedrich was crouched over her, her knee pinning Praxis down, her arm a solid restraint across the top of Praxis's chest. Her face hovered above Praxis, filling the entirety of her view. Kaedrich was breathing hard, her lips parted infinitesimally. She swam in Praxis's view, larger than life, filling every one of her senses. A sprinkle of sweat pricked Kaedrich's face, so near to Praxis that she could see her pores.

Praxis's heart slammed against her ribs. She was breathless, and flush with heat far beyond just that of the physical exertion of sparring. It was too easy to imagine Kaedrich closing the narrow gap that raged between them, and Praxis's mind betrayed her as it spun out each of the hundred tantalizing paths that such a kiss might lead them down. She was so lost trying to draw herself out of these visions that she actually froze when Kaedrich leaned in—but, alas, Kaedrich was not doing it for the reasons Praxis had wished for in the fraction of an instant that she'd begun to move. Kaedrich's head hovered beside Praxis's, their lips parallel but untouching, as she whispered, "Do you yield?"

It should have been easy. Praxis could see the road before her, playing out as if it was already happening: she could turn her head, submit her answer by finding Kaedrich's mouth with her own. She would barely have to even move. She *could*, but even as the idea bloomed effortlessly in her mind, Praxis knew that she wouldn't. And this knowledge, so sudden that it hit her straight in the chest, burned off the happy fog that she'd shrouded herself in, as fast as if it had been lit on fire.

She nodded instead. Nothing more, and then Kaedrich was sitting up, standing up, holding out a hand to assist Praxis in getting to her feet.

Praxis ached all over. She allowed herself to be pulled up, wincing at both the pain and her own cowardliness. Kaedrich was already retreating, stepping over to retrieve her shirt and vest and coat from where they lay neatly folded on a bench.

There was no way to dive back into the moment that had just passed, and even if she could, Praxis never would have taken advantage of it. All that was left for her was to retreat to safer ground, to remember her purpose in coming here in the first place. She took a moment to compose herself, to check the tension running in the wires along the wrist and arm. She took a breath, steadying her nerves. "So," she said, trying to sound as casual as she'd intended to when she first arrived. "Fancy taking a trip to the morgue with me?"

When Kaedrich turned back, her eyebrow was already raised.

*   *   *

IT WOULD BE impossible for Kaedrich's absence to go unnoticed for long.

Oh, the instructors themselves might not notice, and even if they did, they wouldn't care. Skipping lessons was a common enough practice that in any given class there were probably one or two faces missing. It wasn't as if this was a mandatory academy, after all, and given the nobility of many of the students, trying to enforce their attendance to each and every lesson was nigh to impossible. So, although Kaedrich had never skipped out on a class before, there wasn't even a punishment awaiting her for later, or at least not from the academy itself.

But *Marlick* would notice.

Already, Kaedrich was anticipating the sly nudge-and-a-wink greeting that Marlick would give her the next time that they saw each other. She could see perfectly the conclusions that he would draw, just like he'd drawn that morning: that Kaedrich had snuck off for a secret tryst, that this was nothing more than an excuse to spend some "quality" time with Praxis. Kaedrich's stomach clawed at itself as she casually left the building, ducking behind a cluster of her compatriots to avoid being spotted by Marlick at their usual meeting spot. Her mind was racing with excuses, for there was no way that Kaedrich would tell him where they were honestly going, until she realized that she didn't *have* to correct him.

She nearly tripped, thinking this, and yet it was true: if Kaedrich was going to stick with the story Praxis had allowed him to believe that morning, then there was no reason why Kaedrich had to deny whatever sordid escapade Marlick made up about her absence. It was strange . . . here Kaedrich had spent more than a year trying to hide or even outright deny her feelings, only to find herself now in a position of trying to maintain the fiction that everything she'd ever secretly hoped for had come true.

Honestly, she wasn't sure what to feel about that. The idea titillated and horrified her in equal measure; but then, if Praxis was all right with people thinking this about the two of them . . . well, what grounds did Kaedrich possibly have to protest?

On the other hand, it was an easy lie for Praxis to maintain. With Kaedrich's true identity disguised, what difference did it make to Praxis if a few people gossiped about her bedroom antics with a man of Monfort? It occurred to Kaedrich as she walked that Praxis was probably only all right with it *because* of the fiction, and Kaedrich's stomach soured at the idea once again.

She met up with Praxis a short while later, at a platform for one of the short loops that ran above the city streets. Praxis had snuck out of the academy a few moments earlier than Kaedrich, slipping into a back passage that Kaedrich had barely ever noticed before. Her back was turned as Kaedrich approached, and when Kaedrich drew near she could hear Praxis saying something under her breath.

"—lucky there are so *many* of them, or I swear you'd end up on the constable's watch list," Praxis said. She tossed something over her shoulder, a tiny yellow feather that caught and settled against her coat as it fell.

Kaedrich smiled. "Maybe if you didn't make such a fuss over them, he wouldn't like it so much."

Praxis whirled around, obviously startled but trying not to show it. She hid behind her tinted spectacles, the loose earflaps of her deerstalker cap. Brex was curled in her hands, but at the sight of Kaedrich the animal made a happy chitter and flapped his wings once, vaulting out of Praxis's grip. He leaped at Kaedrich, who caught him easily and brought him to her cheek.

Praxis brushed a couple of errant feathers from the sleeves of her coat. "I think that canaries must be related to a bird that lives in Tjalava. There's no other reason why he would want to go after them badly enough to break into houses and cages, when there's plenty of other wildlife around for him to hunt."

"Unless he just enjoys the challenge," Kaedrich said, nuzzling Brex for a moment. She kissed the creature's tiny head, and then tossed him into the air. Brex dove, swiping playfully at Kaedrich's close-cropped hair before he took off in a streak of blue and silver. Kaedrich watched him until he disappeared around the corner of a building, because it was easier in some ways than looking at Praxis. She was grateful when one of the miniature engines arrived overhead a moment later, squealing to a halt. It gave them something solid to concentrate on: maneuvering the tightly wound spiral stairs, the crush of people heading up to board.

A few minutes ago, all that she'd concerned herself with was the practical matter of getting out of the academy, settling how she was going to handle Marlick. Now, that burden lifted, her mind kept betraying her, back to what had preceded it.

Kaedrich hadn't *meant* to show off—well. Not really, anyway. When Praxis had first suggested a sparring match, it had seemed unthinkable. The amount of danger in Praxis even *being* there was enormous, despite how lightly she'd taken it, but to have risked being caught engaging in the academy's very own techniques, in their own hallowed halls, with someone who hadn't gone through any of the ceremonies or the swearing of Falconridge's oath? Sure, the level of mystery and ceremony that they piled on was ridiculous—but they took it seriously, and the consequences for violating their edicts were just as serious.

But then, somewhere along the line, Kaedrich had kind of . . . forgotten about where they were, what rules they were or weren't violating. She had managed to impress Praxis—really, truly impress her, Kaedrich could tell by her eyes—and then one thing had so easily led to another. Praxis's approval was so rarely doled out that it struck Kaedrich's head as hard liquor: lopsided grins, fuzzy thinking, warmth spreading through her belly. Each minor victory encouraged another, more impressive display, another hit from the bottle of Praxis's admiration.

So Kaedrich really didn't *think* about what she was doing. Heat from Praxis's fireballs seared past her skin as she swerved and dodged, each success egging her spirits on. This wasn't a trick, that's what made it extra intoxicating. Her victory here was mere agility, a lightness of foot, a careful eye. Her movements brought her closer to Praxis, and then in a burst of reflexes she'd spotted her opening. Kaedrich had darted, flipping Praxis over in an exercise she'd only recently learned. None of it was planned, none of it was intentional. She grinned down at Praxis, knowing that she'd won, really won, and the biggest rush of all washed over her.

All of that was fine—until she realized that she was, in fact, pinning Praxis to the floor. Kaedrich's grin disappeared, so fast that by the time Praxis's disoriented eyes seemed to settle, she probably wouldn't have even seen it. There passed then a century that was probably only a second, where Kaedrich was painfully aware of the arm that pinned down Praxis's chest, the narrow gap hovering paper-thin between them, the way that she all but straddled Praxis's leg as she held her in place. None of these maneuvers seemed remotely inappropriate when she'd practiced them over and over again with the other students, sometimes in this very room, the instructor strolling lazily back and forth between the rows of paired-off sparring partners. It shouldn't be any different now, but oh, it was. In the haze of her victory Kaedrich felt disconnected from herself, like she was walking through a dream. It felt like a dream: and this is where she would lean over, and this is where everything would change.

She actually started to bend down before she caught herself, and looking back, she was so grateful that reality had finally caught up with her. Kaedrich veered at the last moment, hovering as if she was going to whisper something in Praxis's ear. This was almost as bad, and so she had scrambled, and she said the first thing that her mind offered up: *Do you yield?* The standard protocol in a match like this, the same thing she would have said to anyone else that she'd managed to overcome.

Now they found themselves on the upper platforms, one of the few times that Kaedrich had ever boarded the elevated rail lines that ran around the city. It was a perfect spring day, the air warming around them, the breeze carrying in the honey-lime smell of the bay. The near-disaster of Kaedrich's impulsive choice seemed long forgotten from Praxis's mind, if she'd even noticed anything at all, so that was a small blessing at least. Praxis dropped two coins into the slot as she boarded the car, one for each of them, and slid into the knot of passengers.

There were no seats available in the "hopper" car, as they were known, and so Kaedrich and Praxis steadied themselves on a support pole near the back. It was *like* a train, except that everything was done in miniature: the steam engine at the head was little more than what would pull one of the new self-propelling motors like Havil had shown off, and the entire affair was only a single car. There was a circuit of newer lines along the crest of the city that had no individual engine at all, but relied on a single cable line that the cars clamped onto—it was said to be able to handle slopes that the rest of the trains just couldn't, and Kaedrich kind of wanted to see it, sometime (she'd heard it was eerie how quiet it was), but she reminded herself that this excursion was not for sightseeing. It had a purpose, even if Kaedrich still wasn't sure what said purpose was supposed to be.

Unfortunately, a crowded car wasn't the best place to talk about either their plans for the day (which, knowing Praxis, probably involved "bending" at least a few rules), or the attack that had driven Praxis out of her hotel the night before. Kaedrich was guessing that the attack was what had precipitated Praxis's interest in the morgue. There was already a brief mention of it in the paper that morning; no names, but it had Praxis's signature all over it. Nobody knew what had caused it, or if the room's undisclosed occupant had been an instigator or a target, but there was mention of two bodies having been removed from the premises.

The thought of this dampened the rest of Kaedrich's already waning mood. The car jostled, Praxis's elbow bumping up against Kaedrich around their shared pole, and Kaedrich used the excuse of the motion to steal a glance at Praxis's face.

She was so calm. She was always so calm, and that's what made it easy to forget the trail of accidental deaths that littered the wake of her life.

This probably wasn't fair. Kaedrich knew that underneath her callous exterior, Praxis was both a good person (okay, somewhat reluctantly at times, but still), and that she carried the weight of every death that she'd ever caused. You could almost see them, sometimes, in the stoop of her shoulders when she let her guard down, or the slack pull of her face when she tried to cover the pain of it. She also knew that Praxis had never intended anyone to die, not really. All of them were either accidental or defensive, and considering Kaedrich's recent education, who was she to judge a person's ability to protect themselves or their loved ones with deadly force? All right, so it's not like Kaedrich had ever had reason to use her skills for anything more dangerous than sparring matches, but she didn't kid herself. She wasn't at Falconridge to play games.

Kaedrich knew all this, understood and agreed with all of this. And yet.

It was difficult sometimes, to think that the person that fate had allowed her to fall in love with was also a person that knew what it was like to take someone's life away from them. Perlandra surely must have a strange sense of humor, to have matched Kaedrich's gentle heart against the icy core of someone like Praxis. Kaedrich touched the pin on her lapel, running her fingers down the length of each of the wavy rays in turn

"Something wrong?" Praxis asked. She spoke softly, the better to avoid being overheard. She had taken off her tinted spectacles and was watching Kaedrich's fingers, and Kaedrich stilled them as she hastily withdrew her hand.

"I'm fine."

It was clear Praxis didn't believe this, but she did not press the issue. It's possible that she might have, under different circumstances, but they would never find out; the car began to slow, and Praxis's attention snapped to the windows, her scowl instantly in place.

Kaedrich glanced to see what had drawn her gaze, though it was not immediately obvious. They were coming to a stop right beside a tall building, brickwork stained with ash and age. A broken window passed by their view as the hopper car drew to a gradual halt.

Praxis was already moving, shoving her way brusquely through the crowd. Kaedrich jerked out of her swirling thoughts, hustling to catch up. From the front of the hopper car she could see a thick cluster of people clogging up the streets running below them—while somewhere up ahead, smoke billowed up into the perfect blue sky over Monfort.

THEY WATCHED THE smoke belch into the sky, an ever-expanding cloud of blue-black smog blooming up from a point just beyond view. The stench was already filtering in—it had been the first thing to catch Praxis's attention, before the hopper car had even begun to slow. For several long seconds all of the passengers stood in a frozen silence, everyone trying to figure out where, exactly, in the city the fire might be, and did they have any business or loved ones potentially in harm's way?

"Well," Kaedrich muttered after a moment, "at least I don't need to worry that this one is *your* doing."

Praxis turned, eyebrow cocked high. "I'm the one that's supposed to be sarcastic."

"Do I look like I was joking?"

She didn't.

Praxis scowled. "Shut up," she said. By now, other bits of conversation had started to leak through the shock, and several people were descending upon the driver at the front of the car in a mob-like fashion to find out what he planned to do with them all. Such matters did not hold sway for Praxis, however; it did not matter what the rest of the hopper car did, because her path had unfolded so expertly in her mind that it may as well have been the plan all along.

They made their way aft through the hopper car, Praxis in the lead and Kaedrich following along with fearless trust. There were no proper doors on a hopper car, just a single open archway above a set of three steps, and so they did not even have to draw attention by opening anything. They simply stepped out, as if this was their stop, and everyone else was so distracted with the circumstances that they did not pay much (if any) attention to what was going on behind them.

The tracks were narrow, not even quite as wide as the hopper car itself. For Praxis, this proved somewhat of an inconvenience, but the improved design of her harness system allowed her to step *around* the doorway and set down behind the car without too much difficulty. She was grateful that she had practiced as much as she had, in the weeks since she'd begun using this design, and doubly grateful that her practice had included more difficult maneuvers than simply walking about—it demonstrated, she thought to herself, a remarkable sense of foresight, and she allowed a brief swell of pride at what she perceived as a great step forward in maturity and planning.

Never mind that what she had been planning for was mischief and trespassing; the point, she felt, remained the same.

She took a few careful steps away from the hopper car, allowing room for Kaedrich to scoot around after her. Stale air pressed in, a thousand times worse than a campfire. The smell clawed over Praxis's skin and down her throat, and she spat through the slats of the rail lines, watching it fall like pigeon shit between the people hurrying around on the street below. Great: not only had three of her new shirts been ruined by the smoke of last night's hotel room fire, but now this one would need to be excessively laundered before she would wear it again. Not that Kaedrich seemed to be paying them much mind. But then, Praxis tried to tell herself, that wasn't *really* why she'd purchased them anyway.

This was a blatant lie, but a comforting one. She took a few more steps, curling and shifting her fingers as she made her way to the opposite side of the tracks. The gears controlling her leg caught once, just for a moment, and Praxis flicked her fingers violently to unstick them.

The building that the hopper car had stopped beside had a delightfully abandoned look to it. Praxis leaned across the gap, barely more than a foot or so wide, and braced herself against the wall with one hand as she jiggled one of the windows with her other. The first one she tried was stubbornly stuck, so Praxis shifted her thumb, clicking the gears of her leg back into operation, and sidestepped down to the next one.

This one slid open easily, much to Praxis's delight. She pushed herself up from the wall and stepped back, motioning toward the gaping entrance. "After you."

Kaedrich shook her head. "Oh, no. I'm not the one that just goes barging into rooms without permission."

Praxis rolled her eyes. "That was *one time*," she said. "And I told you, I had my eyes closed the whole while."

"Yeah—how did you even know to do that, anyway? It's been bugging me. I mean, I suppose that you could have guessed I was getting changed but—"

Praxis's eyebrow raised. "You know I can sense people's movements."

"What, so you just—oh gods." Kaedrich leaned back, wrinkling her face as if she'd just stumbled across a particularly vile spider. "Praxis, were you . . . *sensing* that I was taking my clothes—?"

"I think that the point is that I was respecting your sense of modesty, and that you should be happy for my tact," Praxis said. "Now, if we could return our attention to the present for a moment: I know that you don't like 'barging in' to places, but I assure you that in this case there's no one inside, and I . . . could really use a hand climbing through myself."

Kaedrich forced a nod. She still looked a bit flushed and queasy around the edges, but she dutifully moved past Praxis, watching her footing the whole way, and stepped with such ease across the gap and through the window that a flash-flood of jealousy coursed through Praxis's veins.

It was mostly that it was such a large gap that caused Praxis concern. She really wasn't sure which was better: to leave the weight on her disabled leg as she stepped forward, or to *put* all of her weight on it upon landing. She hovered for a moment, trying to settle this, but she didn't want to waste too much time appearing to think about it. Praxis clicked the gears back into place and started forward, ducking to move through the opening of the window.

Briefly, she had a vision of falling through, of tripping and colliding with Kaedrich, the two of them falling to the floor in a graceless tumble. The idea came onto her so strongly that when it *didn't* happen it was almost confusing. But of course, Kaedrich would not let her fall. She took hold of Praxis by the waist, spinning her into the room and setting her into place like a perfect gentleman helping a lady down from a horse. And this, Praxis thought, was in some ways almost as good. She'd taken a stabilizing hold against Kaedrich's shoulders and upper chest out of instinct, and for a moment their hands lingered in place around each other, holding on like lovers not ready to part. Kaedrich's fingers shifted slightly as they held Praxis's waist.

Kaedrich cleared her throat and pulled back, turning to examine the darkened room. Praxis took off her hat and spectacles and stuffed them deep into her coat. She snapped her fingers, cupping a palmful of flame, and held it tall to let the light pour out into the void.

They were standing in an abandoned office. A gigantic piece of cabinetry stood sentry in the corner, its neat wooden file drawers partially opened in the stagnant air. The door to the room was ajar, and Praxis shoved through before they had a chance to talk.

The building may indeed have been abandoned, but it had not yet fallen into decay. Picked clean, yes, emptied out by whoever owned it and then no doubt scavenged already by the homeless and the desperate, but in no way falling to pieces. The hallway was clear and wide, bits of light filtering in from open windows in rooms to either side. Praxis led the way, cupping her flame above her head so that some light would cast behind her. She proceeded with caution, testing her weight against the floorboards just in case, but so far she was finding nothing more ominous than creaks and groans.

"So, does this mean that you know what, like, *everyone* is doing, all of the time?" Kaedrich asked. They were about halfway down the first staircase they came across, and the question burst free as if she'd been holding it in the entire time.

"What? No, don't be ridiculous. I'm not a *god*."

"You act like one, sometimes."

A laugh burst out of Praxis, though she wasn't sure if Kaedrich's comment was more of a joke or jab. She fell quiet, testing out the next step. She shifted her fingers, shifted her weight, and moved forward.

"Well, I'm not," Praxis said after a moment. "There are limits—of distance, and detail, and . . . concentration factors into it, too. Familiarity. I mean, with *you*—" Praxis shut her mouth, her cheeks flaring with heat over the conversation that she'd almost stumbled into. The stairs creaked, the gears along her leg clicked forward. "There's just a lot to it," she added hurriedly, hoping to move things along.

At the mention of herself, Kaedrich had paused. Two steps up from Praxis, her foot already halfway lifted from the stair. She shifted at Praxis's attempts at distraction, rushing to catch up. One hand was running along the railing, such a lightly feminine touch (Praxis should probably point that out, sometime), the other nervously tugging at her shirt collar. "What *about* me?"

With you, I almost feel like I can sense your heartbeat, Praxis was going to say, but thankfully didn't. She kept her mouth stubbornly shut, her teeth grinding together. She increased her own pace and Kaedrich matched it, seemingly without a thought. *When we're alone, you flood my perceptions; I can barely even concentrate on the path in front of me because you flare so brightly in my mind.*

She said nothing like this, of course. Instead she scowled, even though Kaedrich couldn't see it from behind her, and said, "Why are you so interested in this, all of a sudden? It's no secret. For sanity's sake, you were taught how to *confuse* this sense."

"Yeah, but I didn't know that wizards were going around *spying* on people all of the time!"

"Oh, please. Is it *spying* if I'm in the same room as someone who's talking loudly enough for me to hear them?"

Kaedrich fell silent. Her movements stiffened in the way they always did when she was concentrating on something, uncertain how to react. They reached a landing, and turned to descend to the next level.

"Try to understand," Praxis said, her voice softening, "I can't help but be aware of my surroundings, to some degree or another. I don't even think about it anymore, it just . . . *is*."

Kaedrich tipped her head as if conceding the point. Her steps loosened, just a little. "Still," she said after a moment, "you really should *try* not to pay so much attention to it at times. When people are, you know, in . . . bathrooms and—and bedrooms, and . . . things."

"Why, are you planning on doing something in your bedroom that I shouldn't know about?"

It was said without thought, rushing out as a lark. Only once Kaedrich froze in place behind her did Praxis realize what she'd actually asked.

The thing is, it had been more than a year that Kaedrich had been living in Monfort. It was enough time. Just because Kaedrich hadn't mentioned anything, that didn't mean that she hadn't gotten to know someone else— she had not, after all, told Praxis about her job. And sure, Kaedrich's masculine persona would have made things complicated for her, but it wasn't insurmountable; she could have confided her true identity easily enough. For the first time Praxis considered the possibility that she was too late, that the reason that Kaedrich wasn't taking any of the openings that Praxis kept leaving for her was because she was already involved.

Praxis stumbled down the last step. Her flames dropped to the floor and puffed into oblivion as she threw her hands out to catch herself. She fell gracelessly against a wall, landing hard on her shoulder. Praxis cursed under her breath even as Kaedrich rushed forward, already asking if she was all right.

There was no light at the bottom of the stairwell. Kaedrich reached out blindly, fingers waving until she landed upon Praxis's shoulder. "Praxis?"

"I'm fine," Praxis said, realizing she'd been silent on the matter. "I lost my footing." She was talking almost directly into the wallpaper, but even in the dark she did not want to turn around and face Kaedrich, not yet. It was bad enough to be aware of the hesitation in Kaedrich's muscles, the way that she pulled back her hand almost immediately upon learning that Praxis wasn't hurt.

There was, of course, no reason to assume that Praxis's fears were true, but that did nothing to stop them from piling on top of her, so many and so fast that it was a wonder that she didn't collapse underneath the weight of them. She found herself doing a snap-review of the people in Kaedrich's life that she'd met so far—and then realized how few of them there had been, which only lent greater credence to her paranoia. Gods, what if Praxis's cowardice and worries about being overbearing had meant that she'd put it off too long? If she'd missed her opportunity, she'd have no one to blame but herself.

Chapter Fourteen

THANKFULLY, THE HOPPER car had stopped only a handful of blocks from the morgue. They passed underneath the tracks, soon leaving it far behind them as they moved through the ever-thickening smoke and crowd.

Kaedrich's skin crawled, worse the farther they worked their way forward. She tried to tell herself that it was just the fact that they were moving *toward* the fire and chaos rather than away from it or standing still, the two choices that everyone else around them was making. She tried to tell herself that it was just the fact that there was a fire sputtering through the heart of Monfort, that such times always made people uneasy. She tried to tell herself that it was the smoke stinging in her eyes, or leaking in around the handkerchief that she kept pressed against her face. Because it would be irresponsible, in the midst of this swirling chaos, for a large part of her discontent to be related to her own personal difficulties. A good soldier thought not of himself—that was a line favored by her tactics instructor, although he often brandished it like a whip when he wanted his students to stop gossiping and pay attention, and less as an actual lesson. And Kaedrich wasn't exactly a soldier, even if she was getting a soldier's training. And there was no war . . . not exactly.

Though more and more the city of Monfort had taken on a cold, hopeless feeling that Kaedrich thought must be what it felt like to be at war. She had been blind to it before, when there was nothing more complicated in her life than finding the time to actually *write down* the letters to Praxis that she was constantly composing in her head; she felt it now. There was a brittleness in the air, a vague sense of impending disaster hanging just over the horizon. Even now, look: a fire, raging somewhere nearby, and while there was panic and distress, while there were shouts for help or loved ones, there was not a single shred of *surprise*. Something dark had woven itself into the heart of Monfort, something that expected to be trampled, to be dismantled, to be broken.

And could anyone blame them? The ghosts, the ensuing spiritual crisis that had followed, the great recession raining down on them. Businesses were collapsing, empty buildings littering the city like missing teeth. The Crown had done nothing to reassure them; on the contrary, the "broken king" had been useless for more than two years before the crisis had even begun, and the prince ... rumor was that the prince barely left his chambers anymore, frightened into isolation. The ghosts had made no distinction for royalty, and while Prince Hemmerick had tried to keep a calm face in the months immediately following the crisis, the mind can only take so much torment. They say that the Pon had been his only comfort, though Kaedrich had always assumed her words had as much to do with his current state of distress as the ghosts themselves.

They were almost to the morgue, and now they could finally see the reason for the state of chaos. From far beyond the fire, blazing merrily two blocks away, a thick knot of protesters had relocated themselves here, of all places. A knot settled in Kaedrich's stomach, remembering the reports; of course, the bodies would have been brought here, and of course there would be some that would follow.

By the looks of things, though, they weren't getting what they'd hoped out of this pilgrimage. A pile of royal guards stood blocking the entrance, hand in hand to form a human chain. Only one stood in front of his peers, shouting for people to get back.

"You can't hide the truth forever! We will not be kept in the dark!" one of the protesters screamed at the lead guard. He waved his fist in the air, not necessarily intending to hit the royal guard stationed outside of the morgue, though the guard did have to swing his head to avoid the unwieldy flailing.

"That's *enough*!" one of the other guards snapped. He broke ranks with his fellows and waved his gold-emblazoned truncheon in the protester's face, attempting to corral the crowd back at least another couple of steps—though the crowd didn't seem to be taking the idea to heart. The guard frowned. "For Perlandra's sake, can none of you see that this evacuation is for your own *protection*? We cannot guarantee the containment of the blaze—"

"A blaze that *you* set!" This new shout came from somewhere in the midst of the crowd, and it was quickly piled onto, one after another, calls of "Yeah!" and "Merciless pig!" and "Can't keep us out forever!" spitting fast over the heads of the assembly.

"For sanity's sake," Praxis grumbled beside Kaedrich. Her speech was muffled through the cloth of a horribly bright plaid scarf that she'd picked up . . . somewhere (Kaedrich really didn't want to know where). "What do these people expect? That they'll just be able to stroll into the morgue as if the bodies are out on public display?"

"Well, yeah," Kaedrich said, and when Praxis turned, looking at her as if she was insane, Kaedrich managed a small laugh, which broke into a cough against the smoke of the air. "You don't know?"

"Know *what*?"

Kaedrich only shook her head. She kept her handkerchief firm against her face as she said, "Come on. If we're going to bust in, we might as well do this properly."

She tapped Praxis on the elbow, motioning for her to follow, and then led the way through the mass of angry bodies. They kept away from the thickest of the crowd, though to avoid them altogether would mean going several city blocks out of the way. Kaedrich led a meandering path, craning her neck the whole time to act like she was just another onlooker hoping for a better view.

The back corner of the morgue was relatively quiet, just a single guard stationed at the door. Not even one of the royal guards brought in to deal with the situation: one of their regular stock, by the looks of him, in a tired uniform that had clearly seen too many washings. Kaedrich paused along the edge of the crowd, the bulk of which was largely ignoring this minor doorway, and studied the man for only a moment or two. He had his shirt yanked up to keep the smoke out of his nose and mouth, though he was clearly struggling; his shoulders convulsed every few moments with the failed effort of suppressing his coughs. Kaedrich had only been in the thick of the smoke for a few minutes, and already her lungs were scratchy with heat and soot—she could only imagine how badly he felt.

"Wait here," she told Praxis, and cut through the last of the crowds before Praxis had a chance to argue.

The guard spotted Kaedrich about halfway through her approach.

He straightened himself up as best as he could, holding his hand out. The guard dropped his shirt front so that he could speak more clearly, as he called out, "That's far enough, sir, I'm afraid that they've closed—"

"It's all right," Kaedrich cut in, lowering her handkerchief. She ran the last few steps separating them, and motioned quickly at the Falconridge patch sewn over her breast pocket—so quickly, in fact, that she hoped he didn't have enough time to take in more than its general shape. It was certainly impressive looking: a shield behind a falcon's head, rapiers crossed as if mounted to the wall, the whole thing detailed in brassy-colored thread. It lent Kaedrich a nice air of vague authority as she said, "Lt. Darbury—they've sent me to relieve you."

The guard blinked at her, surprise written plainly over his face. Surprise that was fast going to turn to suspicion, and so Kaedrich pressed her handkerchief hard back over her face, coughing into it more than was strictly necessary.

As she'd hoped, this triggered an involuntary sympathetic reaction from the guard. He doubled into his own cough, burying his face in his sleeve. *Come on*, Kaedrich thought, watching him carefully. *Don't you want to get out of this?*

When he was done coughing, the guard hesitated—but only for a moment. He nodded, in acknowledgment and gratitude both. "No one in or out," he said, leveling a steady look at Kaedrich.

"Of course."

The guard nodded again. His eyes were red-rimmed and watery with irritation, and he took no further prodding. He jogged off, folding himself seamlessly into the nearby crowds.

Kaedrich hid a grin behind the cloth of her handkerchief. By the time she refocused her efforts into looking across for Praxis, Praxis had already broken away from the group and sidled up beside her. Kaedrich yanked the door open, hurrying Praxis through.

Praxis was already laughing by the time Kaedrich shut the door behind them. "Oh gods," Praxis said, her laughter slurring her speech. "Kaedrich, I lo—uh . . ." She cleared her throat. "That is, um . . . good job. I'm impressed."

Kaedrich shook her head as she drew the bolt on the door. "I'm getting as bad as *you*."

"Mm," Praxis mumbled, half-agreeing without even seeming to pay attention to what Kaedrich had said. She was angrily yanking the "borrowed" scarf away from her face, her focus already shifted to the narrow corridor around them.

The air inside of the building was clear. Though a bit of smoke had followed them in, and of course a faint layer of the stench of it permeated the whole place, a person could breathe just fine inside of the protective walls of the morgue. Kaedrich stuffed her handkerchief back into her pocket as Praxis dropped the scarf into a heap on the floor.

There was only one way to go, and at the end of the corridor a door opened up directly into the main part of the morgue. And then Praxis could see for herself, why the protesters expected to just be able to walk in whenever they wanted.

Sometimes good enough ideas have unintended consequences, and that is more or less the story of the Monfort Morgue.

It started about four summers ago, after a blitz of hurricanes had struck the Durlish coastline. Torrential rains and terrible winds had knocked a record number of people (and even some small buildings) into the embrace of Abbney Bay, so much that they were fishing bodies out of the water for months afterward. In the first week alone they overwhelmed the old morgue, both in the physical sense of running out of space to put the bodies, and in the enormity of the task of identifying all the bloated corpses that they suddenly had on hand. So someone, somewhere, perhaps even in a fit of dark humor at their grim situation, suggested that they should just open the doors to the public and let them come in and claim their loved ones.

And this is more or less what happened, except that nobody anticipated the sheer titillation that the people of Monfort would experience at being able to come in and examine such gruesome sights for themselves. Within days they were overwhelmed by visitors: some looking to find a lost relative or friend, some wondering if they might spot the occasional neighbor or known shop boy, but most just for the simple disturbing fascination of it all.

These days, it was one of the most flocked-to (and most profitable) enterprises in all of Monfort, the one business still flourishing in the shocked aftermath of the great ghost crisis. Apparently people's brush with death had only *increased* their appetite for the macabre, and the influx of funding and visitors had subsequently expanded the building's elegance tenfold.

So now the dead of Monfort lived on velvet padding, their nearly naked bodies scrubbed clean and laid out in such comfort that many of them had never known in life. They were set out in large glass cases trimmed with silver and gold, four or five corpses to a case, their clothing and any items they'd been wearing neatly folded and presented beside them.

Tiny, handprinted cards gave a brief summary of the circumstances of their death: *drowned in the bay, stabbed in a back-alley, hanged (apparent suicide)*.

Kaedrich hovered near the doorway and explained this to Praxis as she darted, open-mouthed, from case to case in the vast room. Kaedrich herself had been here only once before, being shown around the city by Marlick and Havil shortly after they'd all met. She hadn't liked it then, and she didn't much like it now; it reminded her too much of the displays buried deep in the land of the dead, the final moment of a person's life preserved as a life-sized diorama.

"I would say that it's kind of disturbing," Praxis said, looking across from the far side of a glass case with five gunshot victims inside, "but it's really not *that* different from the Syll's judgment rites. Have you ever witnessed one?"

Kaedrich raised her eyebrow, as if to ask, *Do you seriously expect me to have?*

Praxis turned her attention back to the display case, covering what looked like the faintest blush at the tops of her cheeks. She spread her hands across the glass, staring at whatever random corpse she happened to have stopped in front of. She shrugged. "It's really not a terrible idea, besides. Why *not* let the public come in and report these people's identities? It's better than rotting in a basement for months on end."

"Yeah, but could you imagine actually *finding* someone you know in here? Like, oh, you come in for a stroll and there's your Uncle Garreson with the back of his head bashed in." Kaedrich grimaced. "What if you didn't even know that he'd *died*? I don't think that the trauma is necessarily worth the benefit."

She was speaking off-the-cuff, vocalizing the latent distaste that she'd had for the morgue but had never quite put into words before—but she didn't expect that Praxis would actually be paying much attention to what she said, and she certainly didn't expect much of a reaction.

And yet, at her comments, something hard settled over Praxis's face. Her finger, which had been idly tapping the glass, suddenly stilled. "Death and trauma are unavoidable," she said.

There was something pinched in her voice, and it was only after she spoke that Kaedrich realized what her problem was—of all the arbitrary deaths that Kaedrich could have used in her example, why in the name of Perlandra had she reached for *that* one? During their time in the land of the dead, Kaedrich had gone into Praxis's worst memory. She should have known better.

Kaedrich winced, embarrassed by her own thoughtlessness. "Praxis, I didn't mean to—"

"We're wasting time," Praxis said, straightening up. She was already clutching at the scar on her wrist as she jerked her chin toward the front of the building. "I'll check the bodies in this half of the room, you check the other."

Kaedrich nodded. Though it pained her not to apologize, she allowed the subject to drop. "What are we looking for?"

As soon as she asked it, she realized that she already knew the answer. She almost told Praxis not to bother, but Praxis was already talking. "Burn victims," she said, her voice level and as dead as any corpse in the room with them. "More of my handiwork, you might say."

"Praxis—"

Praxis raised her hand. "Don't." She motioned at the cases nearest to Kaedrich. "Just help me look so that we can get out of here, all right?"

SURPRISINGLY, THERE WAS a time when dead bodies didn't bother Praxis.

When she'd first left Yandosia she'd even worked for a while alongside the stone-shapers of Aul, preparing the bodies of the dead and burning them down with magical flames until nothing but a smooth stone remained. Though the first few days had been difficult—actually *watching* another Aul body smolder and burn, turning slowly to ashes, after what she had been through—there was something cathartic about going through the process a hundred times over. She knew even at the time that she would never *get over* accidentally killing her mentor and tutor in all things magic, but with each new body transformed before her very eyes, it was almost like burning out that part of her. Almost.

At the very least, exposure to so many of them meant that she could look at a body now without thinking only of Moc.

So when she left Aul, a year after she'd arrived, on that front at least she felt almost optimistic. Okay, so the rest of her time on the string of islands had been . . . complicated, at best. And the circumstances of her leaving could not have been worse—Rinn had seen fit to that—but on the long voyage to the shores of Tjalava, Praxis decided that the experience had been a crucible, one that had set her on the path that she was destined to fulfill.

It's *possible* that the terrible food and self-imposed isolation during her trip might have played a factor in these conclusions, but at the time she was too wound up and bitter to consider thinking about the emotional implications of any of her choices. Praxis Fellows, eighteen years old and full of repressed fury and regret, stepped off of the boat in Tjalava, and found herself in the middle of a plague zone.

Nothing could have delighted her more.

She had come to the country to study death, after all. Everything that she had been through in the last few years—toying with life and death and having them toy right back with her—it all wound together into a fat rope, and she felt that if she didn't listen to it, it would tighten around her and choke her to death. It had to *mean* something, or at least that was what she needed to believe at the time.

The appearance of so very many corpses, then, was as great of a gift as the shores of Tjalava could have provided. Praxis gawped over them as she schlepped her way through the coastal city, her suitcase banging against her legs and the strap of her bag digging against her chest. She wiped her brow with the back of her hand; her tidy braid was losing structure in the humidity, random strands plastered to her forehead. Sweat dripped freely down her back, her arms and legs trapped behind the fabric of a Yandosian dress. Even their lightest cloth was oppressive here, but Praxis grinned despite the heat. There were so many bodies that they were piled in the streets, blocking traffic. The stench was unbelievable.

Of course once she arrived at the Yandosian embassy, she was urged in the strongest possible language to stay inside with them. Praxis had sent word ahead, in a postal ship that would arrive a full week before she did, to make her needs known to them; the Yandosian ambassador himself had made the journey from the capital city to offer the services of his private translator, and he could not believe her when she said that she'd be leaving again so quickly.

"But—Miss Fellows!" he sputtered. He kept wringing his hands, and Praxis wondered if he so easily lost his cool when dealing with diplomatic problems. "It's not safe out there! The fever has already felled nearly half the city!"

"And you think that something that virulent will be stopped by the borders of our pocket of Yandosian soil?" She shook her head. "I've already walked through the thick of it—if this virus is going to kill me, it will kill me. In the meantime, I have work to do."

The ambassador's eyes widened. He leaned away from her, almost imperceptibly but just enough.

Praxis nodded at the other man that had been standing silent at his side throughout this whole exchange. "This is the translator?"

The man was young, probably no older than Praxis. He was crisp and polished, and though he seemed to have his own personal style about him, he also had a way of blending into the background. It had taken her a moment before she'd even really registered that he was standing there at all.

"Yes, miss," the translator said, speaking for himself. From his jet-black hair and sandy colored skin Praxis judged him to likely be a Syll, which struck her as odd enough for the job he was doing for them, but he greeted her in her native tongue, and there was not the slightest trace of an accent about him. He pressed his three central fingers against his lips in a Yandosian greeting of great respect, and Praxis raised an eyebrow.

"You can call me Tully."

"Tully," Praxis repeated, trying it out. "Is that short for something?"

Tully smiled. "Something that you likely cannot pronounce, yes. Let's just leave it at that."

Praxis shrugged. "Fine—you'll do."

There was a bit more urging from the ambassador as Praxis made arrangements for her bags to be taken up to the room they'd prepared for her, but Praxis cut his arguments off with a sharp glare that she'd learned from her mother, and that was the end of that. She was, after all, a Fellows, and there was little that he was willing to do to risk her wrath. She told him that she planned to spend the rest of the day exploring this delightfully dying city, and then she and Tully would head off first thing in the morning.

That was the plan, anyway. At least until Praxis started coughing up blood.

THE BODIES THAT Praxis was looking for were nowhere to be found.

Neither were the ones that had been staked up to the front of the Crescent, Kaedrich noticed, though she did not bother reporting this to Praxis, who was busy enough fuming over the absence of just the two that she had wanted to find. (And nor, thankfully, was Lord Wellen here—though *he* had no doubt been identified by Mr. Bundling and moved out by now. The story was in all the papers, the downfall of the once great Society of Magic; Kaedrich had grudgingly written the first draft.)

"I don't understand," Praxis said, storming past Kaedrich in a furious click of gears, "did we *miss* them somehow? Are you sure you looked in every case?"

"Unfortunately."

"Look again, then. Take my side, and I'll take yours."

Kaedrich shrugged. She did not believe that it would help, but if Praxis wanted to look again, they would look again.

It did not help.

At Kaedrich's suggestion, they decided to search the rest of the building. Though she had no reason to suspect there were more private accommodations for the bodies, she could not guarantee that there *weren't*; and it did no harm to poke around, since they were already here. She saw the logic of this settle well with Praxis, and in a back corner, through a door, they found a staircase leading to an upper floor in one direction, and a basement in another.

"I'll take the basement," Praxis said, already moving.

This, then, is how Kaedrich ended up pushing open a door into what appeared from the outside to be nothing more than another office in a long row of offices. Only when she stepped inside, she froze in her tracks.

The room was clearly intended to be something else not long ago, and had been converted in great haste: there stood a bookshelf packed to the gills, and two benches sat wedged into the corner of the room, one flipped upside down and stacked on the other, while a pile of boxes stood sentry on either side of the door. The middle of the room had been cleared, and five great slabs of tables had been brought in and set in a row underneath the overhead lamp. They took up the vast majority of the floor space, barely a foot of walkways around and between them all.

She had found the bodies that they were looking for. All of them—the three that had been staked up in front of the Crescent, and Praxis's burn victims too. They were spread out in a neat row, in various stages of what Kaedrich assumed were autopsies. A few tray tables littered what little space was between the bodies, only instead of serving tea, gleaming instruments were laid out upon them.

Kaedrich took a ginger step into the room, followed by another. She pressed her sleeve back against her face—not to block out smoke this time, but stench. Something chemical was stinging at her nose and eyes, mingling with death and decay. She tried to look at the bodies; she tried *not* to look at the bodies. She inched her way around to the far side, where Praxis's burn victims were. There were boxes underneath all the tables, with a cryptic set of numbers and letters across them that Kaedrich was willing to bet were the call-codes for the unidentified dead. She was about to lean over and pull one of the boxes out when a soft scuff of the heel of a shoe caught her attention.

"Well, well. If it isn't Kaedrich Mannly."

Kaedrich whirled. Tol, Lanali's right-hand goon, the person that had been sent after them more than once, that had tried to kill Kaedrich on multiple occasions, was standing in the open doorway—only this time, he knew who she was.

While the question of how Tol had learned of her identity was a valid one, though, there were a few more pressing issues at hand. Panic flared, but Kaedrich stamped down on it. There were no flowers in here, only the bitter scent of death and decay. In an instant, she reviewed the room in her mind: one exit (blocked), two windows (barred), a variety of tables and nasty-looking instruments lying about, several corpses. Bookshelf, benches, boxes—useless. She carried no weapons on her person, something that felt at the time like the stupidest decision that she had ever made. *Stay calm.*

Kaedrich shook her head. "That's not my name."

Tol smirked. "Sure, sure." He took a handful of steps into the room, clearing a line to the exit in the process. "I should have known that an evacuation wouldn't keep you two out. I assume it's two, and that Miss Fellows will be along shortly? It seems that a person can never encounter one of you without the other being far behind. Isn't that so?"

Silence felt like the safest bet, and so Kaedrich did not rise to Tol's bait. Words can be like weapons in the right context, and there was no way that she was giving him more than he already had in his arsenal. She tried to keep her posture still, her arms relaxed.

He was still moving casually into the room, circling around as he took in a view of the row of bodies that the workers had abandoned in the evacuation. The door was completely unobstructed now, though quite a distance from Kaedrich, with Tol closer to it than she was. The positioning of the tables meant that she would have to either move *closer* to him in order to reach the exit, or attempt to vault over them—possibly slowing her down, and certainly offering distractions as she tried to pull the maneuver off.

Tol reached one of the bodies, the second-to-last in the row: one of the burn victims, splayed open for analysis. Between the extra-tall tables and the significant girth of the dead man's chest, it was a wonder that Tol could see over the corpse at all; he actually shifted onto his toes as he peered into the open cavity that the morgue workers had winched open in the dead man's ribs.

Tol glanced up. "You're not exactly the talkative type, are you?" He shrugged. "That's fine by me—truth be told, I've grown tired of listening to people drone on incessantly. But since I have your attention, Kaedrich, I will offer you one piece of advice. As a friend."

This, Kaedrich almost laughed at. Almost.

"I know that you're in love with Praxis Fellows," Tol said, and now Kaedrich's careful stillness turned into one of frozen terror. Tol brushed his hands together over the dead man's chest, as if somehow just looking at it had sullied them with crumbs and dirt. He wasn't watching the corpse, though, he was watching Kaedrich as his statement made impact, and he smiled, self-satisfied, as he continued. "So here's my advice: if you want any hope of things ending happily between the two of you, you'll both pack up and leave Monfort immediately. Confess your feelings to her, and ride away into the sunset together. Just forget about all of this." Tol was moving on to the final body now, the other burned man splayed open much like the previous one. He glanced into the man's chest, and Kaedrich wondered, fleetingly, if he could see the corpse's heart as easily as he had spotted hers.

How did you know?

She did not ask it aloud—she would never make the mistake of asking it aloud—but this was the question that had been ringing through her mind for a minute already, and this is the question that would continue to haunt her in the days to come.

"After all," Tol continued, brushing his hands over the second man's chest as he had the first, "does any of what's going on here really matter, in the end? When compared to everything that the two of you stand to lose, if you interfere?"

It was a cheap tactic, but damn if it didn't work: as soon as Tol said it a vibrant image had struck her, the sort of thing that she tried very, very hard not to let herself picture anymore. She didn't even have to close her eyes for it to overtake her for an instant or two. It was the living dream that she'd swam in for the first few weeks after coming to Monfort, the one where things had gone differently at the restaurant, the night before Kaedrich had left. One where she *didn't* run into Praxis having dinner with a man, where instead Praxis had been dining alone and greeted her warmly, where Kaedrich had presented the flowers she'd brought and said the lines that she'd rehearsed over and over in her head on the walk over. The life that they could have had, if Praxis was interested.

The fact that it wasn't going to happen didn't make it any less intoxicating. The idea flooded Kaedrich, pinning her uselessly in place, and riding the tide of this image came the terrible fear of Tol's threat: achieving her dream only to lose it again, and all because she'd gotten too curious, too noble-minded.

It distracted her just enough. Just enough that she didn't stop to wonder *why* Tol was brushing his hands together above the open chests of the two corpses, and just long enough for him to finish and then nod to himself, satisfied with his work. By the time the workings of Kaedrich's mind had started up again it was too late.

An acrid, nose-hair-curling stench was already filling the examination room. Kaedrich lurched forward, not even sure what she could hope to do in the face of this, and Tol merely raised his hand. "I would keep your distance until the process is done, if you want to keep your flesh," Tol said. Then he shrugged, as if he didn't really care either way.

Tol was at the door by the time Kaedrich rushed over to the bodies, but she did not even try to stop him from leaving; all things considered, it seemed the least important crisis of the moment. Whatever Tol had done, it was chewing away at the insides of the corpses, curdling their organs until they had crumbled to nothing but dust. Kaedrich lurched to a halt over them; she *wanted* to reach in and rip out the magic that Tol had set in motion, but his final warning rang loudly in her mind. Not that she knew *how* to stop a magical reaction like this—and more likely as not, she probably couldn't—but standing there and just watching it happen felt . . . wrong.

She turned to an instrument tray sitting beside the tables. The tools had been left scattered when the building had been evacuated, and Kaedrich grabbed the first one her eyes landed upon. It was probably some sort of large clamp, its curved protrusions snapping open and shut with a spring-mechanism in the handle, but whatever. Kaedrich plunged it into the dissolving mass of the corpse, snapping madly at anything left solid that she might be able to grab a hold on. The reaction had already spread to the walls of the body's ribs, and now the entire structure of the dead man was melting and collapsing like hot candle wax. "Blast it!" Kaedrich shouted as some slippery thing that she'd managed to grab fell out of her instrument's grasp, spitting and hissing as it struck the dust littering the rest of the corpse.

"What in the seven hells is going on here?"

Kaedrich yelped at Praxis's voice. The instrument slid from her grasp and clattered against the table on its way to the floor. "I—" Kaedrich started, but there didn't seem to be time to sufficiently explain.

Luckily, it didn't seem that Praxis actually required much explanation, not at first anyway. She rushed into the room, the click of gears echoing out as she strained against the maximum speed of her harness. She shoved Kaedrich out of the way, took in the scene before her—and instantly began to swear in Yandosian.

"Is there anything I can—?" Kaedrich started, but Praxis was already on the move.

She lurched to a table closer to the door, where a completely different corpse lay unassaulted by Tol's magic. A woman this time, peels of skin scattered like ribbons flowing off of her; she was stripped to nothing, a sheet covering only her lower half. Praxis flicked her hand through the air beside the woman's body, and a fresh cut split the corpse's side like a seam bursting open. Kaedrich's stomach twisted up, and then heaved even more violently as Praxis dove her hand into the woman's side. With a flash and a sickening *crack!*, Praxis yanked one of the dead woman's ribs out, hoisting it almost triumphantly into the air.

It was not a celebration, though, and there would be no time for one even if they'd wanted. Praxis was back between the two dissolving corpses in an instant, the rib bone held tall over her head. She shut her eyes— there was another flash, and another *crack!* as the rib split in half. She held a half over each of the two corpses, though calling them such was kind of optimistic by that point. Pools of dripping flesh and scattered ash were spilling over onto the floor, and Kaedrich hopped back from the table to avoid being splashed.

So she didn't see, exactly, what happened as Praxis crushed the two halves of the rib in her fist. Bone flecks scattered over what little was left of each body, falling from between Praxis's tightly clenched fingers.

There were several hisses, like butter landing on a hot pan. A bit of smoke, curling up into the already rancid air. Praxis opened her palms, dropping the last of the bones as she lowered her hands over the remains of the corpses. She was muttering under her breath the whole time, her eyes still shut, and her hands got so close to the pool of melting flesh that Kaedrich's heart lurched, sure that she would accidentally touch it.

She didn't.

The process stopped.

Praxis peeped one eye open, then the other as she sagged in a heap of relief. She caught herself between the tables, her elbows plowing into the sides of lipid corpse. She pressed her fist to her mouth, shaking her head at the near-ruin of the bodies that flanked her.

Kaedrich rushed up to her, though there was nothing to be done by this point. Still, she crouched in front of Praxis, who was herself crouched between the tables, and tried to do what little she could.

She pulled out the nearest box, the one she'd been going for before Tol had interrupted her. Praxis watched, confusion and a touch of incredulousness marring her face, but Kaedrich wouldn't be able to help with the bodies themselves, that was going to have to be Praxis's domain. What she *could* do, she thought grimly as she pulled the box top open, was this.

As she'd suspected, the box was full of whatever clothing and possessions had been on the bodies at the time they'd been brought in. Though most of it had been reduced to a charred pile of flecks, the police officers or morgue officials had been careful to include it all. Kaedrich dug through the box's contents, sifting underneath layers of crusted black and ash.

Praxis, meanwhile, had straightened herself back up and was currently ignoring Kaedrich's work. She poked around the puddled goo that remained of the two bodies, prodding at them with her fingers and muttering to herself.

"Hmm," Praxis said several minutes later. Kaedrich glanced up from her spot on the floor, in time to see Praxis rest her hands on her hips. "Well, that's not exactly what I was hoping to find."

Kaedrich pushed herself to her feet. She had already pocketed one or two items that had more or less survived the flames (gods, she really *was* getting as bad as Praxis), and now she steeled herself and looked down at the corpse that Praxis was standing in front of.

The thing was a mess—not that you could have ever called it appealing, being dead, but this was something else entirely. Strings of what was once flesh hung from the curling wicks of half-melted bones, while the pool in the middle of the cavity was now filled with ash and goo. Kaedrich clamped her hand over her face, and not just because of the stench.

But Praxis didn't really seem to be paying much attention to the chest splayed open in front of her. While Kaedrich had been digging in the box, Praxis had sliced open the corpse's arm—not yet impacted by whatever Tol had done to the body—and as Kaedrich watched, she reached her fingers straight in and pulled back the layers of skin and muscle. The exposed arm bone was ordinary, dull white underneath the streaks of red now dripping like raindrops over its surface. "Do you see?" Praxis asked, as if this was somehow an interesting discovery. "It's not silver."

Kaedrich would be the first to admit that she hadn't made a detailed study of human anatomy, but she was quite certain that this shouldn't have been a surprise. "Did you *expect* it to be?"

"Well, *mine* is, so . . . yeah. Yeah, I did."

She said this with such a casual air that at first Kaedrich nodded automatically. As if it made perfect sense. It was only after a moment that the reality of what Praxis had said caught up with her. Kaedrich drew still, an awkward pause hanging between them.

They had never talked about it. Not that there had been time, but Praxis wouldn't have talked about it even if circumstances were different. Despite the fact that the Silvers still plagued Kaedrich's nightmares even now, a year and a half after the ordeal in Vaulaine. The way that their magic had slipped into her mind, twisting around her and smothering out the essence of who she was, until she was doing and saying things that she would never choose for herself. The magic that they needed to save her could only be provided by another Silver and so, without Kaedrich's knowledge or agreement, Praxis had plunged into their lair and let herself be temporarily converted into their ranks. She had come out looking like them: silver hair, silver skin, silver *eyes* that were empty and yet seemed to stare directly into your soul. Kaedrich's stomach twisted up just remembering.

Mine is. Gods, Kaedrich had never even thought to *ask.*

"Praxis . . . I—"

"The thing is," Praxis continued, ignoring the subject entirely, "magic comes from your bones. Did you know that? So if Lanali is trying to impose her *own* magic over someone else, then she *has* to install a stable presence. Otherwise, it's going to be a temporary effect, either fading or . . ."

". . . Or?"

Praxis shrugged. "Or killing. It's the nature of magic—you cannot change the fundamental essence of a thing, the core of who or what it is. Which means that any long-lasting spell like the Silvers needs something to constantly refresh the magical effect. But if she's not mimicking Deeter Vaulsk's technique . . ."

She fell silent, looking with soft contemplation at the arm splayed open before her. Idly, she tapped her finger against it in thought.

A hollow, vaguely metallic sound rang out into the quiet room.

Praxis jerked back, glaring at the bone as if it had suddenly learned how to talk. She leaned in, tapped it again. This time she was prepared for it, and she kept her attention fixed on the bone as the sound repeated itself, echoing out from the corpse and rebounding off of the plain walls. Tap-*clang*, tap-*clang*, tap-*clang*, like a peg-legged man in a suit of armor walking up the stairs.

"Well," Praxis said.

"Well," Kaedrich said.

There was really nothing else *to* be said. They looked at the bone and then at each other.

Without a word, Praxis yanked the offending arm bone straight out of the corpse with a sickening, slurping sort of crunch. Kaedrich yelped, jumping back to avoid the spray.

"Gods! *Praxis!*"

"Come on," Praxis called, tucking it underneath her coat as she headed for the door. "I'd say that it's time that we find out exactly what Lanali has been up to."

Chapter Fifteen

 $\mathcal{P}$ ON LANALI LOVED a good costume.

Once a very, very long time ago, when she was still just a young girl who called herself Frel, there came to the islands a theater troop all the way from Durland. The reason was long since lost to her memory, if she ever knew it at all. The troop was staying for two weeks, performing thrice a day for most of the days. It was all anyone could talk about as their arrival loomed, although at first Frel couldn't see *why*. She had been to plays before, and tended to find them rather dull. "What's the point?" she'd told her father once, when he asked her why she hadn't enjoyed the annual performance of *Lost in the Mists* that the players of their local island cluster had put on. "Everyone *knows* that they're lying."

He stopped dragging her to the usual performances after that, but he still insisted that they go to this one. "How often does an opportunity like this happen?" he asked, as if that settled matters. "These people have traveled here from Durland, Frel. Durland! Can you imagine?"

She couldn't imagine, not really. Durland might as well have been from a fairy tale, for all of the reality that it held to a girl on the sun-warmed beaches of Aul. But she also couldn't imagine disappointing her father, and so she did not protest after that.

It was just the two of them back then, Frel and her father against the rest of the harsh world. Her mother had died in childbirth, the only time that she'd ever fallen pregnant. They lived on a community island with two other small families, both of which were also going to the plays that evening. Frel's father dug out his only suit, the crisp white fabric nearly blinding in the open sunlight. He had taken the time to redo all of his braids the day before, and now he wove them together into a single fat bundle that ran down his back.

Frel didn't have any fancy clothes in those days, so she went as she was. Washed and primped, her favorite pale blue shirt tucked into flowing tan pants. Her own braids had been growing ragged over the past week, and so she twisted them together into a single knot on the back of her head, covering the worst of the mess with a silky scarf patterned with halva blossoms. Her father told her that she looked as pretty as a dream, although Frel dismissed his comment as sentimental mush brought on by his own excitement. Her father had always wanted to travel, always dreamed of sailing off and seeing what he could see, and yet he'd never managed to untangle himself from land enough to actually *do* anything about it. Having someone bring this tiny piece of a far-off land right to their very doorstep was therefore treated as a blessing from the gods. Frel had smiled at him, thanked him, taken his hand as he led her to their island's community boat.

Salk island was packed that evening. Frel and her father wound through a sea of bodies, excited voices chattering over each other in a wash of restless enthusiasm. Frel kept hold of his hand, letting him find a way through, while she kept her attention on the trees, the edge of rooftops. An albino reed crane had been stalking her recently, when she'd go to school or her father's shop, when she'd go sailing or gathering pirlo melons from the grove, and she was afraid that it would manage to find her even here, even now. But as they made their way toward the stage, into tighter and tighter circles of people, there was for once no sign of her great avian nemesis.

They found a place to sit. There was only a single width available in the crowded bench (even that, they were lucky to find), and yet Frel's father remained undaunted. "You can sit on my lap," he said, patting his legs as if she was still a toddler. Frel had frowned, ready to protest—she was not so young as *that*, anymore—but by this point someone was blowing a horn from beside the stage, urging quiet, and there was no more time to argue anything. She sat, wiggling to try to make herself as comfortable as she could on his bony thighs. He held his daughter, encouraging her to settle back against him. "Just look," he whispered into her ear. "Look at how they do things. Isn't it marvelous?"

Frel wasn't sure she would call it marvelous, but as she finally turned her attention toward the stage, she could see at once that they certainly did things *differently* than she was used to. The great circular platform had been divided, the side farthest from them cut off by a wall that someone had erected. Wooden support beams framed a large painting of sorts, though the painting was extremely odd: it looked as if it was showing the inside of a room, with a fake window, and even a fake painting painted into the wall. Frel knew from pictures in her books that it was supposed to be a Durlish room, and the painting-within-a-painting showed pasty Durlish faces. But none of it made any sense to her—for one thing, how was the rest of the crowd supposed to watch the performance? It wasn't until the question was posed in her mind that she realized that all the benches had been dragged around to be able to face this *single* viewpoint, the crowd jammed in until they couldn't see behind the great painting at all.

She was about to ask her father about this when someone came out from behind the great painting itself. The crowd whooped and snapped their fingers repeatedly in approval, her father loudly among them, and Frel bit down her question to watch. The man greeted them in Durlish, which Frel thought was rather rude. Though a common language of trade and politics the world over, it was still only spoken in bits and pieces of Aul; Frel herself understood about half of what the man went on to say, but only because her father had insisted that she study Durlish, as he believed that it would help her when she grew up and did all the things that he would never manage to do with his own life. Frel was scowling, already regretful that she had allowed herself to be dragged out for this, but then the man stepped off the stage and several others replaced him, and soon after something magical happened.

Frel became entranced.

She hadn't *wanted* to. Her sour mood and predisposition against plays made her hate the players, at first, as they hurried into their opening positions. Who did these people think that they were, coming in here and doing things so differently, acting like they knew better? This wasn't how a play was *supposed* to go. Plays were *supposed* to be seen from all directions. Plays were *supposed* to be no more than two or three players, swapping out roles as the story needed. And what was this, these ridiculous outfits that they were wearing? Everyone knew that you wore plain tan robes, with only different types of masks and trailing colored ribbons to represent one character or another, switching as needed. These players were dressed, Frel quickly realized, as if they actually *were* the people they were pretending to be. They spoke and moved and laughed as though they had actually changed skins; and the story presented itself not as a great narrative, the

Orator telling you what was going on at each step of the way, but more like the audience around them had simply walked in on these people living their lives.

It wasn't like anything that Frel had ever seen before, and a few minutes into the process, she found herself intrigued despite herself. A few more minutes gone, and she had almost managed to forget that these people were players at all. By the halfway point of the performance, when the man that had spoken first came back out and announced that they would break for something called an "intermission," Frel jerked as if waking from a dream. She hated that man, suddenly, for ruining the illusion for her—for surely by now, it could not be denied: Frel had lost herself in the story, somehow, somewhere along the way. What the players had been doing up there no longer felt like lying to her. She had started to *believe*.

She had been using magic all of her life, and yet she felt as if she'd just stumbled into a secret world, where a whole new branch of magic had presented itself to her. Here were people that could *really* weave spells, making themselves into whole other people, and Frel desperately wanted to understand how it worked.

For the rest of the theater troop's visit, Frel did her best to make sure she attended every performance. Even if it meant that she had to stand in the very back of the crowd, or climb a tree to be able to see the stage. Even if it meant that she was positioned so far to the side that she was separated from the rest of the crowd, and could see behind the great painting (a "backdrop," she'd heard someone call it once). In fact, this last situation she discovered was the best outcome of all, for here she'd finally gotten some glimpse of the inner workings of their elaborate game. Not enough yet to make sense of what they did to weave such a perfect illusion over the audience, but useful just the same. Frel ended up falling in love— with the story, with the players, with the art. She never had the nerve to approach any of the Durns themselves, even when she spotted one or two of them outside of the theater, just strolling and looking at the different sights of the islands; but she loved them all the same, from a longing distance.

When they left, it felt as if Frel's life had ended. An overreaction, perhaps, but she was just barely twelve years old, and now she found herself without a purpose.

After what felt like an appropriate mourning period, Frel did *try* to recreate some of what she'd lost. She approached some of the people that put on the local plays, inquiring if she could help, if they might teach her some of their own skills. However, it quickly became apparent that whatever the Durlish players had brought with them, they'd taken all of it when they'd sailed away from the islands. The Aul players, by turn, recited their lines in carefully metered bursts. They wore the masks, did what the Orator said they were doing. But none of it felt convincing, and none of it captured Frel the way that the others had.

So Frel abandoned them, retreating to a little cove that it seemed that only she knew about, and there she tried to figure it out for herself. She spent weeks pouring over her memory of their play. She wrote down everything of the story and the dialog that she could remember. She drew pictures. She fashioned little models of the players out of dry straw and scraps of cloth, molding these raw materials with her magic until she had a series of eighteen careful dolls. She twisted bits of light and color out of the air and strung them around like gauzy garlands, turning her cove into a crude recreation of the ballroom where the most dramatic parts of the story took place.

It took her a long time to get the hang of curling her tongue around someone else's words, and longer still before it sounded even remotely natural. Eventually, Frel realized that dressing to the part helped a lot—no, she could not hope to recreate the elaborate ballgowns that the players had worn, but even finding a skirt of a similar color, enhanced with a little bit of magic, stringing some shells together to form a necklace, even these small gestures helped her to lose herself in the role.

How ironic that now, years and years later, her greatest costume was no costume at all.

The Great and Venerated Pon Lanali may have started as just a game, a creation with no more substance than the lords and ladies of the Durlish play from her childhood, but over time it had taken on a far greater depth than that. She looked at herself in the mirror, her black veil folded neatly over her head. Gone was Frel, the girl who dreamed of greater worlds, the girl who tried on a hundred different personalities in the hidden cove. Lanali could not find a single trace of her anymore, not while she wore her practiced smiles, the mask of her own face. She did not even need the veil anymore to feel like Pon Lanali—she *was* Pon Lanali. She knew this down to her core, the single most defining part of her self.

So on the rare occasions when she still had need to be someone else, it was Frel that she went back to. With her door locked and bolted, Lanali removed her veil, washed away her scrub of makeup, slithered out of her signature black dress. She shed her current persona, and slid back into her old skin.

On the street, nobody recognized her. Lanali had exited through a back door that only she was privy to, and slipped out through an equally disused garden gate. Down a brief alley, and from there it was easy to blend in with the passing traffic. Though her height may have singled her out in some circumstances, here nobody batted an eye. Monfort was the capital of all trade in this region, after all, and the sight of an Aul was not *so* unusual. She wore a simple laborer's hat low over her face, and in the middle of the day she could have been a merchant in off the boat, or even an urchin child out looking for work and things to slip into her pockets.

It wasn't so far from where she'd started.

She forced that thought from her mind.

Lanali kept her head down and her walk brisk. Costumes, she had learned, went beyond simple clothing; one had to adopt an entire persona if you intended to be convincing. An Attendant did not have the same gait, after all, as an overworked baker, nor did he exactly match that of a smug nobleman out to meet his mistress. Who were you? Where were you going—and why? It all factored in, and Lanali had made it her life's work to study the weight and pull that each of these factors had on a person's bearing.

In this case her character knew exactly where she was going, even if Lanali did not. She *was* a merchant, she decided, come to Durland with a crew of seventeen in order to trade halva seeds and palla wood for steel bearings. It was only once she'd made the choice that she realized that, if circumstances had been just a little bit different here and there, it was possible that this could have *been* the truth, and not just the latest lie for her to hide behind. It was what her father had always dreamed of, after all. His own ship, trade beyond just the wide strip of the islands of home.

Lanali tried not to think of her father these days. She scowled now, remembering him, and hurried her step.

It took her a while to find Woodland Alley. It was in a portion of Monfort that she never visited as the Pon. Modest, multi-family houses crammed together right along the street, sandwiching a variety of no-nonsense shops that sold everyday items like candles and boots, bread and fish. The sett stones themselves were surprisingly clean and Lanali was almost impressed, until she realized that the reason for it was simply that carriages (and therefore horses) spent little time going up and down this lane. Here, foot traffic reigned supreme, the occasional bicycle for those in a hurry.

She kept track of the house numbers as well as she could, with the limited signs tacked up here and there. Wooden signs, mostly, with hand-painted letters long since fading under the weather. In the end, though, she needn't have bothered, for the protective wards ringing the top floor of one building in particular made it stand out like a tree bedecked for the feast of St. Gildren—at least, to the eyes of someone with magic. Lanali stopped just down the street from it, pretending like she was interested in a shop window display, and focused her mind.

Almost immediately, she flinched and staggered back. The top floor of the building had rebelled against her attempts to sense the interior, like touching an open flame with her magic.

Fine: if that was how Praxis Fellows wanted to play things, then Lanali could run this game just as easily as any other. Glancing around the street with both her eyes and her mind, it was easy enough to spot a hidden corner, just inside of the range of her senses from the building that Praxis was protecting. Lanali allowed herself to be washed down the street, darting out of the crowd just as she approached her hideaway. It was a cramped alleyway, packed almost full with crates bearing the stamp of the shop next door. The smell of aged wood and stale piss assaulted her as she crawled over the nearest crate, settling herself out of sight from the street. Lanali folded herself up, sitting cross-legged on the ground with her merchant's coat pulled tightly around her shoulders, and her cap sunk low over her face. She'd lived in worse. The year after she'd struck out on her own . . . but it wasn't worth remembering that. Lanali would only be here for a few hours—overnight, tops—as she waited, and listened, and felt the presence of the crowd milling thickly all around her.

She may not be able to tell what was going on inside of the top floor of Praxis's building, no. But she could pinpoint exactly who would move in and out of it, and that was almost as useful.

PRAXIS STOOD AT the front window of Kaedrich's apartment, scrutinizing the street below.

Marlick was still out when they'd returned, which was just as well—Praxis hadn't yet explained to him how to get around the layers of protective wards surrounding the top floor, something that Kaedrich would no doubt reprimand her for later. Her own reaction to the wards was a bit terse, though she dutifully whispered her true name into the apartment's keyhole. The magic, when triggered, took a keyword and an impression of the hand gripping the doorknob, and if both matched correctly then the wards granted entrance and sealed themselves back up once the door was shut. All that Kaedrich had to do in the event of someone trying to forcefully coerce entrance into the apartment, Praxis had explained, was to simply get *one* of these identifiers wrong; the first person to walk in would still remain unharmed, but anyone else would be subject to the wards' . . . more defensive properties.

"Don't you think that you're being a little paranoid?" Kaedrich had asked as they stepped inside.

"Paranoia is what it's called when your life is *not* being threatened," Praxis said, brushing past her. "In this case, I thought a basic level of prudence was called for."

"But nobody is after me."

"Not that we know of. Not *yet*."

"See, now *that's* paranoia," Kaedrich said. She shrugged out of her suit jacket, now filthy with a layer of soot and smoke, and dropped it over the back of a dining chair. "Tea? Or, no, wait—coffee? I think I have some somewhere."

Praxis shook her head.

"Suit yourself," Kaedrich said as she retreated into the apartment's tiny kitchen alcove. She rolled up her sleeves and began to wash her hands and face off first, her back to the rest of the apartment—and to Praxis.

Praxis removed the bone from where she'd hidden it underneath her coat, laying it across the arm rests of the same chair as Kaedrich's coat. "Besides," Praxis called, as she meandered over toward the front window, "we can't assume that my staying here is going to keep me hidden forever. They're bound to be searching, even now."

Kaedrich snorted. "There's a cheerful thought."

"It's not about cheer." Praxis peered outside, her attention combing the street from one end to the other. Clinks and shuffles filtered in from behind her, the quiet bustle of a person working in a kitchen. Below, life progressed as normal, and yet there was something niggling at Praxis. It might have been fatigue—then again, it might not.

"Okay, so while we're on the subject," Kaedrich said, talking over the sound of water pouring into a kettle, "we really should settle how we're going to handle tonight."

Praxis glanced over her shoulder, a pert little frown creased between her brows. "Tonight?"

"Yeah," Kaedrich said. She shuffled over to a cabinet and pulled out a small tin canister, dented along one side, and then dug in the drawer below it for a spoon. "I don't exactly have a spare bedroom."

"What's wrong with yours?"

A clatter broke through the apartment as the spoon slid out of Kaedrich's fingers and hit the floor. Kaedrich ducked to retrieve it, but the tin that was still in her hands caught the lip of the counter and tumbled out of her grip as well; the lid popped off as it struck the floor, and a spray of tea leaves danced quickly out of the mouth of the canister.

"It's just—it's more efficient," Praxis said hurriedly, as Kaedrich scrambled to clean up her mess. "I only have to put the heaviest protections on one room, and, well, it keeps Marlick thinking that we—"

"Right, right, of course." Kaedrich nodded, though she still wasn't looking up as she brushed the tea leaves into a tidy pile. "It's fine, of course it's fine. I . . . I don't know, I just wasn't thinking, I guess. I mean, I knew that you were staying *here*, but . . ." She shook her head. "Anyway, it's fine."

Praxis turned back to the window, before the heat blooming in her cheeks could stain them vivid pink. So maybe it was true, then—maybe Kaedrich didn't want Praxis staying in her room because she was already planning to sneak someone else in.

She felt so stupid, all of a sudden. Of *course* Kaedrich would have moved on by this point—not that she'd necessarily ever harbored feelings for *Praxis* to begin with. True, she had seemed . . . quite distressed, to watch Praxis's magically created double die in front of her, but the vacant had never really been Praxis. And while it was flattering and encouraging to see that Kaedrich might have had feelings for the creature, it did not mean that they were so easily transferred to the genuine article.

Besides, all of that . . . gods, all of that was *ages* ago. Kaedrich was young, and Monfort was full of pretty girls to turn her head. Here Praxis had come to the city assuming nothing would have changed at all, but why shouldn't it have? It was a foolish move, a naïve assumption based on nothing more than hope and the obsessive leanings of her own heart. Praxis clenched her fists, a flare of anger at herself springing up so hard that she almost couldn't bear it.

The problem is that she hadn't stopped to disengage the connection between her hands and her leg harness, and so the balled fist also resulted in her leg suddenly kicking wildly out and to the side, as if she was trying to attack an invisible intruder. Her foot hooked with an end table, sending it toppling, and her center of balance failed her. She followed the way of the table, collapsing in a furious, useless heap on the apartment floor.

She was already swearing and had pushed herself up into a roughly sitting position by the time Kaedrich swooped in, steady hands landing on Praxis's shoulders.

"Gods, what happened? Are you all right?"

Praxis ignored the questions, shoving Kaedrich off of her. She flexed her fingers, trying to get her feet underneath her again—only nothing happened. Praxis swore again, clicked her thumb twice to disengage and then reengage the system—still nothing. The normally tense wires running across the back of her hand and up her arm were slack.

She gave a disgusted sigh. "Help me with my coat, will you?" she asked, already shrugging out of the shoulders.

Kaedrich needed no further prompting, nor asked any questions. She took the coat as Praxis slipped her arms free, and provided a small boost while she slithered the hem of the garment out from underneath Praxis's backside. She set the coat aside and pulled a throw pillow off of the nearby couch, which she positioned between Praxis and the wall behind her, creating a kind of seat for her to lean against. She helped to stretch Praxis's legs out in front of her, and did not even ask before she began to undo the row of access buttons running up the leg of Praxis's trousers.

"I can manage from here," Praxis snapped as most of the mechanized leg harness came into view. She batted away Kaedrich's help, and Kaedrich dutifully pulled back and sat on her haunches. Nearby, and ready to spring into action if called upon, but at least her fingers were no longer accidentally brushing against the skin of Praxis's outer thigh.

Praxis ducked her head, tracing the line of tension wires and gears, trying to track down which part had gotten broken or wrenched out of place in her tumble. At least it gave her something else to look at, and an excuse not to talk to Kaedrich at the moment.

Or so she thought.

Kaedrich took a breath. "I'm sorry, I didn't mean to imply that . . . I mean, of course you can stay with me, if you need to."

"I really don't," Praxis said. "I'm perfectly fine on the couch."

"No, but you're right—Marlick would start asking questions, he's like that. I would never hear the end of it if you *didn't* stay with me."

Praxis nodded. This answer should have pleased her—delighted her, really—except that all it really meant was that Kaedrich wouldn't be sneaking anyone else in *tonight*. And okay, yes, there was still nothing in Kaedrich's actions that definitively proved that she did have a secret lover somewhere; but nor did they confirm denial.

Praxis shut her eyes for a second, trying to get herself to shake it off, trying to gather strength. If she only *knew*, really knew, one way or the other . . . but of course that was impossible.

Surely.

Right?

Of course.

Impossible.

Unless . . .

When she went back to inspecting her harness mechanism, she did her best to affect an air of disinterest, like the matter was completely settled and it wasn't important either way. She tugged at the tension wires as they approached her knee, trying to figure out where they went slack. As she plucked at them almost like a musician, she said, oh-so-casually, "Since I am going to be staying here, I just, I want you to know that I'm not trying to interfere with your life. So . . . you know, if you're going out, or . . . if you'll be inviting anyone over . . . you can just tell me, and I'll, I don't know, I'll make sure that I'm not in your way."

Kaedrich raised an eyebrow. "Um . . . thanks?"

Praxis shrugged. "*Are* you expecting anyone?"

"Not currently, no . . ."

"Okay, well." Praxis shrugged again. "Just . . . let me know if anything changes."

"That's . . . awfully accommodating of you," Kaedrich said slowly. She leaned over, peering up at Praxis as Praxis yanked at a stuck gear along her knee. "What are you really up to?"

"Nothing," Praxis snapped. "Gods, a person can't be nice without an ulterior motive?"

"A person can, yes. *You* usually don't."

Praxis gave an exaggerated sigh. "I'm just *trying* to be a good house-guest. I can hardly be expected to know every intimate detail of your social calendar in advance, now can I?"

Kaedrich snorted out something resembling a laugh. "Mine, you probably could. It's not complex."

"Good," Praxis said, before she realized it.

She froze.

Kaedrich was watching her closely now, still leaned over, and Praxis hurriedly buried herself back in her work. She moved on from the stuck gear and found a snapped bit of tension wire farther down her leg, where the system would lift up her ankle.

"Wait," Kaedrich said, sitting back. "Were you . . . were you asking me if I was expecting . . . a *special* guest?"

"No," Praxis snapped. But then she shrugged again. "I mean, it would be fine if you *were*. I don't care."

There was a moment of stillness and silence, a single beat of the clock passing while the rest of the world held its breath.

"I . . . ," Kaedrich started. Her face was twisted up with a tight frown. "No. Gods, no. Praxis, you of all people know why I can't have that kind of arrangement even if I wanted to."

"Yes, well, you could have *told* someone about—"

"No, I couldn't. It's only ever been you." Kaedrich paused, cleared her throat. ". . . That knows about my situation. I wouldn't risk telling anyone else."

"Okay," Praxis said. It was the only thing that she trusted herself to say, a flood of relief closing up her throat.

Kaedrich pushed herself up and went over to the chair with the coat and the bone, moving both of them to make room for herself. She folded the coat neatly over her lap, resting the bone on top with such casualness that it was as if it was merely a rolled-up newspaper. Praxis tried not to look at it, suddenly uncomfortable and not being entirely certain why. It was one thing when *she* was cavalier about the death and destruction that followed in her wake, but somehow the idea of Kaedrich becoming comfortable with it . . .

"Right," Praxis said abruptly. She motioned at her leg. "This can wait. If we're going to try to figure out this whole mess, we really should get moving. Help me up?" Anything to get out of the sitting room and away from the wreckage of this disastrous conversation.

Kaedrich slid instantly out from underneath the coat and the bone, coming over to offer Praxis first her arm and then her shoulders for support. She ducked underneath Praxis's outstretched arm, propping her up, one hand wrapped around Praxis's waist as she began to hop away from the window. "Where are we going?" Kaedrich asked.

"Your bed," Praxis said, and then she froze midshuffle as her poor phrasing caught up with her. "Not *together*, obviously," she added, speaking so fast that she nearly tripped over her words. "I'm perfectly fine handling things on my own—though you could watch—and the bone might make things easier. I mean—!" Praxis paused, visibly wincing. "It's for a *ritual*. A *magic* ritual, and—okay, you know what, I am going to stop talking right now," she said, as Kaedrich very nearly doubled over laughing at the accidental innuendo that Praxis had just spilled all over herself.

"Just shut up," Praxis added, though she was the only one that had been talking.

Kaedrich's shoulders continued to shake off and on with laughter, though, as she collected the bone and helped guide Praxis in the direction of her bedroom.

"Give me that," Praxis snapped as she finally settled herself down on the edge of the mattress. She snatched the bone out of Kaedrich's hands, and only now that she stared down at it did the mirth of the room curdle and fade.

"So, seriously," Kaedrich said, as she leaned against the doorframe, "what exactly is this all for? What are you going to do?"

Praxis ran her hands along the length of the bone, unnaturally clean of any of the blood from its former body. She didn't really want to tell Kaedrich, and yet at the same time she did. "I need to visit an ... old friend," Praxis said finally.

Kaedrich didn't say anything, just watched in silence as Praxis reached underneath the collar of her shirt, hooking her fingers around a heavy old jewelry chain. Praxis hesitated for just a second before she pulled it out, the ancient pendant swinging freely in front of her. Her link to the Beacon of Souls. She had never shown it to Kaedrich before, not the real one anyway, though of course Kaedrich had seen it in the land of the dead. Kaedrich's eyes widened with recognition.

"Are we really that desperate?" Kaedrich asked. Her fingers were clutched tight on her crossed arms, now, the fabric of her shirt bunched up fast in her grip.

"'Desperate'? You make it sound complicated."

"Well, I thought ... I mean, the kind of magic required ..." She trailed off, scuffing at the floor with the toe of her shoe.

Too late, Praxis remembered that for Kaedrich (or anyone else who wasn't the Lady of Souls), the prospect of plunging into the land of the dead was a far more involved ordeal. It had become so normal to her in the last two and a half years that she'd very nearly forgotten—as she'd very nearly forgotten that Kaedrich had been forced to pay a high price for her one journey there. Kaedrich had never told Praxis what that price was, and Praxis hadn't ever mustered up the courage to ask her a second time.

"The rules are ... different for me," Praxis said.

Kaedrich snorted. "Of course they are."

This was too true to argue with, and so for once, Praxis didn't argue. She occupied herself with the process of laying down, of dragging her leg up after her, trying to get more or less comfortable on her back. With the pendant in one hand and the bone in the other, she was ready to begin.

"Give my regards to the Beacon," Kaedrich said. There would be nothing on this side of things for her to see, and so she did not stick around to watch.

A LONG-SUFFERING SIGH filled Praxis's mind to the bursting point, as if an entire army condemned to fight an endless, hopeless battle had all let out their breath at once.

"To what do we owe the pleasure this time, my Lady?"

"Nice to see you again, too," Praxis said as she opened her eyes. Immediately, she averted her attention from the display that appeared in front of her, the same one that always appeared in front of her when she first arrived. Too late; no matter how fast she was, she always caught a glimpse of Moc, slammed against the ice wall at the moment of his death. The very first death that Praxis had ever caused.

But she wasn't here to revisit the past—or at least not *her* past.

Praxis turned around and, as usual, one of the thick shadows that cloaked the walls of the museum had separated itself from the others. Though it had physical form, it had no distinct features, just a blur of shadow in roughly the shape of a person. *Behold,* Praxis thought, *the face of death.* Vague and ill-defined, an endless force that would one day seize you and everyone that you've ever known.

Praxis held out the bone, laying naked across her open palm. She'd been surprised, when she first seized control of the Beacon for herself, that certain types of objects could actually travel back and forth from this realm to the next. It was how she'd gotten hold of the pendant itself—she'd stolen it from Lanali there, and yet it had been clutched tight in her hand when she'd woken up. That first week, still learning how everything functioned, Praxis had tried to take a wide variety of objects in both directions, but only a limited few had worked.

Bones had worked.

The shadow tipped its head as if regarding the offering. "Are you giving us a present, my Lady?"

"No," Praxis said. Though that had sort of been her intention at first, the question had raised hairs on the back of Praxis's neck. Experience had taught her to be cautious with how far she trusted this ancient creature. "I want you to show me who it belongs to."

"Shouldn't you know? You're the one that met him, not I."

"Oh, you've met."

Though it was impossible to tell by the looks of it, Praxis could almost swear that the shadow smiled at this comment.

"Show me," Praxis said again.

Abruptly, the shadow turned and marched out of the central chamber. The rest of the museum that was the land of the dead spread out in all directions, branching off like spokes. Praxis followed quickly, unhindered by her normal system of gears and braces—in this realm she looked however she liked.

The shadow led her down an endless corridor, flanked on all sides by the displays. There was one for every soul in the world, though only the ones that had actually died were illuminated. Praxis tried not to look at them as she walked, neither the ones that were lit nor the ones that lay dark. It wouldn't do her any good to try to peer into the darkened ones even if she wanted to, anyway, because she knew that the contents would keep shifting until the day that the person actually died.

They walked for what seemed like ages, but finally the shadow did stop. Praxis saw the display coming from quite a way off (death by fire was thankfully not that common, compared to all the other means), but that didn't make actually stepping in front of it any better. Still, she forced herself to look at it straight on, to acknowledge the role that she'd had in making this man's display take its final shape. He was collapsed on the floor, fire already engulfing him. His mouth was open as if in a frozen scream. Heat poured out into the museum hallway, a faint sheen of sweat already edging Praxis's brow.

Underneath the display was a simple brass name plaque, and after what felt like a sufficiently respectful moment of silence, Praxis knelt in front of it and traced her fingers across the lettering. Jerrish Drumm.

Praxis glanced up, taking in once more the twist of agony on Jerrish's face. "Well, Jerrish," she said, standing back up. She reached beside his display, where a pair of opera glasses hung from a chain mounted to the wall. "I think that it's time that I see what you've been up to lately."

ON THE COAST of Tjalava, so long ago now that it was hard to remember when, Praxis's fever raged for three weeks. Despite the Yandosian ambassador's insistence that they remain isolated from a disease when it had only infected Tjalavans, he sung quite a different tune when it came to matters of one of their own—*especially* a Fellows. Praxis was rushed into a fine suite in the middle of the embassy, a room cooled by magic to more closely resemble their own familiar climate. The shutters were drawn, incenses that were believed to promote healing were lit. Doctors were summoned, ripped from other patients' bedsides to tend to this, suddenly their most "important" patient.

The ambassador sent out urgent requests through high-level diplomatic channels for additional support staff, additional medical care, additional medicines and healing wizards. More than once, he was seen pacing the hallways outside of Praxis's suite, running his hands through his rapidly thinning hair, muttering to Tully and his aides about how they must *not* allow a Fellows to die underneath their charge. "Do you have any idea what they would *do* to me?" he hissed, his eyes frantic as they danced between the faces of his staff.

The Yandosians did. They knew all too well. They looked solemnly at their hands, their feet, silent and already mourning the potential and brutal loss of their ambassador. Tully didn't, but he *did* know enough to keep his mouth shut.

The ambassador's paranoia, however, did have one unintended benefit, and that was that he was unwilling to send word home to Yandosia, at least until they knew anything for sure. One way or another. His aides questioned this decision in private—didn't the Fellows family deserve to know?, they asked themselves, though what good would that really do? They were too far away to send help, for it would never arrive in time. And it turned out that this decision would ultimately be what saved Praxis from being dragged back into the depths of the ice, though she would never find out, and so she would never have the opportunity to be grateful for the ambassador's own self-interest.

Because of course Praxis was privy to none of this—the doctors, the chaos, the swirling dread that blanketed the Yandosian embassy like a death shroud. She had succumbed to fevered dreams within hours of the first symptoms, and she lay in her massive feather bed thrashing and whimpering, clutching often at her chest as if she wanted to claw it open.

Her dreams were a senseless jumble, few of which she would really recall in more than hazy fragments lurking in the shadows of her fears. Some of it blurred and mingled in with the real world: a fuzzy image of someone leaning over her, injecting something in her arm, became the sight of her mother tending to her after she'd returned from her ordeal on the Qol Nar. A breeze drifting through her suite carrying the heavy stench of incense would become the beginning of a fire on the islands of Aul. Often, she half-woke in a panic, sure that something terrible was happening and unable to be calmed. Always, she missed Rinn.

In the delusion of her illness she had forgotten everything that had happened at the end—the way that Rinn had used an ancient Aul spell without Praxis's knowledge to seed a baby in her belly, the searing hatred that had torn through Praxis when she'd learned what had been done to her, the life force that she'd ripped out of the budding life she was carrying, her need to leave. All that was left was the year that they'd spent together before it, the beaches and the laughter, the sex, having someone curled against her in a palla pod at night to comfort her in her sleep. It did not matter that this was only a tiny fragment of what being with Rinn was like, that in reality there had been plenty of cracks in the foundation of their relationship before it all blew up in their faces. In dreams, Rinn was perfect, the way that she'd seemed in the beginning. Her face wove through Praxis's mind as a constant ghost, laughing and whispering and moaning. She didn't disappear until the fever did.

On the twenty-second day, sometime in the dead of night, her fever broke. Praxis slept a normal sleep for the first time in weeks, and finally Rinn was gone.

But in her dream she was still in Aul. It wasn't an Aul from her own history; this was an island undeveloped for housing, with sharp cliffs behind her and nothing but a stretch of open sea before. The farthest edge of the island chain, the last beach before the world. Praxis was standing in the water's edge, the waves lapping against her knees, water crawling up her long Yandosian dress as it slowly soaked through the fabric.

"It's perfect, isn't it, young thing?"

Moc may or may not have been standing beside her before, but he was now, and in the manner of dreams, suddenly he had always been. He bent into the shifting water, hauling up a trap constructed of wooden slats and so many ropes. He peered inside, smiling to himself, and then held the trap out for Praxis to see. Inside were the flailing legs of at least half a dozen sand crabs, their spiny joints clicking as they stretched and prodded the slats of the trap. Moc tossed the trap into a pile already accumulating on a small raft floating beside him and then took another few steps and plunged his arms back underneath the waves.

"This is what I was doing before I came to your country," Moc said, lifting another trap out of the water. A flood of saltwater tears pooled from the slats, streaming down twisted strands of seaweed. He looked at Praxis. "Did you know that?"

Praxis shook her head. Moc turned, hauling the trap up onto the raft with the others. He looked the way that he did in the end, wiry white hairs sprinkled in with his mane of burnt orange. Though his skin was tanner, closer to the way that he'd been when he'd first arrived in Yandosia and first started tutoring Praxis. While he could never be called pale, in the long years that he'd been there, he had certainly lost some of the extra depth of his wrinkled brown skin. In the dream he was shirtless, the whole litany of his tattoos—the record of his life lessons—out on full display. Some of the older, faded black ink was difficult to see against the sun-darkened shade of his skin as it was supposed to be.

She looked down at her own wrists. Her scar and tattoo, reminders of her two worst mistakes, were already in place.

The next trap that Moc checked was empty. One of the slats had broken off, or been broken off by a creature of sufficient size and determination. Moc sighed, adding it to the pile anyway—it would need mending before it could go back in the water.

"I thought that you were always a teacher," Praxis said, picking up the conversation that had fallen into the waves a moment ago.

Moc began to untie the raft from the post that it had been anchored to. "I was. But this is what my family has always done, and this is what I had planned to spend the rest of my retirement doing." Moc frowned. "Until I met you."

Heat flared in Praxis's wrist. Praxis clutched at her scar, the living fire churning wildly beneath the skin. "I'm . . . I'm sorry," she said. "I'm so sorry."

This is when she knew that it was a dream. Praxis had never been able to apologize to Moc in real life. Not just for her final mistake, the outburst that ended up taking his life; even before that, to apologize would mean to admit that she'd erred in some fashion, and she could never allow her tutor, her mentor, to see fault. Not if she could possibly cover it up, deny it hard enough, sweep it under the rug.

But this was a dream. The real Moc was dead, and he would never know that she'd made such a terrible mistake, and so right there, in the open water, the sunlight pounding furiously against her skin, Praxis apologized, and then she began to sob. In real life, Praxis had long since used up her tears, weeping over what she had done to him, but in dreams they came as freely as they had on the first day after his death. They poured through her fingers and fell into the ocean, salt mingling with salt.

Moc tutted, shaking his head in disapproval. "I don't need your *pity*, young thing."

"Then what do you want?" Praxis asked, gulping around her sobs.

"Salvation," Moc said, and instantly Praxis's face was as dry as if she'd never learned how to shed a tear. He looked up at her, his face softer and more kind than she was used to. He reached up and cupped her cheek. The water from his hand replaced her tears, the smell of the ocean bringing a sense of terrible sadness upon her. "Young thing," Moc said, his voice soft as the wind. "There is a way. You can still save me."

Praxis's eyes widened, in the dream and the real world both, as she woke with a gasp. Nurses instantly fluttered to her side, feeling her forehead, trying to get her to look at them, but her wild eyes barely took notice. "Moc," she whispered, though no one knew what that meant.

When she touched her cheek, it was still damp.

Chapter Sixteen

KAEDRICH HURRIED IN and shut the door, leaning her forehead against the solid pane of wood. One hand still rested on the doorknob, the other clutched tightly around a book and the handle from her shopping parcel. Gods, would she never catch a break today?

It had been like this since the morning. Well, the night before, really—since she hadn't been able to figure out anything useful from the half-melted lumps that she'd stolen from the morgue, and Praxis's foray in the land of the dead turned out to be useless: the memories she was looking for were shrouded in the same black haze that had plagued Lord Wellen, except that they were no longer living memories and therefore couldn't be even partially cleared. That had sent them both to bed in a state of dejection, but today . . . Gods, today was something else.

Kaedrich had jerked awake to find Praxis sprawled across the vast majority of her bed, one arm flung haphazardly over Kaedrich's side. Bad enough that Kaedrich had let herself be talked into sharing the mattress—now she was all but falling off of it, shoved so far to the side that at least half of her body seemed to be hanging numbly over the edge. Kaedrich wriggled out from underneath Praxis's grip, toeing to the windows; Praxis had the curtains tightly drawn, plus an extra blanket thrown over the curtain rail to provide extra darkness. Yet when Kaedrich peeped around the edges, a slice of bright, midmorning sunlight assaulted her face. She staggered back, accidentally yanking the blanket down, and whirled to her alarm clock, only to discover that *someone* had shut the alarm off.

So it was a fast scramble to gather a fresh set of clothing up and attempt to rouse Praxis, who only grumbled and insisted that she'd keep her head under the pillow while Kaedrich changed. A faster scramble as Kaedrich gave up, darting terrified through the apartment toward the shared bathroom with her clothing clutched hard against her chest; luckily, Marlick was still abed, but *still*. There was no time, then, for her usual run, or even *breakfast*, as she was already late for work. Work, which was itself a nightmare—Mr. Bundling was in an even worse mood than usual, though he wouldn't explain why. Then it was a scramble to her classes, stopping just long enough on the way there to pick up several items at a druggist after she'd discovered a hasty list stuffed into her vest pocket. She was restless and distracted through her lessons, got yelled at more than once by the instructors for not paying attention—then Marlick had been summoned to the director's office partway through, so Kaedrich didn't even have him to complain with during the brief downtime between lessons.

Shopping followed. Kaedrich had realized to her shame the night before just how paltry their kitchen was stocked, but she'd forgotten to add more money to her wallet and could only manage a few items. She was almost home—her feet aching from a blister she'd developed by accidentally wearing Praxis's shoes—and was looking forward to nothing more than a hot cup of tea and an evening with a good book, when she rounded the last corner to her block and ran almost literally into Lyana.

"Goodness!" Lyana had said, jumping back, her hand fluttering to her chest. "Kaedrich! *There* you are."

"I'm sorry, I didn't see—I mean, I should have been more careful, I was just, I was going too fast, I—"

Lyana laughed. She reached out, settling a hand on Kaedrich's shoulder to still her protests. "Kaedrich, it's fine—I was looking for you, in fact."

Kaedrich flinched, though she tried not to show it. "Oh. You were?"

"Yes. You've been so impossible to track down lately! Where have you *been* these past few days?"

There was no excuse that Kaedrich could immediately think to offer, though, her already frazzled mind betraying her, and so she just ended up staring somewhat blankly at Lyana.

Lyana raised an eyebrow. "Well, anyway. I've been trying to return your book to you."

"My what? Oh!" Kaedrich said, glancing down as Lyana extended the object in her hand. "Right, my . . . yes. Thank you. Um. Did you like it?"

She hated herself for asking it the instant the question escaped her lips, because of *course* Lyana had liked it. In fact, Lyana had *loved* it, and spent at least five minutes extolling on this part or that, only a tiny fraction of which Kaedrich followed. It took another five minutes before Kaedrich was able to extricate herself from the conversation, and only deft thinking prevented her from falling into another one of Lyana's traps to maneuver her way up to Kaedrich's apartment.

And so: the door, the soft *clunk* of Kaedrich's forehead.

"Did you get the nitric acid I asked for?"

Kaedrich jumped, accidentally clonking her head harder against the shut door. She winced as she turned around, massaging the spot where she'd hit it.

Praxis was standing just outside of the kitchen alcove, both her coat and her newest vest discarded across the back of a sitting room chair. Her new blouse was tailored almost as fit as her vests, though, and she had the top of it unbuttoned as if she'd been working up a sweat. Unfortunately, the *V* of this was drawing Kaedrich's eyes inappropriately downward, and she only caught herself after a second or two of dazed staring.

Kaedrich shook her head, forcing her attentions away. "Did I . . . ? Yes. Yes, I got it for you."

"Excellent!" Praxis said, clapping her hands together.

"You know, most people say 'Welcome home' before they start demanding things," Kaedrich grumbled as she deposited everything onto the seat of the same chair that Praxis's coat was on.

Praxis shrugged. She hurried over, hovering over the chair as Kaedrich began to unbundle the parcel.

"Most people also say, 'Thank you,'" Kaedrich added as Praxis snatched the little bottle she was waiting for out of Kaedrich's hand.

"I say 'thank you' all the time."

"Yeah? Like when?"

"Oh, for sanity's sake, I left you a thank-you *note* the first night that I stayed here."

Kaedrich raised an eyebrow, remembering the two-line missive she'd found that morning, what felt like years ago. *I've gone out . . .* "Praxis . . . you do realize that in order for something to be called a thank-you note, it has to contain the words 'thank' and 'you.'"

Praxis batted her hand. "*Pshaw.* The sentiment was clear."

"No it wasn't!"

"No?" She shrugged. "I suppose at least half of that has to be on you, then. My intentions were right."

Kaedrich pinched the bridge of her nose as Praxis laughed. The clink of her brace played out with the slap of a bare foot across the floorboards, announcing Praxis's retreat back to the kitchen alcove. Kaedrich took a deep breath, trying to steady herself—and immediately wrinkled her nose. "Gods, I hope that's not dinn—" she started as she opened her eyes.

She hadn't looked into the kitchen alcove yet, not since returning home, and now she wished that she hadn't. Kaedrich's mouth dropped open, and she raced toward the alcove, catching her foot on the chair as she stumbled forward. "Praxis, I . . . what did you *do*?"

Praxis raised an eyebrow. "What?" She was leaning over the tiny little chopping block in the middle of the alcove, peering at Kaedrich over a spread of glasses and bowls.

While Kaedrich did not allow herself to keep their kitchen as tidy as she might if she lived on her own (never wanting to draw too much suspicion from Marlick), she did at least manage to keep things in better condition than *this*: every cabinet door was opened, every drawer pawed through. Praxis had a tiny burner set up on the chopping block, a wine glass tipped diagonally over the flames as if it was a makeshift beaker, while a pot bubbled something thick and greenish-gray on the stovetop. The rest of the bowls and glasses on the chopping block were blackened underneath, their contents settling as if they, too, had been subjected to this mad science experiment that Praxis seemed to be involved in. The smell of something burned hung thin in the air—Kaedrich should have noticed it sooner.

"Praxis!"

"Do you want to know why the bullet prevented my healing spell, or don't you?" Praxis asked as she straightened up. She picked up the wine glass from above the flames, swirling the contents before dropping said bullet with a *tink!* into the liquid. "Do you want to know what those bones were actually made of, or don't you?" She shrugged. "I needed lab space. It was this or the bathroom."

"I! But!" Kaedrich sputtered. "You can't just—!"

"I can." Praxis stopped swirling the glass; the bullet spun around the bottom for just a second or two more, and then, much to Kaedrich's shock, Praxis tipped back the liquid as if it was actually wine. The bullet fell into her mouth, too, and for a second Kaedrich wondered if Praxis was going to choke on it—but she just swirled it all around in her cheeks for a moment, then spat it back into the glass.

"Blech," Praxis said, frowning at the concoction.

"What, did you actually expect it to taste good?"

"Well, it *might* have—I did use a bottle of elderberry wine that I found in your dresser, but—"

"You *what*?"

"—it had a much more . . . salty flavor than I would have expected." She snapped her fingers. "I'll bet they were using platinum to treat the bullet. I don't know why, but I'd wager a significant sum that—"

"Blast it, Praxis! You can't . . ." Kaedrich threw her hands up in frustration. "You can't just go around ransacking my apartment!"

A single white eyebrow, arched to a sharp peak. "Wait, are you *actually* upset?"

"Yes! Perlandra's breath, yes! I am upset—what else would I be?"

"I don't know . . . flirting?"

"Flir—I . . . *No*, gods, I wasn't . . . Why would I be *flirting*?"

"I don't know," Praxis said, looking quickly down at the glass still in her hand. She gave it a tiny swirl, though it looked like she was just finding something to do rather than having any actual purpose for the motion. "Maybe you were just trying to keep up pretenses."

"There's nobody else *here*."

Praxis shrugged.

Just like that, all of the angry winds fell out of Kaedrich's sails. A quiet chill fell over her as she watched Praxis fish the bullet out from the bottom of the wine glass. It kept slipping out of her fingers, falling back, and Praxis swore quietly underneath her breath.

"Praxis . . . you, um . . . you didn't *want*—"

"Don't be stupid," Praxis snapped, as if she already knew what Kaedrich was asking. She flicked her fingers and the bullet shot up the side of the glass, where Praxis caught it in midair.

Kaedrich turned away, trying to make herself go back to unpacking her shopping. Her cheeks were burning, her chest aching. *Stupid, stupid.* Of course it was stupid. Of course Praxis didn't want her to be flirting— gods, why would Kaedrich even think such a thing, much less come right out and *ask* it? She couldn't believe that she'd been so careless with her words.

She tried to focus on the parcel, lying half-opened on the chair cushion, but her hands were shaking as she started to paw through it. And it had suddenly gone very quiet in the kitchen alcove behind her, only the faint sound of Brex's snores trilling out from wherever he was hiding for a nap.

"Kaedrich, I—"

The rattle of a doorknob cut her off. Marlick kicked it open with his usual cheerful rush, coming in with a whistle at his lips and no clue about what he'd just interrupted. "Hey!" he said, spotting them. "Kaedrich! Praxis! Just the people I was looking for!"

"Did you expect to find anyone else, in your own apartment?" Praxis asked. There was a *clink* as she set the bullet down, and she was already pouring a new concoction as Kaedrich turned back around. Her face was set in concentrated stone, all trace of mirth replaced with scientific precision.

"Fair point," Marlick said with a snap of his fingers. He paused as he took in the scene before him, the spread of lab work and the upturned drawers and cupboards. "Wow. Kaedrich, when they suggest that you should find a woman who's good in the kitchen, I don't think this is quite what they mean."

"Feh," Praxis called out. "This is much more useful than soufflés."

Marlick shrugged. "Soufflés taste a lot better, though."

"How do you know unless you try it?" Praxis straightened up, a smirk wedged into the corner of her mouth. She held the glass out, the one that had spent several moments being swirled around in her mouth before being deemed "salty."

Marlick laughed, holding up his hand in decline. "Thanks, but I'd rather keep my palate."

"Suit yourself," Praxis said. She set the glass back down, returning to her work.

A tiny knot began to twist itself up in Kaedrich's stomach. She frowned at Marlick, who was still watching Praxis's movements as she went about her business.

"Praxis doesn't cook," Kaedrich said. It wasn't really relevant—and certainly seemed obvious, once she'd spoken it—but she was working fast, trying to divert Marlick's attention with the first thing that had crossed her mind. He was paying, she felt, just a little bit *too* much attention to Praxis's movements.

Marlick chuckled, but Praxis glanced up sharply, her eyes narrowing in on Kaedrich. "I *cook*."

"Since when?"

Praxis was quiet for a second, considering this. "I understand the scientific principles of cooking," she said finally. "How hard could it be?"

"Ask me that again after you've actually tried it. Seriously, have you ever cooked a meal in your *life*?"

"I made you fish."

Kaedrich frowned. "Um, no you didn't."

"Yes, I did."

"When?"

"Remember our first trip together? To Marcovalla? I not only cooked you a fish dinner, I *caught* the fish that we ate."

Kaedrich paused, trying to remember. Their first trip together—it was a strange way to phrase the madcap adventure that had propelled them into the neighboring country of Marcovalla (and eventually, the land of the dead), but Kaedrich supposed that she'd phrased it that way to avoid uncomfortable questions. So much of that journey was a blur in Kaedrich's mind these days, but . . . now that Praxis mentioned it, there was something vaguely familiar about that.

"Right," Kaedrich said slowly, "but . . . hang on, *Brex* caught the fish. And I had to tell you when to douse your flames, or else you'd have charred the thing!"

Praxis waved her hand in dismissal. "Ah, but I *didn't* char it, so it counts. Technically. I believe that you owe me an apology."

"Yeah, that's not happening."

"O-kay!" Marlick said, cutting in with a cheerful clap of his hands. "Well, since the kitchen is obviously, um, out of commission this evening, what's say that the three of us head down to the Cross Street pub for dinner?"

Kaedrich frowned. "No thanks. I don't—"

"On the contrary, we'd love to," Praxis said. She snapped her fingers, and the flames on both her temporary burner and the stove died out with a tiny flash. She cut through the apartment with surprising speed, although it really wasn't that many steps from the alcove to the chair where Kaedrich was standing. Her arm draped over Kaedrich's shoulder in an instant. "Wouldn't we, *sweetheart*?"

Normally, Kaedrich didn't mind that her bones lacked whatever it was that let some people manipulate the world around them in a way called magic; but she wished for it now. The ability to magically reset the day, or transport herself into the comfort of her own bed, or even just become invisible to everyone else, sounded so appealing right then that she almost felt like it could happen if she only wished for it hard enough.

But of course, such magic didn't even exist at all, and even if it did it would do Kaedrich no good. She slumped her shoulders in resignation, Praxis's arm weighing down across them. It felt heavier than it seemed like it should, though maybe that was just the load of expectation that a night out would cost Kaedrich. She forced a twisted smile, looking from Praxis to Marlick and back again. "Of course," she said, "that sounds just lovely."

"But why would you *want* to cook? People work hard to become professionals at it—what, you're saying that I should just take away their job?"

"Praxis, you realize that not everybody can *afford* a cook, right? I mean, that knowledge does exist somewhere in your mind, doesn't it? That things actually cost money?"

"Well, sure, obviously *some* people can't—"

"*Most* people can't."

"—but then, well, they should just get more money. It seems damned inconvenient, having to do all that work for yourself."

"More—! Are you even listening when you talk?"

"Not really."

"Okay, well, at least that explains that."

"Sure, but my *point*—"

"Enough!" Marlick snapped. "Please, for the love of all that is merciful, can we not go *one block* without the two of you bickering and batting your eyelashes at each other?"

Kaedrich glanced back over her shoulder. In the meandering walk to the Cross Street pub, she had almost forgotten that he was there at all, trailing along behind them in much the same way that Brex circled in and out of view above their heads. Of course, he had run back to the apartment early in the trip, saying that he'd forgotten his watch, and so it had been only too easy for the conversation to spring up in his brief absence.

Kaedrich nearly jumped out of her skin when Praxis looped her free arm through Kaedrich's elbow, like a proper lady being escorted by a gentleman. "One block!" Praxis called back to Marlick. "Without bickering at least. Though I make no promises on the eyelashes."

Then she leaned her head against Kaedrich's shoulder, and Kaedrich nearly tripped over her own feet.

It was lucky that the Cross Street pub was not too much more than a block away by this point. Kaedrich's legs ached to rush forward, to feel the sidewalk pounding underneath her shoes, the contract and pull of her long muscles. Anything to get away from this situation, anything to get this evening over and done with faster.

Except that another part of her didn't really *want* to rush through it. Walking openly down the street like this, Praxis curled snugly against her side; it was wildly inappropriate, far too intimate for public view, and yet . . . Praxis's fingers curled around the hook of Kaedrich's elbow so gently, and her hair was brushing against Kaedrich's cheek, the familiar smell of her own soap mingling in with the distinctly Praxis-scent of her scalp. This was as close to her daydreams as Kaedrich was likely ever going to get, and she'd be foolish to deny the gentle thrill that it sent thrumming through her veins.

So it was with mingled relief and disappointment that they reached the pub, and Praxis slipped out of her hold. Praxis opened the doors herself, diving in with far too much enthusiasm for Kaedrich's tastes.

Inside, it was just another weekday evening. The Cross Street pub was a respectable establishment with clean tables, polished countertops, and glass-covered lamps hanging from the ceiling that splashed patterns of green and red and yellow across the patrons' heads. At this time of day there was at least as much food as drink being served, and the warm smell of fried meat and melted cheese assaulted Kaedrich's empty stomach. Her mouth began to water before she'd even realized that she was hungry.

Kaedrich started to make her way toward a table in a relatively quiet corner of the pub, but Marlick grabbed her by the shoulder. "Where are you going? Everyone's this way."

"Every—?" Kaedrich started to ask, as her attention drifted past him. Underneath one of the lamps, smack dab in the center of commotion, she spotted Lucan's golden head; and then, in quick succession, Havil's riot of curls and the thick rope of Tristy's braid hanging over her shoulder. Kaedrich narrowed her eyes. "You planned this, didn't you? This had nothing to do with the kitchen."

Marlick shrugged. "No, but it certainly made things easier," he said, which elicited a delighted cackle of laughter from Praxis.

Kaedrich shot her a glare. "Don't tell me that you were in on it."

Praxis grinned, shook her head. "Sadly, no."

Kaedrich pinched the bridge of her nose. "Marlick—"

"You would never agree to it if you knew. Oh, come on, Kaedrich! You found yourself a *lady*. I can't keep this to myself."

"'Lady'?" Praxis asked, cocking one eyebrow.

Marlick glanced at her, one overlong look up and down. "Maybe not the most ladylike one, sure, but there's no denying the basic facts, miss."

Kaedrich sighed. "This is a bad idea."

"What?" Praxis said. "Are you embarrassed to introduce me to your friends?"

"I—what? No! I just . . ." She trailed off, an awkward pause punctuating her objections.

Praxis sniffed, haughty and disdainful. "Well, I think it's a fantastic idea," she said, and she turned and started to flounce over to the table, her fingers flexing.

"Hey—wait!" Kaedrich called. She lurched forward, rushing to catch up, but Praxis had already broken through the crowd and drawn the attention of the table.

Kaedrich hurried to Praxis's side just as everyone was scrambling to cover their initial reaction at her sudden appearance. "Praxis Fellows," Praxis said, leaning over and extending her hand as if she hadn't even noticed. "Pleasure to meet you all."

Tristy was the first to recover her social graces. She gave Havil a subtle jab with her elbow, and Havil sprang to his feet as if he'd been a jack-in-the-box waiting to escape. Havil, then, gave Lucan's shoulder a swat, but Lucan didn't react at all.

"Miss Fellows, how do you do?" Havil said, continuing on as if Lucan wasn't being unbearably rude beside him. "I'm Havil Thorner. Might I present Tristy Mordoe and Lucan Lebule?"

"We've actually met," Tristy said. She glanced at Praxis's outfit, the trousers and the masculine cut of her coat, and then Tristy extended her hand, fingers curled, as she would to a Monfort gentleman of good standing. Praxis accepted it with the proper form, raising it slightly, though she did not grace a kiss over Tristy's fingers (much to Kaedrich's relief).

"Lovely to see you again," Praxis said, though without any real feeling.

Tristy inclined her head. "Likewise," she replied as she withdrew her hand.

This left only Lucan, still seated where he'd been. Praxis turned upon him, a pleasant-enough smile fixed to her face. He, however, was staring openly up at her, a tiny frown marring the gentleman's tan of his forehead. "Praxis . . . *Fellows*," he said, glancing at the open hand extended in his direction.

It wasn't that Lucan didn't know her full name before this—they'd all heard it at various times when Kaedrich talked about her life before coming to Monfort. Brindlewood was the only thing that she *would* share about her past, and their joint work was one of the only things that felt safe to discuss. But apparently Lucan hadn't really thought much about it, none of them probably had, and now you could see the gears connecting in his mind as he took in the deathly pallor of her southern heritage.

"That's right," Praxis said.

"Of *the* Fellows family?"

"Don't be daft," Marlick said. He had caught up somewhere in the flurry of introductions and was standing next to Kaedrich now; when Kaedrich glanced over, he was all but rolling his eyes. "I mean, look at her," he continued. "Besides, I think that I would know if I had one of *the* Fellows staying as a houseguest in my own apartment."

This line of reasoning seemed to appease Tristy and Havil, who had both looked sharply at Praxis following Lucan's question; but Lucan himself was a different matter. He was still just studying Praxis's icy face, the two of them never once breaking eye contact.

Praxis smirked. "My mother would be so pleased to know that you've heard of us."

Lucan's eyes widened, but it was Marlick that was truly struck by this admission. He caught himself on the back of a chair. "What, you . . . ? Sweet mercy, are you *serious*?"

Praxis leaned forward so that she could better see around Kaedrich as she reached her hand across. "Praxis *the* Fellows," she said. "At your service."

A heavy silence fell over them next, a tiny bubble of stilted quiet in the otherwise lively pub. Then Marlick gulped, quickly accepting Praxis's gesture of goodwill. "P-pleasure, my lady," he said automatically, and Praxis rolled her eyes.

"Oh, now, let's not start *that*," she said. She yanked her hand back and pulled out a chair, settling herself without formality. She glanced once around the tabletop, the opening selection of drinks sitting in front of everyone, and helped herself to the glass with the most liquid in it. "So are we going to have dinner, or what?"

Kaedrich winced. She pulled out the empty chair beside Praxis and sat down, the act of which seemed to be the signal that everyone else was waiting for. Those still standing sat, though with somewhat more timidity than Praxis or Kaedrich, and a variety of nervous glances were exchanged all around the table.

Kaedrich swiped the glass out of Praxis's hand, just before she was able to drink from it. She dropped it back in front of Havil.

"If you must drink, then buy your own," Kaedrich said. She snorted. "For Perlandra's sake, you can certainly afford it."

Praxis rested her hand oh-so-innocently against her chest. "Oh, did I forget to mention? I'm paying for tonight—have as much as you'd like, everyone. My treat." She threw a grin at the startled faces circling her, then leaned in to whisper in Kaedrich's ear. "*Now* they'll like me."

ON THE OPPOSITE side of the city, up the hill and across the peak, back down the outer slopes of Monfort, another establishment that liked to call itself a pub was also doing brisk business that evening.

The sign out front didn't bother with words, because at least half of its patrons couldn't read. Instead, a faded painting of a rosebud creaked as it swayed back and forth in the evening breeze. "The Crimson Rose" was too nice of a name for a place like this, but the original owners (back in the day) had no possible means of imagining what would happen to their once-proud establishment as the grime and corruption spread its way across the old quarter like a plague.

Mr. Bundling stood underneath the sign for a long while, watching the flecked red paint of the rose. He was early, but his contact would be, too—he always was. Abruptly, Bundling flicked his collar up and tugged his hat down, and pushed his way through the doors of the pub.

Ferran was in his usual spot at the far end of the bar. A tall drink sat in front of him, which Bundling knew from experience would still be at the same height by the end of the evening. Ferran was absolutely nothing if not careful: with his time, with his money, with his person. It was one of the things that Bundling was growing to like about the boy, not that such things were really a concern at times like these. Bundling refocused his thoughts as he sat down next to the young man that had been his contact throughout all of this mess.

They didn't speak at first, they never spoke at first. Bundling flagged down the barkeep and ordered the least foul option available in a place like this, then immediately took a long swig from the glass put in front of him. The drink burned Bundling's throat and nearly knocked him onto his ass—he would certainly feel it in the morning if he kept this sort of thing up, but in Bundling's experience it was more important in a situation like this to blend in than to keep one hundred percent of your wits. Ninety, or ninety-five would do well enough. Eighty-five at worst.

"You should be more careful," Ferran said. He wasn't looking at Bundling at all, staring up at a painting above the bar as if it was the most interesting thing in the universe, but there was no doubt as to who he was speaking to. "Tonight, especially. They're out in *force.*"

"Yet you still can't tell me who, exactly."

Ferran shrugged, one delicate shoulder rising and falling. Every detail of the boy was slight and smooth, so much that it was easy to mistake him for younger than his years. He tapped one long finger against the bar, his tidy nail clicking softly on the countertop. "I can feel them. More and more every day. They're going to spread through the city until they choke out the rest of us, Bundling. Like blooms strangled by a persistent vine."

This, Bundling didn't doubt. He kept thinking about Lord Wellen: he'd been so easily cut down—a nobleman, once a respected up-and-coming wizard. One by one, the opposition was shrinking. If they continued to sit here and do nothing, what would become of the rest of the city? Would no one be safe?

Bundling considered his next words carefully. He kept turning his glass around on the countertop of the bar, restless and unsettled. "You don't think . . ." He paused, not at all sure if he wanted to continue this line of thought. Unfortunately, he hadn't been able to *stop* thinking it, not since Kaedrich had first put the idea in front of him. "That is," Bundling tried again, "do you suppose that it's possible that . . . the Pon—"

"*Stop,*" Ferran said. One tiny little lash out, like a kitten's pin-sharp claws, and then he retreated and composed himself. "I'm not speculating on anything, and you'd be best to do the same."

"It's my *job* to speculate," Bundling said, snarling into his drink.

"Then find some other direction to speculate in," Ferran said. "Because that one will lead you nowhere good."

Bundling nodded. So Ferran had his suspicions, too.

Ferran cleared his throat. "You know the fire downtown yesterday?" He asked it like it was nothing, like they were just two men out chatting about the day's news over some drinks.

"Of course."

Ferran was quiet for a little while. Still studying the painting, a portrait of a robust woman sprawled half-naked over a velvet settee. Bundling would have been annoyed by the boy's coyness, except that he was too used to it by now to really care. Ferran was a highly respected lieutenant in the police force, and even being here at all was taking an enormous risk to his career and reputation. He was allowed his precautions, his quirks.

"It was a very odd blaze," Ferran said finally. He talked underneath his breath now, his face tipped over his drink as if he might actually be considering it. "Consumed the building within moments, but then it did not spread beyond the foundation. When the fire brigade got there, they fought against it for nearly an hour without success—and then, abruptly, their efforts just . . . started working. They put it out within minutes."

Bundling arched his eyebrows. "Magic?"

"So it would seem." Ferran ran his finger along the edge of his glass; a tiny bit of beer foam came away, and he licked it off absentmindedly. It was the closest that he would get to actually consuming his drink. "Though that's not what the official reports are going to say."

"No?"

"Hush!" Ferran hissed. Bundling didn't think that his question had been particularly loud, though he *had* worked his way through most of his own drink by this point.

Ferran glanced at the painting, then looked down toward the barkeep as if he was considering waving him over, then finally back to his glass. He shook his head, just enough for Bundling to notice. "Apparently, the chief deems the matter 'unimportant,'" Ferran continued. "If anyone asks questions about it . . . Well, let's just say that most of us know *not* to, by this point."

"But I thought that Lenould was opposed to unrestricted magic use?" *And so is the Pon,* he thought, but didn't say.

Ferran nodded. "He is. Very much so."

"Then why—?"

"That is the question, now, isn't it?" Ferran said. He glanced over his shoulder. "I have to go. Trust no one. Say nothing. They have spies everywhere." He stood up, leaving exactly the right amount of money on the bar beside his untouched drink. Before he left, he rested his hand on Bundling's wrist, his touch as light as a breeze. His delicate face was solemn, his eyes sad. "Good luck," he whispered, and then he withdrew his hand and was gone.

Chapter Seventeen

Unfortunately, Praxis's methods did not have the immediate effect that she was hoping they would. While not *quite* as awkward as the first few moments, their table still remained unnaturally solemn. Lucan continued to stare at Praxis, the muscles of his face twitching as his emotions shifted behind the scenes from one thing to the next; Tristy, meanwhile, was sipping her drink and watching Kaedrich carefully—or rather, the tiny pocket of air that existed between her and Praxis, her attention missing nothing; poor Marlick still looked as if someone had struck him upside the head with a club, and was perched in his chair like he was expecting a bomb to go off at any moment; only Havil seemed unconcerned, smiling benignly at the table at large and stealing long looks at the lengths of tension wire running down the back of Praxis's control hand.

"Fellows," Lucan repeated finally, breaking the silence.

Praxis rolled her eyes. "Yes, I believe that we've established that."

Lucan's attention turned sharply to Kaedrich. "How in the darkness do *you* have an acquaintance with a *Fellows*?"

Kaedrich shifted in her chair, slinking just a fraction lower. "I've told you, we met at Brindlewood Hall."

"Ignore him, Kaedrich," Praxis said. "He's just jealous."

Lucan raised an eyebrow. "On the contrary, my concerns are for *you*, Lady Praxis, not myself."

Praxis laughed. "Oh, really?"

"Indeed." He straightened his shoulders, his whole posture morphing from friend-out-at-a-pub to socialite-on-parade. He rested his fingers neatly on the table, as if holding court at a great house. "Forgive me if I appear to be overstepping my bounds, my lady . . . I only mean that, well, *I* like Mr. Mannly as well as the next man, of course, but do you really want to be seen associating with a person so *very* far below your own station?"

Praxis let this hang in the air for one second, two. Beside her, Kaedrich was sliding even farther down in her chair, her shoulders curling forward more than Praxis had seen in a long time. She noticed, of course, but she kept most of her attention on Lucan; the smug little smile that he was trying to hide behind his Helpful Face, the calculations going on behind his eyes as he wondered: How could he turn this situation to his own advantage? How much ass did he have to kiss?

Gods, Praxis had known these kinds of people her whole life.

Luckily, though, this had given her plenty of opportunity to perfect how to handle them.

"Well, I certainly thank you for your concern, Mr. Lebule," Praxis started, and watched with hidden satisfaction as Lucan buoyed slightly at her words. "Unfortunately, if I started to worry about that sort of thing myself, then it would *also* deprive me of the continued pleasure of *your* charming company."

A tiny silence followed this pronouncement, as Praxis gave him her most charming smile—one she'd learned directly from her mother. Everyone else was staring with frozen shock, and the moment might have dragged on for the rest of the evening, had Kaedrich not burst out laughing right then and there.

Praxis grinned, catching Kaedrich in a half-hug as her laughter sent her toppling against Praxis's side. She kissed the top of Kaedrich's head as Kaedrich shook with mirth against her shoulder.

Though Lucan was scowling, trying to hide his burning face behind his rapidly emptying glass, the jab had served its purpose, and the rest of the table seemed to let out a tiny breath. Several hidden grins and stifled chuckles darted through the group, stopping only as a barmaid appeared in their midst. Kaedrich straightened up and managed to compose herself enough to place her order with the rest of them, dinner and fresh drinks all around, and now things could proceed with a little more breathing room.

Havil was the first to get over his apprehension. Or maybe it wasn't so much that he was over it, so much as the burning curiosity had finally won over his better social judgment—either way, he apparently couldn't contain his enthusiasm any longer. "So what *is* that?" he asked. He was openly staring at the network of wires covering Praxis's hand, though he pointed anyway, as if it wasn't obvious. "Some kind of . . . like, electrical glove? Does it let you send a charge through whoever you touch?"

Praxis glanced down. Her three middle-most fingers were capped with a little rubber dome that provided the base point upon which she could flex the wire cords; rings hugged each of the joints, the wires fed through a feed along the top. There was an additional thick support brace at the point where the fingers connected, where the wires came together and snaked down the length of her hand almost as a single, thicker cord, while a thumb-loop broke off and provided the means of quickly connecting or disconnecting at her wrist. There *was* something vaguely electrical-looking about it, now that Praxis thought of it, though she didn't think of it often. She flexed her hand, watching the tension as the wires pulled over the curl of her fingers.

"Why would I want to do that?" she said finally.

Havil shrugged. "I don't know. Defense against your enemies? Or, if the charge was mild enough, you could use it as a means of disciplining your servants, I guess."

"I don't *have* servants," she said, to a collective look of shocked disbelief.

Lucan snorted sourly into his drink. "What do you call *him*?" he asked, jerking his chin in Kaedrich's direction.

Praxis smirked. "I don't think that I should say, in polite company."

A ring of stifled chuckles and snorts shot around the table—still a bit on-edge, still holding themselves back somewhat, but at least they *were* starting to relax a little. Praxis helped herself to a giant handful of peanuts sitting in a bowl in the middle of the table, in an effort to appear disarming. She let several fall down her chin as she stuffed them in her mouth.

Kaedrich clucked her tongue in mild disgust, and instantly reached over to pluck the fallen peanuts from where they'd landed on Praxis's lap. "Gods, can't I take you anywhere?"

"No, but really," Tristy said, piping up. "I understand that you're out playing at being one of 'the commoners'—I've seen that plenty, at the music halls. But do you honestly mean to tell me that you don't have *any* servants? Not at all?"

Havil raised an eyebrow, temporarily distracted from her control hand. "Yeah, that's a fair point. I thought that you were all dripping with money?"

"Maybe she's disgraced," Lucan muttered. "Kicked out of the family."

Their heads all swiveled toward her now, tipped as if considering this possibility. You could see the way that it made a certain amount of sense in their heads: it would explain, certainly, her ratty coat, the disregard that she would have for associating so closely with someone of Kaedrich's social standing.

Praxis scowled. The remaining peanut mash suddenly tasted bitter in her mouth, and she stole a (nearly) empty glass and spat the rest out while everyone else tried not to look *too* disgusted.

"Praxis is *not* disgraced," Kaedrich said, before Praxis could. She was sitting up a little straighter, her face set into a hard glower in Lucan's direction. "She has far more money and social clout than you could ever hope to achieve, Lucan, and I thank you to be mindful of that."

Lucan raised a single golden eyebrow. "Forgive me," he said, dipping his head just long enough to be vaguely submissive. Then he drained the last of his drink, setting the glass down with a loud *thunk*.

A stale silence hung in the air, everyone regarding their drinks or their hands far more than the other people at the table. Even Praxis, who was staring at the half-masticated pile of peanut flecks in the glass by her elbow.

Kaedrich glanced at the glass and pulled a face. "Praxis, you realize that's disgusting, don't you?"

Praxis shrugged. She snapped her fingers over the top of the glass and dropped a matchstick-sized bundle of flames inside, turning the remnants of both alcohol and peanuts into a brilliant conflagration.

It was a brazen move, and it had the potential to backfire on her in an explosion much more impressive than the controlled burn that she'd just set. Praxis had no way of knowing how Kaedrich's new friends felt about the subject of unrestricted magic use (though she did notice a ruby tie clip glinting on Lucan's chest—slightly scuffed from daily wear), and even if they were largely friendly toward it, her light show could have easily drawn unwanted attention from the rest of the pub. The sweaty crowd pressed in thick against Praxis's back as her flames struck their mark. Her glass flared, catching the expressions around their table as if it was a photographer's flash-lamp: the sour twist of Lucan's mouth, the sparkling curiosity in Havil's deep brown eyes, the nervous sweat along Marlick's brow, the measuring gaze of Tristy's level stare. They jumped, to varying degrees of surprise, as the flames licked up the sides of the glass and teased at the underside of Praxis's fingers, still hovering over the rim.

Praxis toyed a bit of the flames up and away from the others. She flipped her hand, the fire pooling and dancing in the cup of her palm. In the noise of the pub, her actions went unnoticed. Praxis twisted the flames, gathering them into thin ropes that she could weave together into a form. It was the same trick that she used to create her creatures of flame, although far scaled down. She had never tried it on something this small, this fiddly before, and she bit her lip as she focused on the construction in her hand.

When she was done she set it right down on the table—she'd cooled the output, funneling the heat back into herself so as not to set the table on fire—and drew her hand back to reveal her creation. A tiny steam engine, not perfect but reasonably rendered considering the medium she was working with. She snapped her fingers again (purely for show), and it puffed up a tiny hiss of smoke and rolled straight toward Havil, who laughed with delight and clapped his approval.

Praxis smiled, and her fire train disappeared with a showy flash of light.

Lucan, Praxis knew, was a lost cause, at least as far as any action that she could take that evening. But if simple money was not enough to win their affections, then she knew that she could eventually worm her way into the good graces of the others.

WITH NO MORE business to keep him there, Bundling really should have left. Every other time, he had left. He'd been meeting Ferran for two months now, ever since the young man had first timidly approached him, telling him that he had some interesting information to share. And interesting it certainly was: right from the beginning, Bundling had become convinced that there was clearly *some* kind of web threading itself through the whole of Monfort lately, and the police chief was just the latest piece to be woven in.

They'd met roughly twice a week, always on Ferran's terms. Bundling couldn't blame him; he'd probably do the same thing in Ferran's place. A promising officer in the police force, newly promoted, in line to be made inspector in a few years' time—he had a lot more to lose than Bundling did.

Yet for all the information that Ferran had given him—and he *had* given him information, good information, information that had led Bundling down paths to the Governance Council and the courts and social elite of all stripes—there was still so much about the shadow creeping over Monfort that Bundling didn't understand. If it was the Pon, then what did she hope to gain by it all? If it was power that she was after, she could not seek election on the Governance Council. Bundling kept waiting, kept hoping for a breakthrough. There was so much going on in the city these days, but trying to connect it would surely prove the death of him. Even Lord Wellen from the former Society, whom Bundling had pinned such hopes on—what good had he done, in the end? Oh, so they had *tried*. Fat lot of good the Society's trying had done anybody.

Bundling slapped some money down on the bar and turned to go, disgusted with not just the evening, but this whole investigation. The Crimson Rose had filled up even thicker than when he'd come in, whole swaths of stinking humanity packed elbow to elbow like fish in a can. Plenty of drunks, of course, but also gamblers, and opium enthusiasts, whores and the men seeking them . . . and two gentlemen of surprising standing, their blood-red vests catching the light as they consulted with their pocket watches.

Bundling watched them. He sat back down and flagged for a third drink, his head buzzing with anticipation. The gentlemen were discussing something between them, quietly and with their heads dipped. They would regard the crowd, who were largely ignoring them—this was not the sort of place where it was generally safe to mind other people's business—and then lean in and mutter things to each other again. It looked . . . Bundling frowned. It looked more like people out shopping at a meat market than anything else, he had to admit.

Abruptly, the two gentlemen broke off from where they were standing and made their way toward the pub's back room. Bundling's head swiveled like a cat's, craning to watch as they disappeared through a patchwork curtain. It was almost certainly safer to ignore this, and a part of Bundling knew it—but he didn't listen to that voice. He was *tired* of listening to that voice. He was *tired* of poking at this mystery from afar, listening and hoping that some trickle of information would leak its way back to him. He was *tired* of not knowing.

And so Bundling slipped off of his stool, his drink still clutched firm in his grip, and he made his way casually over to the patchwork curtain. There didn't seem to be any sounds coming from behind it at all, good or ill, and Bundling took another long drain from his glass for courage.

He went through.

* * *

THE EVENING PROCEEDED along, and far from being the disaster that Kaedrich had anticipated, it was actually kind of . . . working. Oh, sure: Praxis was still dishing out sass whenever someone asked a question that she deemed too "stupid" for civil discourse, and she continued to nettle at Lucan whenever he tried to out-snob her on some point or another—she was still *Praxis*, after all, and Kaedrich knew that you could never expect her to sit still and get in *no* trouble. But there was a shift in the air, as she chatted and showed off, as she tried first one approach and then another to dazzle and impress. She was putting on her best behavior, like she *wanted* Kaedrich's friends to like her, like it *mattered* to her for some reason.

And so Kaedrich watched, the heavy knot in her chest loosening, as Praxis worked another type of magic on the table, a rough sort of charm that sprang mostly from surprised laughter at something unexpectedly brash that she'd pull, but . . . it *worked*. She got Tristy laughing hysterically more than once, and melted some of Marlick's terror at realizing who he'd been entertaining for the last few days. She indulged Havil's questions about the brace and gears that controlled her leg, extending her hand to let him examine the mechanism at the base of her thumb that engaged and disengaged the system at will. Dinner came and went, of course, and drinks replaced empty glasses—Praxis taking coffee, the rest of them growing steadily drunk.

It was late into the evening when Lucan got up, excusing himself as he wove toward the thick of the pub. Most of them barely noticed that he left (Praxis was in the middle of a long and, as far as Kaedrich could figure out, entirely fictitious tale of her near-death adventures in Tjalava that stole the rest of their attentions), but Kaedrich kept a wary eye on him as he slipped through the crowd.

Kaedrich followed suit a moment later, pausing only long enough for Praxis to pull her down and plant a fast kiss on her cheek, telling her to not be long. Kaedrich forced a nod. Her whole face burned as she followed the path where Lucan had gone, through the twisting crowds of barmaids and laughing patrons.

She found him a moment later, standing at the wide slab of bar and frowning into a full glass in front of him. "Hey," Kaedrich said as she approached. "You know, we could have had someone bring that to you."

Lucan rolled his eyes. "I wanted to stretch my legs," he said, in a way that clearly indicated both that this was a lie and that he didn't care that it was obvious.

"Listen, about Praxis—"

"Yeah, you've got yourself a real 'charmer' there, Mannly," Lucan said with a snort.

Kaedrich waved this off. "You know that she doesn't really mean it when she's rude, don't you? I mean, she doesn't care about things like social class."

"Good lord," Lucan said, turning to stare incredulously at Kaedrich. "You really believe that, don't you? Of *course* she cares," he added, before Kaedrich could argue. "They all care. They wouldn't be aristocracy if they didn't."

"Yandosia doesn't have an aristocracy," Kaedrich said. It was true, though it wasn't really an argument to Lucan's base point, and they both knew it. She had read all about it in a book, though, the cultural hierarchy of the world beneath the frozen pole. The Fellows were mentioned by name. More than once.

Kaedrich shook her head. "Anyway, Praxis isn't like the rest of them."

"Bullshit." Lucan turned, pointing back toward the table. "You see the way that she's holding court over there? One look at that table—one— and you know who's in charge. You think that's a coincidence? You think that it's just because, what, she's so *enchanting*?" Lucan snorted messily into his drink. "Honestly, she's not."

Kaedrich screwed her mouth into a tight line. She had no immediate counterargument to Lucan's assessment, and it vexed her that she could see where his line of thinking had come from. Praxis *was* the focal point upon which the world around her turned, and not just here. She tended to dominate whatever social structure she found herself in, but it had nothing to do with wealth or status, or even her ability (or lack of same) to enchant her audience. Kaedrich had always attributed this effect as what naturally followed when a strong woman knew her own mind; it was, in fact, a trait that she had often envied, and longed to figure out how to achieve for herself.

But now Kaedrich watched, as Praxis swept her arm wide to punctuate some high point of a tale, and for a moment all that she could see was the way that Lucan saw it: the nobleblood lording her status over the rest of them, the laughter that greeted her carefully modulated to appease the ego.

"Believe it or not, I'm not trying to insult her," Lucan said a moment later. "Everyone knows that I have plenty of reason to encourage this little distraction of yours, if it keeps you away from my sister."

Kaedrich grimaced. "I'm really not—"

"Yeah, yeah." Lucan waved his hand. "I'm not worried about you, really, so much as I am about her. So obviously, I think that anything that dissuades Lyana's interest is a good thing. But as your friend . . ."

Lucan fell silent, and for a split second Kaedrich was almost disappointed that she might not get to hear what it was that really concerned Lucan. Then she remembered both that they were discussing his assessment of Praxis's character, and that Lucan was the type that became an *honest* drunk—and Kaedrich was suddenly sure that, whatever it was that he had been mulling over, she wasn't going to like it.

Sure enough: "I'm just worried that you don't realize what you're getting into. Her kind, they can't help but feel superior to the rest of us, Mannly. It's in their blood. She's going to play with you for a while, and if you're just looking for a bit of fun then fantastic, enjoy yourself. But you're not, are you?"

Thankfully, Kaedrich was saved from the burden of answering when someone collided against her back. The impact shoved her against the bar, knocking into Lucan's elbow; Lucan, then, shouted at both Kaedrich and the man that had run into her in the first place, and by the time idle threats were exchanged and insults issued, it seemed as if Lucan might have lost his train of thought. He resumed his drinking with a sour expression, but that wasn't uncommon by any stretch of the imagination.

Ordinarily, Kaedrich would try to stay with him. Lucan had a tendency to disappear when he drank too much, which the others attributed to him slipping off with an attractive lady—though Kaedrich, for reasons she couldn't quite put her finger on, tended to doubt that explanation. She often felt it was her duty, in a group situation, to keep an eye on him. The weight of obligation pressed down on her now, and she felt it, trying to pin her in place, trying to keep her nearby. He seemed flighty tonight, spinning his empty glass on the bar over and over again.

She returned to the table anyway. A cloud of guilt followed her, so thick that you could almost smell it, but being a nanny to Praxis took up so much of Kaedrich's effort that she didn't really have anything left for the rest of them. When she got back, she found Tristy doubled over with a fit of giggles, and Havil and Marlick looking somewhat queasy. Praxis, as ever, was smug and content, as if everything was going exactly as she'd planned—and, knowing her, it probably was.

Kaedrich yanked her chair out, sat back down. The shade of warmth and optimism that she'd managed to cultivate had disappeared with the speed of a summer storm, replaced by her earlier grumpiness. No, it wasn't that the evening was *horrible*, but at this point she just wanted it done.

Playing this game of pretend, letting Praxis touch her knee or kiss her cheek, listening to people's opinions about a relationship that didn't even exist . . . it was messing with her head. Once or twice, she'd almost started to forget that it *was* a game.

"Well, this has been fun," Kaedrich said, jumping into a momentary pause in the conversation, "but I think that we should probably be heading back by now, don't you?"

"So soon?" Marlick asked. Kaedrich turned, curious. She had expected a protest, but she did not expect it from him; on the contrary, after his embarrassment at learning exactly who Praxis was, Kaedrich would have assumed that he'd be the first to agree to call the whole evening over and done. Instead, he nearly jumped out of his skin at the idea, scrambling for his pocket watch. He regarded it, and then gave a nervous laugh. "What's the rush? The night is still young."

"I'm afraid that won't do any good, Marlick," Praxis said. "I've learned that there's no point in arguing with Kaedrich once he's made up his mind."

Kaedrich whipped her head back toward Praxis. "Since *when*?"

Praxis glanced at her, considering. She shrugged. "Well. I didn't say that I always *listened* to myself, now did I?"

Despite everything, the game had to be advanced.

Lanali prowled through her own house as if she was a petty thief. Her senses were perked to their fullest extent, impressions of her followers melting through the walls of Dreamfield House and entering her mind like a headache. She darted from shadow to shadow, folding herself into empty rooms whenever someone drew too near. She was once again dressed as a merchant, having interrupted what she hoped would be her final errand as Frel, and could not afford to be seen. Not here.

Ordinarily, Lanali wouldn't dare dream of leaving the safety of her chambers looking like this—but she was in too much of a hurry to waste time changing. This was vital, more important even than the death of Praxis Fellows.

This was the key to everything. Finally, and after all of this time, she had it.

If her information proved accurate.

Which is where Tol came in—except that Tol was not in his room. The realization of this hit Lanali as she reached the fourth floor landing. Lanali stopped, gripping the railing at the top of the stairs as a flare of anger coursed through her veins. The railing split, long cracks trailing down from her clenched fingers. Where *was* he? She did not have time to waste chasing him down, not now. She did not—

He entered into her range of perception, two floors down.

Lanali raced down the stairs. Like a breathless lover, unable to contain herself any longer. She found him on the stairwell outside of the last library and pushed him inside before he had the chance to say anything. They tumbled into darkness, the door snapping shut behind them.

He said nothing. Stillness oozed off of him, so intense that his impression started to blur into the background. Ghosts of moonlight danced through the gaps in the room's velvet curtains, catching only a slice here and there of his strong profile, his braids, his controlled stance.

"The regent of Melmont," Lanali said. She offered no explanation; Tol did not need one.

"Lord Shillingly? We ruled out that contingency," he said.

"We were wrong. We may have been wrong."

"That seems unlikely," Tol said. "The Lady Trelina's fate is well known, and well pitied."

This was true, she *was* well pitied. Her title, as well as her family's seat on the King's Court of State, were currently being held by her uncle until the time when Lady Trelina would marry. Her uncle: a man who had, himself, married into the family line ages before Lady Trelina's father had been killed with no male heir, and who had absolutely no incentive to approve a match for the lady. (Lanali couldn't blame him— circumstances of the late Lord Melmont's death were so natural and innocent that Lanali immediately suspected the uncle of arranging it himself.) Thus, it seemed to polite society, would Lady Trelina go forever unwed, doomed to grow old as a spinster despite her wealth, her status, her alleged beauty.

Except:

"There may be a godfather."

This was difficult even for Lanali to believe, but there it was. The gossip had reached her ears as she rode the hopper cars toward her destination, a package held tight in her lap. The night swirled sickly-sweet around her, the honey-lime smell of the bay particularly strong. A pair of young, high-society ladies occupied the seats in front of Lanali, their pointed profiles and sloping necks catching the lights that flashed into the hopper car as they trundled by. They were trilling on about nothing in particular—parties and social calls, marriage prospects for all of their friends, whom to invite to a charity ball that they were hosting to make themselves look good—when the conversation turned, of all things, to Pon Lanali herself.

"Yes, but he's been going up to the Pon's house lately—you know, the one on the hill?"

"So?" A graceful shrug. "Lots of people do. I've received invitations."

"The difference is that you've had the good sense not to accept."

"You know, you really should give this up. I understand that your brother lost his position—"

"This isn't about Brythard *or* the Society." She paused, leaning over as if to collect something that she'd dropped. When she spoke next, she kept her voice low, hoping that only the two of them could hear. "I've just never liked her, all right?"

Her friend frowned. "The Pon?"

A curt nod. Then the lady laid her hand on her friend's shoulder. "Only, please don't tell anyone that I said so directly."

"Of course," her friend said. She gave the lady's hand a gentle squeeze.

The lady sighed. "Thank you. It's bad enough, having a brother that refuses to abandon the magical arts at a time like this. The last thing I need—"

"I understand."

"I'm not sure who I can trust with this anymore. All of our old friends have abandoned us. The Westbautons, the Rightens, the Dufranes—"

"Of Melmont? I thought that Lord Shillingly was one of the last holdouts *against* the Pon."

"He is, so I'm told. Only he'd never say so openly. I think that he's afraid of offending Trelina's godfather—did you know, *he* actually owns half of the deed on Chelling Manor?"

Her friend arched her eyebrows. "Really?"

Another nod. "That's what Lina says. Apparently, he used to be thick as thieves with her father. Helped to save the family from ruin, or something."

"She never told *me* that."

A shrug. "She's always liked me best. It's not my fault."

Their conversation fell into frivolity after that; though Lanali purposefully missed her own stop and tailed them at a discreet distance back to an opera house near the coast, just to be sure. Then she'd retreated back to Woodland Alley, finished her business, checked her watch. Praxis Fellows was not due back for a while yet—if Lanali hurried . . .

She felt the time pressing down on her now, in the library. She did not have time to waste convincing Tol.

Luckily, he did not need convincing. Loyal Tol—Lanali's heart almost threatened to swell in affection as he said, "Do we know anything about him yet?"

"Only that he was the best of friends with the late marquess. If true, it shouldn't be difficult to verify."

"It might," Tol said, "depending on whose interest would be served in keeping the truth quiet."

"I trust you to work around that problem," Lanali said. She watched the weight of this settle over him: *trust*. Of course she trusted him, but it was important to say it sometimes, to keep him from getting hopeless. She put just the right softness into the word, just the right gravity. Tol had been in love with her since forever—since the beginning, since he didn't even *know* her, since she was nobody. She cupped his cheek, feeling the seconds tick by beneath her. If it was anyone else, she never would have wasted time like this; but Tol . . . if she lost his loyalty, her entire bedrock would crack.

"Don't fail me," she whispered, and Tol reached up and wrapped his own fingers around hers. He pulled her touch away, and under different circumstances, Lanali could see that he would have kissed the back of her fingers. That he wanted to. That he would have trailed his lips down each of her digits in turn, nuzzled her palm, worked his way to her wrist, the inside of her arm, pulled her close as he inched slowly, so slowly, up toward her neck.

He didn't, of course. He wouldn't.

"Never," Tol said. He dropped her hand.

They left the library in silence.

Chapter Eighteen

*H*AD EVERYONE GONE INSANE?

This was the only explanation that Kaedrich could come up with, because she knew what both Praxis and Marlick were like when they were drunk, and this didn't come anywhere close. They walked home together, the three of them side by side by side. Praxis had her arm linked through Kaedrich's as if Kaedrich was a proper gentleman escorting a lady down the street; she was whistling a merry tune and grinning at people as they passed, even going so far as to point out what a *beautiful* night it was, and look!, how full the moon is!, and doesn't the bay smell *wonderful*!, and other trifles that Kaedrich didn't even think Praxis ever noticed. She laughed at almost everything, drinking in the night air, throwing her head back to look at the stars that clustered thick and brilliant over Monfort.

Marlick, meanwhile, dragged his feet and kept his head down. He didn't respond to anything that Praxis or Kaedrich said to him, not with more than a murmur of agreement or a huff, anyway, and he kept glancing around anxiously when he thought that no one was paying attention. His hands were jammed into his coat pockets, his shoulders drawn up as if he was fighting against a cold and bitter wind.

There was no sign of Brex this time, but that wasn't surprising. He'd probably be out hunting until dawn.

As they rounded the last street corner, Kaedrich didn't think that she could ever be so happy to see the narrow building of her little apartment. She quickened her pace, dragging both Praxis and Marlick along with her like two distracted toddlers. It took all of her self-restraint not to bound up the steps two at a time, and she only just remembered, in her haste, to lean down and whisper her name into the doorknob before she let them all inside.

Home. Perlandra be praised.

"Are there any cakes?" Praxis asked, already veering toward the kitchen, while Marlick edged into the sitting room as if he was afraid it might explode. Praxis skirted around her mess and opened the breadbox, peering in disappointedly, but Kaedrich was already making a beeline for her bedroom. Anything to put this day behind her. Kaedrich's thoughts turned longingly toward her pillow, as her mattress seemed to call her forth all the way across the apartment and through the door.

And then she stopped, just inside of the room, because of course Praxis had managed to make a mess of it, too. Kaedrich closed her eyes, gathering her strength for a moment. Miscellaneous clothing lay scattered across the floor, on top of which were assorted books, a handful of papers, and even a plate with a nibbled-off crust smeared with jam. There was, for reasons passing all understanding, a broom laying down upon the bed as if it had grown weary and simply decided to tuck itself in. And a potted plant, sitting on top of Kaedrich's dresser.

It was the plant, more than anything else, that irritated Kaedrich. No doubt part of some experiment that Praxis was running in the kitchen (perhaps the oil of it provided some chemical reaction, who knows?), except that now it would undoubtedly fall to Kaedrich to care for and maintain it as long as it was here. "And you say you don't have servants," Kaedrich muttered as she picked her way across the detritus on the floor. Naturally, Praxis had left it nowhere near the sunlight of the window.

Kaedrich drew closer, leaning in to examine it. It really was an ugly little plant. Already, it looked half-dead, and what life it did have was spiny and grotesque. A nest of twisting vines surrounded a central stalk, tiny little vomit-green leaves dotting the lengths. Spines rose from the top of the stalk, thin white barbs that caught the lamplight. Kaedrich raised her voice, turning slightly toward the open door behind her. "You really couldn't have found something more attractive to help you?"

From the rest of the apartment, there was a slight bang of a pot or a metal door snapping shut, and then, "What?"

"This plant," Kaedrich called. "It's hideous."

"What plant?"

"What do you mean 'what plant'? The plant that you left on my dresser!"

Another small clang, and then the shuffle of footsteps. "I didn't leave anything on your dresser," Praxis said, her voice rising and falling as she moved through the apartment.

"Oh, come on," Kaedrich said. She turned back to the plant, scoffing at how ridiculous it was that Praxis couldn't remember buying such an unattractive thing.

She was just reaching toward it when she heard a sharp intake of breath from behind her, and Praxis's voice crying out, "Kaedrich, don't touch—!"

The bedroom door slammed shut between them. Kaedrich jumped, her fingers brushing against the outermost nest of vines; she started to whip her hand back, but before she could even blink, a vine had shot out and wrapped itself fast around her wrist.

Kaedrich froze. Praxis was already pounding on the door, shouting through it, asking if she was all right, calling her name, but Kaedrich did not dare move at first, did not dare speak, barely even breathed.

When a moment passed and nothing further happened, Kaedrich cleared her throat. Still nothing. "I'm . . . I'm fine," she said, tentatively, and then again, louder to be heard over Praxis's panic, "I'm fine!"

And she was, because look: there were no flowers growing on it, and clearly a plant could not fire a gun.

"Did you touch it?" Praxis asked. She slammed against the door. "Gods, tell me, please, that you didn't touch it."

Kaedrich looked at the vine, wrapped so tightly around her wrist that her fingers were starting to grow cold. "I didn't touch it," she said, because really what was the point in increasing Praxis's terror? "What do I do? Is there a way to kill it?"

A strangled laugh came through the door. "I don't know. Probably, but I don't . . . I don't know. Can you open the door from your side? I can't get through out here."

Kaedrich looked over her shoulder, glancing at the distance between her and the door. There was no way that she could reach it, not without moving, and moving was still on the bottom of her list of things to do at the moment.

The plant, however, had other ideas. There was a faint rustle, and Kaedrich whirled her head back, staring in horror as the other vines began to uncurl from around the central stalk.

It was a split second decision: Kaedrich yanked her hand away, hoping that she could rip the plant right off of the dresser and send it crashing to the other side of the room. But at the slightest movement, the rest of the vines suddenly lashed out, staking themselves into the dresser as an anchor. The dresser jerked slightly, but that was it. The wood split with a series of hideous snaps, the vines shooting down through layers of clothes and drawers, finally crunching out the bottom and rooting themselves straight through the floor.

"What was that?" Praxis shouted through the door. The knob rattled, the hinges creaked underneath some outside strain.

"Nothing," Kaedrich called. "It's fine."

Except that it wasn't, because in the distraction of all of this backfired attempt to free herself, Kaedrich hadn't even noticed that the vine lashed to her wrist had begun to twist, the end slithering up her arm. Kaedrich tried to wrench herself free again, but the vine only gave her so much slack; she could thrash around, uselessly, but she was tethered to the plant as surely as if she was part of it.

Enough, she thought to herself, stamping down on a chill of panic. She glanced at the bed, but she was too far away to reach the gun underneath her pillow—all that she could grab was the corner of the blanket, and though she gave it a few tugs with some vague idea of dragging either the sheets or the head of the bed toward her, there wasn't enough space in the room to be moving furniture. The window, too, was out of reach, so she could forget about breaking the glass and using one of the shards to cut herself free. The only things that were near her at all, really, was the mess that Praxis had left behind: the clothes, the books, the dirty plate—

—and a butter knife, lying across the top of it.

Sadly, it was not a *sharp* knife, but Kaedrich was not going to whine over missed fortune. She dragged the plate toward her with the toe of her shoe, and then leaned over to retrieve the utensil.

Praxis, meanwhile, was still trying to force her way through the door, and still shouting through it, though Kaedrich had tuned her out by this point. Marlick's voice had long since joined her, in smaller muffled tones, and Kaedrich supposed that it was nice to know that she had people on her side, even if they were of no immediate help.

She had the butter knife now, but the vine had snaked itself all the way up her arm. Her fingers were numb, the rest of her arm quickly following suit, and maybe that was why she didn't even feel the spines at first, why she didn't think to even look. It was only when she turned back and tried to get her frozen fingers to grab at the length of vine trailing off of them that she spotted the ribbons of blood pooling out from her shirtsleeve.

Kaedrich shrieked before she could stop herself. Skeletal-looking spines, identical to the ones coming up from the plant's central stalk, had grown out of the plump vine and stuck themselves like needles through her skin. A rush of queasy dizziness punched her in the gut, and Kaedrich had to catch herself against the edge of the dresser to keep from passing out. She didn't know if she could *actually* feel them now, or if it just felt like she could because she was aware of them, but either way, she watched and felt (or imagined) with horror as the spines burrowed underneath her skin, threading along the bone as they, too, traveled up her arm.

She succumbed to a brief panic then. Hacking at the stalk that tethered her, Kaedrich felt a surge of victory when her butter knife sank partway into the thick curl of vine. Her triumph was short-lived, however, when further ends began to uncurl themselves from the mass surrounding the central stalk. More of the spines were already growing as they lashed out, whipping through the air at Kaedrich. Kaedrich twisted aside, brandishing her knife as if it was a sword. Her blade struck several of the spines, though one darted through her defenses and left a deep puncture wound on her hand.

A part of her noticed, briefly, that the pounding on the door and the sounds of Praxis's shouts had fallen silent, but she did not have time to worry about it. More vines were uncurling from the central stalk, every single one of them by the looks of it. Those that weren't otherwise occupied grounding the plant to the dresser thrashed in the air around the plant, occasionally striking out at Kaedrich when she would lunge forward with her butter knife, but . . . but mostly, they were acting more *defensive* than anything else. Kaedrich stopped her attack long enough to take a large step back, as large of a step as she could with her arm immobilized and bound to the plant, and sure enough, nothing immediately followed her. The stalks that she'd been fencing with retreated to a perimeter around the central stalk, joining the others like a swarm of bees protecting the hive.

Pain flared in her shoulder, the vine beginning to inch across her collar bone. Kaedrich took a steadying breath, watching the mass of vines as it writhed over and around the pot. She went to grab her pin for a dose of courage, but the vine crawling up her had already reached it, and she was not about to risk getting her free hand tangled up. Instead, Kaedrich closed her eyes, offered a brief prayer to Perlandra, and dove toward the pot before she could change her mind.

The vines attacked, thick and fierce. Spines dove into and probably even through Kaedrich's hand (she did not dare to look), but the basic fact is that ultimately, a human running on a surge of adrenaline is stronger than a potted plant. Several of the spines snapped, breaking off as Kaedrich hacked away at the central stalk in a furious rage. She was screaming senselessly, in pain and anger as well as to bolster herself, her fingers growing slippery with ooze that was spurting out of the stalk.

When she felt the knife slip through the opposite side of the plant, she did not dare believe it. All of the vines convulsed, digging their spines deeper into her in one last burst of self-defense, and then they all collapsed, each and every one of them sagging and falling to either the dresser or the floor. The central stalk toppled, like a tree falling over, while the trunk crumbled to dust and sank into the potted soil.

Kaedrich blinked. She almost laughed—she was taking a breath— when the pot itself rattled, and a new green sprout broke through the surface of the dirt.

There was no time to hesitate. Kaedrich stabbed at the deep, fragrant soil. The knife may be blunt, but the force of her attack was more than enough. An inhuman wail pierced the room as Kaedrich's knife struck something partially solid. She drove it deeper, and then even deeper, as the wail reverberated off of the walls, rattled the windows, raised the hairs on the back of her neck.

And then it just stopped.

Kaedrich stood there, breathing heavily. Her hand was wrapped tight around the handle of her knife, sunk so deep into the potted soil that her fist was partially punched down into it as well.

Slowly, so slowly, Kaedrich uncurled her fingers from the knife handle. Ooze was already pooling up from the surface of the dirt, a gray slime that coated Kaedrich's hand and dripped from her fingers as she gingerly pulled her arm out of the tangle of dead vines. She was covered with the plant's spines, so thick that her arm resembled nothing so much as an upset porcupine. Kaedrich tried not to look too closely as she plucked the spines from her hand, her wrist, her arm. The numb fingers of her other hand kept stumbling over the job, until finally she had to just give up. She'd managed to get maybe a third of the spines out, and certainly the worst of them. Her other arm, however, the one the vine had coiled up and shoved the spines deep underneath her flesh . . . she did not trust herself with that one, not in this state anyway. The end of the vine had snaked all the way up until it was now teased against the base of her neck, and Kaedrich tried not to think about what would have happened if it had continued its path. She plucked the knife out and cut the vine that tethered her to the main knot of dead plant.

Sufficiently untangled, Kaedrich turned her attention to the door. She was not so lucky as to find it magically unlocked, and now a fresh panic threatened to seize her: she did not like how quiet it was in the sitting room. Kaedrich kicked at the door, but of course if *that* was going to work, it would have worked when Praxis tried it from the other side. Kaedrich was tempted to slam her fist against it and call out for Praxis, but what would that really accomplish aside from wasting time? If Praxis was able to answer her, she wouldn't have stopped shouting through it in the first place.

Kaedrich turned away, trying once more to figure out what she had to work with. Somehow, she did not think that her butter knife would help her this time. She glanced at it ruefully. She'd dropped it on the floor once she was done with it, and it sat there now in a puddle of the plant's ooze, smoke curling up from the edge of the pool, and—

Wait. Smoke? Kaedrich rushed over, and sure enough, the ooze was beginning to eat straight through the wooden floorboards. Several droplets nearby had already bored holes straight through, and as she glanced up, she saw more damage, sprinkled on the dresser, wherever the ooze had struck wood.

She did not think, she just did. The pot was lighter in her hand than she expected it to be, but it soared with a satisfying arc through the air, and when it struck the door, the crash was magnificent. Shards of pottery went flying in all directions, dirt sprayed from the point of contact like a brown firework. Thick layers of ooze splashed around the door, already hissing and smoking as they began to chew through the wood.

Unfortunately, as the ooze seeped through and formed holes, its own smoke was not the only one to come pouring through the openings.

IT'S BEEN SAID that one of the more irritating facts of life is that *knowing* you shouldn't panic is not the same thing as *not panicking*. Praxis felt this keenly as the door to Kaedrich's bedroom slammed into her face.

Even before she tried the doorknob, she knew that it would fail. Doors were not magically rigged to slam shut if they were intended to be reopened that easily—but that didn't stop her from trying it anyway, several times, jiggling the handle more fiercely with each attempt. She shouted at it, shouted through it, kicked at it with her free leg and then maneuvered to give her harnessed leg a try. Her hip was screaming at her, but

Praxis ignored it, barreling against the door with everything that she had. Hearing Kaedrich's voice was somewhat of a comfort, but it didn't stop the fact that she was trapped in the room with a plant that Praxis had only ever read about in vague accounts that didn't tell her much, but what they did was never good. It was native to Marcovalla, in one patch of Marcovalla in particular. They were not easy to get your hands on (Praxis should know), and she did not like to contemplate what it meant that someone had managed to get it inside *Kaedrich's bedroom* without Praxis knowing about it.

She hated that someone had gotten through her wards so seamlessly that they hadn't even been broken. She hated that she had allowed her guard to drop, that she hadn't immediately sensed that something was wrong the moment they'd walked through the door. She hated that Kaedrich wasn't moving to the other side of the room, as far from the plant as she could get. She hated the door sitting between them. She hated how useless she sounded, like a damsel in an old story book, calling "Kaedrich! Kaedrich!" as if Praxis was waiting for her knight to come charging in and save her. She even hated Marlick, for no particular reason other than the fact that he was out here with her, and Kaedrich was not.

Praxis was trying to break the hinges off of the door when Kaedrich shrieked. It had been obvious for some time that Kaedrich had been lying, that she was somehow stuck in place, but Praxis had taken what marginal comfort she could in the idea that Kaedrich had continued to sound so level and calm—how bad could it have been, if she was holding it together that well? At the sound of her cry, though, Praxis's efforts turned vicious. She had already tried throwing fire at the door, attempting to blast it away, and that hadn't helped, so for the last few seconds she'd been heating the metal of the hinges. She cut off the flames with a stamp of her fist slamming shut, and threw ice at them next. The sudden change in temperature should have been enough to shatter the metal, even with magical protections, and yet when she started pounding at them with a chair leg that she'd ripped off a moment earlier, the hinges remained stubbornly intact.

She was quickly running out of ideas, and Marlick was being a useless lump—sitting on the couch, his head between his knees as if the whole matter was making him queasy. Praxis threw the chair leg across the apartment just to vent some of her frustrations, and it collided with a delightful crash into a table lamp.

Marlick leaped to his feet. He'd narrowly avoided the hurtled chair leg himself. "Watch it, will—" he started, but the rest of his admonishment was cut off by a series of *pop!-hiss* sounds, a dozen or more of them peppering the entire apartment.

Praxis whirled, as a yellow-gray gas began to creep across the floor like a rolling fog. A large collection of it seemed to be pooling out from underneath the remains of the chair that she had ripped apart, and so Praxis kicked it aside, gritting her teeth against the pain in her hip. She held her breath and flexed her fingers until she could crouch, rummaging through the thickening gas. Her fingers brushed against something and when she picked it up out of the depths, it revealed itself to be a sickly looking little seed pod, pouring out a noxious cloud like a constant, terrible fart.

"We have to get out of here!" Marlick shouted. He was already scrambling over the back of the couch in his haste to reach the apartment door.

Praxis threw the seed pod aside, coughing and waving away the cloud that it had left in front of her face. "Bollocks to that," she said. "We still need to get Kaedrich free."

"Bollocks to *that*!" Marlick snapped. "It's every man for himself!"

He had already reached the door by that point, but of course it had sealed itself up the same way that Kaedrich's bedroom door had. Praxis tried to ignore him as he raced behind her, toward the window, but she couldn't help telling him, "That won't help you. All the exits are probably locked down at this point."

She didn't even want to think about how that was possible, not yet. No doubt she'd flay herself alive over it once the crisis was over and done with, once Kaedrich was safe (she did not dare allow herself to consider that *this* outcome might not come to pass), but for now she at least had enough self-preservation not to waste time wondering how her own careful protections had been so flagrantly circumvented.

It wasn't clear if Marlick didn't understand her, Praxis's accent slipping toward the impenetrable, or if he didn't care for what she said. There was a smack as Marlick tried throwing something at the window, though the glass did not break. Marlick muttered something in frustration as he raced back across the apartment, but Praxis was already concerning herself with just the one door again by this point. She pulled her collar up in front of her face—she probably should have woven an air pocket over her mouth earlier, but by this point all it would serve to do is trap a portion of the gases inside, concentrated for her convenience.

Kaedrich's scream cut through the shut door, deep and primal. Half battle cry and half blood-curdling terror, it ripped a fresh wave of panic from Praxis's chest. Praxis slammed against the door, trying to force it open through sheer strength of will as she shouted for Kaedrich. It was no surprise that Kaedrich couldn't hear her, though, and in the cacophony it was also no surprise that Praxis didn't hear Marlick—not at first.

It was a loud crack that finally caught Praxis's attention. No doubt just the latest of a long line, if what she saw when she turned her head was to be believed.

For Marlick had grabbed an ax from somewhere, and was currently engaged in the laborious process of chopping a hole straight through the wall.

"What the . . . ?" Praxis started, wheezing slightly, and Marlick glanced back but did not even stop.

"You said that the *doors* were sealed." He was shouting through a thick scarf as he heaved the ax back, readying another swing. "You never said we couldn't make another."

The brilliance and absurdity of this struck Praxis dumb for two critical seconds. Marlick kicked into the opening he'd made for himself, the thin outer layer of wall folding underneath his heel. Then Praxis lunged forward, ripping the ax from his grip—but he did not protest, for he was already halfway out of the apartment by that point.

He tumbled out into the hall and did not stop to wait for her, did not come back to help. Praxis let him go without comment, already turning back toward Kaedrich's bedroom. The room was wedged off to the side, the architecture sadly leaving only a small bit of exposed wall beside the door. Praxis did not know if Marlick's trick would even work here, given the space constraints, but it was better than standing around doing nothing.

Unfortunately, her thoughts were starting to grow murky as she stared at the faded wallpaper. She blinked, and the image momentarily split itself into twins, the painted flowers doubling and then coming together once more. She hadn't kept a good hold on the collar over her face, and between her panic and the deep breaths that had preceded her shouting, there was no doubt that she'd gotten several strong lungfuls of the gas that was clouding her vision.

Still, she'd be damned if she ran. Praxis stood there, trying to make her breaths as shallow as possible as she bent over and grasped the handle of the ax in both hands.

The first time that she tried to lift it, it stubbornly remained on the floor, as if its weight had tripled in the brief time since she'd put it down. The second, the handle slipped from her grasp as easily as if it had been coated in butter. When she went to grab it a third time, she ended up missing the handle completely, her hand swiping through empty air. Her fingers were numb and heavy, and the force with which she'd reached for it unbalanced her. She tried to catch herself, but her legs had gone rubbery, and she ended up slumping against the very wall that she'd been planning to attack.

Praxis squeezed her eyes shut, trying to gather strength. Her lungs were burning, her eyes were burning, her nose was burning. Even the wound on her hip was burning. She coughed a couple of times, but it only made things worse; her breath caught in her chest, and she wheezed in a raspy lungful of gases. The effects were hitting her sudden and strong, as if it had taken a minute to reach her bloodstream but now that it *had* . . .

If it took her this badly, this fast, then how long did she have before she collapsed entirely? How long before Kaedrich was trapped in there with no hope of rescue?

Praxis shoved herself off of the wall, but rather than standing resolute and coming back fighting, this served only to tip her the opposite direction. She sagged back, collapsing against the edge of the sitting room couch.

And then there was a loud *crash*, like glass or pottery breaking, and the door in front of her began to hiss and spit. Curls of smoke bored through the wood, snaking up to mingle and mix with the hazy gases of the rest of the apartment. As the holes in the door grew larger, light from the bedroom lamps poured out like some kind of celestial apparition, and then soon a face peeped through the opening, and Praxis nearly cried in relief and joy and despair all wrapped up in one. She collapsed to the floor, the last of the strength draining from her limbs.

The next few minutes she experienced in bits and pieces: Kaedrich hauling her up, dragging her alongside as they headed for the exit Marlick had hacked for them; nearly tumbling down the stairs as gas billowed out behind them into the rest of the building; a glorious burst of fresh night air, which she drew in through heavy, ragged gasps; Praxis's own special whistle for Brex, coming from Kaedrich's lips. Marlick reappeared, helping to maneuver Praxis into a back alley, out of sight. It was hard to tell whether his hands or his voice were shaking worse, as he took in the state of the two of them. It was all that Praxis could do not to shove him away, not to curse him for abandoning Kaedrich like that—if she had more strength, she might have. As it was, it was difficult enough to stay upright, even after being leaned against a brick wall. A nervous chitter came peeling in from above, a heavy thump landing on Praxis's collarbone. Praxis winced as what felt like a tiny needle pierced her neck, Brex settling in immediately in an effort to purge a toxin from her blood. Praxis blinked heavily, trying to clear her thoughts as well as her vision.

"Praxis? Can you hear me? Talk to me," Kaedrich said. Her voice seemed to be coming from somewhere far away, though she was standing right in front of Praxis. She reached out and propped each of Praxis's eyelids open in turn, peering intently for a reaction.

Praxis swatted Kaedrich's hand away. "I'm fi—" she started, slurring her speech, but soon all words failed her as she took in the sight of Kaedrich.

She wanted to look.

She didn't want to look.

Kaedrich shifted, turning so that the arm that was the most covered in a network of vines was farther out of Praxis's line of sight. Her hand, pincushioned with needle-thin white spines, she tucked behind her.

"Are you—?"

"It's not as bad as it looks," Kaedrich said. She cast a glance both ways down the alley; Marlick had stationed himself at one end as a lookout, but that was obviously little comfort to her. She turned back to Praxis, calm and appraising. "If you're feeling up to it, we should keep moving. There's no guarantee that whoever set up that attack isn't still nearby."

Praxis nodded. Her jaw brushed against Brex, still nestled snug into the curve of where her neck met her shoulder. Even just that small movement made Praxis's head spin, but Kaedrich was right, they couldn't stay here. Praxis's thoughts were refocusing now, clicking back into gear one tiny piece at a time. She motioned for Kaedrich to come closer—Praxis still wasn't up to moving about on her own, not yet.

"I just wish I knew where we could go," Kaedrich said as they began to shuffle toward Marlick.

"Oh, don't worry about that," Praxis said. She hadn't even thought about it before she spoke, but of course as soon as the words were leaving her mouth, she knew exactly where they would go. "Turn left," she said, as they reached the end of the alleyway. "And just keep going straight until I say otherwise."

Kaedrich grunted as they maneuvered slowly around the corner. She kept casting nervous glances over her shoulder, even with Marlick now serving as an extra set of eyes. "Where exactly are you taking us?"

"Someplace safe," was the only answer Praxis gave. At least, she hoped that it still was. She could picture the house, the basement, her memory of it perfect after all of these years. She'd left it behind so quickly that she didn't even have a chance to pack—and though she'd left it sealed up and warded against intruders, the truth is that she had no idea what state she'd find it in. There was no reason to bother Kaedrich with any of this, however. At the moment, it was still their best bet.

"I'M SORRY," TULLY SAID, six days after Praxis recovered from her fever in Tjalava. "I don't quite understand. Is this some sort of Yandosian colloquialism?"

Praxis shook her head. "Nope."

She marched through the halls of the Yandosian embassy, her bag in hand (the suitcase she'd left for Tully to carry). For six long days she'd been bedridden as she ate and rested and let the doctors and other wizards fuss over her miraculous recovery, and for six long days she'd been mulling over her dream. The appearance of Moc, the fact that none of it was built on the scaffolding of memory, the pure visceral details that it had contained. The details had been too perfect. A fish had nibbled on her toes, the smell of the ocean made her vaguely sick with regret. The sun had burnt her skin even in the little time that she'd spent there—a faint pink sheen had adorned her cheeks that first morning after she'd awoken. And then, lying there, people hovering all around her with looks of astonishment and relief. She'd survived; where so many others had perished, Praxis Fellows had survived.

Six days was the absolute limit. She was wasting time. Praxis had shooed everyone out first thing in the morning, slipped on her laborer's dress with the medium-high collar (she'd have to purchase something cooler, and quickly, but for now she was still safely entombed in the embassy's artificially cooled walls and she had left all of her clothes from Aul behind her), and trapped her hair into a complicated looking braid that tumbled halfway down her back like a vine ripe with fruit. In spite of—or perhaps because of—her recent brush with death, every inch of her teemed with life. Even the air around her felt charged, and refreshingly sweet. She was a little unstable on her feet, but her weakened muscles ached to be used. She practiced walking around and around her suite for an entire hour, and then when she finally felt somewhat stable she opened the door and she summoned only Tully, refusing anyone else. "Oh good," she said, once he was found and brought to her rooms. She pointed to her suitcase. "Carry that one for me. We're leaving."

"Where to, madam?"

Praxis grinned at him. "Someplace where we can bring someone back from the dead."

"I'm sorry, I don't quite understand. Is this some sort of Yandosian colloquialism?"

"Nope."

Tully was still catching up to her a moment later, both in step and in reasoning. "Perhaps I am just not quite translating correctly, then," he said as they entered the lift. "Because it sounds to me as if you're saying that you plan to reanimate a corpse."

The lift attendant shot them a somewhat nasty glance before he realized his breach of protocol, and exactly who he was looking at. His head spun forward again so fast that it was a wonder he didn't strain his neck.

"I am not planning to reanimate a corpse," Praxis said, to the apparent relief of both Tully and the lift attendant. The gilded doors of the lift rattled a bit as they set down, one floor below where they'd been. Praxis squeezed through the opening before the attendant had even finished pulling back the gate. "I'm talking about a complete restoration of an expired life."

As expected, this left a pregnant pause in her wake, which Praxis ignored as she cut through the embassy lobby. She had timed her "escape" to coincide with the Yandosian ambassador's lunch hour, though no doubt someone had gone running for him by this point. Her doctors had insisted that she stay put for another week, and Praxis still had a lingering cough that sometimes caused a stitch in her chest if she breathed too heavily—like, say, after rushing through a building—but she'd be damned if she sat put any longer.

She squinted as she stood on the front steps, and shaded her eyes against the oppressive Tjalavan daylight. The streets had grown quieter in the few days that she'd been cooped up, the piles of bodies so disordered now that they were more like heaps of dung collecting in the drains.

The door opened up behind her, Tully's measured presence now hovering just off from her shoulder. "Madam, forgive me—I am not aware of what kind of instructions you received on the subject of magical arts, but I'm afraid that you've been sadly misinformed."

"Get me a carriage or something," Praxis said, ignoring him. "I cannot walk in this heat."

There was little traffic on the streets. What few carriages were being drawn were utilitarian by the looks of them, pulled by beasts that Praxis had never seen before, but looked more or less like the drawings of things called "horses" that she'd read about in books. Though she'd always pictured them a little taller, more sleek—these things were as short as dogs, stubby tails flicking in irritation.

Tully had dutifully moved in front of her, watching the traffic meander back and forth across their path. He was wearing a loose-fitting one-piece garment that somewhat resembled a dress, except that it was sewn together along the hem, with only two openings for his feet. The outfit was off-white with swirls of pale blue and yellow colliding like starbursts. The fabric fluttered and snapped against his legs like sails in the wind.

"Anyway, what does a translator know about magic?" Praxis asked, lacing her voice with an obvious sneer. She was still bristling from his doubts, the way that he had dismissed her quest out of hand. Who was he to question her word on, well, anything? A *servant*. That's all that a translator really was, when you got down to it.

Tully turned, his brow drawn low and straight across his face. Without so much as a word, he glanced at the Yandosian embassy looming behind Praxis, its bright white face shining out like a second sun over the crowded rows of buildings that surrounded it. Tully flicked his wrist as if he was throwing something at it; despite herself, Praxis jerked in reflex as a whirl of darkness flew over her head. It collided with the embassy's façade somewhere on the second floor, a billow of thick, black haze blooming out from the point of contact. The haze spread until it stretched all the way across the street, covering them like a thick canopy. Praxis lowered her hand, the sun no longer blaring against her eyes.

She stared at Tully. He stared at her.

"There is no way to revive people from the dead," he said finally.

"According to whom?"

"According to everybody. Every school of thought, every study of magic, every book ever written. Symposiums and colleges of magic and scholars throughout the ages have tried it. It cannot be done."

Praxis nodded. "Well, that's certainly good to know, Tully, and I thank you for your candor. But do you know what that tells *me* about it?"

Tully said nothing.

"It tells me," Praxis went on, "that the discovery of how to do it has yet to be made."

Tully shook his head. "You are a foolish girl."

"And *you*," Praxis said, "are out of line. Now get me a carriage before I pass out from this infernal heat."

*   *   *

SHE WAS NOT LATE, but it was already *too* late. By the time Lanali returned, Praxis Fellows had already come back early and left again. A screech of frustration ripped down Woodland Alley—though nobody thought anything of it, because it was generally assumed to be the sound of a cat in distress.

On the street, a patch of moonlight caught a discarded newspaper. Crumpled white wings stretched over the tightly-locked stones. Lanali stomped on it, grinding the paper underneath the heel of her boot.

Chapter Nineteen

Contrary to what they liked to say, the Royal Society of Magic was not the first of its kind; but it was the most prestigious and, up until recently, the oldest surviving institution for the study of magic in the whole of Durland. Though it had been interrupted, like all other magic endeavors, during the Marcovallans' rule, it had been quick to reestablish itself, preening and pretending as if it had an unbroken history.

To join it required three things: that you be wealthy, that you be male, and that you pass the entrance exam. The first requirement, Praxis had managed with no difficulty. The second, she had bullied her way through, thanks to a combination of diplomatic agreements and the quirk of Yandosian law that viewed all of their wizards as men. The third, she'd had to fight for—they did not want to administer the exam to her, even after grudgingly conceding that, according to a strict reading of the rules, she did *technically* qualify to take it. Despite that, they'd done everything in their power to keep her from passing: changing the appointed time and place no fewer than fifteen times in an effort to make her miss it, nitpicking every act of magic she performed for them, making it the longest and most grueling exam that they could possibly dream up.

They did not formally acknowledge when she aced it. Nor, to Praxis's infinite frustration, did they grant her full membership status, and any protests that she made in the face of this decision were met with contempt. *Technicality be damned, madam,* they'd said to her more than once, for they would not be budged on this point. She had passed, and paid her dues, and so they would allow her to use their facilities, to read their books, to experiment in their labs—off-hours from anyone else's work, with certain areas of both study and location cut off entirely, and under the stipulation that she may not attach the name of their illustrious organization to any work that she would be doing.

This turned out to suit Praxis just fine, especially once she decided to stop respecting the boundaries of where she may and may not go, and it might have worked out amicably on all sides if they hadn't then stolen her research and published it under the name of one of their own; a frustrated, then-middling lord of the Society named Eagleburns.

That was the first strike in their subsequent, private little war, but it was far from the last.

Praxis tried not to think about it too much as she let Kaedrich and Marlick into the basement entrance of Calswell House, though it was difficult to keep such thoughts tucked away where they belonged. This had been the place she'd staked out for herself after that first breach of her security and trust. The Society had a number of buildings to its name, scattered throughout all of Monfort, each one serving different functions. Calswell was treated mostly as a lecture hall in those days, a place where young wizards could get a taste of what might await them should they prove very, very lucky. The basement was disorganized and little-used, and it took them almost an entire month before they even noticed that Praxis had taken it over for her own purposes.

The house was abandoned now, stripped of ownership and sitting around empty until someone decided what should become of it next. Protective wards lay in tattered strips around the sidewalk and the tiny patch of back garden, invisible to the eye but swirling like dead leaves around Praxis's ankles. All but the ones that protected the basement, anyway, which Praxis noted with a tiny swell of pride warming her chest.

Inside was a time capsule. Gas sputtered back into the lamps, and it was as if she had just come home after a long evening out. Her large worktables, filling most of the space, were covered with half-finished experiments; chalkboards held thoughts that she had either forgotten or completed. There was a narrow bed with a sagging mattress in one corner of the room, covered in patchwork blankets and bits of abandoned clothing. A few plates even lay scattered here or there, the remains of her dinners long since eaten by rats or turned to dust.

It was clear from the look on Kaedrich's face that she recognized the signs of Praxis's habitation, though Marlick was moving about and examining things with a much more confused and repulsed expression.

Brex, meanwhile, swept through the door and made his way to the ceiling beams with a happy, familiar chitter.

"Make yourselves at home," Praxis said as she finished coming down the short staircase from the entrance. "Though I'd advise that you use extreme caution in the rest of the house until I've had a chance to secure the building."

"What is this place?" Kaedrich asked.

Praxis made her way over to the narrow bed, shoving some of the debris aside. "It used to belong to the Society." She threw a ratty shirt onto the floor to act as a tarp, and then motioned for Kaedrich to come closer. "Let's get your arms cleaned up."

Though she'd have to face it soon enough, Praxis allowed herself another moment or two to avoid looking at the mess of vines and spines that made one of Kaedrich's arms look like an ivy trellis, and the other like a cactus. She motioned for Kaedrich to sit on the bed, and then Praxis perched beside her. Praxis's hip ached in relief as she sat down, but it really wasn't her own injuries that were concerning her at the moment.

"I'm afraid there's no way for me to make this less painful," Praxis said, turning her attention to the mess of Kaedrich's arms. Her stomach heaved, but she struggled to keep her expression neutral; the last thing that Kaedrich needed was to see how much this distressed her.

Kaedrich half shrugged, lifting the shoulder that wasn't crawling with vines. "I'll manage."

"If it helps, you can grab my leg—I'm not going to feel it anyway."

The offer was out of her mouth before Praxis realized it, and by the time it caught up with her it was too late. She bit her lip, turning her head in what she hoped was a thoughtful and studious way.

There really was no other way to do this than just to begin. Each spine needed to be withdrawn like a needle, each vine carefully unwound. Praxis wasn't that familiar with this particular plant, but she was trusting Brex's unconcern to mean that Kaedrich at least hadn't been poisoned, which left only simple extraction.

Simple, ha. Praxis almost laughed under her breath at the idea. As if this delicate process wasn't going to take hours.

The arm that had been wrapped up was closer to Praxis, so she started there. Marlick quietly excused himself, heading upstairs, as Praxis took the end of the vine that trailed from Kaedrich's wrist.

Kaedrich winced as Praxis started to thread the first spine out. Her other hand twitched—it looked, for a second, like maybe she was going to go ahead and squeeze Praxis's leg after all, but her hand was too covered in the spines not to impale Praxis in the process. Instead, Kaedrich looked at the room, probably to distract herself. Her eyes roved hungrily over all the details that lay scattered about.

"How long did you live here?" Kaedrich asked after a moment.

Praxis didn't answer at first. It wasn't something that she'd really considered before, and she found herself doing some math in her head before she spoke. "Oh, ages. It must have been . . . I don't know, three years? Four? Something like that."

"I had no idea that you'd been in Monfort that long."

"Those were only the last years. I was here a little longer than that, even."

"So what happened?"

Praxis frowned. "You know what happened," she said. She dropped a sickeningly long, blood-coated spine onto the shirt on the floor, and began to unwrap a bit more of the vine. The plant had dug so tightly into Kaedrich's skin that it was leaving wavering lines in a spiral all around her forearm.

"Not really," Kaedrich said. "Not entirely."

"I'm not sure what you think you're missing. I smote the nose off of my patron, they kicked me out. It's not terribly complicated."

"What did he do to deserve it?"

"What makes you think he deserved it?" Praxis asked. She started teasing another spine loose. "Maybe I was just a wild, reckless mess of hysteria, acting out with more power than I deserved to wield. A testimonial to the idea that women can't be trusted with that level of magic."

"Gods, is that really what they said?"

Praxis huffed. "That's what your friend *Bundling* said." Her eyes flicked up, taking in Kaedrich's reaction to this.

Kaedrich's face softened. "I'm sorry. He . . ." She shook her head. "No, there's no defending it. That was wrong of him."

"It doesn't matter," Praxis said, suddenly self-conscious. She turned her attention back to her work. "Ignoring the broader implications about women in general, he might have been right—about me, anyway."

"Praxis. You can't really believe that."

"I didn't, at the time. But you have no idea how much magic I actually have, Kaedrich. Far more than I deserve—more than anyone deserves." Praxis went quiet. She closed her eyes. Her senses were so heightened from the adrenaline of earlier in the night that she could probably do this entire process with her eyes closed; that's how much she had, thrumming through her, constantly ready to burst out at the slightest provocation.

Her eyes were still closed as she threaded out the next spine. She sensed the hitch in Kaedrich's chest, the slight hesitation in her muscles. Kaedrich reached out, resting just her fingertips against Praxis's leg, not close enough to accidentally stab her, just enough. And though Praxis couldn't *feel* it, she was flooded with the impression of Kaedrich, the solid pressure against her fingers, the grubby texture of Praxis's trouser leg.

"Well, if that's true," Kaedrich said, "then I'm glad you're the one that got stuck with all of that extra magic. I wouldn't trust anyone else with it."

"How can you say that, though?" Praxis whispered. She made herself look up now, made herself look Kaedrich directly in the face. Gods, why did she have such a kind face? She really did trust Praxis, wholly and completely, which only made it harder for Praxis to say, "You know what I'm capable of."

She was, perhaps, the only other person who truly *did* know. She had witnessed Praxis's memory of the death of Moc, she had been there when Praxis had lost control and turned a room that they'd been held prisoner in into an inferno. Others, occasionally, found out the depth of Praxis's magic—Kaedrich was the only one that had ever survived it.

Kaedrich nodded slowly. Was she remembering these things, too? If so, Praxis did not know how she could be sitting there so calmly, still unafraid. Still trusting. "I know," Kaedrich said. "But so do you. And I'm not saying that your power isn't dangerous, but . . . there are lines that you don't cross. You could use it for personal gain, and you don't. You could kill anyone that opposes you, and you don't. You *respect* it. You're a good person."

Praxis looked away. Kaedrich's assessment of her burned as hotly as Praxis's cheeks. *A good person.* Had anyone actually ever described Praxis that way before? Intelligent, sure; skilled, absolutely. Gifted, stubborn, arrogant, brave, a royal bitch; all of these she'd heard. She'd even been called beautiful now and again, but *good*?

It wasn't a concept that she was used to associating with herself, and the fact that Kaedrich saw a glimmer of it made her head spin. She tried to shake it off, to dismiss it as nothing more than Kaedrich's generosity of spirit, being kind to someone smaller and weaker than herself. Praxis dropped another of the spines on the floor, and unwrapped the next section of vine. She was only about halfway up Kaedrich's forearm by this point.

The problem is that Kaedrich's words had lodged themselves into Praxis, and she found herself mulling over them as she worked. It was nice to know that someone saw her like that, she guessed, but Praxis knew better than to believe it herself. Just because someone *said* that she was a good person, it did not make it so; only Praxis could make that true, and so far she hadn't done a very good job of it.

But then, no sooner had she thought this than another voice rose up from somewhere deep inside of her: *Well, what if you tried?*

KAEDRICH DIDN'T EVEN want to know what time it was when she finally crawled into bed that night. It had taken ages to pluck each of the long barbs from her hands, Praxis healing up the skin as she went, and even once that was finally done, Praxis had insisted upon sweeping the house before she'd allowed Kaedrich up the stairs. "But Marlick has already been up there for hours," Kaedrich had said, though Praxis only snorted.

"Yes, but that's because it's 'every *man* for himself,'" she said, as she curled her fingers up one careful step at a time. "Stay here until I'm done. You can sleep in the bed, if you're tired."

Kaedrich didn't have enough energy to argue the point, so she waited (though she did not sleep—she did not even trust herself to sit back down on the mattress). When Praxis was finally finished, she led Kaedrich upstairs herself, showing her to an empty bedroom. It was so late by then that Kaedrich hadn't bothered to look around, nor to unbind her chest, nor even to take off her shoes; she collapsed face-first into the mattress the instant Praxis shut the door behind her, and slept like the dead.

Until searing pain began to stab at her arms.

Kaedrich woke up midflail, already lashing out at her perception of an attack. Her arms felt as if they were being ripped apart again, as if she hadn't yet escaped the plant. She threw herself from the bed, already slashing her hand through the air, but it collided with nothing. There was nothing to fight against, because she was alone; heavy moonlight spilled in through the parted curtain, and there was no one else in the room.

But *something* had clearly happened, because when she glanced at her arms, fresh blood was already seeping into her shirtsleeves. Her hands were riddled with punctures and gashes.

She raced back to the bed, ripping the sheets off. It was more cloth than she needed, and the bundle was unwieldy as she wrapped it in a tangle around her wounds to stanch the bleeding. In her panic, she had thought that the gashes ran up and down the full length of both of her arms, but now that she was taking the time to deal with it, she saw that only one arm was completely covered, while the damage to the other was largely centered around her fist and forearm. And this is when enough of the fog of sleep lifted, and she realized that the cuts and punctures that she was tending to now were in the exact same pattern as the ones that Praxis had healed earlier that night. It was as if Praxis's magic hadn't taken effect, or rather that it *had*, but only temporarily. But Kaedrich had never known Praxis's healing spells not to work before, or—no, that wasn't entirely true. There was a single bullet, and a vicious tear that was probably still healing on Praxis's hip.

So at least this might help explain one mystery, though Kaedrich took little comfort in it now. Pain was still screaming in her arms, piercing straight down to the bone. She dashed out of the room, fumbling for a moment with the doorknob as she tried to keep her arms bundled up in the sheets.

Praxis had stayed in the basement, amid the remnants of her former life. She was already awake and scrambling to get up as Kaedrich burst in, almost as if she'd known that Kaedrich was coming—but then, Kaedrich realized, she probably *had*.

"What's wrong, what's happened?" Praxis asked. She threw a ring of flames toward the ceiling to light the room, not wanting to take the time to find a proper lamp. She was up and on her feet, more or less, though leaning heavily against the worktable nearest to her narrow bed. The bits and pieces of her leg brace and controls lay on a nearby chair.

Kaedrich drew to a halt, embarrassed. She'd panicked and had gone running for Praxis, but now that she stood there in front of her, it seemed foolish, the threat smaller and sillier than it had been a moment ago. She felt like a child, fleeing into the arms of her parent after waking up from a nightmare. Praxis even kind of looked the part, her face still bleary from sleep, dressed in a nightgown that she must have left behind here years ago. Kaedrich flinched.

"I . . . nothing, I'm sorry. I didn't mean to scare you—*wake* you. I didn't mean to wake you. Or scare you. I—"

"Gods, Kaedrich, your arms!"

Kaedrich glanced down. The sheets hadn't exactly stayed tidy in her haste, and now blood was trailing from her shoulder down onto the pristine white, mingling with streaks already there.

"Get *over* here," Praxis said, and Kaedrich did not hesitate. She was grateful at least that Praxis hadn't asked her to sit down on the bed again.

Praxis was leaning her hip against the worktable, temporarily steadied, and she pulled the sheets away from Kaedrich's battered arms and dropped them to the floor.

Earlier that night, healing up Kaedrich's wounds as she worked, Praxis had merely slid her fingers up past the cuff of Kaedrich's shirt, or prodded through the tears in the fabric. Once they'd freed enough of the fabric from the spines skewering it in place, Kaedrich was able to remove her suit jacket; and when they'd gotten to her shoulder, Praxis had Kaedrich open her shirt enough to slip her arm out. But by that point it was so late that Kaedrich was too exhausted to be embarrassed, and besides that, her undershirt provided enough modesty that it wasn't exactly like there was an *issue*.

But now it was almost morning, and even as she stepped up beside Praxis, Kaedrich was already growing wary about the prospect of repeating the process. And so, almost as if she could read the jittery thoughts in Kaedrich's mind, Praxis took a different approach, and ripped the entire sleeve off of the arm that carried the worst of the injuries.

"Hey—!"

"You'll need a new one, anyway," Praxis said. Her hands were already sliding over Kaedrich's arm, her fingertips first warming and then cooling as they traced across her skin. Her whole face was drawn inward in concentration and concern, working as quickly as Kaedrich's wounds allowed. Kaedrich felt the familiar tug of her skin, softening and stretching under the command of Praxis's magic. Warmth spread through her, deeper than the early effects of the healing spell. She found herself watching the little furrows between Praxis's brow, the set line of her mouth. Active magic distracted Praxis, which in turn gave Kaedrich one of the only times that she could get away with openly studying Praxis's face. As a result, Kaedrich was developing a somewhat unhealthy relationship with healing magic—it was terrible to need it, a clear result of having gotten into trouble that she should have tried to avoid, and yet . . .

Kaedrich made herself look away. This was hardly appropriate, and so she tried to fix her attention on the room at large. Tried to ignore the sting of her arms, the blissful relief that replaced it as Praxis worked her way along. Besides, it's not like the room wasn't fascinating; each table, each shelf, each corner held a treasure trove of insight into a slice of Praxis's past. Everything from the smattering of notes and diagrams, to the bits and pieces of clothing still left strewn over the furniture, was an insight into the woman she'd been before they met. There was even, Kaedrich spotted, a tiny collection of picture frames in the far corner of the room—too distant for her to make out the details, alas—though now she was determined to find her way over there at some point, have a look for herself. She had to wonder: how quickly had Praxis been forced to leave this place if she'd abandoned them for anyone to find? There had to be more to the story than what Praxis had told her last night, but somehow Kaedrich didn't think that further prying would yield better results.

"We're going to need to keep an eye on this," Praxis said eventually. She was still looking at her work, still healing up each gash and puncture with meticulous concentration. "I don't know what properties of that plant caused these to reopen, but I can't guarantee that it won't happen again."

"That's going to be somewhat problematic," Kaedrich said. When Praxis glanced up briefly, confusion written on her face, Kaedrich added, "What, are you planning to follow me to work and classes?"

Praxis frowned. "Don't be ridiculous. You're staying here."

"No, I'm not."

A tiny flare of heat passed from Praxis's fingers to Kaedrich's arm. Hotter than the warmth of a healing spell, more a flash of irritation made manifest. Praxis shook her shoulders as if trying to shrug off an unpleasant thought. "We don't have to talk about this now."

"We might as well," Kaedrich said, "because I'm not going to change my mind. I won't hole up somewhere and stop living my life just because someone attacked my apartment. I have obligations."

"Oh, so you plan to just *carry on* as normal then?" Praxis sniped.

"Yeah."

Praxis frowned. "That's the stupidest thing I've ever heard."

"It's what you would do, if the situations were reversed."

"Which is why I know how stupid it is." Praxis glanced up sharply. "Kaedrich, if someone is after you—"

"They're not after me," Kaedrich said. "They're after you, and you know it. I was just in the way."

Praxis's mouth tightened, but she did not immediately argue the point. Kaedrich pressed on.

"Besides, if we stay here, don't you think that's just going to double the chances that someone finds us? I can't be seen walking in and out of here all the time. It's not safe for you."

"All the more reason for you to stay put."

"I *can't*." Kaedrich shook her head. "I don't expect you to understand, but I have a job. I have lessons that I can't just walk out of. I'm already falling behind on my studies just spending so much time—" She drew short, just before she actually *said* "spending so much time with you." She didn't want to make it sound like she was blaming Praxis. "The point is that I have a life here. You said so yourself. That means that I have places that I need to be, and things that I need to do. Ignoring it is not an option."

Praxis was unusually quiet in the wake of this. Her fingers still traced along the path of Kaedrich's injuries, sealing them up underneath her touch, but her thoughts seemed divided now, warring expressions twitching the corners of her mouth and eyes.

"*You* should stay here," Kaedrich continued. "Lie low for a while. You have plenty to do, trying to sort out what everything that we've learned means. Unless you have a better plan of what to do next," she added, raising her voice to stop Praxis's argument before it even started.

Praxis's signature scowl, so familiar, was more than answer enough.

There was nothing but silence for a few minutes. Plenty of protests seemed to run through Praxis's mind as she finished healing Kaedrich's arms, but none of them got far enough to be said aloud.

Her fingers lingered as she finally reached the last of Kaedrich's cuts. Or maybe Kaedrich had just imagined it—that was certainly possible. Praxis retreated, looking away as she pushed herself off of the table and hopped around until she was standing on the opposite side of it. A wide swath of scattered lab equipment stood between them, and Praxis seemed to be surveying them as if figuring out what would be useful to her now, with this latest set of mysteries.

Kaedrich ran her own hands over her arms—one bare, one with the sleeve pushed halfway up. Her skin was smooth and cold now, a tautness stiffening her range of motion. "Thank you," she said.

Praxis ignored this. She was already brushing aside a new workspace, beakers clinking together as she swept them off to one corner of the table.

Kaedrich turned to go.

"What are you going to tell them, then?" Praxis asked suddenly. "I mean . . . if I'm not staying with you anymore . . ."

Heat flooded Kaedrich's cheeks. Of course: their cover story had been that they'd just become a couple.

"I guess I'll just say that it didn't work out," Kaedrich said. She tried to tell herself that it didn't hurt to say it, that she was relieved not to have to keep up such uncomfortable pretenses. She made herself look back at Praxis. "It's the easiest explanation."

Praxis stared at her for a second. Her expression was painfully blank, a perfect mask of impenetrability. She gave Kaedrich a stiff nod as she returned to her work. "Fine. I suppose that works as well as anything," she said, and then there was nothing more to say on the matter.

Kaedrich went upstairs.

Chapter Twenty

Even half-drunk and all-terrified, Bundling managed to keep his wits about him. *Your mother was right,* he thought to himself, *You really should have become a detective instead.* It had been his oldest dream, his dearest wish—but he could never pass the physical exams to become a police officer, and before he could afford a place to set himself up as a private investigator, his mother had gotten sick. He'd needed money, he'd needed it fast, and he had a decent enough way with words. Bundling had told himself that he'd only stick it out at the newspaper long enough to save up for his own office, but people have a tendency to *settle* in whatever is familiar. As soon as Bundling's ass had hit the chair in the Daily Witness for the first time, he knew—he *knew*—that he would never get up again. Not for good, anyway.

Oh, but look at him! Such wasted talent. What other reporter would have maintained his cool, as he was drugged, as he was slumped unceremoniously over someone's shoulder, as he was tossed into the back of a cart that jostled hard underneath him, his head clonking against the wood. *I am a rock,* he thought, his head muddied, as they lurched to a stop. How long had they been traveling? It felt important that Bundling figure that out, so that he could track down this place again, once he had made his daring escape.

Because he was going to escape. Of course he was. He would let his captors keep him just long enough, until Bundling had all of their secrets, and then he would burst out of this place, this place that smelled of stale piss and hay fields. And then he would take them down. Bundling's thoughts were clearing a little by this point, the drug wearing off, and with each new sense kicking back into high alert, he tried to pay extra attention. His eyes were covered, his tongue thick, but he could listen. He listened to the sounds of the countryside, the city far behind them. He listened as heavy boots clomped him up a set of stairs, one, two, seven, twelve steps on the staircase. He smelled: the sweat of the man carrying him, a thick application of cologne only doing so much to mask the time it had been since his last bath. Someone was cooking beans, somewhere nearby, the smell drifting away the farther up the stairs they got. He felt the surprisingly soft touch of a blanket as he was thrown against something—a bed?—and then the blindfold was yanked from his head. Bundling blinked, and squinted, and blinked again. It was dark, and they had taken his glasses. The world blurred as it grew away from him. A faint slice of moonlight, coming in from a tiny window. A wooden chair, casting shadows across a bare floor. Bundling saw someone retreating through a door, and heard the heavy *thunk* as it closed, the click and clink of several locks.

He sat up, still somewhat dazed. His hands were bound behind him, his ankles lashed painfully together. But that was okay. He would figure this out. He got to his feet, hopping across to the window. An empty field, he didn't need his glasses to know that much. A full moon overhead. The stars had disappeared, the sky turned gray with the first streaks of morning. No sign of anything, or anybody else, just the world stretching out into nothing. A blob that might have been a tree in the distance.

Panic scuttled up the back of his throat. Bundling tried to swallow it down, but it sat lodged where it was, like the lump of a bad cold. *This is where I'm going to die,* he thought, and immediately tried to unthink it. *No,* he told himself firmly. *No, this is a temporary setback. You are Erstan Bundling. You will escape. You will bring this whole thing to print, and then everyone will know.*

He turned away from the window. The smallest details, he told himself. Look at everything.

Remember everything.

* * *

IN THE MORNING, they still didn't speak to each other. Kaedrich had fallen back asleep, and woke up again without incident. Her arms were sore, traces of raw pink running along each of the lines that Praxis had healed, but they had not reopened. She left without comment.

Kaedrich wore her tattered suit jacket back to the apartment. She knew that she looked frightful, but what was there to be done? The jacket, even with bloodstains and rips all up and down the length of both arms, was still the marginally better alternative to being seen in the state of semi-undress that a man without a coat was viewed as. Especially with one sleeve of her shirt missing, she'd have been taken as a barbarian for sure. At least this just indicated that she'd been in a scuffle of some type—and she was hoping that the underlying quality of her ruined clothes would grant her actions a touch of heroism, rather than signaling her as someone that had stumbled into a senseless brawl.

She held her head high, walking side by side with Marlick down the city streets. He, at least, had fared all right, his clothes only rumpled from being slept in. She tried to ignore the raised eyebrows that were rippling out from them as they went, just like she tried to ignore the uncomfortable chill breezing through the holes of her sleeve.

Her arms itched.

She missed Praxis already.

Which was silly, because it's not like Praxis was actually *going* any-where, and it wasn't as if they had *actually* broken up—because in order to end a relationship, you had to first be in one. That was kind of the whole point.

This logic did nothing, however, to clear the weight that had locked around her chest, that made it hard to breathe, that closed up her throat. But maybe it was better for her to appear unsettled, maybe that would help to sell their story to Marlick and the rest of them. After all, they'd all bought into the lie; they wouldn't just accept that Kaedrich had decided to walk away without being at least a *little* upset about it, would they?

They were almost all the way home before Marlick broke the silence hanging over them. "Listen, I'm . . . I'm sorry."

A sour knot twisted in Kaedrich's stomach. *Here we go.* "It's fine," Kaedrich said. She was already sweating, afraid that she wouldn't play out her part well enough. How much heartbreak was expected from her? How cold was she supposed to be? How soon was too soon to "get over" Praxis? She had little enough experience listening to women cry about men, but how was it supposed to work from the other side? Her friends hadn't exactly been helpful in that regard—Lucan was the only one of them that had gotten involved while Kaedrich had known them, and of course his manner tended to run toward, as he called it, "one and done."

There was no denying it: Kaedrich was on her own here.

"I mean," she continued with a shrug, "it's not like things were ever going to work out with her long-term. Not that I was looking for that. But, you know. If things were reversed and I had been wealthier than she was, *maybe* we would have been accepted, but there's no way . . ." Kaedrich scowled as she trailed off. She hadn't even meant to venture down that thought path, but now that she had, she realized just how true it was. The fact that Kaedrich was a woman, they would hide—the fact that she was *black* . . .

Marlick frowned. "Um. I didn't—"

"Anyway, it doesn't matter," Kaedrich said. She quickened her pace, her mind still whirring angrily. "I don't care. I had my fun with her, and now it's over."

"Okay, but that . . . wasn't what I was saying 'sorry' for."

Kaedrich's cheeks flushed. "Oh."

"Though I think maybe you're not quite as fine with this as you like to say that you are," Marlick said. "If that was any indication."

Blast. Kaedrich's flush deepened, and she turned her face away so that she didn't have to look at him. Was there even a point in denying it? She doubted that Marlick would believe her if she tried, and besides . . . she actually *wasn't* fine with it. The certainty of this struck her like a fist to the gut. It didn't matter if it had all been a lie. (It *had* all been a lie, hadn't it?)

"Fine, so . . . what did you want to tell me, then?" Kaedrich said, trying miserably to change the subject.

(Hadn't it?)

Marlick didn't answer immediately. They stepped aside, making room for a group of protesters on their way toward the center of the city; a cluster of large signs were leaned back against the shoulders of almost every single one of them, and Kaedrich tried her best not to read their slogans or hear their excited chatter, not today.

When they had finally passed, Marlick sighed. "I'm sorry, for—for what happened at the apartment."

He was unusually jittery as he said it, though he had been much the same the night before and all of that morning. Kaedrich couldn't exactly blame him for being shaken up. If anything, Marlick's reaction to the attack was the healthy and appropriate response; Kaedrich didn't really want to think about what it meant that she *wasn't* more upset about this.

"Marlick, you have nothing to apologize for. Besides, it was you that broke through the wall, wasn't it?" While removing all of the plant matter from Kaedrich's arm, Praxis had relayed, more or less, what had happened in the rest of the apartment.

Marlick shrugged. "Yeah . . ."

"Then you *saved* us. Think nothing further of it."

"But—"

"No," Kaedrich said. "Listen, take it from me: you can drive yourself crazy remembering these kinds of situations, trying to figure out if there was anything that you could have done *better*. You dealt with it at the time in the best way that you could, and we're all fine and healthy in the aftermath. That's all that you need to concern yourself with."

Kaedrich fell into silence, shaking her head. A few short years ago, she would have been the kind of person that needed this type of reassurance. She pictured her younger self, terrified of being branded a coward but more terrified of danger. That Kaedriella wouldn't have recognized herself now.

Marlick did not immediately argue with Kaedrich's logic, but nor did he seem particularly convinced. It didn't matter, though—he would have to deal with it in his own way, in his own time. Besides, they were almost back.

They rounded a corner, the last corner before home. The building came into view in the distance. It looked so ordinary in the fresh light of day, as if nothing strange or dangerous had ever happened within its walls. The disconnect between Kaedrich's memories and the tranquil sight before her was jarring. She quickened her pace, eager to get in and assess the damage, to begin picking the pieces back up and putting some order back into her life.

It seemed that their landlady, however, had other ideas.

How, exactly, she had known that Kaedrich and Marlick were coming was a mystery. She was already waiting for them, sitting on the top step, just outside of their door and the splintered hole that Marlick had chopped through the wall. Her arms were crossed as they rested on her knees, and she drew her brow together as the two of them tromped up the stairs.

Kaedrich saw her first, came to a sudden stop. Marlick bumped into Kaedrich from the step below, muttering a complaint until he looked past Kaedrich and saw what the problem was.

"Shit," Marlick muttered.

"'Shit,' indeed, Mr. Darbury," said Mrs. Davish. She nodded at

Kaedrich. "Mr. Mannly. I don't suppose that either of you would care to account for what happened here last night?"

Kaedrich and Marlick glanced at each other, then back to Mrs. Davish.

"I . . . ," Kaedrich started.

"It was . . . ," Marlick added.

Then they both fell into awkward silence.

It wasn't that they couldn't attempt to explain the situation to Mrs. Davish. She was, in Kaedrich's experience, a generally kind and reasonable woman, not hung up too much on social convention and what the neighbors were going to think. She also had the impressive track record of being once widowed and twice divorced, the latter of which was not an easy accomplishment for a woman. In short, she was exactly the kind of person that you would want to confess the details of an attack to—except that, when they'd first gotten the apartment, it had taken some effort to convince her that having two students of the Falconridge Academy of Arms in her building wasn't going to bring trouble along with it. Reputations preceded them, stories preceded them, but Mrs. Davish had agreed to ignore all the warnings that she would no doubt get from concerned friends and family, and took a chance on them.

The look on her face now made it clear that Marlick and Kaedrich had not fulfilled their end of the arrangement.

Silently, Mrs. Davish held out a single piece of paper, the end drooping so that the number at the bottom of a long tally was clearly visible. "This is what the repairs are going to cost," she said. "I expect the two of you to cover it. Without complaint."

Kaedrich took the paper from her, still staring at the final total. It was well over what she had saved up, far more than she'd have ever dreamed that such repairs would cost. She fleetingly considered asking if Mrs. Davish had gotten a second opinion, but one look at her landlady shut those thoughts up tight. Kaedrich pressed her lips into a firm line, nodding once in acknowledgment.

Mrs. Davish nodded. "Good." She got to her feet, brushing off her long skirt with the backs of her hands. "Oh, and I'm sorry to say this, but I'm afraid that I'm going to have to insist that the two of you leave my building. By the end of the day."

Kaedrich's gaze fell to her feet, but Marlick's head jerked up. "You can't do that!"

The trouble, of course, is that she could. Mrs. Davish held up a single finger, silencing Marlick's continued protests as efficiently as if she'd cut them with a blade. "It's either you, or the tenants beneath you—they refused to stay in the same building, and I can't blame them. Frankly, you brought this on yourselves." Her face softened. "I am sorry. You're good boys. I just can't have this sort of thing happening under my roof."

She squeezed by them, patting Kaedrich on the shoulder as she went.

"End of the day," she repeated, as she disappeared down the steps.

THE DIFFERENT CITIES of Tjalava were connected not through a series of roads, but rails.

Young Praxis had never been on a train before, and admittedly she was kind of intimidated by the prospect. She stood to the back of the waiting crowd as Tully made arrangement for their passage, trying to imagine what it would be like. She told herself that there was nothing to be afraid of; but Praxis had read about trains. She'd read about derailings, and accidental collisions when two were set upon the same track in opposite directions. She'd read one account of a fiery explosion from an overheated engine striking some obstacle that had fallen across the tracks—she could not recall at the time what the circumstances were, but she remembered the drawing that had accompanied the account, flames as if from the deepest hell springing up to engulf the train, plumes of smoke trailing up and up forever. The illustrator had used so many crosshatched little lines to create the smoke that it nearly blacked out the upper portion of the page. Once, she'd even read an adventure novel all the way from Durland, which featured gangs of hijackers and bandits, so many wild unsavory types running about in the open plains that gunmen had to position themselves all along the forward compartment to ward them off.

It turns out that she had nothing to worry about, though, except for the banal complaints of a lack of privacy and "appropriate" accommodations for a woman of her status. Instead of seats, the trains had nothing but rows and rows of slabs stacked two high along the walls, lined with padding and blankets. These served double-duty as both benches and beds, and staking claim to the expanses of territory was a complicated social dance that Praxis did not understand the rules to. She ended up wedged into a narrow gap between two large and boisterous families, Tully somewhere across the way and about a dozen feet down the train car. Praxis drew her feet up onto the bunk with her, hugging her knees to her chest. She did not even have enough space to lie down.

Not that she was going to get much sleep, even if there was more room. Nobody seemed the slightest bit interested in sleeping. Games, stories, and music filled the car, everyone joining in to whatever interested them irrespective of what group of travelers they were originally with. At one point, at the front of the car, someone even started a small magical fire near a window that they'd propped open, and began cooking up whatever provisions people had stowed away in their luggage. The smells of roasted meat, seared fruit, and a thousand tangy spices that Praxis had never encountered before embedded themselves into her clothes and hair. Tully threw himself into the fray, laughing and eating and singing along with the best of them, but Praxis kept scowling and shaking her head whenever anyone tried to draw her in.

Meanwhile, day turned to night, and night turned back into day, and the jungle slipped by outside of their windows. They had to stop a couple of times, to beat back the wilderness that had crawled too thickly over the tracks. Rainstorms, Tully explained, had an almost explosive effect on the local flora, far too sudden for regular line maintenance to take care of the problem. "Nature will always win out, in the end," he said with a shrug when Praxis complained about it, but what did she really know about nature? The only plants that she'd known as a child were potted.

People used the stops to jump out and stretch their legs—and once, when there was a river within sight, about half of the train spilled out and stripped down to their undergarments, splashing and shrieking in delight at the respite from the heavy heat. Praxis watched through the windows, sweating in the tin can of the train car. A young Tjalavan woman brought her back a cloth soaked in the cool water of the spring-fed river, and Praxis stared at it, unsure, until the woman motioned more forcefully for her to take it. Tully hadn't returned yet, and so Praxis couldn't have said a proper "thank you" even if she wanted to; she tried to smile instead, but it came out as more of a grimace and the woman laughed brightly at her as she walked away.

They had to switch trains four times to reach their destination. Praxis emerged feeling much like the clothing stuffed into the bottom of her suitcase: battered and twisted up, smelling more strongly of sweat than she wanted to admit. She had her hair wound into a tight braid that she'd wrapped around her head and wove in place with a stray bit of ribbon, but loose tendrils were falling down against her neck like wet snakes. Praxis swatted at them, muttering that she should just cut it all off and be done with it—but her complaints stopped dead in their tracks as she looked up.

She'd already seen a couple of Tjalavan interior cities as they passed from train to train, of course, and so she had *some* idea what to expect. But admittedly, she'd always been so distracted jogging to keep up with Tully, her heart racing from both exertion and the fear of missing their next train, that she'd barely glanced at the marvel of architecture and engineering around her.

It was nothing like the coastal city, the welcoming port that was designed to both withstand hurricanes and set tourists at ease—this was Tjalava proper. Massive stone pillars, at least as wide as a mine shaft, sprang up from the jungle floor like tree trunks and spread as far as the eye could see. They shot through the canopy, the city they were supporting hidden above the leafy roof. Lifts bolted to the side of the pillars were carrying up people, cargo, animals—anything that the city needed, really, a constant flow of traffic. The lifts were eerie in their silence, and Praxis wondered aloud at the type of magic being used to power them, but Tully had only laughed and said that there was no magic, just something that he called "electricity."

Tully was beaming at her when she finally drew her attention away. "What?"

"Science," Tully said, still grinning. He started to make his way through the crowd, walking backwards so that he could keep an eye on Praxis. "See, you're always complaining—but I knew that you'd like it once you got here. Come on. There's so much more."

Praxis hurried to keep up. Tully led her through the foot traffic, past sellers' carts loaded down with silks and books and jewelry, past what looked like a preacher of some sort as he led a small group in hummed prayer, hanging back as they allowed a small caravan of caged up animals to cross their path. Lampposts were set up at regular intervals, bright white lights helping penetrate the unnatural darkness of the city's canopy. Praxis boggled at all of it, bumping into carts and people as her attention strayed more than once. "This way!" Tully called back, waving her forward when she got distracted looking at a pack of small animals being led by on a multi-ended leash.

He was waiting for her at the base of one of the lifts. It already appeared to be full to Praxis's estimation, and yet when she met up with him, he motioned for her to get inside. Praxis's eyes widened, and she tried to mutter apologies as people miraculously wedged farther into the corners. There was no personal space, though Praxis was getting sadly used to that, after the trains. Tully darted in with her, literally pressing into her side as she held herself rigid to avoid doing the same to the man next to her.

Tully chatted happily with the people around him, as if this was nothing. The lift gave an alarming lurch as it set off, and Praxis only just avoided shrieking in alarm. She hugged her bag against her chest, trying to look up more often than down, though either option was giving her a wave of vertigo.

Praxis could never remember being so happy as she was when the lift finally jerked to a stop and the gate sprang open. She leaped from the pack of other passengers, shoving them out of the way as she broke free. At the moment, she didn't care that the sun was pounding down on her with unrelenting cruelty, that it was so bright she could barely see. She was just grateful for space, and air, and the safety of something solid underneath her feet.

Tully caught up with her a moment later, resting his hand lightly on her elbow. "Managing all right, there, miss?"

Praxis waved off his concern, though she wasn't entirely sure that she *was* all right. She shaded her eyes and squinted, trying to get a sense of her surroundings, but all that she could really make out was the impression of being encircled by low-slung stone buildings.

"Come on," Tully said, guiding her gently forward. "I think before we settle in, there's one stop that we should make first."

"I don't understand," Praxis said a few moments later, as Tully guided her down a labyrinthine path of winding bridges and sweeping arches. A network of cables ran from building to building, strung along like clotheslines. "How do you know this place so well? It's my understanding the ambassador's work keeps him primarily at the capital and the coast."

Tully nodded. "That's true. But I do get vacations, once in a while. And when I do, I always come home."

"But . . . Syll is—"

"*Not* my home," Tully said. He laughed under his breath. "My grandparents are from Syll. Don't tell me that you think that everyone who looks the same all come from the same place."

"Of course not," Praxis said quickly, because it felt like the right thing to say. Though, in truth, it had never occurred to her *not* to assume that. She looked around now, still squinting in the sunlight, suddenly wondering if any of the uniformly dark faces around her originated from someplace else.

Abruptly, Tully came to a stop in front of a low, wide building on the edge of the city. Behind it lay nothing but a carpet of rolling greenery, the jungle as seen from above.

The building turned out to be a shop, and Praxis couldn't figure out why he had insisted on dragging her here. Surely finding their hotel was a higher priority? It wasn't even as if the shop sold particularly useful items: it appeared to be a glassblower's workshop, long airy shelves lined with vases and sculptures as if laid out for a gallery show. A few cabinets in the corner housed stemware and drinking glasses, and a row of crystal bells stood near the door, but other than that . . .

Tully made a straight line for the shopkeeper. She was an older woman with a broad, smiling face, and she exchanged rapid-fire greetings with Tully. He clearly knew exactly what he was looking for, and the woman nodded easily at his request. She glanced at Praxis, gave a single belly laugh that shook all of the wrinkles of her face and arms, and then ducked underneath a counter to retrieve something.

"Is this really necessary?" Praxis asked. She glanced at a nearby sculpture, what appeared to be a stylistic representation of a naked woman holding up a sphere.

"Trust me," Tully said as he accepted a small wooden box from the shopkeeper. He asked her a quick question in Tjalavan, but the woman only laughed again, shaking her head. She pointed at Praxis, and made another fast remark to Tully, who nodded and placed his hand gratefully on his chest. *"Ploya,"* he said to her.

Praxis sighed. "Are we done? I really didn't come here to sightsee."

"Obviously not, because you're not going to be seeing much of anything with those spoiled eyes of yours."

"Excuse me?"

"Not without this, anyway," Tully said, as he held the box out to her. "The ambassador finds these most helpful."

"I see," Praxis said, though she didn't really. Not until she opened the box, because there, nestled on a padded bed, was a pair of spectacles with lenses tinted so deeply that they were almost black.

"For the sun," Tully added, when it was not immediately apparent.

"Oh . . . oh! Really?" Praxis glanced up, not quite sure yet if somehow this was part of an elaborate joke. A year she had spent in Aul, baking underneath the tropical sun, squinting so hard that sometimes she actually had to shut her eyes against it. Nobody had ever suggested that there might be a simple, tidy solution to her problem.

When Tully offered no hint of mirth at having gotten her, however, Praxis drew the spectacles out, handing the box back to him. She walked to the door and slid them in place, bracing herself just in case it still proved to be a falsehood. She took a deep breath, stepped outside.

The world spread out around her, full and more comfortably present than anything that she'd seen since leaving Yandosia. Pots of flowers glowed vibrant pink and blue and yellow, insects with colorful wings flitting from bloom to bloom; the red-orange roofs of the buildings were warm and friendly; the swishing wrap dresses of passersby no longer hurt to look at. Nothing, in fact, hurt to look at, and Praxis's throat closed up in a flood of sudden gratitude.

"You're welcome," Tully said, squeezing past her and out the door of the shop.

Praxis cleared her throat. "Well," she said. "I guess I'll keep you around for a little while longer."

Tully rolled his eyes. Praxis could actually see that Tully rolled his eyes.

He started off again, striding comfortably into the sea of bodies. "This way, miss."

Chapter Twenty-One

MARLICK PACED THE length of the antechamber to the director's office, back and forth from one door all the way to the other. The last time that he had been in there was when this whole mess had started. Marlick kept trying not to think about it, and kept failing.

He should have known that something was wrong with the situation from the very beginning, but he'd been so chuffed about having been selected for this, his "special" assignment, for being asked by the director personally, that he'd been blinded to the potential dangers. And Director Tarlock had painted it as such a simple thing, no problem really. He'd shown Marlick into his office, drawn out the visitor's chair and patted the seat. Once Marlick had settled, Director Tarlock himself perched casually on the edge of his desk. He explained that, as part of the preparations for the upcoming Trials, they were going to be performing certain tests. These were to remain absolutely secret, for they dealt with loyalty and fortitude, and any foreknowledge of what was to come would ruin the results. Did he understand?

Of course Marlick understood; he understood that the director was trusting him, and him alone, with something important, and that Marlick must not let him down. He understood that this was his chance to prove to Director Tarlock that he was not just some stupid kid, a soft, know-nothing son of an antiques dealer, here on a whim before swearing off violence forever.

The assignment itself couldn't have been easier: Director Tarlock was going to send someone to the apartment that evening, an Aul merchant, who was going to make certain preparations for the upcoming test. All Marlick had to do was let this person in at the appointed hour, and then make sure no one returned to the apartment until the work was completed.

Marlick's trepidation started as soon as he saw her. There was something cold and sharp about the merchant's eyes, a vicious hunger that only increased as she stepped inside and took a long look around. She didn't look like a merchant, though her clothes did fit the broad category. In her arms was a nasty-looking potted plant. She did not answer any of Marlick's questions, or indeed even speak to him at all, only glared at him until he left.

Marlick had run to catch up with Praxis and Kaedrich on their way to the pub after that, already feeling queasy.

Now he turned, and began to pace back the other direction once more. The director's secretary sighed and rolled his eyes. He was an even more thickset man than Marlick; he barely fit into his tailored suit, and he adjusted the pinch of his trousers as he sat waiting. "Are you sure you wouldn't prefer to take a seat yourself, Mr. Darbury?"

Perhaps Marlick should have, if for no other reason than to avoid pissing off the secretary, but he was too jittery to sit. He'd barely slept the night before, barely eaten, barely stopped shaking. Marlick had finally given up on sleep around three in the morning, curling himself in supplication on the floor and begging Perlandra not to send him to the Shadowlands for his transgressions. This may or may not technically have been the right form of prayer—for all of his father's wishes, Marlick really wasn't that well-versed in the traditions of his faith—but if sincerity counted for anything, then it would do the job. His guilt burned like acid through his guts. Walking back to the apartment with Kaedrich in the morning had been an exercise in self-restraint of monumental proportions, and he had no strength left to continue forcing a veneer of calm.

Thankfully, it was at this point that Director Tarlock strolled in.

He barely paid Marlick any mind, stopping to confer with his secretary for a moment, accepting a file that he reviewed for almost a full minute, placing a lunch order for later. The only acknowledgment that he gave Marlick came at the end, just as he was walking into his office: a single crook of his finger, come with me.

Marlick scooted in, stepping aside just as Director Tarlock snapped the door shut behind him.

"What can I do for you, Mr. Darbury?" He was already walking around his desk, already regarding the papers spread across its surface.

"Sir, I—About last night—the assignment? It—"

"Yes, I've received a report," Director Tarlock cut in. "Shame that things were not more successful."

"'Shame'—!" Marlick started, then clamped his mouth shut. He had planned this out so much more eloquently in his head. He closed his eyes and took a deep breath, in through his nose and out through his mouth. "You lied to me."

"I most certainly did not."

"How can you say that?!" Marlick said, the last of his reserves crumbling underneath him. "This isn't what I thought I was agreeing to! She almost killed my friends!"

"And if she had succeeded?"

Marlick sputtered. He had come to the director's office, he realized, with the scant hope that Director Tarlock would, if not openly *deny* the actions that had been taken, then at least claim ignorance of them—that the academy itself wasn't directly involved, that it had been a terrible misunderstanding, or that the Aul merchant had been acting outside of their authority. But now . . . Marlick stared at Director Tarlock, who had settled down in the chair behind his desk and steepled his fingers underneath his austere nose.

He'd *known*. He'd willingly sent someone to their apartment, willingly ordered Marlick to let her in, willingly allowed these actions to befall Kaedrich.

Marlick's knees started to buckle, and he sat heavily in the chair opposite. He dug his hands through his hair, twisting the ginger locks in his tight fists. *"Why?"* he asked. It was the only question that mattered anymore.

"That's not your concern. All that we require of you, Mr. Darbury, is your cooperation. Now, then: tell me what has become of the woman."

Marlick grew carefully still, as if there was a wasp in the room. Slowly, so slowly, he drew his hands down from his rumpled hair and looked up. "What?"

"Praxis Fellows," Director Tarlock said. "Tell me where she is."

Instantly, a picture of the abandoned house where they'd stayed drew itself up in Marlick's mind. He shoved it violently aside, burying it somewhere deep in his thoughts. "I don't know," he said instead. "She disappeared right after the attack. I haven't seen her since."

He tried to keep himself steady as he gave his lie. Praxis Fellows? *That's* what all of this was about? Marlick supposed that it made sense—after all, what could anyone possibly have against Kaedrich? Praxis, however . . . one of *the* Fellows . . . The family had to have plenty of enemies, but for the life of him, Marlick could not figure out why in the world Falconridge would be involved in targeting her.

It didn't matter why, though. Marlick realized this in an instant: he would protect her, from the academy or anyone else, for as long as she mattered to Kaedrich. He had done this, he had brought this upon them, but he would do it no longer.

The director shrugged. "Then find her."

"What?"

"You heard me," Director Tarlock said. He glared across the desk, every ounce of his authority lending shadows to his face. He had always been an intimidating figure—tall, commanding, brusque—and certainly he had made all of his students nervous many times. But never before did Marlick remember being *terrified* of him.

Marlick swallowed, his throat suddenly gone dry. "Sir, I don't think—"

"I'm not asking what you think," Director Tarlock said. "Find Praxis Fellows; find her quickly. Or else you may discover to your infinite dismay that your position at this school is not as secure as you'd like to believe."

Mr. Bundling wasn't at work that morning, but that was just as well as far as Kaedrich was concerned. She spent the time that she would normally be writing up a draft of his articles at a luggage shop, wincing as she handed over the money for several large trunks to be delivered to her apartment.

Her former apartment, she supposed. Kaedrich tried not to think about that as she signed the receipt. In truth she didn't even know how many trunks she was going to need to fit all the stuff that she'd managed to acquire, but the price of even these was more than enough to send her into a panic—there was no way that she was shelling out for more. If anything wouldn't fit, she would simply sell it; which was not a bad idea anyway, given the circumstances. Kaedrich's stomach clenched, thinking about the enormity of the bills now hanging over her. She hadn't gotten an opportunity to discuss their outstanding debt with Marlick yet, though fairness dictated that Kaedrich should really foot most of it herself. It was *her* houseguest that had been the intended target of the attack after all, and there's no reason that Marlick should have to be punished for something that he had no hand in creating.

She supposed that she could ask Praxis for money, but she knew that she wouldn't. For one thing, she did not want to admit that she'd now been kicked out of her apartment. But more than that, if Praxis knew how bad the situation was that she'd gotten Kaedrich into, she was very likely to pull something rash in an effort to assuage her guilt. Kaedrich didn't know what, but neither was she willing to risk finding out. Right now, she needed Praxis focused. Kaedrich . . . well, Kaedrich would survive. She would always survive.

Classes seemed to take forever. Between her and Marlick, they made so many disruptive mistakes that at one point they were sent out of the room so that the rest of the students could finish without further interruption. Kaedrich sat on the floor just outside of the classroom, soaked in sweat, and leaned her head back against the polished wall. A headache was building up at the base of her skull, tendrils of pain reaching forward toward her temples.

"Do you know where you're going to stay yet?" Marlick asked. He was standing several feet away, trying to look as if he was examining the details of the hilt of his fencing foil. His voice was small and scared.

"Not really," Kaedrich said. "You?"

Marlick shrugged. "My uncle has a place here—I'm sure he'll let me stay until I can figure out something better. I would ask you to join me, but . . ." Marlick glanced up. "He's . . . not exactly the type of person that *you* would get along with." He looked pointedly at the rich brown of Kaedrich's exposed arms, her sleeves rolled partway up.

"Ah."

"I'm sorry," Marlick said. "I wish he wasn't like that, but—"

"Forget about it. I'm fine. I'll be fine."

She had to keep telling herself that, lest she start to believe otherwise.

The rest of the day was a tangled mess of logistics and scrambled packing. Kaedrich's trunks were delayed in arriving at the apartment, and even after she'd finally received them, it didn't take long to realize that they wouldn't hold everything. How in the world had she acquired so much *stuff*? That was the biggest frustration that hung over her as she once again emptied everything out in an effort to repack more efficiently. It was the only safe thing to feel at the moment, because if she dared look at the situation from any greater distance than that, she felt sure that she would burst into tears.

In the end it took all the trunks, plus a suitcase, plus two overflowing bags and a handful of miscellaneous objects carried in awkward armloads, but Kaedrich managed to wrangle all of her stuff out of the door by the appointed deadline. She and Marlick stood on the sidewalk as their respective luggage was loaded into two separate carriages. They shared a brief wave, the most that either of them could bring themselves to offer in parting, and left it at that.

That night Kaedrich checked into a cheap inn along the border to the old quarter. She was not yet willing or desperate enough to actually cross the line (she would never be able to hold on to the slim amount of respect that she'd earned if she did), but nor was she stupid enough to try putting herself up in the heart of Monfort. She lugged her stuff in herself, stacking it high along the far wall of her tiny room, where it towered over her ominously as she got ready for bed and settled onto the lumpy mattress.

At least the injuries on her arms hadn't reopened. She hung onto that one small favor the gods had granted her, touching her pin where it rested on the wobbly nightstand.

Kaedrich was too sore and too tired to bother going for a run the next morning, so she took her time getting ready instead. She treated herself to a bath, even though it meant waiting in line at the communal bathroom and using secondhand bathwater that had gone cold. She dressed herself with extra care, for she would not put forth such a disheveled appearance as she'd done yesterday. When at last she was ready she still had more than enough time to cross the city and arrive at work early, and she strolled through the front doors of the Monfort Daily Witness in a surprisingly good mood, given the circumstances.

Mr. Bundling wasn't in his office. Again.

Kaedrich waited around for a few minutes, sitting at her cramped tea tray and trying not to read too much into his absence. He was normally at work before Kaedrich, yes, and it was now the second day in a row that he'd broken his pattern, but it didn't necessarily mean anything was *wrong*. He might have been caught up in an investigation. He might have been ill. He might have made an excuse to stay home and spend some "quality" time with his wife—there were lots of explanations, really, any number of them to choose from. There was no reason to jump to conclusions.

Fifteen minutes later she was at the front desk, leaning against the counter.

"This *again*?" the Witness's secretary asked. She huffed as she shifted a stack of papers, thumbing through them for several moments.

"I'm sorry, but this time I'm certain something's wrong. I can *feel* it."

The secretary sighed. She leaned forward onto her elbows, lowering her voice to a conspiratorial whisper. "Look, I really shouldn't be saying anything, but the real trouble isn't so much that he's not here now, as that he's missed *two* deadlines. They were due last night. If you ask me, he's probably just avoiding Jemson's wrath."

Kaedrich swallowed down a nervous lump that had lodged itself in her throat. Mr. Bundling might occasionally be a little flaky, but the one thing that he never did, *ever*, was miss a deadline. Kaedrich had been called in too many nights to help him polish up a draft to believe that he'd ever purposefully be so careless.

"Has there been *any* sign of him?" Kaedrich asked, already fearing the answer.

The secretary reached back and scratched her head, a single carefully done nail slipping underneath the mass of hair twisted up in a knot. "Not that I know of? But Kaedrich, there are lots of reasons why he might not be here—not *all* of them bad."

"But *some* of them are."

The secretary screwed up her lip and half-rolled her eyes in a sort of face version of a shrug. "I can't really deny that."

"Then give me his address."

"What?"

"His address."

"Oh no," the secretary said, raising her hands and backing up in her chair. "No, I can't. I'm not allowed." She turned back to her work, shaking her head.

"Please?"

"No."

"Look, I'm worried about him," Kaedrich said. She glanced around the open office, but the pool of minor writers and editors were all hunched over their own desks. No one was paying any attention to the curved desk of the secretary. "I just want to go over and make sure he's okay."

"He's *fine*," the secretary snapped.

"Is he? Has he *ever* missed a deadline before?"

She ignored Kaedrich. A staff writer walked in the main doors and she glanced up and gave him a nice smile, a polite nod as he passed by on his way to his office.

"What if something *has* happened to him?" Kaedrich asked. She'd slipped around while the secretary was temporarily distracted, and now

Kaedrich leaned over the back of her chair. She pinned the secretary at her desk, holding the chair firmly in place as she whispered in her ear. "What if he needs our help, right now, and we just sit there doing nothing? Are you really willing to risk living with that kind of guilt?"

The secretary heaved a sigh. "Oh, for Perlandra's sake," she muttered. She shoved her chair back with enough force that Kaedrich let her go.

There was an enormous bank of filing cabinets along the back wall of her alcove, and the secretary marched straight over to them. "Don't come near me," she said, keeping her voice low. "They'll suspect if they see you over here."

Kaedrich leaned back against her desk instead, and crossed her arms. She waited as the secretary pulled open a drawer, rifled for a moment with the files inside. When she came back over, she slapped the file down on her desk and sat down to work.

"Don't you dare take it," she said, "but it's open to the right page."

It didn't take more than a glance for Kaedrich to read what she'd been looking for. "Thank you," she whispered, pushing herself back to her feet and rounding the desk.

The secretary glanced up. "Thank me by finding him," she said. Her eyes had gone soft, her mouth pinched into a concerned line. "And bringing him back safely."

Kaedrich nodded. "I'll do my best," she said, as she let herself out the front doors.

THE WALK TO Mr. Bundling's house took longer than Kaedrich wanted. He lived in the middle strip of Monfort, in a narrow little street that was bustling with housewives and children. Right away, Kaedrich knew that she'd found the right place, because the door was opened by a woman that matched Mr. Bundling point for point: the same overly small nose, upturned at the tip; the same muddy-brown hair slicked straight back off of the forehead, though hers was longer and gathered into a fat braid that hung over her shoulders and trailed all the way down to her waist; the same slack-faced expression of utter disinterest in whatever it was you happened to be saying.

"Yes?" she asked, sighing the word out as if it had personally offended her.

"I'm . . . I'm sorry to disturb you, ma'am, but I'm looking for Mr. Bundling. Erstan Bundling," Kaedrich added, like this woman needed the clarification.

The woman's lip curled up. "Heh. Yeah, me too. Useless waste of a husband. What are you, one of his boys?"

"His . . . I'm sorry, his what?"

"Like you don't know," Mrs. Bundling said. She poked Kaedrich in the chest, so hard that Kaedrich actually stumbled down a step.

"Hey—!"

"You got a lotta nerve, showing up here and asking for him like this," Mrs. Bundling said. "But I tell you, he's not here. Probably still with one of you pretty boys, so I'd start by asking the rest of your friends. Ask them, and when you find him, sprawled in the gutter somewhere, pants around his ankles, you tell him for me, you tell him: I ain't gonna put up with this anymore. He thinks I don't know, but I got *proof*. Tell him if he doesn't come home now, that proof is going to find a way to the magistrate. I'd get the house, I'm sure of it, what with him being a filthy—"

"Ma'am, I swear to you, I have no idea who he might be with right now. I'm *not* one of his 'boys.' I work for him at the Daily Witness."

Mrs. Bundling sneered. "Sure you do."

Kaedrich sighed. "Can you please just tell me when the last time that you saw him was?"

"Night before last," Mrs. Bundling said. She put heavy emphasis on each word as she spoke them, breaking them into their own sentences; it seemed to Kaedrich as if she'd been bottling it up, just waiting for someone to ask, so that she could make a big stink about each and every night Mr. Bundling had missed.

Kaedrich would have had more sympathy for the woman, except for the fear that rooted her to the front steps at the knowledge that Mr. Bundling had been missing for that long. Gods, anything could have happened to him in the meantime.

"Thank you, ma'am," Kaedrich said as she forced herself back down the steps to the sidewalk. She raised her fingers in a half-salute, what would have been a hat tip if she'd been wearing one. "I'll do my best to find him for—" but the door was already closing in her face.

THE SKY WAS a scrub of dismal gray as Tol cut across an overgrown lawn. Flowers swayed underneath a rippling breeze, bursts of color that had grown too tall. In the distance was a house, small and sturdy and brick. Its location was known only to some dozen or so men, most of them either currently inside, or stationed out of view in a defensive perimeter.

The house, like so much else, was seized property. It used to belong to a wizard—not a member of the Royal Society but skilled just the same. A healer, who up until recently had been quite a thriving member of his community. He'd had an office in the local village, though he kept his home address private.

It had been disturbingly easy to ruin him. A few choice speculations over the people that he hadn't been able to save (that no power, magic or mortal or godly, would have been able to save, but nobody needed to know *that*); a few questions asked too loudly in the village pub about what exactly the wizard *did* in his spare time; a few farming and cooking tools treated with Tol's new formula to prevent healing magic, so that the next time someone injured themselves on them and sought out his help . . .

A complaint was filed, an investigation held. The wizard, now locked in the Monfort prisons, had his land and property seized by the Crown, and from there, gifted to Lanali. Done, and done. It had barely taken any of Tol's time or talents to arrange.

Once in a while, he felt the smallest twinge at the back of his conscience. Barely there at all, really, like a tickle at the top of the throat that you ignored because surely it wasn't enough to herald the beginning of a cold. Then he would glance down at his hand, at his tattoo of a wave. He had made his choice. Always, this was what he told himself. He had made his choice.

He glanced at it now, his fist curling and uncurling in perfect harmony to the thundering of his feet as he rolled across the lawn like an angry storm. A day. A day! The incompetent fools had kept their prisoner for more than *an entire day* before they'd thought to inform either him or Lanali.

A single day (and two nights, really) might not seem like much, but Tol knew that even a single day could mean the difference between success and failure. (By the tides, he'd managed to find out everything he needed to know about the regent of Melmont in a day.) And there was no telling if people were already out looking for the man, but no doubt they would be soon.

He blew into the house, the door crashing open and shut behind him. Kinnly, the lead of this particular contingent of Lanali's men, leapt to his feet. What had once been a comfortable living area was now littered with stray boots and coats, old cigarette stubs and empty bottles and filthy coffee cups. At Tol's appearance, a handful of playing cards and a racy magazine were stuffed underneath chair cushions by the rest of the guardsmen.

Tol assessed it all slowly. He needn't bother—he'd spotted everything of note the instant he set foot in the room, but it was good for the men to see him see it. It was good for them to sweat over it, to meet his eyes one by one and worry which of their sins he was reading on their faces.

They expected him to either start yelling or start throwing punches, and so Tol did neither. Kinnly had raced to stand before him, spine ramrod straight, and he'd already begun to blunder through a handful of general apologies when Tol's sharp glare cut off his words as surely as if it had taken his tongue.

"Show him to me."

Kinnly nodded, his head bobbling like a cheaply made wooden doll. He led Tol up the stairs, to what had once been the bedrooms. It was such a shame, really, because it actually was a charming house and had clearly held a family that loved both it and each other. Cheerful cream wallpaper lined the upstairs hall, neat little rows of daisies seeming to smile at them as they passed. A decorative table at the landing of the stairs held a book that had been set down in passing, a bookmark about halfway through. There was a family photograph mounted to the wall, a portrait of a man and a woman and a baby nestled in an oval frame. Tol felt the brush of each of these things and more, like a knife grazing against his skin. They were everything that he was never going to have.

But he'd made his choice.

All of the doors had been boarded over, extra locks and chains transmuting bedrooms into jail cells. Kinnly went straight to the one at the very end of the hall and pulled out a jangling set of keys. He went through a long and overcomplicated process as he undid each of the latches and locks in turn, and then he swung the door open.

Tol knew from experience that most of the time, the men had packed people in three or four or six to a room, but this one held just one occupant. Hands and feet bound, mouth gagged, a sickly, sagging bruise blooming underneath one eye ("That wasn't our doing—he came in like that," Kinnly was quick to point out), the man was nonetheless instantly recognizable.

Tol pinched the bridge of his nose. "Mr. Bundling, I do apologize for this grave mistreatment."

Bundling snorted around his gag. He made some sort of muffled argument, though of course his exact words were lost to the gag clamped between his teeth.

It had been easy for Tol to hope that the reports were inaccurate. That perhaps the person they'd taken prisoner had just *looked* like Erstan

Bundling, and therefore that the men had gotten scared over nothing. Tol hadn't believed this hope, but it had clung to him like a bad odor as he'd made his way out of the city, dispatched to clean up someone else's mess.

The message had come to Tol first, and then *he'd* had the distinct pleasure of having to tell Lanali. She had sat in stony silence as she listened to Tol's report. If you didn't know her, you might have thought that it meant nothing to her, but Tol recognized the way that her fingers played with the edge of the chair's armrest, tracing the patterns of the carved wood with forced languidness; holding her face still always made her restless.

It would have been different if the procedure was ready, but it wasn't. Drumm and Cranish had been willing volunteers, but Lanali had still never had the slightest bit of success in converting someone that wasn't already eager for it.

Tol dropped his hand as he turned to Kinnly. "Leave us."

Kinnly quirked his eyebrow, but ultimately shuffled out of the room. Tol waited for several long moments, giving Kinnly the opportunity to listen at the door and give up on the idea of hearing anything interesting. When he finally shuffled off a little ways down the hall, Tol sighed.

"We can't risk a high-profile disappearance," Lanali had said, just before Tol had set out. *"Even our man at the police cannot contain something like that."*

Tol had nodded, because he knew that Lanali was right, and he knew the routine: a knife to the throat, the man's pockets turned out as if they'd been picked clean. The fact that Bundling already had a bruise on his face would lend a nice sense of authenticity to the whole deal. They'd abandon his body on a street corner in some unsavory part of the old quarter, and that would be that.

Tol drew out a knife. Bundling's eyes widened, and he jerked back in the chair that he was lashed to. His feet kicked out, and the chair teetered back onto two legs.

"Oh now *really*, let's not have any of that," Tol said. He rushed forward, grabbing the chair and stabilizing it even as Bundling tried to scoot it farther back into the corner. "We're both gentlemen, Mr. Bundling," Tol added, raising his voice as Bundling tried shouting something through his gag. "Can we not have *some* dignity in death?"

Bundling kicked again, narrowly missing Tol's shins.

Tol shrugged. "I guess not," he said. He grabbed Bundling by the hair, yanking him back. A flick of Tol's wrist, a spray of red decorating the nearby curtain. He held Bundling in place until the wet sucking, gurgling sound came to an end, until the man stopped convulsing underneath his grip. Tol threw the man's head forward as he released him, and stepped wide away from the mess of the body as he drew out a cloth for his knife. In some ways it was a pity, Tol thought as he began to wipe the blade clean. Bundling had such potential to be useful, if circumstances had been different. But Bundling had made his choices, leading him here, and so had Kinnly and the rest of the men. And so had Tol, such a long time ago now.

Tol glanced at his tattoo, speckled with a light mist of Bundling's blood. He wiped his hand off on Bundling's shirt as he headed for the door.

Chapter Twenty-Two

"YES, HI, I'D LIKE TO report a missing person," Kaedrich said.

The policeman behind the desk glanced up and snorted disdainfully. "You don't say."

Kaedrich opened her mouth to answer, but no answer came out, so she closed it. She nodded.

A shout erupted from somewhere behind Kaedrich and she whirled, her hand flying to her hip, where she'd started carrying a sheathed dagger. But the shout had nothing to do with her: two police officers had just entered the building, dragging a drunken man between them, and he was cursing in their faces. Kaedrich watched the scene, wide-eyed. The drunk man was probably middle-class, judging by the suit that was more or less a match to Kaedrich's, though he'd obviously been in one hell of a fight. One sleeve of his jacket was torn off at the shoulder and hanging halfway down his arm, and there was a hole ripped in the knee of his pants, through which Kaedrich could see blood oozing from a fresh scrape. A yellow-brown bruise was already blooming on the man's filthy cheeks. The policemen dragged him right past Kaedrich, so close that Kaedrich reeled back from the smell of him, cheap booze and vomit and piss all mixed together. The drunk thrashed and yelled the whole time, pausing his tirade only long enough to hock a mouthful, which he spat arbitrarily out at the room in general; it landed with a sickening *splat* on the desk near the officer that Kaedrich had been speaking to, a man with a brass badge reading *Harrington*. Harrington, for his part, didn't even flinch. He grabbed a stained cloth and brushed the desk, as if this sort of thing happened all the time.

This was Kaedrich's first time actually being inside of a police station and, Perlandra willing, it would also be her last. She tried to avoid them, as a general rule. Quite aside from the simple fact that Monfort police officers were known to be aggressive toward men who looked like Kaedrich, men who were far too dark to ever pass for merely having spent too much time in the sun, there was also the little matter of Kaedrich technically doing something illegal just by passing herself off as a man. The way she looked at it, why tempt the fates?

But this time, she felt that she had little recourse. Mr. Bundling was gone—likely having suffered the same fate as all the other people that had disappeared recently, but even if not, his circumstances couldn't possibly be good. Respectable men did not simply up and vanish.

Her first thought, of course, had been to go to Praxis. She almost did just that. Kaedrich had gotten more than halfway across the city, heading straight for the abandoned Society house, when she stopped herself abruptly, right in the middle of the street. Ignoring the fact that Praxis had yet to make any headway in determining what had happened to the others that had disappeared, did Kaedrich really want to draw attention to her job at the newspaper? They hadn't talked about it since the day that Praxis found out that she *had* a job, and while Kaedrich wasn't willing to believe that Praxis had forgotten about it, she didn't exactly feel like bringing the subject up again. How was she supposed to explain to someone like Praxis about the need to be financially independent? And what was she supposed to *do* about the situation, anyway, that Kaedrich couldn't do for herself? This was a straightforward situation: someone was missing; all you had to do was look.

Harrington sighed. He reached underneath his desk and drew out a battered ledger, which he slapped down heavily. He ignored Kaedrich as he lifted the cover, which was only barely attached to the book by this point. A pen was lying on the desk, a pool of ink underneath the tip; Harrington picked it up and shook it once, twice, then dipped the tip in an ink bottle near his elbow. "Name?"

Kaedrich plucked nervously at the pin on her lapel. "Do you . . . do you *need* my name, to file a report?"

Harrington rolled his eyes. "Not *your* name, kid—the *guy*. Cripes, you want to do this or not?"

"Oh! Yes, of course. Um. Bundling. Erstan Bundling."

"You mean the newspaper man?" Harrington shook his head. "Forget it. He's not missing."

"What? You mean, you know where he is?"

Harrington shot Kaedrich an incredulous look. "What do I look like, a mystic? No," Harrington said, holding up a single finger, slightly crooked, to silence Kaedrich before she could start. "Take it from me, though— those types, they're always nosing around where they don't belong. He'll disappear for a few days and then come back claiming he's got the scoop on some big, important story. Flighty, is what it is."

Kaedrich frowned. "I really don't think that's the case this time."

"And you would know this because . . . ?"

"Well . . . his wife doesn't know where he is."

"Ha! Yeah, I'll bet she doesn't." Harrington slammed the cover of his book closed, and dropped the pen carelessly back on the desk.

"But—!"

"Kid: can you *prove* that he's missing?"

"I . . . I don't even know how I would do that."

"Exactly," Harrington said. He leaned over to look behind Kaedrich, perhaps hoping that someone else was requiring his attention; but the main room of the station was empty except for a smattering of officers, a bored-looking prostitute sitting on a bench, and a man beside her that was dressed up identically, right down to their flashy-looking garters and the fake mole on their chins. They'd been waiting since before Kaedrich had shown up, and likely would be held long after her departure.

When Harrington's attention returned to Kaedrich, it was clear from the look on his face that this matter was considered a complete waste of time. Kaedrich edged away from the desk, knowing well enough when not to prod the matter. The last thing that she needed was to get a policeman irritated with her, looking for an excuse to lash out. She turned and made her way toward the door, trying her best to look purposeful even as the man dressed as his prostitute friend blew a wet kiss in her direction.

Outside, it had started to rain, a heavy spring cloudburst that soaked the street and sent everyone running for shelter. Kaedrich sighed, muttering "blast" under her breath. She *had* an umbrella, but it was currently buried in the bottom layer of one of the trunks towering in the corner of her hotel room.

There was nothing for it, however. Kaedrich was not going to stand around on the front steps of the police station all day, not when every minute might be the difference between life and death for Mr. Bundling.

It was an unusually melodramatic way of looking at things, a mood that Kaedrich was not ordinarily prone to, but that morning she couldn't exactly help it. She dove into the curtain of rainwater. A chill instantly doused her head, and the water made short order of the fabric of her suit jacket.

With nothing better to go on, Kaedrich's vague idea was to head back to Mr. Bundling's house and begin to ask his neighbors if they'd seen where he went on the day he'd disappeared. Hopefully, she'd be able to trace his steps from sighting to sighting, all through the city if she was lucky. She didn't really expect it to be that easy, but you never knew. Perhaps he was missing simply because no one had thought to follow him yet.

Kaedrich stopped at an intersection to wait for a gap in the traffic. Rain bounced off of horses' shifting hides, and ran like heartbroken tears down the heavy, oil-slicked cloaks of drivers, and sprayed out from the wheels of carts and carriages and the occasional passing bicycle. A motocarriage trundled past, lost in its own private cloud, the rain turning instantly to steam as it hit the furious engine. Kaedrich turned to watch it go, and spotted a policeman standing at the base of a streetlamp just down the road.

It was nothing, she told herself, but she kept her head down anyway. Kaedrich turned forward once more and strode through a narrow gap in the passing traffic. Not too fast, lest the officer think that she had something to hide, but not too slow lest she appear to be loitering. One wrong move, one wrong *look*, that would be all that it would take—not necessarily even that.

She stuffed her hands into the pockets of her suit jacket, just for something to do. Her shoulders curled forward, from the chill and the rain and the unease. She edged her way up the sidewalk, skirting people who had been smart enough to bring their umbrellas. The rail lines hung fat over the next block, and Kaedrich took her time down this street, savoring the scant protection from the rain.

But at the next corner, she made the mistake of turning back. And there he was again: a lone policeman, this time paused as if inspecting the contents of a haberdashery's window.

Was there proof that it was the same man? It was hard to say. Both times he had been spotted from a distance, and both times Kaedrich did not let her gaze linger overlong in his direction. She turned away again, dashed across the street. She did not even really care anymore if she was headed the right way—the right way, right now, was simply *away*.

Kaedrich kept her pace brisk and her head down as she tried to lose herself in the spotty crowds.

She did not look back at the next intersection, nor the one after that. She turned down a side street, narrow and zigzagging as it cut up the slopes of Monfort. She climbed it like a staircase, skipping over the scrubby bushes planted between the cutting lane.

The top of the street spilled out into a wide alleyway between two enormous and opposing temples. Kaedrich turned left, for no particular reason, and maneuvered around refuse and the occasional huddled form of a beggar. Too late, she realized that she should probably be checking some of those faces as she passed, just to make sure Mr. Bundling hadn't gotten beaten up and left somewhere to bleed to death. She paused at the end of the alleyway, considering whether it was worth it to go back. It felt as if she'd lost her pursuer, so maybe it was?

Even if it wasn't, though, Kaedrich didn't know how she'd be able to live with herself if she *didn't* go back and make herself check; what if one of them *was* Mr. Bundling, and she hadn't helped him when she could? She spun around, back toward the mouth of the alleyway, and a policeman was staring right at her.

Kaedrich couldn't help it, she yelped. The policeman grabbed her by the arm, dragged her roughly into the shadows of the alleyway. Somewhere in her haste, the rain had let up, though cold drops still peeled from the rooftops and landed in heavy splatters along the sett stones. Kaedrich's foot splashed into a puddle as she was thrown forward; she hit the wall, her hands scrambling over cold bricks.

If he was going to arrest her, he was certainly going about it oddly. He had released his hold on her and now she had a straight shot down the alleyway. Her thoughts were already sprinting that direction, but something in the pit of her stomach held her back. What if the policeman was just toying with her, what if he wanted her to run? Kaedrich—the real Kaedrich—had been shot as he'd been running for his own freedom. There were no flowers in the alleyway with her, but that didn't mean that she couldn't be taken down, that she couldn't get a bullet lodged into her back, or her knee, or her shoulder.

She pushed herself off of the wall. She faced the policeman.

He jerked his chin at her. "You said the newspaper man was missing?"

Kaedrich didn't know what she was expecting from this man that had tailed her here, but she knew one thing for certain: whatever she might have come up with, this wouldn't have been it.

She didn't answer him, not right away. She was still trying to decide what the potential dangers were—though right now, just standing there, he didn't *seem* particularly threatening. His face was young, and surprisingly delicate, like a doll or a dancer. His hands were loose by his sides, just hanging there like he didn't really know what to do with them. He neither scowled nor glared nor sneered at Kaedrich, instead watching with a placid expression that bordered on disinterest.

"What's it to you if I did?" Kaedrich asked finally.

"That's my business," the policeman said. His face softened. "But needless to say, I have an interest in knowing what happens to him. Please. You said that he was missing?"

One of you pretty boys, Kaedrich thought before she could help it. She shook the words from her head. "Yeah, I . . . I did. He is."

The policeman sucked the air in sharply through his teeth. He held his fist up to his mouth as he turned away, almost as if he was biting down on some terrible lament. "How long?" he asked, still facing the wall.

"Two nights," Kaedrich said. "Though I don't know how much of the day before that."

The policeman swore. He ripped his helmet off and threw it against the wall, letting it clatter to the wet stones. "I *told* him to be careful," he muttered, or at least that's what Kaedrich thought the words were. It was hard to tell from where she stood.

Abruptly, the policeman spun back. "You have to look for him."

"Yeah, that's what I was going to do. Though it would go a lot better if I had some help."

"No," the policeman said. He shook his head fiercely. "I *can't*. But listen, go to the old quarter. Widow's Row, a place called the Crimson Rose. That's where he was that night. Just . . . just ask around. See if anyone saw what happened to him."

Kaedrich went cold. "The old quarter?"

"That's right. Widow's Row. You know it?"

Kaedrich made herself shake her head. No, she didn't know it, but that's okay—she could find it. What *wasn't* okay was the knowledge that Mr. Bundling had likely fallen into the exact same trap that had ensnared Lord Wellen before him. Kaedrich's stomach twisted up, remembering what Praxis had said about Lord Wellen's experiences.

"So you'll do it?" the policeman asked.

The words "of course" were halfway out of Kaedrich's mouth before she caught up with herself. On the one hand, yes, of course—of *course*. Someone was in trouble, and Kaedrich was in a position to do something about it: of course she would.

On the other hand . . . people in the old quarter didn't take kindly to some man showing up in their midst and asking questions. Any man, whether he wore a policeman's uniform or not. And there may have easily been a time when Kaedrich dressed as if she belonged in a place like that, but these days her mid-priced suit would immediately label her an outsider—untrustworthy, contemptible, suspicious. She'd have to stop at her hotel room along the way and try to change into something cheaper, dirtier, but even then . . .

Unless . . .

Kaedrich glanced down. While they'd been talking, she'd instinctively crossed her arms over her chest, always so afraid of being caught out in the rain like this. She'd have to change anyway, yes, and the people that she'd be speaking to were likely to get riled if a *man* came around asking questions.

But Kaedriella did not have to ask them as a man.

She looked back at the policeman, still standing there, waiting for her answer. Already, a tiny thrill was running through Kaedrich's body. "I can't do it," she told the policeman, who immediately frowned and opened his mouth to argue. Kaedrich held up her hand. "But I think that I know just the person to help us."

IN THE TIME since Kaedrich had left, an eternal day and a half ago by now, Praxis had managed to burn her hand on her own flames, stub her toes no fewer than five times, drop and break a glass beaker, pinch her finger in a door, and nearly chop her thumb off when she'd tried to slice up an apple.

The knife dove into her flesh, striking tendon and bone. Praxis swore profusely at the blood pouring from the joint of her hand, her thumb stinging like the tongue of the second devil himself. She wrenched the knife out and wrapped her whole palm around the wound, sparking magic to life and feeding it down.

Healed up, she wiped her hand off on a napkin and threw the knife across the room so that it landed with a *thud-THWAAAANG* in the wall. Nothing was going right, now, not a damned thing. Not her investigations (either the one into the disappearances *or* the one into the question of the plant that apparently wrought havoc with healing spells), and not her meager attempt at lunch, and not the political climate of Monfort (if the paper that she'd stolen from her temporary neighbor was at all to be believed). The Crown had just unilaterally cut a whole swath of social services, under the guise of it being a cost-saving measure, and the already suffering were now going to suffer even more. The Governance Council and the Crown were shooting a variety of angry jabs at each other across the pages of the Daily Witness, each blaming the other for the problems in Monfort.

But none of that mattered to Praxis now. The most not-right of all, of course, was Kaedrich herself. The absence of her hung over the entire house as a thick fog. Rain pelted the windows, a storm system that had been accidentally dragged in yesterday by Praxis's ill temper—downpours had been cropping up all day and all night and all day since. Praxis stopped in front of one of the windows now, peering out. What did it matter if someone saw her anymore? She didn't care. She watched the gray skies for signs of Brex. He had insisted on being let out about twenty minutes ago, despite the spitting drizzle that continued long after the major downpour had subsided. He had reentered her awareness at around the same time that she'd been accidentally almost chopping off her own thumb, but he was so small and prone to distraction that it was hard for Praxis to ever pin down his exact location.

She spotted him now, barreling toward the window. He made a straight shot for Praxis's heart, and Praxis was not at all sure that he wouldn't have burst in right through the windowpane if she hadn't swung it open in time.

"Hey, hey, calm down little fella," she whispered to him. He had slammed into her chest and Praxis had cradled him out of habit, pinching the scruff of his neck as she spoke. She eased the window shut as Brex wrestled free of her protective grip. He was still damp from the earlier rainstorms, and he shivered as he climbed up her shoulder and pawed at her face. On his front paw was a scrap of cheap paper, rolled into a tiny scroll and tied to him as if he was a carrier pigeon.

Praxis frowned as she slipped the paper off of him. It was small enough that she could unroll it with one hand, rubbing her thumb and forefinger together. Meticulous writing stared up at her, each letter perfectly formed, and Praxis's breath caught in her chest. She would have known who it was from even if it hadn't been signed.

P, it read, *I need help with something. Please meet me in the alley at the corner of Stefford Lane and Market Street as soon as convenient. (Don't worry, I am in no danger.) -K.*

A surge of delight jolted through Praxis. She threw Brex at the ceiling, where he squawked once in protest before fluttering to land on a high shelf beside some dusty canisters. Praxis all but flew out of the kitchen, moving as fast as her brace would allow her. She cut down the hallway and the basement stairs, making a beeline for a package resting on her bed.

Though her first inclination had been to run straight to the location Kaedrich had given her, Praxis held herself back. Fresh blood soaked through the cuff of one shirtsleeve, a burn bore a hole in the other. She had taken off her vest last night and slept directly in her shirt, not wanting to put on the nightgown and remember the awful circumstances of the last time she'd worn it; but now the whole garment was covered in wrinkles, and one lapel refused to lie flat. And while normally none of this would bother Praxis one bit, these were hardly normal circumstances.

The package was wrapped in delicate paper that had been scented with lilacs. Praxis undid the knot and lifted the top sheet, revealing an expertly folded shirt and vest. Despite sulking and brooding in the basement for most of yesterday, doing what she was supposed to and trying to sort out the puzzle pieces of everything that had happened since coming to Monfort, she had snuck out for a fast trip to the shops. Her pants still weren't ready—it was more than just cutting a line down each leg and adding in a row of buttons: one leg was going to be wider than the other, just enough to accommodate Praxis's unusual situation, but still tapered and fitted so that they would appear slim and hopefully wouldn't draw notice to their uneven construction. And of course her new coat was a special order, being sewn wholly from scratch to Praxis's exacting specifications. But he had a number of new shirts and vests for her, and Praxis had accepted them happily. Despite her outward pessimism, perhaps she knew on some level that Kaedrich would be reaching out to her eventually.

Or maybe it had just been wild, blind hope. That was just as likely.

Praxis yanked off her shirt, practically ripping the buttons off in the process, and dropped it into a heap on the floor. She reached for the new one, but paused when a distinct funk toyed at her nostrils. Praxis checked her armpits, scowling as she reeled back. Did she have time to take a bath? How would she even go about it, in an abandoned house like this, trying to haul the water all by herself? She doubted that the Society had added proper plumbing to the facility before they'd left—they tended to avoid modern advancements, seeing science as a potential rival to their own "glorious" achievements.

There was a narrow dresser in the corner of the room, barely large enough to be useful. Praxis made her way over and began to pull out drawers, pawing through their contents. A random mishmash of memories assaulted her as she placed each item: a turquoise hair comb that she'd bought after her first week in Monfort, determined to celebrate but too angry to figure out how; a ticket stub to a play, where Praxis had made such extensive eye contact with the lead actress that she'd tumbled off the stage; a folded letter that Praxis dared not think about.

And here, at the bottom of the drawer, she found it: a bottle of expensive perfume, only barely used.

Praxis scooped it up, just holding it for a moment. She'd worn it only a handful of times, back when she was trying to impress the sister of her last patron. This had been during a heady, predatory time in Praxis's life; she had no interest in long-term romantic entanglements, laughed openly at the idea of love, and in the spirit of all the men that surrounded her at this infernal Society, she had taken it upon herself to attempt to bed women for sport. Given the utmost need for discretion, Praxis had thankfully never managed to lure more than a handful of them back with her, but one of them, the fates had decided, would be the young Miss Levington.

"What did he do to deserve it?" Kaedrich had asked her the other day. Of course Kaedrich would have assumed that the attack on her former patron was justified, and for a long time Praxis had told herself that it was, but in truth the blame for it rested entirely on Praxis's shoulders. She had broken Miss Levington's heart, used her and cast her aside, and all her brother had done was try to defend her honor.

In the aftermath, Praxis had told everyone that he'd made an aggressive pass at her. What else was she supposed to say? She couldn't admit the truth without doing exactly what Lord Levington had threatened to do, which was expose her taste for women. Cutting his nose off had certainly been enough to get him to shut his mouth, but then people were demanding answers, and so Praxis lied. She lied and she lied and she lied, so often and so well, for so long, that maybe a part of her had even started to believe it.

This scent, then, wasn't anything that Praxis liked to associate with herself anymore, but Kaedrich had no idea what it meant, and it was better than reeking. *Besides, it worked once,* she thought, and then immediately threw the bottle back into the drawer, horrified at herself for the idea.

A sponge bath, then. Just enough to get her underarms, not so long as to cause a real delay. She could manage that. Gathering up her shirt and vest, Praxis marched back up the stairs in search of some soap.

* * *

Across the square, temple chimes began to spill out through the vibrant afternoon. Kaedrich glanced out from her spot in the alleyway, already recognizing the cheerful, three-toned pattern of them. Her chest twisted up as the front doors opened, and a wedding party spilled out onto the street.

There was nothing terribly unusual about this, of course. Springtime in Monfort—it was a popular time for love and weddings. Still, it was nice to know that even in the midst of all the economic ruin and political upheaval, all the schemes and plots unraveling all around them, that people were still going on with the happiness of their lives. Maybe if Kaedrich was still presenting herself as a woman she might have heard more gossip about marriages and babies, all the tidy rituals that held society together, but in her current life it was easy to forget sometimes the simple fact that life goes on. No matter what else happens, life will go on.

She leaned back against the alley wall, watching as the wedding party grinned and laughed, everyone talking excitedly over each other. An open-topped carriage was pulling up now, bedecked in flowers and ribbons, small bells tied to the horses' tails. The couple was lucky the sun had come out again, the last of the clouds burning off by lunchtime. The honey-lime smell of the bay was particularly strong, lending a wonderfully joyous perfume to the day. The groom climbed up first—a very fine young man, all crisp in his wedding suit, tall and strong and grinning from ear to ear as he helped his new wife up beside him. They kissed each other, right there in the middle of it all, as if they couldn't possibly contain their happiness another second; and when they broke apart, the bride gave her husband such a smile that it tore a ragged hole straight through Kaedrich's heart.

She turned away. She looked at her hands: the neat trim of her nails, the smooth brown of her skin. There was really nothing to see there, not to anyone else anyway—except that every time *she* looked at them, all that she could see was the ghost of a ring that never should have existed in the first place.

It had been part of an elaborate trick, she told herself. She had to tell herself this, because otherwise it was too easy to fall into believing it. Back when the magical vacant had been posing as Praxis's double, as Praxis from the future, it had needed to convince Kaedrich of the truth of what it had been saying; so the creature used its magic and conjured up a man's wedding ring, and slid it into place on Kaedrich's finger. And Kaedrich had spent an entire day, more or less, convinced that she'd been handed a piece of the future, that something *other* than her death was now set in stone.

Forgetting something like that was impossible, even if she wanted to. Even if she *needed* to. Kaedrich touched the spot where the ring had sat, massaging her finger as if working out a deep hurt. She had thought about it a lot since then, how her outward appearance as a man would actually let something like that work—except for the fact that there was only one woman that she'd ever tell about her true identity, and that one woman . . .

Well. It wasn't worth thinking about.

"You all right?"

Kaedrich jumped at the sound of Praxis's voice. Her hand flew to her chest, a tiny squeak escaping before she could stop it. "Gods, you scared me."

"I'm sorry—I didn't mean to," Praxis said. She was standing not far down the alleyway, in a new purple shirt and diamond-patterned, green-and-blue vest that cinched in to accent her waist. Gods, why did she have to pick *now* to change her standard outfits? This was the last distraction that Kaedrich needed at the moment.

Kaedrich drew her attention away. "No, I know," she said. She shook her head—she hadn't even heard Praxis's approach, between the ambient noises of the square, the tolling of the wedding chimes, the swirl of her own thoughts. Without meaning to, she glanced across at the wedding party, still clustered around the couple's carriage. They were only just setting off, the snap of the reins and the tinkle of the horses' bells jostling into the happy chatter.

She felt Praxis leaning around her, peering out into the square beyond their darkened alleyway. "Something wrong?"

Kaedrich shook her head again as she averted her gaze. "I was just watching."

The tiniest of frowns creased Praxis's forehead, as if she was confused; then the cheerful commotion seemed to draw her eye, and she suddenly grew very, very still. "Oh."

"Yeah, I know it's stupid." Kaedrich shrugged. "I don't know, it's just strange sometimes . . . Thinking about everything that I gave up, to pass myself off as . . . myself. If you know what I mean."

Praxis forced a nod, though she was still watching the procession, as the wedding carriage circled gaily once around the square, everyone waving and laughing. Coming up to get a better view, she'd stepped so close to Kaedrich, and now Kaedrich could study every tiny flex of muscle in Praxis's jaw and around the eyes as she watched. Praxis licked her lips, her tongue flicking so fast that it was almost impossible to spot. She jerked her chin at the scene unfolding on the square. "Is that what you want?" she asked. Her gaze broke away, pinning Kaedrich against the wall so fast that Kaedrich didn't have time to stop staring.

Kaedrich's cheeks burned as she looked down. She stuffed her naked hand into her pocket, as if somehow Praxis could see the memory of the ring that she carried there. "It's not a question of want. It's not going to happen, not without giving up everything else in my life."

"But if you could?"

"It doesn't matter," Kaedrich said firmly. When she looked up, she forced a smile and the sort of polite, useless laugh that runs underneath small talk. "What about you? Think you'll ever get married?"

Praxis didn't answer at first, though she did take a step back, as if she'd only just now realized how little space she'd left between them. She shrugged as she leaned against the opposite wall of the alleyway. "Probably not. I doubt it."

It was the answer that Kaedrich expected, but it still stung. Kaedrich cleared her throat. On some level, she couldn't believe that she'd actually stumbled into this particular conversation, but on the other she supposed that maybe it was better to have this stated openly, the better to dissuade any foolish ideas that might pop into her head. She forced her voice light and breezy. "Not the kind of life for you?"

"I don't know," Praxis said. There was something so straightforward and honest in her answer that it stopped Kaedrich's thoughts as suddenly as if they'd been hit by a train. Praxis went quiet for a moment, like she was actually considering the question in depth, like they were actually *talking* about this and not just wasting words. Her whole face softened, her attention shifting out of focus. "Even if it was, though, I don't think it would happen. There's . . . there's only one person that I'd ever imagine spending my life with, and . . ."

She bit her lip. Fell silent.

Kaedrich took a breath, trying to hide the way it shook. "And . . . ?"

When Praxis looked up, it was like a switch had been thrown. The transition was so sudden that it made Kaedrich's head hurt. Praxis smirked, all thoughtfulness retreating back to the depths that it had slipped out from. "And that would be me, of course. I mean, come on. Who else would *want* the job? I'm not exactly . . . warm and cuddly."

"I . . . suppose," Kaedrich said, and when Praxis flinched at the comment she added hastily, "but you have plenty of other good qualities! You're smart, you're brave, you're loyal, you're—"

"Which qualifies me to be a good soldier, maybe."

"—beautiful," Kaedrich finished over her.

A tiny pause fell into the alleyway. Even the outside noises seemed to still and stop, one infinitesimal moment of perfect silence ringing into the world.

"And kind," Kaedrich added hurriedly, hoping to move on and distract Praxis from her blunder.

Praxis laughed. "Kind?" She glanced briefly skyward, like the idea was too ridiculous to contemplate. "I don't think that's how most people would describe me."

"That's because you cover it up," Kaedrich said. She watched as Praxis's head lowered, her eyes returning to a level plane with Kaedrich. "You pretend you're all surly all the time so that people will think that you're tough and strong, but you always watch out for the people that you care about. And you *try* to make sure that nobody innocent gets hurt when things go wrong."

"I don't think that's—"

"You're sweet to animals. You never raise your voice to children."

"Please stop," Praxis said softly. Her head had continued to lower while Kaedrich was talking; she was staring at the ground by this point, her face contorted as if Kaedrich had physically hurt her.

"All right," Kaedrich said. "I'm sorry. I only . . . I only wanted to show you that you'd make a lovely wife, and . . . and any man would be lucky to have you."

A bitter little smile twisted up Praxis's face. She was still looking down, still trying to compose herself. She nodded. "Any man."

Kaedrich swallowed around a knot in her throat. "Yeah."

Praxis shut her eyes. It was clear by now that Kaedrich had done *something* wrong, although in the flustered blundering that she'd just gotten herself into, who could say exactly which part of that ramble had been the offense? And so Kaedrich just stood there for a while, afraid of saying the wrong thing and somehow making matters even worse. She could only watch as Praxis rallied herself, shaking it off and replacing the vulnerability with calm detachment.

"So," Praxis said finally, as if nothing had happened at all, "what did you want me for, anyway? Your message made it sound important."

Her message—in the wake of everything, she'd almost forgotten that this meeting was her idea in the first place. Kaedrich remembered the situation with a sick twist of her stomach, shamed at having let herself get distracted in the first place. "It is important," Kaedrich said, but then she paused, because she really wasn't sure how Praxis was going to take this. "I, um . . . I need you to go dress shopping for me."

Chapter Twenty-Three

"*I* DON'T UNDERSTAND," Praxis said, about twenty minutes later. "People just . . . they just hope that the dresses fit?"

They were standing outside of a secondhand clothing shop in a remote section of the old quarter. Old dressmakers' dummies, each with a piece missing here or there, stood in the shop window, bedecked in sun-faded clothing that had obviously sat there for years.

"A lot of people are more or less the same size as each other," Kaedrich said. "And if the fit is *too* bad, they can always make a few alterations themselves."

"Themselves."

"Yes."

Praxis narrowed her eyes, pulling down her tinted spectacles so that Kaedrich would be sure to see the expression. "Is this another lesson in not having to depend on servants?"

"It's cheaper, Praxis. Not everyone can afford a tailor. You did realize that, didn't you?"

"Of course I did," Praxis said, but too quickly.

"Look, I promise that it's really simple. You go in, you try on a dress that looks more or less the right size, you buy it. If it fits you, then it should fit me well enough. Only . . . make sure that it's, you know, a bit larger than you need, in . . ." Kaedrich paused. She waved her hand vaguely. "The upper region."

Praxis's eyebrows shot up. She took a moment to pointedly look at Kaedrich's flattened chest, hidden by bindings, shirt, vest, and suit jacket. "What, seriously?"

"It's nothing personal," Kaedrich said, the undertones of her cheeks tinting coral pink.

"I should hope not. I'll have you know that there is nothing wrong with my 'upper region,' thank you."

"I never said that there was."

Praxis made a slight "hmm" of discontent, her mouth twisting up. She glanced at the shop, then back at Kaedrich, her attention still lingering more than it probably should on the way that the suit jacket hung over Kaedrich's chest. She couldn't imagine even getting her own chest as expertly hidden as Kaedrich had, never mind . . . if that was true . . .

Kaedrich coughed, and Praxis snapped her attention back up. "What?" Praxis said, a little more defensively than she'd like. "I'm impressed, okay?"

She didn't elaborate on which part, exactly, had impressed her.

"So you've got it?" Kaedrich asked. "You're okay with it?"

Praxis rolled her eyes. "This isn't exactly complicated, Kaedrich. I think that I can manage to buy a dress."

"Best make it two, though, just to be sure that at least one of them will fit."

Praxis laid her hand dramatically over her heart. "Oh, well, now you've gone and made it too much. I couldn't possibly manage *two* dresses."

"Shut up," Kaedrich said, and Praxis laughed.

"Don't wait up," Praxis said, breezing past Kaedrich as she let herself into the shop.

The inside was every bit as dingy as the outside; poorly lit, smelling vaguely of sweat, the shelves sagging in the middle as if even holding up what little folded piles they were asked to was more than they could bear. Praxis kept her coat buttoned up to hide her new shirt, suddenly grateful that she didn't yet have her new coat. As she took off her tinted spectacles, folding them with one hand and stuffing them in a pocket, she nodded at the proprietor. The shop was run by a scrawny middle-aged woman with a long scar down the side of her face.

Praxis tried to keep her look of disdain hidden as she surveyed the options. So this was what it was like to be poor? All but begging for the scraps cast off by the moneyed, pieces that looked as if they'd seen three or even four owners before landing here. Despite knowing what Kaedrich wanted the dresses for, Praxis couldn't help but feel a pang whenever she picked one up and considered presenting it to her. She could do so much better, if only she'd been allowed to consult with a proper dressmaker. It had taken Kaedrich years to reach the point where she didn't have to shop at a place like this herself, and the thought of her having a dress from here *now*, even if only as a temporary disguise, felt like a giant kick in the shins.

Still. Praxis had been asked to do a job, simple as that, and she was going to do it properly. If only because Kaedrich had been the one asking.

Kaedrich didn't wait up, though it was not because Praxis took an especially long time. Even with sorting through the options to find the two least-soiled dresses that still had the proper fit, it didn't take her quite an hour. Praxis waited as the proprietor tied them up with used twine, not offering any wrap to keep them clean, and then she walked the long way back to Calswell House. Despite the sharp aching in her hip, Praxis took her time. It felt better to be overcautious, to make sure that no one could trace her movements.

When she did finally arrive, pain still flaring, Praxis could think of nothing but getting off of her feet. She let herself in through the basement door. The cold brush of the wards washed over her as she stepped inside, like passing through a waterfall; she had to fight the urge to shake herself off as a dog would, because it was difficult to convince herself that she was not really wet.

"How'd it go?" Kaedrich asked, before Praxis had even shut the door behind her. She was waiting in the basement, amid the scattered supplies of Praxis's experiments. Brex was perched on her shoulder, throwing himself whole-body at her neck in his effort to rub against her.

The sight of the two of them was a snag on Praxis's heart, as if someone had caught it with a fishing hook. Here, in Praxis's temporary hideaway, it almost felt like returning home after a day at work to find something like a family waiting for her.

Praxis scowled. She tossed the lumpy bundle of dresses to Kaedrich. "Fine. I hope those will do, because it was the best that they had."

"I'm sure I'll manage," Kaedrich said. Brex hopped off of her shoulder, vaulting the short flight to the top of Praxis's head. Kaedrich had already cleared a space on the narrow bed, and now she laid the bundle down and lifted each dress in turn.

Praxis sat on a stool by her worktable, watching Kaedrich work. What must it be like, Praxis wondered, to consider the prospect of presenting yourself as woman (however temporarily) after playing a man for so long? Did Kaedrich even remember how to play the part?

Her musing was cut short, however, by Brex clawing at her head. "Ow!" Praxis muttered, reaching up to untangle his paw from the snarl that he'd created in her hair. "Watch it, will you?"

Brex chittered, slipping his paw free and going straight back to mussing up the short locks. Praxis brushed a stray piece away from her forehead— the front was getting overlong at this point, bits starting to hang down across her eyebrows—when a thought struck her. She glanced at where Kaedrich was now holding one of the dresses against herself, getting a sense of size.

"Hey," Praxis said. "Um . . . what are you going to do about your hair?"

Kaedrich laid the dress down, picked up the other. She didn't even bother to turn around. "I'll cover it. It might not be perfect, but it'll hide it well enough."

"Did you want me to grow it for you?"

Kaedrich stilled. The second dress was pressed against her, one sleeve running down the length of her arm. "You could do that?"

Praxis shrugged; she didn't know why, as Kaedrich wasn't looking at her, but she shrugged just the same. "Yeah. I mean, you might not want to bother, since you'd just have to cut it again after. But—"

"Yes." Kaedrich turned, still clutching the dress to herself. "Gods, yes. I don't care if it's only for a day. Please do it."

"Okay," Praxis said. She tried to clamp down on the sudden swell of pride that rose at the sight of Kaedrich's eager face, but part of it kept tugging at the corner of her mouth. To cover, Praxis ducked her head and snatched Brex off, who squawked indignantly as she tossed him up to find a place to settle somewhere else. Praxis stood up, the pain in her hip be damned, and patted the seat she'd just left.

Kaedrich threw the dress down and darted forward, sitting so fast that Praxis was worried that she would topple the stool out from under her. She sat up straight, her shoulders perfectly level, her head tall.

"Right," Praxis said. "Fair warning: this is probably going to make you a little lightheaded. And you're going to be hungry after it's done, so just bear that in mind. Um, you've eaten since breakfast, right?"

"I had lunch before I met up with you."

"Good. You're going to be grateful for that, in a minute."

Kaedrich nodded. "I'm ready," she said, and then all that was left was for Praxis to do it.

Which, staring at the back of Kaedrich's head, suddenly felt like a bigger deal than it had a moment ago. She had offered the favor without thought, hoping to impress Kaedrich, and only now did she realize that she'd actually have to follow through with it.

It wasn't that it was terribly complicated magic. Growth was essentially the same thing as a healing spell, and Praxis could practically do that in her sleep. It's just that, as she reached out and laid her hands on Kaedrich's head, it felt very *personal*—more so than it really should. Perhaps it was just Kaedrich's eagerness, the delight that was radiating off of her at the prospect. Or maybe it was just the velvety softness of Kaedrich's head, the warmth coming off of her scalp.

Praxis took a breath, detaching herself from the situation. She clicked a spark of magic to life behind her eyes, guided it down through her fingertips. She started to drag her fingers down, but the hair that was building underneath her touch had other ideas; it sprang forth in a riotous burst from Kaedrich's head, jumping up and out as much as anything else. A soft "oh!" escaped Praxis's lips, a quiet laugh of surprise trailing after it as she tried to contain the sudden influx of curls.

She didn't know how long to make it, so she let it unfurl until the weight of it began to drag down the ends. A cascade of tightly looping curls spilled around Kaedrich's head and shoulders by the time Praxis managed to stop it. Her hands were buried up past the wrists, and Praxis giggled at the novelty of it as she drew them out. She had to be careful not to get her mechanical glove tangled up in it, curls stealing back in every time that she thought she'd managed to escape them.

Praxis could not stop staring. The curls sprang and danced underneath her touch, piles upon piles of them, and she pawed at the tousle for a while with her unencumbered hand. She didn't even realize that she was doing it, so entranced by the explosion of beauty. Nor did she see when Kaedrich reached up, touching her hair for herself; they only seemed to realize when their fingers met through the curls.

Praxis drew herself away, her cheeks flushing. She was on the verge of apologizing for overstepping her bounds, a rare mutter of "sorry" already working its way to her lips, when she saw the jerk of Kaedrich's shoulders. A quiet sniffle followed, and then before Praxis knew it, Kaedrich had buried her face in her hands. Her hair tumbled forward.

Praxis froze. Her life experience thus far gave her limited practice when it came to dealing with someone who was crying, and especially so when she didn't even understand what the problem was. If she was being honest, normally it just made Praxis angry; who did they think they were, allowing themselves to be so weak and vulnerable in front of another person, forcing her into the role of comfort-giver?

She was not angry now—her chest clenching up, as if the sight of Kaedrich crying was enough to wound a part of her, too—but nor did she know what to do about it. She watched with a surge of actual *jealousy* as Brex swept in and landed on Kaedrich's lap, soft chitters of reassurance already rippling out from his tiny chest.

Praxis started to reach out, her hand hovering just behind Kaedrich's shoulder. She drew herself back. "Did I mess it up?" she asked instead. "Is your hair not supposed to be like that?"

Kaedrich shook her head, her piles of curls bobbing gently. "No, it's . . . it's fine. It's perfect," she said. She must have drawn her hands down at some point, maybe to cradle Brex, because her voice was muffled only by the stuffiness of her nose. She kept her head bent forward. "I'm sorry, I just . . . I never thought that I would have my hair back, and . . . I guess I was wrong—I wasn't ready."

"Oh," Praxis said uselessly. "Um. Okay then."

It wasn't really okay—nothing that made Kaedrich cry would ever be okay in Praxis's book—but what was she supposed to do at this point? She could not go back and undo her magic, to give Kaedrich more time to prepare.

Kaedrich got up then, skirting past Praxis as she made her way to gather up one of the two dresses. Brex fluttered up to the ceiling beams, curling up for a nap. Then Kaedrich slipped up the stairs, heading somewhere else to change. Praxis tracked her movements without even really meaning to, as Kaedrich made her way up the stairs, through the main level, up the central staircase. She let herself into one of the empty bedrooms, and this is where Praxis *tried* to rein her attention back. It only sort of worked.

Praxis busied herself with her work, but she kept getting flashes of Kaedrich's movements. Praxis lit a flame underneath a makeshift burner, and Kaedrich leaned in toward what was probably a mirror, gingerly touching her curls as if afraid they would disappear at any moment; Praxis started grinding down a sample of the bone, pummeling it into dust with a mortar and pestle, and Kaedrich undid the buttons of her shirt; Praxis surveyed the label of the tiny selection of chemicals that she'd managed to scrounge up, and Kaedrich gathered her hair behind her head, tying it out of her way. When Kaedrich started to unwrap her bindings, Praxis focused hard on pouring out a bit of aqua regia into the powered bone, purposefully humming to herself to try to block things out—but she *felt* the sigh of relief as Kaedrich's breasts settled into themselves, and Praxis jerked, spilling a portion of the aqua regia over her hand. Praxis swore furiously as she shook her hand off, flinging the remaining bits of acid across the room to hiss against whatever they struck.

Maybe it is *kind of creepy . . .* she thought, wincing as she healed up her skin.

Cleaning up and healing herself did at least provide more of a distraction. Praxis doused the flames, still not trusting herself with fire at the moment, but to her relief she was able to pull her sense back at least a little more successfully than she had before. By the time Kaedrich left the room and started back toward the basement, Praxis was almost surprised.

Praxis felt the hesitation in Kaedrich's steps as she approached. Kaedrich hung back at the bottom of the staircase, then plunged into the room all in a rush.

Because she knew Kaedrich was coming, Praxis had already turned. She'd been readying herself to give some smattering of encouragement— a gentle tease, perhaps, or a generic you-look-great—but any semblance of command over spoken language disappeared from Praxis's head the instant Kaedrich came into view.

Rather, the instant Kaedriella did. For the person standing just inside of the doorway bore no traces of that careful façade. And now Praxis saw the full extent of what Kaedriella gave up every single day, just to grab what little respect she could from these people. It wasn't just the physical effort, though looking at her now, it boggled Praxis's mind that one could ever become the other. There was something honest in this look, in the way that Kaedriella carried herself as she smoothed out her skirt and stepped over to pick up the spare dress. Despite the veneer of discomfort at being seen like this, a fluidity of truth ran underneath, and Praxis knew: this was Kaedriella as *herself*, this was who she wanted to be. With her mass of curls, smoothed tightly back over her head and unfurling in a glorious billow to frame her face, and a comfortably worn dress swishing around her legs. Kaedriella skipped the last of the distance, turning with a bit of a twirl to let the skirt bloom out like a dancer.

"So, I shouldn't be more than a few hours," Kaedriella said, and even her voice was a little bit different: softer around the edges, one word melting into the next. She was folding up the unused dress as she spoke, smoothing it against herself. "Would it startle you too much if I just let myself in when I come back? Or should I try to send word ahead?"

"It won't matter—I'm going with you."

If it was anyone else, anyone less practiced in studying the art of Kaedriella's movements, the slight pause in folding the dress might have gone unnoticed; Praxis noticed.

"You don't want me to go," Praxis said.

Kaedriella shook her head. "I didn't say that. It's just . . . if anyone sees me, sees us—I don't want any association between this me, and . . . *that* me, you know?"

"Oh." She supposed that she couldn't argue with that. Praxis glanced down, watching absently as Kaedriella's hands folded one piece of the dress over another. A single sleeve kept worming its way free of the rest of the pink bundle, trailing down Kaedriella's leg and needing to be collected over and over again.

It slid free again, fell down again. Praxis held out her hand. "Give me that."

"No, it's fine, I've got it," Kaedriella said.

"No, I mean, *give* me that," Praxis said. Kaedriella glanced up quizzically, but Praxis only held her hand flat, ready to accept the dress. "If that's what your concern is," Praxis continued, "then let's make sure no one recognizes either one of us."

THE WHISPERS HAD failed her.

For days now, Lanali had every ear that she could trust pinned to the ground, listening for the slightest sign of where Praxis Fellows had gone, the slightest ripple—nothing. Tarlock's plan to use the Falconridge boy to find her had failed. Her network of rumors and informers had failed. Her own efforts, senses constantly perked as she went about her business of meeting with wealthy and important people, had failed. Discreet inquiries had failed.

Lanali knew that Praxis Fellows couldn't have left the city, but wherever she was, she was certainly doing a good job of going to ground. Which was exactly what they *did not need* right now—so close, they were so close, and they could not have her out there, free and scheming . . . waiting.

It was all a waiting game. A game within a game, so many games that Lanali was starting to lose track. She pinched the bridge of her nose, trying not to smell the infernal incense, as she waited in her receiving room. Someone, an eager follower wishing to suck up to the venerated Pon, had brewed her a calming tea and left it on a tray by her elbow, but Lanali's stomach turned at the thought of it. She pushed it aside.

Not everything was cause to despair, however. Tol's investigations into the regent of Melmont had turned up such perfect information that Lanali was tempted to give credit to providence—and now . . . Lanali drummed her fingers on the armrest of her chair. Now, if all went well, Hendril would be returning soon with *very* good news.

So it was that Lanali held herself still. Kept herself calm. She ignored the tea, doing a breathing exercise that someone had taught her years ago, and tried to be patient. At the appointed hour, Davil poked his head in and tidily cleared his throat. "Lord Hendril to see you, ma'am. With Lady Trelina of Melmont."

Lanali smiled. Controlled, but with a trace of genuine pleasure lacing the edges. She waved her approval and the butler scuffled out, and a moment later Hendril strolled in to take his place. His chin was held high as he led a young woman along on his elbow.

Well, no. Calling her that was really an exaggeration that Lanali was not comfortable making in the privacy of her own mind. The person that Hendril brought before the great and venerated Pon was a *girl*, a tiny wisp of a thing that was barely taller than Lanali herself. But at sixteen she was old enough to be married off, by Durland's standards anyway, and that was all that counted.

The girl stood before Lanali now, golden and shimmering with youthful optimism. Her smile was so sweet that it made Lanali's teeth hurt. Plus, she giggled constantly. She giggled when she was introduced to the Pon. She giggled when she and Hendril took their seats on the sofa opposite Lanali. She giggled at Lanali's questions, though she did at least have the courtesy to answer them when she was done. Yes, she was familiar with the Pon's teachings. Yes, she was an only child. Yes, her godfather technically held the legal power over her, even though she didn't live with him. No, she had no objection to going against her uncle's wishes—in fact, judging by the gleam that had entered her already sparkling blue eyes, going against her uncle's wishes was undoubtedly the very highest of *her* wishes. That, and no doubt a handsome, wealthy husband. Really, Lanali was giving her everything that she'd ever wanted.

Hendril played a polite smile as the girl leaned over and rested her head briefly on his shoulder. He was not as good of a liar as Tol, but he *was* a member of the aristocracy, and lying was a basic survival skill in their circles, too. When he looked at the girl, it seemed sincere enough. He laughed at something that she said, and kissed her lightly upon the nose.

It had taken Lanali a while to convince him to do it. She'd assured him most ardently that it need not change matters between them, though Lanali still hadn't decided if she would bother keeping that promise or not. When that still didn't seem to convince him, she'd "confessed" to him in a tearful whisper that she was incapable of bearing children—but that, as the lover of the Pon, some of her Grace had passed on to him. It was therefore imperative, she said, that *he* make a fruitful union, for all of their sakes, so that some part of her divinity would be left to the future generations.

The story was so ridiculous that even Lanali wasn't sure he would buy it, but she had apparently underestimated Hendril's loyalty as a true Devout: he literally fell to his knees at the idea, swearing that he would do everything in his power to fulfill this, the greatest honor of his life.

So that was good to know.

Lanali smiled at the two of them now, and bestowed nothing but blessings upon their impending marriage. They spent about an hour making arrangements. The joyful event would take place here, in Dreamfield House—quickly, and with the utmost discretion, the better to avoid her uncle.

Their business finally concluded, Lanali went to the window and waited until the two of them exited the great house. They strolled easily down the front walk together, his elbow holding her steady as they descended the steps. A carriage was already waiting for them at the street, and as Hendril paused to help his giggling bride inside, he turned back toward the building. He looked straight into Lanali's window, though he did not appear to see her. Lanali held herself steady—if she flinched back, shying out of view, the movement might draw his attention.

She knew that Hendril would have preferred a different bride to fulfill his great honor, but what she had told him the other day was true, in a Lanali sort of way: Lady Trelina Dufrane of Melmont *was* valuable to them and important to their cause, just not for the reasons Hendril believed.

Of course, Lanali wouldn't have even bothered with all of this fuss if Lord Shillingly or another one of the justices of the King's Court of State that still opposed her would just change his damned mind—but alas, that had yet to happen, and they were fast running out of time. Lanali knew that her game would be challenged, and she was not about to let victory slip from her grasp on account of a technicality.

The carriage trundled off, and Lanali turned away from the window. Her hand rested idly on her cheek, her mind spinning with all the threads that she had to keep hold of.

Ever since the ghost crisis, things had been different. Not just because the populace believed that Lanali had saved them from oblivion, though that certainly helped her cause. *Lanali* had been different. Something had happened to her, in the gardens beneath the realm of the Beacons, something that she couldn't quite remember; but ever since then, she'd felt drawn somewhere. It was like destiny itself had thrown her a life rope, and she was struggling to keep hold of it in a sea that was constantly trying to drag her down. She was meant to do something now, something important.

She had to find . . . something. She didn't quite know what—much less where to look for it—but she knew with all of her heart that she had to pursue it. But to do that, she needed resources. Vast and powerful resources, far outstripping the reach and scope of what any individual person could wield, no matter how rich they were.

In short: she needed control of the Crown.

And it was so close, now, so close that she could almost taste it.

The whisper of footsteps approached from behind her chair, carefully weighted so that they were just enough to announce their presence.

"So I've been thinking about our failures," Tol said. As usual, he'd been hovering just out of sight somewhere nearby—his presence had grown so familiar in Lanali's mind that sometimes even she forgot that he was there.

"*Your* failures," Lanali snapped through gritted teeth. "I will never fail."

Tol snorted. "That's the Pon talking. Not you."

Lanali threw herself from her chair, rounding to face him head-on. The air of the room thickened and darkened, a tiny storm roaring against Tol. *"I am the Pon!"*

"Yes," Tol said with the tiniest of sneers. He batted his hand at a fast-encroaching storm cloud, dissipating it as if it was nothing more than smoke. "In the meantime, I think that I've figured out some of why our efforts to rid you of Praxis Fellows keep . . . encountering difficulty."

Lanali scowled. She took a breath, willing the storm back. Within moments, the afternoon light was once again pouring through the windows. "She is my great nemesis," Lanali said. "It's no surprise. The fates are testing me."

"Good gods," Tol laughed, "you don't honestly believe that, do you?"

Lanali raised a single eyebrow and Tol leaned in, peering cautiously at the structure of her face. It's possible that they hadn't been this close in years, and from here Lanali could see the first flecks of gray beginning to creep into Tol's hairline, the ever-deepening lines that spidered out around his lips.

She turned away before he could offer his verdict. Lanali strode back to her chair, settling as if she had never been disturbed at all. "If you have something useful to say, then say it and be done."

There followed thereafter a lull, and for the briefest moment it seemed as if perhaps Tol was going to withhold his thoughts; but they both knew that Lanali would never beg, and Tol would never have brought it up if he didn't intend to speak his mind.

He came around Lanali's chair, so that he was once more within her line of sight. His hands were folded neatly in front of him, and he was idly tapping his wave tattoo with his opposite thumb. "It occurs to me that— aside from a *distinct* lack of patience—our biggest problem has simply been a matter of playing on the wrong side of the board. At best, we've made our gambits on neutral territory; at worst, they've been played out across her own squares. What we need," he went on, pausing slightly for dramatic effect (which Lanali only barely restrained rolling her eyes at), "is to lure her onto our own turf. Someplace where we can control all the elements at play."

"She would never fall for something like that."

"She might," Tol said. "Every player has their weak spots."

Rule twelve.

Lanali paused, considering the argument presented to her. Tol's suggestion was risky, yes—not just because there was no guarantee that Praxis could be manipulated into such a move—but when had Lanali ever balked at the idea of taking risks? She would not be where she was, *who* she was, if she was afraid of a tricky game. She tipped her head, neither agreeing nor dismissing the idea. "What did you have in mind?"

Tol smiled. Beatific, patient—and utterly uncooperative. He knew the value of his proposal, and was not going to give it up for free.

Lanali huffed. "*Fine.* You can have the job back—does that satisfy you? Make you feel sufficiently important?"

He did not rise to the bait. He dipped into a grateful bow, courtly as any of the high lords of Durland. "You will not regret it."

"I had *better* not," Lanali said. "Because this is your very last chance. I swear to the gods, Tol, if you cock this up again, I am going to install Hendril in your place—and then, you can answer to *him*."

The subtle tightening of a fist. Tol's polished smile was brittle around the edges as he met her gaze.

Lanali smirked, openly pleased with herself; and so, in the language of their trade, they understood each other. She waved her hand in dismissal.

Chapter Twenty-Four

PRAXIS CHANGED WITH remarkable speed, and they set off right away. To further the disguise, she was leaving most of her brace and control system behind: she'd locked the knee joint straight to give her something stable to lean against, and found a battered cane in the corner of the servants' quarters. She'd even started to grow out her own hair, but had barely added an inch before passing out from hunger.

Kaedrich, of course, took no end of joy in chiding Praxis for ignoring the advice that she'd just given her, and Praxis, of course, had scowled and muttered "shut up" as she'd gone in search of a hat or something. In the end she tried wrapping her head in a large scarf, which Kaedrich had to take off and reapply for her in order to get it to lay correctly over her hair.

She looked more than a little ridiculous in the end, more old-woman beggar than anything else, adding an extra hobble to her every step, though for their purposes it would suit them just fine. They sent Brex off hunting and snuck out the basement door. Kaedrich felt that it was probably stranger for her to see Praxis in a dress than it was for Praxis to see *her* in a dress, but she couldn't figure out a way to ask, and so she'd kept her mouth shut. Besides, how do you define the relative strangeness of something like that?

It wasn't *exactly* the first time that they'd had this experience, though it was the first time that they'd gone through it in the real world. When they'd first worked together, when they'd ventured into the land of the dead and stopped Lanali, they'd briefly entered an illusion drawn from Praxis's memories. Her childhood home under the ice, some ball befit to honor a queen. The illusion had placed Praxis back in the style of clothes that she'd grown up in, and whatever magic ruled over the process had bedecked Kaedrich in an appropriately styled ballgown of her own. So it wasn't as if either one of them was completely unprepared for the sight of themselves now, although there was some question in Kaedrich's mind as to the accuracy of the illusion they'd shared.

This was different. This was a dress that Kaedrich felt at home in; and somehow, even though it was a million miles from the palace beneath the ice where Praxis had lived, behind the veneer of the image they'd crafted for her, somehow the plain-spun clothes here seemed to suit her a little better, too. They stepped out into the world together, two unremarkable-looking women walking down the street, and no one batted an eye.

Given the circumstances, she knew that she really shouldn't be enjoying this so much. They were, after all, out on serious business. A man was missing, subject to who even knew what kind of potential horrors. A relatively good, relatively honorable man, a man that Kaedrich liked and respected (though, admittedly, a little bit less now that she knew what he'd said about Praxis all of those years ago). A man with a wife, with responsibilities, with maybe the power to answer some of the questions that had been plaguing the city for months now. People were counting on Kaedrich to find him, and she had every intention of doing her best.

But.

She couldn't help it. Being out like this, being free in her own skin again, being able to *breathe*, being beside Praxis, all of it lent a festive air to their walk through the city. Like they were two friends, the best of friends, headed out for a night of entertainment and fun. It was hard not to take Praxis's hand, harder still not to grin. She didn't even try to keep all of the skips out of her step. Her dress swung around her legs, a delightful breeze chilling her calves. She'd borrowed a dusty pair of Praxis's old boots, abandoned from the days when Praxis had lived in the Society house, and the click of tiny heels in tune to Kaedrich's steps was like a long-forgotten song. She had forgotten so much of what it was to walk about as a woman, to be seen as a woman. Some of it was nice: the unspoken solidarity with the others of her gender, being able to stop and say hello to adorably small children without people thinking you were strange.

On the other hand, there were things that she hadn't missed at all, the leering and even the less obvious gazes constantly sizing you up like something offered for Sunday brunch. There were things that she hadn't even realized were there until she'd gotten used to being without them, like the way that men would just keep walking toward her and expect *her* to always get out of *their* way (if she'd been a noble-born lady, it would have been different, gentlemen needing to adhere to the all important rules of etiquette—but as it was, even the men of her own social class treated her as if she was subservient to their very existence). Never had the world felt more sharply divided, and Kaedrich went through the city with an oversensitive awareness of the genders around her. Even the children, too young to be dressed differently, were still handled with slight adjustments depending on whether they would grow up to be a lady or a gentleman. Kaedrich watched it with the hairs raising along the back of her neck; this stuff was imprinted from birth, and for *what*? She made a perfectly respectable man, if she said so herself. She made a perfectly respectable woman. It meant nothing. The distinctions felt meaningless.

"Are you doing all right?" Praxis asked, and Kaedrich realized that she'd lost a bit of the enthusiasm from her gait.

She nodded. "I'm fine. Just thinking about everything. Doesn't it ever drive you crazy?"

"Many things drive me crazy," Praxis said. "You'll have to be more specific about which ones you're referring to."

Kaedrich laughed. They were edging their way through a thick crowd at the moment, and she focused instead on simply avoiding the elbows and errant feet, the tips of jutting canes and parasols and corners of boxes being carried back and forth.

She never did end up elaborating. They spoke little as they made their way across the city. Looking the way that they did, they felt that it was wiser to take the usual, long way around to the old quarter, rather than cutting up and over the crest where the high society lived; they'd likely be arrested if they even attempted the shortcut. It was a well-worn path along the inner curve of the city, to a point where the slopes came down low enough to be crossed, and then a journey nearly as long back along the outer curve. The smell of Monfort proper faded away as they rounded to the outer curve of the crater, the air now filled with a mix of industry and grime and stale dirt. Kaedrich glanced nervously skyward as they walked— the time that it had taken to meet with Praxis, get the dresses, change, make the slow journey here, every piece of it added up. The sun was not yet so low as to streak the sky with pinks and orange, but it would be doing so soon. If she'd known how long it was all going to take, she might have journeyed here as her usual persona and done her best regardless, but it was too late to lament about her choices now.

Finding Widow's Row took some doing. Neither Praxis nor Kaedrich were particularly familiar with the portion of the old quarter where it was located, and they ended up getting turned around a good half a dozen times before the faded sign for the Crimson Rose came into view.

They agreed to split up. One woman listening eagerly to local gossip would go unnoticed, even if she was gently asking questions that led around to a particular topic more often than not; but two would smack of specific intentions. And women with any kind of purposeful agenda were never trusted.

Praxis immediately started to head into the pub, but Kaedrich caught her sleeve.

"I don't think that's really the best idea, do you?" Kaedrich asked, raising her eyebrow pointedly.

Praxis sighed. "I'm *not* heading in there to get 'boshed,' if that's what you're thinking."

Kaedrich said nothing, though her silence spoke plenty as to her doubts.

"Oh, come on!" Praxis said. "Seriously? Have I ever broken my word about this to you? I promise that I'm going to behave myself. All business."

"If that's the case, why do you seem so insistent? Why don't you comb the street, and I take the pub?"

"Because, of the two of us, who do you really think is more likely to know how to talk to the people in there?" Praxis asked.

"I've had plenty of experience in pubs now, Praxis."

"Yes, yes," Praxis said, waving her hand in dismissal, "you're a much more worldly young m—*woman* than you were when you were just a simple country girl. I know. And yet." She held her arms wide, indicating that Kaedrich should take a good long look at her.

The trouble is that it was hard to argue her point. Despite the fact that they were both now wearing dresses of roughly equal low quality, they wore them completely different. Kaedrich's was a buttery yellow with tiny white flowers and cream (or possibly just aged) trim around the cuffs and neckline; it fell smoothly down the length of her body, any rips cleverly hidden, and she'd managed to find a ribbon that more or less matched it to tie back the mass of her hair. Praxis's, on the other hand, was baby pink except for the faded stain down one sleeve, and the fresh splatters of mud soaking up the hemline; it had been buttoned poorly, and one sleeve was hanging down longer than the other. There really was no question who the rum-soaked regulars in the Crimson Rose would be more willing to simultaneously talk to and ignore. And that was, after all, the whole point.

"All right, fine," Kaedrich said finally. "You're right. Just . . . promise me that you're not going to get into any trouble in there. That you'll be extremely careful—I don't want you to end up like the rest of them."

"Shall I make a Wizard's Oath?" Praxis asked.

Kaedrich rolled her eyes. "I don't think that's necessary."

"Good," Praxis said, "because we don't have time for all that fuss, and I highly doubt there are any willing virgins around to serve as my sacrifice."

Heat flushed up to Kaedrich's cheeks. "You . . . you are joking, aren't you?"

"I guess we'll never know," Praxis said. She grinned, already turning, leaning heavily on her cane for support.

Kaedrich stood and watched her go. The swish of her skirt as she let herself in the door, the faint trail of what might have been perfume lingering in the air behind her. A funny little knot had twisted up Kaedrich's stomach, hitting her at the same time as her blush. Maybe it was foolish, but Kaedrich hadn't really given much thought to the question of Praxis having former lovers. But there was something so easy and dismissive in the way that she'd joked about virgins, the tone of someone so far beyond the question that it had ceased to carry any weight at all.

Kaedrich shook herself. She turned away from the pub, trying to draw herself back to the present, back to the task at hand.

She got to work.

As Kaedrich had hoped, the streets surrounding the Crimson Rose were packed with gossip—and, also as she'd hoped, no one was paying the slightest bit of attention to a low-class woman going around collecting it like scraggly roadside flowers. Women's gossip, after all, was hardly considered a thing of value, so who was going to object?

Though trying to extract the useful bits of it was like attempting to wend free a single thread from a densely woven tapestry. Kaedrich kept having to reverse the conversation, trailing it down a twisting path that seemed to be going nowhere. It was exhausting, honestly, tittering or fretting alongside the women of the old quarter, acting as if she had no particular agenda for asking. The one upside was that it didn't tend to take much prodding to get them to express concern over the string of recent disappearances—but trying to divert it back to *this* disappearance, trying to discern if anyone had seen anything in particular *this* time, well, that was proving to be a little more troublesome than she'd expected. She wondered if it had anything to do with the fact that the victim this time hadn't been "one of their own," instead a moderately dressed man slumming it up from the middle reaches of the city. Like any other social group, these women tended to care less about what was happening outside of their borders, even if those borders were loosely drawn and occasionally cut through back alleys as if on a dare.

"Serves him right, struttin' in here with his fancy money," one of the women, a young nursing mother sitting out on her stoop, said. There was a small group of them, three all told, stacked almost on top of each other in the tightly neighboring doorways. Kaedrich had stopped by to coo over the children a few minutes ago, a shifting mass of little ones that toddled in and out of the doors and disappeared underneath their mothers' skirts. She was surprised to find the youngest of them still up and allowed out after dark in a place like this, but the middle mother had shrugged one shoulder, the baby at her breast gently rising and falling in line with her indifference. "They have to learn sometime," she'd said, and that was all that was spoken of that.

When Kaedrich had asked next if they were afraid of being out here all alone in the darkened street, the mother on the left had let out a hearty cackle. She was the smallest of the group, so slim and so young that for a moment Kaedrich hadn't thought she was one of the mothers at all, but rather a girl playing at being one. "No one dares bother *us*," she'd said, and the other two had nodded vigorously.

So Kaedrich had expressed a desire to feel as secure as they did, and asked what made them so confident, because she'd heard that just two nights ago a man had been taken right from these very streets—and a businessman at that, someone from the inner slopes of Monfort.

"Feh," the youngest, smallest mother had said.

"They're all soft as milk-dough," the one on the right said.

"Not *your* milk-dough," the youngest said.

"Serves him right," the middle one said, "struttin' in here with his fancy money."

The youngest nodded. "Yeah, tha's true as I ever heard."

"'Course you know who I'd really like to see get who's coming-to?" the middle one asked. She popped her baby free of one breast, and shifted it easily to the other. "The fancymen."

"Oooh, yes, the fancymen!" the youngest agreed, while the one on the right nodded. She was quietest, the right, stockier and with a somewhat rough face.

Kaedrich settled on an overturned bucket sitting nearby. One of the children came up and climbed unceremoniously onto her lap, and Kaedrich wrapped her arms around him. "Who are the fancymen?"

This got a merry laugh from each of the mothers. Cackling from the youngest, who slapped her bony knee; a deep guffaw from the middle; and a surprisingly girlish giggle from the stocky one on the right.

"The fancymen think they're so smart," the middle one said.

"Think they're better'n us," the youngest added.

"I'd like to see them try to do half as much as we do in a single *day*," the middle continued, "and then we'll see if they're still looking so fancy when it's over."

The youngest cackled again. "Lord, can you imagine the fancymen scrubbing down a floor?"

"Or throwing out the shitbucket?"

"Or wiping a bottom?"

"Well, now," the middle one said, "let's be fair. I imagine they'd be happy to wipe a fancy lady's bottom."

"Like anyone would let them near it!"

"Hey, for the right price?" the middle one asked. She rocked her hand back and forth like a shifting scale, as if to indicate that it could go either way in that case.

The one on the right shook her head. "The fancymen have been coming for ages now," she said, speaking directly to Kaedrich at this point. "Always in pairs."

"Good point," the youngest said. She sat up straight and grinned, like she'd just thought of the world's most amazing joke and wanted everyone to know it. "Maybe they're wiping *each other's* bottoms."

She and the middle one dissolved into raucous laughter at that one, but the one on the right merely shook her head again.

"No, what *I'd* like to see," the middle one said, after she'd finally composed herself again, "I'd like to see their trick for keep them coats so nice and clean. Down here night after night, and I know they don't drive no carriage in 'cause I've seen 'em walking the streets same as the rest of us, right? So they's got to be getting all kind of muck on them, but you don't even see no stains on their *boots*! Lord, if I could bottle that!"

"Yeah," the youngest one said, leaning forward and cupping her chin in her hands, and even the one on the right gave a wistful sigh.

They fell into a thoughtful silence after that, including Kaedrich, mulling over what she'd heard. She glanced down at the child that had crawled into her lap; he had curled up against her and fallen right asleep, his back in a curve along the crook of her arm as if she was a sling. All up and down the street were people skulking from one place to another, trying to avoid each other, but the mothers that Kaedrich had found herself with were right: no one was daring to bother *them*. A warm comfort extended from their front stoops, feeling almost like it would if a crackling fire lay by their feet. Yet no such fire existed, the stoops thrown under the cloak of darkness. It had to have been magic.

The boy in Kaedrich's arms shifted, and Kaedrich shifted in response to him, trying to keep his head propped up. "When did the fancymen first show up?" she asked, hoping that it wasn't too direct.

But if the mothers could tell that Kaedrich was specifically interested, they didn't care. The middle mother waved her free hand vaguely. "Three months ago? Near enough, at least."

The youngest nodded. "It was during that storm—you remember."

Right around the same time as the first of the disappearances, then. Kaedrich shivered. "These men . . . I don't suppose that you've gotten a glimpse of their forearms at all? Only, if they have a sort of silvery rash—"

"Ha! So you have seen them!" the youngest said. She swatted the arm of the one in the middle. "You see, I tolds you it weren't just us."

"Ow," the middle one muttered. "Quit hittin' me every time you think you're right, will you?"

The youngest one smacked her again.

"Ow!"

"I *tolds* you—"

"Yeah, yeah."

"Wait," Kaedrich started, trying to cut in before their argument could continue, "you mean that in all of this time, people this obvious . . . no one else has been seeing them?"

The middle one shrugged. The one on the right sighed. Only the youngest spoke.

"It's not that they don't see them, it's just that no one else . . . *notices* them, you knows? Like, you point to them and folks'll say, 'Oh yeah, that fella?', but then they'll just carry on like there's nothing about them. But there *is*."

"We *know*," the middle one said with a groan. This was obviously a tired argument. She reached over and patted the knee of the youngest one, three weary pats right in a row. "We know."

"Well, if we *know*, then why're we never doing nothing about it?"

The middle one smiled, her teeth flashing in the dark. "Oh, but we are," she said. She turned, looking straight at Kaedrich. "We're telling our friend here. Ain't we?"

"Ohhhh," the youngest said, like she finally got it, and even the one on the right had turned now. All three of them regarded Kaedrich with steady, open faces, as if this was nothing, as if they did this sort of thing every day.

And Kaedrich supposed that maybe she should have been unnerved by this, their apparent insight into her purpose, their faith in her ability to solve it, almost like they'd been sitting on the front steps waiting for her to show up, like they'd *known* that she would. The street had fallen quiet all around them, nothing but the softest *nup-nup* of the baby suckling on its mother.

The thing, though, is that Kaedrich trusted magic. Maybe she didn't before, and maybe all the rest of the country around her was losing what little faith they'd always had, but somewhere deep down in Kaedrich's bones was a belief burning so pure that it ran iron-red in her core. So she didn't get nervous at the idea that they had a plan for her, nor question how they'd gleaned their insight. She met their expressions straight on, still hugging one of their sons snug against her chest.

She nodded. "Yeah, I think I can do that."

The middle one grinned. The youngest clapped, making her look even more like the toddlers at their feet. The one on the right gave her a shy smile as she reached into the pocket of her thick work apron. "Take this," she said, drawing something out and passing it over.

Kaedrich leaned forward, being careful not to wake the boy in her arms. She found herself holding half of a fork, four long tines glinting as she turned it over. The handle had been snapped off, and a hole bored through the thick part where the tines all met. A dirty piece of twine was threaded through the hole, turning the thing into an ugly sort of necklace.

"The fancymen do *not* like silver," the one on the right said, answering Kaedrich's unspoken question. "Though I sold the handle to pay for food. Sorry."

"Don't ever be sorry for that," Kaedrich said. She slipped the twine over her head, tucking the piece of fork underneath her dress for safe-keeping. "Thank you."

The mothers nodded, one after another in a neat little row, like chickens bobbing for grain. Kaedrich stood up carefully, passing the still-sleeping boy over to the youngest mother, who'd extended her arms for him as soon as Kaedrich had moved.

They didn't say goodbye, and when Kaedrich reached the end of the street and turned back to look for them, they were gone.

Chapter Twenty-Five

THE FIGHT BROKE out about thirty seconds before Kaedrich walked in the door.

Of course, Praxis thought bitterly, just as she ducked to avoid the first swing of the man's fist. She had already sensed Kaedrich's approach a breath earlier, but by that time the tension in the room had nudged just beyond the tipping point, and the resultant fallout would inevitably spill forth regardless of what Praxis had done next.

"Go hang," she'd said, and then ducked as a meaty fist went *swoosh* over her head. If it was going to happen anyway, then Praxis would be damned if she didn't at least get the last verbal jab in before all of the hells broke loose.

Contrary to what colorful tales and adventure novels liked to paint, the entire pub did *not* all spring into chaos at once. The crowd closest to them—the ones that had been paying the slightest bit of attention, anyway—all sprang back, avoiding the flying of three chairs as everyone at Praxis's table leapt to their feet. And this did create somewhat of a ripple effect, the next layer shouting "oy!" and "watch it!" as they suddenly found themselves trampled by the hasty retreat of the innermost circle; the layer after that turned their heads, wondering if whatever had disrupted their neighbor's drink was going to be crashing into them as well. But at first most of the pub remained seated, and only the bartender himself surged *toward* the brawl.

Though by the time Kaedrich stepped in, catching the door in confusion as one of the patrons went fleeing out into the street beyond, things had somewhat . . . *escalated*. Who could really say why? It didn't matter why. Praxis did her best to avoid flying glasses and swinging arms, veering as she drew parts of the crowd between her and the men that she'd inadvertently insulted at the start of this whole debacle. "This is not my fault!" she called when Kaedrich tentatively popped her head inside, her eyes somehow instantly finding Praxis in the chaos and narrowing accusingly. And that was . . . sort of true. Partially true, anyway, almost certainly no more than fifty percent her fault, for a particular definition of "fault." She did not force those men to engage her in conversation, nor did she mean to cause offense when she'd suggested that his manners were probably the result of being dropped on the head as a baby.

There was no time to explain this to Kaedrich, however. Praxis grabbed her by the wrist and yanked her down in time to avoid being struck by a chair that was sailing across the pub. They ducked underneath a nearby table, their heads clonking in the scramble.

Kaedrich winced at the sound of something loud crashing nearby. "I asked you to be discreet!" she said, all but shouting to be heard over the calamity.

"Yeah, and why do you think I'm not using magic right now? You're welcome!"

"That's not what—!" Kaedrich started, but cut herself off as the table above them shook with the weight of two men slamming into it. Kaedrich's eyes widened in alarm as she scurried out from underneath. She raced for a relatively quiet corner of the room.

Praxis muttered under her breath as she slithered out from underneath the table. She hauled herself up, unsteady on her cane after so much practice with her brace, and veered across the pub toward Kaedrich with as much grace as she could muster. The one upside was that it seemed that the drunken oaf that she'd offended had gotten distracted in the ruckus; she spotted him halfway across the room, trading sloppy punches with a new partner.

"Satisfied?" Praxis asked, when no one came immediately to attack her on sight. In fact, the two of them were being so utterly ignored that if they wanted, they may well have been able to stay on the sidelines and place bets on the winners—not that Kaedrich was likely to go along with such a ploy (and that was a shame, really, for Praxis could have easily thrown some subtle magic in to manipulate the situation in their favor, and no one would have to be the wiser).

"No," Kaedrich said. "We're never going to find anything useful now that—watch out!"

They both ducked again, as a bottle struck the wall over their heads. Glass and dregs of liquid rained down over them.

Kaedrich sighed as they straightened up. She carefully brushed broken glass off of herself, shaking it out of her hair. "Right, well, if we're just going to be wasting our time, then we might as well—"

She cut herself off. Her eyes widened, though she quickly turned her head away from whatever she'd seen.

"What—?" Praxis started to ask, but Kaedrich shook her head.

"Over there," she muttered. A slight jerk of her hand, which could have been nothing more than another attempt at getting bits of glass off of her dress, but Praxis didn't think so. Praxis turned, following the vague line of direction that Kaedrich had indicated.

The pub was chaos, but it was easy enough to see what had caught her attention. Two men, dressed far nicer than anything else normally seen in these parts, were standing at the top of the stairs and looking down at the scene with pinches of distaste written plain across their features.

"Don't *stare*," Kaedrich said. She snagged Praxis's arm, and Praxis looked away from them. Praxis left a thread of interest behind, however, her magic teasing out until she could get a small sense of them as individuals, rather than merely pawns shuffling through a large crowd. She felt as they moved down the stairs, edged around the fight that was finally beginning to wind down. Felt as they moved toward the door.

"Shall we . . . ?" Praxis asked, already knowing the answer. Kaedrich had slipped around her, following the men at a discreet but stubborn distance.

Praxis grumbled, hurrying to follow. Her hip ached from the added pressure of supporting her body without the help of her leg brace, and she was far slower on a cane than she should be. "Slow down!" she hissed, though of course Kaedrich didn't listen. And nor should she, really: the men were already moving ahead, and if Kaedrich was to slow down and wait for Praxis, they would surely lose them.

It didn't matter for long, though—because just as Praxis was about to give up and send Kaedrich on ahead of her, the men abruptly stopped.

It was hard to know what had tipped the fancymen off, because Kaedrich was sure they were being reasonably discreet. Perhaps it was just a wizard's sense, an understanding that they were being followed, and no matter *how* good of a job they were doing, the fancymen would always be able to tell.

This was as good of an explanation as any. Praxis grabbed Kaedrich's arm, though Kaedrich did not need a wizard's sense to know that something was wrong. The fancymen had turned down a side street, which ended up being nothing more than a dead-end lane, and when Kaedrich rounded the corner she'd found them idly leaning against the wall.

No amount of backtracking was going to help her now, though she followed her first instinct to jump back, out of sight. She and Praxis darted around the corner and pressed themselves against their own wall, looking at each other with flickering panic and uncertainty. Kaedrich breathed in deeply, but all that the alley smelled like was filth and decay. Besides, Kaedrich knew that if the fancymen made a move to follow them, then Praxis would know about it, so Kaedrich felt reasonably all right with pausing for a second to figure out what to do next.

"I have no idea," Praxis said, whispering an answer to Kaedrich's unspoken question. "This was your crazy plan, remember?"

"Can we take them?"

Praxis laughed under her breath. "I'd rather not make the attempt if I don't have to. I'm not exactly at my best right now, remember?" She motioned with her cane.

Kaedrich nodded. "Okay, so we wait them out. Back off long enough for them to come out of hiding, then—"

"Shit!" Praxis said. She grabbed Kaedrich's hand. "We don't have to wait that long. Run. Run!"

Kaedrich pushed herself off of the wall. Praxis released her grip, all but throwing Kaedrich's hand away, and Kaedrich hurried down the street. It was only when she got near the end that she realized that Praxis wasn't keeping up, and when she turned back she found that Praxis hadn't even *tried*. Instead, Praxis had positioned herself almost directly at the intersection between the side street and the main, directly in line with the fancymen.

Kaedrich sighed. She ran back, but Praxis whirled, throwing a line of flames to leap up between them. "Just go!" Praxis shouted through the fire. "I'll hold them off!"

"Oh no you don't! Take this fire down right now!"

"No!"

"Fine!" Kaedrich shouted. "Then I'm coming through anyway!"

She did not give Praxis time to argue. Kaedrich took two large steps back, giving herself a tiny bit of run-up room. If she hesitated, she might not be able to drum up the courage, and so instead Kaedrich shut her eyes, muttered a fast prayer, and shot forward.

The sight of the flames almost managed to halt her in her tracks. A flare of terror burst through Kaedrich as she leaped up. She was plunging straight for them, and she squeezed her eyes shut in panic. Heat flared near her, licking fast at her skin—but just as it was starting to hurt, the heat vanished. Kaedrich opened her eyes as she came crashing back to the ground. She tumbled forward into a controlled somersault. Her skirts made the maneuver a little more tricky than it should have been, but Kaedrich was on her feet again just as the street cut out around her.

By now, at least, Kaedrich was familiar enough with magic to know a black haze hex when she stumbled into the middle of one. So she did not panic as she stood up in total darkness, and she did not panic as a flash of something magic sparked through the air nearby.

Praxis shouted something, though it was either not Durlish, or it was so slurred as to be unintelligible. A whip of flames cut through the dark, disappearing as fast as they'd been created.

The sounds of several pairs of shuffling feet cut through. One of them was coming for her, and it did not take a wizard to know that wizards had a significant advantage in an arena where you couldn't see. Kaedrich shuffled backwards, trying to be both careful and hasty, as she scrambled with the neckline of her dress. Her fingers snared on the twine of the necklace that the women had given her, and she yanked it off from around her neck. Kaedrich paused, listening to the noises of the street: the continued sounds of a fight, playing out nearby, and the rapid footfalls that weren't even trying to hide their approach.

Grasping the bit of broken fork in her fist, Kaedrich swung out. Her first strike didn't connect, and nor did her second, but she heard the sound of someone lunging, and on instinct she turned in toward it.

Kaedrich's fork made contact with something solid, and sank in deep. An angry scream cut through the fog. The fork jerked in her grasp, the fancyman obviously trying to yank himself back. Kaedrich tried to pull her fork out, to keep it for another strike, but it slipped out of her fingers before she could get it. "Blast!"

The fancyman was shouting something now, angry incoherent screeches that must have drawn the attention of his companion. In an instant, Praxis's familiar grip had settled on Kaedrich's elbow, her voice right in Kaedrich's ear. "*Now* will you run?"

* * *

IT WAS WITH enormous relief that Praxis felt Kaedrich start to move. Praxis kept a firm grip on her, guiding them slowly but steadily out of the haze of Praxis's own creation. Their attackers, for whatever reason, were making their own hasty retreat in the opposite direction. After several long minutes, they had cleared the range of Praxis's black haze hex, the night reopening around them.

Kaedrich jerked her arm free. "We shouldn't have let them go."

"We're lucky *they* let *us* go," Praxis said. She massaged her hip, which she'd wrenched painfully in an attempt to worm out of their grasp.

"But Mr. Bundling—"

"Is not worth *your* life," Praxis said. She cast Kaedrich a sidelong glance. "I'm sorry, but he's just not. We'll try again tomorrow."

Kaedrich went quiet. Which wasn't exactly a ringing agreement with Praxis's plan, no, but at least it wasn't an argument.

They took the hopper cars most of the way home, ignoring the dirty looks thrown at them by the rest of the passengers. Several people edged away, as if the very presence of two unescorted *women* from the old quarter would sully their fine clothes. For a moment Praxis considered pulling her shawl off, smoothing out her hair, holding herself straight, and telling them in her haughtiest voice exactly where they could place their twisted noses. If what others told her was to be believed, her current state of dress would not hide her pseudo-aristocratic upbringing, so she might as well use her powers for good, for once.

And she might have done just that, if Kaedrich hadn't leaned her head against Praxis's shoulder and let out a weary sigh. But there was no way that Praxis was moving now, no chance that she would risk disturbing this moment of quiet between them. The hopper car trundled underneath their seats, rocking them like a babe in a cradle. Outside, the sun had long since set, and in the darkened hopper car, just then, it was easy to forget about the other passengers sitting rows away. It was easy to imagine that it was just the two of them, tucked away somewhere alone.

"We're not going to find him, are we?" Kaedrich asked after a moment. She spoke softly into the fabric of Praxis's dress, fiddling with the cuff of the sleeve. There was a loose thread that she kept trying to tuck out of sight.

It took all of Praxis's mental effort to speak. "Of course we are."

Kaedrich's head shook with a faint laugh. "It's not like you to be the optimist."

"It's not like you to be the pessimist."

"Right now it's hard not to be."

"Don't say that," Praxis whispered. She shifted her hand, easing the cuff of her sleeve out from underneath Kaedrich's picking, and turned her palm up. Kaedrich's hand settled effortlessly into hers, their fingers interlacing and holding each other firm. "We'll find him," Praxis continued. "I said that we'll go back out tomorrow, and I meant it. Tomorrow, and the day after that, and the day after that, and we'll scour the entire city if that's what it takes. We'll turn it inside out. Together."

It was meant to be comforting, and yet as soon as Praxis had said it, she felt Kaedrich go still beside her. Tension replaced the sleepy looseness of Kaedrich's muscles. She picked her head up from Praxis's shoulder, and Praxis took a breath, ready to apologize for whatever had offended her, when she found herself looking right at Kaedrich. Kaedrich had picked her head up but only to turn it, to stare at Praxis, and she was so close, noses brushing with each jostle of the hopper car.

"Why are you being so nice to me?" Kaedrich asked.

And there were so many ways to answer that, that Praxis didn't even know where to start. *Because I would do anything to make you happy,* she wanted to say, or *Because you would do the same for me.* Because Praxis couldn't imagine *not* helping Kaedrich. Because seeing the dejection in Kaedrich's face pierced at Praxis's heart. *Don't you know by now?* Praxis wanted to ask her. *Because I love you.*

"Because . . ." Praxis started. She paused, licked her lips. "Because . . ."

"Bleaker Street!" the conductor shouted.

The hopper car jerked to a stop. Praxis and Kaedrich tumbled forward, breaking apart as they caught themselves on the seat in front of them. Lamplight from the platform splashed in, staining everything orange-yellow, and all around them, people were standing up and sneering in their direction.

"This is our stop," Praxis mumbled, though Kaedrich must have known that because she was already on her feet. She helped Praxis up, helped her retrieve the cane that had gone flying from her grip. Several of the other passengers looked on, affronted that someone of their status would be getting off at the same stop.

They shuffled out into the night air, warm and oddly dry for that time of year. The rest of the passengers that had gotten off with them were already hurrying down the platform's long staircase to the street below, and Praxis let them get ahead. She took her time, her leg and her cane *clunking* from one step to the next, Kaedrich hanging ever-faithfully behind her.

At least she didn't need to look at Kaedrich for a few minutes. Seeing her as a woman was messing with Praxis's head, making things that seemed like terrible ideas before look somehow just a bit more reasonable now.

They followed one street to another, cut down a set of narrow steps as the slope descended toward the coastal ring. The question of Praxis's motives seemed to have been forgotten, but in the silence anything could crop back up again. So Praxis cleared her throat, hoping to deflect the conversation before it had a chance to ensnare her once more.

"On the plus side, Bundling's disappearance at least fits the profile of the others."

"How do *you* know what the other disappearances were like?"

"Hey now," Praxis said. "I've been brought in to investigate, and I'll have you know that I've been investigating." She shrugged, seeing the incredulous look on Kaedrich's face. "Now and then. When I get the chance."

Okay, so it was once, but she didn't need to exactly admit that. One trip to the old quarter by herself, in the jumble of the first few days after her arrival. She'd nosed around, tracked down the people that had made the initial reports of the disappearances, listened to their sob stories. Gods, the sob stories. Praxis felt sullied just remembering the time that it had taken people to blubber them all out.

"Anyway," Praxis said after a moment, "like I said, it fits. So that's one mark in our favor."

"You think that's *good*?" Kaedrich said. Her attention snagged on the boarded up window of a passing storefront, but she dragged herself away from it as quickly as she'd begun. More shops were closing every day now. This was nothing new.

Praxis shrugged. "Sure it is. It makes it easier to understand what's happened."

"If we knew what was going on with the other ones, maybe."

"We know enough."

Kaedrich laughed under her breath. "Yeah? Like *what*?"

"For one thing," Praxis said, "we know that all the victims have reappeared eventually, whole and alive, and they lived for up to two weeks after their return. Which means that Bundling should, too."

This observation was met with a taut silence. Eventually, Kaedrich gave a nod.

"And once he does," Praxis continued, "we can get our hands on him immediately, and then *maybe* we'll finally get some answers to all of this mess."

"In time to save his life?"

Praxis hesitated. "Hopefully, yes."

She knew even before she said it that it wasn't what Kaedrich was hoping to hear, but there was no avoiding it. Praxis was not going to lie about something like this, was not going to try to soften the truth just to make Kaedrich feel temporarily better. They would try their best, yes. It might be enough.

"Do you think . . . ," Kaedrich started, but she trailed off midthought. She shrugged and turned away, watching the shopfronts again. Most of them were still open, hoping to entice people in until the last possible minute of the day.

"Do I think what?" Praxis prodded.

Kaedrich didn't turn back as she spoke, so the question was posed to the shops. "Do you think that he's going to be all right in the meantime?"

"I wouldn't go so far as to say 'all right,' no," Praxis said with a shrug. "Sorry. But given that Lanali's apparently been trying to recreate the magic of the Silvers for herself, 'all right' seems a bit much to hope for."

Kaedrich flinched. A part of Praxis wanted to take back her words, but what would be the point of that now? The conversation had soured the bubble of softness from earlier, and Praxis wanted nothing so much as to hurry back to Calswell House and forget about the evening they'd had. Despite herself, she found her mind drifting toward poor Bundling's fate, imagining the kind of things that he might be going through right now. She may not *like* the man, no, but he didn't deserve to be turned into a Silver for Lanali's amusement. No one did. The extra weight in Praxis's arm seemed to increase as they walked, dragging her mood down to trail behind her in the filth of the street. In her pessimism, "all right" seemed a bit much to hope for—in any of her endeavors.

"THEN IT'S A good thing I'm here, isn't it?" Praxis had asked, years ago. She pushed her short sleeves farther up her arms, leaning back as she fanned herself with a handful of ancient scrolls that had been smoothed flat for ease of use.

Across the table from her, Tully glanced up. "What?"

"You said that no *man* has ever been able to crack the secret."

A tiny crease appeared between his eyebrows. "A fault of your language, not mine. You will not succeed—certainly not due to the flower of your sex."

"Leave my flower out of this. My *brain* is going to solve it."

Tully shook his head. He did not argue—he did not need to. His dismissal of Praxis's abilities pooled off of him like the faint lines of sweat trailing down the sides of his face and neck. Though he had been a true and able translator so far, he had never believed in her quest.

That was fine. Praxis wasn't looking for anyone to believe her. The only person's approval that she sought was the only person whose approval she had *ever* sought, and if she was successful then he would be the first to know.

It had been two months by this point, more or less, and every day was the same. Praxis was living comfortably in a hotel in the middle of the city—Tully had insisted that she would be more than welcome to stay in his family's house, but after her experiences in Aul, Praxis was in no hurry to lodge with *anyone's* family. Instead, she stayed in her hotel, and she had Tully meet her in the lobby every day just as the sun sank below the canopy horizon. Although the darkened lenses he'd given her were helpful if she *had* to go out in the daylight, the omnipresent heat of the middle of the afternoon was still more than she could tolerate. In the end it was simply easier to sleep through the worst of the day, and conduct her business at night.

"I cannot believe that you choose such an unnatural way of life," Tully said to her, after three weeks of putting up with her odd hours. He was yawning as they walked along the emptying streets.

"*Pfft.* There is nothing natural about the sun."

"People are going to start thinking we're *kinjin* if we keep this up. Vampires," he added when she looked confused.

Praxis laughed. "Vampires are a myth."

"True," Tully said. He shot her a meaningful look. "Anyone who believes that there is an escape from death is surely believing a lie. Yet some of us insist on clinging to it anyway."

Praxis hadn't answered him, and since he'd made his point, he didn't push the issue.

They worked in the libraries of the famous cloud shrines. The northern edge of the city was carved straight into the side of a mountain range, and the cloud shrines were on platforms farther up the slope. A mountain river broke out of the rocks a little above the shrines, cascading down as a waterfall that they collected and sent as a narrow canal between the network of buildings. At the edge of the shrines' platform they'd formed another waterfall, which fed into a branching set of canals that provided both running water and electricity throughout the entire city like a circulatory system. (A third waterfall sent whatever was left over crashing into the jungles below, where a basin had formed and leaked out into a natural river.) In truth, it wasn't so much normal *clouds* that hid the walls of the shines from the view below, as vapor from all the different waterfalls, droplets turning to mist as they tumbled from one level to the next to the next. But since when did a thing like truth matter in the naming of things?

To get from Praxis's hotel to the cloud shrines required crossing over the canal network at three separate bridges, and then climbing a narrow set of steps built right near the main waterfall. Cool mist constantly drifted over the steps, which made for a pleasant break from the heat, but also a treacherous climb—everything turned slick underfoot, and especially at night, you had to use extra care to navigate to the top. Tully often used this as an argument for shifting their timetable back to the daylight, but Praxis would not be budged. Instead, she raced up the steps as quickly as she could, hitching her skirts high so that she could vault up two or three at a time. Sometimes she even slipped, nearly falling off the high platforms, where, Tully assured her, she'd have surely met her death— unless she *happened* to know of a spell that could slow a person's descent, which of course she did not, though the idea of it intrigued her. He'd meant it as a reprimand. What he didn't know is that these near misses were only serving to fuel the bubble of belief that Praxis was growing as to her own immunity toward death. Every night now she was getting more reckless. A crackling energy was building just underneath her skin, and the only thing that ebbed it was these occasional brushes with her own mortality—or seeming lack thereof.

It could not be denied: something was going to break soon. Praxis felt the certainty of it, seeded deep in her bones.

And then one day she woke up, and she just knew—suddenly *knew*— exactly what her next move had to be.

Her eyes flew open. Her scar was flaring, the heat of it leaching out to flush the rest of her skin. The glare of the afternoon sun snaked around the edges of her curtains, vivid slices that seared at her vision. Praxis threw her hand over her face as she stumbled out of bed. She rang for one of the hotel's handmaids, dressed quickly, stuffed her tinted spectacles over her face as she cut a mad dash across the city. Her hair was still in the braid that she'd worn to bed, and it thwacked against her back as she ran, loose pieces of hair flying around her head and sticking to her sweaty neck. She was probably attracting any number of stares and startled looks, but Praxis did not care. She knew what she was doing now. She *knew*. The fire of her scar was racing as fast as her heart.

It didn't take long to find the house of Tully's family. He'd told her where it was in case she changed her mind and ever wanted to visit, and though the only part that she remembered was which region it was located in, once she got there it was only a matter of following her sense of his location. Praxis stopped short in front of a home that looked impossibly small. For a fleeting moment she was convinced that her intuition had somehow led her astray, but no, he had managed to imprint himself upon her senses in their months together, and there he was, lying just behind this wall, in the corner.

She skipped the door and rapped straight on the wall itself, right over his head. "Tully!" she shouted. "Tully, wake up!"

On the other side of the wall, Tully fell out of his bed as he jerked awake. Praxis sensed him stumble to his feet, tripping as if he was tangled up in sheets or else over items scattered on the floor. She moved to stand in front of a steepled window at the same moment that he did, and by the time he yanked the curtains open she was already grinning.

"Come on," she said, and waved him along, "come on, come on, we have work to do."

Tully blinked, scrunching his face up and squinting. "Miss Fellows? What are you—What time is it?"

"I don't know." Praxis shrugged. "Hot. But that's not the point; this can't wait."

Tully groaned. He was already making like he was going to collapse back onto the nearby bed, and so Praxis leaped up and reached through the high window, grabbing him by the collar of his shirt. Or probably pajamas, but she wasn't going to bother looking. "No, no, no, no, no. No sleep. We've slept too much. Work. Inspiration. Now."

Twenty minutes later (it might as well have been twenty *hours* for the speed that it felt like it took to pass), they were crossing the threshold into the archives of the cloud shrines. "Where was it, where was it, where was it?" Praxis was muttering to herself, hurrying with little rabbit-hop steps down the long aisles. The archive was massive. Praxis cut straight through the main library, where she'd spent hours pouring over thick volumes, and ran to the depths. In this room, stacks of diamond-shaped cubbyholes were built so tall that standing on the attached ladder to reach the top left even the most seasoned expert a little shaky. Praxis was craning her neck this way and that as she moved, turning around in a series of circles on her way down the length of the room. Tully shuffled some distance behind her, still occasionally yawning.

She found what she was looking for. In a cubbyhole about halfway up one of the shelves, tucked into the corner of the heat-soaked halls. Praxis wiped her hands down on her skirt to remove the sweat before she gingerly plucked the scroll off of its stack. The depths contained all the oldest writings, volumes that gave even Tully some difficulty.

Tully was already seated at a table, his head propped up by his fist. He jerked awake as Praxis slapped the scroll down in front of him.

"It was this one, I'm certain of it," Praxis said. She peeled the scroll open, laying ceremonial stones along the corners to hold it down. The ancient paper crackled slightly, unhappy about being disturbed again so soon after she'd pawed through it the last time. Praxis jabbed her finger at the text, the curling letters familiar but unreadable. "Start somewhere there—it was in the middle, something about dreams."

Tully sighed, but he did what he was asked. He muttered under his breath as he read, and his fingers trailed over the scroll. He did not touch it, leaving just a whisper of space. Underneath his guidance, the words began to shift and rearrange themselves, letters slithering from one configuration to another. The round and merry script of Tjalavan slumped, words seeming to collapse sideways against their neighbors as if they were too weary to stand, and soon the slanted print of Yandosian took their place.

Praxis was reading over his shoulder as he worked. "That's it!" she shouted a moment later. She ripped the scroll out from underneath his grasp—several letters now appeared smudged, halfway through their transformation, though the effects wouldn't last more than an hour or so. She retreated to the other side of the table, settling down to read as if she was a beggar presented with a seven-course dinner. She grinned up at Tully, having spotted what she was looking for. "Dreamer's death," she said.

Tully shrugged. "What about it?"

But Praxis was already standing back up, already rerolling the scroll and stuffing it hastily down the front of her blouse. "Come on, come on," she was saying again, her same manic refrain. She grabbed Tully's hand and dragged him to his feet. "If we hurry, we might just have enough time to make it before sundown."

"Make it—? Miss Fellows, what are you talking abou—"

"We're going to the jungle," Praxis said. "You're going to help me die."

Chapter Twenty-Six

Praxis must have noticed the growing hesitation in Kaedrich's muscles the closer they got to the Society house, because no sooner had they tromped into the basement than Praxis said, "You know, there really isn't a rush for you to leave. Why don't you go ahead and enjoy being dressed as yourself for a while longer?"

Kaedrich was turned away from her at the time, so she did not even try to hide the initial grin that this brought to her face. She gave what she hoped was a mild shrug of indifference. "I suppose I could, yeah."

"Good," Praxis said. Kaedrich was surprised to hear a sigh of relief in her voice, but when she turned back all she found was Praxis motioning at one of the large worktables. "Because honestly, I'm having trouble sorting all of this out. I don't suppose . . . ?"

Kaedrich nodded. "Of course." Of course Praxis would have been happy for the extra help—of course it wouldn't have been anything *more* that was making her pleased that Kaedrich had stayed. Kaedrich tried to keep the disappointment from her face. She squared her shoulders and went over to have a look at the mess sprawling over the tabletop. It seemed that Praxis had assembled most of the bits and pieces of what they'd found and learned over the course of this mixed up jumble of investigations, but trying to put it into any kind of coherent order was clearly too much organization for her. Kaedrich smirked.

"Well, if you'll excuse me, *I'm* going to go change," Praxis said. She was already gathering up the scattered clothes and pieces of her leg harness from where she'd left them in her haste.

"Oh . . . I could go upstairs for a minute, let you—"

"No, no." Praxis waved her hand as she moved toward the stairs. "There are plenty of rooms in the rest of the house, I'll manage. You stay. Maybe you'll have better luck with all of that than I have."

She was gone before Kaedrich could argue. Her deliberate footsteps thumped up the stairs one at a time and trailed along the floorboards over Kaedrich's head, but in their wake a sense of utter isolation fell on the basement. Kaedrich glanced at the table, a physical manifestation of everything that they had yet to accomplish. Their failures drifted like ghosts in the empty room.

She had to admit that there was no helping Mr. Bundling tonight —Kaedrich had no idea how to contact the policeman until their pre-arranged meeting tomorrow morning, and despite the presence of "the fancymen," that brought them no closer to being able to track him *down*. Following the fancymen had proven impossible, and though Praxis had gotten a glimpse of a cottage during her visit to the land of the dead several days earlier, the obscurity that Lanali had shrouded over it meant that they had no idea where to start looking. Though Kaedrich didn't like sitting still at a time like this, she had to admit that motion would be pointless without a direction; all she would do is expend meaningless effort under the guise of making herself feel better, and that wouldn't do Mr. Bundling any good.

So she turned her attention to the jumble in front of her, like she'd said that she would. The surface was littered with a bit of everything: beakers as Praxis attempted to break down and understand the chemical properties of the bullet and the plant that had attacked Kaedrich; a map of the city, pins sticking up like metallic trees in a thickening forest that spread over the twisting streets; scraps of bone, ground down or sliced into thin discs; the melted lumps of metal that Kaedrich had retrieved from the box in the morgue.

There had to be a pattern to all of it. *Something* linking all of these disparate pieces together, *some* means of connecting it back to Lanali in a way that people would believe. Kaedrich had to believe that, because otherwise what was the point of all of their efforts?

She decided to start with simple organization. Praxis wasn't exactly known for her tidiness; and in grouping like with like, there was a certain meditative quality for Kaedrich. For a while she almost lost herself in the efforts, and eventually she even picked up a spare sheet of paper and began to make her own list, random questions that nagged at her while she was sorting things out.

Kaedrich worked for a long time, though it was hard to tell exactly how much. Long enough for her shoulders to grow stiff, for her neck to begin to ache. Her stomach gave a thin wail, and Kaedrich straightened up. The world came back to her, slowly, and somehow a bit more manageable than it had been before. She stretched her back and shoulders, her joints popping. Her pocket watch was folded into her pile of men's clothes, and she got up from the stool and went to find it.

On her way, she passed by the collection of framed photographs that had caught her attention that first morning, when the cuts all over her arms had reopened. (Thankfully, though the injuries had come back a little since then, they'd reappeared only as angry red lines, somehow already scabbed over. One or two of the deeper wounds had bled when they'd first shown up, but it was nothing that Kaedrich felt she couldn't handle on her own, and nothing that she'd wanted to bother Praxis with.)

Kaedrich glanced at the staircase. She hadn't heard or seen any sign of Praxis since she'd gone upstairs to change, but if Kaedrich was going to allow herself to snoop—and Kaedrich did not kid herself, that was exactly what she was doing—she did not relish the idea of being caught out.

All was quiet, however, and so Kaedrich allowed herself to lean over and examine the photographs.

To her amazement, most of them were not portraits. Though Kaedrich understood that sometimes pictures were taken for other reasons, she had never known a person to collect and display them like this. It was rare enough to get a picture taken at all, and most people did not want to waste it on anything other than their loved ones.

So really, it should not have come as a surprise, and yet it did. Kaedrich poured over them anyway, as much as if they'd been faces. There was one that showed a mountain range, white snowcapped peaks underneath a smudge of gray sky, and another was a moss-covered stone building somewhere in a jungle. One was so hazy with smoke that it was difficult to make out the details inside of it at all. Another showed an empty room, an ostentatiously decorated chair so covered in glimmering gems that it may well have been a throne.

The few portraits that she did have were no more illuminating. Praxis, posed stiffly on the deck of a sailing ship, a trim dress blurring around the hem as the wind no doubt toyed with it; she was surrounded by a group of sailors, bearded men with dark skin and thick beards. A distance shot of Praxis in front of a building in what looked like it could have been Monfort, the familiar spiral rooftops spread out behind her. There was one that wasn't actually a photograph at all, but rather a painted portrait, and that one Kaedrich picked up. It had been tucked in the back, hidden behind so many other frames that even its splash of bright colors had been hidden behind the sea of black and white.

That one nearly took her breath away. It was an oval painting in an oval frame, so expertly done that it could have easily passed for real life. In it was Praxis as a very young woman, done up to look like a queen; a high collar spread out behind her and dwarfed her head, and she was swaddled in a ballgown that spilled out to take up the rest of the frame. What little background you could see was white and icy blue, no doubt the depths of Yandosia. Gems trailed over her entire dress, twisted in ribbons up her high collar, dotted her hair. It wasn't that Kaedrich had never seen anything like this before—the memory that she'd stepped into in the land of the dead was from this same time—but even that was . . . different. Praxis may have looked more or less like this, but she was still *Praxis*, the same woman that Kaedrich knew, and they'd struggled together to free themselves from the memory.

The version of her in the picture . . . that was something else. A frozen moment of time, one in which Praxis was clearly settled into her role in life. The artist had captured her perfectly: the faint trace of boredom in her eyes, the superior tilt of her chin, the practiced smile. This Praxis never would have looked at Kaedrich twice.

A loud crash from upstairs caused Kaedrich to jump. She nearly dropped the painting, catching it only at the last second. Kaedrich hastily set it back on the shelf and was already sprinting toward the stairs by the time Praxis's shouting and cursing caught up with her.

Kaedrich hitched her skirts up and vaulted up the steps, raced down the twisting hallways. She followed the trail of shouts and the ever-thickening stench of smoke, her heart pounding. A dozen images filled her head, everything that could be going wrong right now: Lanali's people, broken into the house; Praxis fighting for her life; the place beginning to burn down around them. Gods, why hadn't Kaedrich checked on her earlier? What had distracted Praxis; why hadn't she come back down to the basement? Kaedrich should have *known* that—

But when she burst through the door, there were no attackers. Brex squawked madly, swirling through the thick smoke of the room, and Praxis was somewhere in the depths swatting at something as flames leapt up in front of her like angry lions. Kaedrich lunged forward. She grabbed a cloth for protection and wrapped it around the handle of the source of the flames, a frying pan on a heavy stove. She ran across the room with it, plunging the frying pan into a sink full of tepid water. Steam leaped up toward her face, and Kaedrich jerked back as a symphony of hisses and pops erupted from in front of her. She could not see at first, just a wall of heat and damp blotting out her vision, smoke stinging at her eyes. Brex was still squawking like crazy from the ceiling, though even he seemed to be sensing that the worst of the disaster had passed.

"Gods," Kaedrich muttered as she turned around. She swiped at her brow with the back of her sleeve. "What in the darkness were you *doing*?"

Though even as she posed the question, a sense of understanding was beginning to creep up her back. Kaedrich took in the sweep of the kitchen: a pile of unevenly chopped vegetables sitting on the counter beside a spilled sack of flour; a stockpot bubbling and rattling its lid on the stove, trails of liquid running burned down the sides; a fat, battered old cookbook propped against a tin canister, held open with an egg slouching against its pages. Praxis was staring sheepishly at the mess on the stove, the pools of congealed *something* hissing as they fused against the hot surface. She was actually wearing a stained cook's apron that she'd no doubt found somewhere in the cupboards.

"It's *supposed* to be dinner," Praxis said finally, as Kaedrich approached the stove, "only I think it's malfunctioning."

Kaedrich lifted the lid off of the stockpot and reeled back. Whatever it was that Praxis had intended to make in there, it clearly wasn't that anymore—a grim sludge, vaguely green but mostly brown, was blorping and sputtering as thick bubbles broke the surface. "What was this even supposed to *be*?"

Praxis pointed at the cookbook, and Kaedrich picked it up, glancing at the three recipes displayed therein. Kaedrich bit down on a smile. "Right . . . You realize that these are all sauces, don't you? None of this is intended to be eaten alone."

"I . . . ," Praxis started, and then she screwed her mouth up in distaste. "I knew that. Obviously I knew that. That's what the liver and game hens were for." She motioned, vaguely, at the blackened lumps that Kaedrich had thrown into the sink.

It took all of Kaedrich's self-restraint not to laugh openly in Praxis's face. She shut the cookbook, tucking it away underneath the countertop. "Okay, seriously, if we're going to get anything to eat tonight, I think that you should let me take over."

Praxis sniffed indignantly. "And how do *you* somehow just know how to do this?"

"Hey, I may be playing at being a man these days, but I was raised as a woman, remember?" She spread her arms wide, her true form making her point for her.

"Yeah, well, so was I."

"No," Kaedrich said. "You were raised as a *lady*. There's a big difference."

Praxis scowled. She clearly wanted to argue the point, though Kaedrich knew already that she'd won. Kaedrich held out her hand, and Praxis grudgingly undid the ties of her apron. She did not immediately hand it over, however, clutching it against her chest for a moment as she took in the results of her own misguided efforts. There was obviously something gnawing at her, and she fought against herself for a moment, wringing the apron tightly as she thought it over.

Kaedrich took a step forward—to start cleaning off the stove, since there was no way they were getting any cooking done on that mess, and so as not to rush Praxis's internal struggle—but Praxis held up her hand as if to stop her.

"Will you teach me?" Praxis asked, all in a rush.

The question had clearly taken enormous effort for her. She bit her lip now, staring at Kaedrich anxiously as she waited for a response.

Kaedrich blinked. "You . . . you want to know how to cook?" Honestly, she could not have been more surprised if Praxis had said that she was renouncing magic and devoting her life to Perlandra.

Praxis forced a nod. Just once, and then something seemed to settle in her mind, and she nodded again, twice, and more enthusiastically. "I do," she said. "I . . . I want you to teach me how to cook. And . . . I don't know, laundry? That's something people without servants have to do for themselves, right?"

"Sure it is."

"Okay, then. That. And . . . whatever else you think I've been lacking, by growing up in . . . what did you call it? An 'ice palace'?"

Kaedrich shrugged. She couldn't recall specifically ever referring to Praxis's home by those terms, though it sounded like something she'd have said. "You do realize that if *that's* your criteria, then you're going to have a *lot* of catching up to do, right?"

"Probably," Praxis said. "I mean, if you say so, then sure. I wouldn't know. But I want to. I don't . . . That is, I'm not . . ."

She fell silent. She looked down at the apron still twisted up in her hands. Praxis had probably never even held an apron before, much less put one on and tried to cook something. She looked so out of place with it, like a child trying on her mother's dresses. Lucan's words came back to Kaedrich as she watched. *They can't help but feel superior to the rest of us, Mannly. It's in their blood.*

Kaedrich frowned. *Nonsense,* she thought to Lucan, days too late. If Kaedrich had accepted the life and the mindset that she'd been born into, she never would have ended up where she was today. Neither would Praxis. The circumstances of your birth colored your impressions of the world, certainly, and if you didn't stop and question them, you could go your whole life assuming that all of your bad behaviors were normal. And maybe you would always carry a sliver of that experience with you, blinding you to certain advantages that you received, but Praxis was *trying* to see around hers. Kaedrich was not going to discourage that.

"Right, then," Kaedrich said. She went over and found a rag in a nearby drawer, which she tossed over to Praxis. "Put that apron back on. The first thing that you're going to need to do is learn how to clean up your own messes."

"No," Praxis laughed, shaking her head. "No, that can't possibly be true. Tell me you're making that up."

"I swear on my bones that I'm not," Kaedrich said. She sighed, slouching farther into the stiff cushions of the divan. She was sitting sideways, her bare feet propped on one armrest and her back against the other. She'd long since released her hair from its confines, and it pillowed around her head as she shifted position. Her face went soft and contemplative as she stared at the half-empty glass balanced on her stomach. Despite herself, a smirk and the whispers of a giggle fought against her lips. "It took *weeks* to get the stink out."

This, of course, sent Praxis into a fresh round of her own laughter. She clamped her hand over her mouth, trying not to find mirth at the expense of a childhood Kaedriella, but the more that she tried to stamp it down, the more forcefully it escaped her chest.

"Gods, I can't believe that you would do something like that," she said once she had regained enough composure to speak. "I wish I had known you then."

Kaedrich smiled in a sleepy way, her eyes unfocused as she stared into the depths of her memory. "No, you don't. I was a bratty child, and you would have already been nearly grown. You'd have *hated* me."

"Ha! You want to compare bratty child stories? I promise that I'd have out-bratted you three times before breakfast."

"And you're still doing it," Kaedrich said, grinning as she raised her glass in a toast.

Praxis stuck her tongue out. "Shut up," she said, though by that point they were both dissolving into giggles.

Somewhere from the depths of Calswell House, a clock that may or may not have still been running correctly tolled out three o'clock. They'd been in the back sitting room since sometime after midnight, the remains of their wine bottle dragged in with them as they stumbled in and slumped on whatever sheet-covered furniture was available.

But then, they hadn't even gotten around to dinner until nearly eleven. It had taken Praxis ages to return the kitchen to a clean enough state that Kaedrich would even consider letting her cook in it again. Praxis had tried to argue that it hadn't even been that clean when she'd *started* messing it up, but that logic hadn't made a difference. Kaedrich sat on a rare empty counter, munching on one of the apples that Praxis had bought with the vague idea of preparing some kind of tart, and from here she offered direction and the occasional bit of advice as Praxis scrubbed and scoured, rinsed and dried and mopped.

"You know, you could get down here and *help* for once," Praxis had snapped at one point. She'd been cleaning up a greasy, filthy puddle that she had no idea how she'd even made, sitting on her knees (an effort in and of itself, given her brace and control system) and cursing her earlier insistence on learning how to do all of this nonsense.

But Kaedrich had only laughed at her, and taken another crackly bite of her apple. "What," she asked around her mouthful, "like the way that you've always volunteered to help me?"

That had shut Praxis up, though not without a scowl and a long-suffering sigh.

Learning how to make dinner, by comparison, had almost been a pleasure. Kaedrich had rummaged through the spartan pantries, looking for things left behind in the Society's haste to evacuate the property, and had stumbled upon a sack of oats that she deemed still fresh. Praxis was grateful she didn't openly question the presence of the new fruits and vegetables, the results of Praxis's trip to the market the day before, when she'd been out and had the grand idea of looking for an excuse to cook for Kaedrich in the first place.

Praxis had expected many more ingredients to follow, but Kaedrich only drew out a handful of staples: milk, a little bit of sugar, a cinnamon stick that she'd found who-knows-where. One of the apples. Praxis stared at them incredulously for a moment—what in the world was Kaedrich expecting her to make with these? Okay, so she was wizard, but that didn't mean that she could perform kitchen magic.

"You don't need magic when you're making oatmeal," Kaedrich said.

Praxis raised an eyebrow. "Oatmeal?"

"What, you expected me to start you off with something complicated? No," she continued, ignoring the look that quite plainly told her that, yes actually, that was what Praxis expected, "if you can't handle the basics, then you'll never manage anything. Trust me. Oatmeal."

So oatmeal it was. Kaedrich kept a careful eye over Praxis's shoulder, but just like the cleaning, she made Praxis do all the work. When it was done, Praxis held her breath as Kaedrich dipped her finger straight into the pot and took a sample. Kaedrich nodded. "Not bad," she said. "A little runny, but not bad."

They ate in the dining room, bunched together at one end of the long table. Kaedrich had found a bottle of old, cheap wine as she'd been rummaging, and she produced it with a flourish as Praxis dished up.

"I thought that you didn't like me drinking," Praxis said, hesitating as she accepted a glass.

"I don't like you *abusing* it," Kaedrich said, "which is all that you ever did before. But Brex is out hunting, and you're under my supervision for the evening." She smiled, tapping their glasses. "I'd say we're safe."

Praxis poured the very last of the wine out now, shaking the bottle as if proof was required that it was really empty. She set the bottle on the floor beside her chair, staring up at the ceiling of the sitting room. In order to avoid drawing attention from the street, they'd left the lights off and fire empty, with only the moonlight for company as their eyes adjusted to the dark.

A long stretch of silence followed their latest bit of laughter. The house was utterly still around them, only the subtle whistle of the occasional gust of wind batting at the windows.

"Why don't we do this more often?" Praxis asked finally. She spoke into her glass more than to Kaedrich, though it was obvious who the question was directed toward.

Kaedrich tossed a grin across the room. "Do what, have dinner? I don't know about you, but I try to every night."

Praxis rolled her eyes. "No, not *dinner*. *This*. Just . . . being together, without work, or some stupid crisis propelling us from one disaster to another."

"That does seem to be our routine," Kaedrich admitted. She shrugged. "I don't know. Just one of those things."

Praxis continued to stare at her wine, as if drawing courage from the bottom of her glass. "It's only that . . ." She hesitated. "I . . . I love spending time with you."

Another silence filled the room. Praxis scowled at herself as she drained the last of her wine; so close. So, so close, and yet . . .

Coward, she thought, and she was right.

When Kaedrich did speak next, it was so soft that Praxis had a difficult time figuring out what she said, though it sounded like "Tell me something."

"What?"

Kaedrich cleared her throat. "Tell me something," she said again, more confident and yet also somehow shying back around the edges. Praxis had the distinct impression that it was only the beginning of a thought that she'd decided not to finish.

"What do you want me to tell you?" Praxis asked. She was nervous, suddenly; her hands went clammy around her empty glass. Right here, right now, if Kaedrich asked her openly . . . even with her cowardice, Praxis didn't know if she had it in her to lie to Kaedrich's face.

But to Praxis's simultaneous relief and disappointment, Kaedrich shrugged in dismissal. "I don't know. Tell me anything. I've been talking all night—tell me a story. Tell me something about you that I don't already know."

"I . . . I'm really not much of a storyteller."

"Nonsense. You make stuff up all the time. Pretend you're doing that, except this time make it true."

Make it true. As if it was that easy, as if being honest was simply a matter of just opening your mouth and letting the truth tumble out. Praxis had no idea where to even start.

"Come on," Kaedrich prompted after a moment. She yawned widely, stretching out her arms as she set her glass on the floor. Her legs stretched next, each tiny toe spreading, her skirt riding up her calves as she tented the armrest with the bend of her knee. She'd slouched completely down on the couch now, her head snuggled against the flat cushion beneath her as if it was a pillow. Her eyes closed. "Tell me a bedtime story. Tell me anything."

Anything. The prospect was so enormous that it was dizzying, like the first time that Praxis had stood underneath the night sky. She'd squinted up and tried to see if she could find the face of her *sare l' dell* somewhere in the jumble of points that crowded overhead as thick as a snowfall, even though by then she was already too old to believe in such romantic fairy tales. Now she sifted through her memories, trying to find something that was suitably entertaining without also being maudlin or macabre. She thought about her childhood, her lonely adolescence, the long string of countries that she'd visited one by one on her mad quest to understand all of the magic in the world. All of it was important to her development as a person, she supposed, though searching it now for moments of joy and pleasure, there were few that Kaedrich didn't already know, because there were few that didn't directly involve her.

"Well," Praxis said, after several long minutes in deep contemplation, "I suppose there is one thing. Have I ever told you about . . . ?" But she trailed off, because just as she looked up to begin, she'd seen Kaedrich's mouth drift open, the faintest whisper of a snore escaping her lips.

Praxis shook her head, though that was just as well. The memory really didn't make for a good bedtime story anyway.

So she sat there for a while instead, a long while, the night stretching on and on around them. Kaedrich's chest rose and fell, her breath deepening the further into sleep she drifted, but Praxis wasn't even remotely tired anymore. Here in the peace of the night, she could have sat up forever, just watching Kaedrich sleep.

Here's a better story, then, Praxis thought while she counted Kaedrich's breaths in the back of her mind, thirty-six, thirty-seven, thirty-eight. Deep and steady and even. *About a girl that was trapped in the ice for so long that she didn't even realize her bones had frozen. Her laugh was the bitter wind of the tundra, and it would snap out across the open drifts whenever people tried to tell her about love. There's an old song, older than memory, and it tells of the Yandosian heart, about a fierce and terrifying love that blooms only once in a thousand thousand couples, and it wends them together until their blood courses through each other's veins, until the beats of their hearts run on opposite shifts to keep them both alive at once. And the frozen girl would scoff because hers barely beat at all, much less enough to help sustain another whole person, and if it wasn't true for her, then how could it exist in anyone else either?*

"But do you know what happened, Kaedriella?" Praxis asked, her low voice drifting like the sigh of the wind, or the lullaby of dreams through a still and empty night.

If Kaedrich did, she did not answer. She snuffled in her sleep, her nose scrunched up and her hand swatting at her face. Sometime in the quiet, a curl had fallen across her cheek; it shifted slightly underneath her efforts, and Kaedrich sighed and stilled once more, though the end of the curl still lingered as a feather touch against her skin.

Praxis sat up, clicking her thumb as she stood. The tick of gears echoed in the empty room as she crept over the distance between them, so loud in the otherwise silent house that Praxis worried it would wake her.

It didn't. Kaedrich slept on, a faint smile playing at her lips. Her face was so relaxed that it took on the air of a celestial painting, a holy relic that sent people crashing to their knees in worshipful supplication. Never before had Praxis wished for artistic ability; lacking that, she paused for a moment, just trying to commit the image to her memory instead. This, she decided, was going to be the image that she would forevermore associate with Kaedrich. The utter peace of her, every muscle free of care. The soft curve of her cheek, the line of her neck.

Praxis lifted the curl, setting it aside with the rest of them. "I can see why you miss your curls so much," Praxis whispered, and then, before she could question herself, she leaned over and laid the gentlest kiss on Kaedrich's forehead. When she sighed, her breath mingled in with Kaedrich's. "This isn't going to mean anything to you, I suppose," she continued, watching the gentle dance of Kaedrich's dreaming eyes tucked snug beneath their lids, "but I just want you to know . . . I believe in those stories, now."

OF COURSE, WHEN Praxis said that she was going to *die*, so many years ago in the jungle, that didn't necessarily mean she was planning on, well . . . *dying*.

Not in a literal sense, anyway.

Not technically.

Not quite.

(It was complicated.)

"And when you die—"

"I'm not going to *actually* die, Tully. Don't be so dramatic."

"When you die," Tully repeated, steady and even, "who do you think is going to get the blame? Hmm? You think that there aren't going to be consequences to this?"

Praxis shook her head. "I won't die. Not really."

"You might."

"Not if you administer the antidote on time."

This was, of course, assuming Praxis was able to *find* the antidote.

The existence of it was a kind of long shot, Praxis was willing to admit that—it wasn't even part of the ritual surrounding *dreamer's death*, but something else she'd read about, and it had seemed like a good idea at the time. Now, she wasn't so sure. She'd been crawling through the thick of the jungle for more than an hour by this point, sweat and grime and dank air clinging to her skin and turning her hair into wet ribbons that stuck against her forehead and neck, that trailed down her arms and got stuck in her armpits. Though she'd braided it before setting out, the humidity had seemed to cast a life-breathing spell into its depths, so that it snaked out and let itself run wild. This, without even counting the discomfort of the thousand insect bites covering every bit of her exposed skin, without even counting the blisters on her feet and the mud squelching down into her shoes. Without even counting the cuts along her arms and face, razor-sharp plants slapping her as she tried to wriggle through dense chunks of foliage.

Tully may well end up being right anyway, but not in the way he thought. The jungle might find a way to kill her without the help of *dreamer's death*.

Tully followed behind, deftly moving a branch out of his way. "You don't get it, do you? Death cannot be *tamed*, Miss Fellows. Not by you, or anyone else. It *wants* to win. It will *always* win."

"Not this time."

"Yes, this time. Every time. It's a force of nature—it cannot be stopped." He paused as they maneuvered through a particularly thick patch of vines. Praxis hopped up to examine what might have been an animal's nest nestled in the low branch of a tree; but either it wasn't, or it had long since been abandoned, and she huffed in indignant disgust.

Tully held out his hand to try to help her down, but Praxis ignored it. He sighed. "You think that people haven't tried this before? Do you really think that you're the first person who's been driven so mad by grief that you'd do anything to try to undo it?"

"I'm not grieving," Praxis said. *At least, not for Moc,* she thought to herself, though she dared not say it. She hated that she even thought it, that the image of Rinn's face had flashed in her mind. Gods, would Praxis never be rid of her? She trudged on.

"Okay, then what's this about?" Tully asked.

"I hardly think that I need to explain myself to you."

"You'd better, if you want my help."

Praxis's rage was swift and fierce. She did not even have to consciously summon the spark of magic behind her eyes—it darted to her fingertips before she'd even felt it, fire springing to life over her palms as she whirled on Tully. She grabbed him by his tunic and slammed him against a tree, her fist smoldering, her free hand burning ominously in front of his face. Dead leaves drifted down, shaken free by the impact. "How *dare* you speak to me like that! Who do you think you are?"

"I don't know. Your friend, maybe," Tully said, as he shoved her off. "Though for the life of me, I cannot think why."

Praxis made a face. She snapped her palms shut, tamping out the flames, and made a disgusted sound as she turned away. A *friend*. What did that get her, exactly? Being close to people had never done her any good so far, and more importantly, it had been even worse for the objects of her affection: Moc had died, her family had lost her, Rinn had gotten her heart broken. Praxis whirled back, and yanked the stolen scroll out from where Tully had tucked it into his belt. The pain in her scar was raging as she slammed the scroll against him. "I don't need a *friend*," Praxis said. "I need a translator. So why don't you do something useful, and tell me what we need to get this ritual over with."

"But we haven't found the antid—"

"I don't care. I'm tired of waiting, and they're probably a myth, any-way. I mean, you've lived here all of your life—have *you* ever heard of a creature that can purge any toxin from your system?"

Tully hesitated. "Not . . . not outside of a story, no."

"Exactly. So let's just move on."

"Then how, exactly, are you planning on *not dying*?"

Praxis shrugged. "You're the one that was so convinced I would die regardless."

"That doesn't mean I want you to kill yourself on purpose!"

"Oh, please," Praxis said. She pulled a smashed lump out of her pocket, a sodden mess that used to be a five-pointed flower. She'd picked it up maybe half an hour ago, while Tully wasn't looking. "Let's not pretend that either of us ever cared about the other."

"I care," Tully said. "Sylls do not believe in apathy."

"Too bad for you, then." Praxis stuffed the wilted flower into her mouth whole—Tully's eyes popped, a strangled cry of alarm escaping his throat. Bitter taste filled Praxis's mouth, vapors instantly released and pouring down to her lungs. Praxis coughed on it a little, though she stubbornly kept her mouth shut. Flames snapped to life in her palms as Tully surged forward. "Don't you dare," Praxis snarled at him, doing her best to keep her mouth shut while she spoke.

"Miss Fellows, please—! You're not supposed to—"

"I know damned well what I'm not supposed to do," Praxis said. Like stuffing the flower straight into her mouth. There was a whole recipe, written out in Tully's scrolls, with measurements and heating times, to condense the flower and change the nature of its essence. Praxis blinked, her vision already blurring. Her flames crackled in her palms, the light of them nearly blinding in the fallen darkness. What would happen to a person if they ignored the recipe and ingested the flower directly? She supposed that she would find out. She swallowed the rest of it in a heavy lump.

"—don't know what you're doing," Tully was saying, when Praxis finally shifted her focus back. Her thoughts were growing murky, her limbs heavy. A pain was beginning to stab at her fingers, as if someone was driving needles up underneath her nails.

"You'd . . . better get . . . translating," Praxis said. She staggered forward, her flames dousing themselves as she fell to her knees. Tully was somewhere above her now—how, exactly, did she end up on the ground?—but maybe it was below; it was hard to tell with the world spinning so fast. She shut her eyes, just trying to keep from vomiting, and his voice rang on and on, elongating and rising until it was nearly the same pitch as a mosquito's whine. She felt like she was falling, and floating through space, and hovering snug as a baby back in her mother's womb. Her body jerked; she tasted dirt. And then everything was oddly silent, the whole world holding its breath.

A chuckle broke the reverie. "Hello, young thing."

Chapter Twenty-Seven

THERE WAS NO warning for the storm that blew over Monfort the following morning. One moment, the skies were a hazy blue, the sun warming the back of Kaedrich's shoulders as she walked up the steep streets toward the commercial level. In the next, a layer like ash swept in. Thick as smoke and black as soot, it was tempting to believe that an apocalyptic fire was raging through the city—but there was no smell to it, no heat, and soon a downpour had broken free of its bonds and was flooding the streets.

Like everyone else, Kaedrich had started running. Not in panic, but simple haste. With the collar of her jacket upturned and her head ducked to keep the rain out of her eyes. She dashed through the familiar streets, her feet plunging into sudden puddles. Water pooled down her neck, snaking underneath the collar of her shirt and soaking through the fabric underneath. The intensity of it should have felt angry, a storm brought on by rage as pure as if it came from the gods; but it didn't feel angry. Instead, there was something pointed and profoundly *sad* about it, like a thousand hearts breaking all at once.

Kaedrich shuddered as she stepped into Drewer's Books. The lonely rain pounded against the windows so hard that it drowned out the jingle of the bell used to announce her arrival. She peeled off her coat and hung it on a rack by the door, where already a small pool was threatening to overrun the tiny tray set up to catch the drips. Water trailed behind her as she made her way through the shelves. Her shirt was clinging uncomfortably to her chest, and she kept her shoulders slumped in an effort to hide the minor swells contained in her bindings.

She had expected that stepping back into her male façade would be uncomfortable after so many hours without it. With the one exception of a time when she'd been sick and laid up in bed for nearly a week, Kaedrich hadn't dropped the act for that long since she'd begun five years ago—and that time hadn't even really counted. She'd been miserable, coughing and running a fever, and desperately afraid the entire time that someone other than Praxis would stick their head in to find out how "he" was doing. Yesterday had been different. Yesterday had been . . . well, wonderful, yes, but in the manner of a dream or a night out at the opera. Transient, and all the more beautiful for the fact that it wouldn't last. It was *meant* to be temporary. So in some ways, it was easier for Kaedrich to cut her curls off than it had been to get them back in the first place. She reached up now, running her hand across the velvet of her shorn head. In the warmth of the bookstore, her hair was already drying.

With nothing else to do, Kaedrich began to browse the long shelves. She was grateful that the policeman she'd encountered had suggested a bookstore for their next meeting, though she hated being idle at a time like this. Each of the many hours of Mr. Bundling's disappearance were dragging on her, stacked together into a precarious weight on her back. She tried to lose herself in the warm smell of dust and old books, and that helped some. But only some.

The problem is that the policeman was late.

Kaedrich tried to deny it at first. She told herself that she was early, and that was true: she'd been looking for an excuse to leave the Society house ever since she'd woken up with a jolt to find herself sprawled on a sofa in the sitting room. Brex had been rattling furiously against the outside of the window, and Kaedrich had stumbled up and nearly tripped over Praxis—fast asleep, naturally, and on the floor for no reason that Kaedrich could figure—to let the creature in. He'd barreled into the room with dizzying speed, made even more dizzying by Kaedrich's blooming hangover. She'd expected that he would head straight to Praxis to begin purging the aftereffects of the alcohol from her system, and so it had come as quite a shock when she felt him pummel against her own shoulder instead, twin fangs piercing her neck. Kaedrich had yelped, and hopped around the room with quite a lack of dignity, until Praxis had finally thrown a sofa pillow at her and yelled at her to shut up.

While the effects of Brex's help were remarkable in their speed and efficacy, it still left Kaedrich more than a little rattled. She'd chopped her hair and hurried back into her normal persona, and left the house with only a hastily shouted "We'll catch up later, yeah?" as she scooted out the door.

So the fact that she had to wait some time for the policeman to show up was not a surprise. But then nine o'clock came and went, and okay, it was easy enough at first to dismiss his slight tardiness. He might be one of those people who are perpetually late. His watch might be running a little slower than Kaedrich's. He might not *have* a watch. He might have been delayed on police business. All of these seemed like perfectly reasonable explanations in the first five, ten, even fifteen minutes past nine.

They began to wear thin at about twenty after. By this point, Kaedrich had long since made two complete loops through the bookstore, and the clerk was beginning to give her shifty looks. Kaedrich dutifully ignored them, reviewing once again the shelf of old historical tomes from the Syll peninsula (covering the three-thousand-year Imperial Age, before the teachings of Habernese took root). And while normally this might have proven fascinating to her, several titles perhaps tempting the tightness of her purse strings, Kaedrich's anxiety made it such that she could barely even read the gold-stamped titles swimming in front of her. She picked up a book and put it back down, and picked it up and put it back down, and picked it up, opened it, stared blankly at the engraving on the first page, and then shut it and put it back down again. The rain pounded harder on the roof of the bookstore, and the newly installed electric lights flickered on the walls, and the clerk huffed and had just come around his oak desk when the door to the shop slammed open.

It was lucky Kaedrich was standing so near to the front of the shop already. Everyone turned—Kaedrich and the clerk, the nearby gentlemen in their dripping top hats, the moneyed academics who were pawing through first editions with damp fingers and ill-regard, the one woman that had positioned herself in the corner, her purple-striped walking dress and little button-sized hat oddly dry in the face of it all. Everyone turned, and everyone saw the ghostly-faced policeman step in, his wild eyes flashing past each of them one by one.

They settled on Kaedrich, much to the apparent relief of the clerk. The door was still open, the downpour framing the policeman in a backdrop of flashing silver and gray; he jerked his head and disappeared into the rain almost as quickly as he'd entered.

The clerk was sputtering. No doubt he'd been hoping that the policeman would "handle" Kaedrich for him, and Kaedrich tried not to feel *too* insulted as she bolted for the door. How much would it mess with the clerk's head, Kaedrich wondered, to have her chasing a policeman? This thought amused her as she retrieved her jacket, but all mirth disappeared underneath the freezing rain.

For a moment, standing on the street corner, it was hard to even figure out where the policeman had gone. There was little in the way of foot traffic out anymore, everyone hiding and huddled—she could see a few faces peering out of doors and windows, squinting up at the sky as if the thick layer of unnatural clouds would give them any indication as to how long it was planning to stick around.

Even Kaedrich had to admit, at times like this, she could sort of understand where people's suspicion of magic came from. Storms of this nature sent a chill down her spine, for dragging in the weather was never a sign that anything good had come.

She spotted him a little ways down the road. His black helmet was bobbing steadily away from her, neither slowing nor stopping to see if Kaedrich was keeping up. Kaedrich dashed down the open sidewalk, swerving around an abandoned flower cart and a stack of wooden crates left half-unloaded from the back of a carriage.

He was around the next corner, brooding underneath a striped awning that flapped and splattered at the onslaught of the pounding rain. He had taken his helmet off and sat upon it like a handy-made stool, his head bowed forward and his hands clasped 'round the back of his head. With his lithe frame and the compact nature of his pose, he could have been a lanky child hiding in the alleyway. His hair, which Kaedrich remembered as being tidy, combed, and oiled, now fell in locks to hide the side of his face.

Right away, Kaedrich knew that Mr. Bundling was dead.

This understanding hit her like a sock to the gut. Kaedrich's stomach flipped, and if she'd had breakfast it might have made a reappearance. She stood in the rain at the entrance to the alleyway, unable to approach the policeman. Guilt locked her knees, questions about what might have happened differently if she'd acted faster, if she hadn't called off her search the previous night, crashed over her like a tide, only to recede just as quickly once she looked back at the policeman; for whatever Kaedrich was feeling, the policeman was feeling it a thousand times worse.

The only thing that she could think to do was go over and rest her hand on his shoulder, but that felt too feminine for some reason. She forced herself to approach, clearing her throat as she parted through the curtain of rain hanging off the awning. In some respects the policeman was like a wounded dog, and Kaedrich did not know whether her presence was going to alarm him, either into flight or attack. Hopefully neither, but she remained delicate and light on her feet as she crouched down beside him.

"Where?" Kaedrich asked. It seemed the only safe question available to her—forcing the policeman to admit to Mr. Bundling's death outright would be too cruel.

The policeman raised his head up just enough so that he could speak without mumbling into his knees. "They found him near the Crimson Rose. His throat was . . . That is, they . . ."

Feminine or not, Kaedrich touched the policeman's sleeve. If nothing else, she needed him to understand that he didn't have to finish either of those sentences. Besides, Kaedrich really wasn't sure that she wanted details. She just kept picturing Mr. Bundling—alive, normal, sitting in his office or berating Kaedrich for some minor spelling error. It didn't seem possible that one day he'd been fine, and the next he was just *gone*, still and lifeless as raw meat. Kaedrich tried not to picture what his display in the land of the dead must look like, and her stomach twisted up when she realized that it would be lit forever now, frozen in that exact moment.

She hoped, at least, that he hadn't been afraid.

The policeman took a minute to compose himself. His shallow breathing gradually grew deeper, and slowly he was straightening up. Kaedrich backed off, standing and retreating to the farthest edge of the little awning's protection from the rain. The weather, too, was pulling back a little. Kaedrich glanced out at the rain, the way that it had respectably pulled itself together, but was still falling steady and somber to match the brave expression on the policeman's face. Who *was* this unlikely ally that Kaedrich had stumbled upon—apart from who he must have been to Mr. Bundling? He couldn't have been a member of the Royal Society, not with the social ranking of a policeman, and yet Kaedrich was given to understand that manipulating the weather was beyond the raw power of an average wizard; even within magic there were strengths and weaknesses, betters and lessers. You never escaped that.

"Well," the policeman said finally, a meaningless filler word to indicate that he was trying valiantly to move on. He rose to his feet, brushing down his soaked uniform. Steam rose in tiny puffs where his hand passed over the fabric, leaving it marginally drier than it had been. He looked at Kaedrich, his emotions shutting down as he filed and tucked them back into their socially-approved corners of repression. "Thank you for helping to bring this matter to my attention, sir. And . . . for being willing to help look for him. I'm sorry I wasted your time."

"No, hang on—we're not *done*," Kaedrich said.

"I'm afraid that we are."

"But there has to be more that we can do! We have to prove who did this. We have to stop them, before—"

"Are you *mad*?" the policeman asked. "That's exactly the kind of half-witted thinking that led Bundling to his doom. Now he's been dumped in an alleyway in the old quarter as if he was nothing more than yesterday's table scraps, and it's obvious to any officer with eyes and half a brain that he didn't die there, but the chief refuses to investigate. Do you *see*, now? They're *everywhere*. They've already won."

The policeman took a deep breath in the wake of his tirade. Kaedrich let the matter hang for a moment, gave him time to settle himself again. She supposed that she should be surprised that the police chief refused to investigate Mr. Bundling's death, but by now she really wasn't.

They've already won. Kaedrich could understand where the policeman was getting that idea, especially in the wake of Mr. Bundling's death, but she refused to accept it. There was always something more that could be done. There was always a fight still left, in the face of evil and injustice.

Maybe she wouldn't be able to convince the policeman of this—and that was fine, really. It didn't make her happy to lose a potential ally so soon after finding him, but Kaedrich probably had enough resources as it was. If he wanted to hide away from the truth, that was his business. Kaedrich and Praxis had already stopped worse; surely they could do it again.

"They haven't won yet," Kaedrich said finally, and the policeman snorted at her optimism. "They haven't won, and I'll tell you why: because I won't let them."

The policeman rolled his eyes. "And that's exactly the kind of thinking that will get you killed."

"Maybe," Kaedrich said. Her honesty startled the policeman, who turned and looked at her as if she was something that he had never seen before. Kaedrich shrugged; the memory of flowers tugged at her mind, so sharp that she could almost smell it there on the street. "It'll happen sooner or later, and if this is my time, then this is my time. But if my death *is* going to catch up with me, then you can be sure I'll die defending something I care about."

*   *   *

THE CLOCK WAS TICKING.

This statement was true in multiple different ways. First off, there actually *was* a clock ticking: a large grandfather clock, standing in the corner of Mr. Tarlock's office. It had belonged to his father, and his father before him, and his father's father's father; a whole line of fathers, so the story goes, keeping the clock safe as the family moved from house to house in the turbulent days of Marcovalla's rule over Durland. Taking it apart, and putting it back together again; a symbol of the Tarlock family resilience and ability to rebuild and redefine itself. The top of the clock had a bird's head carved into it, and it was from here that the academy's symbol was created, in the hopes that the spirit of resilience would continue on in their students. Sometimes, those same students liked to point out in a thoroughly smug tone of voice that the bird was not, in fact, a falcon— something about the beak shape—and it used to bother Tarlock. He'd looked it up once, and dammit, they were right.

He'd given up caring, though, in the years since the ghost crisis. What difference did it really make if the symbol represented the bird perfectly? Didn't those students realize? One day, they were *all* going to die, and it wouldn't change a damned thing if the school that they attended to learn defense had the proper bird's beak on its seal. It would not save them. Nothing would save them.

Clock's ticking.

The clock was ticking on Pon Lanali's instructions, as well. Tarlock tugged at his new gloves, making sure they were securely in place. They were quality gloves, made of the finest leather, handstitched by the best glove makers in Monfort. And yet they brought Tarlock no joy. He was acutely aware of the fact that the littlest finger of his left hand wasn't bending—because it was no longer there. Stuffing took its place, packed in so thickly that anyone gripping his hand shouldn't notice. His attempts to get Praxis's location out of young Mr. Darbury hadn't panned out, and Tol had made sure Tarlock knew the consequences of failure. Tarlock had to grudgingly respect this, even as his hand ached day and night, even as the skin streaked red, and oozed where the missing digit was supposed to be.

Tarlock glanced up. The clock was ticking on Mr. Mannly, too; he was supposed to have been here fifteen minutes ago. Tarlock knew little of Mannly, though he did know this: the boy was punctual, almost to a fault. So if he wasn't showing now, then what did that mean? Had he figured out that something was going on? Had Darbury said more than he should have? Tarlock tried to bite down on the flicker of panic that ran up his spine, if this newest plan didn't work. He reached into his desk drawer and took out a tiny bottle, topped with an eyedropper. The smell was terrible as he twisted open the cap—it stung at his eyes—but he suckered up an eyedropper's worth and loosed ten, fifteen, twenty bitter drops onto his tongue. He closed his eyes and shuddered. The drops helped his nerves and the pain, both, and lately he'd been going through more of the stuff than he cared to admit.

The door to his office burst open. Tarlock hastily shoved the bottle back into his desk and slammed the drawer as Mr. Mannly, out of breath and somewhat wild-eyed, came in and braced to a halt in front of Tarlock's desk.

"S-Sir! I'm-so-sorry-I'm-late-your-message-didn't-arrive-until-I-had-already-left-for—"

Tarlock held up his hand. His stuffed finger was slightly crooked, he noticed, and he motioned for Kaedrich to sit in the hope that the motion would hide this error.

Kaedrich sat. He wore the usual expression of apprehension and fear that most of the students wore when they sat across from Tarlock, and this raised Tarlock's spirits a little. At least the boy did not suspect anything. Tarlock's opinion of him wouldn't matter if he had.

"I'm afraid there's been a problem," Tarlock said. "With your tuition."

"A . . . a problem?"

Tarlock waved this off. "Yes . . . I'm told it's nothing major—some paperwork that needs to be updated. But apparently, my secretary has been having trouble getting hold of . . ." Tarlock glanced down at the file that lay open and ready on his desk. As if he didn't already know what it said. "Praxis Fellows? That is the name of your benefactor, is it not?"

Kaedrich hesitated before nodding. "That's . . . that's correct."

"Excellent." Tarlock picked up a pen. "I assume that *you* know how to get in touch with her?"

He stared at a paper on his desk, his pen poised and ready to write. When Kaedrich didn't say anything, Tarlock looked up.

Kaedrich cleared his throat. "I'm afraid that she's . . . um, unavailable at the moment. She's . . . at sea."

Sea, my barnacle-covered ass, Tarlock thought. What he said, though, was, "That's most unfortunate."

"I could take the papers," Kaedrich said. "And—and have them sent to you as soon as she's had the chance to update them."

"I'm afraid that won't do," Tarlock said. "Strictly confidential, you see. I have to ensure that they are viewed by no one but the payer, and until then they need to remain on the premises."

"I see," Kaedrich said.

Tarlock put his pen down. He folded his hands on his desk and leaned in, hoping that he appeared thoughtful and concerned for the future of his student. "I'm going to be honest with you, Mr. Mannly. If we do not get this straightened out in time, and receive our next payment by the end of the month, your education here is not going to be allowed to continue."

"Well . . . how much is the payment, then? I'll take it on myself, if I have to."

Tarlock ticked his eyebrow up. He glanced at Kaedrich in a very *pointed* way as he said, "Five thousand."

Kaedrich's eyes bugged out.

"Per semester," Tarlock added, and the poor lad across from him looked to be on the verge of passing out.

Tarlock sighed. "I understand that this is a difficult situation that I've put you in. If there's *any* chance that Miss Fellows can be reached before the month is out—"

"I'll see what I can do," Kaedrich whispered.

"Excellent," Tarlock said, nodding. "Excellent. Have her swing by my office anytime—my secretary will know where the paperwork is, if I am not in. Whatever is convenient for her."

Kaedrich nodded. In his stunned silence, the tick of the clock echoed prominently through the office.

It was always ticking, Tarlock thought as he dismissed Mr. Mannly. On all of us.

IN HER DREAM, Praxis hadn't moved. She stood, disembodied, over the prone figure of herself as she lay curled in the tangle of plants along the jungle floor of Tjalava. Tully hovered over her, frantically checking her pulse and her breath and spreading the scrolls in the dirt. He cupped a flame in his palm, illuminating the page in the thickening darkness of the jungle.

And Moc stood right behind him.

"You've gone through an awful lot of trouble to see me, young thing," he said.

Praxis's throat closed up. The dream version, the one she could feel. "I had to. I owe you."

"Did you?" Moc sneered. "And did you also 'have to' use the fabled *dreamer's death* in order to do this?"

"It . . . seemed like the only way."

"No," Moc said. "It seemed like the *easiest* way. It was the first way that you found that might have done what you were looking for, and so you took it—rather than waiting to see if another option presented itself, rather than doing the research, rather than consulting with experts, rather than—"

"That doesn't matter," Praxis said, her temper rising. "I'm *here*, aren't I? You're *here*."

Moc shook his head. "It always matters. I would have hoped that you'd learned to be a little less impulsive over the past few years, but I can see that you haven't changed a bit. Still arrogant. Still reckless. Still with absolutely no regard for the larger implications of what you're playing with."

Praxis's fists clenched, and her scar flared. "I don't have time for this. You can hate me all you want, once I've saved your sorry ass."

"Saved me? Is that what you think you're doing?" Moc laughed, deep from his belly. "Tell me, young thing, do you have any idea what this magic entails? Or did you just charge in headfirst and hope that everything would sort itself out in the end?"

"Neither—this time, I'm doing the sorting myself." She marched around, being mindful to step on neither the other version of herself nor Tully's notes, and took hold of Moc's hand. A fast binding spell sent a thread of light darting around both of their wrists before fading into the aether, though Praxis smirked in self-satisfaction as the tug of it still rested tight against her skin.

Moc nodded. "Okay, I'll grant you that's kind of clever. Unconventional thinking, certainly, though a hundred points off for sheer *stupidity*. Do you really think something like that is going to work here?"

"I guess we'll see now, won't we?" She looked down at Tully, who had shuffled over until he was kneeling right beside Praxis's real head. His hands were shaking as he rested his fingers over Praxis's forehead. Tully closed his eyes and began to mumble something deep underneath his breath, no doubt an ancient incantation that he'd found in the gibberish of the scroll.

Praxis grinned. Any minute now, and she'd be waking up. Any minute now, and her magic—strong and vibrant, more powerful than anything the ancient monks had worked with in their experiments—should pull Moc right out of this world, and drag him back into the land of the living. Any minute now, and Praxis will have not only single-handedly rewritten some of the fundamental laws of life and death, but managed to finally, *finally* undo her single biggest mistake. Then, maybe, she could have some peace in her life. Then, maybe, she could release the fire that she'd trapped inside the scar on her wrist, constantly raging as a living tattoo.

Any minute now . . .

Any minute . . .

Tully's magic finished. He peeped through one eye, nervously glancing at Praxis. He leaned over, his ear to her breath. He swore.

Moc was laughing again. Tully threw himself to his feet, kicking at a random tree, and then he scrambled back to his scrolls. Frenzy was burning in his eyes as he tried to figure out what had gone wrong, what *hadn't* worked.

"Okay, but," Praxis started, "that doesn't mean that it won't work *next* time. Just . . . just give him a minute, let him figure out what he did wrong, and then—"

"He didn't do anything wrong," Moc said. He turned toward Praxis, wrenching his hand free. The binding spell snapped, falling like ash to the jungle floor between them.

Praxis boggled. "But—but that shouldn't—how did you break—?"

"Because it's not a *real binding spell*," Moc said. He was sneering at her now, his whole face filled with disgust. "Don't you understand? Nothing here is real. Nothing that you *do* here is real. And nothing that your friend does to save you will touch you—that's the secret of the *dreamer's death*, young thing. That's the part he can't translate. There is only one way to save yourself, only one way to save anyone in this thrall, and it cannot be done from outside."

"Then tell me."

Moc smirked. "Are you sure? You're not going to like it."

"Tell me."

"Death," Moc said. "Death is the only release."

Praxis snorted. "Oh, fantastic. Thanks so much for the help." She turned away, hovering over Tully's shoulders as he reviewed the scrolls. Only bits and pieces of it were translated into Yandosian, but she'd be damned if she sat around and did nothing. Maybe there was a formula; some *thing* which transcended language barriers that she could use to figure a way out of this.

"What's the matter?" Moc asked. "I thought you would be pleased. I gave you the solution to your riddle."

"Yeah, not exactly keen on killing myself, thanks."

"Did I say that it had to be *your* death?"

Praxis looked up sharply. "What are you playing at?"

"This is no game, young thing, and I am not 'playing' anything," Moc said. "The magic you've trapped us in has restored enough of a sense of life into me that taking it away again should be enough."

"'Enough'?"

"To save you."

Praxis threw herself back. "Oh, no. No. Absolutely not."

"Praxis, I've been dead for a long time."

"I did *not* go to all of this effort just to kill you again! Don't you understand? I . . . What I did, it's . . ." Praxis shut her eyes, took a haggard breath. "I can't *live* with it anymore. I can't. You have to make it. You *have* to come back."

"Then there is only one option."

Realization stabbed her in the chest. One death, to release one life. Tears pricked at her eyes as she blinked them back open. It's not like she didn't know that this—dying—was a possibility when she'd started the whole process. She stepped back over to Moc, looking down at him. He was exactly as she remembered, the same mix of wisdom and tenacity and biting affection. If she died for him, she wondered, would the excess of her magical energies be passed on to him? She hoped so—he'd certainly do a lot better job with it than she ever had, or ever would.

She nodded. "All right," she said. "You can . . . you can have my death."

A bark of laughter slapped her in the face. "No, young thing. It's not that simple. You cannot bargain *your own life* for mine."

"But you said—!"

"Yes." Moc grinned. "A death is required." He turned, looking beside them. "It's a pity, really—the boy seems nice."

Praxis gasped. "*What?* You think I—No! No, I can't—I *won't*—kill Tully! There has to be another way."

"It would be nice if there was," Moc said. "But reality is what it is. You want me to live, young thing, someone else has to die. That's just how it works."

"But . . . but Tully!"

Moc shrugged. "It's up to you. I can stay dead. *Or* he can take my place. But whatever you do, make your decision fast—or else the magic you've caught the three of us up in is going to drag us *all* down."

"But I . . . I . . ." Praxis sputtered, unable to finish her sentence. She looked from Moc to Tully, Moc to Tully, as if somehow either of them was going to give her a better answer. As if she hadn't done this to herself, through her stupidity and carelessness, through her blinding grief and raging guilt. Her scar flared, hotter than she'd ever felt it, and she cried out and collapsed to her knees, clutching at her wrist. The world around her, already dark with night, dimmed further still, as the trees and undergrowth, the stars above, all rumbled and fell away. Only a tiny patch of ground remained, encircling them; everything else was a gaping void, darkness blacker than the depths of the mines.

Moc crouched down next to her. "There's not much time, young thing. Either one of us dies, or we all do. Which is the worse outcome? Honestly?"

Praxis shook her head. She could not even begin to make this choice. Moc, her mentor—or Tully, who may have eventually been a friend, and had Praxis ever even *had* one of those before? Tully, who was certainly too young to die, and who certainly did not deserve this, being a pawn in Praxis's very messed-up game of deadly Cloak and Crowns. Praxis squeezed her eyes shut, rocking herself on the damp ground, paralyzed with indecision.

The warmth of Moc's hand settled on Praxis's back. "Praxis. It's okay. Let me go."

"No," Praxis mumbled. She was huddled over so far now, talking into her knees, and Moc sighed and rubbed her back some more. He had rarely ever acted like this in real life—reassuring, paternal even, a gentle presence to soothe her tortured soul—and the feeling of it now overwhelmed her. His hand, so real and warm and solid, with flesh and bones and a living pulse thundering through his veins. Praxis gulped down a sob. "I can't," she said, still talking to her knees. "I can't . . . I can't kill you again, I can't."

"Then make the choice."

She sat up. Turned around until she could look Moc in the face. "You would really ask that of me?"

Moc shook his head. "No. I'm willing to die again. But you have to kill one of us, and I cannot make the decision for you."

Praxis nodded slowly. "What do I need to do?"

"I think you already know," Moc said. He leveled her with a heavy look, holding it until understanding clicked into place. Praxis's eyes widened. Moc nodded.

"I don't know if I can do that on *command*," Praxis said. If she was right about what he meant—and she was sure that she was—then shifting her perception until she could actually *see* the life force energies around her was something that she'd only ever done in fits of desperation. It was advanced wizardry, far beyond her skill, and so deep in the realm of what was considered "dark" magic that no one would ever dare to teach her if she'd asked. Which she never would, because who even *wanted* that kind of power? After knowing what it felt like, the hole that it ripped in your own soul.

But if that was what it took to save them . . . *Two out of three lives,* Praxis thought to herself. *It's not the worst.*

She shut her eyes, looking deep inside of herself. Her first attempt failed, and so did her second. The ground rumbled on her third attempt, reminding her of how little time she had left to pull this off, but that knowledge did not help her in her fourth. Praxis sighed in frustration, shut her eyes for a fifth time. She tried to remember some of the feelings that she'd used to dredge this up with before. Betrayal and rage and nameless panic. Fear. Fear of death, fear of a life she did not want. She tried to make herself afraid now, really deep-down-to-the-bones terror. The idea of dying didn't do it—but the idea of failing Moc again, of killing Moc *again* . . . A tremor of fear rippled through her belly, and Praxis stoked that, growing it until it filled her up. She could not fail Moc again, she could not, she could not, she—

She opened her eyes. Her tiny world, reduced to just the three of them, was glowing brilliant orange. Praxis's own life, enhanced far beyond the measure of what it should be, reigning a supreme glow over Tully's healthy hue, and Moc . . . a flicker, that was all that he had left. The smallest stub, nestled deep in his core.

Praxis knew now that he was being optimistic before: his own energy would never have been enough to save someone else.

She turned to Tully. Blissfully unaware of his fate, he had moved back around to try another spell on Praxis. Another one that would fail. There was only one way to save her, only one way out. Praxis fought against the sting of tears as she reached her hand out, as the first tendrils of Tully's energy uncoiled and handed themselves over to her willingly. They wrapped around her hand, and she grabbed them like a leash, her stomach convulsing as she remembered the last time that she'd done this.

"I'm sorry," Praxis whispered, though of course he couldn't hear. He would never hear her remorse.

She shut her eyes and yanked before she could talk herself out of it.

The Praxis on the ground gasped. Praxis felt the rush of air, how it forced itself into her lungs. She felt the dirt underneath her cheek, the ache in her muscles, the thundering of her heart, the shaking of her limbs. She flew up into a sitting position, her eyes popping open quite without her telling them to. She wasn't sure that she wanted to see, not yet, the crumpled form of Tully slumped on the ground beside her.

"Miss Fellows!"

A squawk and a flutter of wings distracted Praxis; she jerked in alarm, her hand flying to her neck. Something small, iridescent blue and silver, was fluttering away from her and coming to rest on . . . on . . .

Praxis blinked as the creature settled itself on Tully's shoulder.

"Tully?"

Tully laughed in open relief. He sank back on his heels and then fell to his rear in the dirt, not even caring, as he looked at Praxis. "Don't *ever* do that again, okay, Miss Fellows?"

"But . . . you . . . That is, I . . . I . . ." Praxis whipped her head around, side to side, gaping at the dense jungle that surrounded them. "Where is he?"

"Huh?"

"Where is he?" Praxis repeated. Panic filled her voice, and she scrambled to her feet. She checked the undergrowth nearby, ripping aside vines and leaves in a frenzied search.

"Miss Fellows, what are you talking about? Who are you looking for?"

"Moc," Praxis said. Her chest squeezed up around her heart, so tightly it was a wonder she didn't pass out. "I can't . . . I don't . . ."

"Hey—*hey*," Tully said. He had stood up, too, and now he rested his hand on her shoulder. He turned her to face him. "Look at me. Praxis, look at me. Whatever you saw in there, it wasn't real. Do you understand? None of it was real."

Praxis shook her head. "No, but it—I—he was there, and I—I could save him, and . . . and . . ."

"No," Tully said. "I translated the rest of the scroll. I don't know exactly what you were hoping the *dreamer's death* was going to do for you, but it wasn't a way to bring somebody *back*. All it does is reveal to us our true nature. Nothing more."

Praxis froze. Tully was still looking at her, concern and compassion written plainly across his damned soft face. She didn't want to believe him, but in an instant she knew that what he said was true. *Our true nature.* Praxis almost couldn't breathe. A deep ache burned in her wrist, tamer and yet somehow harsher than the usual fire.

She had killed Tully. Maybe not in real life, but that didn't matter. She'd made the decision, and she could not deny it—just like she couldn't deny the sharp pang in her chest, a fierce *disappointment* that it hadn't worked. Tully was here, and Moc wasn't.

Nothing more, he'd said, as if understanding her true nature wasn't enough to kill her all over again.

"Are you okay?" Tully asked, and Praxis nodded. She wasn't, but what good would it do to admit that?

"So . . ." Praxis cleared her throat. "So, how *did* I survive, then?"

Tully grinned. "Thank this little guy," he said. He whistled, and a flutter came down from the trees. The same bundle of fur and wings that Praxis had seen before, in the first confused moments after waking. The creature landed in Tully's open hands. It turned and looked up at Praxis, and Praxis could have sworn that it was glaring at her accusingly.

"How—?"

"There's a ritual, everyone knows it just in case. I thought that it was a myth, but . . ." He shrugged. "I tried it—it worked. He seems to like me, well enough to save you when I asked him anyway, but . . . I think maybe you'd find him more useful than me."

Tully held the creature out to her, but Praxis recoiled. "Me? Why not just let him go?"

Tully blinked at her. "Don't you know the legends? Once one of their kind crosses over, helping humans, it isn't welcomed back into its pack anymore. The price you pay for its help is to tend to it, give it a new home."

Praxis shook her head. "I can't. You do it, then, if it must be done. You're the one that called it."

"They'd never let me," Tully said. "The embassy would take it away immediately. They'd want to study it. These things . . . they're so rare. I'm sure they'd kill it, just to find out more about it. But *you* . . . surely you could keep him safe."

A lump formed in Praxis's throat. She didn't deserve to tend for something so small, so precious, not after what she'd done. She looked at the creature, nestled comfortably in Tully's palms, and it looked at her. It blinked. Frankly, Praxis wasn't even sure that she deserved to live anymore, but . . . she was the reason that this animal had lost its home. Another victim of her ill-considered endeavor, only this one she actually could save. If she was willing to. If she had enough of a heart left to do it.

She wasn't at all sure if she was up to it, but she held out her hand anyway. Tully passed the creature over, and it squawked a little indignantly as it climbed onto Praxis's upturned palms. It turned its head up, peering intently into Praxis's eyes. Its ears were back, and the faintest hint of a hiss was coming out of its mouth.

Praxis raised the creature up, until their faces were level. "I'm sorry," she told it. It perked its head to the side, considering. "I know that I'm probably not your first choice, and I understand that, but I promise . . . for you, I will try to do better . . . little Brex."

Chapter Twenty-Eight

"EXCUSE ME, PARDON ME! I'm sorry, I'm—watch out! Coming through!"

Kaedrich darted around a group of workmen who were repairing a storefront, scaffolding and tools spread everywhere across the sidewalk. She veered and ran straight into the traffic of the street, startling a horse and getting shouted at by at least three separate people in two different languages. She waved in what she hoped was an apologetic manner, though it may have accidentally come across as a rude gesture. Oh well—she did not have time to worry about it. She jerked to the side as a motocarriage cut her off. Blast it, she did not have time for this! The crowd thickened around her, and Kaedrich bit her lip as she was forced to slow her pace. "Excuse me, excuse me, sorry, pardon me." She ducked underneath a protest sign, throwing back her apologies as she ran through a narrowing gap that she'd spotted.

"Sorry" was fast becoming her most commonly uttered word these days. In the last week, she must have shouted it a thousand times a day as she ran from one place to another, always late or on the verge of late. Kaedrich barely glanced at the traffic as she ran across the intersection, veering around a baby carriage at the last possible second. The mother pushing it shouted in alarm. "Sorry!"

When she was late for her jobs: "Sorry."

When she was late for classes: "Sorry."

When she had to beg for another day before her weekly hotel bill was due: "Sorry."

And always, on the streets: "Sorry, sorry, sorry."

Boy, was she sorry.

Sorry that she'd gotten herself into this mess. Sorry that she didn't seem to have a probable solution—at least, not any time soon. Sorry, in the dark stretch of night, in the few hours that she had to toss and turn on her paper-thin mattress, not sleeping, that she'd ever come to Monfort.

Sorry that she'd ever even *asked* about the cost of tuition.

She should have just kept her mouth shut. All right, so there was a problem with the paperwork. Kaedrich didn't need to have *asked*. She could have just nodded, and then taken what Director Tarlock had said back to Praxis. And Praxis, without a second thought, probably would have marched straight down to Falconridge and shouted at somebody until the problem was fixed.

Which was, in and of itself, exactly the problem.

Because Kaedrich did not want Praxis getting involved in this.

Maybe it was nothing. Maybe there really was a snafu involving the payments that Praxis sent in every quarter—gods, the *enormous* payments that Praxis sent in every quarter—but something about the whole situation just didn't sit right with Kaedrich. The timing of it was impossible to ignore completely. Just after Praxis had gone to ground, and the very first thing that Director Tarlock had asked of her was Praxis's location? He just *happened* to need it *now*?

Every day since then, Kaedrich had studied him, trying to spot either additional red items in his clothing, or the same silvery "rash" she'd spotted on the arm of the man that had killed Lord Wellen, and every day she failed to find any. But.

It just wasn't worth the risk. And so this was Kaedrich's life now: four jobs (the newspaper, having fallen through with the untimely death of Mr. Bundling, had shown their "appreciation" by kicking her unceremoniously out on the street), classes in every tiny slice of downtime, running ten different directions over the city. It still wasn't enough money, and so she'd stolen away to the Scorpion's Stable more than she liked, to try her luck at Fiddler's Dash. At night, exhausted, she dragged herself back to the grubby hotel room, emptied her pockets, and tallied up her current savings. With her eyes scratchy from lack of sleep, she ran numbers by the light of a candle stub, for it was too expensive to buy oil for a proper lamp. Last night, she'd decided to do without the candle—she sat cramped in the window, squinting in the full moon.

Light or no light, it would never be enough. Kaedrich could run herself ragged for a whole *year*, and it would never be enough.

At the corner, she turned down a side alley. She knocked on Tristy's door. She was out of breath constantly these days, and when the door opened up, the first thing that Tristy said was, "Gods, Kaedrich, you look awful."

"Thanks," Kaedrich said. She wasn't even trying to be sarcastic anymore—she didn't have the energy. She pushed her way past Tristy, because she didn't have time to waste on pleasantries. "Is it done?"

"It's done."

Tristy shut the door behind Kaedrich, and too slowly, she moved across the room. Kaedrich started tapping her foot, caught herself, and made herself stop. She crossed her arms instead. She was jittery, impatient, stiff, hungry. A steady drizzle had settled over Monfort in the past week, the perfect match for her mood.

"Can I get you anything?" Tristy asked. "I made coffee, and I think I still have some cake from the other day."

Kaedrich's stomach growled. "No," Kaedrich said, as she clutched herself around the middle.

"Kaedrich—"

"I don't have *time*," Kaedrich said. "Can I please have it?"

Tristy clucked her tongue. Though she did at least open up her wardrobe. She pulled out something on a hanger, a simple cloth thrown over it for protection. "Will this do?" Tristy asked, as she drew the cloth away with a flourish.

It was Kaedrich's best suit. She'd given it to Tristy a few days ago, to see if Tristy could find a way to make it look just a little fancier, using some costuming tricks that she'd picked up working in shows. Tristy had grinned, so flattered to be asked, and assured Kaedrich that she was sure she'd find something to do to it.

She had. Bits of what looked like green silk now lined the lapels, with a matching twist of silk poking out of the breast pocket like a folded handkerchief. The suit itself had been cleaned and pressed, and Tristy had accented some of the piping of the plaid lines with an additional thread of yellow-gold. She'd added some fabric to give the hem of Kaedrich's pants a nice wide cuff, the current fashion, and pressed sharp creases down each of the legs. A bit of spit and polish brightened the buttons from a dull brass to what looked more or less like gold.

In the right lighting, it could almost pass for something expensive.

Tears pricked at Kaedrich's eyes, and she hastily wiped them off, muttering something about dust. "It's perfect," Kaedrich said. She dug into her pockets. "Thank you."

"You're welcome," Tristy said. Kaedrich held out some money, but Tristy closed Kaedrich's hand around it. "Don't bother. Consider it my good-luck gift."

"Tristy, I can't—"

"You *can*. Please. For me." She tipped her head to the side, considering Kaedrich. "You do know that we're all worried about you, right?"

Kaedrich nodded. She'd barely seen any of them, so consumed with just trying to keep her head above water. Even at the academy, it felt like she never had time for so much as a "hello." She certainly never took the time to go to the Cross Street pub anymore.

Tristy reached out, rubbing Kaedrich's arm. "Hey, when the Trials are over, what's say that we all make time to go and celebrate, all right? Like we used to."

"Assuming I even pass," Kaedrich said with a snort.

"Doesn't matter," Tristy said. She handed Kaedrich her suit. "You'll pass . . . but we'll go either way. Yeah?"

Kaedrich nodded. "Yeah, okay," she said. Though even as she took the suit, and a small bundle of what smelled suspiciously like wrapped-up cake, ready-to-go, she doubted how much she actually meant it. Crown Day, and the Trials, were two days away, and Kaedrich could not even begin to think beyond them. The Trials themselves would determine whether or not she qualified for her next year at Falconridge, but there was a bigger, simpler reason for not wanting to consider the aftermath: the tuition deadline was two days later. Which meant that Kaedrich had, essentially, four more days to live—for it did not seem possible, short of divine intervention, that there was any way to raise the rest of the funds in time. And then . . . well, she did not like to think about "then." She tried to push aside thoughts of the poorhouses, recently instituted in Monfort, all the horrors that Mr. Bundling shoved into an article that had never made the papers.

Four days. Kaedrich swallowed down the rising knot in her throat.

Perlandra have mercy.

MONFORT WAS CRUMBLING. Everywhere that Praxis looked, she could see it. Fires tore up isolated buildings, leaving swaths of rubble in the middle of an otherwise normal street. A constant flow of people were moving to the old quarter, where as a result rents were skyrocketing at levels previously unheard of in that portion of the city. Beggars lined the streets, seeping farther out into the rest of the city every day. Earlier that week, one of the hopper cars skipped its tracks and crashed into a nearby shop, and the people of Monfort had barely *blinked*. Protests had bloomed like mold, spreading everywhere. Occasionally, they turned violent, but the police and royal guards did nothing unless the citizenry targeted someone with sufficient capital and social clout. The city felt like it was being held together now by hope and spit; one of these days, Praxis felt, it would simply fall away into the sea, swept out like the tides. Its skeleton would be left to rot on land, a monument to something that was once great.

Of course, some of this was just her rotten mood leaching into her perception of things. She knew that, but she couldn't bring herself to care. Pessimism was the name of the game these days. If Kaedrich had been around, she might have been able to brighten things up, to infect Praxis with some of her sunny optimism—but that was a large part of the problem. Kaedrich *hadn't* been around. Not for a week now, not since she'd stopped by in a rush to inform Praxis that Erstan Bundling had been found dead, and that no, she didn't want to talk about it, and no, she didn't have time to stay and eat some oatmeal. She'd been cagey, constantly glancing at the door behind her, and she had not come by Calswell House again since.

So Praxis had spent her week doing what she usually did when Kaedrich wasn't near: she sulked. Oh, on the surface, she still continued her investigations. She ran more tests of the bullet and the remains of the bones that she'd taken from Lanali's not-exactly-Silvers, and she scoured the streets for more clues about what Lanali's next move might be, and she returned repeatedly to the Crimson Rose to nose about, ask questions, get kicked out for being drunk and disorderly, and . . . absolutely nothing had happened. Her investigation was stalled.

Once, she did reconsider the idea of simply breaking into Lanali's house. She'd gone so far as to stand outside of it, in the shadows, peering up at the towers and the widow's walk, the spiral rooftops. The protections on it were subtle, but they were nestled deep into the house's very *bones*. Praxis could get through them, sure. They were not designed to keep people *out*. They were designed to tag and track. If Praxis set foot inside of the property, even in the gardens, she'd be lit up for Tol and Lanali to find no matter where she ran to. Clever, twisted, nasty magic.

Praxis had to admire it, even as she cursed it.

But at least now she had some small thing to look forward to, some tiny sliver to lift her spirits. Crown Day, the annual celebration of Durland's independence from Marcovalla, was coming up, and with it, the Falconridge Academy Trials. Praxis had never given two whits of care to either one of them the last time that she was in Monfort, but she'd be damned if she was missing her opportunity this time. She'd broken into Bundling's office and rifled around until she'd found his invitation— for always, prominent reporters were invited to spread the word about how elegant and fantastic it all was, and it's not like he was going to be *using* it—and the last of her preparations was nearly complete. She'd already stopped by the tailor, and now she carried a large box carefully through the streets. Her heart skipped a little faster, imagining Kaedrich's face when she saw. Maybe this was her chance, Praxis thought to herself. Kaedrich would do fantastically at her Trials, and Praxis would be waiting for her, ready to finally lay it all out. She'd started counting down the days, and as the time drew nearer she found her fog of grumpiness lifting. She was actually devolving into a giddy girl, a person that she'd never been in her youth. She wondered if something could be done about her hair. She wondered if she was over-thinking things.

She wondered if she'd actually be able to survive the evening.

There was only one way to find out.

Praxis was as ready as she would ever be.

THE MORNING OF Crown Day dawned with a blood-red sky, and news that the prince had almost been killed.

An exaggeration, the royal guard was saying. Prince Hemmerick had never been in any real danger. The assailant, whose identity was not being revealed, had been captured inside of the palace walls within moments. A glorious testimony to the efficiency of the royal guards. Long live the Crown. Etc., etc., etc.

It was a blatant attempt to downplay the very real danger and incompetence of the situation; but still, even in the current mood of Monfort, this story might have worked, and ultimately been forgotten about, had it not been for the prince's decision to flee the city.

"There's an argument to be made for his decision," Lord-Councillor Braynish said. He was in his office, in the Crescent. He did not get to partake in spring recess, but that was fine with him—his home was here, his life was here. Red light still streaked in from outside, bathing everything in a rosy hue. He'd been in the building since before dawn, roused from his bed by the whole situation. As the head of the Council of Security, any relocation on the part of the Crown was organized, in part, by his office.

Sitting across the way, Pon Lanali smiled beatifically at him. "Shepherds do not vanish," she said.

Braynish ground his teeth together. Ages ago, he had asked the Pon to stop using her muddled way of speaking around him, as a personal favor—her habit of using synonyms that didn't quite fit, of rearranging words so that they were *almost* in their proper order, drove him crazy. But Lanali had only smiled at him, apologizing for her poor understanding of Durlish grammar, and reminding him of her heritage from an island nation far from here. Braynish didn't buy that for a moment, but he had accepted defeat gracefully; he knew that he would not be getting a confession out of her, not then.

Unfortunately, this meant that even now, after so long knowing each other, after so many meetings, he still had to parse through her botched grammar and twisted expressions. Though he had noticed an improvement in recent months, a distinct upswing in her apparent "understanding" of syntax and vocabulary. This latest proclamation was downright *normal*, if a little metaphorical for Braynish's taste.

He shook his head. "It's not our place to question the Crown's decision when it comes to his own personal safety."

"Is it not?" Lanali shrugged. "Perhaps should be. Perhaps . . . his safety, more important to him than that of people's."

Braynish went quiet. In the office, the only sound was the wind brushing against the windowpanes, a tense whisper that he heard all over the city these days. *Change,* it seemed to be saying. Change was coming.

Braynish wasn't stupid. He knew what Lanali wanted, even if she was always careful to avoid saying it directly. And, privately, Braynish felt that she was dangerously close to getting her wish. Her sentiments had been repeated to him already at least half a dozen times this morning, by the most influential members of the Governance Council. Rumor had it that a handful of lawyers were already looking into . . . technicalities.

Which meant that the time for subtly was over.

He sat forward, crossing his hands on his desk. "What do I get out of the deal?" Braynish asked.

Lanali blinked at him. From behind her veil, her face was as controlled and impassive as ever. "There something you covet?"

"I covet many things," Braynish said. "And if you're going to be in a position to grant them, then I promise you I will take full advantage of that. But I can't help you get there if you don't trust me with the truth."

Lanali raised an eyebrow. "My utterances always bear truth. I am Pon."

"Perhaps," Braynish said. "However, if you want my help, you're going to have to do something for me: I want you to drop the voice. Right now, or else I am siding against you with everything at my disposal."

Lanali said nothing. The wind picked up outside, shushing against the glass.

Braynish waited. He was good at waiting. He could wait out anything, anyone. He could wait out the wind. He was still as a statue, watching Lanali.

She reached up. Folded her veil back. Her face underneath was a little older than Braynish expected it to be, the first lines sneaking in along her forehead and next to her eyes. "What assurances do I have that you won't go against me anyway?" Her voice rang through the office, as clear and polished as a diva.

Braynish smiled. He pulled out a sheet of paper and, ignoring her for a moment, wrote something down. When he was done, he tapped his pen against his desk, three sets of three firm taps each, and then set the pen down. He slid the paper over to Lanali.

He watched as she read it. Her brow pinched, just a little, so subtle that he might not have noticed it if her veil was still hiding her expression.

"We need each other," Braynish said. There was no going back now. "What would you like me to do?"

Lanali folded up the paper. She slipped it into her dress. "Make sure the Crown Day celebration at the palace goes forward," she said. "I know there are rumors that it won't."

Braynish raised an eyebrow. "More than rumors. It's been canceled."

"Well, *un*-cancel it," Lanali snapped.

"Why?"

Lanali waved her hand. "The details aren't important. Suffice it to say, there are people that I need occupied for the evening, and the Crown Day celebration has a way of proving . . . quite engrossing. Besides," Lanali said with a smile, "you're going to be there, aren't you? Consider this the perfect time to *mingle* with some of your fellow noblemen. In case there's . . . anything at all . . . that you'd like to discuss with them."

Chapter Twenty-Nine

A STRING OF CARRIAGES snaked away from the palace entrance for more than a mile. Kaedrich was probably the only person in attendance to arrive on foot. She watched them as she passed by one carriage after another, jammed up in a slow-moving line, bored drivers sitting atop them that watched her with envy as she strolled along unhindered.

Kaedrich was just relieved that it was all still happening. When the news of the prince's departure had broken, the very first question people had asked was whether the celebrations were still taking place. She'd gone down to the academy that morning, first thing, to find a mob of students in the main hallway, all buzzing with the same worries that she had. The Trials, after all, had started as a means of prospective students vying for consideration to be in the king's royal guard—and though there was no technical *requirement* these days that those who passed would join up, a number of Falconridge graduates continued into the service.

Director Tarlock had sent his secretary to address them, which hadn't exactly been reassuring. *Everything's fine, no worries,* was the general message of his impromtu speech, but Kaedrich had wondered the entire time that she was walking here tonight, if there was even a point. Would there even *be* a Crown Day celebration for the Trials to take place in?

But apparently the lack of a royal presence was not seen as a good enough reason to cancel a party after all. And now Kaedrich was going to get to see the palace up close.

Despite everything, it was a wonder to behold. Built in the early years after Durland's liberation from Marcovalla, the palace was designed to be one of the great wonders of the modern world. Great sweeps of architecture rose from the ground in such a way that it looked as if the palace was a natural outcropping of the ridge of Monfort. There were huge expanses of glass walls, towers that shot toward the stars, balconies that curved along at upward spirals. A garden second to none sloped down from the outer walls, resplendent with waterfalls and fountains, and flowers of every shade and hue.

Kaedrich slipped around the carriages, making her way carefully up the drive. The front entrance was well in view now, and dread knotted Kaedrich's chest as she approached. The guards at the door were well trained, and did not seem to regard Kaedrich with any particular sense of wariness—still, she could feel an invisible undercurrent to their casual glance, a hidden question as to what someone that looked as she did was doing here. They took in the apparent incongruity of her appearance: the fine suit, looking better than Kaedrich could reasonably afford under the circumstances, with Praxis's gifted cufflinks dotting her wrists, contrasting in their mind against the darkness of her skin. Only once they spotted the seal of the academy on her breast pocket did she make sense in their mind, though it was clear they didn't necessarily agree with the school's decision to accept her among their ranks.

But Kaedrich was determined to enjoy this evening, so she did her best to ignore them as they parted, allowing her access to the hallowed halls. They did not open the doors for her, she noted, but that was fine. The less showy of an entrance that she made, the better off she would be. Kaedrich slipped into the palace without fanfare, without notice.

She had worried beforehand that it would be difficult to navigate her way around, but in fact it couldn't have been simpler. The crowd was funneled down the main halls, easily directed into a series of large rooms laid out with places for eating and places for dancing. Gold and glitter seemed to be the theme of the evening, and Kaedrich found her suit feeling oddly shabby by comparison. Never before had Kaedrich had the opportunity to observe this level of Durland's upper-crust up close, and she found herself thinking back to the ballroom that she'd seen in Praxis's memory. The styles were so different that it was hard to compare, but the opulence put on by the people in the palace was certainly giving the Fellows a run for their money. Immaculately tailored tuxedos gleamed as brightly as the ballgowns they accompanied; hair had been swept and arranged so perfectly that it did not even appear real. As for the building itself, it bedazzled at every turn: electric lights brightened the rooms to their full sparkling height, everything polished and gleaming, while strings of exotic flowers trailed as streamers over the heads of the assembled guests. Kaedrich paused for a moment, closing her eyes and taking a deep breath, and was soon calmed—these were not *her* flowers. She was not to die tonight.

Thus assured, she made her way to a long table, laden down with more food than Kaedrich had ever seen before in her life. Though she knew that she shouldn't load down on too many platefuls before the Trials, she could not help but nibble a few treats around the edges. The taste of ginger-lemon exploded across her tongue, and Kaedrich closed her eyes to savor it. If this *was* to be her only time in the palace, her last chance at living the academy life (and she was growing quite sure, by now, that it would be), then she was going to enjoy it while she could.

She helped herself to a drink, but a respectably tanned hand reached over and snatched it out of her grasp. Kaedrich turned, incredulous but already knowing what she would find.

"What?" Lucan asked, as he took a long sip from the glass he'd stolen from Kaedrich. "You're the one performing at the Trials tonight, not me. If either one of us is supposed to stay sharp . . ."

"You're an ass."

Lucan shrugged. "Yeah, but everyone knows that. So," he said, glancing around, "where's your date?"

Instantly, Praxis's face flashed in Kaedrich's mind. She shook her head to clear it. "I don't know what you're talking about."

"Oh, don't tell me that the two of you have had a spat. Come on, Mannly. The first woman you've managed to bed since I've known you—hells, what am I saying, probably the first *ever*—and you let her get away from you this quickly? I mean, if it was *me* . . . But you're not like that."

Kaedrich could only stare at Lucan at first. Surely news of the collapse of her fake relationship must have spread by now? She tried to remember the last week. She'd been so swamped just trying to keep herself afloat financially, scraping together as much money as she could in a mad effort to afford the tuition deadline and the repairs to her old apartment. In her mad scramble, had she even seen Marlick since the day they'd gotten kicked out? A flutter of panic coursed through her—but if something had happened to him, wouldn't she have heard?

Then again, she'd thought that Mr. Bundling was probably fine, too. And look how that had gone.

Kaedrich swallowed around the knot of dread in her throat. "Marlick didn't tell you, then?"

Lucan groaned. "Gods, *seriously*? I was joking, but—shit, Mannly, what is wrong with you?"

It was a fair question, Kaedrich felt. However, she was in no mood to dig into the nature of exactly why she couldn't keep Praxis, especially since it had all been pretend *anyway*, and especially when she was now filled with worry about other things.

"Have you seen Marlick, by the way?" Kaedrich asked.

Lucan hesitated a second, clearly not sure if he should let Kaedrich change the subject that easily. Then he shrugged, one lazy shoulder hitching up as if he couldn't care less. "No, but I don't expect to. Initiates usually go into isolation. Didn't you hear?" he added, seeing Kaedrich's confused look. "He quit the academy. Said if he's going to join the cloister, he might as well get it over with."

Kaedrich's eyes bugged out. "Wait, are you serious?"

"Why would I lie about something like that?" Lucan asked, frowning as if he'd just spotted an insect crawling up his sleeve. He was already half-turning away, his attention snagging on the passing backside of a young woman with blond hair and a shimmering blue dress.

Kaedrich let him get distracted and go; she doubted that she would learn anything more from him, not once he'd picked a target for the evening. She made her way farther through the party, trying to reconcile Marlick's decision against his constant opposition to the idea before. She was quite certain there had to be more to his choice than that, but at the moment, she couldn't imagine what had convinced him.

Her time for introspection was cut short, however, by someone tapping her on the shoulder.

"I was hoping that I could catch you here," Lyana said.

Kaedrich forced a smile as she turned around. She inclined her head politely. "Miss Lebule."

Lyana was already beaming as she returned Kaedrich's acknowledgment with the slightest of curtsies. "Mr. Mannly. I feel like we haven't seen each other in forever."

"I've been busy," Kaedrich said.

It wasn't a lie, though in the moment it felt like one. Kaedrich hadn't even thought of Lyana in days.

"Well, I hope that you're not too busy to enjoy yourself tonight," Lyana said. "Have you seen the rest of the palace?"

"No, just a few rooms."

"Oh, it's amazing—you simply must have a tour. Come on, I'll show you some of the best parts."

"Um, I'm really not sure if I should," Kaedrich said. "I mean, the Trials—"

"Aren't going to start for another hour, silly." Lyana laughed. "I promise that I'll have you back before you're needed. Now, follow me. I insist."

Kaedrich glanced around—though what she hoped to see, what helpful distraction or excuse she wanted to find, even she didn't know. In the end, there was nothing to do but accept. She allowed Lyana to hook onto her elbow, though Lyana was the one leading the way.

Of course she wasn't lying: the palace was amazing, and Lyana knew her way around it as well as if it was her summer home. Under her expert directions, Kaedrich strolled through the rest of the party while Lyana chattered on brightly about the various paintings on the walls, the age of the rooms, the type of marble passing by underfoot. Lyana accepted drinks for both of them off of a passing tray, and Kaedrich sipped just enough out of hers to mellow the tight knot of anxiety that was twisting up her stomach worse than menstrual cramps.

Eventually they moved through a massive archway and found themselves outside, at a balcony overlooking a packed courtyard. Just as inside, the sloping gardens and patios were bedecked with only the finest. Flowers filled the air with an inviting perfume, while candles in fat glass vases had been dotted everywhere. The music from the orchestra spilled out from behind them and spread over the lawn, muffling the lilting conversations and peals of laughter to a gentle wash. Even the night itself was on their side: the faintest touch of cool in the air, just enough to calm the flush of the dancers, while a dazzling spray of stars twinkled like fairy lights overhead.

Lyana moved to stand right along the balcony, and Kaedrich followed suit. They stood there with their drinks, looking out at the splendor of the evening. Lyana set her glass on the stone railing, nestled in between a carefully twisted vine dotted with white and red flowers.

"Oh, this is much better," Lyana said. "So much easier to breathe out here, don't you think?"

Kaedrich nodded, though she was having an equally uncomfortable time outdoors as in. She reached up to fiddle with the pin on her lapel, trying to garner strength.

A faint shriek was followed by a *boom*, and Kaedrich and Lyana jumped. Kaedrich's hand flew toward the dagger at her waist, but before she had even reached it, she realized that there was nothing to be startled by; they'd begun the fireworks display. Lyana held her breath as the next one shot into the sky, laughing and clapping as it burst over the distant waters of Abbney Bay. "I just love fireworks," Lyana said, eyes still turned upward as color splashed across her face.

"Yeah, they're—" Kaedrich started, and then her voice dropped, ". . . great."

She had made the mistake of looking down, at the assembled party guests in the courtyard. People were continuing to arrive, an entire sea of faces and dresses swimming in and out of view. So any one individual shouldn't have stood out, and yet Kaedrich's attention had landed on her as if she was under the gaze of a limelight.

Of course Praxis had come. And now Kaedrich saw what she'd meant when she said that her new outfits had been a "work in progress," for the clothes that she appeared in now were a far cry from the rags that she'd worn when she first came to Monfort: gone were the last of her scrappy trousers, the scuffed shoes—even the signature battered coat.

In their place was an outfit that could have only been for Praxis. New pinstripe trousers piped with a whole rainbow of colors had been tailored to hide the bulk of her leg brace. A delicate silver shirt was cinched in by a dark vest that glimmered like the night's sky. A midnight-blue cravat had been twisted and repurposed as a neckerchief, off-centered so that the ends trailed at a jaunty angle over her chest. As for the new coat . . . Kaedrich had never before seen its like. Her slate blue had been replaced by the same deep midnight shade as her cravat, but dotted with a similar, starry sheen as the vest. A Yandosian-style collar fanned up to frame her head, while the torso hugged tight along the curve of her body and arms; it billowed out at the wrists and waist, spreading behind her half like the sweep of a mighty cape, and half like the trail of the finest dress. When she stopped, it took a fraction of a second to settle around her, and when she started up again it moved as if it was liquid rippling and pooling underneath a moonlit night.

Kaedrich was glad that Lyana hadn't noticed her. Lyana was still absorbed in the fireworks, gasping in delight at each new burst of turquoise and yellow-gold. But Kaedrich didn't even see them, could not tear her eyes away from Praxis. It wasn't just that she looked amazing, though of course she did—it was that she looked wholly and completely like *herself*, defying social convention and daring anyone to tell her that they had a problem with it. She moved through the crowd with her own gravity, her head tall and sure.

Lyana sighed dreamily beside Kaedrich. "I think this is the best show yet. Kaedrich, isn't this just the most beautiful thing that you've ever seen?"

"Yes," Kaedrich said, still staring as Praxis laughed effortlessly at something that someone had said to her. "Yes, I think it is."

The feeling of Lyana's hand alighting on Kaedrich's shoulder jerked her out of her reverie.

"Kaedrich? What are you . . . ?" Lyana trailed off, already turning to see what had caught Kaedrich's attention.

"It's nothing," Kaedrich said quickly. She hastily set her drink down and took Lyana's arm, trying to turn her back. It felt vitally important, all of a sudden, that Lyana not see Praxis, that she did not catch Kaedrich staring.

But Lyana was proving stubbornly resistant to Kaedrich's efforts to redirect her. She kept twisting her head, scanning the glittering crowd below. Any second now, she'd spot that distinctive white head, and then—

"Would you like to dance?" Kaedrich asked.

It was, truly, the only thing that she could think of, the only thing that might prove enough of a distraction to Lyana.

And sure enough: Lyana's face lit up as she returned all of her attention to Kaedrich. She was fighting an obvious grin as she lowered her eyes demurely. "Of course, Mr. Mannly. That would be delightful."

A surge of guilt coursed through Kaedrich, but what was there to be done now? The offer could not be rescinded, not without causing an enormous offense.

Kaedrich took Lyana's hand, and led her back into the main ballroom. Past the outer ring of wallflowers, chatting couples, and people craning their necks hopefully to spot their next partner, to the empty edges of the dance floor. Her head was still full of Praxis; she saw her everywhere now, in a thousand shades of the crowd around her. The swirl of a skirt became the edge of Praxis's new coat, a flash of a white flower in someone's hair was momentarily the curve of Praxis's cheek, a laugh ringing out was in response to one of Kaedrich's untold jokes.

Kaedrich nearly jumped when Lyana cleared her throat. She was holding her arms out, poised and ready for Kaedrich to take her hand, to wrap her arm around Lyana's waist. Kaedrich swallowed as she took up her position with Lyana on the dance floor, and then she froze. She stared at Lyana, a cold dread rooting her in place.

"Lyana—Miss Lebule, I . . . Forgive me," Kaedrich stammered, "but, I just realized, I . . . I don't actually know how to dance."

Rather than being offended, however, Lyana actually giggled. Which only made Kaedrich's shame worse—did she somehow think that Kaedrich had been so eager to hold her that she'd blurted out the need to dance, before the reality of it caught up with her? Gods, if only she could have the last few minutes back, to do them over again.

Lyana smiled at her. "Don't worry, I'm a very good teacher."

"Not so good, I think, as to teach me *that* in five seconds." Kaedrich nodded her head to indicate a couple nearby, spinning past with such grace and harmony that a cold sweat broke out along Kaedrich's back.

"True," Lyana said. "But we'll start off with something much simpler, and work our way up from there."

"I don't—"

"Follow me," Lyana said. She took a step back with her left foot, and Kaedrich jerked forward, nearly trampling Lyana's skirts in the process. But Lyana only shook her head, still smiling gently, patiently, as she stepped to the side. "That's it. We're just going to make a nice little square, see? Forward, side; back, side. Just like that."

Kaedrich's cheeks burned and her mind whirled as she struggled to regain her composure. Lyana had already guided her through one square and now she repeated her steps, and Kaedrich tried to follow what she was actually doing this time. She stared at their feet until she realized that it might look as if she was staring at Lyana's chest, and then she forced herself to look, with a stilted grin, at Lyana's face instead.

Lyana laughed, and shook her head. "Don't look so nervous. It's fine, you're doing fine. This is very simple."

And it was, Kaedrich was forced to admit to herself. They repeated this first, basic pattern, over and over, and Kaedrich's muscles slowly began to relax into the rhythm of it. If they hadn't been in the middle of a group of people, all moving through steps so much more complicated than theirs, it might have even had an element of fun to it.

Lyana, however, didn't seem bothered by this in the least. "Good," she said, as Kaedrich smoothed out her motions. "Good, exactly. One two three, one two three, see?" She smiled at Kaedrich. "Now we just need to match it to the music."

Kaedrich nodded. She paused when Lyana did, listening to the pattern of the orchestra. Lyana was tapping her shoulder, matching the beat of the music until it seemed like Kaedrich had found the pattern for herself.

"And . . . now," Lyana said, as she eased back, and Kaedrich did not need to wait for her guidance to step forward. Lyana grinned. "Perfect."

Despite herself, a swell of pride flooded through Kaedrich. She almost grinned at the small accomplishment of their first lesson, but it was still taking most of Kaedrich's concentration to keep herself moving along the unfamiliar steps. They kept up that pattern for a while longer, letting Kaedrich get comfortable with it, and she was. Slowly but surely, she was. She took a deep breath, trying to calm her frazzled nerves, trying to relax into what she was doing. She looked up, taking in the glamour of the ballroom—wanting, perhaps, to soak in a bit of the experience.

Praxis was watching them.

A jolt of terror threw off all of Kaedrich's timing. She tripped over her own feet, and started to fall forward; she managed to catch herself, but in the process she'd thoroughly trampled on Lyana's toes, and now *she* was hopping back, wincing in pain, and Kaedrich was spilling over in apologies, and by the time she looked back up, Praxis had disappeared.

"I'm—I'm so sorry!" Kaedrich said, again. "I think—that is, maybe I've had enough dancing lessons for now."

Lyana nodded, still wincing as she took first one careful step and then another. Kaedrich offered her arm, and Lyana leaned on it heavily as they broke off from the main dance floor.

They found a quiet corner, and an empty chair sitting in line of the breeze from the doorway. Kaedrich settled Lyana in it, still offering apologies at every opportunity.

Lyana held up her hand. "Kaedrich. Really, it's fine. You should have seen it when I taught Lucan to dance. I don't think that I could walk for a week, he stepped on my feet so much."

"Knowing him, though, that might have been on purpose," Kaedrich said. She tried to smile at Lyana, to lighten the sour mood that had fallen over them, and Lyana smirked.

"That's true," she conceded. She shook her head. "Brothers can be such a pain. Oh! Um, present company excluded, I'm sure."

Kaedrich glanced away. "It's fine," she told the nearest potted plant. "I'm not a brother, so you can't offend me."

"Oh," Lyana said. She shifted uncomfortably in her chair. "I thought—"

"Well, well, if it isn't the happy couple."

Kaedrich froze at the sound of Praxis's voice. She couldn't even look at her for a moment, though she was hard-pressed to pin down exactly the reason why not. Instead, without turning around, she said, "Praxis."

Lyana nodded an acknowledgment of her own, following suit. "Miss Fellows, how lovely to see you again."

"I'm sure," Praxis said. "Kaedrich, you never told me that you were such an . . . *accomplished* dancer. Tell me, who's your teacher?"

Now Kaedrich turned. A narrow frown knit her forehead together, and she stared at Praxis for a moment, uncertain if she was trying to be rude or not.

Because it was impossible to tell from Praxis's face. She held herself at a cool distance, an empty glass hanging from her fingers. She was watching Kaedrich and Lyana placidly, as if it didn't matter to her who was in front of her, or what they might talk about.

Lyana straightened up in her chair. "I'll have you know that Kaedrich is a very quick study," she said, and Kaedrich supposed that it was sweet that Lyana had risen to her defense, though it would have been better if she hadn't. Because now a slim, controlled smile was pulling at Praxis's lips, and the sight of it terrified Kaedrich.

"Is he?" Praxis said. "Forgive me, I didn't realize that you had just started. All of your Durlish dances seem like beginning moves to me. In Yandosia, the process is so much more complicated and . . . intimate." She tossed a wicked grin at Kaedrich. "You should study *that* sometime, if you really want to impress."

"I—" Kaedrich started, not even sure where her sentence was going to go.

Thankfully, Lyana cut her off.

"Yes, I'm sure that your culture is *quite* fascinating," Lyana said, a hint of disdain coloring her voice. "Tell me, do all women there have such . . . interesting fashion sense?"

Praxis glanced down at herself, as if she had forgotten what she was wearing. She ran a hand along the cut of her jacket, down her hips and out. "Nope," she said happily, shaking her head. "Just me. Do you like it?"

The faintest of wrinkles appeared on Lyana's nose. "I don't think that you should be asking me that so directly."

"Good point," Praxis said, waving her hand in dismissal of Lyana. She turned. "What about you, Kaedrich?"

Kaedrich's eyes popped, startled by having the conversation wheel on her so directly. "I—What?" she stammered.

Praxis grinned. "I thought so."

"Oh, *please*," Lyana said. She actually rose to her feet now—either her toes had stopped hurting, or else she was indignant enough at this point not to care. She hooked her arm through Kaedrich's elbow as she continued, "If you think that looking like a cross between a harlot and a clown is going to win you Kaedrich back, then perhaps you need to go back under the ice for a while to cool your head."

Stunned silence rang in the wake of this pronouncement. Praxis actually took a step back, her eyes wide. "Wow," she whispered, and Kaedrich couldn't blame her. Such an open declaration of hostility and aggression would have been a shock from anyone in this room (well, except maybe for Praxis herself), but to have Lyana spit those words out was enough to unbalance anyone. Praxis's cheeks had tinted, just slightly, on the tops, and Kaedrich's chest twisted up in sympathy for her.

"Lyana, please, it's . . . it's not like that," Kaedrich said. She tried to shoot Praxis a look, to let her know that she understood, that she knew that Praxis hadn't dressed like that to impress her. She couldn't imagine the embarrassment, having something like that just dropped out in the open. Kaedrich's thoughts were grasping for anything, now, that might sway Lyana, who had shot Kaedrich an incredulous look. "Really," Kaedrich continued, "even if Praxis *wanted* to—which she doesn't, I promise—she knows that there's nothing between us anymore. We're done. Isn't that right?"

A thin, brittle smile twisted Praxis's lips. "Of course. Well," she said, glancing at her empty glass, "if you'll excuse me, it looks like I'm due for a refill. Lovely talking with you, Miss Lebule. Kaedrich." She turned as if to go, but lingered for just a moment. She reached out, touching the cuff of Kaedrich's suit. "Nice to see that my emeralds have held up," she said, and on *that* note, she left.

Kaedrich shut her eyes, groaning inwardly at everything that had just happened. Once again, she found herself wishing desperately for the ability to go back and redo the last small portion of her life, to keep herself from stumbling down this particular path. How was it possible for everything to have gone so badly in such a short amount of time? And she still had the Trials to get through, no less, though it was seeming less and less likely that she would be passing.

Still, at least it couldn't get any worse, right?

Lyana cleared her throat. "Kaedrich," she began, picking her words carefully, "what exactly did she mean by *her* emeralds?"

Or not.

Chapter Thirty

WHOEVER WOULD HAVE thought that such a little thing as cufflinks would prove to be such a big deal?

It had taken several long minutes for Kaedrich to extract herself from Lyana—and in the end, it wasn't so much that she'd managed, as that Lyana declared that she was over-warm and needed some fresh air, and that no, Kaedrich did not have to escort her, thank you.

So that was something that Kaedrich was going to have to deal with, another mess to sweep up sooner rather than later, but at the present moment she had more important things to worry about: Praxis was missing from the party.

At first, Kaedrich tried to tell herself that she was overreacting, and jumping to conclusions that didn't necessarily follow from the information at hand. There were several large rooms and a handful of corridors to search, after all, not to mention the multi-tiered courtyards and sweeping back gardens decked out in romantically dim lights. There were any number of places for Praxis to have disappeared to. Or technically she could have just left, though Kaedrich doubted that very much once she overheard one server complaining under his breath to another about a guest swiping drinks straight out of people's hands.

All of the hairs on the back of Kaedrich's neck stood up. She tried to shift closer to the servers, hoping to learn more, but they were called away in separate directions before she could hear anything else. Gods, if

Praxis decided to *really* break her sobriety and go full-on Praxis-Drunk in a place like this, with all of these important people to insult . . .

Kaedrich's stomach knotted at the very idea. *Don't panic,* she told herself, even as she increased the speed at which she was slipping between merry party guests.

She searched the rooms in turn, keeping half an ear out for shouts of offense or alarm. She climbed the steps to the balconies, getting a look at the rooms from above. She took a quick tour through the gardens, though the only things she found between the hedgerows were a few distracted couples that she backed away from before they could notice her presence. She spotted Lyana, out on the patio, gossiping with a flock of other young ladies of quality. Laughter trailed away from them, and Kaedrich attempted to not let paranoia flood her, the idea that Lyana had decided to laugh at *her*. The laughter ebbed and flowed as Kaedrich slipped by unnoticed, until the music inside finally drowned them out.

There was a corridor outside of the main ballroom, largely empty. Kaedrich had the impression that perhaps the toilets were down this way, and perhaps Praxis had drank enough by now that she'd need them? It was a long shot, Kaedrich knew, but she slid down the hall, nodding formally at the occasional lord or guard as she went. Plush turquoise carpet sank underneath each of her footsteps, and the eyes of the line of kings glared down at her from a row of paintings on both walls. The occasional door broke up the display, roped off with thick golden cords.

Except for one.

Kaedrich groaned inwardly. A single door along the hallway was cracked open, the cord that was supposed to be blocking it off hanging limply from its hook.

She sidestepped, making it look as if she was interested in studying a nearby painting in greater detail, as an important-looking couple strolled past arm in arm. The polished voices rang down the hallway, oblivious, ignoring Kaedrich. Kaedrich waited until they were well out of sight, and then she slipped through the partially opened door for herself. She hooked the cord properly across the opening and gently shut the door behind her.

And now her pulse shot up, because she suddenly realized that she'd just let herself into a private wing of the palace—and oh gods, all the things that could happen to her if she was caught! Kaedrich froze. She glanced longingly back at the door, an instinctive desire to do the right thing urging her to go back into the designated guest areas of the palace. But on the other hand, if she was right (and she was sure that she was), then Praxis was somewhere up ahead, wandering deeper into the bowels of the palace, half-drunk and getting into Perlandra-only-knew what kind of trouble.

There really was no choice.

Taking a deep breath, Kaedrich began to scurry down the long corridor. She kept to the sides, all the more ready to dart into a closet or a room if there was the slightest sign of anyone coming. But so far, this portion of the palace was even more deserted than the hallway that Kaedrich had just left. Which meant that if Praxis was here, it should be fairly easy to spot her—especially if her tipsiness was making her careless. And so it was: Kaedrich rounded a corner and sure enough, Praxis was skulking about at the end of a wide hallway. *"Praxis!"* Kaedrich hissed.

Praxis whirled, eyes wide and flames springing to life in her palms. At the sight of Kaedrich, she snapped her hands shut and the flames puffed out. She scowled. "Keep your *voice down*!" Praxis said, all but shouting the words. They echoed down the hallway, tumbling as they bounced from wall to wall.

Kaedrich raced toward her, though Praxis was already turning back to whatever she was doing, giving the flaring hem of her new coat a haughty swish. Praxis was moving slowly and deliberately, running her fingers over the wood paneling, up along the gilded frames of all the portraits, tracing the nose of a bust as she passed by.

"You're not supposed to be here," Kaedrich said softly as she caught up. "What are you *doing*?"

"Nothing," Praxis said, too quickly. Her cheeks were flushed, though she kept her face turned in such a way that she was clearly hoping would hide it. "I . . . investigating. Obviously." She cast a sidelong glance. "What are *you* doing here? Your girlfriend is going to wonder where you've gone."

Kaedrich sighed. "Blast it, Praxis, you know that she's not—"

"*You* might believe that, but clearly you haven't gotten the message through to her yet."

"I . . ." Kaedrich frowned, pinching the bridge of her nose. "Yeah, I know. Listen, it's complicated. Lyana—she outranks me socially, you know that. I can't just up and insult her by telling her that I don't want her."

Praxis laughed under her breath. "Are you sure that's really what's holding you back?" She curled her fingers, taking another careful step away from Kaedrich. "Maybe you aren't quite as certain of that as you claim you are."

"What?" Kaedrich's whole face scrunched up in distaste. "Gods, no. How can you even think that?"

"Why not?" Praxis asked, stopping and turning back to Kaedrich so suddenly that Kaedrich nearly ran into her. Praxis was frowning deeply, and tiny gusts of wind kicked at her clothes and hair. "Is there something wrong with her?"

Kaedrich blinked. "Well . . . no, I guess not."

Praxis huffed. "Exactly. There's *nothing* to object to about her."

"But—"

"Isn't she young? Isn't she pretty? Isn't she polite and sweet and *charming*? Why *wouldn't* you choose her?"

"Praxis, I—"

"She can *dance*, for sanity's sake, and I just, I—fuck." She closed her eyes and took several deep breaths to steady herself. Her voice had been pitching both higher and louder as she'd been talking, the letters slurring together into an ever more densely accented jumble. She flung her hand angrily and muttered something to herself in Yandosian, and the smell of alcohol wafted from her.

Okay, so it was obvious she'd had a few drinks, and Kaedrich decided that clearly Praxis didn't know what she was talking about anymore. "Come on," Kaedrich started to say, intending to lead Praxis back to the party, where she could sit and breathe the night air and sip some water. She'd just taken Praxis's shoulder when the first of the voices broke in, galloping up the corridor towards them.

Praxis and Kaedrich exchanged a nervous glance. Throaty male laughter was fast approaching, and here they were standing out in the open, in a hallway clearly beyond the bounds of where guests to the palace were allowed to wander. "We should—" Praxis started, but Kaedrich had already surveyed the hallway and spotted exactly what she needed.

"With me, quickly," Kaedrich said. She dragged Praxis forward, darting across the hallway to where a discreet door was tucked into the wall paneling. Wherever it led, it was better than being caught where they didn't belong, and so Kaedrich threw herself and Praxis inside and shut the door behind them just as the men's voices were rounding the corner.

Inside, it was pitch black and stuffed full—a closet, probably, for there was hardly any room, and what felt like a shelf was digging into Kaedrich's ribs. Praxis's sour drink-breath was full in Kaedrich's face and their arms were twisted up awkwardly between them, pressing against each other. When Praxis took a breath, her shirt brushed against the back of Kaedrich's hand. "If you—"

"Shh!" Kaedrich hissed. She wiggled her arm free and pressed her fingers against Praxis's lips to shut her up. The voices were drifting closer outside of their little hidey-hole, and Kaedrich rested her ear gingerly against the door to listen.

A tangle of low voices ambled up the hallway. It was a good thing that she was only trying to track them and not eavesdrop, because most of what they were saying was an unintelligible blur. Kaedrich heard three— or maybe four, it was hard to tell—distinct voices in the group, pinging off of each other as they rumbled higher and lower in waves of disagreement and resolution. They were not walking with any particular haste. They passed right by the door, and Kaedrich held her breath, terrified. ". . . be better to act now while everyone is already assembled?" she heard one of them say.

"No," came the steady reply. "We mustn't, not until we've received word that the vote is secure. If we act before they're ready . . ."

The remainder of his argument fell into a wash of low murmurs, and soon the group was retreating beyond the range of the hallway.

Kaedrich let out her breath. She leaned her forehead against the door in relief, and it was only then that she realized that her fingers were still resting against Praxis's lips. They were ridiculously warm underneath her touch, scrunched into a half-pucker from her interrupted speech.

Kaedrich jerked her hand back, thwacking her elbow hard into one of the closet's shelves. "Ow!" she muttered, grabbing her elbow where it had struck.

"Are you okay?" Praxis whispered. "Do you want me to heal it?"

"No!" Kaedrich said, harsher than she'd meant to. She cringed, though Praxis wouldn't have been able to see it. "I mean . . . I'm fine. Thank you, but I don't need any help." She didn't even want to think about pulling off her suit jacket right now, rolling up her sleeve, all in the tight confines of this closet, with Praxis right there, and—

Kaedrich shook her head. She reached for the doorknob, but Praxis's hand wrapped around hers, stilling it.

"If you really don't want her, you should tell her," Praxis said, picking up the thread of their earlier conversation as if nothing had happened. "It's not fair to keep her hoping."

Kaedrich sighed. "I know, I know. You're right, I should, but . . . I don't want to hurt her. It's not her fault."

Praxis was quiet for a moment. Her fingers squeezed around Kaedrich's hand, so subtle that Kaedrich wasn't even sure that she'd done it at all, or been aware of it even if she had. "I understand, but rejection . . .

isn't the worst thing in the world," Praxis said finally. "It's better than constantly living with this knot of dread and hope tied up together, never knowing if you're just being foolish, always bracing yourself for the moment when you realize that nothing's ever going to happen. If you don't want her . . . just get it over with. It's the kind thing to do."

Kaedrich nodded. Then she realized that Praxis couldn't see her in the dark, so she took a breath to say "I know" again, instead; then she realized that Praxis probably *had* known that she'd nodded after all, that her sense of surroundings had no doubt given her that knowledge. She shut her mouth. Just how detailed was this sense, anyway? Could she tell the way that Kaedrich's eyes kept seeking her out in the dark, even knowing that she couldn't find more than the faintest outline as her vision adjusted? What about the wild thundering of Kaedrich's heart, so loud as the blood pumped by her ears? The knot in her stomach, exactly like Praxis had described, dread and hope tied up together? She'd gotten it exactly right, as if she was pulling the feeling from Kaedrich directly.

Would it really be better to know, though? Kaedrich wasn't so sure. She used to think that she knew—she was so sure, when she'd first come to Monfort, that all the sweet lines that Praxis's fake double had fed to her had come out of Kaedrich's own head. It was the certainty that had carried her through the first few difficult weeks, yes, and gotten her set up, gotten her into her apartment, enrolled in the academy, applying for jobs. The sting of loss had motivated her to always keep moving, keep moving, because if she stopped it would wash over her and threaten to pull her under. And over time the movement had just become natural.

But then Praxis had shown up again. And despite everything that Kaedrich had been telling herself over these last two weeks, a door that she'd long since forced shut had crept open on her while she wasn't looking. Every sidelong look, every laugh, every time that Praxis had taken Kaedrich's hand while they'd pretended to be a couple . . . Kaedrich had been telling herself, over and over again, that it had all meant nothing, that it was just her own wishful thinking coloring her perception. Still, despite herself, the hope had bloomed in her chest once more. She hadn't been watching, hadn't wanted to admit it, but here at the Crown Day celebration, trapped in some random closet, she had to be honest with herself: she wasn't really sure anymore, if it was only her own longing.

Which is precisely why Kaedrich said nothing, in the empty minute that followed. It would have been too easy, their faces hidden in the dark, to ask, too easy to find out—and having just gotten a flutter of that hope back, Kaedrich was in no mood to lose it again so soon. She elbowed the question roughly aside, forcing it back into the recesses of her mind. Her hand found the doorknob again.

"Kaedriel—"

"I have to go," Kaedrich said. "The Trials are going to be starting soon."

TOL PATROLLED THE ROOFTOPS.

Up and over the crests, around the spirals, along the rail of the widow's walk, stalking like a cat on the prowl. He gave a wide berth to the electrical wires, installed last year when Lanali was gifted Dreamfield House; they vibrated against his sense of the surroundings, a cold tickle running down Tol's spine.

The air was cool and clear around him. A perfect night—he could see all the way down to the bay, where silver ships glinted like fish in a crystal pond. The rippling water reflected the glimmer of the fireworks bursting up above, alternating turquoise and yellow-gold. At the very peak of the crest of Monfort, the pinnacle of the city, the palace was lit up against the backdrop of the starry night. Its lights spilled down the slopes, dotting the rooftop of Dreamfield House in alternating depths of shadow.

Somewhere in the distance, six temple chimes were ringing.

Tol closed his eyes. He breathed in the honey-lime perfume of the city.

It was done.

The last piece was in position. The last move before the endgame. Tol stood on the rooftop and looked out over the city, as still and watchful as a gargoyle.

In all of this time, all of this effort, Tol had never *truly* believed that they would succeed. And they still hadn't, he reminded himself. But . . . they were so close . . . It seemed impossible that anything could mess things up now. Every piece was in play, every card matched up.

The only thing that he hadn't been able to secure was Praxis Fellows, but that was hardly a surprise. If anything, Tol would have been shocked and suspicious if his plan had *worked*. Using the ransom of Kaedrich's tuition to lure Praxis out was weak, he admitted that readily, but anything more aggressive was too dangerous. Lanali liked to dismiss Praxis's abilities, but Tol never would. He knew that dealing with her was like dealing with a firecracker in the middle of a dry forest. The slightest wrong move, and Tol felt certain Praxis would declare an all-out war against them.

Which is partly why he was *here*, at Dreamfield House. There would be no conflict, not tonight. Not with so much resting in the balance. The wedding, going on deep in the halls below, was being handled with the utmost discretion and delicacy, and it was no coincidence that it was taking place on the same day, at the same *time*, as the most showy and ostentatious event in the whole calendar of Monfort's social elite. Tol knew how it would look, the tempting target that the Crown Day celebration would be. Many times, he and Lanali had discussed how best to use it to their advantage, and in the end it turned out that the best way to use it was not to use it at all. Let Praxis assume that they would go— while the *real* work of the evening took place here. Quietly. Privately.

But Tol remained behind. He trusted this plan as well as he trusted anything, which was to say: only as far as he could spit. If Praxis *did* somehow catch wind of the impending nuptials, if she *did* show her face . . . well, Tol was prepared for that. In the meantime, he waited. He watched. He listened to the temple chimes, and he watched the fireworks, and he tried not to think about the fact that, several floors below him, he had just given Hendril everything that the man could ever want.

Everything that Tol could never have. A wife; a future.

Tol glanced down, grounding himself on his wave tattoo. He traced the line of it with his finger.

They were so close now . . .

IF PRAXIS WAS anyone else, it's likely that she'd insist that Kaedrich could wait one more minute, that Praxis be allowed to finish her sentence.

Not that she knew what that sentence was going to be. It wouldn't have been a confession. It wouldn't have been an open declaration of her feelings. It wouldn't be something as simple as: *I really wasn't talking about Lyana just now.* But she had started to say *something*, and that was further than she'd ever gotten before.

But she didn't. Of course she didn't. Instead, Praxis had only nodded, and allowed herself to be dragged back to the main halls. They didn't speak along the way, and Kaedrich disappeared as soon as she'd deposited Praxis back into the outskirts of the ballroom. "Don't even *think* about getting drunk while I'm gone," was Kaedrich's parting remark, and Praxis huffed with indignation as Kaedrich disappeared into the crowd. Praxis fluffed herself, as if her metaphorically ruffled feathers could be settled as easily as if they were real. Shame burned through her cheeks, which she knew had to be flushed crimson already. Look at her: she was a ridiculous old woman, strutting around and playing at youth, acting as if she could turn Kaedrich's head if only she was *shiny* enough. Her clothing felt like Lyana had described it, a cross between a clown costume and a whore.

This entire evening was a disaster of epic proportions. Praxis set off through the party once more, snatching glasses off of passing trays as she went. *Nothing between us.* Why had Praxis even *asked* Kaedrich to tell her? Hadn't Kaedrich said what she'd felt already? Every time Kaedrich's words to Lyana floated through Praxis's head, she chased them away by downing another drink. *Nothing. Not like that.* It wasn't helping, but in the grand tradition of jilted hearts everywhere, she kept trying. She forced her way through the crowd, her shoulder colliding with arms and elbows, shouts of indignation following in her wake. Another drink, swiped directly from the hands of a party guest, and then she traded the empty glass with a replacement from a waiter's tray. She knew that she was causing a fuss, and it's entirely possible that soon she might be asked to leave, but she didn't care. What was the point of staying now? Wine soured on her tongue, the fizz of champagne burned its way down her throat. *We're done.*

Done, and they hadn't even started—not for real, not properly anyway. Two glorious days of pretend, that was all that she'd gotten. Not even that, because on the second day Kaedrich had gone out to work and the academy and the rest of her life, leaving Praxis at home to tinker with her blasted *experiments* and to try to figure out what Lanali was up to now.

All of that effort, all of that time, all of that snooping, and in the end, what had it gotten her? Praxis had thought that she was doing something so important, but maybe she was only fixating on it so much because she was too scared to do what had *really* been important—to tell Kaedrich, finally and openly, exactly how she felt.

And now it was too late. *We're done.* Kaedrich was gone, had run back to the rest of her life just like she always did. That had to mean something. Couldn't Praxis take a hint? How much more direct did Kaedrich need to *be*?

"Miss? Miss! Excuse me!"

Praxis blinked. She'd been so lost in her sour mood that she hadn't noticed as a server approached her. He tapped her on the shoulder and she turned, irritation and confusion vying for equal control of her face. "Yes? What?" she snapped.

The server did not even flinch at her ire. "I have a message for you," he said, already drawing a slim little envelope out of his suit jacket.

Praxis raised an eyebrow. She was in no mood for games this evening.

She snatched the envelope away, glancing at her own name written in an unfamiliar hand, and by the time she looked back up the server had disappeared into the crowd like a zebra into its herd.

She bit her lip, considering. Tucking her glass into the crook of her arm, Praxis sliced the letter open and pulled out a single sheet of paper, almost as thin and fine as tissue. It only took her a second to read it. She went still. Her heart had leapt into her throat, and she read it again, and then again, or at least the last line, at least the postscript of the missive.

She snapped her head up, scanning the room for a clock, but she needn't have bothered: somewhere in the depths of the palace, a chime was tolling, ringing out the top of the hour. Praxis dropped her glass, not even caring if it shattered, and raced out of the ballroom as quickly as her brace would allow.

The Trials were starting, and somewhere, somehow, Kaedrich was in trouble.

Chapter Thirty-One

IN THE MAIN reception hall, roughly a dozen of Falconridge's students were lined up in order of rank. They stood underneath the only balcony of the room, the main stage from which Prince Hemmerick would be delivering toasts and speeches to the assembled guests, if he was still in residence. The students were positioned out of his sight on purpose, the idea being that only by proving themselves were they worthy of the honor of being seen. This might have been a good thing in Kaedrich's mind, except that it meant that (being directly underneath the seat of the prince) they were full-on in the limelight for everyone else.

At least it wasn't the entirety of the assembled guests. The Trials were the primary honor of the evening, and as such, only the elite of the elite were allowed to attend. Kaedrich scanned the crowd, mingling along the long wall opposite herself and the other students. Opulence reigned supreme. Feathered headdresses and glittering jewels adorned the women, while the men were loaded down with so many sashes and military or nobility honors and rankings that they might as well have been wearing armor. Though she didn't know any of them personally, she did recognize a wide number of nobility and members of the Governance Council. She even spotted Lord-Councillor Braynish, the man that she and Praxis had helped to save in Vaulaine, standing between a member of the Court of State and Lord-Councillor Westingly, the speaker of the Noblemen's Arm of the Crescent. They were largely ignoring the Falconridge students, talking quietly between themselves—it looked like an important discussion, but then, Kaedrich supposed that a group like that could make anything seem like an urgent matter of state business.

Kaedrich searched the room as discreetly as possible, but of course she did not see Praxis. Which was good: if Kaedrich's goal was to keep Praxis away from Falconridge and Director Tarlock, then leaving her behind in the rest of the party was exactly the right move. Still, a part of Kaedrich had expected Praxis to show up anyway, and now that she hadn't ... Kaedrich told herself that she was not disappointed. Praxis had never been involved in this part of Kaedrich's life, so it did not have to sting that she wouldn't be here to witness Kaedrich's success or failure. Even if this was her last and only chance to prove herself in the eyes of Durland's high society, even if this was the last and only time that she would ever compete under the Falconridge banner, literally hanging from the vaulted ceiling all up and down the room. Even if this was the highest honor of her entire life, and she knew it, and it would never come again.

It was fine. It was what Kaedrich had wanted.

Kaedrich took a breath, and tried to draw herself back into her own concerns. This was the moment that she'd spent months preparing for. She did not have time or mental space to waste being distracted by feelings of rejection. She ran through the early, ritualistic parts of the Trials that would come first—muttering underneath her breath, repeating words that had become second nature to her.

By the time a bell sounded a few minutes later, she had almost managed to calm herself down. Director Tarlock stepped out of the sidelines, his shoes clacking across polished wood in the sudden hush that had settled over the crowd. A wide space had been cleared in the middle of the room, a single electric lamp shining down on it from above. Even in this room, surrounded by such airs and graces, he cut an imposing figure. He walked with the authority of a general, every footstep planted as surely as if staking new territory for the Crown. He turned to address the audience, his back as straight as a toy soldier.

He cleared his throat. "Lords and ladies, honored guests—allow me to welcome you to another year of Falconridge's distinguished Trials.

"I know that some of you have been wondering if we would be going forward with them this year, and that was a fair concern. What is the point, after all, of trying out for the king's guard if there is no king present to impress? Well. Allow me to be the first to assure you that while our illustrious monarch is unable to be with us this evening, he remains well-represented here tonight. He has sent to us not only the honored judgments of the First Guard, but"—he motioned upward, his arm striking a dramatic angle as it jutted toward the balcony over Kaedrich's head— "he has also graciously allowed his seat to be filled this evening. This place of honor has been given to someone of the very highest level of trust and respect, not just to the Crown itself, but to the people of Durland!"

Uh-oh.

"My lords," Director Tarlock went on, pausing for effect. "My ladies . . . To bear witness to these esteemed proceedings, I present to you the Most Revered, the Wise and Honorable . . . Pon Lanali!"

Miss Fellows—

So sorry that I won't be able to enjoy your company this evening. Alas, important business detains me elsewhere. Know that my thoughts, as always, are with you, and take solace in the knowledge that I am sure that we will meet again soon. —Tol

P.S. I hope that your friend enjoys the present that I arranged for him. May his Trials be everything that they deserve to be.

"I'm sorry, miss," the guard at the door said, "but your card is a standard-issue invitation. Only guests with the appropriate pass are allowed entrance into the Trials."

Praxis shook her head. "No no no, you don't understand, I *need* to get in there. It's vitally important, don't you see?"

The guard gave her a pitying, condescending smile. "I understand, miss, I really do. Unfortunately, rules are rules."

"No, but I—"

"Miss, please."

"No!" Praxis shouted. "That's *ridiculous*." She drew herself up to her full height, assuming her most haughty Yandosian expression. "Do you have any idea who I am?"

The guard shrugged. "No, actually. Which means—no offense—that you can't be as important as you say you are. I've been a palace guard for near on forty years. I'd know you, if you mattered."

Praxis took a single step back, honestly startled. This was not even remotely the response that she'd been expecting. She sighed in exasperation. "Fine," she said, drawing out her purse from somewhere deep in the folds of her new coat. "Fine, you want to play it that way? How m—"

"Let me stop you right there," the guard said. He folded his hands directly over hers, stilling them as she reached inside of her purse. "I will warn you, miss, that attempting to bribe a palace guard is an offense punishable by five months behind bars."

"You're *kidding*."

"I'm really not," he said, and the look on his face made her believe him.

Praxis glanced at the door behind him. She glanced back at him. To either side of him, two more guards in identical uniforms stood by, ready and waiting. And while Praxis had little doubt that she could force her way through these three, how many more lay beyond? Not to mention that as soon as she started to use force, ten kinds of hell would be raised, along with every alarm in the palace. Did she really want to start that level of a fight? Did she really think that she could protect Kaedrich from whatever Tol had arranged while trying to battle against the entire force of the palace guard?

For once, Praxis's better judgment won out. She forced a nod, and withdrew her purse. "Thank you," she made herself say. She turned and stalked off, down the hall, until she was around a corner and out of sight. Okay, but there *had* to be another way in—a servants' hall, a secret passage, *something*. These kinds of buildings, there was always another way.

All Praxis had to do was find it.

THE STUDENTS RAN through the ceremonial aspects of the Trials with the usual flourish, and then the real show began. Kaedrich, now divested of her jacket and tie, watched from her place on the sidelines. A knot had cinched tight in her stomach the moment that they'd started, and now it showed no signs of abating. Quite apart from Lanali's presence—which would be enough to tense Kaedrich up all by itself, no doubt—what she was witnessing tonight was only one step below a slaughter.

Not literally, of course. The Trials were all ritual, nonlethal, totally safe.

In theory.

In practice, Kaedrich was finding that the tests were a lot more . . . *aggressive* than she'd been led to believe. Perhaps it was because the stakes were so high: failure to advance meant an immediate expulsion from the academy, after all, though you'd still be responsible for any open tuition that you'd pledged to the school. Not that most of the students had to care about this last part. Kaedrich shouldn't have even had to care about this last part, not if the fates were kinder, not if everything was going the way that it was supposed to. Not if she could talk to Praxis, explain the situation, let her go in and sort out whatever legal technicality had hung up the payments in the first place.

Kaedrich tried to push this weight out of her mind. She would pass—she had to pass—and she would do whatever it took to raise the money for her next year's tuition. Eventually, whatever crisis was brewing in Monfort would blow over, and then, if it was still too much, Kaedrich could approach Praxis for help. All she had to do was hang on, for a little while longer. All she had to do was make it through tonight.

Not that the guards were going to make that easy for her. Kaedrich winced, nearly sick as one of her fellow students miscalculated his opponent's move, and was literally *thrown* across the room. A collective gasp went up from the audience, several of whom had to leap out of the way as the young man went crashing against the wall. Murmurs of shock rippled through the room, and the hairs on the back of Kaedrich's neck raised as a realization settled thick on her shoulders.

This wasn't normal. Even if the rules of the competition were technically being followed, the royal guardsmen were taking things to a whole new level this year. Kaedrich could see it, in the hungry, predatory glower in the eyes of the guardsmen, and she could see it in the way that the nobles scattered along the edge of the room seemed to sit up straighter, their interest actually *hooked* for once. They wore expressions of open delight and surprise, so wrapped up in the proceedings that they had dropped the false disinterest that was part of the uniform of their rank. Even Lord Braynish, normally so controlled, had sat on a chair and leaned forward, enraptured by the spectacle before him.

This was blood sport.

Kaedrich glanced at the opposing line of students that had already finished: four of them, now that the young man was being collected from the wall, all failures, all holding bundles of ice to their face or cradling an arm that looked suspiciously broken. The rest of the young men in line with *her* were looking distinctly green underneath their gentlemen's tans, the understanding of their fate having caught up with them.

The next student was called forward. A man named Denkin, someone Kaedrich shared a handful of classes with but had never really spoken to. Kaedrich touched her pin, sending a silent prayer to Perlandra that he would fare better than the rest of them. Her attention was locked in now, as riveted as everyone else.

Except that her interest was selfish and professional—she had to know what kind of tactics the guardsmen were using, where they differed from the gallant sparring that the students had been trained in. Kaedrich took note of everything: the speed of the guardsmen, bordering on unnatural; the deadly determination in the set of their jaws; the techniques of their vicious uppercuts; the patterns of their footwork. Sweat ringed her collar as she tried to cram more than a year's worth of techniques and fighting styles into her brain all at once. The concern that she'd felt for her fellow students fell away, replaced by a cool evaluation of their likely injuries. How would Kaedrich keep going, if she suffered the same? What would she do differently, to avoid falling into the same traps?

One by one, the rest of the Falconridge students took their place. One by one, they were wailed upon by the royal guardsmen. Two of them actually did manage to take a proper swing, landing contact solidly in the abdomen of their opponents, and violent cheers went up around the perimeter of the room. These few winners were led away with the fanfare of a reigning prizefighter leaving the ring, but the rest of them dropped, again and again and again.

Kaedrich was the last one left. She did not wait to be called forward. She blinked in the sudden brightness, which obscured most of her view of the surrounding guests. The only other part of the room with good illumination was the king's balcony. Lanali peered down, her veil folded back over her head for once. It was the closest that Kaedrich had been to her since facing her down in the land of the dead, and it struck Kaedrich now that the experience there hadn't exactly been real. Kaedrich stood tall, staring Lanali square in the face. Did Lanali even remember her? Did she have any idea who Kaedrich was?

It didn't matter. She would now.

Traditionally, each student stepping forward was petitioning for consideration into the king's service and the royal guard; as such, they were each given a ribbon with their name stitched into it. This ribbon was tied to their upper arm at the beginning of the ceremony, then taken off and tied to a post along the edge of the combat area to mark their intention to compete for the king's approval. If they lost, the ribbon was torn off by the guard that had beaten them and fed into a flame burning nearby. If they won, it remained in place.

Kaedrich pulled the end of her ribbon. She felt the whole thing loosen, the tail fluttering down the length of her arm. She did not take her eyes off of Lanali as she held the ribbon aloft, displaying it underneath the gaze of their would-be sovereign—and then tucked it neatly into her pants pocket.

Gasps rippled through the assembled crowd. Lanali's brow contracted, just slightly, her lips pressed into a firm line of stately disapproval. Kaedrich turned her back, taking up her starting position, as loud grumbles of outrage and discontent continued to circle.

These comments were quickly cut off, however, as Kaedrich's opponent stepped into the pool of light. Hush swept in, everyone's breath held fast.

This had to be a joke. The man across from her was dressed in the bright teal of the royal guardsmen, yes, except that his uniform was stripped of ornamentation, reduced to its barest essence. A plain set of black trousers; a simple, military-style coat cinched in at the waist. The only thing to indicate his rank was a patch sewn into the upper portion of his sleeve—the captain's seal, personally tailored to reflect the talents and attributes of each new man to hold the post.

The captain of the royal guard gave a polite and formal bow to Kaedrich, as if this was so routine that it was hardly worth noticing. All Kaedrich could do for a moment was stare at the emblem on his arm, her thoughts exploding all at once. What was the captain even *doing* here? Shouldn't he have gone with the prince when the Crown went into hiding?

A bell was rung from the shadows surrounding them, and Kaedrich jumped. A fast sweat broke out over her body. Her questions didn't matter now. She'd been preparing to face down a guardsman, yes, but the *head* guardsman? That was a level beyond anything she'd trained for, anything she'd witnessed here tonight, and she couldn't help but think that Lanali had something to do with this. Kaedrich wanted to steal a look at her, perched over the proceedings in her place of honor, but she did not have time. Kaedrich jerked to the side before she'd consciously realized that anything was happening, and the *whoosh* of a heavy fist ran past her ear. And then, suddenly, it didn't matter that this was unfair, that the fight was designed for her to lose, that they were even at the Trials, in the palace. It didn't matter what was going on, who was around them. Kaedrich's focus narrowed in, her world reducing in scope until there was only herself and her opponent. She forgot about everything else as she skittered back several steps, avoiding his next advance. And the next. The next.

In the quiet, her body reacted out of instinct. Her mind was silent, her attention as sharp as a blade. Kaedrich danced backward, keeping out of his reach as she assessed his fighting style. He did not waste his movements; every strike was calculated, forceful. He gave not even a scrap of energy to showmanship or razzle-dazzle. There was no way that Kaedrich was going to wear him down or wait him out, but neither did it seem as if she was likely to get a strike of her own through his fortress-like defenses. When she tested, his blocks were as sudden as a stone wall.

In short: she was not going to win this fight. Not by a long shot, not even close. He was chosen to humiliate her, to save the most spectacular of the academy's failures for last, and what was worse is that everyone in the room was realizing this. Kaedrich felt a subtle shift in the atmosphere. The guests had been rooting for her fellow students, yes, but with her defeat assured, they had quickly shifted. They smelled blood, and by the gods, they were going to enjoy getting it.

Losing their faith was just enough of a distraction. Kaedrich didn't even see the blow that landed on her side. Pain exploded across her ribs, and she went reeling back. She only just ducked to avoid the next punch, though she felt the air of it compress as his fist swung hard over her head. Kaedrich sprinted for the far corner of their combat area, clutching her side, not caring for a moment if this made her look the part of a coward.

Of course the captain was fast on her trail. Kaedrich veered at the last moment, leaving her foot stuck out behind her. It was hardly one of the sanctioned moves of honorable combat; nonetheless, she felt a tiny surge of victory as her opponent caught on her heel and stumbled forward.

He caught himself before he hit the floor, as Kaedrich fully expected. That was fine—she did not need him down, merely off guard. All that was required at her rank for a victory was one solid hit to his abdomen, and Kaedrich quickly spun back, her fist already swinging.

The captain caught her punch in his hand, crushing down his grip. Kaedrich cried out, her bones grinding together. She buckled, falling partially to her knees, and the captain turned and threw a solid punch across her jaw.

She fell back. The captain let her go, releasing her hand with an almost playful shove backwards. Kaedrich landed hard on her backside, toppling quickly until she was sprawled across the floor. Her head clonked on the polished wood, her whole body screaming in agony. The captain towered over her, his arms spread wide in victory. From her place on the floor, the captain appeared to be a god over Kaedrich. Celestial light poured down on him from behind, throwing his face into shadow as he acknowledged the undignified whoops and cheers of the crowd.

The captain turned, still acknowledging his praise. As he turned, he stretched his arm to wave to someone in the audience, and it was this motion that pulled his shirtsleeve back. Just an inch or so. Just enough.

The bloom of a silvery "rash" caught the light. In the exact same spot as the man who'd killed Lord Wellen, though whether it was indicative of his guilt in that crime, or just related to their replacement arm bones, Kaedrich couldn't say. All that she knew, lying there, was that this man, the head of the royal guardsmen, the prince's top adviser when it came to the safety and security of his person, was one of *them*. The "fancymen." Lanali's men.

Every single one of Kaedrich's muscles protested as she pushed herself up: first onto her elbows, pausing to catch her breath, and then sitting upright. By the time she'd staggered into an unsteady crouch, the crowd had realized what she was doing, and a new silence had begun to breeze through the room.

The captain turned around just as she'd drawn herself up to her feet. His grin of victory had never once left his face, and he actually laughed at her now. "Gods, haven't you had enough?" he asked.

Kaedrich shook her head. "Doesn't look that way, does it?"

She threw herself toward him, a wild and entirely uncoordinated attack against a mountain. The captain sidestepped, barely even trying.

Kaedrich could feel the audience losing patience with her. The fierce determination that she'd put forth initially had been a good show, solid and honorable, but this . . . this was unseemly. Her next several lunges brought forth groans of exasperation, and one or two members of the crowd threw in heckles and jeers. She knew that she should probably stop, but the idea of simply *giving in*, of losing to one of Lanali's foot soldiers . . . It wasn't something that she was prepared to do. Even if it meant fighting until she dropped, even if it meant fighting with her last breath. She threw another attack at him, nearly grazing his arm this time.

"Done now?" the captain asked, as he blocked and then dodged. "Come on, kid, be a man about this. I've won."

"We're done when I say I'm done," Kaedrich said. She tried a kick, and the captain grabbed her by the ankle and threw her down—except this time he followed, pinning her in place much like Kaedrich had done to Praxis in the training room, what felt like a lifetime ago.

His posture was not quite as textbook as Kaedrich's, however, and the butt of his elbow ended up mashing down hard on Kaedrich's trapped breast. Kaedrich bit down on the scream that had ripped up through her throat. It was a fast enough reaction to fool the audience, but unfortunately the captain was not stupid. Kaedrich watched in horror as his expression froze. He glanced from her face to her chest and back to her face again, narrowing his eyes infinitesimally.

It was not the distraction that Kaedrich had been hoping for, but damned if she was going to waste it. Fueled by the rage of being found out, she drew all of her remaining strength together, coiling like a serpent, and lashed out.

Her shoe connected hard with the soft flesh between his legs.

The captain's eyes bugged out, and then his whole face crumpled together in sick agony. He recoiled out of instinct, releasing just enough of his grip over Kaedrich for her to slither out from underneath him. She shot to her feet, and he staggered to his. Hatred burned through his eyes, and he lashed out at Kaedrich, ready to rip her to shreds, but it was her turn to leap aside. A flutter of panic raced through her chest—it felt as if she'd just enraged a bull, and her instincts turned toward thoughts of running. She darted aside, but there was nowhere else to really *go*. She found herself next to the pole that she was supposed to have tied her name to, the two remaining ribbons fluttering lightly overhead. The captain was all but *charging* at her now, and so Kaedrich did the first panicked thing that she could think to do.

She grabbed the pole, sturdy underneath her grip. She vaulted herself up, holding on to it, and screamed as she thrust her legs out into a kick as if from the depths of the Shadowlands.

Her feet struck him clean in the chest. The jolt was every bit as hard on her as it had been on him, and the force of it swung her back. Kaedrich barely managed to hold on to the pole as she hastily set herself back down, and so she was occupied and denied the pleasure of seeing the captain begin to fall.

The crowd let out a collective gasp. In Kaedrich's mind, the first tiny flicker of awareness to what she had managed to do was sparking, but in the moment she did not pay it any attention. Rage at Lanali, at everything that she had done, transmuted itself into rage at the captain, and so Kaedrich ran unthinkingly forward, her fist connecting with the underside of the captain's jaw as the last of his balance failed him.

He toppled. His body struck the ground with a thud that sent shudders through the soles of Kaedrich's shoes.

Nobody said a word. The whole of the room lay silent, breathless. There *was* no audience, as far as Kaedrich was concerned, no witnesses to her victory save but one. The captain lay on his back, his eyes fluttering in a daze, and Kaedrich marched up and planted her foot straight onto his chest, pinning him in place. She turned, looking up into the balcony, toward the place of honor. The face of the prince was gone, but Lanali was watching, and Lanali had seen, and Lanali *knew*.

Kaedrich drew out the ribbon from her pocket. She felt the texture of her name, stitched into place. *Kaedrich Mannly.* Without taking her eyes off of Lanali for even a moment, Kaedrich dropped the ribbon across the fallen captain. "Next time, it's you," Kaedrich whispered. She knew that Lanali couldn't hear her, not from this distance, but it didn't matter. The words were intended more for herself, as a promise, as a pledge. Lanali may be enjoying her seat of power now, but it would not last. Not if Kaedrich had anything to say about it.

The audience burst into riotous applause. Kaedrich turned, spreading her arms as she dipped into a grateful bow. Though she knew that her victory would be seen as a massive boost for Falconridge, tonight Kaedrich knew that she had won for herself. Her shirt, plain white and free of the academy's markings, caught the light as she bowed and basked in the admiration of the assembled guests. Tonight, in this moment, she felt that she could accomplish anything. Tonight, in this moment, she felt that she could fly.

Chapter Thirty-Two

IN A CORRIDOR outside of the main reception hall, a wooden panel fell to the floor. Praxis's feet stuck out of a crawlspace near the ceiling, her new shoes covered in dust. She winced, wiggling awkwardly until she fell out of the crawlspace and landed somewhat unsteadily on her feet.

The effort hadn't been easy. Between the pain still flaring in her hip, and the restricted movement of her brace, Praxis had more dragged herself along than crawled—but in the end, it had been worth it. Despite the filth on her fine clothes, despite the effort, despite the strain that she'd put on her aggravated hip wound, it had all been worth it.

She'd seen Kaedrich do something impossible.

Okay, so her view was extremely limited, peering through a wooden grate near the ceiling, in an access shaft designed more for working with the chandeliers than for observing what was going on below, but still. Panic had been replaced by pride, a swell of it that had closed up her throat as the captain of the guard had fallen. Praxis had gone through all of this effort in an attempt to save Kaedrich from a threat, and in the end it turned out that she needn't have bothered, that Kaedrich had the situation well in hand.

Praxis could not have been more delighted.

She kicked the panel aside now, not caring if she left signs behind of where she'd been. The hallway was empty, but she could hear excitement and commotion from up ahead, where news of Kaedrich's victory was spreading fast. Praxis edged up to the end of the hall, peering into the room beyond. Now that the Trials were over, the guards at the door were gone, and access between the rooms flowed freely.

People were swarming Kaedrich. Thrilled chatter pinged left and right, and Praxis stood tucked in the shadows and watched for a while, letting Kaedrich enjoy her moment of glory. When Kaedrich finally managed to extricate herself, Praxis was waiting: she grabbed Kaedrich by the elbow, whisking her off into a side room like a street magician making coins disappear. Kaedrich started to yelp, but Praxis threw her arms around Kaedrich in a hug, embarrassment and propriety and awkwardness be damned.

"Gods, you're amazing," Praxis whispered.

"Ow—thanks—ow."

"Oh! Sorry, sorry," Praxis said. She hastily pulled herself back, as Kaedrich clutched at her side, the point where the captain had landed his first solid punch.

"It's okay," Kaedrich said. "It's just . . . a little tender, that's all." She tried to smile anyway. "You saw it, then?"

"Of course."

Kaedrich bit her lip as she looked away. She shrugged. "It's just . . . I didn't think that you were there."

"I was there. You were amazing."

Kaedrich laughed. "It was mostly luck."

"That doesn't matter. You took advantage of the luck."

Kaedrich looked up, and now it was Praxis's turn to be shy. Dammit, why was this so complicated?

Praxis cleared her throat. "So, um . . . do you want me to . . . ?" She waved her hands vaguely at Kaedrich.

"Oh! Yeah, that would be nice, thanks," Kaedrich said. She fussed to untuck the hem of her shirt, and raised it up, just enough so that Praxis could get to the bruise forming at the bottom of Kaedrich's ribs.

"Seriously, though, that was . . ."

"Amazing?" Kaedrich offered with a cheeky grin, and Praxis swatted Kaedrich's shoulder with her free hand.

Kaedrich winced, from what looked like more than just the pain of her quickly healing bruises. "Thanks," she said, though she didn't look at Praxis as she said it.

"What's wrong?"

Kaedrich hesitated. She glanced through the door to the hall beyond, then lowered her voice even though, tucked away like this, they were more or less alone. "It's just . . . he *found out*."

Praxis frowned. "'Found out'?"

"Yeah," Kaedrich said. She raised her eyebrows meaningfully, and glanced down at herself for a second. Praxis hastily pulled her hands away; they'd been lingering against the soft skin of Kaedrich's ribs, and she thought for a second that Kaedrich was trying to reprimand her for it. But then understanding struck her hard and fast, as if Praxis had received one of the same punches that had left their marks on Kaedrich. Praxis's eyes widened, and Kaedrich nodded at her. He had *found out*.

"I'm not sure what to do," Kaedrich said eventually. She shrugged as she lowered her shirt. "Not that there's anything *to* do, I guess, although it feels wrong to just sit here and *hope* that he doesn't tell anyone." She began to tuck her shirt back in, straightening out the fabric. She was back to not looking at Praxis, as if somehow this was Kaedrich's fault, that her carelessness had let this happen. As if she was *embarrassed* with herself.

Praxis reached up. She traced her fingers along Kaedrich's jawline, the skin warming and then cooling underneath her healing touch. Gods, how she wanted to be able to do this without the excuse of Kaedrich's bruises. "Leave it to me," Praxis said, soft and comforting.

Kaedrich looked up. Their eyes met, locked in on each other for perhaps the most *direct* look that they'd shared all evening.

Praxis's breath caught in her chest. Looking at Kaedrich, it was as if all of the protective layers that Praxis armored herself in fell away, that the gap between their hearts had vanished, that there was no more sharp divide between separate entities. Praxis's head spun. Her breath came back to her in a rush, her blood suddenly thundering through her veins. A strange sense of rightness passed over her, like the world had aligned itself properly for the first time. Her fingers were still lying gently against Kaedrich's jawline, the bruise long since gone. She hastily pulled herself back, embarrassed, and it was only once they'd separated again that Praxis realized what had caused the odd feeling of imbalance that had made her dizzy: her sense of Kaedrich had shifted, and in the span of a moment, Praxis's heart had skipped—stopped and started, so fast that she hadn't noticed. It was settled by this point, beating at a rate that wasn't quite what she was used to . . . but that perfectly aligned, now, as a back-and-forth song with Kaedrich's.

Praxis looked away. She did not dare trust herself, in this moment, to do anything. To speak, or move; to try to address what had just passed between them. If indeed anything had. Maybe it was all her—had Kaedrich even noticed? Praxis tried to tell herself that maybe she was imagining it, but every time she closed her eyes, every time she focused on Kaedrich, their counterpoint hearts rang as loud as temple chimes in her mind.

Shit, Praxis thought.

Kaedrich cleared her throat. Praxis looked up, hope flaring in her chest. "I . . ." Kaedrich started, but then she frowned as she trailed off.

"Yes?"

"I . . ." Kaedrich tried again. She took a breath. "I should probably find Lyana. There's—there's something that I need to tell her."

"Oh," Praxis said. Ice seemed to freeze through her veins, and in an instant her heart had stuttered again, beating once more underneath its own shaky rhythm. She shrugged, trying to play it casual. "Of course. Go on, then. Don't let me keep you."

Kaedrich nodded. She glanced once at Praxis, her attention lingering just slightly too long. "I'll be back in a little bit, okay?" Kaedrich said.

Praxis shrugged. "I'll be here."

Which was true, although . . . there was one thing that she needed to take care of first.

Jakalone Montrey, captain of the king's royal guard, did not get where he was today by allowing people to sneak up on him. He may not have a wizard's sense of his surroundings, unlike his predecessor, but he did have excellent ears, and even better reflexes.

In the streets outside of the palace, he knew that he was being followed. He'd chosen to leave the party early, for obvious reasons, and had quickly set off down a little-known side street used mainly by service personnel. He'd barely gotten twenty feet down the lane when he heard the first scrape of a shoe, an odd little *clink* following softly in its wake.

Montrey did not react to this, not at first. He strolled along, various parts of his body aching but with his head held high, and he did not allow himself to appear as if he had noticed the sound. There was a junction coming up, with a nice wide intersection, and there he would make his move. A flicker of anticipation coursed through his veins. Someone had picked the *wrong* night to attack him, that was for damned sure.

He kept an ear out, tracking the person that was tracking him. Whoever it was, they were good—Montrey almost lost the sound of them, once or twice, though always there was that little *clink*, the telltale sign that gave his pursuer away.

He reached the intersection. He stopped, looking up at the stars for a moment, and then fished into his pockets as if he was distracted looking for something to smoke. In reality, though, he was wrapping his hand around the hilt of a knife, and by the time the padding footsteps caught up behind him, Montrey was already whirling.

There was a flash of fiery orange. The knife wrenched itself out of Montrey's grip as if a hand of the gods had reached down and seized it for themselves, and it went clattering to the ground somewhere in the shadows. Montrey pulled his arm back, instinctively blocking his face with one hand as he thrust a straight punch with the other. He could not see at first, temporarily blinded by the flare that had stolen his knife from him, but he felt something searing hot coil itself like a serpent around his wrist and yank it safely downward.

A rope of flames had snared him. It snaked out from his wrist, running like a leash back to the hands of its master. Hatred burned through Montrey's chest, as fast as if a second blaze had been set alight. *Damned wizards,* he thought. He almost spat at the ground between their feet, but a wizard wasn't even worth that much, in his book.

Especially not this wizard. Though she'd changed her clothing slightly from the image that the Pon had circulated, the *look* of her was unmistakable: Praxis Fellows.

As soon as Montrey realized this, a surge of raw determination blanketed his mind and quieted his thoughts. *Rule number one,* a voice whispered to him, pulsing straight through to the core of his soul. *Kill Praxis Fellows, and bring me her head.*

He was reacting so quickly that he didn't even know what he was doing. He felt his muscles compressing and stretching, though it was as if someone else was guiding them. He did not know that he was going to jerk back until he did it, he did not know that he was going to try yanking on his leashed arm and throwing another punch with his free hand until he had clenched his fist. He threw himself in a raging fury, as if every piece of his mortal being was filled with the hatred from a divine.

But flames had surrounded him, as tall as his neck. Every time he tried to lash out, they nipped at him like a pack of snarling dogs. Even then, the need to destroy Praxis Fellows tried to drive him forward. Heat and pain flared against him, and his instincts fought against each other as he pulled back into the safe center of the ring. His soul ached, as if the war itself was physically tearing him apart.

He did not have to struggle for long, however. Montrey had only been encircled by flames for a moment when Praxis Fellows stepped right into them, and Montrey froze. Rarely had he seen anything that had actually scared him before, and though he would never admit it, this was one of them: the fire licked around her, as steady as if she was a part of it, and she did not burn. Montrey had gone up against a lot of wizards in his time, and many of them had used flames; *none* of them had ever had that much direct contact and come away unscathed.

Power crackled around Praxis as she reached forward. Montrey backed up, scrambling to get away from her, but the flames were tightening now. In the choice between facing Praxis and burning alive, Montrey almost chose the latter—but he did not get that chance. Praxis's hand clamped onto Montrey's face, and in the time it took to gasp, a thousand images had ripped through his mind. Everything that had happened that night, from arriving at the party, to the humiliating fight with the dark Falconridge student, to this very moment. Montrey's stomach pitched.

He found himself on the cold ground, his thoughts piecing themselves together as if waking from a dream. A breeze shifted over him, and Montrey shivered. He pushed himself up, shaking his head to try to clear the fog. Where was he? Had the boys somehow managed to get him drunk? But he was dressed in his uniform, and he never drank while on duty. Montrey frowned. He was covered in sweat, his shirt soaked through, and he ached in places that he distinctly tried to *avoid* aching in. He looked up. The palace loomed over him, lit up against the night. A firework exploded behind it, and with a jolt he realized that it had to be the evening of the Crown Day celebration, that he was supposed to *be* there right now, that he was scheduled to fight in the Trials—and that, however he had ended up in this side lane, he was clearly missing it. Montrey threw himself to his feet, scrambling toward the palace, wishing like hell that he wasn't too late.

THE PARTY SWIRLED around Kaedrich as if she was moving through a dream. Nothing quite felt real: the laughter pinging around her, the glimmering dresses, the lingering notes of the orchestra winding down for the evening. She just kept going over her conversation with Praxis, trying to figure out what had happened.

Because *something* had happened. An odd little moment, dragged on too long; a strange feeling in Kaedrich's chest. She might have dismissed it as her imagination, except that she'd been looking straight into Praxis's eyes, and she *knew* that Praxis had felt it, too. Which meant . . . what?

That was the problem. She really didn't know what it meant, except that Praxis was right: she had to find a way of telling Lyana the truth. Or a version of the truth that she could understand, anyway, a means of letting her down without revealing *too* much, without insulting her pride.

Gods. What had she gotten herself into? Kaedrich's stomach twisted up just thinking about the challenge ahead of her.

But first things first. She had to *find* Lyana, in this sea of ballgowns, before she could find a way to tell her that she wasn't interested. Which was difficult enough under ordinary circumstances, but now, with Kaedrich's head spinning and buzzing, her thoughts being pulled in a thousand different directions, her task felt nigh to impossible.

So it was good, and not, that she found herself waylaid by something entirely different.

In her distraction, Kaedrich's shoulder collided with someone else's. Panic coursed through her as she bounced off of them, wondering exactly what ranking of important person she might have royally offended. "I'm sorry!" she said, so quickly, turning back, and then surprise replaced her fear. "Havil!"

Havil grinned. "Kaedrich! Gods, there you are. We've been trying to find you all evening."

"We?" Kaedrich asked, but then the question was answered immediately. Tristy appeared from behind one of the party guests, delight upon her face.

"Oh! There, I told you we'd find him," Tristy said. And then, to Kaedrich's surprise, she sidestepped and looped her arm through Havil's waiting elbow. A tiny gemstone caught the light, a glimmer from Tristy's finger.

Kaedrich's eyes widened. "O-kay . . . I guess there have been some . . . developments lately."

Havil blushed, and Tristy laughed. "Not as many as you might think," she said. "*This*"—she motioned between herself and Havil—"isn't exactly new, we've just kept it from everyone because Havil's family wouldn't approve. I'm sorry we had to lie to you—to all of you. I hope that you understand."

"I do," Kaedrich said. She tried to pour every ounce of sincerity into her voice, to make sure they knew that she meant it. Because gods, if anyone understood the need to lie to protect herself, it was Kaedrich.

"Anyway," Havil said, "I'm afraid that we can't stay. We really just stopped by to say goodbye, and to wish you luck."

Kaedrich frowned. "Goodbye?"

They gave a collective shrug, perfectly in sync. "We're leaving Monfort," Havil said.

"I'm sorry we won't be able to have our celebration after all," Tristy said.

"It's just," Havil said, "the city really isn't what it used to be—"

"And I have family up north that would be happy to help us out, so—"

"We're heading up in a couple of days," Havil finished. "Before my parents can throw too big of a fit."

Kaedrich blinked. "Um . . . wow. That's . . . I'm sorry, that's a lot to take in."

Tristy smiled. "We know." She stepped forward, raising herself on her toes to place a quick kiss on Kaedrich's cheek. She tipped her head, studying Kaedrich. "But some things are just too important to ignore any longer. You know?"

Kaedrich swallowed down a lump in her throat. "Yeah," she said. "Yeah, I know."

Chapter Thirty-Three

You did the right thing, Praxis told herself as she stepped back into the party. *The right thing. Exactly the right thing.*

If she said it enough, she might start to believe it. She snatched a wine glass and threw it back. The memories that she'd stolen from the captain of the royal guard shouted in her mind like rowdy neighbors. Praxis reached up, massaging her temples, but of course this did nothing to soothe the ache in her head. She had someone *else's* memories trapped up there, and that was . . . well, that was never supposed to happen. She didn't even know that it *could* happen—all that she'd been trying to do was go in and attempt to recreate Lanali's fog. The trouble was twofold: not only did Praxis not know *how* Lanali had done it, but then once she was there, once she was seeing what the captain had seen, once she was feeling what the captain had felt . . .

He was going to tell Lanali about Kaedrich.

And, well. *That* couldn't be allowed to happen, now could it?

Praxis had reacted without thought. She'd ripped the memories straight out of his head, watched the captain's eyes roll back in their sockets, watched him collapse. In her haste, she'd accidentally stolen the entire day from him. She left him in the street, scurrying away before he could rouse himself.

"Oh, Miss Fellows!"

Praxis flinched. Back in the party, she'd been trying to use the drinks to dull herself to the cuts of the evening, but it wasn't working. She turned around, acutely aware of every tuck and pull of her muscles, of the notes pinging around the room, of the thick smell of combined perfumes and sweat from a hundred different party guests. Acutely aware of how radiant Lyana looked, and of every tiny imperfection of her own appearance. Acutely aware of the tension humming through her every muscle and nerve; she was surprised that the air around her wasn't buzzing and crackling with restless energy.

Lyana smiled at her: young, fresh, brimming with self-confidence. Her teeth reflected the glamour of the party, as bright as diamonds. The very sight of her made Praxis bristle.

Praxis drew herself up to her full height, making every effort to keep her temper in check. "I'm afraid that I don't know where Kaedrich is, if that's what you've come to ask," she said.

She watched with hidden satisfaction as this struck Lyana across the face. The girl's lips compressed, just enough to be noticeable. "*Thank* you for your concern," Lyana said, "though that isn't what I came to talk to you about."

"Oh." Praxis shrugged, and took an exaggerated pull from her glass. The wine poured like heat down her throat, spreading out to stoke Praxis's hurt and humiliation and desire. When the glass was empty, she deposited it on the tray of an unseen waiter. "Then what did you want?"

Lyana's lips curled up, though there was no goodwill in her smile. "Only to apologize for judging your new clothes so harshly. I was just talking to my friends, and"—she motioned behind herself, where Praxis noticed for the first time that a handful of young women, maybe five or six if she bothered to count them individually, were clustered in a loose semicircle at Lyana's back—"we've decided that your forward-thinking and individualism is to be *applauded*. Tell me, what tailor was it that was willing to take on such a unique order?"

Praxis groaned inwardly. Oh, she had known girls like this her whole life. A titter slipped free from one of Lyana's so-called friends, and several of them were openly smirking at Praxis, amused by the whole thing. Praxis gritted her teeth. *Do not engage,* she thought to herself. *Do not.*

"Dermont," Praxis said simply. "Excuse me."

But Lyana sidestepped, blocking Praxis's exit with (she had to admit) masterful grace. "Oh, but of course," Lyana said. "On Selman Street, isn't it?"

"That's right."

Do not engage, do not engage. She took another step, and Lyana countered.

"Yes, I've heard good enough things about him. I, of course, go to Miss Halison's for my dresses—but I don't suppose that you'd know anything about finding a good *dressmaker* in this city, would you? Tell me, did you stumble into Dermont's by accident, mistaking it for a shop for ladies?"

A trill of polite laughter went through the assembled crowd. Praxis shut her eyes for the briefest moment, surely looking no longer than a drawn-out blink. Something was uncoiling within her, old muscles yearning for use. She knew that she was slipping before the words were even out of her mouth, but she did not care. She smiled pleasantly—too pleasantly.

"Not at all," Praxis said, her voice as smooth as silk, just the right edge of her aristocratic accent folded in. "Though I admit, the idea of going out *to* any sort of shop for one's clothes is somewhat embarrassing for me; my family employs a team of the finest tailors and dressmakers to cater to our needs. Not that you would know anything about that. Still, I suppose it is good to get out in the world and see how the little people do things, wouldn't you agree?" She raised an eyebrow, looking pointedly down at Lyana's gown. It really was a fine dress, and a shame to be subjected to Praxis's next barb, but what could be done? The box had sprung open, the demon set free.

"Although," Praxis continued, "I do have to say, yours *has* done a remarkable job, Miss Lebule. I never would have guessed that you'd be allowed in a place such as this, and yet here you are! What a lovely disguise that dress must be. Why, it's almost possible to imagine you as a lady of status. *Almost.*"

Lyana sputtered, exactly as Praxis had wished for. Praxis did not even try to hide her glee.

"How *dare* you, madam!" Lyana said. Her voice was just a tiny bit too loud, and now one or two uninvolved heads had turned curiously in their direction. "I'll have you know that my *father*—"

"Is the senior most superior *ass-licker* of the unimportant masses, yes. How wonderful for you." Praxis tutted, rolling her eyes in disdain. "Don't flatter yourself, girl. These people invite you to their parties as an act of *pity*, a way to make themselves look charitable in the eyes of their true peers. Isn't that right?" she asked, and several of the girls around them took a wide step back. A few others glanced, suddenly, at their drinks. One nodded outright.

Praxis smirked. She leaned in close, stage-whispering to Lyana. "Just between you and me, sweetheart, I would forget about your little rebellious infatuation with Kaedrich, and try to sink your claws into someone with real status while you're still pretty enough to draw their eye. Believe me, you're going to need it later."

And then she straightened up. Her gaze had already shifted off of Lyana, ignoring the results of her efforts as if such concerns were utterly beneath her notice. A wash of smug superiority buoyed Praxis's spirits for perhaps the first time all evening, and she turned away with a delightful swish of the hem of her new coat. The party around her seemed suddenly more alive than it had before, the music popping, working its way into the shift of her hips. All of her senses had been tightly focused a moment ago, dulled by drink and concentrated on cutting down her rival as efficiently as possible, and now they ballooned out again to cloak the room.

Kaedrich was right there. Praxis felt her presence, whipping her head to catch up with her awareness. She'd been standing behind and just to the right of Praxis for who knows how long, but certainly long enough to hear the last several barbs that she'd exchanged, certainly enough to have seen. She was just staring at Praxis, her face blank but carefully tight. Stillness radiated off of her.

I told you that someone needed to tell her, Praxis thought, and while her advice to Lyana hadn't quite been in so many words, it should have done the job at least. She gave Kaedrich a casual shrug, letting the wine in her veins and the thrill of victory block out her cares. Let Kaedrich deal with this however she wanted to, now, but at least the first crack had been struck. Praxis blew a showy kiss in Kaedrich's direction as she set off, once more, for the nearest circulating tray of drinks.

ALL RIGHT, so not *everything* had been a complete waste this evening.

The night wound down quickly after that. Praxis helped herself to some of the last of the food as groups began to disperse into the empty night. Lyana, apparently, was in no mood to stick around, and Praxis saw Kaedrich trying to soothe her for several minutes before shuffling off and returning a moment later, a wrap in hand that matched Lyana's dress.

Praxis followed them out, sticking to the shadows. She watched as Kaedrich helped Lyana into the carriage. Praxis waited until her ride began to trundle off, Kaedrich's hand raised in a parting wave. Music still trickled out from the palace, swelling and collapsing in waves as people let themselves out into the night. All of the drinks from the evening had settled over Praxis, a comforting fog holding the earlier stings at bay; she grinned now, nothing left but delight at her victory over Lyana. "That was fun!" she called as she unfolded herself from her hiding spot. "I can't remember when I've had a nicer evening."

Kaedrich flinched at the loudness of Praxis's voice, but she did not turn around. The set of her shoulders only hardened as she began to walk away.

"Hey, wait!" Praxis hurried after her, only just remembering to control her leg harness as she set off. Her fingers curled and stretched as she walked, and for the first time it occurred to Praxis that it was almost like she was plucking at an instrument, playing herself, and this thought made her laugh as she caught up with Kaedrich almost a block later. She clapped her free hand on Kaedrich's shoulder, but Kaedrich threw her off.

"Don't," Kaedrich said, as Praxis hurried to regain her footing. "Just . . . gods, just don't."

Praxis frowned. "Hey—hey!" She tried to clutch at Kaedrich's sleeve, but it jerked out of her grip before she'd even caught it. "What did I do?"

Kaedrich laughed, but it was not anything like the normal melodic laughter that Praxis was familiar with. This laugh was sour, and lashed out as a cold slap at Praxis. Her happy buzz shuddered at the impact, a tiny piece breaking off around the edges.

"You really can't figure it out, can you?" Kaedrich asked. "I suppose that I'm not honestly surprised."

"Well, are you going to *tell* me, then, or—?"

Kaedrich abruptly stopped walking, long enough to grab Praxis by the elbow and drag her into the narrow alley between a temple and the guardhouse for the estate next door. "You were horrible to her! And you *humiliated* me in there, Praxis! Don't you *get* that?"

"Let go of me," Praxis snapped. She wrenched her arm free, massaging her elbow. It didn't really hurt—the pain that she really wanted to be purged was a sharp jab to her heart, but that one she was stubbornly ignoring. She rolled her eyes in the face of it. "You're exaggerating."

"Am I? Tell me, you think that I'm going to be welcomed back into the Lebules' social graces after *my guest* said such terrible things to their daughter?"

"I wasn't *your guest*," Praxis sneered. "I had my own invitation."

"That doesn't matter, and you know it. Perlandra's breath . . . I've worked *so hard* here. So! Hard! You have no idea, the amount of effort I've put into fitting in, and now—!" Kaedrich stopped short. Her breath was darting fast through her chest, her whole body shaking underneath the effort of keeping herself still.

The choice to apologize bloomed in front of Praxis. She could see it, so real and so near that all she had to do was reach out and grab it. *I'm sorry.* Was that so hard? Two little words. And yet, in her own embarrassment, knowing that Kaedrich was right, knowing that she'd fouled everything up for her, she couldn't bring herself to pluck it.

She stomped on the blossom instead, plowing straight ahead in her protective anger. "It's not my fault if your new 'friend' can't handle being told the truth."

A crack of laughter broke the night. "Oh that's rich, coming from you," Kaedrich said.

"What's *that* supposed to mean?"

"Only that you *love* making other people live up to their own bitter truths, but try getting *you* to admit to one and it's a whole other story." Kaedrich shook her head, a wash of pity contracting her face. "Have you ever told the truth in your life?"

Praxis scowled. "You're talking nonsense. I tell the truth all the time."

"You're lying." Kaedrich laughed. "Gods, you're lying to me *right now*. Don't you see it? You're more afraid of the truth than anything else! How do you *live* like that?"

"I'm not afraid of anything!"

"Then prove it!"

"Fine!" Praxis shouted. Drink and bitterness sat coiled in her belly, stirring at Kaedrich's insinuations. Praxis, a coward? A *coward*? It was one thing for her to think it herself—it was quite another to hear it coming from Kaedrich. Heat flared in Praxis's cheeks. "Fine," Praxis said again. "You want the truth? Do you *really* want the truth? Here's the truth!" And she cupped Kaedrich's face in both of her hands and kissed her before she could *not*.

If it had been planned, it never would have happened. Terror and elation clung to her in equal measure and in the first second, two, she could not move, too shocked by her own actions to realize what she'd done. Then the reality of it caught up with her, but before she could sabotage it for herself Praxis grabbed at her delight, like a rope thrown to a drowning woman, and suddenly she remembered how this was supposed to work. She broke apart and dove back in, years of buried fantasy springing to the surface and playing out in time to the wild pounding of her heart. For a while there was nothing else, just the perfect working of Kaedrich's mouth acting in tandem to her own. Instinct drew Praxis forward, as she released Kaedrich's face and grabbed her waist, her hips, their bodies colliding somewhere halfway between them. Kaedrich gasped at the impact, stealing a fraction of Praxis's breath for herself, and Praxis caught Kaedrich's lip between her teeth. She slid her hand past Kaedrich's suit coat, underneath her vest, working at the stubborn tuck of her shirt. Her hand settled, momentarily, on the hidden curve of Kaedrich's side, the triumph of finding warm skin, and then Praxis froze.

What in the seven hells was she *doing*? A kiss was one thing, but this—pawing up Kaedrich in an open street, vaulting over boundaries left and right, surging forward without the slightest hesitation . . . Did she think, somehow, that she had some *right* to Kaedrich's body, that because she'd longed hard enough, long enough, that somehow granted permission? Gods, maybe Praxis had been right to hold herself back, maybe she really *was* no better than Rinn.

There was her truth.

She jerked back, opening up a rush of air between them, horrified and disgusted with herself. Kaedrich's eyes fluttered open, like waking from a dream, her lips still parted from the kiss Praxis had interrupted. For a moment they just stood there, staring at each other, and Praxis knew that there was no undoing what she'd done.

A braver woman might have stayed. Even then, a tiny part of her knew that it was possible that there might have been *some* way forward from here, that the steady application of the right words and care might have been able to salvage the friendship that Praxis had just sent crashing to the ground. She didn't listen to that voice. That voice was among the chorus that had gotten her into this trouble to begin with, and Praxis wanted nothing more than to never hear that voice again, any of those voices again.

It's possible that Kaedrich started to say something—a subtle intake of breath, the beginning of a word—but Praxis did not wait long enough to find out. She threw a black haze hex at the ground between them, darkness billowing up so thick and fast that all of the world was blotted out in an instant, and in this black cloud that perfectly matched the inner workings of her own head, Praxis rushed from the street corner as fast as her legs would carry her.

Chapter Thirty-Four

PRAXIS HAD *KISSED* HER.

This was Kaedrich's first thought upon waking in the morning, and the underpinning to every task that she completed by rote as she prepared for the day. Getting dressed, and Praxis had kissed her. Going for a run, and Praxis had kissed her. Scraping the last dregs of jam across stale bread, ripping off a bite with her teeth, forcing down old coffee, and Praxis had kissed her. Heading out, and Praxis had kissed her. It should have elated her. It should have sent her dancing soundlessly through the hotel. It should have washed away every sour thought, cleared the skies, filled her heart with joy until it burst.

It didn't.

Kaedrich remembered the frozen shock, pinning her in place, all of her thoughts failing her. It did not make sense, it did not make sense, it did not make sense, and then it did. A spark of desire flared up and coursed through her as every inch of her body came alive at once, from the top of her head to the tips of her toes, and especially the parts nestled firmly between the two. She was fleetingly aware that she'd been angry a minute ago, though for the life of her she could not remember why. She thought of nothing else as she kissed Praxis back, hard, mashed lips and flitting tongues fighting for dominance over each other. She remembered the perfect bubble that had seemed to spring up around them, the intoxicating rush in her head, the warmth of Praxis suddenly pressing against the entire length of Kaedrich's body. Praxis's hands flew at her with expert precision, sliding up her back, directly across the length of the bindings that were suddenly far too tight for Kaedrich's ragged breath. Her other hand at Kaedrich's waist, the outward curve of her hip.

Then Praxis had sprung back, as if she'd just touched a hot stove. Her face was contorted into a look of abject horror, that struck out at Kaedrich's heart and curdled every scrap of warmth left flooding through her veins.

But what had Kaedrich expected? Whatever drink or rage or wayward thought that had driven Praxis forward, it would not survive the insurmountable fact that Kaedrich was a woman. Nothing could change that, and the minute Praxis had come face-to-face with it she had recoiled. She had left, and Kaedrich staggered back to lean against the wall of a nearby building, gulping down lungfuls of damp, bitter, chill air.

It was still cold in the morning, unnaturally so, and the slub of gray sky pressed thick against the crest of the city. Frozen fog poured down the streets as if they were riverbeds, pooling at corners and spilling over the hold of short dividing walls. Kaedrich trudged through it, up to her knees in the mist.

If she hadn't gone along with the kiss (thrown herself into it, really, she was forced to admit), would things have been better? Surely they must have. Praxis had made a mistake, all right, but it was a fleeting action in the heat of a sour argument—it could be forgiven, even forgotten in time. *Kaedrich* was the one that should have known better. In retrospect, her duty as a friend was so clear that it burned her cheeks with shame to think that she could have done any differently: she was supposed to have pulled back immediately, holding Praxis at arm's length until she'd come back to her senses. Instead, Kaedrich had taken advantage of Praxis's obvious lapse in judgment, allowing her own secret wishes to spur her onward. Realizing this knocked the life out of Kaedrich's legs, and she stumbled on the open street, catching herself against a lamppost. Gods, had she no decency?

There were no temples of Perlandra in the immediate vicinity, not that Kaedrich knew of anyway, though at the moment she sorely wished for one. She would have thrown herself inside, begging the gods for mercy. She would have stationed herself in a heap in the middle of the soulbearing alcove and sobbed right on the marble floors, not even able to speak of the mess that she'd wrought on every corner of her formerly ordered life. Ever since Praxis had come to Monfort, Kaedrich had been trying to find some balance between her past and her present, but the problem is that with Praxis, there was no balance. Praxis *was* her life, or at least she would be, always, if Kaedrich ever had any choices in the matter—but she didn't. The one clear and shining thing that Kaedrich wanted for certain, the only solid point that Kaedrich knew how to anchor herself to in this world, and it just happened to be the one thing that she *could not have*. And yet she had allowed everything else to fall to ruin in stubborn, stupid pursuit of it.

She would have torn her love from her chest right there, if that was how it worked. Instead, Kaedrich clung to the lamppost, ignoring the curious looks that the rest of the morning rush was throwing her as they washed by. She didn't even notice as a carriage slowed, right beside her, nor did she hear the voice calling to her from inside—not at first. Lyana had to actually have the driver dismount, and tap Kaedrich upon the shoulder before she started, whirling, and finally settled on the sight in front of her.

Lyana motioned for the driver to open the door, and she stepped out onto the sidewalk. "Goodness, Kaedrich. You look terrible—are you all right? Has something happened?"

If the situation had been even slightly less wretched, Kaedrich might have laughed at the question. *Has something happened?* But she couldn't laugh, couldn't do anything. She stared blankly at Lyana, hardly knowing what to say.

"Come on," Lyana said gently. She took Kaedrich by the shoulders and led her toward and into her carriage, and Kaedrich followed numbly because what else was there to do? It was only once they were settled into place, and Lyana rapped for the driver to start up again, that Kaedrich remembered that Lyana had no reason to be so nice to her, not anymore.

Kaedrich rubbed at her face, hardly knowing where to start. "Gods, Lyana, I . . . I'm so sorry."

Lyana frowned. "For what?"

"For—everything. Last night."

"Ah," Lyana said, and much to Kaedrich's surprise, she actually brightened at the topic. "That's why I came to find you—your friend came to the house this morning, during breakfast. She apologized to me for her terrible behavior, in front of my entire family. *And*, she's issuing a formal letter of repentance in the evening edition of the Witness."

Kaedrich shook her head. "Wait, that's . . . that's not possible."

Lyana sat back, smug, and drew a folded paper out of the reticule on her lap. "I assure you, it is. Here, look, she's given me the receipt for it, which includes a draft of the letter. See for yourself."

Kaedrich could not even take the paper, not at first. Lyana had to actually press it into her grasp, and even then it took a few attempts before Kaedrich could unfold it and smooth it out enough to read. She leaned toward the window of the carriage for better light, taking in the neatly typed lines before her.... *unabashedly rude... my behavior was inexcusable, and so I do not beg the lady's forgiveness... actions were mine, and mine alone... only wish to offer my sincerest and most humble apologies...* It took ages before Kaedrich could get herself to read the lines in their entirety, and even then she didn't believe it. She read the letter three times over, trying to sort it out, and then she read it another three times just to be sure. *Praxis A. Fellows,* it said at the bottom, and the signature on the receipt certainly matched, but—surely it was a joke. A trick of some sort. In nearly three years, Kaedrich had rarely known Praxis to apologize at all, and certainly not in such an open and declarative voice—and *never* in writing!

She could not even begin to process what it meant, that Praxis had done so now.

"You see?" Lyana said eventually. She carefully took the letter from Kaedrich's hands, folding it back up and whisking it out of sight. She grinned. "I have to say, it impressed my father terribly, especially once he found out who she was. Gods, Kaedrich, why didn't you ever say that you had such connections? It would have made things much easier for you. He's talking about having you to our next dinner party, by the way, and that you should bring your guest."

"Dinner?"

"Yes." Lyana smiled, watching Kaedrich carefully.

"I . . . I honestly don't know what to say."

Lyana laughed. "Well, you could start by inviting me out somewhere. Since your standing has just improved, I'd say that no one could reasonably object."

Kaedrich froze. "What?"

"Just that if there's . . . anything that you want to ask me . . . I mean, I'm not exactly *courting* anyone, so my social calendar—"

"No. Lyana, I'm sorry, but . . . but no."

Now it was Lyana's turn to pause. The carriage jostled, turning a corner, and Lyana's mouth pinched in just enough to crinkle. She folded her hands neatly in her lap. "Kaedrich, I realize that I'm being forward with you, but you cannot honestly tell me that you're not *interested*. I mean, I'm not trying to be indelicate, but even with your association to a Fellows, someone of your rank isn't exactly in the position to be turning down an opportunity like this."

This was cold, but also true. Or at least it *would* be, if Kaedrich was really who everyone thought that she was, if she could ever actually court a young woman, or take a wife, or make a family together. "I realize that," Kaedrich said. She paused, trying to pick through her words before she spoke them. The last thing that she wanted to do was destroy her social standing when she had, apparently, just managed to avoid doing so. "And I really am flattered. It's just . . . I don't have what you're looking for in a man. Trust me."

There. That wasn't, technically, a lie.

For a moment, nothing happened. The carriage jostled on, and Lyana just watched her, seemingly indifferent to this declaration. Kaedrich's heart began to stir, a hopeful flutter—maybe she would accept this, gracefully?

Lyana's eyes narrowed. "It's because of *her*, isn't it? Gods, you're actually going to go crawling back to her, aren't you? *Aren't you?!*"

Her question was so sharp that it broke through the carriage like a gunshot, making Kaedrich jump. "Lyana, no, it's not—it's not like that. It's not a choice between you."

"Of *course* it is," Lyana snapped. She clutched at her side, the stays that restricted her agitated breath. With nowhere else to go, her exasperation heaved her labored breaths up, and Kaedrich very delicately averted her attention from the aggrieved rise and fall of Lyana's bosom.

"Perlandra forgive me, I've been such a fool," Lyana said. Kaedrich tried to reach across, intending to offer some type of comfort, but Lyana jerked away from her. "Don't touch me! Stop the coach. *Stop the coach!*"

Her shriek was apparently enough to get the driver's attention, for they jerked to the side and came to a shaky stop a moment later. Lyana did not wait for him to come around; she fumbled with the door latch herself, throwing her body out of the coach and staggering into the crowded sidewalk. Kaedrich scrambled out after her, apologies already bubbling up to her lips.

Lyana snapped her hand up, cutting Kaedrich off before she could even properly begin. "Save your breath. I was willing to give you a chance, Kaedrich, despite your . . ."—she paused, taking in Kaedrich's appearance; her eyes settled on Kaedrich's face, the rich brown of Kaedrich's skin reflecting for an instant before Lyana's lids narrowed to slits—"deficiencies. But I can see now there is no helping you. Go, then. Cavort with *wizards*. I hope that you enjoy your last day together, because as soon as the election is finished, there will be nothing left of her kind—or those that betray their own by siding with deviants."

Kaedrich froze in the wake of this tirade. The insults themselves were surprising, though perhaps not as much as they should have been—Lyana was hurt, after all, and lashing out at any obvious point of attack. She watched with an oddly cool detachment as Lyana spat at her feet, because that really wasn't what had stilled her. "Lyana, wait," Kaedrich said, grabbing her by the elbow as Lyana turned to leave. She wasn't going to apologize, or even begin to salvage the shaky kind-of-friendship that had once existed between them. Her reputation, temporarily saved by Praxis's apology, now lay ruined at their feet, and Kaedrich would have to deal with that later—for now , , , "What election, exactly?"

Lyana sneered. "Haven't you heard? Oh, wait, no, someone in *your* position surely wouldn't have. My *father* heard about it last night, straight from the head of the King's Court of State."

"Heard what?"

For a second, Kaedrich was worried that Lyana would keep it from her, purely out of spite. It seemed like she was considering it, as she smirked and held herself at a careful distance. But apparently, in the end, gloating about her secret knowledge wasn't *quite* as much fun as seeing the damage it would do firsthand, and so Lyana shrugged. And said, "The Governance Council is being recalled from break early. They're to vote on the matter of revoking the Crown's claim of legitimacy. Once they do, they're going to need a replacement head of state to oversee the transition of power, until a new heir can be found and a fresh Council assembled."

"Perlandra's breath," Kaedrich muttered. "Lyana, are you *serious*?"

Lyana laughed, sharp and cruel. "Oh yes. And somehow, I don't think that your little *spell whore* is going to like their top choice for replacement." She smirked again, shifting the collar of the cloak that she'd been wearing. Kaedrich hadn't bothered to even really *look* at Lyana's dress before now, but suddenly she couldn't see anything *else*. She didn't know how she had managed to miss it so far.

Though the base dress itself was a rich ivory, all the details, the trimming and the lace overlays, the ruffles skirting the hem, the neat little bow up by her neck—every bit of it was blood red.

Kaedrich's eyes widened. A chill seized hold of her, which had nothing to do with the cold fog still twisting up around her feet and legs. "Please tell me that you don't mean her," Kaedrich said, nearly breathless.

Lyana's grin was so cold, freezing the morning air even more than it already was. "Of course I mean *her*. Who else?"

Kaedrich turned and ran, propelling herself down the street without a conscious thought. Maybe there was something else Kaedrich should have done, or said, but at the moment she could think of nothing, could do nothing other than this. Her only focus was on finding Praxis. It did not matter anymore, what might have passed between them, how awkward seeing her would have been under ordinary circumstances—nothing mattered now, in the wake of this revelation, nothing except for seeking allies and finding some way, any way, to stop Lyana's tale from coming true.

Pon Lanali must never, under any circumstances, be allowed to be elected as head of state. Not so long as Kaedrich had any breath left in her body.

PRAXIS RETURNED TO Calswell House to find that her ward had been broken.

The careful circle that she'd constructed hung around the perimeter of the house, the tension gone slack. Though it had no visible indicator, Praxis could feel the snapped ends of the ward trailing down the back steps, fluttering in the breeze like a cut ribbon.

She kept her distance for a few minutes, surveying the house from the tiny green at the corner of the street. There were no outward signs of distress—though even the ward itself was a warning, not defensive, so she did not expect to be able to see anything obvious. Nonetheless, she approached with caution, all of her senses perked to detect the slightest disturbance. Through the back door, toeing it open, flames already prepared in her free hand.

The house appeared as empty as it ever was, but Praxis felt the flutter of an impression, just on the edge of her awareness. Someone was in the basement; they had broken into her inner sanctuary. She inched down the hallway and then the stairs, being mindful of her step. By now, she knew every creaky board, every loose stair. Praxis hovered just outside of the basement door, but the familiarity of the presence had broken through the fog that the shock had caused her. It flared impossibly bright in her mind, a perfect impression of the woman standing just inside. And yet, Praxis didn't dare believe it, couldn't believe it, as she let herself into the basement.

"Kaedrich."

Though it was barely even whispered, Kaedrich turned at the sound of her name. She was standing in a swath of lamplight that softened her face, and as she stilled, Praxis's breath escaped her chest; for in the first heartbeat of recognition, a flood of memory had rushed up to swaddle Praxis. Her impulsive kiss, the taste of ginger-lemon still lingering on Kaedrich's lips, the feeling of everything in the world finally being exactly how it was supposed to be. Praxis hovered in the split second before shame and embarrassment would crowd in, absorbed by the sight of Kaedrich, ready to fall to her knees in sheer wonder at how perfectly *beautiful* the woman standing before her was.

She didn't, of course. The clock ticked forward, Praxis looked away, and every scrap of dread that had been building all night crashed into her mind as one, like obnoxiously loud and grating party guests upending all the furniture. Nausea ripped at her gut, and Praxis only just managed to remain standing. Her careful speech, the expertly crafted excuses and apologies—where had they gone? She scrambled, mind flailing, but she could find only fragments of what she had intended to say. Praxis swallowed, her mouth suddenly too dry. Maybe the fact that she had forgotten what she wanted to tell Kaedrich didn't even matter, for could she bring herself to speak at all?

In the end, it was Kaedrich that broke the silence, though not at all in the way that Praxis had wished that she would. "They're giving the crown to Lanali," she said.

Praxis whipped her head up. "What?" It was such a sudden jar from where her thoughts had been just a moment ago that Praxis couldn't even process it at first, so utterly convinced that she'd misheard what Kaedrich had said. While she recognized each individual word, they seemed unable to fit together into a coherent thought, like someone had cut up phrases from a newspaper and splayed them out across a table all jumbled up together.

"I heard it from Lyana," Kaedrich said, already pacing the room, "but I took the time to check in at the Witness. I might not have a proper job there anymore, but I still have a few connections. Everyone is being really tight-lipped about it, but it's . . . gods, Praxis, it's *true*. There's to be a vote, *tomorrow*. They'll make it official then."

"No, that's . . . that's not possible."

"It *is*. And while I wish that we had time to stand here and be incredulous and disbelieving about it, we just flat-out don't. We need a plan, right now. What can we do?"

Praxis's eyes widened. She leaned back, as if somehow distancing herself from Kaedrich's words made the situation a little farther away, too. "I don't know," Praxis said.

Kaedrich shook her head. "That's not an acceptable answer. I don't care if your ideas are only vague and ill-formed—we need any ideas, and we need them *right now*, so that we can hammer them into something better."

A strangled laugh escaped Praxis's throat. "What makes you think I have *any*? Why is it my responsibility somehow?"

"Because you've been working to take her down!"

"Yeah, well, I haven't exactly found anything I can use, now, have I?" Praxis shouted. Her breath was ragged in her chest as she stepped into the room, steadying herself against the dresser. "Believe me, Kaedrich, if I had any ideas, I'd have acted on them already. You of all people should know that I am often too impulsive for my own good."

It wasn't until she said it that Praxis realized she'd been speaking only *half* about the situation at hand. The other half was the closest that she could come to expressing her regret over what had happened the night before. Carefully, she stole a glance in Kaedrich's direction, wondering if she had picked up on the unintended double meaning of her words.

Only it was impossible to read Kaedrich's stoic face this morning. If she was thinking about it at all, then it clearly brought her no joy.

"All right, fine," Kaedrich said. "In that case, let's get moving."

Praxis frowned. "Where are we going?"

"To see your 'friends' from the Society of Magic. Oh, don't give me that look," Kaedrich said, holding up her finger and instantly cutting off Praxis's argument before it could even start. "This is no time to be choosy. You don't have any ideas, I don't have any ideas. I'm betting they probably don't, either, but maybe between the group of us we can figure *something* out."

Chapter Thirty-Five

Don Eagleburns shook his head. "The bottom line is that it doesn't matter. Even *if* we can manage to convince a few people to listen to your mad rantings—I'm sorry," he added, obviously not sorry at all, "but that is how they're going to be seen—it still won't do any good. Lanali is simply too powerful at this point for the majority not to vote for her."

Praxis bit down on her tongue, physically holding herself back from insulting him. So far, this meeting was going exactly as Praxis had expected it to. Just getting inside the building had been a process, involving several polite knocks from Kaedrich, a lot of waiting, and finally Praxis breaking their ward and busting in the door. That hadn't exactly gone over well with the apprentices she'd found in the hallways inside, though thankfully Weevish had come running in and calmed them down before Praxis had to resort to anything violent (well, more violent than a broken door, anyway).

"What are all of these people doing here?" Praxis had asked as Weevish sighed and waved for her to follow him back to the Dons.

Weevish had shrugged. "You said to get everyone out of the city."

"Yeah, but . . . I didn't expect you to actually *listen* to me."

Another shrug. Praxis stepped around an apprentice loitering in a doorway with a heavy book hanging open in his hands. Their faces may change from year to year, but these boys were all the same.

"Okay, so we block the vote," Praxis said now. She looked around the table, taking in each of their faces in turn. The former Dons, who'd only just agreed to see her. Weevish stood by in the corner, while the Lord-Dons Trew, Eagleburns, and Trimbly all shared a table. Apparently, they were all that was left of the former council. "Right?" she said. "I mean, there has to be some way to disqualify her from being considered."

All eyes turned to Don Trew, the one member of their small group that used to actually sit upon the Governance Council. Don Trew shrugged. "There *is* obviously a list of candidates, and I suppose that it would be possible to influence whether or not someone gets added—if we were talking about anyone else. But frankly, there is no chance in all the worldly hells that Lanali won't be on the ballot. If she *wasn't*, there would be an open revolt!" he added, talking over the beginning of Praxis's protestations. "She's the people's savior, and they're not going to allow her to be blocked from consideration. I'm sorry. It's just not possible."

Praxis scowled, though of course he was right. With the truth of the ghost crisis buried and known only to a select few, there was nothing that would dissuade the people from thinking of Lanali as the next best thing to a god. Naturally, she would be their top choice to lead them.

Her scowl only deepened the longer that the silence dragged on, the longer that she sat with it. She turned to look beside her at Kaedrich, fleetingly hoping that she'd have a better idea of what to do, but Kaedrich wasn't looking at her; her own lips were set into a hard line.

Instantly, Praxis remembered the way that those same lips had felt pressed against hers last night. She turned away, cursing herself for thinking about such things at a time like this, though her heart was already racing. She hadn't said anything on the matter to Kaedrich this morning, and not just because all of *this* had exploded around them. Kaedrich was right: trying to get her to admit her own truths was nigh to impossible, even if she routinely demanded the same of others.

That was the biggest problem, though, wasn't it? Hiding the truth. It hadn't done Praxis any good in her personal life, and it wasn't doing Durland any good either.

"What if . . ." Praxis started, but then she hesitated. She'd been keeping the deeper truth about Lanali from the Dons for a long time now. Once, she'd told herself that it was for their own good, but . . . oh, hells, what good was this secret doing *anyone* anymore? Maybe Kaedrich was right, maybe they needed to *tell people*, the way that Kaedrich had tried to tell Bundling.

Praxis cleared her throat. "What if there was a way to prove that Lanali didn't do what everyone says she did? She didn't solve the ghost crisis—in fact, she *caused* it."

Praxis was expecting scoffs, and she got scoffs. A whole ring of them, all the way around the table, as well as an eye roll, a huff, and the exasperated shake of Don Eagleburns's head.

"Oh please," Don Trew said. "Miss Fellows, we all know that you don't like Lanali, but that doesn't mean that she—"

"I was there."

A bark of laughter escaped Don Trimbly. "Were you? And you expect us just to take your word for it? You expect the *people* to just take your word for it?"

"You have no proof," Don Trew said. He chuckled to himself. "Unless you can summon up a ghost to claim witness for you."

A scrape of gruff laughter circled the room, but Praxis wasn't paying attention. Her focus had snapped to Don Trew at his jab, the gears of her brain whirring madly. "What did you say?"

Don Trew hesitated, his mirth broken by her sudden interest. "I was merely pointing out the folly of trying to prove your case. There's no—"

"No, I got that. The other part, the part about . . . summoning."

"You're *not* going to summon a ghost," Don Trew snapped. "Even if you could—which you can't—it wouldn't do you any good."

For once, he spoke the truth: a ghost wouldn't do any good. Praxis fell silent, and leaned back in her chair. She reached up toward her shirt collar, her fingers idly touching the necklace chain hidden underneath. The links were warm from being up against her skin. "No, a ghost won't work. But what if there was someone . . . else . . . that I could summon? To claim witness to Lanali's actions."

Don Eagleburns shook his head. "It would have to be quite the extraordinary witness."

"Is the Beacon of Souls extraordinary enough for your tastes?"

A slight pause followed this proclamation—just enough—and then their disbelief broke the room like a series of firecrackers going off. "*Really,* Miss Fellows," and "This is what we get for listening to a woman!", and "Do you honestly expect us to believe that?", as well as just a general commotion of huffery and righteous indignation. Praxis let it crash around her, flooding the room as their haughtiness grew louder and louder, and then she slowly stood up. They were still mostly ignoring her, concerned more with saying their own piece than with listening to any counterargument that Praxis might wish to make. But she didn't wish to make one, not really. She glanced once at Kaedrich, and Kaedrich nodded at her, and then Praxis pulled the necklace of the Beacon of Souls out from its place beneath her shirt.

She held it out, the pendant swaying slightly over the middle of the table, as each of the gentlemen noticed, sputtered, and fell into resentful silence.

Don Eagleburns snorted, the first to break the quiet. "A *trinket*. It proves nothing—certainly not the existence of *Beacons*."

Though it wasn't clear how much even *he* actually believed that, and how much he said it because he needed it to be true. Despite themselves, their attention was fixed on the shifting glow trapped inside of the Beacon's pendant. Praxis let herself watch it along with them for a moment: the way that the shifting glow would claw its way up the sides of the pendant, collapse back down to the base, and then start the process all over again. Even if you didn't have the slightest idea what it might be, the sight of it was entrancing. It *wanted* to be watched. It *needed* to be watched.

"There's a ritual," Praxis said. She paused, but no one seemed, for the moment, to be interested in interrupting her. "I can bring the Beacon into our world, for a limited time. Enough to bear testimony against Lanali. Right now, she has a power hold because nobody knows what really happened. Her whole routine is built on showmanship and lies. If we could reveal the truth to the world—"

"It still wouldn't work," Don Trimbly said. He smacked his lips, shaking his head for extra emphasis.

Just like that, whatever spell Dons Eagleburns and Trew were under was broken. They blinked, coming back to themselves. They were nodding, murmuring agreement.

"It might!" Praxis said. She spoke quickly, before their skepticism could once again overrun them. "At least enough to throw her authority into question. Maybe even enough to delay the vote."

Though the room did not immediately agree with her, for once there was no sharp argument thrown back in her face, either.

Praxis pressed on. "What's the alternative? Do nothing, and let Lanali come to power? Try to oppose her, and spark a *real* revolution? *Kill* her?"

"There are worse ideas," Don Trew muttered.

"You'd never get near her, though," Don Eagleburns said, shaking his head sadly.

"More's the pity."

"We're *not* going to go around killing people," Praxis said. "Especially not when there's a perfectly viable alternative in front of us."

Don Eagleburns sighed heavily. "Miss Fellows—" He shook his head, waved his hand. "Praxis," he started again, and now Praxis knew that she was in trouble. "There is not a single one of us in this room that is a friend of the Pon, but to be frank, what you're suggesting is madness. I have no doubt that you believe you are capable of pulling this off, and maybe—maybe!—you are. But it won't help."

"I will not stand by and do nothing."

Don Eagleburns shrugged. "Do what you feel you must. But don't expect anyone here to help you. I, for one, am not going to risk my neck on a fool's errand."

"Hear, hear," Don Trew added. He got to his feet, sweeping his gaze once over the rest of them. "We've wasted enough time on these follies. We should be making preparations to flee, not squandering our chances to get out while we still can."

General noises of agreement circulated the room, cut off abruptly by a loud snort of disgust. "You would really be so cowardly?"

All eyes fell to the chair beside Praxis. Or rather, to its formerly silent occupant.

Kaedrich hadn't said a word throughout the proceedings, watching with professional detachment as the wizards squabbled the matter among themselves. There was, perhaps, a brief moment where the rest of them wondered if Kaedrich had even spoken at all—except that *someone* had just insulted them, and the only other person that might have done so had merely scowled.

Kaedrich stood up, meeting Don Trew on his own level.

Don Trew bristled. "Are you addressing *me*, boy?"

"I am. This isn't a problem that you can just ignore. What you men decide to do here is going to have widespread repercussions for everyone—and you're trying to tell me that your answer is to run away, and save yourself?" Her face wrinkled in obvious disgust. "How could you be so selfish? Knowing there was something that you could do, and not doing it?"

A glower snapped into place, shifting Don Trew's entire countenance. His spine drew rigid, his mouth and hawkish brow drawn into parallel lines slashed across his face. "You are obviously not capable of under-standing the complexities of this situation."

"I understand fine. People's *lives* are at stake."

"*Our* lives are at stake!" Don Trew snapped. He closed his eyes as he drew a steadying breath. "We are among the most wanted people in all of Monfort—even setting *foot* in the capital right now would be a death sentence. If your *friend*," he said with a sneer, "wants to throw her life away on a doomed attempt at stopping the inevitable, then that's her choice. The rest of us will not go down so easily."

Don Eagleburns nodded. "Finely said, Clemence." He stood up, and so too did Don Trimbly. Only Weevish remained where he was, tucked aside but watching the proceedings with open trepidation.

Kaedrich took a breath, but Praxis stilled her with a hand to her shoulder. "Don't waste your time," Praxis said. She was already putting the necklace back on, tucking the pendant out of sight. She stood for a moment, staring down each of them in turn: the Lord-Dons Eagleburns, Trew, and Trimbly, even quiet little Weevish off in his own corner. She should have known better than to hope for anything useful out of these men.

They turned and left without another word, Praxis leading the way down the long halls of their crumbling house. Apprentices jumped aside as she stormed past.

"I'm sorry," Kaedrich said from beside her, just as they were passing through the front doors.

Praxis shrugged. She was already slipping her tinted spectacles into place. "Don't be," she said, her mouth twisting up in disgust. They set off down the front walk. "It was a good idea. It's not your fault that they're all a bunch of filthy, weaselly, useless lumps of—"

Footsteps broke through Praxis's billowing rant, sharp and slightly uneven on the crunching gravel.

"Miss Fellows! Miss Fellows, a moment!" Weevish called, his voice growing louder as he approached.

Praxis came to a stop with a sigh. "If you've come to talk me out of this . . ."

"I haven't," Weevish said. He was puffing slightly as he caught up with them. "On the contrary, I . . . I'm going to help you."

"Really?" She made no effort to hide her surprise. She looked Weevish up and down. "What about the wishes of the Society?"

Weevish huffed. "There *is* no Society anymore, despite what those gentlemen might want to pretend. I, for one, am not content to be a coward. I'm familiar with the ritual you spoke of—that is, I've read of it. You'll need another wizard to assist you, will you not?"

This, Praxis could not even attempt to deny. She tipped her head in a half-nod of acknowledgment.

"Then let me help."

"I thought that you hated me."

Weevish shook his head, the hint of a smile playing across his face. "I will not deny that, from a strictly clerical point of view, you have been the single biggest nuisance of my career—*and* I'm not terribly fond of you personally. No offense."

"None taken."

Weevish sighed. "But . . . you are a far more talented wizard than any two of them put together. And I believe you. I want to help."

Praxis raised an eyebrow. "Okay then. Do you know what we'll need to perform it?"

Weevish nodded.

"Then gather the supplies, and bring them to Calswell House back in Monfort," Praxis said. She tossed him the key, flipping end-over-end as it arced between them.

Weevish scrambled to catch it. He stared down at it with a frown, his thumb running over the bow of the key, the Royal Society's stamp embossed in the metal.

He did not ask, though he clearly wanted to, how Praxis had gotten it.

"I will," Weevish said. Then he glanced up, concern written plainly on his face. "Only . . . forgive me, but where do you plan to get the—the host?"

"Oh, don't worry about *that*," Praxis said, waving off his concern. Weevish did not look convinced, but Praxis ignored him as she pulled out her pocket watch, snapping it open. "Now, if you'll excuse me," she added, leading Kaedrich by the elbow, "the two of us have a funeral to attend."

"Florina *Madgar*?"

It was a name that Kaedrich hadn't heard in years, and now the mention of it brought on a flood of old memories. The Madgar estate had been the first place that she'd ever visited with Praxis, back before they even really knew each other. They'd sought out Lord Redly Madgar, Florina's husband, because he was an old friend of Praxis, and she thought that he might be able to assist them in their efforts to breach the land of the dead. Kaedrich remembered Lady Madgar, how stiffly she moved, the steady glass of her eyes. *That's what you get for marrying a dead girl, Redly,* Praxis had said.

Kaedrich shook her head. "I don't understand. If Lady Madgar . . . That is, if she's already been, well . . . dead . . . then . . . ?"

Praxis had been looking out the window of the train car, watching as they gathered up speed just beyond the city limits. She turned back now, her face a practiced blank. "There's only so long that you can delay the inevitable. Florina . . . she wasn't technically *dead*, so much as she was . . . frozen."

"Frozen."

"At the point just before death. Redly managed to grab her just before it took hold, and he used the power of his own soul to breathe the approximation of life back into her."

Kaedrich gulped. "Do I want to ask how—?"

"He carved out his own heart. Quite literally, and gave it to her." Praxis frowned, turning to examine her fingernails. "You wouldn't believe the amount of blood."

"What, you were *there*?"

Praxis nodded. "He needed someone he could trust, to finish the enchantment. And then, of course, he was in no position to stitch his heart into her chest. I had to leave him there . . . I didn't expect him to . . ." Praxis lapsed into silence, staring off at nothing. She cleared her throat. "The point is that the magic was always going to run out eventually. It was only a matter of time."

There was nothing that Kaedrich could immediately say to this. She was sorry she'd even asked. The train jostled underneath them, carrying them out to the countryside, and Kaedrich folded up the newspaper that Praxis had given to her, the one with Florina's obituary printed inside. *Beloved Wife and Mother.* Kaedrich couldn't bring herself to read the whole thing.

She passed the newspaper over, and Praxis tucked it underneath Brex's cage. He was curled at the bottom, sniffing happily at Praxis's hand as she wrapped her arm around the bars. Praxis smiled down at him, wiggling her finger for him to swipe at. When she glanced across the small compartment at Kaedrich, she was actually smiling. "It's just like old times again, isn't it?"

Kaedrich looked away. It was true that a lot of their early relationship had been spent in a shared train compartment, sitting across from each other as they journeyed first on a wild adventure, and then just the daily slog of commuting back and forth to Praxis's makeshift laboratory. Sitting here with her, with Brex, was painfully familiar, like dipping back into a blissful memory of childhood; and yet, in the way of nostalgia, it also stung like a splinter when she prodded at it. There was an innocence to those times—back before Kaedrich had begun to realize her feelings for Praxis, when they were just friends and colleagues. It wasn't that Kaedrich would actually go back to that, if she could, but no, this was not like old times again. The weight of everything that Kaedrich wasn't saying, the memory of their stolen kiss, was so present that it coalesced into almost a physical form, a third person sitting in the compartment with them.

They didn't say more than a handful of words for the rest of the trip, though thankfully the journey was only a little over an hour. They slowed on the outskirts of a quiet village along the western coast, just north of Monfort. *Welcome to Fennington,* read the sign as they approached, a large green post with curly gold letters. Kaedrich leaned forward, peering at the jagged line of roofs, a single temple rising tall on the far end of town. It didn't look anything like the last place where they'd gone to visit the Madgars, and at first Kaedrich worried that they'd accidentally booked the wrong train. Then again, perhaps they were just passing through?

Except that Praxis was already making herself ready, checking the latch on Brex's cage, tucking the newspaper into a deep pocket of her new coat.

"Where are we?" Kaedrich asked.

Praxis glanced at the window. "The Madgars gave up their estate about two years ago. Redly never stayed in one place for too long, not since . . ." She shrugged. "People tend to talk, and once rumors go around, it's hard to keep up relations with the neighbors. I have to admit, though, I never expected him to find someplace so . . . quiet."

It *was* certainly that. As the train pulled through the last quarter mile to the station, there was almost nothing of note to see. A handful of buildings clustered in the center of town: a post office, a tavern, several houses, and a scattering more spread in a loose tangle behind them. Beyond that, no sign of anything but open fields and clear skies. Only a few people milled around, lingering to chat. A dog lay on the station platform, his tongue lolling easily out of his mouth; he glanced at the train as it approached, but gave no particular sign that he cared.

Praxis took Brex herself, ignoring Kaedrich's offer of help. They were the only two people to depart.

"Gods," Kaedrich said, stepping out into a flood of sunlight, "it's far too nice out for a funeral."

Praxis hung back, staying underneath the overhang of the platform. She was frowning at the wide sunny street, as if it had personally offended her and now was asking for a dance. "Yes. I'm kind of surprised that Redly's mood didn't bring in a storm. I fear what his mental state is going to be, but I suppose you'll find out soon enough."

"Me?"

Praxis nodded. "I can't go. I . . . don't do funerals."

"But I thought the whole point—!"

"Is to arrange a meeting with Redly." Praxis reached into her coat and drew out a folded paper, which she held out to Kaedrich. "Give him that. Tell him I need his help. Try to gauge his mood, if you can. I'm not sure how he's going to react to hearing from me."

Kaedrich shook her head in disgust, but she took the note and tucked it into her vest pocket. She turned away without further comment, strolling into the village as Praxis opened up Brex's cage.

It didn't take long for her to get directions to the cemetery, which was itself only a five-minute walk from the village center. Surrounded by a neat little fence overflowing with blooming flowers, today the gate was open and inviting. Kaedrich let herself in, keeping to herself as she worked her way toward a small gathering of people on the opposite end of the cemetery. She had expected a larger crowd, a bigger production, and so for a moment she was worried that she had stumbled into the wrong funeral—was there another cemetery in this little village, or had Praxis gotten the day and time wrong, perhaps? But then someone in front of her shifted, bending down to whisper something in a little boy's ear, and there by the graveside was Lord Madgar, his twin daughters lined up neatly beside him.

Kaedrich remembered him as a man that radiated youth and vitality. True, they had only met once, but in the halls of the sprawling estate that he'd lived in at the time, he had clearly been in his prime. Not a single hair had been out of place, and his full beard was trimmed with military precision. He had smiled easily, laughed often, doled out thoughtful and contemplative advice. While Kaedrich knew that he had interest in some of the darker, less savory magics, she had always been fond of him.

The man that looked up now, and met Kaedrich's eyes, may as well have been a stranger. Though he'd clearly gone through some effort to clean himself up for his wife's funeral, his appearance could only politely be described as "rumpled." His hair hung limp, in need of a trimming, a lock falling across his eyes; his beard was rough and wild; his clothes were still well-tailored, but poorly matched, as if he'd picked them out himself without much thought to his choices. He looked at Kaedrich for a long, uncomfortable moment, not the slightest spark of recognition in his eyes, and when he drew his attention away, it seemed more out of habit than as if he had anything better to look at. Kaedrich shivered, despite the warm breeze.

It was a lovely service, short but moving. The Attendant was the only one to speak, standing at the head of the open grave, his mellow voice drifting over the cemetery. It didn't really matter what he said—it sounded sincere, and it made Kaedrich sad in a vague sort of way. Lord Madgar stared at the ground during the entire proceedings, his hands folded neatly in front of him, not moving even when one of his daughters reached over and tried to hold him. As Lady Florina Madgar was lowered into the ground, the other of the twin girls stepped forward, a tiny paper program trembling in her grip. She began to sing, a sweet little melody that Kaedrich herself had sometimes sung as a child. The girl's voice was high and perfect, sounding much too innocent to fully understand the depths of what the girls had just lost.

Kaedrich turned, slipping out of the gathering with as much discretion as she could manage. The song chased after her, nipping at her heels even as she fled the gates. She darted around a corner of a nearby shop, disappearing down an alley, and leaned her back against the brick walls. The bands around her chest felt tighter than they had that morning, cutting off her breath.

She would have no way of knowing when her own mother died. It seemed silly, to be concerned with such a thing at a time like this, but suddenly she just couldn't stop thinking about it. Really, it may have happened already; Kaedrich wouldn't know. When she'd first fled she'd stayed far away, out of reach should the debt collectors get word of her survival, and later . . . One of the first things that Kaedrich had worked on, as she'd been learning how to write, was a letter to her parents, but how was she supposed to breach the subject now, after years of silence? The weight of it had felt enormous, and so she'd just kept putting it off, and putting it off, and eventually it had slid to the back of her mind.

It seems she did that a lot. Was that to be her legacy, then? Kaedriella Mannly: she put off the things that really mattered. Her mouth twisted up, along with her stomach, thinking about it.

The funeral broke up a few minutes later. Kaedrich heard the crowd dispersing, the soft clatter of their voices dragging her out of her own thoughts. She crept to the end of the alleyway, watching as everyone filtered out of the cemetery. The girls were led out by a tall woman in a crisp black uniform, the three of them boarding a waiting carriage. They left a moment later, without Lord Madgar.

When Kaedrich reentered the cemetery, Lord Madgar was the only one left. He was standing exactly where he had been, his hands still clasped in front of him, as if he hadn't even realized that the service was over, that it was time to leave. There was a cluster of trees nearby, casting shade over most of the surrounding plots, but Lord Madgar stood in the lone sunbeam that broke through the gentle boughs. Kaedrich kept her distance for a minute or two, but he did not appear to be doing, well, *anything*. And so Kaedrich approached, cautiously, ready to excuse herself if he seemed to need it.

He didn't. He looked up at the sound of Kaedrich's footsteps, mere whispers over the thick spring grass. "So she sent someone in her place, did she?" he asked. His voice was deadened, like he didn't really care either way.

Kaedrich cleared her throat. "Lord Madgar, I have a message from Praxis Fellows." She drew the note from her pocket, holding it out.

"I know," Lord Madgar said, though he did not take the paper, not at first. "What has it been, two years? Three? And *today* she breaks the silence?"

"Keeping in touch is not one of Praxis's strong suits."

Lord Madgar huffed. "No." He snatched the note out of Kaedrich's hands, flipping it open right there. It was barely an instant for him to take in the two or three lines scrawled across the page. When he looked back up, the first shade of emotion that Kaedrich had seen from him all day crossed his face—irritation. "She honestly expects to bother me now? *Now?*"

"I'm sorry," Kaedrich said. "I would have tried to talk her out of it, but I'm afraid that it's important."

Lord Madgar's fist clenched over the note, the paper crumpling in his tight grip. "And *mine weren't?*"

"I . . . I'm sorry, but I really don't know what you're referring to."

"No," Lord Madgar said, sneering. "I don't suppose that she would have told even you, would she? Why risk ruining your good opinion by admitting that she chose to ignore a friend in need?"

Kaedrich glanced at her hands. Of course there would be more to this situation than Praxis admitted—Kaedrich felt foolish, suddenly, to have accepted the surface-level story of what they were doing here. "I'm sorry," she said again, though what was she even apologizing for this time?

Lord Madgar sighed. "No, it's not your fault, lad. By all means, please do escort me to Miss Fellows. I would appreciate the chance to bring this matter up with her directly."

PRAXIS SET HERSELF up in a corner booth of the local pub. It was tucked away from the rest of the afternoon patrons, with high-backed benches that afforded a modicum of privacy. She ordered herself a simple lunch, and she settled in to wait. She was prepared to wait all day, if necessary.

It wasn't. Within the hour, Kaedrich was back, Redly Madgar trailing behind her like a stray puppy.

Kaedrich spotted her first. Without even speaking, Praxis knew that her initial meeting with Redly hadn't gone well, and that the conversation they were about to have was going to be uncomfortable at best. Still: Praxis shifted her fingers, standing up, and waited for them to approach.

Redly shoved roughly past Kaedrich, marching straight up to Praxis's table. Before Praxis could say anything, do anything, he grabbed her glass and threw the contents all over Praxis's face and the front of her shirt.

Thankfully it was just water, but Praxis still stood there for a moment, blinking, before she picked up her napkin and began to wipe her face off. "Nice to see you, too," she said, as she took her seat.

"You're lucky I threw a drink, and not a punch." Redly sat, throwing himself into the opposite bench with enough force to rattle it against the wall.

Praxis sighed. "I know that you're angry with me, but—"

"Angry? No, Praxis. Angry is what happens when one friend offends another. It's temporary." Redly leaned forward, the table practically cutting him in half. He jabbed his finger against the tabletop as he spoke. "You're the best gods-damned wizard I know, and when my *wife* starts to deteriorate, you ignore *every single one* of my requests for your help."

"There was nothing to be *done* by that point," Praxis said. "Redly, I'm sorry, but mortal magic can only go so far. You know that!"

"You could have tried." Redly sat back, crossing his arms. "You could have *tried*."

Praxis looked down at her plate, long since emptied. A faint trace of crumbs littered the surface, a smear of grease. She had no counterargument to Redly's point. She *could* have tried. She'd been with him at the beginning, helped him hold Florina just on the brink of her death. Besides Redly, she knew more about what was keeping Florina in the world than anyone.

She could have tried.

"So what did you want *my* help with?" Redly asked. "I'll admit, I'm going to enjoy telling you 'no.'"

Praxis drummed the fingers of her left hand along the table, the ones that didn't control her leg. She had envisioned this conversation going in a lot of different ways, and knew that there was a chance that Redly was going to be upset with her. But somehow it was different to face him for real, to sit across from all of his grief and pain, and ask him to be a better friend than she had been.

Thankfully, this is when Kaedrich slid into the booth beside her. "Have you been following what's been going on in Monfort lately?"

Redly snorted. "In case you haven't noticed, I've been a little busy."

"Pon Lanali is going to get elected as a temporary head of state, to oversee the formation of a whole new government."

"I think someone mentioned this, sure." Redly shrugged. "What difference does it make? Governments rise and fall."

"Lanali was responsible for the ghosts," Praxis cut in, before Kaedrich could elaborate further. She kept her voice down, leaning in to speak. "You were right, when I came to you for help—it was a Beacon. She'd stolen control of it, and was letting ghosts out to scare people into listening to her teachings."

Redly rolled his eyes. "Yeah, sure."

"It's the truth," Kaedrich said. "We were there. Remember? We were looking for a way to get into the land of the dead?"

"What makes you think I even care?"

"I don't," Praxis said. "I really don't expect you to care, not after what you've just suffered. But in order to convince people of what we're saying, we need proof of our claims, and in order to do *that* we need to summon the Beacon of Souls itself—to speak for itself. Which means that I need a body. A soulless body."

Redly stared at her for a minute, his head tipped. His hair was falling across his forehead and down into his eyes, which crinkled up along the edges as he actually broke into a smile. A smile, so incongruous to what Praxis had been expecting that at first she felt a flutter of hope—until he started laughing, snorting and laughing and nearly choking over his own tears, doubling forward until his head banged against the table.

Kaedrich glanced sideways at Praxis, as if uncertain how to proceed. "Um . . . should I . . . ?"

"No," Praxis said, not even caring what Kaedrich was offering to do. "Redly, I'm serious."

Redly snuffled, choking down the last of his laughter as he sat up. He rubbed at his eyes, digging his fingers deep into the sockets. "I know that you are. Gods help me, but I know that you are. That's what makes it so funny." When he dropped his hand again, all the mirth had disappeared from his face. "The answer is 'no.'"

"Redly—"

"Not that I care, but how would you even go about something that stupid, anyway? You cannot be so arrogant as to assume that normal wizardry would allow you tap into such a power. I mean, if you wouldn't even try to help Florina because you're convinced that it would fail, then you can't possibly expect me to believe that you think you can somehow summon a *Beacon*. Assuming you're even right, and by the way I'm not convinced that you didn't just make all of that shit up."

"It's true, I'm afraid."

"Maybe—*maybe*. But there's more to it than that, isn't there?" Redly leaned in, staring Praxis directly in the eyes. Their noses were so close, both of them bent over the table, that from a distance it might have looked like they were about to kiss each other. "What's the part that you're not telling me?"

"That's all there is."

"Bullshit." Redly sat back, slumping against the back of his bench. "Come on, Praxis. There are gaps here. You say Lanali seized control of the Beacon, yet now you can somehow summon it into the world, to, what? Inhabit my body for a while?"

Praxis shrugged. "More or less, yes."

"But how are you supposed to do that if Lanali has—oh." Redly raised his eyebrows. When he spoke next, his words were slow and deliberate. "Lanali doesn't *have* control of it anymore, does she?"

"No," Praxis said quickly. "We took care of that. But she's still dangerous, and we still need the Beacon to—"

Redly snatched up Praxis's empty glass, hurling it across the table—it would have hit her straight in the head if she hadn't ducked aside, and now instead it shattered against the wall behind her. Bits of broken glass exploded out, kicking against the back of Praxis's head, landing on her shoulders, trailing down her neck, as somewhere in the distance a bartender shouted, "Oy! None of that!"

Kaedrich scrambled out of the booth, running to the bar to smooth things over, and maybe fetch a cloth or something to clean up the mess. Praxis didn't bother watching her to try to find out. She needed all of her focus on Redly, in case he lashed out with something more potent than the table settings. The sky outside had grown quickly dark, wind rattling the windowpanes. Redly's eyes were glassy and deadly.

"That's why you've been ignoring me all of this time, isn't it?" Redly said, through teeth clenched so tightly that it was a wonder words could escape at all. "*You're* in control of it now, and you didn't want me to find out. Did you?"

He was practically shaking with rage now, his fury whirling through him. What was Praxis supposed to do? She did not want to lie, for once, and yet she could not deny that this was *exactly* why she had ignored Redly since the ghost crisis. "Can you blame me? Look at you!"

Redly shut his eyes, as if he could barely contain himself and needed every last scrap of concentration to maintain his self-control. "Just answer me this," he said, still not looking at her. "Could you have saved her?"

Praxis didn't answer right away. She picked at a bit of dried food stuck to the tabletop, chipping away at it with her thumbnail. It was a little more complicated than that, she wanted to say. There were rules, and even if the Beacon had the *power* to do something, it might not be able to do so. It could not violate its oath—except, of course, under direct orders from the Lady of Souls. But even then: it would be the last order that the Lady would ever give it, the command itself stripping her of her powers over the ancient creature.

It wasn't worth explaining all of this to Redly, though, assuming he would even take the time to listen. He had asked her a straightforward question, and he wanted a straightforward answer.

"I don't know," Praxis said. And then, quieter, she added, "Maybe."

Redly opened his eyes. They were surprisingly clear, surprisingly calm. It was almost more unsettling than when they'd been brimming with hatred and resentment—Praxis did not trust this peace. "Maybe," he repeated.

Praxis nodded, and Redly stood up. "Redly—" Praxis started, but all Redly did was hold up a finger.

"Go to the darkest hell, Praxis."

Chapter Thirty-Six

THE HOUSE WAS nice, about a mile outside of town and set back from the lane. The gardens were probably lovely, but Kaedrich couldn't see them well in the dark. Though even in the dark, she could tell that the property wasn't anything like the one the Madgars had lived in when she'd last gone to visit. It wasn't just the size; there was something plain and modest about this building, with neat little shutters and rows of cheerful flower boxes, nothing showy or ornate. Even the number bolted to the door was unadorned, and standing there, ready to knock, Kaedrich was forced to wonder if she'd been given the correct address at all.

No one answered.

There was a low light flickering from behind the curtains of one of the front rooms, and so someone was clearly home. Under normal circumstances, Kaedrich certainly would have respected that person's privacy, would have backed off down the lane and maybe tried again tomorrow. The idea of disturbing anyone was bad enough, but to disturb a new widower, his wife's grave still fresh—! It spoke volumes to the seriousness of their goal that Kaedrich tried the doorknob and, finding it unlocked, let herself into the house.

She had missed the last part of Praxis's argument with Lord Madgar, but Praxis, for once, had gone ahead and outlined the whole thing, in the quiet comfort of the hotel room that she'd booked in order to wait and see if Redly might somehow change his mind. The decision to keep the truth from her friend had clearly worn on Praxis's conscience, and while she didn't explain exactly her reasons for keeping it to herself, it was obviously a messy, complicated choice where nothing that you did would ever be quite *right*.

"So you think he will change his mind?" Kaedrich had asked, as Praxis shrugged out of her new coat and sank onto the edge of the bed.

Praxis had shaken her head. "I doubt it. Why should he?"

Why should he, indeed? It was possible that nothing that Kaedrich (or anyone) said or did at this point would make the slightest bit of difference, but she couldn't just sit there and do nothing. "Is there anyone else we could ask?" Kaedrich said. "Could *I* do it?"

Though of course she couldn't. She'd known it before she asked it, but it had to be asked.

So now it was down to this. Kaedrich pushed the door to the Madgar house open, poking her head into the tiny foyer. "Hello?" she called into the dark. "Lord Madgar? Are you home?"

Because the idea of doing *nothing* was not something that Kaedrich was content with. The thought of Lanali, standing tall over the governing body, presiding over a whole new organization that would rule over Durland . . . it was literally the stuff of nightmares.

She toed her way into the foyer, and shut the door carefully behind her. "Hello?"

Still no answer, and so Kaedrich made her way toward the room where she'd seen a little bit of light.

It turned out to be a sitting room, or at least that's what it was supposed to be. Nothing in the house was serving the purpose that it was supposed to right now, though, because someone had gone through and trashed every room, one by one. The sitting room was no exception. Paintings were torn from the walls and smashed over furniture, which was itself overturned, the stuffing half ripped from their cushions. Glass and porcelain littered the floor, crunching underfoot. One stretch of wallpaper had been ripped down the middle, a long ribbon trailing out into the sitting room floor. Even the poor rug was not immune to the rampage, flipped up and stabbed through with a lamp.

In the middle of it all sat Lord Madgar.

"Hello?" Kaedrich said, as she stepped gingerly around a smashed-up globe. "Lord Madgar? Redly? Can you hear me?"

He was sitting still as a statue, right on the floor. One leg was tucked underneath him, the other sprawled out at an uncomfortable angle, as if he'd simply collapsed into this position and had not bothered to move.

He was staring into a crackling fire, the source of the light that Kaedrich had spotted. His knuckles were bloodied, and a single cut ran down the side of his face. He hadn't bothered to heal any of it.

"Redly?"

"She was right," he said. Redly nodded, slowly, still staring at the fire.

Kaedrich approached with care, being sure not to move too quickly as she settled down next to him. "What do you mean?"

"Not to tell me. I've been sitting here . . . and I've been thinking, I've been trying to picture the most horrific thing that I could have done, to gain control of the Beacon for myself. To save her. I've been think-ing . . . Would I have tortured for it? Killed for it? . . . Raped for it?" Redly turned, meeting Kaedrich straight on. "There isn't *anything* that I wouldn't have done. I'm not a cruel man, but gods, there isn't . . . *any-thing* that I wouldn't have done." He frowned. "Does that make me a terrible person?"

"You must have loved your wife very much," Kaedrich said, artfully ignoring the question.

Redly turned back to the fire. "I suppose I must have." He took a breath. "But you know, I became so obsessed with saving her, over the years . . . I had to wipe her memory so many times, in the process, and now that she's . . ." He waved his hand. "I just keep wondering how many of our days I took from her. How many times did I tell her that I loved her, only to erase it later?" He lowered his voice, barely a whisper at this point. "Did she even know it at all?"

"I'm—" Kaedrich started, then stopped. The words *I'm sure she must have*, comforting and trite, had been right on her tongue but she bit them back. She wasn't sure of anything, certainly not the feelings that had been in Lady Florina Madgar's heart.

Luckily, it didn't seem as if Redly was looking for an answer—at least, not from Kaedrich. He reached out, feeling the heat pouring off of the fire. His hand was so close that Kaedrich feared for it, but she did nothing. He was a wizard, after all; he could heal.

If he wanted to.

"In the end," Redly continued, "all we have is time."

Kaedrich bowed her head. She knew this better than most. Her fixed death had given her a drive to absorb as much knowledge and practice as she could, because she never knew where it was waiting for her. Was this her last month? Was the next? On a practical level, maybe it wasn't that different from anybody else's experience—but it *felt* different. Somehow, the idea of it being inescapable made it more . . . real.

And yet: for all of her determination to make the most out of her time left, there was still one thing that Kaedrich had forever shied away from. Kaedrich's chest twisted up. *Did she even know it at all?* This, in the end, was the thing that tormented Redly Madgar—more than the prospect of living without the woman he loved, there was the simple fear that she had died without knowing the depths of his feelings for her. *Did she even know it at all?* Without prompting, Praxis's face flashed through Kaedrich's mind, and she was forced to admit that, no, she didn't. Not even the kiss would have done it—there were so many ways to twist interpretations of what had happened between them, so much room for doubt.

Praxis didn't know. In all of this time, all of these opportunities, and through all of it, Kaedrich knowing that her chances were narrowing day by day—and still, Praxis didn't know.

Gods, what a coward Kaedrich had been. Shame flooded her face as she sat in quiet vigil with Redly. For all of Kaedrich's life she'd wanted to avoid being branded a coward, and yet look, here she'd allowed her fears to silence her on perhaps the most important subject of all. Denying it, burying it, hiding it. *You're more afraid of the truth than anything else,* she'd said to Praxis, but look what she had gone and done.

It didn't matter anymore what the fallout would be. Something about that was going to have to change.

KAEDRICH DIDN'T RETURN to their hotel room until a little after two in the morning. Praxis hadn't even tried to go to sleep in the meantime. She stationed herself in a chair by the window, keeping watch on the street so that, by the time Kaedrich had her key in the lock, Praxis was already yanking the hotel room's door open from the other side. "Well?" she asked, drawing Kaedrich into the room. "What did he say? Is he going to help us?"

"I don't know. I hope so. I told him when our train was leaving for Monfort, and I wrote it down and left it by his nightstand because I doubt that he'll remember by the morning. But I really don't know what he's going to do."

Praxis took a sharp breath. This wasn't actually a surprise (in fact, in some ways, it was more surprising that the answer wasn't an outright "no"), but it still stung. Praxis turned away, curling her fingers as she went to sit on the edge of the bed.

For years now, she'd been telling herself that she was doing the right thing—that if Redly ever found out that Praxis was the Lady of Souls, he would force her to use the power of it to help Florina. She had avoided him completely, because she did not trust herself to see him. She owed him, after all. He had helped them during the beginning of the ghost crisis, pointing them in the right direction and fighting off an attack side by side with Praxis. As a result, he still had three ghosts trapped inside of his clockwork heart, forever rattling away in their cage, chipping away at it bit by bit. Praxis could have gone to him, could have released the ghosts and used her Beacon to return them safely to the land of the dead—but doing that would have exposed her new power, and then . . .

It was easier to ignore him. She could not risk her own empathy betraying her.

Or at least that was her justification, all of this time. Now, she kept going back to Redly's question, straightforward and pure: could she have saved Florina?

She didn't know. Everything that she'd understood about mortal magic told her "no," but the Beacon wasn't exactly mortal magic. She did not *know* the depths of its powers, or the range that her status as its Lady granted her. Maybe she could have found out, maybe she could have tried. In which case, did her decision to keep to herself make her responsible for Florina's death?

A gentle touch settled on Praxis's knee. Kaedrich had come around sometime while Praxis was swirling in her own remorse; she crouched in front of her now, and took up both of Praxis's hands in hers.

Time paused, or maybe it was only Praxis's heart that drew still. It was impossible to say how long Kaedrich just looked at her. There was something solemn in her expression, yet her eyes remained gentle and as kind as ever.

Oh gods, she's going to do it.

Praxis's heart kicked back into motion, slamming so hard at the top of her chest that she felt it all the way up through her constricted throat.

Kaedrich took a deep breath. "Praxis, there's something I—"

"I should go check on Redly," Praxis said. She sprang to her feet, stumbling around Kaedrich in a graceless flail of arms and legs. She only remembered to reengage her leg harness about halfway through, catching herself against a chair.

Though Praxis did not turn back, she could *hear* Kaedrich's frown as she spoke. "What? Praxis, he's asleep."

"Exactly! I should be there when he wakes up. Maybe I'll have better luck now that you've spoken to him." She hurried across the hotel room, to where her coat was hanging from a peg board by the door.

Kaedrich stood up. "Can't it wait?"

"Best not," Praxis said. Her hands shook as she stuffed them down the sleeves of her coat. "No telling what he's going to do, once he comes 'round. I might miss my opportunity."

Kaedrich huffed under her breath. "Yeah, I hate it when that happens."

This jab did not go unnoticed. Praxis hesitated, her grip already on the doorknob. A part of her was screaming at herself in rage, *What are you doing?!*, but the larger part knew that she couldn't handle this right now. Not with the sting of Florina's death still burning in her mind, not with the threat of Lanali coming to power hanging so heavily over them. Not so soon after having pushed the bounds of Kaedrich's body, without so much as a thought to whether or not it was what *Kaedrich* wanted.

I'm sorry, Praxis thought, and she was. So sorry, for so much. The words were already in her mouth, curdling on her tongue the longer that she stood there, not saying them. Praxis swallowed them back down as a bitter pill, and she opened the door.

SHE DIDN'T GO to Redly's house like she said she would, but nor did Praxis return to the hotel room. Instead, she walked. Through the entire village, up and down every little street, sweeping like a ghost past every sleeping house and shuttered storefront. Brex flitted in and out of view overhead, and Praxis walked until she was too exhausted to walk any farther. She walked because she had nowhere else to go, and she walked because she was not allowing herself to think.

It was only once the sky began to stain the first shades of pale gray that she sat down to rest. She leaned against the base of a tree just outside of town, closing her eyes while Brex perched protectively on a branch above her head. She slept for an hour, or maybe two.

When she returned to the hotel room, Kaedrich was ready to go. They didn't speak, just checked out and paid, walked in silence back to the train station to wait. Praxis whistled, settling Brex back into his cage, and then the three of them sat on a bench and watched the minutes tick by on the station's hanging clock.

So they would have to come up with *some* other plan, though neither of them had any ideas immediately forthcoming. The shrill whistle of the tracks announced their train's impending arrival, and when it shuffled into place in front of them they dutifully boarded. They were both already seated, Brex nestled into his usual spot beside Praxis, when the door to their compartment rattled open.

Redly stumbled in, throwing himself into a slump on the seat next to Kaedrich. He slouched so low that his knees practically touched the padding on the seat opposite, and he crossed his arms in a huff over his chest. His eyes were puffy and bloodshot, his suit a rumpled mess, his hair unkempt and uncombed. He glared across the compartment, the hatred of his eyes burning into Praxis. "Don't even *think* of thanking me," he said. "Because I am in no way doing this for you."

Praxis shook her head. "I won't."

"Why, then?" Kaedrich asked. It was a question that Praxis couldn't dare get away with.

Redly shrugged. At first, it seemed that was the most that they were going to get from him; his attention wandered to the window, the bough of a vibrant green tree fluttering easily in the breeze. "I still have two daughters, don't I?" was all that he said.

Chapter Thirty-Seven

THE TRIP BACK to Monfort seemed to take a year. Redly Madgar refused to speak once the train was underway, not even to Kaedrich; instead he folded himself against the wall of the compartment, shut his eyes, and pretended to sleep. Praxis and Kaedrich didn't dare talk—for one thing, anything they said would be listened to, and for another, what was there to say to each other right now? Every topic felt like a bomb waiting to go off. Kaedrich watched the world slip by outside of her window, thinking about how close she'd come to admitting her feelings, and then wincing inside at the sudden wall that she'd run into instead. How was she supposed to take that? Did Praxis have a guess about what Kaedrich was going to say, and didn't want to hear it? But if that was true then, what, was Kaedrich being rejected without even first having the chance to express herself? Or maybe Praxis thought that Kaedrich was going to talk about their blundered kiss, and was hoping to avoid the subject? Maybe she just wanted to forget that it had ever happened.

Such is the manner in which Kaedrich's thoughts swirled, spiraled, and ultimately looped back around on themselves in the long ride back to the city. By the time they arrived, her stomach was twisted up into a thousand knots, and she had no idea how she'd ever try to broach the subject again—if, indeed, she ever should.

She probably shouldn't.

And yet.

Kaedrich shook her head at herself as they disembarked. Gods, how much more pain did she need to put herself through before she just gave up already? Hadn't she been humiliated enough? Hadn't she suffered enough? At what point did her persistence just make her a fool?

When they got back to the Society house, Weevish was waiting for them. A nervous look pinched his face, and he kept running his hands over themselves as if he was washing them, again and again.

Praxis wasted no time. She threw her hat and coat aside as she entered, waving vaguely at the rumpled man strolling in behind her. "Weevish, Redly Madgar. Redly, Weevish."

Redly and Weevish exchanged a brief glance, though neither bothered with any of the standard social protocols like, "Hello," or, "Pleasure to meet you." Weevish flinched back underneath Redly's deadened, empty stare, and Redly's eyes slipped off of him after barely a moment. They were both already following Praxis as she wove through the Society house, gathering things in her arms as she went. A candelabra from a shelf, a white sheet yanked off of a draped chair, an empty cage just big enough for a rat.

Kaedrich had hung back for a moment when they first entered the building, releasing Brex from his own cage. The animal chittered nervously and immediately streaked up the stairwell, disappearing from view. Kaedrich frowned, then hurried to catch up with the rest of the somber party.

"There were, um . . . a few substitutions that I had to make," Weevish was saying now. He skipped along nervously beside Praxis, still wringing his hands. "Some of the things that are called for . . . well . . . in polite society—"

"We're not being polite," Praxis said. She paused in front of an old liquor cabinet. Most of the bottles were missing, but a few remained tucked in the back. In the haste that the Society had exercised in evacuating the building, they'd left a lot of useless little bits and pieces behind, and apparently that included the cheap stuff. Praxis tucked her hodgepodge supplies underneath her free arm, clicking the thumb of her control arm as she reached in and plucked an impossibly tiny bottle off of the shelf. It was only once she turned back, taking a breath to continue speaking to Weevish, that her eyes fell upon Kaedrich.

Praxis hesitated. The look that flashed over her face—was it possible that she'd forgotten Kaedrich was even there? After all of these years, everything they'd been through, when faced with a true crisis and surrounded by wizarding allies, did Kaedrich's presence really matter that little to her?

Praxis stuffed all the assorted bits and bobs that she'd collected into Weevish's arms. "Kaedrich," she said, "I need you to clear out of here for a while."

Kaedrich raised her eyebrows. "You can't be serious."

"I am, and I'm afraid that I'm going to have to insist. This isn't going to be safe for you."

The absurdity of this almost made Kaedrich laugh. Kaedrich, who had seen more than her share of risk over the years? Kaedrich, who had been threatened at gunpoint, who had jumped from a moving train, who had gone up against Silvers and wizards and the Beacon of Souls itself? Kaedrich, who had brought them the news of this latest danger in the first place, and gotten them to form a plan of action?

Kaedrich shook her head. "I'm not leaving."

"You have to."

"No. Perlandra's breath, Praxis, I'm not a child. I've been to the *land of the dead*, I think I can—"

"That's exactly *why* you need to leave," Praxis cut in. "I'm not questioning your bravery, Kaedrich. I'm going to be bringing a portion of the land of the dead here, and I cannot have anything familiar around that it might try to cling to. You're a risk. You need to leave. We'll meet you at the Crescent, by the hangman's tree."

All of the air seemed to rush from Kaedrich at once, as if she'd been kicked to the ground so hard as to lose her breath. She *felt* herself deflate under Praxis's level stare. The idea to argue rose and then immediately collapsed in her mind. There was no arguing. Praxis was not joking.

She couldn't speak, so she just left. Even and steady footsteps, no outward sign of the discontent swirling through her. She did not even slam the door.

Praxis watched her go, but more than that, she kept a mental tether on her, tracking her movements as she cut through the house in a barely contained rage. Her sense of Kaedrich had only gotten stronger since coming to Monfort, and more so since the Crown Day celebration; Praxis felt as if she could *see* Kaedrich now, through the many layers of walls, as Kaedrich began to wend her way through the narrow streets of Monfort. She waited until Kaedrich was a full block away, and she might have waited even longer, if Weevish did not clear his throat.

"Um . . . I'm no expert, of course, but that doesn't seem to me as if it's actually a risk."

Praxis shot Weevish a glare. Outside, she could still feel Kaedrich retreating, working her way toward the edge of the city. "How much longer do we have?" Praxis asked, ignoring Weevish's comment.

Weevish shoved the armload of collected objects into Redly's somewhat reluctant hands, and dug until he found his pocket watch. His face blanched. "Three hours."

"Then let's not waste any more time." She turned to Redly. "Ready to meet the face of death?"

LANALI STOOD IN front of a mirror, practicing her smiles.

People sometimes make the mistake of thinking that a smile is one of the most straightforward expressions of all, but in fact there are an almost infinite number of variations: there was the mischievous grin, the bemused smirk, the forced smile; there were flirty smiles, and half-smiles, and brave smiles; there were smiles that were intended to soothe, smiles that were intended to provoke, smiles that were supposed to mean one thing to one person and something else entirely to the next. Lanali ran through her usual litany, trying each one on and making sure they all still fit properly. Here she was pleased, here she was secretly angry, here she was in love.

It steadied her to have something to concentrate on, something that was entirely within her control. Though she had done everything that she could to ensure the success of the impending vote, the ultimate outcome was now in the hands of the fates.

And Praxis Fellows was missing from Monfort.

Lanali tried not to dwell on this. She had not seen the symbol of the white bird for days now, in either dreams or omens—surely that had to be a good sign, didn't it? It would be naïve to think that Praxis had no plan for opposing her, but perhaps this meant that such oppositions were destined to failure.

Still, Lanali had her spies out everywhere. Every ear that could be trusted with a shade of the truth was tuned for news of Praxis Fellows, every eye was peering in earnest throughout the city. The Crescent itself was under her tight control, her personal guard scattered on every level.

She had nearly finished running through her smiles when a knock rapped on her door. Lanali wiped her face clean, regarding herself in the mirror. *"Enter,"* she said in Aul.

She watched the door open and shut in the reflection. The top of Tol's familiar red hair appeared behind her shoulder a moment later.

It was still several hours until the Council would assemble, and so there could only be one reason for him to disturb her solitude. Lanali's face scrunched inward, an open display of distaste. "Where?"

"We're not sure, exactly. But it's not all bad." He took another step, two, forward. He wore a smile of pleased expectations. "Do you remember how I wanted to lure Praxis into our territory?"

Lanali's eyes narrowed. "You propose that we allow her to come *here*?"

"She is coming here whether we wish to allow it or not," Tol said. "Of that, you can be certain. What I suggest is that we make sure we're ready for her. We can still salvage this—if we're careful."

There was obviously no arguing with this. The vote was mere hours away; there was no time to track her down, no time to stop her en route. Lanali glanced down at the dresser underneath the mirror, and froze in place. Gentle, midmorning sunlight dappled in through the nearby window, dancing and shifting as it filtered through trees and curtains.

A patch of sunlight, reflecting pure white off of the polished dresser, was fluttering in the shape of a bird at flight.

Fear stabbed at Lanali, and she reached out behind her without thought, waving her hand sightlessly until Tol's warm grip found it and steadied it in place. His hands were always softer than Lanali expected, soft and careful and gentle. She squeezed his grip, and he squeezed her back. "Make your preparations," Lanali said, never once taking her eyes off of the flight of the bird, heading toward her whether she wanted it or not. "Make whatever preparations you want, except for one detail."

"What's that?"

Lanali turned. She could still *feel* the bird's presence, flapping at her back just as strongly as if it was manifest. Everything came down to this.

Tol was watching her, steady and curious. He wore no smiles anymore, either practiced or natural. He brought Lanali's hand to his chest, flattening it against his steady, solid ribs. The tempered beat of his heart filtered into her palm. "What do you wish of me?"

"Stay with me," Lanali said in Aul. She said it fast, before she could think better of it. *"Send whoever you wish to deal with Praxis—send them all, send the best—but you . . . If they fail, if she reaches me . . ."*

Tol bowed his head. His braids brushed over his cheek, a curtain falling across his face. In fear, the two of them might as well have been back on the islands, back where their collaboration had first begun. They were afraid then, too. And Tol had stayed by her side.

"As you wish, my Pon."

* * *

BEFORE THEY BEGAN, Praxis, in an uncharacteristic display of good sense, took a number of precautions. She made sure that Brex was safely contained in another part of the house. She verified that Kaedrich was, indeed, still somewhere beyond even the haziest reach of her senses. She had several buckets of water prepared and standing around the perimeter of the basement, where they were set to perform this act. She made sure that Redly had a filling meal beforehand, and though he rolled his eyes at it, she made him lie down and rest during their preparatory efforts so as to conserve his strength.

She also paid one final visit to the Beacon of Souls.

"Welcome, my Lady."

Praxis opened her eyes, already turned to avoid seeing Moc's display, and jerked back in surprise. The central chamber was filled with shadows.

Of course, it normally was; but normally, they clung to the walls and ceiling like heavy drapes, blotting out the illusion of sunshine that filtered in from the arching stained glass windows overhead. Normally, they filled in the gaps. Normally, they coated the floor as a thick mist. Normally, they would only create a solid form when Praxis started speaking to them, and even then it was a lazy, almost reluctant transformation. One would detach itself from the rest, limbs and a head rising idly out of the mass.

This time, the room was full of forms. A thousand empty faces stared back at her, not a single scrap of darkness hanging back against the walls. They encircled her as a tight pack—she couldn't look at Moc's display now, even if she wanted to. Only the tall pillar in the middle of the room remained unobstructed, and that more by sheer height than from the shadows' lack of numbers. At the top, the glass orb that matched her pendant writhed and twisted, shining out over the heads of the shadows.

"Um . . . I take it you already know what I'm planning, then."

The orb of the Beacon flared, just for a second, and Praxis could almost *feel* it purr its pleasure at the idea.

"Oh, yes," said the shadows. They spoke as one, nearly a hundred from all points around the chamber. Their excitement bristled off of them, palpable as it raised the hairs on the back of Praxis's neck.

Praxis nodded carefully. "Okay then. That makes things a little easier, I guess—don't need to bother explaining it to you. I would like to lay out some ground rules first, though."

A shudder of discontent rippled through the assembled crowd. "Rules?" they asked.

"Yes, rules. I am not going into this without all of us knowing exactly where we stand. First off: you have to promise me that no harm will come to Redly as a result of your . . . presence."

"The vessel will not be damaged."

Praxis grimaced at their phrasing, but she supposed that it would have to do; Beacons did not, after all, have the capacity to hold a mortal's true name in their mind, and they did have to call him *something*.

"Second: no matter how tempting it may be, you may not use this opportunity as a chance to betray me, manipulate the situation to your own advantage, or otherwise attempt any form of an escape or change of leadership. I *am* your Lady, and I will remain so during the *entire time* that you are inhabiting mortal form. Are we absolutely clear on this point?"

At this, every single one of the shadows surrounding her bowed their heads in unison. "My Lady," they said, "such an idea did not even occur to us."

They were incapable of outright lying to her, and so Praxis had to accept this as the truth—though she still didn't entirely trust it. "All right, well . . . good. Don't think about it now, either."

"No, my Lady."

Praxis nodded. "Very well. Now, I want to be direct on how this is going to proceed. After the ritual, we are going to head straight to a building called the Council's Crescent. There may be opposition to us getting inside, or getting to the room where we're headed. If that happens, you keep yourself and Redly safe until the danger has passed. Once we're inside, you're going to be called upon to give testimony as to Pon Lanali's actions in regards to what we refer to as 'the ghost crisis.' You will answer these questions as honestly as if you were speaking directly to me, understood? If I so much as *think* that you're trying to twist your words in order to help her—"

"We have no interest in helping the Pon," the shadows said with, if Praxis wasn't mistaken, a distinct sneer in their collective voice. Their ranks tightened at the mention of her name, as if they were forming a wall against the very idea of Lanali.

"See that it stays that way," Praxis said. "Oh, and one more thing. This is important. I'm assuming that you remember Kaedrich Mannly."

She did not need the Beacon to answer verbally; its stiff silence was more than enough. Praxis supposed that it was only understandable that it would have a less than warm reception to Kaedrich—she had, after all, not only played a critical role in returning it to being under mortal control, she'd all but crippled it by allowing it to share the experience of a mortal life from her mind. It didn't matter that it was by the Beacon's request. It did not forgive easily, if at all.

"She's going to be there with us," Praxis went on. "But it is absolutely vital that you do *not* refer to her with feminine pronouns. My understanding of this ritual is that Redly is going to be aware of everything that happens to his body, and *no one* must find out that Kaedrich is really a woman."

The shadows shrugged. "It makes no difference to us what terms mortals use to distinguish each other."

"And I'm glad that you have no objections, but I need to hear you swear it. I will not, under any circumstances, proceed if I do not have your solemn word on this matter. At no point will there be any hint in your speech or manners that Kaedrich isn't a man. Do you swear?"

There was the slightest hesitation at this, just a breath. But far from concerning her, this actually served to calm Praxis's nerves a little. She did not think that she would trust the answer if it came too quickly.

One shadow stepped forward, head already bowed. "My Lady," it said, "You have our absolute word on this point. There shall be no mention."

"Good," Praxis said. She nodded her approval. "All right, then. I think that we're ready to begin."

It was a nasty ritual, full of Old Magic: the sacrificing of small animals, the exchanging of blood, lots of incantations and darkness and fire. Most of it was probably useless trappings, but with the fading of belief in Beacons came a distinct lack of study of the magic used to manipulate them, and Praxis wasn't willing to risk skipping an important step simply due to her own arrogance and distaste. There were enough risks as it was, pulling something like this off, working from a spell that had been translated and retranslated, passed down in dusty tomes that no one really cared about or bothered to proofread. (Case in point: the list of acceptable animals included a "smell goat," which Weevish insisted could well have been a particular breed from the Ashmorre highlands known for their somewhat cheesy aroma. Praxis had scoffed. "They mean a *small* goat," she said, but since they had access to no goats at all—small or smelly— the question had remained academic, and they had to choose something else instead.)

Praxis grimaced her way through most of it. The stench was horrific, even without the cheese-goat, and more than once she had to fight to keep the bile from rising in her throat. Weevish, to his credit, had approached the matter with the professional detachment of a well-trained surgeon, at times even appearing less ruffled than Praxis. That came as somewhat of a surprise, as she'd expected him to remain at the edges of their cleared workspace in the basement, and she found herself oddly comforted by the wide stance that he took beside her, the clear bellow of his voice.

Which left only Redly: the ritual afforded him little dignity, sitting cross-legged under a bright burst of flames, stripped to nothing more than what essentially amounted to a ceremonial loincloth, the panel into his carefully guarded clockwork heart on full display. Frost covered the glass in a tight latticework of dusty tendrils, a permanent reminder of the three ghosts still rattling around somewhere in the depths of his mechanical masterpiece. Praxis offered, before they started, to release them and use her abilities as Lady of Souls to send them back to the land of the dead, but Redly had staunchly refused. He seemed to view them as something of a penance, though what he felt his crimes were, it wasn't entirely clear. Praxis could, of course, have forced the issue and done it without his consent, but preparations had taken a disturbingly long time, and she was starting to get worried about the clock. She told herself that she would do it later, once all of this business with Lanali was finished and Redly was back at Calswell House recovering.

She couldn't help staring at it, though, as she and Weevish ran through the tedious process that the Watchers had supposedly set down millennia ago. Redly kept his eyes closed, his breathing steady. Whether he was preparing himself or simply bored, it was impossible to tell.

The ritual concluded with a flourish. A wet ripping sound cut the room as Praxis yanked the remains of their slaughtered sewer rat in half while Weevish warbled a low chanting and set off a series of carefully timed bursts, ringing their entire group in twelve points of flame. Droplets of blood splattered Praxis's face and she reeled back, shutting her eyes instinctively to avoid getting anything in them.

But she did not want to miss anything, so she forced herself to peep them back open, first one and then the other. She blinked, trying to get the droplets out of her eyelashes.

She found herself staring down at Redly, who was staring up with an expression equal parts bemusement and superiority.

"Brilliant," he said sarcastically. He started to clap, each one drawn out for maximum effect. "Nicely done. Only next time, maybe try doing something that *actually works*? Gods, Praxis, of all the—"

A gust of wind cut him off, as cold as if it had sprung up from Yandosia. The twelve flames encircling them turned instantly black, casting everything into a terrible, monochromatic glow. The pendant around Praxis's neck, on prominent display as instructed for the ritual, rattled irritatedly against her chest for several seconds, and Praxis couldn't help it—she yanked it off, in terror and apprehension, and threw it without direction into the middle of the circle.

Rather than striking anything, though, the pendant swerved in midair. It sailed over Redly's head (though he still ducked to avoid being snared in the chain's loop), coming to rest at a point just above and behind him. And then they all watched, gaping, as the pendant grew in size, larger and larger, the chain dangling below it snaking to the ground and turning to stone.

The central pillar of the land of the dead, made manifest. No longer was the pendant a pendant: the orb sitting atop the pillar now writhed faster than Praxis had ever seen it before, whirling so hard that for a moment she was worried it would somehow shatter the glass entrapping it.

It did not. Instead, the black flames flared, rising high enough to lap against the crossbeams of the basement ceiling, and in one swift moment that happened as fast as a blink, twelve shadows in their human-shaped forms stepped forth from the hearts of the fire.

For the next breath, time hung suspended. Praxis had time to take it all in: the Beacon, as whole and real as anything, its pillar chipped with ancient cracks; Weevish, staring open-mouthed at the scene before him; the twelve shadows, identical and yet somehow distinct to Praxis's eye, standing like foot soldiers prepared for battle; and Redly. Redly, looking so small and vulnerable in the center of it all, his face full of nothing but naked terror. Perhaps he didn't think that it would really work. Perhaps the reality was worse than he'd imagined.

Perhaps he saw an impression of his wife, shimmering somehow through the depths of the shadows.

He didn't want to go through with it, not anymore. Praxis saw this, in the eternity that the rest of the world was waiting in, holding their breath. The shadows hovered, holding themselves back, and suddenly Praxis understood that they would not act without her final command. That nothing would, that all of time was waiting for her now, to make this one choice. Redly was staring at her, frozen like the rest of them, but his eyes were wide and pleading. *Don't do it.*

But what other choice did they have? He had accepted his fate the minute he'd stepped onto the train with them, and the stakes were simply too high to turn back now.

"Take him," she said, and all at once the world snapped back into action. The flames sputtered back to life, the frozen wind returned to swirl around the perimeter, and Weevish gasped as the shadows plunged, one after another, into Redly.

Redly screamed. He howled. Raged, and cursed, and threw himself to his feet, clawing at his chest, his head, his skin, as if a thousand insects were burrowing through him at once. Weevish paled, shrinking back for the first time since the whole process had begun, but Praxis stood tall. She would not allow herself to flinch away from what she had done. It would have been convenient if she could attribute her coldness to an inheritance from her mother, or merely a stoic resolution in the face of what awaited them, but unfortunately for Praxis, she gave herself none of these comforting lies. The impassive slack of her face was all her own, and she studied what was happening to her friend under the full brunt of knowledge that she'd done it willingly.

This is what she did not want Kaedrich to see.

The shadows had completely engulfed Redly by this point, losing their form as they shrouded him in darkness. All that was left was the sound of him, which had faded to a dull whimper by this point, and then that, too, stopped, as abruptly as the whole process had started. A hollow, sucking noise broke the stillness, and the shadows snapped inward, imploding and compressing, and when they were done there was only one figure left. A shadow, standing where Redly had been, its head bowed and its arms laid open by its sides in gentle supplication.

It was far more defined than it should have been, though—Praxis could make out a nose, distinct ears, even the faintest trace of what might have been eyelashes. She did not get the chance to study the creature in depth, however, as in the next instant the black flames flared to blinding white, and when Praxis was able to open her eyes again they were just in the basement. Weevish's original fires flickered idly around them, the pendant had returned to its normal size and dropped with a clatter to the floor.

And Redly was back, in the same position that the shadow had been.

Except . . . even as Praxis edged forward, Weevish peeking curiously around her shoulder, she knew that it wasn't exactly Redly, not really. Not anymore. His clockwork heart continued to tick forward in perfect rhythm, his breath steady and even, a faint sheen of sweat lining his pale skin—but there was something distinctly *not* human about him, difficult even to put a finger on.

Praxis reached out, gingerly tapping his shoulder. "Redly? Can you hear me?"

Redly looked up. Or, more accurately: the Beacon looked up, raising Redly's head in order to do it. It blinked at her. Something flashed deep in the point of Redly's pupils, and Praxis's stomach twisted up as she realized that they reflected out as perfect replicas of the orb of the Beacon.

The Beacon quirked Redly's mouth up in a half smile. "My Lady," it said to her, and then frowned at the sound of a mortal voice coming out of its mouth. It smacked Redly's lips, cleared his throat. It looked down at Redly's body, taking it in with a detached sort of curiosity. "I do believe that we are going to require clothes," it said.

Chapter Thirty-Eight

KAEDRICH STOOD ON the edge of the grounds, not quite sure if she wanted to approach.

She'd walked all the way out of the city, to a quiet strip of land where the last of the industry gave way to a series of farms and vineyards, where the road became muddy and rutted and the traffic passing in and out of Monfort didn't even look twice at the humble buildings sitting back from the road.

One such building was squat and wide, ancient bricks covered in vines. Unlike its neighbors, there were no fences to mark the borders of its sprawling gardens. An explosion of color spread over the ground, with no strict division between wildflowers and those that had been cultivated, between the trellises loaded down with grapevines and the meandering rows of vegetables. One of the trellises was currently being tended to by a young man in gray coveralls with a shining bald head, and it was here that Kaedrich's attention became fixed.

Kaedrich took a deep breath. She cupped her hands around her mouth. "Marlick!"

Marlick started at the sound. A grapevine sprang up, out of his grip, as he turned. He squinted into the distance. His head was gleaming with sweat, a pale egg that hadn't yet tanned to match the rest of his body.

He shook his head as he trudged over.

"So it's true, then?" Kaedrich asked, once he'd gotten close enough that she didn't need to shout. Kaedrich didn't know why, but she didn't feel comfortable crossing over the threshold of the cloister's grounds, even if they weren't marked, even if they preached about letting in visitors whenever called upon to do so.

Marlick shrugged. He reached up and ran his hand along his now-bald head. It was beyond strange seeing him like this, even if it's where Marlick's life was inevitably supposed to take him. Kaedrich supposed that a part of her had never believed that he would *actually* go through with it—that instead, he'd find some way of changing his father's mind, or would outright disregard the family's wishes and strike out on his own. Kaedrich tried to picture it: Marlick, soon to be going silent for half a year, scrubbing floors and praying and studying ancient texts inside of the foreboding walls of the cloister. His new look certainly helped to sell the idea, but it was still a stretch of the imagination.

"It's true," Marlick said eventually. "I couldn't stay there. Falcon-ridge . . . it isn't what I thought it was, Kaedrich. It's not what you think it is."

"Yeah, I found that out the hard way."

Marlick flinched. "I'm sorry. I heard about what happened at the Trials." Despite himself, it was easy to see a grin trying to break through Marlick's meditative veneer. "Wish I could have been there to see the look on their faces, though," he added, unable to contain himself. "Was it seriously *the* captain of the royal guard?"

Kaedrich's cheeks flushed, embarrassed and proud at the same time. "It was seriously *the* captain, yes."

Marlick let out a low whistle. Then he shook his head. "Well. I always knew you were more than capable."

"No you didn't."

Marlick laughed. "No," he admitted. "That's true, I didn't. Congratulations. I'm impressed."

"Thanks," Kaedrich said. She stuffed her hands into her pockets, weighing the decision that she'd made in coming here. While she knew that Praxis's plan would benefit from all the extra help that it could get, a part of Kaedrich felt guilty about the idea of asking Marlick to get involved. Especially now, especially seeing him trying to make a fresh start for himself.

But she'd already come all of this way. And the situation *was* dire.

"Marlick . . ." Kaedrich started, "there's something that you should know."

So Kaedrich told him. About Lanali, the truth of what she'd done; about what was happening in Monfort right now, the remaining members of the Governance Council pouring back into the city; about how word of the vote was spreading, and unfortunately for them, loyalty to the Pon was amassing like a rolling storm cloud. While she talked, Marlick led them over to a fallen tree that served as a bench, and he just sat and listened, dumbfounded, to the whole of Kaedrich's story.

When she finally drew to a halt, what felt like years later, Marlick leaned back, his face upturned toward the sun. "Gods," he said. "I . . . I don't even know what to say to that."

"Just start by telling me if you *believe* me."

"Hell yes, I believe you," Marlick said. He turned back to Kaedrich, looking as if even the very question was cause for personal offense.

Relief flooded through Kaedrich. For a moment she was tempted to throw her arms around him, but she held herself back. She settled for momentarily shutting her eyes as she composed herself. "Thank you."

"But I'm not sure if anyone else will."

Kaedrich nodded. "We know. That's why Praxis is going to summon the Beacon of Souls, to speak for itself."

"She can *do* that?"

"She's already working on it," Kaedrich said. She reached into her pocket and checked her watch; there was still time. "Basically, we want to demonstrate to everyone that Lanali isn't who she claims to be. If we interrupt the vote, perhaps we can get enough seeds of doubt going to delay the Crescent's actions. Get people asking questions. Demanding answers. Even if they still want to disband the Council, revoke the crown—just so long as they don't give it to *Lanali*. The people deserve the chance to know the truth."

Marlick went quiet. He was looking at the dirt, his hands knitted together between his knees. It was a look that Kaedrich was plenty familiar with, whenever Marlick was trying to make a serious decision.

He's going to make a good Attendant, Kaedrich suddenly thought. Calm and patient, unwilling to rush into something without listening to all sides. The idea made her smile, the first flutter of optimism that everything truly was going to be all right in the end.

"Will you help us?" Kaedrich asked.

Marlick didn't answer at first. "Yeah," he said after a moment. He nodded. "Yes. All right. Let's do this."

Kaedrich grinned. "Excellent. Now all we need is to get the others, and then—"

"Wait," Marlick said. "Others?"

"Well . . . yeah. Lucan, Tristy, Havil—"

"They won't help you," Marlick said.

"What are you talking about? Of course they'll help. Havil and Tristy haven't left *yet*."

Marlick shook his head. "No, that's not what I meant. Havil's a coward, and Lucan's loyalties when it comes to the Pon are questionable at best—you know where his family stands on the matter. Tristy . . . I mean, she'd probably come with us, but do you really want to ask a woman to put herself on the line like that?"

"*Praxis* is taking a stand."

"That's different, and you know it."

"No," Kaedrich said, bristling. "I don't. If a woman wants to fight for something that she believes in—"

"You *can't* ask Tristy," Marlick snapped. He shut his eyes as he took a deep, calming breath. "Please believe me. I can't tell you why, but you don't want to put Tristy at risk right now. It's not safe for her, and besides, what's she going to do? Dance and sing at them until they surrender? She's not exactly a soldier."

Kaedrich felt the urge to sag her shoulders, though she steeled herself against the impulse. It did not help that she was still angry at having been banished from the Society house where Praxis and the others were making their preparations. She'd known even at the time that Praxis was lying, her reason flimsy, but there was no point in fighting it. What Praxis said might not have been the truth, but what she'd *meant* was: *I won't do this until you're gone.*

So now here Kaedrich was, trying to make the best of it, trying to use her time toward furthering their goals, and she was coming up with next to nothing. Sure, Marlick's help was more than welcomed—but *one* additional pair of hands, *one* additional sword, would do them little good if they came up against any actual resistance in reaching the main chambers of the Crescent. And Kaedrich did not delude herself: she expected resistance. More resistance, really, than they'd likely be able to handle even *with* all of her friends on her side, but somehow their absence made things seem hopeless in a way that they hadn't before. Kaedrich's stomach squirmed—apparently, she'd be putting her training to good use after all.

Marlick sighed. "But . . . I might be able to find a few people who can help."

"Who?"

Marlick jerked his head, indicating the ancient cloister behind them. "Who do you think?"

Kaedrich's eyes widened. "Marlick, no. We can't."

"I think that I have a little better idea of whether or not we can than you, Kaedrich."

"That's not what I meant. It's just . . ." Did she really have to say it? "Marlick, the oaths—"

"Did I say anything about asking the *Attendants*?" Marlick said, grinning. "Listen, I've gotten to know some of the other initiates, and there's a few that know how to handle themselves, all right? None of us are sworn-bound yet, and believe me when I say that there is no love for the Pon within these walls. I think I can round some of them up for you."

Kaedrich blinked. Initiates of Perlandra—it wasn't a wholly terrible idea, given Lanali's distaste of the faith. While she had never been openly hostile to it the way that she had with magic, it was clear her teachings did not all fall in line with Perlandra's gospels, and the temples had been losing people every year since she'd taken hold in the public eye. And yet . . .

"I would never ask you to do something that would get you into trouble here," Kaedrich said.

Marlick shrugged. "I don't hear you asking. Just tell me when and where."

Tears stung at Kaedrich's eyes, and she had to look away. She wiped at her face, muttering something about dust on the wind. Gods, Marlick. Why had she never truly appreciated him before? When this was over, she was going to find some way to make it up to him, somehow, but for now she just nodded. "Okay," she said.

"Okay," Marlick said.

And so it was settled.

THE GOOD NEWS: everybody in Monfort was descending upon the Crescent.

The bad news: *everybody* in Monfort was descending upon the Crescent.

While a good turnout would certainly help them when it came time to make their case, this level of crowds meant that it was almost impossible to get through to the damned building at all. Even just finding Kaedrich in this sea of humanity would have taken hours, if not for Praxis's constant awareness guiding her forward like a compass needle.

Kaedrich had brought company with her. Marlick, now oddly bald-headed, and several equally bald young men that she introduced cryptically as "people Marlick knows." Praxis considered protesting, but one look from Kaedrich stilled her tongue before she'd even started. Praxis bit her lip and nodded, once, instead. Besides, it was not a terrible idea to have extra hands, in case things got complicated.

They slipped behind the Crescent, to a basement door tucked into the corner of the gardens. Weevish nodded at the guard standing beside it, who dutifully turned his back to examine a rosebush as their group let themselves in the building. Brex breezed over Praxis's shoulder. "How . . . ?" Praxis started once they were inside, but Weevish shook his head.

"I still have *some* friends, Miss Fellows."

Indeed he did, for they did not encounter a single person as they worked their way through the basement level, or up into the surrounding network of musty corridors. None of the excitement of the day had reached this remote part of the building, though you could already hear the faint roar of the crowd somewhere far above.

Weevish led the way, at least until they reached the upper levels. His knowledge of the Crescent failed him somewhat once they emerged from the mole-like tunnels of the lower passages of back offices and record rooms, and so Praxis took over from there. She drew up a map in her mind, carefully avoiding the patrols of guardsmen and servants darting continuously through the halls.

They were actually doing well, and that should have perhaps been the first indication that something was wrong. But Praxis was so wrapped up in just trying to find a clear path that she did not take the time to question their good fortune. They only had a few more floors to go before they'd reach the wings of the councillors' offices, and a rare flicker of hope spurred her senselessly onward.

They burst through the doors and into the next room—not even really a room, so much as a wide junction between several different corridors. Wedged into a corner of the building, one curved wall boasted nothing but windows, while three other doors led off of the junction in different directions. Praxis hurried through, ushering everyone else in behind her. The sickly smell of exotic flowers leached down from bouquets in fat vases that rested on inset shelves above every door and window; already, it was working its way deep into the fabric of Praxis's coat, clinging like cigar smoke to each strand of her hair.

Kaedrich was the last one in, the door slamming shut behind her with just a little more force than Praxis felt was strictly necessary. Never mind, though: Praxis was already guiding their ragtag group across the middle of the open room, when the sound of a second door slamming stopped them all in their tracks. And then another, and another. Four times total, each of the doors that branched off of the junction slamming closed. Just before the last one had shut, Praxis tried throwing off a tightly wound funnel of air to wedge into the doorjamb, but even that did nothing— the air burst apart as the door struck it, slamming shut with an ominous click that was clearly a lock sliding into place.

The sure and certain knowledge that they had walked into a trap clawed up Praxis's throat, as fast as if she had vomited it into her mouth. Marlick swore beside her, beating her to it. Brex chittered nervously from above. A flutter of arguments and exclamations began to spring up, and Praxis whirled back around. "Enough!" Though she understood the need to express their shock, outrage, fear, she needed quiet—she needed Kaedrich. Kaedrich could be strong and steady in the face of something like this, a calming presence that Praxis found herself sorely lacking at the moment. As she'd turned she'd already begun to seek her out, but to Praxis's surprise Kaedrich wasn't in the tight knot that surrounded her.

Instead, she was standing right inside of the first door, as if she had come to a halt the instant she'd set foot in the room. She wasn't even facing them, turned back as she stared up at a bouquet of the noxious flowers that sat planted over the door. She was entirely still, entirely fixed on the curl of the petals, her hands gripped tight over the hilt of her sword and the butt of her gun. She may as well have been a statue.

"Kaedrich?"

Kaedrich didn't seem to notice Praxis's approach, not even as Praxis's hand alighted on her shoulder.

"Kaedrich?"

When she did turn back, she did it slowly. Like waking up from a long sleep, Kaedrich's attention went first to Praxis's hand, pinching the fabric of her suit coat, and traced the line of Praxis's arm until the two of them met eye to eye.

A nameless fear staked Praxis in place. There was something slack and deathly serious in Kaedrich's empty face, a hollow resignation that Praxis couldn't identify. This, more than fear of Lanali coming to power, more than terror at the sudden trap they'd found themselves in, made Praxis want to turn and run. "Kaedrich, are . . . are you okay?"

The question itself seemed to settle something in Kaedrich's mind. She took a deep breath, gave Praxis a solid nod. "I'm fine," she said, shrugging out from underneath Praxis's tender grip. Kaedrich took a couple of steady steps forward, taking in the situation at a glance. Her attention swept the room, even and appraising: the doors, the windows, the angles. "You," she said, snapping her fingers and pointing at one of the men she'd brought with her, "get over and guard the southern doors. You: check the windows, make sure nobody is going for the surprise angle. Weevish, Marlick, spread yourselves out, don't give them any reason to cluster in one direction. I'll take the eastern doors. Praxis, I'll need you central—try to provide whatever distance coverage you're able. We're not going to know which direction they'll strike from until it's too late, I'm afraid."

Kaedrich was moving the whole time that she was talking, barely glancing at the people around her as they scrambled to get into their assigned positions. Nobody questioned her authority. Even Brex swept the room, following her and easily fluttering to land where she pointed for him. Kaedrich strode the perimeter of the room like a general surveying the battlefield. She crossed briefly over to the windows, glancing out for herself, then circled around and checked all the doors in turn, looking back into the room to observe the incoming angle of approach from each of the doorways. By the time she'd finished telling people where to go she'd also finished with her inspection, and now she found herself back near where she'd started, standing beside Redly and Praxis.

Her attention settled on Redly first—or rather, the Beacon inhabiting him. She appraised him up and down. "I know that Lord Madgar has magic, and that you do in your natural state, too. I don't suppose that you'd be much use to us combined?"

The Beacon shook Redly's head. "His body knows how, but I lack the knowledge to properly control it."

"And your own magic?"

"Useless, until I release him."

Kaedrich nodded, as if she'd been expecting as much. "Fine. Marlick! Never mind what I said—come here. You and you," she said, pointing, "cluster some of those chairs together, for a barrier around Redly, and then get back to your posts. Marlick, you're in charge of his defense."

"You got it," Marlick said, already guiding the Beacon over to the fort of chairs being rapidly assembled.

"Kaedrich, *wait*," Praxis said. She grabbed Kaedrich by the elbow, turning her attention back. "Tell me what's wrong." She had not forgotten the terrible expression that had passed over Kaedrich's face, the resignation that had driven a stake of terror straight into Praxis's heart.

But Kaedrich shook her head. "Please don't argue with me right now. I doubt that we have much time before they show up, and I need you to trust me."

As if summoned by her words, a handful of shouts began to filter in through the doors of the junction—though due to the shape of the room, it was impossible to tell exactly which direction they were coming from. Maybe they were coming from all of them.

Praxis's throat closed up. "I do trust you."

Kaedrich gave her a sad smile. Her hand rested on Praxis's, still pinched around her elbow. She traced the lines of Praxis's fingers as if entranced by the sight of them. "I need to tell you something before this starts," Kaedrich said, her face softening even as running footsteps and more shouts filtered in from outside. "I . . . should have done it a long time ago, but—"

"Kaedrich!" Marlick shouted. He pointed to a door, which shuddered as it was struck from the outside.

That was all that it took. The gentleness in Kaedrich's face snapped off, so suddenly that Praxis could almost believe that it had never been there at all. She dropped Praxis's hand, pulling it off of her elbow as she stepped away. "Get into position," Kaedrich called over her shoulder to Praxis, even as she sprinted off to her own post by the eastern doors. They flew open just before she reached them, a flood of patrolmen and bodyguards in red coats pouring in through all of the doorways at once.

ONE OF KAEDRICH'S instructors liked to say that there was an *artistry* to fighting. He was in charge of hand-to-hand combat, an elderly Tjalavan that spoke so quietly that every one of his two dozen students would have to lean forward to make out his words at all. He would seat all of his students in a circle around him, and he would make them watch from every angle as he went through a long series of exercises: his hands flowing first past his chest, into a graceful arc above his head, twisting up as he raised a leg here, took a step there. His motions flowed as smoothly as water, each form morphing seamlessly from one to the next to the next. No one, at first, could figure out what these performance-art motions had to do with learning how to clock a man upside the head, and a handful of boys scoffed and left the room, declaring his lesson a waste of their time. Even Kaedrich, dutifully taking notes in a book resting upon her knees, did not see the connection.

The instructor continued on his movements, and another one of the students stood up, disgusted by the lesson plan—and this is when the instructor shifted almost infinitesimally, grabbed the lad by the elbow, and flipped him onto his back as smoothly as a fisherman slapping his catch upon the chopping block.

Everyone else in the room jumped to attention, spines rigid, eyes popping, but the instructor barely paid them any attention. "Without form," the instructor said, his foot lodged deeply against the student's throat so that the boy could not speak even if he wanted to, "none of you will ever get beyond the level of a drunken brawl."

The fight that broke out in the fine halls of the Council's Crescent now was as complicated as a dance, and no less elegant. Partners were spun and exchanged, moves played out in tandem. From above, coats flared like the blooming of dresses. Though none of the people involved knew it, their timing was almost precise enough to put to music. The crack of guns and the clash of swords played out as a steady percussive beat.

Kaedrich focused on the motions, because she dared not think beyond them. She threw herself into the fight, all of her training pouring through her, melting and forging into a single blade of determination. Any lingering questions that she had about the morality of killing another in combat had locked themselves down somewhere in the back of her head, because at the moment such considerations were a luxury that she did not have; hesitation was death, not just for herself, but for the rest of her companions. Right now, they did not need her for her kindness, they did not need her for her morality, they did not need her for her assurances and planning. They needed her for one purpose, and one purpose only: to fight.

So she fought. Their opponents had started shooting the minute they stormed in the doors, and from there, all sense of restraint had been severed. Kaedrich had lined up her shot, her trigger finger instinctively timing itself against the sweep of Praxis's magic; their opponents' bullets, peppering the air, went flying upward, and in the path that Praxis had opened up, Kaedrich's bullet sailed straight and true. Her shot struck its mark just a hair's breadth after the spray of bullets that Praxis had redirected lodged themselves into the walls and ceiling.

That was the first man that Kaedrich downed—wounded, but not yet dead—though it would not be the last. In the battle that followed, she did not keep count. She was aware only of the steady pounding of her own heart, the protection of the Beacon in Redly's fragile mortal body, the warm and stable presence of Praxis at her back.

The two of them operated as a single, seamless unit. Praxis's magic swept the room, as she threw discarded glass, as she formed enormous creatures of fire, as she brought a chandelier down upon the heads of the guardsmen; and Kaedrich's bullets or sword would follow in her wake. They did not need to tell each other where to target, when to strike. Kaedrich ducked, and Praxis threw a fireball over her head. Praxis flicked her hand, and Kaedrich dove toward the opening she was creating before it had even started to form. They came together, back to back; split apart; came together again. Always, they found each other in the chaos. Always, one would protect the other. Brex shrieked and dove, responding equally to either of their wishes.

The process took less than ten minutes, though each of those minutes may as well have contained an entire year. To Kaedrich, it felt as if she had always been there, as if the whole of her life had been spent in this single room, at this single task. She was born here; she would die here. For all of her life, her muscles worked unendingly. People fell all around her, one by one, but she did not, and Praxis did not, and Redly, housing the Beacon in his frail, mortal body, did not.

And then, as suddenly as it had begun, the battle ended.

A great hush settled over the room as the last of their opponents fell. Kaedrich whirled, not daring to believe it. Marlick stood tall atop the fort of chairs they'd built, though he hopped down now, and wiped the sweat from his forehead. Their small party seemed fine, but Kaedrich swept across the fallen bodies, both those of their enemies and two of the initiates that Marlick had brought, checking fervently for any signs of life. Weevish was also down, though he was breathing and showed no obvious sign of injury, and so Kaedrich held hopes that he would make a recovery in time. Which was great, but that wasn't what she was primarily concerned with at the moment. She peered out of the windows, shut each of the doors, lifted the edge of bodies with the toe of her shoe, trying to find whatever it was that she was missing.

Because she *was* missing something, she must be. There had to be another strike coming, or there had to be another guardsman rushing down the corridor, ready to throw himself into the fray. She ordered Marlick and the remaining initiate to try the hallways, to check for additional guards, and they sprang to action. So far, there was no sign of pursuit, but that had to be a trick. The battle could not be over, because Kaedrich was still alive.

That was how this ended, with her death. That was how it was always going to end.

Kaedrich stopped. She had made a complete loop of the room and come back to stand near Praxis, who was crouching as she made some hasty repair to her leg harness. Redly—the Beacon—had crawled out from his protective fort and was hovering idly nearby, regarding the spread of bodies as if it had never seen such a thing before.

They had won. They had protected the Beacon, defeated their enemies, and now all that was left was to wait for Marlick's return, proceed to the main chambers, do what they had set out to do from the beginning. Kaedrich should have been flooded with giddy, dizzying relief, and yet.

And yet.

The smell was exact. The flowers were not just *any* flowers, they were not just *similar* flowers. There were exactly the right number of them, to create exactly the right level of flower-to-gunpowder smell. As each shot was fired, as each of the three vases had fallen and released a fresh burst of perfume, they had been bringing the room closer and closer to perfect, and here it was, she was sure of it, only one shot away at most. Kaedrich was saturated in it, the smell that had stayed locked in her heart for almost three years. It flooded her, surrounded her, drowned her in its tangy embrace. This had to be the moment, and yet their enemies were dead and Kaedrich was not.

She did not dare believe that it was possible to be mistaken on this matter. She held no hope. Kaedrich had made her peace with this moment a long time ago, and on the contrary her skin was crawling now, her stomach writhing like a serpent. Where *was* it? Why wasn't it *here*? She paced in a tightly wound circle, a saber cat freshly snared and unused to captivity. If something didn't happen, and happen *soon*—

A whisper cut through the room. If her senses weren't perked for the slightest shift, Kaedrich might not have even noticed it. It was barely a sound, less than a tiptoed foot might make across carpet, but it was enough. The scrape of a weapon being lifted from marble. Kaedrich was moving, collecting a gun that someone had dropped somewhere, for her own was long since emptied. Her muscles reacted before her brain caught up with what was going on, and by the time she looked up she was already taking up her position, had already lined up the perfect shot. Someone was down but had not been killed, and they'd propped themselves upright on their fallen comrades, a pistol raised straight for Praxis's head.

Kaedrich did not flinch. She stepped between the two of them and fired.

* * *

IT WAS THE noise that made Praxis look up; the crack of a gun, so loud that it rattled her skull. One of the guards jerked to the side, a spray of blood haloing him as he collapsed in the heap of his own broken body. Everything had happened so fast—Kaedrich must have seen him and leaped into position without thought, a crack shot on barely a moment's notice. She stood protectively a few feet in front of Praxis, and as she lowered her gun, Praxis called out, "Nice shooting."

Kaedrich didn't say anything, but that was all right. Praxis was already turning her attention away when the first red drop splashed onto the marble tiles. It landed by Kaedrich's feet, so small that it shouldn't have even been noticed in a room as large and cluttered with blood and bodies as this was now, and yet Praxis couldn't stop staring at it. Time drew to a gradual halt, the rest of the world fading and falling away, until all that remained was the sight of that tiny drop: a splash of red against a sea of pure white. It disconnected itself from the world so expertly that at first Praxis was not even afraid, that was the thing, she was more confused than anything else. The word "blood" floated freely through her mind, bumping into her thoughts without actually connecting.

This is what would haunt Praxis later, that for a moment or two she sat and did nothing. Not that there was anything to be done, even then, but action would have made it easier to live with.

Another drop joined it, then a third. Time clicked back into place as Kaedrich's gun slid from her fingers. It struck the floor first, her knees following suit, as Praxis realized with a jolt that it wasn't a single, enormously loud gunshot that had caught her attention. It was two shots, simultaneously fired.

Chapter Thirty-Nine

INSTINCT FOUGHT AGAINST Kaedrich's better judgment as she tried to get herself *not* to look down at the wound clamped underneath her fingers. What difference did it make if she could see it, or what it looked like? The air was thick with the perfume of the exotic flowers twisting far overhead, and the lingering tang of gunpowder sat lodged in the depths of her nostrils. She knew what it meant—she'd known what it had meant the instant they'd stepped into the room. Once you've smelled the death creeping out of your own display, you did not forget it.

She let herself collapse; first to her knees, then falling back into a pair of arms that had rushed up behind her. She thought that she heard her own name, cried out in terror, but it was hard to say, the moment oddly quiet as a heavy silence blanketed her mind. The sloped ceiling spun overhead, the bright light of late afternoon putting on shadow plays across the white-and-gold molding of the walls.

It was funny: it did not hurt as much as she would have expected it to. Perhaps it was the peace of her acceptance, the fact that she was not trying to fight it, or perhaps it was just that death was already beginning to wrap its fingers around her, dulling her senses. Kaedrich's head rolled back, her eyes beginning to flutter shut.

"Oh, *no* you don't!" Praxis's voice, loud and sharp, cut through the haze, and Kaedrich snapped back to herself. "Hang on, Kaedrich—stay with me, come on."

Kaedrich blinked, and the world suddenly resolved back to itself. The distant scrape and shuffle of the world moving on around her, Brex's anxious cry, sweat and blood mingling in with her death-song smells, the prickle of dirt and debris clinging to her skin. A searing pain tearing through her gut as Praxis swore and prodded at the wound, her healing touch already trying to knit Kaedrich back together.

"Praxis," Kaedrich said, or at least she thought that she managed to say it. She was cradled against Praxis, being rocked softly but desperately back and forth, as a constant mutter of, "It's okay, it's okay, it's going to be okay," washed over her. And that was a soothing lie to hear, but it didn't make it true. Kaedrich knew it, even if Praxis didn't yet.

"It's okay, it's okay," Praxis muttered some more. Her fingers were constantly flexing, her whole face half-focused in the way that she always looked when she was working deep magic. It was nice, at least, that she would be here, that she would be the last thing that Kaedrich would see, even if Praxis's face was filled with panic. "It's okay, it's okay," always, again and again, and then abruptly the mantra stopped. Her whole face stopped. Her fingers stopped.

So this was it, then, the moment that Praxis realized that she'd fail. Kaedrich wondered, fleetingly, if the bullet had been treated to prevent healing magic. It seemed that it must have been, though Kaedrich supposed the reason didn't matter. She saw the realization hit Praxis, how all the air seemed to rush out of her at once. Her lips parted, her eyes flitted to Kaedrich's for a second before scurrying away, back toward the gaping wound that she couldn't fix.

"Praxis," Kaedrich said again, and this time she knew that she'd managed it, however faintly. She grabbed Praxis's hand, stopping her from trying when there was no point to try. "It's okay." Though hers was not spoken in reassurance, the promise that everything would be all right, and they both knew it. Kaedrich blinked again, darkness washing in and out like a tide.

Praxis shook her head. "No, it's not. I . . . I can't stop . . ." Her breathing was coming rapidly, and her blood-soaked hand slid from Kaedrich's and fluttered to clamp over her own mouth.

Full and proper pain seized Kaedrich, then, rushing up from somewhere deep inside of her. She clutched at Praxis, crying out, and with it came a burst of fury and regret, all of the repressed despair that *should* surround death. Knowing that it was coming hadn't made it any better— she was scared now, and angry at herself, and suddenly she was so alone, even with Praxis's arms wrapped tight around her shoulders. She had known what was coming—maybe not which day, maybe not exactly what time, but she had *known* it, seared to the core of her soul, and what good had that knowledge done her? She'd squandered the time that she'd had, hiding away from herself, never acting upon the deepest wish of her heart.

And then, in her head, a tiny voice rising from the thickening depths: *You're not dead yet.*

Kaedrich tried to take a deep breath. It caught in her chest, a fresh round of pain flaring from her ribs. She forced her eyes open, forced herself to look at Praxis. This was not even remotely the way that she wanted things, but it was the only chance she had. Finally, in the end, it would have to do. "It's not your fault I'm dying," she said, surprising herself, but maybe it had to start there.

"You are *not* dying," Praxis said, the force of her denial so strong that it seemed to pound into Kaedrich like a tidal wave.

"Praxis—"

"No, you listen to me," she said. She cupped Kaedrich's cheek, her slicked thumb leaving a trail of hot blood across Kaedrich's skin. "You are *not* dying," she repeated in a whisper. "I will not *let* you die, do you hear me?"

Kaedrich shook her off. Sentiment did neither of them any good at this point, no matter how ardently Praxis wanted to believe that. They were wasting time. Kaedrich could feel her mind slipping, her body shutting down piece by piece. "Just shut up," she mumbled, her words slurring together as her lips began to numb. "I have to . . ."

Did she have to? A sudden wave of doubt struck her: would it do Praxis any good, living with this final confession, or would it just make things worse? But then she looked at her. Praxis was just waiting, her breath held tight, her lower lip bit fast in her teeth, her eyes ringed a puffy red.

Had Kaedrich ever seen Praxis cry before?

There was no question, not anymore. But Kaedrich was already slipping, even as she tried to lift her arm and bring Praxis's head down over hers. She couldn't manage more than a whisper by this point, and she needed to make sure Praxis heard it, if she could get the words out at all. They swirled around in Kaedrich's mind, as tight and furious as a miniature squall. Everything else was falling away, piece by piece, the entire world crumbling down to nothing, but there was still this, there was always this: *I love you.* It was tiny and enormous all at once, and it was the only thing left as the last of her thoughts collapsed, as the last of her breath collapsed. She may or may not have managed to say it in the end, her body failing her, but she felt it all the same, *I love you, I love you, I love you,* as the world slipped out from underneath her.

KAEDRICH'S BREATH CLUNG to Praxis's ear, settling with a gentle sigh. Praxis squeezed her eyes shut. The hot track of a tear cut down her cheek as she shuddered to take a breath. "Kaedrich, I . . ."

But Kaedrich was utterly still. Not a single flutter of pulse from her neck, nor a single rise from her chest. Her face was slack, her lips slightly parted. Her eyes fixed on nothing. An unmistakable, flat peace had settled across her, some intangible spark lost to the winds.

Praxis stared. A thick blanket of denial had rushed in to swaddle her mind, and so on some level the figure still draped in her arms was not Kaedrich, of course it wasn't. It couldn't be, because this person was dead; Kaedrich did not die. Something soothing in her head, not so much a voice as a feeling, was telling her not to believe it. And yet, at the same time, Praxis felt a split run down inside of herself, a second self crowding in, this one with a clear and singular voice: *Kaedrich is dead.*

Kaedrich is dead.

Kaedrich is dead.

"No," Praxis said, more as a way to shut up the ringing sound in her mind than because she had anyone to tell it to. Kaedrich is dead. "No." Kaedrich is dead. "No." Kaedrich is—

"No!"

She started screaming next, because there were no words to capture the grief that tore through her at that moment. It might have started as another "no," but it morphed into a nameless, ageless howl, deep and primal. The sky overhead turned instantly black, and a wave burst out from her, pummeling the room at large. The walls and floors trembled, cracks splintering out from where she sat, glass raining down from the curved skylights, and Praxis's scream continued to ring through the entire Crescent. It chilled the spine of everyone that heard it, and then it broke out through the walls of the building, sweeping across the center of Monfort like a rolling storm. It rang on and on, far beyond the length of mere lung capacity, and when it did finally come to a gasping halt, eons later, an otherworldly silence continued to ring out in its wake.

Praxis collapsed over Kaedrich's body. Her arms were still clamped tight around Kaedrich's shoulders, and she buried her face in the crook of Kaedrich's neck, breathing in sweat and gunpowder, chesterwood soap, the fragrant perfume of the flowers that had fallen to the floor underneath the pounding of Praxis's despair. She was ready to stay there forever, curled in place around Kaedrich, for even the idea of getting up, of letting go of her hold, was beyond the realm of consideration. It didn't matter what came next: she would stay here, with Kaedrich, and let the world go on around her, the two of them slowly turning into a statue, a monument to their loss. The building could collapse around them, the country could fall to ruin, the world itself could implode underneath some apocalyptic disaster, and Praxis would always be there, holding Kaedrich.

So when a hand settled itself firmly on her shoulder, words bouncing off of her—they might have been something like "we have to go"—she went to throw it off with such force that the person making the gesture should have been sent careening across the room.

He was not. His hand remained fixedly in place, an anchor lashed to her body. And only now did Praxis consent to release her grip somewhat, if only to tear around and see who dared to disturb her eternal resting place. She was ready to kill whoever it was, her eyes burning with a thousand hatreds, but when she turned around she found herself facing Redly.

Or, no.

Not Redly.

The Beacon. *Her* Beacon.

Praxis's eyes widened.

"We have to go," the Beacon said through Redly, even as Praxis scrambled to her feet. "I'm sorry, but there's nothing we can—"

"Bring him back," Praxis said. She was clawing at Redly's shirt, his suit jacket, the neat little knot of his cravat. Her fingers danced as madly as her eyes. "You can do it, you can fix this. You can bring him back to me." She could hear the manic cracking in her own voice, but it did not matter—a grin began to split across her face. "Do it, do it. Quickly, now," she said. She dragged him down, the Beacon in Redly's body, dragging him until they were both huddled over the fallen form of Kaedrich. What used to be Kaedrich, and what would be again. She wrenched Redly's hands forward, resting them across Kaedrich's forehead; she wasn't sure if that was what was needed at all, but it didn't matter. It felt fine. It would be fine.

Kaedrich would be fine.

The Beacon looked at her, out of Redly's eyes. His face was soft, and somehow impossibly sad. It drew Redly's hands back, slithering out from underneath Praxis's grip. "My Lady, I'm sorry," he said. Praxis was already shaking her head, but the Beacon touched Redly's hand to his own forehead. "I can feel it. Kaedrich is already here. There is nothing that I can do to release him."

Praxis reared back. "Don't tell me that," she said. As if somehow it was that simple, as if the Beacon was merely a disobedient child. "Don't tell me that! You're the Beacon of Souls—what is the *point* of you if you cannot do what needs to be done?!"

"My Lady," the Beacon said, raising Redly to his feet, "There are limits. I'm sorry that you do not like them, but what you are asking is beyond the bounds of my oath."

"Your *oath*," Praxis said, spitting the word out in a twisted sneer. She vaulted up, so fast that she nearly wrenched the gears along her leg out of place. She grabbed the front of Redly's shirt and yanked him toward her, close enough that her rage was the only thing that he could see. A crackle of lightning broke overhead, as loud as a gunshot, but even that did not mask the sound of her voice. When she spoke next, it was as if a hundred voices were pounding against him at once. "*Your oath is to me!* If I order you to break it—"

"Then you will no longer be our Lady!" the Beacon snapped, and silence cut the room. "You know that. *Those* are the terms that the old god laid out. *Those* are the terms that bind us to this place, that bind us to each other."

"But you *can* do it."

As soon as Praxis said it, she knew that it was true. No mortal magic had the power to reverse death, true, but the Beacon was not mortal. What had Tully said once, all of those years ago? Death is a force of nature? That may be true, but it turns out that it was also a living, sentient being, with a mind and a will all of its own, with full command of its powers. The Beacon *was* death, personified—and it answered to one voice.

Her voice.

No matter what else it was capable of, it could not disobey her direct command.

The Beacon clenched Redly's jaw, tighter and tighter, his teeth grinding together so hard that it's a wonder they did not crack. "Additional guards are already coming," he said instead, "We need to move quickly. If you have any hope left of stopping Lanali—"

"We can do that, *after* you've brought Kaedrich back."

Redly's eyes narrowed. "Oh? You think so?" He shook his head. "The kind of power that you're asking of me can only be achieved from my own realm. I would need to abandon this mortal shell in order to do it."

"Then go—"

"And *only* the Lady of Souls could summon me back again."

Praxis took a step back. She still had a hold on Redly's shirtfront, but at arm's length now, and he looked suddenly more like Redly than the Beacon. So small, so . . . mortal. The Beacon was staring at her through Redly's eyes, and somewhere buried down there she could feel Redly staring at her as well. "The Lady of Souls," Praxis repeated. She didn't know why she said it, because it's not like she needed confirmation. She understood the Beacon perfectly the first time. The Lady of Souls, a title that she would renounce claim to the instant she ordered the Beacon to retreat and perform this act.

She could not look at it anymore, the Beacon or Redly, both of them watching her through the exact same mix of pity and sympathy. They knew that it was not a choice, that this was too important to simply walk away from, that if they did nothing they may well never get another chance to stop Lanali. She would gain her power, seize control of Durland, and with it? One could not imagine, but the very idea was enough to send deep shudders down anyone's spine. The two of them knew it, and you could tell that their hearts (if the Beacon was indeed even capable of having one) were breaking for her underneath the weight of it.

They knew that she was going to have to walk away.

"No," Praxis said, but her voice had gone faint, more a child's protest than a declaration of fact. She shook her head, as if that would help. Praxis dropped her grip, moving numbly over to Kaedrich's body. She knelt down beside her, the sole focus of Praxis's attentions. Kaedrich's blank eyes were still open, staring up at nothing. Everything about her was muted and flat now, all the life and vibrancy sucked down into the depths of the domain of the Beacon of Souls. Praxis closed her eyes, and she could see the display as perfectly as if she was actually there: Kaedrich in a copy of Praxis's own arms, the two of them huddled so close that finally they may as well have been one. The display would preserve that moment forever, unchanging, never aging or withering, never dimming.

And Praxis saw, without even meaning to, the way that time would spin on. How she would shuffle through her life, the Lady of Souls, retreating to her realm more and more often, planting herself as an almost permanent statue in front of this display, ignoring her duties, ignoring her life.

When she opened her eyes, Kaedrich was still dead. Praxis ran her hand across Kaedrich's forehead, and leaned over to plant a kiss on the smooth expanse of skin. As her lips hit their mark, Kaedrich's final words came rushing back to her: *I love you.* Praxis breathed in the smell of Kaedrich, the soap and the sweat both. *I love you.* It was the only thing that she'd wanted to hear, for years now, the only thing that she cared about. They had done so much for each other, sacrificed so much, all building up for this, only to have it snatched away right at the beginning. And as Praxis sat back, brushing Kaedrich's eyes shut, she knew that Redly and the Beacon were right: there was no choice here.

But they were wrong about what the answer was.

Praxis pushed herself to her feet. The heat trapped in the scar on her wrist reversed and flared cold, a thousand tiny icicles of pain stabbing like needles as a warning into her veins. Praxis gritted her teeth; she would not listen, not this time. Perhaps it was true, perhaps she did not deserve to wield this kind of power—it did not matter. She *had* it. It hummed around her, warm as a fever.

Sometime during all of this, the Beacon had moved off as if to give her a moment of privacy, and now it stood idly fidgeting with the cuff of Redly's sleeve. Praxis took her time as she walked over, stepping around the bits of broken glass and used bullets that littered the floor. She stopped directly in front of him, her face still and deathly serious. The Beacon glanced up, Redly's eyebrow raised.

"Bring him back."

The Beacon bristled. "My Lady, I would beg you to reconsider. If you order me—"

"I know. Bring him back anyway."

"I don't think you really mean that," the Beacon said. "Not with what's at stake."

"I really do."

"Are you so sure of that? Tell us, my Lady, what would Kaedrich think of—"

"Kaedrich is dead!" Praxis shouted. Her voice cracked at the end, but not before the force of her declaration had struck the Beacon with a fury of a tightly wound storm. Redly's body flipped through the air, landing half a dozen feet away. Praxis took a deep, stabilizing breath as the Beacon struggled to push Redly's body upright.

"Kaedrich is dead," Praxis repeated, more calmly this time. She began to stride toward the Beacon, the air crackling around her. "I will not let that stand, do you hear me? So I am only going to say this once."

The Beacon glared up at her, through Redly's face, already knowing what was to come next. It had managed to drag itself to Redly's knees, but it stopped when Praxis finally reached it. It knelt before its Lady, its head already bowed in resentful supplication.

Praxis leaned over and tipped its chin up, to make sure that it was looking her directly in the eyes. She straightened up, her back ramrod straight, shoulders held firm. Her eyes could cut ice—not even her mother had ever looked so commanding. Her hold on the Beacon was like the taste of blood in the air. "My name is Praxis Adello Fellows," she said, her voice ringing out through the chamber and *daring* anyone to defy it. "Lady of Souls and Watcher over the realm of the dead, and by the power of the *gods* that created you, you will obey me. Bring Kaedrich back." Praxis's lip curled up at the corner. "Now."

The Beacon flinched.

Darkness welled up out of nowhere, cloaking the walls, blotting out the skylight, sweeping across the floor. It poured in thick, pressing closer and closer around them, thicker than a black haze hex, the air stale and cold as it poured down Praxis's lungs. The shadows from the halls of the dead swarmed. They cloaked Kaedrich's fallen form. They squeezed a tight circle around the room, compressing and piling together, until the only things left visible were Praxis herself and the Beacon in Redly's form, glowering at each other.

The Beacon nodded Redly's head, just once, as it drew itself up. "As you say, my *Lady*, so shall it be," it said, through Redly's gritted teeth. "And on your own head be it."

The Beacon raised its arm—its own arm this time, somehow, the darkness welling up and forming a separate body for itself in the middle of Redly. Redly himself collapsed, the darkness swallowing him whole, the entire room plunging into a swirling mass of shadows.

A hurricane of wind rushed in, pouring through the destroyed glass of the open skylight. Praxis couldn't see a single thing as she shuffled her way through the midnight storm, but she didn't need to see to know exactly where she was going. She would always be able to find Kaedrich. Even if the gods themselves crept back into the world, and flipped it upside down, and made the day night, and the night day, Praxis would be able to find Kaedrich. Wind buffeted her in every direction, tearing at her clothes and hair, but nothing would stop her. She marched straight to Kaedrich, and just as she reached her the wind disappeared, as quickly as it had come. Darkness swept from the room, oppressive afternoon sunlight suddenly taking its place.

Kaedrich gasped in a lungful of air.

Her eyes fluttered for just a second, as Praxis rushed down and gathered her head into her arms. "Kaedrich?"

Kaedrich gave a heavy sigh, a smile playing at the edges of her mouth. She did not say anything as she slipped into a deep sleep in the crook of Praxis's arm.

But that was fine—she was *alive*, whole and gloriously, impossibly *alive*! Her pulse fluttered softly in her neck, her breath expanding and collapsing in her chest. Nothing else mattered now. Praxis ran her hands across Kaedrich's wound, the skin already healed so cleanly that it was as if nothing had ever happened. She grinned, watching Kaedrich sleep, feeling so overwhelmed that she wanted to throw her head back and laugh. Kaedrich had never looked more beautiful, curled against Praxis, a life as new and precious as a babe. Kaedrich. Her Kaedrich. *Alive.*

She could have sat there, cradling this new life forever, but that was not to be. A searing pain struck Praxis's shoulder, jerking her to the side. Kaedrich slid from her arms, and Praxis scrambled to block her protectively from whatever might be happening.

"You filthy, stinking hypocrite!"

Redly, back under his own control, was staggering to his feet—or trying to at any rate. His foot slipped out from under him, but not before he had managed to throw another burst of flame in Praxis's direction.

Praxis threw her own flame, both of the shots smothering each other where they struck. "I'm sorry!" It was unclear, even to her, exactly how much she meant this, considering that she wasn't sorry for what she'd *done*, in the end.

"Don't waste your breath," Redly said. He threw another burst of flame, easily countered. Redly was still trying to get to his feet, though it seemed his feet had other ideas. The process of the Beacon leaving him, Praxis knew, would result in weakness and a sense of muscle confusion, and he was never supposed to be facing that in the harsh unfamiliarity of a room in the Crescent. There was a bed already made up back at Calswell House, where she'd planned for his recovery.

Nothing, it seems, was going the way that they'd wanted it to.

Praxis stood up. "Redly, please listen to me." She approached him cautiously, one hand full of fire, just in case. "I didn't mean to—I couldn't just—"

She ducked, avoiding another spray of flames. "You think that I don't understand?" Redly said. His voice began to crack as a laugh escaped his chest. "You think that I wouldn't have done exactly the same thing? I don't care that you saved your beloved, Praxis—I care that you *didn't let me save mine!*"

With that, he threw himself upright, lunging for Praxis. She twisted, trying to get out of the way, but not in time. Redly collided with her side, the one controlling her leg, and they went down in a graceless tumble. Praxis snapped her opposite palm shut, dousing her flames, as Redly scrambled up and off of her.

He grabbed a sword from where it lay in the middle of the rubble, and Praxis braced herself for the idea of dodging a swing—but he wasn't headed for her.

Instead, Redly made a mad run for Kaedrich.

It was clear from his motions that he didn't have the slightest idea of how to *use* a sword, and that was assuming that his limbs would cooperate and do what he told them to do. But even a randomly flailing weapon had the potential to steal away everything that Praxis had worked so hard to save, and there was simply no power in the world that would allow her to let that happen again.

Praxis managed to push herself to a sitting position as she threw a rope of flame at Redly's back. It struck him square and true, wrapping deftly around his chest. He cried out, knowing what was going to happen next, and so he took his only recourse: he threw the sword, trying desperately to get it across the last remaining distance between himself and Kaedrich's slumbering form.

But Praxis had already jerked him away, using the fat rope of flames as a lasso. The sword fell rather pitifully out of his grip as he was yanked aside. Praxis pulled the flames back, releasing him as he sailed effortlessly across the room and crashed into a painting on the opposite wall.

Redly groaned as he hit the floor. The painting fell on top of him, but he was too weakened by this point to even bother throwing it off. Blood ran down the side of his face, another trail pooling from his nose onto the polished marble floor. He grimaced, turning his head just in time to see Praxis's approach. She had no flames ready, nothing but pity splashed across her face.

He still had enough strength left to summon another burst of flame, but she dodged that as easily as they both expected her to. "Don't think that I won't stop trying to kill you," Redly snarled as Praxis drew nearer.

"Don't make *me* kill *you*," she countered. "Redly, we've been through too much for this."

"*I don't care!* I swear, Praxis, with the gods as my witness, I will never stop trying to destroy you for this. Do you hear me? *Never.*"

Praxis took a deep breath. "Fine," she said. She bent down, only enough to drag Redly up by the scruff of his shirt collar. She slammed him against the wall, the same spot where the painting had been. Redly was already fading in and out of consciousness, though no doubt he would recover from his injuries, given time. Praxis could already hear the sound of approaching footsteps, shouts and orders as a pile of guards began to approach the sealed doors. She didn't have time to waste. "Redly, I know that you will never believe me, but I am sorry," she said. "For . . . what I did to you, and what I'm about to do, both."

Redly sneered. "Just do it."

Praxis nodded. And then she punched him in the face.

The weight of her arm, the bone of silver, made contact with a sickening thud. Redly's head whipped to the side, striking the wall. She did not think that the blow would prove fatal to him (or at least, she hoped it wouldn't), but it did serve to knock him out cold.

She dropped him where he stood. Redly collapsed in a heap of disgrace, his once-fine clothes tattered and bloodstained. There was a steady pounding at the door now, a fresh contingent of guards attempting to bust their way through, and Praxis hurried back over to where Kaedrich lay. Gathering her up took some effort, and in the end she had to content herself with throwing Kaedrich's sleeping form over her shoulder like some damsel in distress.

But looks didn't matter, because no one was going to see them.

Praxis went to the wall of windows, the glass long since shattered. Abbney Bay sparkled far below, warm and inviting, dotted with ships. It took her a second to arrange Kaedrich, a bubble of sealed air fitted over her nose and mouth. Another minute to get herself over the lip of the windowsill, Kaedrich still slung over her shoulder. The doors were cracking now, long splits breaking down the wood paneling.

Praxis did not bother to wait around.

By the time the guards burst in a moment later, there was no one left to attack.

AT THREE O'CLOCK EXACTLY, the clock tower in the heart of the Council's Crescent began to toll out its melancholy song. At three oh-one, the session was called to order. Every seat was taken, every space between them filled with bodies. All of Monfort's landowners, commoners and lords alike, piled in elbow to elbow and hip to hip, each vying for attention, each with a voice shouting to be heard. It took until nearly three twenty to settle everyone down enough for business to commence. By a quarter after four, the Crown was revoked, the Council was dissolved, and a temporary government elected to oversee a fair transition—to what end, no one quite knew yet. At four thirty, a vote was held for the person that would be chosen to oversee this peaceful transition. It hadn't even formally begun when red handkerchiefs began popping up all throughout the packed hall. More than three-quarters of the assembled citizens, spilling out into the surrounding corridors, spilling out into the surrounding courtyard, spilling out along the streets branching from the great Crescent. It didn't matter that only a small fraction of them were eligible to vote, technically, although who was to decide at that point what "technically" counted for, anymore?

The people had spoken.

And at five o'clock on the dot, a set of doors opened up on a small balcony. The balcony overlooked the courtyard, the heart of the Crescent, the great walls of the stoic building cradling the assembled populace as a loving embrace. Two guards flanked the sides of the balcony, one much shorter than the other, but nobody was here to see them. A figure clad all in black stepped out through the doors, and a riotous spread of applause and cheers swept the courtyard, the streets. It felt as if the whole of Monfort was whooping and crying out as one, as Lanali looked out over the people.

Her people.

She raised her hand, demure and reserved, as the crowd began to chant out as one: "The Pon! The Pon! The Pon!"

Behind her veil, Lanali smiled. For once in her long and twisted life, there was nothing false or practiced about it.

IT WAS NEARLY two in the morning by the time a carriage pulled up in front of Brindlewood Hall.

One figure emerged, circling around and frantically speaking to the driver, throwing a pile of money into his lap. Bone-white hair caught the moonlight as the woman made a mad scramble up to the front door of the great house.

There was no time to make proper arrangements. Kaedrich still lay unconscious in the back of the carriage, and Praxis had no doubt that they were already being pursued. She met Mr. Vandervoon in the foyer— he hadn't been sleeping, how could he, ever since he'd heard?—but Praxis could not waste more of their time with a detailed explanation. She handed over a domed cage, Brex squawking indignantly as Quaith accepted it. "I . . . Won't you need him?" he asked, but Praxis shook her head firmly.

"He won't be able to manage, where I'm going. It's better for him if you look after him. Please."

"Of course," Quaith said. He hugged the cage closer to his chest, the enormity of the trust that Praxis was placing in him almost knocking him off of his feet. "Where . . . where are you going to . . . ?"

"It's safer for you if you don't know," Praxis said. She was already moving for the door. "I didn't even want to come here—I'm sorry for the danger I've put you in, but I needed someone to look after Brex."

"It's all right," Quaith said. "We'll keep him safe. I promise."

Praxis shut her eyes, her gratitude and relief pouring off of her in an uncharacteristic display of emotion. "Thank you."

"There is . . . ," Quaith started, but Praxis was hovering on the front steps now, waiting. "I'm sorry, I won't keep you, but I just . . . is Kaedrich with you? Did he make it out all right?"

The corner of Praxis's mouth ticked up. "He did. He is. We'll be fine."

"That's good," Quaith said. He let out a sigh that he didn't even realize that he'd been holding. "Well. Good luck. To both of you."

Praxis nodded. And then she turned, rushing down the front steps and back to the waiting carriage.

Chapter Forty

𝒢RESH AIR FILLED Kaedrich's lungs. Warm with the promise of another impending summer, full of hope, and tinged with salt.

She opened her eyes.

She was in a . . . bedroom? Cabin? Hotel room? It was hard to tell, especially because she did not remember coming in here, nor laying down on the bed that she found herself in the middle of. She blinked, her head swimming, trying to get a sense of her bearings.

Wherever it was, it was comfortable. Cheerful yellow paint lined the walls, and a single window across the way was propped up a crack, the fresh air drifting in, bringing the smell of the sea. Nothing but blue lay beyond the glass. Her bed was dressed with crisp white sheets and a soft yellow blanket. There was a small dresser, with a mirror bolted to the wall above it, and a nightstand with a basin of water.

And a single chair, with Praxis slumped over in an uncomfortable-looking sleep. The chair was right beside the bed, wedged as close as it would go. Praxis's foot, the one with the harness, was plopped up onto the bed, her shoe mashing up against Kaedrich's pillow. Her old slate-blue coat, battered as ever, lay folded up over Kaedrich's feet.

Kaedrich held her breath, watching. She dared not disturb what looked like a deep, long-overdue sleep, but not even five seconds later, Praxis shifted. Her eyes blinked open, once, twice, settling directly on Kaedrich. She smiled, sleepy and content. "Kaedrich. You're finally awake."

"Looks that way," Kaedrich said. "I, um . . . how long?"

"About two days."

Kaedrich's eyes widened. "Two . . . ?"

"You'll be fine," Praxis said. She sat up, easing her foot off of the bed. Praxis pulled the basin off of the nightstand and into her lap, soaking a cloth full of water and wringing it out. She put the basin back, and had shifted to sit on the edge of the bed before Kaedrich had even realized it.

"Where are we? What happened?"

Praxis pressed the cloth against Kaedrich's face, the cool dampness calming her nerves only a little. "We're on a ship, the *Relentless*," Praxis said. "It'll take us to the tip of Tjalava, and then we'll book passage aboard a cargo vessel the rest of the way."

Kaedrich frowned. "The rest of the way where?"

"Yandosia."

"*What?*"

"Easy," Praxis said. She nudged Kaedrich back against the pillows, which Kaedrich had hastily sat up from. "Easy. I promise, I'll explain everything. But you have to believe me when I say that it wasn't safe for us to stay in Monfort."

Kaedrich slumped back, her head bonking against the headboard. "Oh gods. The Crescent. We failed, didn't we?"

Praxis was oddly silent, twisting the edge of the cloth around her finger, over and over again. "We didn't *fail*," she said. "We just . . . There wasn't enough time. It didn't work."

Kaedrich squeezed her eyes shut. A wave of guilt rolled over her, twisting up her stomach. "It's my fault, isn't it? If I hadn't fallen . . ." She couldn't remember much, the whole day blurring into a single ribbon of dream-like sounds and images, but she could remember that much, at least. It came to her suddenly, along with the guilt. "If I hadn't fallen, we would have had time to make it. Wouldn't we?"

"**No**," Praxis said, so firmly that it startled Kaedrich into opening her eyes. Praxis reached over and brushed the damp cloth across Kaedrich's clammy forehead. "You are *not* to blame for this, do you understand me? The meeting had already started—it was too late. Lanali knew that we were coming, and she made sure to get the support that she needed before we got there. There was *nothing* that we could have done, Kaedrich. The plan had failed before we'd even begun."

Kaedrich tried to nod, to take some measure of comfort from this. She had to believe Praxis, because she certainly couldn't remember how things had all gone down. Her memories of the day were so disjointed, it was impossible to sort them out. She remembered fighting, she remembered a sense of . . . fate? Like she had always been meant to be there, like there was no escaping. She remembered being shot, and a smell . . .

Gunpowder. Flowers and gunpowder.

She should be dead.

She looked over at Praxis. Unless . . . was it possible that Kaedrich had been wrong? That she hadn't been facing her death, after all? That there was another day, somewhere else, with the same smells waiting for her?

There had to be. Because the magic that she'd bargained with was perfectly clear, when she'd struck her deal: there would be no escaping it.

Relief flooded through Kaedrich, so strong that she started to cry.

"Hey," Praxis said, smudging the tears off of Kaedrich's cheek. "What's wrong?"

Kaedrich shook her head. "I thought I was going to die."

"Ah." Praxis sat back, gathering up one of Kaedrich's hands in her own. "Now, see, I promised you that wasn't going to happen."

"Did you?"

Praxis raised an eyebrow. "You don't remember?"

"No . . . ," Kaedrich said, her voice trailing off. She swiped at her damp face, trying to calm herself. "I don't remember much, after . . . after I was hit."

"Oh." Praxis licked her lips, her eyes darting to the side. "Well . . . that's understandable. You just rest. Don't worry about it." She reached over and smoothed her hand against Kaedrich's forehead, her fingers almost as cool as the cloth that she'd set down by the basin.

Kaedrich dutifully let herself settle back against the pillows. She knew that she should probably rest and regain her strength, that much was true, although there was something nagging at her. Still, she closed her eyes, breathed evenly in and out. Praxis continued to sit on the edge of her bed, Kaedrich's hand held fast in hers. Her thumb ran steadily over the back of Kaedrich's hand, back and forth, and Kaedrich tried to remember. She remembered falling. She remembered Praxis, desperately trying to hold on. She remembered . . .

Oh gods.

Kaedrich sat up, her eyes suddenly wide and wild. She pulled herself back from Praxis, sliding up until she bumped straight into the headboard. "Praxis! I . . . you, I . . . you have to forget about what I, what I said . . . when I was . . . when I . . ."

Praxis folded her hands in her lap. "When you said that you loved me?"

"Oh gods," Kaedrich said, burying her face in her hands. "I'm sorry, I didn't, I"—she laughed nervously, as if somehow she could brush it all off—"I thought I was going to die, I didn't—"

"Are you trying to tell me that you didn't mean it?"

"I . . ." Kaedrich drew her hands down, looking anxiously across at Praxis. She was just sitting there, expression blank, watching Kaedrich closely. Kaedrich's face flooded with heat as she ducked her head. She could not openly deny it, not right to Praxis's face, no matter how much a part of her might want to. "No," she mumbled, "I . . . I meant it." She looked back up. "But I know that it can't—I mean, I'm obviously not expecting you to—!"

"Kaedrich, I—"

"And I understand, you know, that you're not—I'm not trying to get—"

"Kaedrich—!"

"And I would never want to do anything to ruin our friendship, so I think it would be best if we just forgot that I ever—"

"*Kaedriella!*"

Kaedrich took a deep, gasping breath, stuttering to a halt. *"What?"*

"I . . . ," Praxis started, and then it was her turn to fall short. She shook her head, instead. "Oh, shut up," she said, as she leaned over and drew Kaedrich's lips to hers.

The kiss was so far outside of what Kaedrich expected to happen that she couldn't move, couldn't think, couldn't even quite operate her lips enough to kiss back. Her eyes sprang open and she forced them shut. It was—but Praxis was—but they had—but this! Oh, this.

This held no secrets, no hidden meanings draped over it to hide the truth. *Here's the truth.* She should have believed it the first time. Praxis's lips were soft as a dream as she shifted, coaxing, and again, honest and pure, until Kaedrich found her mouth responding out of instinct. And then it didn't feel so much like a dream, as they broke apart and came together again, a joint force this time. Then it was just this: the two of them, together and somehow *right*, the promise of a new beginning blooming all around them.

"I love you, too," Praxis whispered, her kisses trailing down the length of Kaedrich's throat.

And then neither of them spoke much for a very long time.

* * *

HOURS LATER, PRAXIS stood along the rail of the *Relentless*, staring out at the choppy seas. The top button of her blouse was undone, her coat hanging open and flapping like a flag at port. Her tousled hair was buffeted by the sea breeze, the familiar whip of the wind that accompanied a ship setting out across the oceans. The smell of Kaedrich lingered around her like a heady perfume as she stared down at the object in her hand.

It was the pendant of the Beacon of Souls. Heavy and old, the glass orb at the heart of it still swirled with a misty black, a single point of light glinting out from its depths. By all accounts, it looked exactly the same as it had before she'd struck her bargain, except that now it no longer responded to her wishes.

She'd tried, a couple of times, in the tense day that she'd spent after getting herself and Kaedrich safely stowed aboard the *Relentless*. She'd laid down, closed her eyes, attempted to settle into the depths of the Beacon's realm with the same ritual she'd used a hundred times. Nothing had happened.

It wasn't that she had expected a different outcome, of course. She knew what would happen the instant she'd ordered the Beacon to break the bounds of its oath, and she was not going to cry over the results. She had Kaedrich back—wholly and completely, beautiful and vibrant and alive. Praxis had only tried the ritual at all because she'd needed to be absolutely sure, before . . .

The railing was cold underneath her grip. Painted metal, slick with the mist kicked up from the sea. Praxis leaned over the rail, stretching her arm out as far as it would go. Her fingers uncurled one by one. She watched with a surprising detachment as the Beacon's pendant slid from her palm and disappeared into the waves below.

And then she stood back, breathing in the salt air. There was a delightful edge to it, a chill that helped to cool her skin. She watched the empty stretch of sea, the water and sky nearly identical in color as twilight muted the beauty of both. Praxis had never really expected to be heading this far out into the ocean again, had never really considered the prospect of returning to the ice after all of these years. But if that was the safest place that she could think of to bring Kaedrich, then that was where they would go.

"There you are."

Praxis turned, smiling, at the sound of the voice. Already, the Beacon was receding from her mind. Such a little thing, so easily forgotten when compared to all that she had gained. She reached her hand out to Kaedrich. "I was just thinking about you."

Kaedrich hesitated, accepting Praxis's hand only after a moment's consideration. She had been asleep when Praxis left, the cabin littered with sheets and empty plates. They'd both been starving, in two distinct ways, and had spent all day alternating between satiating both of their needs.

Now Kaedrich was up again, cleaned and fully dressed; her suit was neat and perfect, the knot of her tie expertly done. Kaedrich let Praxis intertwine their fingers. She stared at the folded interplay of the two of them, tangled up together. "I didn't know where you went," Kaedrich said. "I thought, maybe . . . that is, I worried that you might have regretted—"

Praxis drew herself to Kaedrich as if in a dance, locking their lips together in a kiss that sent her reeling. Kaedrich stumbled back, twisting her head away even as she fought against a grin. "Gods, Praxis. People are going to stare."

"Then let them stare," Praxis said. She wound her hands around Kaedrich's waist, hugging the two of them together at the hips. "I'm done hiding from the only thing that matters to me. And I regret *nothing*," she continued, leveling her eyes at Kaedrich, *her* Kaedrich, the Kaedrich that she almost didn't have anymore, "and I mean absolutely *nothing* that I have done lately." She grinned. "Except, perhaps, that I didn't do this sooner. Does that satisfy you?"

Kaedrich bit back a smile. "It'll have to do, I suppose," she said, pertly kissing the tip of Praxis's nose. "Though I might require additional assurances later—later!" she shouted, shoving Praxis off. "Gods. You're horrible!"

Praxis's grin had never once left her face. "You have no idea," she said. But she turned back to the sea, keeping Kaedrich's arms wrapped around her from behind. Kaedrich rested her chin on Praxis's shoulder, the two of them staring out into the open water. The last light of day was slipping into nothing, stars beginning to peek out overhead, and they just stood there like that, for a long time, watching it all go by. Waiting, together, to see what was going to happen next.

MEANWHILE, THE PENDANT of the Beacon of Souls sank farther into the depths of the Violet Seas. It had swirled near the top for a while when it had first struck, in the tumultuous eddies of the ship's wake. Tossed about, the chain getting tangled and then freeing itself again over and over in one glorious dance. After that, for a while, the pendant sank straight down, unfettered by ceremony. Several hundred feet below, it caught another eddy, and then it was knocked out of *that* by the churning flurry of a passing school of fish. It slid between their bodies, the fish wholly unaware of the power that it wielded, of the fact that they, too, had a place reserved for them in the museum of the dead.

The pendant sank. Deeper into darkness. It grew colder with the depths, but that didn't matter to the Beacon. Nothing in the mortal world could affect the pendant, not heat nor cold, wind nor rain nor the salt of the oceans. Even if it was found, even if someone tried to break it or forge new links, even if someone wore it against their skin every day for the rest of their life—nothing would affect it, nothing except for a wizard, a pinch of luck, the proper slice of magic. So it had been a safe move, casting it into the depths like that, because no wizard lived underneath the ocean. There was no magic that would let a human survive these depths, nothing to give them gills, nothing to protect them against the pressures that grew against the curve of the pendant's orb.

And so, eventually, the pendant struck the ocean floor. A puff of silty seabed bloomed around it, clouding the dark water. The chain settled as a graceful afterthought, nestling artfully beside the faint glow of the swirling orb.

A crab scuttled by. Twisted and unrecognizable to anyone that dwelt on land, it prodded the sea floor with its narrow pincers. Dead and decaying flesh would often litter the soft sand, falling from the waters above. Occasionally even an entire fish corpse landed in its territory, though it had been days since it had found one of those; still, it searched, always waiting, always looking. The crab scuttled closer, probing deep into the seabed. A flicker of something that came close to curiosity passed through the crab, as its pincer clanked against the solid glass of the pendant. It tapped against it, testing the size and shape, scraping its pincer over the surface. But this was not food, and so the crab began to move away, to new territory.

Abruptly, the crab found itself flipping end over end, tumbling through the water as if a large predator had swiped at it. Its legs flailed madly. At one point, facing just so, it was almost blinded by a flash of light coming from the strange new object, the thing that wasn't food. A fresh ripple shot through the water, sending the crab spinning a little bit farther.

That was all that the crab had to do with the pendant after that, settling back on the ocean floor a moment later, scurrying away so fast that it kicked up trails of silt behind it. But the pendant itself, in the deepest depths, continued to pound at the waters that surrounded it, flashing and flaring. Silently screaming into the empty sea.

THE SOUND OF a metal door closing rang through the prison cell. It felt like it was late, the middle of the night maybe, but who could even tell anymore, in a place like this? The ground reeked of sweat and urine, the sun could not reach him, and the only people that he'd seen in two days were not so much people as the hands of a burly guard that slid a metal plate through a slot in the base of the door.

Not that he had bothered to eat any of it. The plates still sat where they'd been left, the moldy bread gnawed to crumbs by the rats. There was no point in eating, no point in sleeping, no point in trying to escape.

No point in opening his eyes as a pair of footsteps moved into the cell with him. They clacked elegantly across the stone floor in the soft, one-two pattern of women's heels. Just like his wife used to move. Oh, of all the cruelties they could have thought up, why ever did they have to send a woman? Did they not realize that he was in enough agony?

"Wake up," a woman's voice said. She nudged his knee with the toe of her shoe, and when he did not bother to respond, she nudged it again, harder. "All right, fine," the voice continued, "If you'd rather pretend like you can't hear me, then I suppose we can play it that way. Although, if you continue to ignore me, then I cannot help you."

He grunted. "I am beyond help," he muttered into his chest. And it was true. Look at him: chained to the wall of a dungeon, held like some common pickpocket. The irons dug into his wrists, but he didn't even care. At least if they let him die, it would finally be over.

The woman clucked her tongue. "Oh, I don't think so. I have always believed in second chances. And you . . . you should believe in them, too."

"Oh?" he asked, despite himself. He raised his head, finally, just a little. Just enough to pop one eye open. He snorted, messy and undignified. "Why's that?"

Pon Lanali leaned over, her signature veil folded back over her head. She grinned at him. "Because, Lord Madgar . . . I think that together, you and I . . . together, we can find Praxis Fellows."

The adventure continues in . . .

THE BEACON CAMPAIGNS • BOOK FOUR

Available Now

PHOTO BY CORIE KELLEY

About the Author

Jenn Gott spent most of her childhood tromping through her parents' woods, and the rest of it making up fifty imaginary friends at a time. She has never let them go—these days they're just called "characters," and they spend more time on pages than in her head. She is still happiest living in the woods, with her equally nerdy husband and their spoiled snuggle-cat.

🌐 jenngott.com
🐦 @gottwords
📷 @jenngottbooks
✉ jenn@jenngott.com

Sign up for the latest news and updates at:
jenngott.com/newsletter